LIVING NIGHTMARE

Kathi looked up suddenly, trying to break the cord of fear that the voices stirred in her. It was Sheri Walker again and someone else—someone called the Tiger—and the shrill voices were invading her mind until there was no place for her to think on her own anymore. How could she think when they were screaming at her over the sound of the train? Her eyes were fixed on David's face, praying silently that he would find a way to silence the voices, to jolt her out of the nightmare and let her be herself again.

Now her whole body was shaking and she had the crazy impulse to move—to run toward the oncoming train. Her knees bent slightly, as ready as a runner for the sound of the starting gun, and her hand reached forward as if it were being pulled toward the track. The only thing holding her back was the taut line of David's gaze, the lifeline that held her eyes fixed with his.

Don't look away, David, she pleaded silently. *Please don't look away. Keep me from doing it . . . keep me safe. Please, David! Keep me . . .*

But he was turning, not reading the anguished plea on her lips, the terror in her eyes . . .

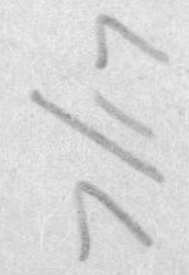

Books by Joanne Fluke

Hannah Swensen Mysteries

CHOCOLATE CHIP COOKIE MURDER
STRAWBERRY SHORTCAKE MURDER
BLUEBERRY MUFFIN MURDER
LEMON MERINGUE PIE MURDER
FUDGE CUPCAKE MURDER
SUGAR COOKIE MURDER
PEACH COBBLER MURDER
CHERRY CHEESECAKE MURDER
KEY LIME PIE MURDER
CANDY CANE MURDER
CARROT CAKE MURDER
CREAM PUFF MURDER
PLUM PUDDING MURDER
APPLE TURNOVER MURDER
DEVIL'S FOOD CAKE MURDER
GINGERBREAD COOKIE MURDER
CINNAMON ROLL MURDER
RED VELVET CUPCAKE MURDER
BLACKBERRY PIE MURDER
DOUBLE FUDGE BROWNIE MURDER
WEDDING CAKE MURDER
BANANA CREAM PIE MURDER
JOANNE FLUKE'S LAKE EDEN COOKBOOK

Suspense Novels

VIDEO KILL
WINTER CHILL
DEAD GIVEAWAY
THE OTHER CHILD
COLD JUDGMENT
FATAL IDENTITY
FINAL APPEAL
VENGEANCE IS MINE
EYES
WICKED
DEADLY MEMORIES
THE STEPCHILD

Published by Kensington Publishing Corporation

THE STEPCHILD

JOANNE FLUKE

KENSINGTON BOOKS
www.kensingtonbooks.com

KENSINGTON BOOKS are published by

Kensington Publishing Corp.
119 West 40th Street
New York, NY 10018

Previously published in a mass-market edition by Dell Publishing in May 1980.

ISBN-13: 978-0-7582-8983-4
ISBN-10: 0-7582-8983-9
First Kensington Mass Market Edition: August 2017

ISBN-13: 978-0-7582-8984-1
ISBN-10: 0-7582-8984-7
First Kensington Electronic Edition: August 2017

10 9 8 7 6 5 4 3 2 1

Printed in the United States of America

PROLOGUE

A tear rolled down her cheek even though she was trying to be big and brave the way she'd promised. She couldn't help it. She didn't want to be here on the train, going to a new Mommy and Daddy. She wanted her real Mommy and Daddy back, and so did Baver. He cried so hard when they took him away.

Dorothy Miller gave her husband a pleading look as she noticed the tears in Sheri's eyes. She knew the anguish the little girl must be feeling, leaving for a new home only days after being separated from her baby brother. Dorothy didn't agree with the adoption system one bit, but her opinion made no difference. The agency claimed to have only the good of the child in mind, but Sheri was too young to understand that.

"Why don't I take Sheri Bear out onto the observation platform for a couple of minutes," Irvin Miller suggested, responding to the plea in his wife's eyes.

Dorothy watched a flicker of interest cross the child's face, and she nodded. "Bring her in when we pass Carlson's Crossing, Irv. We don't want our big girl to catch a cold right before she meets her new Mommy and Daddy," she cautioned.

"I won't catch a cold," Sheri promised, standing up quickly and tugging at Irvin's hand. "Let's go!"

Dorothy flashed her husband a grateful look as they left. She was terribly worried about Sheri. This was the first sign of interest the little four-year-old had shown since her brother was taken away. Perhaps everything would be fine after all, but Dorothy couldn't suppress a sense of foreboding. It was always bad business to separate families; someone would suffer for it.

Several of the passengers turned to smile as Sheri pulled Irvin down the aisle. She was a beautiful child with her long golden hair and big blue eyes. Dorothy just wished that she had been able to talk the orphanage into letting her stay with them permanently. All the protests they'd made hadn't been one bit effective when it came to keeping Sheri's little brother, and now they'd lost again. Dorothy knew in her heart that both children would have been happier together with them, but she and Irvin were too old to qualify according to the agency's rules. There was something wrong with Christian charity when it meant breaking up families, and nothing anyone could say would convince Dorothy otherwise. Father O'Malley had told them that the Lord moved in mysterious ways, but Dorothy was convinced that the Lord needed a good talking to when it came to adoption rules. She and Irvin could have given both children a good home if only the orphanage had listened to reason.

Darkness was beginning to fall as Sheri walked out on the platform. The wind whipped around her, and she tightened her grip on Uncle Irvin's hand as he pointed out at the tracks. She followed his finger with her eyes and saw a rabbit running fast in the circle of light cast by the train. Baver would love to see the rabbit, she thought sadly.

Tears welled up in Sheri's eyes again. She had a big job to do now. She had to find Baver, so they could go look for Mommy and Daddy. Mommy and Daddy were hiding somewhere, just like a trick. All she had to do was get Baver and find them.

The tears came faster now, and Sheri held Uncle Irvin's hand even tighter. She wanted to stay outside a while longer with the wind rushing past her face. But most of all she wanted to forget where they were taking her. If only everything were the way it used to be . . .

The engineer was alert as the train neared Carlson's Crossing. He was always nervous when he came to this particular intersection; it was a bad one, hidden by a sloping curve in the road. Everyone who lived out here knew about it, but he still had visions of some out-of-state motorist zipping around the curve and right into the path of his train. He gave his standard warning blasts, and then another just to calm his nerves. No one could fail to hear the piercing whistle.

There were lights in her rearview mirror. They were coming closer. The car bounced on the winter potholes that hadn't been filled in yet, as she took the curves faster than the posted speed. The car lurched, and there was a frightened whimper from the child beside her, but she couldn't slow down now. She had to get away from him. He was following her, chasing her, but she would never let him catch her. She was a good driver, and the car was powerful.

Perhaps she'd go home later and have it out with him again, listen to the endless accusations. But not tonight. Tonight she would escape him, drive until she sobered up a bit and felt able to cope with the whole rotten world. Didn't he know that was why she drank? So that she could cope with things instead of being afraid all the time?

"Mama!" the child whimpered, the small voice rising to a terrified scream. "Mama! There's a train coming!"

"S'all right, honey," she said, gritting her teeth and managing to keep the heavy convertible on the road. "Don't worry about a thing. Mama's going to take care of that bastard! Just see if I don't!"

"Mama, I'm scared!" The child's voice broke into her thoughts again. "Please, Mama! Not so fast!"

"Quiet!" Her teeth were chattering now, so loudly that they sounded like firecrackers in her head. The top was down and it was cold, the wind whizzing past their heads in icy blasts. She should have put the top up, but they hadn't had time. There hadn't been time to do anything except run, and that was just what she was doing. She'd lose him somehow and drive to Grey Eagle, have a little warm-up drink in that nice little rustic bar her father had liked. They'd have food for Kathi, and she could feel the warmth of the liquor in her body again. Then her teeth would stop chattering. But first, she had to get away from him. He was following her . . . both of them were . . . he and that shameless whore. Damn him!

"Mama! The train!"

The child was terrified, and for a moment the woman paused, looking in the rearview mirror, and lifted her foot from the accelerator. Then she grinned, and her foot thumped down all the way to the floor. The car leaped forward. They would beat the train, and he would be stuck there at the crossing. He'd be stuck, and she'd be free to go on and drink as many doubles as she wanted tonight—without his nagging reminders and polite warnings about her drinking. He could sit there at the crossing until hell froze over, for all she cared; he'd never catch her tonight. Tonight would go her way. Was one night out of so many too much to ask?

Out of the corner of her eye, she saw the child cover her face with her hands. No cause to worry; they were going to make it. They were going to beat that train and then they'd be free. There was a road right past the crossing, and she'd turn off there so he'd never find her. It would serve him right, the sanctimonious bastard. For once, she'd beat him at his own game.

The car's headlights were not visible until they were almost upon the crossing. The engineer felt his heart leap in his chest, and he gave another shrill blast on the whistle to warn the speeding convertible. He leaned forward jerkily as he peered into the wedge of light, and then he hit the brakes and offered up a quick, wordless prayer. That crazy damn fool was going to try to beat the train!

* * *

She heard the scream as the brakes ground against the metal wheels. For the first time, fright penetrated her hazed mind. Of course they were going to make it, but . . . my God! She'd be playing right into his hands if they didn't. He wanted her out of the way, so he could take up with that whore of his. He'd be happy if the train hit her. Then he'd have everything he'd ever wanted, except the money. He'd never get that . . .

The engineer hit the whistle again, but the car kept on coming, like an insect charging an elephant. It took time for the tons and tons of metal to stop, and he didn't dare lock the brakes in place, or they'd derail for sure. There was an instant when time stood still, and he could see the determined face of the woman behind the wheel and the little girl in the seat next to her, her mouth opened in a frightened scream. Reality faded, and he was watching the whole thing in slow motion, hearing the sickening crash, seeing the flicker of the stop-action frames behind his eyes as the car spun and disintegrated, flames ballooning up from the wreckage like hungry demons.

The train swayed for a moment, the giant metal beast fighting to right itself on the metal girders of the rails. There were screams from the passengers as they were thrown from side to side in the car. He heard the screams and knew his own mouth was open, screaming too, although he could not hear the sound of his own voice. The train tipped at a crazy angle, and something sharp struck his head.

God, no! They were falling, lurching, and rolling as the train left the tracks. The giant, lumbering baby was severed from its shining metal cord. Then the blackness came up to meet him, and the screams of the passengers faded until everything was cold and silent. The moon was bloodred, but he no longer saw.

She was there and then she was not, the force of the crash lifting her in painful arms and hurtling her into the brushy darkness along the side of the tracks. There was another girl lying very close to her, but she was not crying. Her blue eyes were open, and she looked like a broken doll. There was pain, she hurt everywhere, and she screamed out for someone to help her . . . to take her to Mama! The bright orange light hurt her eyes, and the noise was so loud, no one would ever be able to hear her. The Tiger had promised; he had promised that the train wouldn't ever come off the tracks, but it had, and it had hurt her. Her dress was torn, and all dirty and sticky with something that looked shiny black in the flickering light. She'd get a spanking for that. The dress was new and now she'd got it all dirty.

"Good God! The poor little thing!" She could see big hands covering the other girl with a blanket, pulling the blanket over her face.

"Christ! Over here!" a loud voice called out, and then she was lifted gently, carefully, but it didn't make any difference. Everything hurt.

"Easy boys. Looks like she's in a coma," a low voice said, and there was a sting in her arm like a bee bite. Something warm and heavy was pressing her eyelids down, so she didn't have to see the flickering orange lights anymore. Everything was dark, the hurt was all gone, and she wished that she could remember why she was crying. . . .

CHAPTER 1

Kathi Ellison shivered a little as she pushed the shopping cart into the meat section and examined the steaks. It was always so cold in this part of the store, and her feet were wet from the rain. Usually David went shopping with her, but she hadn't asked him today because she wanted to pick out something very special for dinner tonight. It was their first anniversary. She had moved in with David Carter exactly a month ago, and tonight they were going to celebrate.

The tall, blond coed made a wry face as she mentally added up the price of the items in her shopping cart: fresh mushrooms, broccoli, a loaf of San Francisco's renowned sourdough bread, and two steaks. Even though Vivian and her father were always cautioning her to eat right, Kathi was sure they wouldn't approve of the way her allowance was being spent this month. And they would certainly disapprove if they knew what occasion was going to be celebrated in Kathi and David's small, off-campus apartment. The Ellisons had no idea that their daughter was living with David, and Kathi wasn't about to tell them now. It wouldn't be right to make her father worry when the senatorial election was less than a month away. No one would find out that Doug Ellison's daughter was living in sin. She was still listed in the college register as being a resident of the girls' dorm, and her former roommate collected all of Kathi's mail and messages. Kathi knew that she'd eventually have to tell her parents—but after the election, not before.

Carrying her purchases in a large sack, Kathi skipped over puddles as she hurried back to the apartment. She wanted to beat David home today and have their anniversary dinner ready to eat by the time he came home from the library. She hadn't even mentioned the fact that it was their anniversary. David would be surprised. She hurried a little faster as she thought of how pleased he would be.

Even though Kathi's yellow rain slicker covered her long legs, and her hair was tucked carefully under the matching rain hat, she was still soaked by the time she got to the apartment building. The lobby door shut behind her, and Kathi fumbled in her purse for her keys, wiping her feet carefully on the welcome mat outside the apartment door. She didn't want to track up her freshly cleaned floor, which she'd done an excellent job of waxing, even though she wasn't used to housework. Even Sally, the Ellisons' maid, would have to admit that Kathi was turning into a good housekeeper.

Kathi had just located her key when the door swung inward, and strong arms pulled her into the apartment.

"Oh, David!" Kathi gasped. "You scared me. I didn't think you'd be home for at least another hour."

"I got through a little early," David explained, taking the bag from her and setting it on the table. "Hey, you're soaked to the skin. Let me help you out of those wet things."

Kathi gave a pleased giggle as David helped her out of her raincoat, and then proceeded to tug off her college sweatshirt as well.

"That's not wet!" she protested. "What are you doing?"

"My mother always said to take a hot shower after you've been out in a cold rain," David advised, trying to look solemn. "I just got home a few minutes ago myself, and I haven't had time to take mine. We could save on water if we took a shower together."

"Always practical, aren't you?" Kathi teased, ducking under David's arm and running toward the bathroom. She didn't have to look to know that David was following her. As far as Kathi was concerned, the shower was a perfect place to start celebrating their anniversary.

"Oh, David! We're going to drown!" Kathi laughed and gasped at the same time. Their wet bodies were slipping together under the heated spray, and she gave another shriek as David fondled her playfully. "You're a sex maniac, that's what you are! Nothing but a—"

Her protest unfinished, David's strong arms were lifting her, carrying her dripping wet from the bathroom to a towel spread out on the bed. So he had planned it! The towel was ready and waiting for them on their big double bed.

As David's body covered hers, there was a singing

in her veins, and the breath escaped from her lungs in an explosion of soft, loving sounds. His hands touched her moist skin, and a burst of heat shimmered through her body.

"How's this?" David asked, his voice husky as his head lowered and his lips found the secret places to kiss. "And this? And then this?"

"Yes—" Kathi heard her own voice joining his as he caressed her. She raised her arms and put them around his neck, pulling him down to her. "Now, David . . . please," she whispered.

He raised up, spreading her legs gently. Filled with an aching tenderness for her, he leaned forward again, kissing with lips that trembled.

"I love you, Kathi. . . . I love you."

She could feel it start to happen. Her body seemed to melt, and her heart was pounding in her throat—or was it his heart? Their lips were open, their mouths joined, breathing in the same air, together so tightly that they seemed to be one person. Then they were moving together, pulling back and joining again, over and over. Her hands were grasping him now, pulling him deeper, deeper, deeper, until the sweetness began to seep into her, and at last they fell back onto the pillows, exhausted, still holding hands.

A long time later, Kathi heard the rattle of drops against the windowpane, and she gave a fleeting thought to the sodden bag of groceries sitting on the table. It was early, still plenty of time for their celebration later, or had this been the real celebration? She smiled and snuggled closer, drifting off to sleep entwined in his arms as she listened to the rustle of the branches outside, and felt the warmth of his body protecting her.

It seemed as if she had always felt the pain, throbbing and stabbing behind her closed eyelids. She opened her eyes tentatively, and then winced as the dim, dusky light coming in through the window told her it was long past time to start dinner. David was still sleeping, and she rose from the bed, hoping not to wake him until she could take some aspirin and get rid of her pounding headache. It felt like a migraine. Vivian had described them often enough for Kathi to recognize the symptoms.

"Hot water," Vivian had claimed. "Always take aspirins with hot water. They work faster that way."

But the sound of the water rushing from the tap seemed to be roaring in Kathi's ears. This was no ordinary headache; it was a bone-crushing, blinding, stabbing pain that made her want to scream in agony. Strange images were running through her mind, and for a moment she wondered if she were still asleep and dreaming. The visions were blurred, but she could see them clearly enough to realize that she didn't know the faces.

A short, plump woman with curly gray hair was standing at an old-fashioned stove, stirring something. Then he was home, her uncle, lifting her up and hugging her tightly. He set her down in a rocking chair, and she realized she was not alone in the big chair. Her little baby brother was with her, swinging sneakered feet that didn't even touch the floor.

Kathi whimpered and held her head tightly between her palms, one hand over each temple as if she could imprison the images with her fingers. What in the world—? She didn't have a baby brother, or an uncle, or an aunt. She must still be dreaming. If only the headache would stop, she could shake her head and make the confusing images disappear.

With shaking fingers, Kathi snapped on the kitchen light. There . . . that was better. She was beginning to really wake up now, and her headache was going away. Her head was clearing, and the faces fading, until she saw only the red Rubbermaid dish drainer and the dishes she had left from breakfast. There was a lingering feeling of uneasiness that made her turn and look quickly behind her, but, of course, there was nothing there. She must remember not to get up so suddenly again. There was something very frightening about the half-awake, half-asleep state she had experienced.

"You've been studying too hard," Kathi chided herself aloud. "David's going to write his master's thesis about you if you flip out on him!"

She laughed as she dumped the mushrooms into the sink and began cleaning them. David probably wouldn't mind at all if she went crazy and volunteered to be the subject of his thesis. Then he wouldn't have to run all the way out to the state hospital to interview patients. And she wouldn't have to pay for expensive psychotherapy either. She had her own handsome shrink right in the apartment.

"No way!" Kathi sighed, laughing at herself. She wasn't flipping out, and she wouldn't be the subject for David's thesis. He was always bugging her to tell him her dreams. She really would have cooperated but she couldn't remember them. Of course, she remembered this one, but for some reason Kathi didn't think she'd mention it. She couldn't really think of a good reason for not telling David, but some things were better off forgotten, and Kathi had the distinct feeling that her experience today fell into that category.

CHAPTER 2

Kathi let the book slip down to her lap, no longer seeing the words printed on the page. There was something wrong, and she knew it. She had never been this preoccupied and absentminded before. Just last week, when she had got the first headache on their anniversary, she had joked about it, but now it was no longer a joking matter. The headaches were coming more frequently, and aspirins didn't seem to help. They were strange headaches, coming on suddenly and disappearing abruptly, leaving her disoriented and shaking. There was definitely something wrong, and she had to figure out what to do about it.

With an impatient sigh, Kathi slipped off her reading glasses and closed the book. She simply couldn't study anymore tonight. The best thing to do was to get a good night's sleep and hope she didn't have any more bad dreams. That was probably the source of her whole problem—not enough sleep and too much worrying about her upcoming exams.

A smile turned up the corners of Kathi's full lips as

she turned and looked at him. David was asleep, lying there with his hair tousled like a small boy. A wave of tenderness rushed through her, and she reached out to brush his hair back from his forehead. At times like this, she felt almost maternal toward David.

"Hm?" David questioned, sitting up with a jerk. For the space of a second, he looked angry, ready to attack whatever threatened his peaceful sleep. Then recognition came, and with it, an apologetic smile.

"Hey," David mumbled, grinning. "You scared me, honey. Don't tell me you're finally through studying?"

Kathi nodded, almost wishing that she had let him sleep now, but she had promised to wake him when she was through. She reached up to flick off the light, and before her hand had lowered again, David was reaching for her, his body sleepy-warm. Kathi felt a knot of fear in her stomach.

She shook her long, honey-colored hair and made a deliberate effort to force the invading chill from her mind. "And just what is it that you think you want?" she asked, trying to make her voice light and teasing. The frightened look in her eyes belied her light voice, but the room was too dark for David to see that.

"You know what I want." David's voice was deep and husky. He was fully awake now, and he felt her body shiver against his.

For one fleeting second, Kathi thought of resisting. Over the past few days, when David reached for her, she had felt a growing fear. The fear was almost worse than the headaches because it was so unfounded. There was no reason to be afraid of David. She loved him!

Kathi knew that she could have pulled back, and David wouldn't have pressed her, but it wasn't her nature to deny a need from the man she loved. She pushed back the fear, and met his warm lips with her own. It was going to be fine this time, just like it had been before the headaches started. Nothing bad was going to happen.

"Mmmmmmm." She sighed, kissing him a little harder. This was better. The panic was firmly pushed aside now, and she knew she'd been studying too hard, worrying about her midterms. It was Sunday night, the fifteenth of October, and by Wednesday her midterms would be over. Then she had until the thirtieth, when classes resumed, to relax and vacation. But how could she relax when the election was only a little over three weeks away? Kathi knew how important the election was to her father. Being a United States senator had always been Doug Ellison's dream.

Kathi could feel the tension build in her slender body as she thought of all the things that could happen to keep her father from winning. How could she think of the election at a time like this, when David was kissing her and stroking her? Somehow her doubts and fears were all tied up with the coming election, and David, and what would happen if the voters found out that she was living with David without being married. Was that what was making her anxious and tense? But she couldn't think about that now. She had to think of David and forget about everything else, and maybe then everything would be all right.

The night sounds were heavy in Kathi's ears, but soon the swooshing of the cars on the street outside was erased by the sound of her own quickened breathing. David's lips were on her breasts, warm and familiar, teasing her nipples until they felt as if they'd burst with heat. There was a pounding in her head, and it drove out all thoughts. His hands were sliding down her body, touching her, making her gasp with awakening desire. Then he was over her, and in her, pushing her back and forth in the familiar rocking motion that reminded her of something else . . . something not quite as pleasant that hovered on the fuzzy edge of her awareness.

She moved more quickly, stepping up the rhythm as she tried to concentrate on David. But suddenly, she was cold. Her passion evaporated in a chill wind, leaving her caught in the middle of something she could not finish. The warm, wonderful embrace of David's arms was like a vise now, holding her down, making her feel as if she were smothering under his heavy weight. And that awful rocking rhythm went on and on, until she wanted to strike out at him and scream in terror.

Still, Kathi forced herself to pretend. She opened her eyes, made out David's face in the dim light from the street, and smiled, a tightening of her facial muscles that felt false. Her hips moved automatically, accepting the lie, denying the fact that something was keeping her from being his completely. Why was this happening?

It seemed as if it would never end, the jiggling, bouncing motion. Even though there was a pleasant smile on her face, her teeth ground together in anguish. The barrier was still there, the fear that remained nameless. And there was nothing she could do about it. She hated him for bringing her to this sharply honed edge of fright, and she loved him desperately at the same time. It was getting worse, more terrifying by the minute.

* * *

The dream started slowly, with a feeling of foreboding that invaded Kathi's exhausted sleep. It was a feeling of something she had lost or forgotten, surfacing in the dark, heavy curtains of her slumber. At first, it was not terrifying, just a vague uneasiness that made her roll over and snuggle a little closer to David's warm back. But that only seemed to make the uneasy feeling grow, as if he were part of the nightmare. With a sharp indrawn breath, she rolled back to the far corner of the bed, huddling on the edge of the mattress with her legs and arms curled inward for protection.

Now there was a heavy sound, gathering in momentum like a harsh panting. Louder and louder it grew, until Kathi felt her body tremble, and she hugged herself into a ball, tighter and tighter, to keep it away.

"It's gonna be fine, Miss Kathi . . . see? There's nothing gonna get my baby. Sally's gonna chase all those bad dreams away if I sit right here. Now you go back to sleep, lamb, and I'll watch over you."

But Sally was gone, and she knew it. Sally wasn't here; there was only David in the big, comfortable double bed. Only David to ward off the nightmares, but his presence seemed to invite the terror.

The dread crept over her in numbing, icy waves. She tried to open her eyes and stop the dream, halting it before it went too far. If she could just open her eyes, she would see the mahogany dresser at the foot of the bed, her doll collection sitting there, real and tangible. Of course it was only a dream . . .

But her eyes refused to open. They seemed to be weighted down, sealed against the comforting reality of the familiar room. The dream was pulling her down, and the gathering horror drew her mind deeper and deeper into that unfamiliar black place. She was helpless, caught in the hideous pattern unfolding before her closed, locked eyelids. Her body was frozen. She could not move. There was someone with her, whispering in her ear like the rushing wind.

She tried to listen, but the whisper was drowned out in pain and screaming, contorted faces and bodies hurtling into the air, the shattering force of the ground coming up to meet her small body, and the splintering noise of bones snapping in her arms and legs. There was the deafening squeal, like a wounded animal, as metal met metal again and again in a series of horrid grating, screeching screams. Then . . . mercifully . . . there was only the blackness.

Perhaps there had been a small sound; David was not sure. He opened his eyes, suddenly alert, and felt the rigidity of Kathi's body huddled there. It was happening again. He reached for the light, turning to gather her into his arms and give her what comfort he could.

"He's gone! My Baver is gone!" Kathi cried out in a child's voice. "The bad people came to take him away!"

"Kathi," David soothed softly. "Wake up, honey." He stroked her shoulders and hugged her as she started sobbing, still entrapped in her nightmare.

"It's all right, baby," he assured her again. "Open your eyes, Kathi. It's just a dream . . . see? You're right here. It's just a dream."

David saw her struggle to cast off the dream. Her eyelids flickered, and then her blue eyes were open, wide with fear. There was a wild, anguished look on her face that made David's heart thud anxiously in his chest.

"Just a dream, honey," David repeated softly, stroking her as gently as he could. "You just had another nightmare, Kathi. There's nothing to be afraid of. You're awake now."

The fear left her gradually, and the terrified expression changed to gratitude. "Oh!" she gasped. "Oh, David . . . I . . . I was dreaming again, wasn't I?"

David nodded, not trusting himself to speak. His earlier suspicions were realized. In the past few days, Kathi had the nightmares every time they made love. It must be guilt . . . unless there was some sort of physical cause for it.

David had been puzzling over the dreams ever since Kathi had mentioned them, trying to tie the clues together. There seemed to be no specific time of night for the dreams, nothing that preceded them to set them off except for one startling revelation that he had proved tonight. Sex set off the nightmares. It was the only constant. David felt guilty for experimenting with Kathi tonight. Of course he always wanted to make love to her, but tonight there had been an ulterior motive. Now that it was over, David felt like a first-class bastard. But at least he knew.

"This has got to stop, baby," David said firmly,

cradling her in his arms. "We're going to the doctor tomorrow, and you're going to get a complete checkup."

"Oh, David," Kathi protested, fighting back tears. "There's nothing wrong with me. It's just nerves, that's all. I'll be fine just as soon as midterms are over and Dad's won the election. Really!"

"It won't hurt just to go in," David insisted. His voice was soft, but he was determined to get Kathi to the doctor tomorrow, even if he had to drag her.

"Maybe they can give you tranquilizers, or something, to make you stop worrying. That wouldn't be so bad, would it, honey? Just until the pressure's off."

Kathi smiled despite herself. David knew full well that she didn't even take aspirin unless she had an awful headache. She hated pills. She wished that she could level with David, tell him that she'd always had nightmares, even when she was a child, but that would make him worry even more. And they had been getting worse lately. The dreams had been growing ever since she'd moved in with David. How could she tell him that? He might think that she should go back to the dorm, and she just couldn't do that. How could she ever give up the only man she'd ever loved, just for a few nightmares?

Kathi opened her mouth to try to dissuade David, but then her mouth closed again as she read the worry in his eyes. David's determination was obvious. She would have to go in and see the doctor, even though she knew that there was nothing physically wrong with her. It was hopeless. But Kathi knew that she couldn't share her deepest fears with David. He would never understand. No one would.

"I . . . well . . . all right," she agreed, sagging

against him. "You're right, of course. It won't hurt just to go in."

David returned Kathi's feeble attempt at a smile. Then he held her carefully as she began to relax. The nightmares never came twice on the same night, so she would be all right now. His strong fingers rubbed the tension out of her back, stroking and massaging until she calmed down and her breathing became regular and deep. A little more and she'd be asleep, and then he could try to piece together the pattern. It was like a giant jigsaw puzzle, and now he had another minuscule part of the pattern to fit in.

"He's gone. My Baver's gone! The bad people came to take him away!"

He could still hear the childish voice, high and thin with fear, and he shivered in spite of the warm room. David knew his insistence that Kathi see the college doctor was purely academic. He really didn't think that her problem was physical, but it was a first step. After they'd eliminated the possible physical causes, perhaps she'd be more cooperative about sharing her thoughts and feelings with him. Kathi was a very private person, and that made it even more difficult for David to know her secret fears, the same fears that must be causing her nightmares.

It took all the self-control David had to hold her quietly. He wanted to get up and pace the floor, have a cigarette or belt down a drink, anything to stop the thoughts from forming in his mind. At first, Kathi's nightmares had been only bad dreams, an occasional awakening in the middle of the night with the traces of tears still on her cheeks. She had laughed about them the next morning.

He hadn't even known about them at first. She'd been able to wake up on her own, sit up in bed and make sure that she was right here in their own room, and then go back to sleep. She'd confessed that only a few days ago. Now all that was changing. The nightmares were becoming more frequent and more intense. It had taken almost two minutes to wake her tonight. What would happen if he couldn't wake her at all the next time?

He forced himself to relax his tight muscles. He could sweat out the night hypothesizing, but it wouldn't do any good. They had to discover the cause of Kathi's nightmares. If only she could remember them, they might have a clue. At least the doctor was the logical place to start. And after that . . . he'd just have to think of something.

David cursed himself for being so helpless. He looked at Kathi, so small and fragile under the covers. He had to protect her . . . see that she got the proper care no matter what the problem was. She had entrusted herself to him, and it was up to him to keep her from harm. He'd accepted that responsibility when he first told her that he loved her.

Carefully, he untangled Kathi's arms from his neck and slid noiselessly under the blankets, cuddling her spoon-fashion until the sound of her quiet breathing lulled him into a restless sleep.

CHAPTER 3

"He said there's nothing to worry about. It's probably just anxiety about midterms," Kathi said clearly, forcing her voice to sound cheerful as she spoke into the phone. "He told me that when the tension lets up, the nightmares ought to disappear. If they don't, I'm to come in again after midterm break."

Kathi's face turned pink as she listened to David's anxious reply.

"Yes . . . of course I told him everything, and you were right about the pills, David. He gave me something to take every morning, and I'm getting the prescription filled right now."

After a slight pause, Kathi nodded, even though she knew that David couldn't see the nod. She could picture him pacing at the end of the telephone cord, back and forth across the gray-carpeted living room, while he talked. David was a pacer and a telephone cord twister. She could hear the tiny crackling noise in the receiver as he twisted the cord in his fingers.

"Yes, I'm relieved too," she said, her face hot with

the lie she had told. A truck sped past the telephone booth and she leaned forward, hugging the receiver tightly so she could hear David's voice. She wished that she could tell him the rest of it—how she'd used Bev Smith's ID card to make the appointment and what the doctor had really said—but that was her secret, another secret she had to keep from David.

"Well, Miss Smith . . ." The doctor had cleared his throat. "It's a bit early, but we can take a blood test and see what happens. Pregnancy is definitely indicated. Nausea, headaches, a sudden weight loss . . . all quite common complaints in early pregnancy. I'll give you something to relax you for a few days, and you can call in on Wednesday for the test results. If your pregnancy is confirmed, I'll refer you to an organization on campus for young women in your situation."

Kathi nodded again, staring through the glass door at the items arranged for display in the drugstore window. David would want to get married right away if she told him, but she wanted to wait and make sure. It wasn't the best way to start a marriage, and nothing could be done until after the election anyway. U.S. SENATE CANDIDATE'S DAUGHTER MARRIED IN SHOTGUN WEDDING. That would ruin her father's campaign for sure.

And what if her other fears were true? The dark fears she had pushed back for so long? What then? Would David still want to marry her if he knew that?

"Hmmmmmm?" Kathi asked, missing David's question entirely, as her gaze rested on an advertisement for the new sporting good shop opening next door. "Oh, yes, honey . . . I'll be home just as soon as my prescription's ready."

She quickly replaced the phone in the cradle, fumbling a bit because her eyes were still fixed on the poster in the vacant storefront. WALKER SPORTING GOODS. Walker . . . Walker . . . the letters swam in front of her eyes, and a blinding pain made her clutch her head in both hands. A prickle of fear ran down her spine.

The tapping had been going on for some time. Kathi blinked as she saw a man and a woman waiting to use the phone. How long had she been standing here?

At first the man looked angry that she was just standing there with her palms pressed to her temples, and then his forehead wrinkled in a distressed frown. Her vision blurred, and she could see the two of them receding into a tunnel, as if she were looking the wrong way through a set of binoculars. The man's voice was weak and faraway sounding, like a record played at the wrong speed.

"Can I help you, miss?"

"Can I help you . . . help you . . . help you?"

"No, I can do it myself, Auntie! Please . . . let me do it all! I can do it right. I know I can!"

It was kind of him to be so helpful. His handkerchief was crooked. It was the kind cleaners provide when they press a suit—a pocket-size piece of white cardboard with the cleaner's name on it, and a bit of white linen sewn on top to simulate a handkerchief. When the cardboard was properly positioned, only the folded linen edge was visible, and there was an instant handkerchief in the pocket, exactly what every well-dressed man should have.

Kathi gave the man a little smile. If he had to blow his nose, it would be difficult with a cardboard handkerchief. Then she reached out to open the door and smiled again to let him know that she was just fine. Her mouth opened and words came out, words she had never heard or even thought before.

"Walker, Sheri Walker. W-A-L-K-E-R. She taught me how to make the letters. My growed-up name is Sharon Elizabeth Walker, but nobody calls me that unless I do something naughty, and I live at four-oh-two Elm. I did that good, didn't I? Auntie says I will be very good in first grade!"

"Miss?" the man asked again. "Are you all right, Miss?"

The woman pulled her companion aside as Kathi stepped out of the phone booth.

"Hippies!" she hissed. "Probably high on something! There ought to be a law, Herbert!"

Kathi wanted to protest. She hadn't said that! Someone else had spoken through her mouth, and now the nice, helpful man was frowning and looking at her suspiciously, his face a mask of disapproval. But Kathi was afraid to open her mouth again, for fear that other voice would come out and say even more outrageous things. She clamped her jaws tightly shut and hurried past them, her head pounding fiercely.

She could feel them staring at her as she rushed into the drugstore, sank gratefully down on a luncheonette stool, and ordered a glass of water from the tired-looking waitress. Her head hurt dreadfully, and she pressed her hands tightly against her temples again, closing her eyes with the pain. What had made her say a silly thing like that? Was she dreaming again?

"Hey, honey. Want a couple of aspirins?" the waitress asked, leaning over to wipe the counter. "He gets 'em free, you know. Those big drug companies give him a ten thousand-count bottle with every order. You look like you've got a beaut coming on."

"Oh, yes, thank you," Kathi mumbled, accepting the aspirins that the waitress shook out into her hand. She gave a little laugh even though she felt more like crying. "I've been studying too hard, I guess."

"I know just what you mean," the waitress commented, shifting her weight to one hip and leaning on her hand holding the cloth. "My brother-in-law's the same way. Stays up all night studying and then he expects to work all day besides. They say an education's important, but my sister don't think so. She has to keep the kids quiet while he studies. You know they can't even have the TV on when he's reading? He's depriving them kids, that's what he's doing!"

Kathi nodded, making an effort to listen through the pounding in her head. She had to hurry and pick up her prescription before her headache got worse. It was beginning to feel like another migraine, and all she wanted to do was go home and crawl under the covers in her own bed. The waitress was trying to be nice, but Kathi wanted to scream at her to shut up . . . to leave her alone so she could finish the glass of water and get her pills. She had told David that everything was fine, and somehow she had to keep up that charade. But nothing was fine now.

Kathi didn't notice the waitress's shocked expression as she got up in midsentence and went to the pharmacy counter to pick up her pills.

The cold air outside helped a bit, but her head was still reeling, and she concentrated on putting one foot in front of the other, stopping and waiting at the traffic lights, and walking in a straight line, so some passing policeman wouldn't think she was high on drugs or drunk. Was this what it felt like to go crazy? Were they going to find her right here on the Berkeley campus, with the carefully landscaped grounds and the tall, familiar multiwindowed buildings, and lock her up?

And who—she had to know—who was Sheri Walker?

CHAPTER 4

"I think we've got it in the bag!" Harry Adams shouted exuberantly, slapping Doug on the back. "Jake Roman promised me that he'd support you for the campaign. You know what that means, Doug? With Jake's support, we'll pull in all the Republican voters that supported him!"

Doug laughed in excitement. That really was good news! He had hoped that Jake would support him, but it had been a long shot. Jake was retiring this year after twelve years in the Senate, two full terms which had made him very popular with the voters. The people of California respected his name and his voting record. If Jake's support was certain, Doug had the race all but won.

"That's great!" Doug exclaimed, hugging his short, balding campaign manager. "You worked a miracle, Harry. I still don't know how you did it."

"Let's just say that your perfect record convinced him," Harry replied, winking. There were some things you didn't come right out and admit to a moral man like Doug Ellison. There was quite a bit of under-the-table dealing in any election. Harry knew that Doug didn't approve, but it couldn't be helped. The less Doug knew about his talk with Jake Roman this morning, the better.

Harry's mind reviewed the interview in detail. One of his unimpeachable sources had told him about Keith Baxter's wife. There was positive proof that the opponent's wife had spent a summer, twelve years ago, drying out in a private sanitarium in Oregon. Harry knew that Doug would never stoop to using that information to his own advantage. Doug was an honest man, and politicians who were honest lost votes. It was as simple as that. What Harry discovered about Mrs. Baxter would never have been used to Doug's advantage if it weren't for Harry's little meeting this morning. If Doug even guessed how Harry had got the information, he'd be livid. He knew for a fact that Doug would fire him if he ever found out about the private detective Harry had hired.

Harry grinned, unabashed. His fancy maneuvering had paid off. Doug would never find out why Jake was suddenly endorsing him instead of Keith Baxter. That would be Harry's secret. He was a smart campaign manager, and there was a hell of a lot he left unsaid. If Doug thought that Jake had finally realized his virtues, so much the better.

At least there weren't any skeletons in Doug's closet. Harry had checked that carefully. He had gone over his employer's life in minute detail, not taking anything for granted, examining even the most trivial-appearing fact. He had accounted for almost every waking moment of Doug's life, from birth to the present, and there was no hint of any scandal. It was hard to believe that a man could be such a paragon of virtue, but Doug seemed to fit that description completely. At first, Harry didn't believe it. He tried to dig up some dirt, any dirt that could be thrown at his boss. There was absolutely nothing. Harry still couldn't believe it, but Doug had never been in any trouble, and his family was perfect. Kathi was a model student and Vivian, a perfect wife. Even the former Mrs. Ellison had come from a very good family.

At first, Harry was a bit leery about Doug's second marriage. It might be a little incriminating to marry one's secretary. There weren't even any rumors about that though. Doug had waited a full year after Roma's death before he had married Vivian. That was proper. Vivian had been an excellent mother for Kathi, too. There was nothing out of the way in Doug and Vivian's relationship. Doug's whole life read like a storybook of a successful, hardworking, professional man. He was a self-made man from humble beginnings, the perfect image for today's voter.

Harry had shrugged when he got the results of the investigation on Doug's life. He was a born skeptic. Perhaps that was why he was so well suited for his job. Campaign managers learned never to take anything at face value. Harry dug into every corner. He regarded himself as a judge with one strange twist. Doug was investigated like a criminal, guilty until proven innocent.

Now, after long months of research, Harry had found nothing to color Doug's perfect record. He was a dream candidate, but Harry found it difficult to believe in dreams. He couldn't help but feel that there must be a flaw somewhere, something he hadn't dug into thoroughly enough. He still had men working on it. It might be a shot in the dark, but he wasn't quite satisfied. There was bound to be a scandal somewhere, something that might jeopardize Doug's campaign. It was up to him to find it before the opponent did. He had to protect Doug from any mudslinging, and the only way to do that was to know exactly what kind of thing the opponent would use, pick up on it, and whitewash it first.

"You're pretty quiet for a guy who's just managed to get the campaign in the bag," Doug chuckled, snapping his fingers under Harry's nose.

"You know me," Harry responded sourly. "I'm never sure of anything until the last ballot's been cast and the counting's over. Even then, I don't relax until you're declared the winner. I may have flashes of confidence, but they disappear in a hurry when my brain engages."

Doug laughed at Harry's cryptic comment. "You're a born pessimist, Harry. No one can ever accuse you of counting your chickens before they're hatched."

Harry smiled ruefully. "That's just the way I am," he offered philosophically. "I just wish I knew what dirt the opponent will dig up about you. It would help if we got a lead on what tack they're going to take. How about it, Doug? Are you sure there's nothing in your record that they can pick up on? Think it over carefully now. Is there anything that you've done in the past you wouldn't want anyone to know? A traffic ticket that's been fixed? Maybe a maiden aunt who ended up in the funny farm? Anything at all?"

Doug held up his hands in a gesture of submission. "You know my life even better than I do." He smiled. "As far as I know, there's nothing that's not a matter of public record. No old bodies buried under my front porch, Harry. I know you'd love to have something to worry about, but I honestly can't think of a thing you don't already know."

"How about Kathi, Doug?" Harry continued relentlessly. "Is there anything about Kathi that the opposition might pick up on? A boyfriend who's not quite her type? A little pot party, or anything like that?"

Doug's normally ruddy face flushed deep red. "Don't bring Kathi into this," he snapped. "She has nothing to do with it. Kathi's life isn't being questioned here. My record is all that counts!"

Harry sighed. He knew he'd better back off a little. Doug was pretty sensitive when it came to Kathi and Vivian.

"I'm sorry, boss," Harry said to placate his angry employer. "You know Keith Baxter fights dirty. I just need to get the jump on him. If there's anything about Kathi that he might use, I'd better know it now."

Doug sighed. Harry probed so deeply into his private life that sometimes he felt like he was on trial. He knew that was why Harry was so good, but it still irritated him, even though Harry had given him plenty of warning.

Doug remembered their first interview. He, as nervous as the first time he'd accepted a case, and Harry, hard-bitten and inscrutable.

"Yeah. I'll take it," Harry muttered, squinting intently at Doug. "I'm warning you though. If I'm your campaign manager, I'm going to be even closer than

your conscience. If you're not going to level with me on everything, you'd better find someone else right now."

Of course, Doug had hired Harry. Harry Adams was a winner. He'd never handled a candidate who didn't make it. Harry was right though. He was closer to Doug than his own conscience. Sometimes Doug felt as if Harry knew everything about him. He wouldn't be surprised if Harry knew precisely what he'd had for breakfast this morning and exactly how many minutes it had taken him to shave.

Doug shifted a bit in his chair. This kind of thinking was only irritating him further, but he managed to smile pleasantly, with great effort.

"I really don't think there's anything about Kathi that Baxter could use," Doug said haltingly. "I hate to admit it, Harry, but Kathi and I haven't been too close ever since she moved to Berkeley. I know she'd tell me if she got into any trouble though." He flashed Harry a searching glance. "I'm sure you've found out everything about Kathi's life, Harry. I hear that your men are remarkably thorough. Maybe *you'd* better tell *me* about my daughter. What's she doing lately, Harry? Anything I should worry about?"

Harry flushed. Doug's words were partially teasing, but there was an undercurrent of sharpness that made him wince. He thought about the reports that had come in on Kathi Ellison. She was still registered as living in the dorm, but Harry's investigator had discovered that she'd moved most of her things into a third-floor apartment a mile from campus. The apartment was rented in a boy's name, David Carter, a psychology major at the college. So far, Harry didn't think there was anything to worry about. There was nothing wrong with having a little fun as long as Kathi was discreet about it. He could always run up there and talk to her if it looked like she was getting careless.

Of course, Harry had immediately ordered reports on David Carter. They were favorable to Harry's way of thinking. He came from a good family, mother and father retired—she a former teacher, and he, an Army Corps engineer. No brothers or sisters. David's scholastic record was excellent. He'd been on the dean's list for three consecutive semesters, and he was up for some sort of graduate fellowship next year. He was active in the honor society on campus, and he had several recommendations from his instructors that were downright complimentary. At least Kathi had chosen a nice guy to shack up with. As long as the two kids were careful, Harry didn't anticipate any problems from that quarter. It would bear watching, though, and Harry intended to do exactly that.

Harry looked up to see Doug watching him expectantly, then he remembered Doug's question. He bet he could tell a few things about Kathi that Doug didn't know, although there would be no sense in mentioning anything about Kathi's new living arrangements to her father. From the irritated expression on Doug's face, it wouldn't be wise to mention that now.

"Kathi's fine," Harry muttered, turning on his heel and marching back toward his temporary office in Doug's suite. He stopped in the doorway and rubbed his chin thoughtfully. His stomach was rumbling.

"Are you going out for lunch or having something sent up?"

"How about a corned beef on rye?" Doug suggested, knowing that Harry hated his favorite choice in sandwiches.

"Sounds fine," Harry mumbled absently. "Order me one too, will you? I've got some calls to make."

Doug chuckled as the door to Harry's office closed. His good humor restored, he called in the order for one corned beef and one ham and cheese. Then he leaned back in his chair and clasped his hands behind his head, his eyes resting on the photograph of Vivian displayed prominently on his desk.

Vivian had objected when Harry demanded she pose for an office picture.

"That's trite, Harry," Vivian laughed. "I thought the only men who had pictures of their wives on their desks were the ones going around pinching secretaries and taking dips in the office pool."

Doug remembered Harry's grin as he had nodded in agreement.

"That may be true for executives," Harry conceded. "This is different. The press will pick up on your picture like hotcakes. Just go do it, will you, doll?"

Harry had been right, as usual. Now Doug was known as a family man to any reporter who had been allowed in his office. Harry knew his business.

Doug stared at the portrait critically. It was damn good. The photographer had picked up the highlights in Vivian's rich brown hair, and her deep green eyes sparkled. Vivian was a remarkable woman. She hadn't aged at all. She was every bit as beautiful as she'd been when she walked into his small law office in

Little Falls and applied for the job as his secretary. That was over twenty years ago and, yet, Vivian appeared unchanged. A few more lines on her face perhaps, and a streak of gray in her hair that made her mutter to herself in front of her dressing table, but Doug thought the slight signs of her aging had made her look more sophisticated. Obviously, other women thought so too.

Doug's mouth turned up in an amused grin as he remembered Vivian's best friend, Mary, appearing one day with a streak of gray in her hair, carefully applied by her beautician in an attempt to copy Vivian. As the wife of a politician, Vivian was now considered a trendsetter. Doug supposed that half the women in Los Angeles would streak their hair when Vivian was the newly elected senator's wife.

Thinking about Vivian made Doug reach impulsively for the phone. He could call her and see how things were on the home front. No . . . she probably wasn't home. Vivian was quite popular at bridge games and women's teas. He wouldn't disturb her now. Even if she were at home, she undoubtedly would be getting ready for one of her afternoon groups.

Doug's eyes turned back to the picture again, and he felt a slight twinge of uneasiness. Vivian had been pushing herself awfully hard lately, making appearances at women's groups all over California. She had thrown herself into the campaign, making speeches and holding meetings of her own to help the effort. Vivian had always been interested in politics in the past, but it had taken Doug a long while to decide to take a stab at it. The moment he'd mentioned that he was thinking about running for the senate, she'd gathered information like a squirrel gathering nuts for the winter, signed up volunteers among her circle of friends, and spearheaded the whole campaign aimed toward women voters. Because of Vivian's efforts, his popularity with women had blossomed and grown to the point where Keith Baxter didn't even have a chance at the women's vote.

The afternoon meetings and late-night campaign planning had taken their toll, though, and Sally had reported that Vivian was tired and out of sorts lately, surviving on a few hours' sleep and running on her store of nervous energy. Doug would have been worried if Sally had been alarmed. She knew Vivian better than anyone else. Sally was practically a member of the family, the first and only housekeeper they'd ever hired. It was a comfort to Doug, having someone in the house he could rely on to give an accurate report of Vivian's state of health. He knew what trouble it could cause if a busy politician's wife got lonely and depressed. And Lord knew he wasn't home enough to really be much of a husband to Vivian in the past few months. Many a candidate's wife had ended up taking tranquilizers or drinking to fill up the lonely hours when her husband was out of town campaigning. He was lucky that Vivian had more sense than that. She was a strong woman, perfectly capable of controlling her emotions without any sort of crutch. She'd been a brick when he'd been in trouble. Without Vivian's good sense, he might have made some disastrous mistakes. At least he had a wife who would could be calm and rational during a crisis. No, there was absolutely no reason to worry about Vivian. She could handle anything that came up, probably better than he could.

Doug leaned back and closed his eyes. He was exhausted today, probably because of the late meeting last night. First, there had been the flight to Sacramento and the speech there, and then the red-eye special back to Los Angeles and a windup in the campaign headquarters. No wonder he was borrowing trouble, thinking about all the things that could go wrong and make him lose the election. He was just too tired to think straight.

The swivel chair creaked softly as Doug leaned back a little farther. God, he was tired. It would be so nice to take a day off and spend some time in the mountains with Vivian. They could drive up to Arrowhead and do a little skiing like they used to do. But there just wasn't any time now, not with the election only three weeks away. The instant he'd got involved with politics, he'd started waving his leisure hours good-bye. At times like this, Doug felt as if he were dealing away his time—time for a comment here . . . a handshake there . . . an interview for this person . . . a meeting with that person. There was no time left for the people he loved more than anyone else in the world, Vivian and Kathi. To succeed in political circles he had to give up something, the same as in everything else. In the city you had to give up nature, in a marriage you had to give up privacy, and in politics you had to give up little pieces of yourself, carefully doled out in meetings and speeches, making your life smaller with each passing encounter. It was almost like bleeding, and Doug sometimes wondered what would happen when he was bled dry.

"Jesus!" Doug groaned, slamming his hand against the side of his head to clear his muddled thoughts. This kind of thinking was ridiculous. He didn't have one reason for being depressed. Jake Roman had promised his support, and everything was going like clockwork, even if Harry did get his goat sometimes with his infernal questions about Kathi and Vivian and his past.

Doug shook his head like a dog coming in from the rain. He stretched his neck from side to side and then around in a circle to force his tight muscles to relax.

"Everything's going like clockwork," he murmured, as if hearing the words spoken could make him believe that they were true. Then he propped his elbow on the desk, took a deep breath, and reached for the speech he was scheduled to make that night.

CHAPTER 5

Kathi waited until David left the apartment before she picked up the phone. She called home at least once a week, and Vivian would worry if she didn't call. Today, there was another reason for Kathi's call too—some information she had to get for the doctor at the health service. It was going to be difficult, asking questions without giving Vivian cause to worry about her, but the doctor had been very definite about needing the answers to his questions. Kathi wasn't sure how she was going to bring the subject up. Vivian always seemed to get upset when she asked about the accident, but she had to know how long she had been in the coma after the concussion. Dr. Jackson seemed to think it might have some bearing on her terrible headaches.

Kathi's palms began to perspire as she dialed the familiar number. She wished that she didn't have to bother Vivian at such a critical time, but it couldn't be helped. Dr. Jackson at the health center was waiting for the information. This was all getting so complicated, that Kathi wished she had never mentioned the headaches and nightmares to David. They might have gone away all by themselves. It was nothing more than strain. David and the doctor were just getting alarmed over nothing.

The phone call came in the middle of the bridge game. Sally knew that Mrs. Ellison didn't want to be disturbed, but this call was an exception. She hurried across the solarium with surprising grace for such a big woman. Sally never wasted any time when the message was from Miss Kathi.

Vivian looked up as Sally bustled to her side. Sally spoke softly and Vivian nodded and then stood up.

"Sorry, girls," she apologized. "I have to take a phone call."

She motioned to Rita, who was sitting out. "Why don't you take my hand, Rita? I don't know how long this is going to take."

Rita DuPont settled into Vivian's chair, and Vivian winked at Mary Lewis, her partner. She knew that Mary hated to play with Rita, but it couldn't be helped. Sally had said that Kathi sounded upset.

Vivian sighed as she walked toward the study to take the call. It was probably something simple. Sally tended to exaggerate Kathi's moods, always worrying about her "little lamb." She clasped her hands nervously every time Kathi called, almost as if she expected something terrible to happen. Of course, it never did. Vivian found it hard to imagine that Kathi was in any trouble now; she had never been in a speck of trouble in her whole life. She was a model child, too perfect, Vivian sometimes thought. It made Vivian's occasional flash of temper seem black and ugly in comparison with Kathi's perfect emotional balance.

Vivian laughed to herself as she crossed the expensively decorated room. She and Doug should feel proud of raising a daughter who stayed out of trouble. Very few of their friends were so lucky. She was always hearing gossip about teenage pregnancies and drug problems. Hardly a day passed that she didn't hear about this son or that daughter who had got into some sort of trouble. Thank God, Kathi had turned out so well.

Vivian sighed. She really should be content, but there was something eerie about raising a perfect child. She almost hoped that Kathi had done some minor thing, perhaps cut a class or got a bad grade. It would help to know that her stepdaughter was less than perfect. Perhaps Kathi would seem more normal if she got into a little scrape once in a while.

"Hello, darling," Vivian said as she picked up the phone. She listened for a moment, and then she felt her legs growing weak. She slumped down in the Chippendale chair next to the phone and lit a cigarette. This time Sally had been right. Kathi did sound upset.

"You haven't been studying too hard, have you, dear?" Vivian asked, noticing that her hands were shaking. Her face felt flushed and then cold. "You sound a little nervous."

"I'm fine, Vivian," Kathi's voice answered, sounding falsely bright to Vivian's discerning ear. "I . . . I just called to ask you a question. You've heard me talk about my roommate, Bev—"

"Yes, of course, dear."

"Well . . . her sister had an accident, and she's been in a coma for a couple of days. I told Bev that I'd been in an accident too, when I was little. Bev wondered how long I'd been in the coma before I came out of it."

"Just let me think for a moment, dear," Vivian responded, hoping that her voice sounded appropriately calm. Her mind was spinning at this unexpected question. She didn't even want to think about Kathi's accident, much less discuss it with her, but she had to answer.

"I believe it was four days, dear," Vivian finally replied. "Yes . . . four days. Is Bev terribly upset about her sister?"

"Oh, yes!" Kathi answered quickly. "You know, it's really strange about that accident, Vivian. I know I was four years old, but for a long while I couldn't remember it at all."

Vivian took a deep breath. "The doctors explained it to us at the time, darling," Vivian replied, forcing herself to stay calm. "You were severely traumatized. It's not unusual to block out memories that are painful. But you say you remember more now?"

Vivian heard her voice rise sharply but she couldn't help it. She gripped the receiver tightly, waiting for Kathi's answer.

"Yes, a little more," Kathi admitted. "I can remember

lying in the hospital, and just the other night I remembered the rescuers finding me."

Vivian tried to think of something else to say, but her mind didn't seem to be working. Suppose Kathy remembered more?

"That's really all I called about," Kathi continued. "Tell Dad I'm rooting for him, and I read the San Francisco papers every day. He's getting good publicity up here. The polls today had him leading with seventy-one percent of the vote."

"Wonderful, dear!" Vivian said, trying to concentrate on what Kathi was saying. Did she dare ask any more about Kathi's memory? Or should she leave well enough alone and pray that Kathi didn't remember any more?

"I'm sorry I got you away from your bridge game, but Sally insisted," Kathi went on. "I know it was a silly thing to call about, but Bev was really upset, so I promised I'd ask. I'm sure her sister's going to be all right."

"Call and let me know, dear," Vivian insisted. "You know you can call anytime at all, and your father and I are always glad to hear from you."

Another few moments and Vivian replaced the phone in the cradle almost as if she were holding a bomb. She finished her cigarette in quick, nervous puffs before she even thought of attempting to get up from the chair. What if Kathi did remember? The doctors had been so sure that her memory would never return, but now Kathi claimed that she had recalled the rescuers and her recovery in the hospital. My God! What if Kathi remembered everything?

How could they possibly explain? And the worst thing was, there wasn't a damn thing they could do to stop Kathi from remembering.

Vivian ground out her cigarette savagely as all her bottled-up fear turned to anger. Why now? For the first time in her life she had started to relax, to live without the awful fear of discovery, and now it was back again, worse than ever. And coupled with the last tense weeks of the campaign, it was more than Vivian could bear. She'd have to call off the rest of the bridge game now. She simply couldn't cope with a bunch of silly, chattering women after Kathi's call.

"Damn!" Vivian spat out the word forcefully. Somehow, she had to get hold of herself and go back in there to face her guests, to act as if nothing extraordinary had occurred, just a little complication that meant calling off the game early. She couldn't let her friends know that anything was wrong. She had to play the part of a winning candidate's wife while she waited for the other shoe to drop, knowing that her whole life would be changed if Kathi remembered just a little bit more.

It was a full five minutes before Vivian regained her composure. A satirical smile crossed her face. And she had been thinking that Kathi was too perfect! It was ironic, but Vivian didn't really appreciate that kind of satirical, cosmic humor. She could have lived quite comfortably with Kathi's perfection, if only she'd known the alternative.

Vivian's hand touched the phone again. Doug—should she call him? He could comfort her, tell her not to worry, that everything would be all right. But what about him? Wouldn't that just add another worry to his growing concern? No, this wasn't the time to tell him. For all she knew, this might frighten Doug enough to make him back out of the race. And then all of her work would have been for nothing. There was no sense upsetting Doug unless Kathi remembered more about the accident. She would pretend that everything was normal if he asked about Kathi.

Vivian sighed deeply. At times she felt so much stronger than Doug, although she'd never admit it to him. He had problems of his own right now. There was the campaign and the heavy schedule of speeches that Harry had arranged. She could cope with this by herself if she had to, and Vivian knew she had to. Her instinct to protect Doug was fierce—almost maternal—at times like this. Doug had a boyish quality that he had shown only to Vivian, and it was that innocence which she had to protect now. To everyone else he was strong and powerful, but she knew what depths of anxiety he could suffer when things were not going well, how he turned to her for strength. She would be his rock. She would handle this alone.

Resolutely, Vivian rejoined the group and made her announcement. If any of her friends were upset at the abrupt termination of the bridge game, they didn't show it. Playing bridge with Vivian Ellison was a definite advantage socially, and any disappointment they felt at having the afternoon end prematurely was carefully masked. Of course they understood. No one would dream of asking Vivian what it was that had come up to end the game so suddenly. That would have been tactless; Vivian's friends might be catty and outspoken, but they were never tactless.

After the girls had gone, Vivian hurried upstairs and shut the bedroom door behind her. She had told Sally that she felt another migraine coming on, and that seemed to satisfy the elderly housekeeper. There was a tightening in the back of her neck, and she did feel a trifle dizzy. It would be wise to try to rest a little and get her thoughts together, if that were possible. Doug wasn't coming home until late, and Sally had instructions to serve him a hot meal when he came in. Everything was arranged. Now all that remained was to get herself under perfect control.

Vivian gave one glance at the bed and went straight to her dresser, fumbling under the gloves and scarves to find her bottle of pills. She sighed, hating to take them. They made her light-headed and sleepy, but she needed something to force her to relax. Nothing else would work at a time like this.

A moment later she was in the connecting bathroom, running a glass of water. Her hand was shaking so hard, that two of the pills dropped into the deep pile of the bathroom carpet. She searched for them frantically, patting the rug with her hands and combing her fingers through the thick pile. If Sally found them, she'd know something was wrong, and she would tell Doug. He mustn't guess that there was anything bothering her. It was up to her to protect him.

Her trembling fingers finally located the pills, and she washed them both down with a glass of water. With the help of the tranquilizers, she'd be asleep by the time Doug got home, and he would assume that she was tired from the afternoon's entertainment.

Vivian stretched out on the white satin bedspread and closed her eyes. There was a feeling of dread in the pit of her stomach, and there was no way she could not think about it. The harder she tried to dwell on something else, the faster her mind returned to the telephone conversation, reviewing every word in detail, hearing every nuance of meaning behind the carefully chosen phrases. Kathi's slight return of memory was a premonition of something worse to come. Fear prickled at the base of her spine.

How much would Kathi remember? She had been very young, yet some people could recall things that had happened when they were two or three years old.

There was a metallic taste of fear in Vivian's mouth. Perhaps they had made a mistake. She and Doug should have said something to Kathi earlier. Before, when there was still time, they should have prepared her. Now it was too late. It was over, and to make a clean breast of it now might only hurt Doug's political career.

The prestige of being a senator's wife . . . Vivian had to admit that her social goal played an important part in her desire for Doug's success. To come up from the life of a secretary and achieve the prestige of being a senator's wife had been in the back of Vivian's mind ever since she and Doug had first discussed his going into politics. She had pushed him; it was true. But her own social position wasn't all of it. Her husband's mattered too; his goals matched her own, and Doug's hopes and aspirations were hers. Both of them wanted that seat in the Senate, and they would get it. Vivian would do everything in her power to see that Doug won the election. Nothing could spoil her plans now.

Vivian took a deep breath and tried to concentrate on something peaceful. She attempted to meditate and think of nothing, setting her mind free like her yoga teacher had recommended. The curtains of time swung back, and her mind floated in a lovely green garden filled with her favorite flowers and trees. There were no palm trees or succulents in her garden, none of the famed California plants that turned pale green in the winter, making California's claim of "green all year long" a fact. These plants were different, only flowering and green when the weather warmed from frosty to humid. She was back in Minnesota again, when she had first met Doug, and the lilacs were in bloom.

Twenty years old and in love with a married man, she was still Vivian Sundquist, Doug's legal secretary. It was a sunny morning in late May, and she was living at home with her mother. Vivian snapped the flower-laden branches off the gnarled lilac trees in her mother's backyard. They were white and pale pink and lovely purple, with a smell so sweet. She carried them to the office, and put them in a vase on her desk so Doug could smell them too.

The vase was clear blue glass and beautiful. It curved upward, with fluted edges, and held the flowers proudly. It was the color of his eyes when he had kissed her that first time so long ago, and she had run back to her mother's house in confusion, wondering whether she should quit her job and move to Minneapolis, just to get away from him. But she had stayed, because to leave was to condemn herself forever to a life without him. It was wrong to love him so desperately, the handsome young lawyer with a wife and daughter, but for Vivian Sundquist, he was the man of her dreams. He was a man who would go someplace in the world, and if things went right, he would take her with him.

Then they were in his office, the door carefully closed. They had to be discreet, for it wouldn't do to have Roma find out about them. Doug's law career was just beginning, and a scandal would ruin it forever. There were weak moments, when Vivian wanted to plead with him to divorce Roma, to move to another town, another state, and start over with her as his wife. But there were important reasons why Doug couldn't do that, and Vivian knew them all. There was the money Roma's parents had left to her, the money that had been used to set up Doug's law practice and to feed and clothe them while he was gradually building up his clientele. There was Roma herself, weak and helpless, unable to cope with life after her parents had died.

Roma didn't care what Doug did; Vivian was convinced of that. But there was the child to consider—beautiful, bright little Kathi—the strongest link in the chain that kept Doug the prisoner of a loveless marriage. Roma had her expensive bottles of scotch to keep her company on the nights that Doug worked late at the office, so she would never find out about the passion that Vivian shared with Doug. Roma's own passion was in the bottom of a bottle, swimming deeply under all the amber liquid . . .

The door burst open. Roma was there, tugging a badly frightened child by the arm.

That was the last image Vivian saw before she dropped off into a soft dark place that had no memories.

CHAPTER 6

It was Tuesday morning, and Kathi glanced at her watch, walking a little faster as she neared the Liberal Arts Building. She was tired, more tired than she'd ever been in her life, and this exam was bound to be a tough one. With her purse clutched under her arm and her long blond hair flying in the wind, she broke into a run, hurrying the last hundred yards to the entrance of the building. She had been up all night studying—supposedly studying—although, in truth, she had been ready for today's test before the weekend. The studying had been an excuse to stay out on the living room couch, drinking coffee, and turning the pages of her books while David went to bed. After what she'd told him about her doctor's appointment, she couldn't risk having another nightmare. It was better to keep herself awake with coffee and nap on the couch later. Then, if she did have another nightmare, David wouldn't witness it. He'd believed her when she claimed she had told the doctor everything, but Kathi had deliberately withheld some information from Dr. Jackson. How could she have confessed what she'd learned only days ago? That she'd had the headaches and nightmares immediately following their lovemaking. There was no way Kathi was going to mention that to any doctor. She was too afraid Dr. Jackson would advise her to see a psychiatrist. The newspapers would love to find out about that and blow it all out of proportion, putting the skids on her father's campaign.

Kathi glanced at her watch and started to run faster, racing toward the building. Her head was whirling almost as fast as the bright, brittle leaves swirling around her feet. She had to stop thinking about David and concentrate on her upcoming exam. There wasn't anything she could do about lying to David anyway. Or about lying to the doctor.

Kathi was panting as she raced up the steps and entered the building. It was warm inside, and she could feel the dampness on her neck as she took her seat in the classroom and slipped out of her fall coat.

It was unseasonably cold for the middle of October. She'd have to stop at the dorm soon and pick up the rest of her winter clothes before Bev left for break week. Then she'd be moved out—lock, stock, and baggage—but Bev would cover for her. It was only until after the election anyway. After that, she could change her mailing address, and she might even tell her dad and Vivian, if the time seemed right. Depending on how the pregnancy test came out, perhaps she and David would be married right after the election.

It didn't matter to her, but it would matter to her parents. She had to think of her dad's career, and Vivian. She owed it to them. They'd both been marvelous when she was growing up, giving her everything she'd needed and supporting her with love and concern. She certainly wouldn't dream of telling them anything about the nightmares. She could remember how upset they'd got when she used to have nightmares as a child. This was something she had to keep to herself.

"Write as rapidly as you can," Dr. Thompson announced, picking up the test papers from his desk and giving the class a stern glare. He looked like a crane, tall and thin, dressed in a dark suit, peering at their expectant faces over the rims of his wire-framed glasses.

Then his eyes met Kathi's, and he gave a flicker of a smile. She was his best student, eagerly responding in class, even to the most difficult questions. She would do well on this midterm. His smile broadened in encouragement as he saw Kathi looking at him. She was one student who was always attentive, although she looked a little dazed this morning, probably exhausted, but that was only natural for midterm week. He wished he could have told her not to study too hard. Her face was white, and there were dark circles under her eyes. These college kids never did get enough sleep.

"You may begin as soon as you get your test paper," Dr. Thompson said, his eyes wandering back to Kathi's face again. "I doubt that you'll have very much trouble with this particular question. We've discussed it in class on several occasions, and I expect a high percentage of brilliant papers."

There was a slight titter from the class, and Kathi's lips curved in a smile as she glanced at her exam. The old dear! She might have known it! He'd stressed Steinbeck heavily in the last few class meetings.

Analyze The Pearl *in terms of various levels of meaning (ecological, sociological, mythological, symbolic).*

Kathi read the question carefully and opened her blue book, staring down at the blank, lined paper. This should be a snap for her, but somehow she couldn't seem to start writing. English literature was Kathi's major, and she had read and reread *The Pearl* in preparation for this midterm, yet the words didn't flow from her pen as they usually did. She couldn't seem to concentrate on the question in front of her at all. Something was blocking her, keeping her pen motionless as her mind spun helplessly.

With a sigh of exasperation, Kathi closed her eyes. She would try the little trick David had taught her. She would relax and let the images come into her mind. That would jog her memory, so she could answer the question.

She imagined Kino and Juana as they awoke at dawn. Juana was rising to tend the fire, making corncakes for Kino. Evil . . . evil was entering the simple dwelling in the form of a scorpion, moving down the rope that supported the baby's hammock. Evil that would change their lives . . .

"No! I want Mommy and Daddy!"

"Don't cry, Sheri Bear. It's only a joke. They're only playing a joke on everyone. It's not Mommy and Daddy in those big boxes. They put dolls in the boxes to fool everyone. Mommy and Daddy are working on a secret, and they'll be back just as soon as they can."

"Dolls . . . yes. But where are they? Where are Mommy and Daddy? Are they really down in the

ground with the other dead people the way Auntie said?"

"No, they're far away, just like I told you. Now you have to keep this secret I told you, Sheri Bear, the secret about Mommy and Daddy and the big dolls. Mommy and Daddy will be back soon, and then they'll surprise everyone except you, because you know. You'll have to act surprised, because everyone else is fooled. Auntie and Uncle, and even Baver, are fooled by the big dolls."

"I could tell Baver. Then he wouldn't cry so much. Can I tell Baver about Mommy and Daddy's secret?"

"Oh, no . . . you can't do that. Baver's too little to keep a secret, and girls keep secrets better than boys anyway. If Baver knew the secret, he'd tell Auntie, and she'd make me go away. Then I couldn't bring messages from Mommy and Daddy anymore. Then you'd be all alone, and you don't want to be all alone, do you?"

"Miss Ellison? Miss Ellison? Are you all right?"

Kathi looked up and blinked in confusion. How long had she been sitting like this? Professor Thompson was standing over her with a concerned expression on his kindly face.

"Oh, Dr. Thompson! Yes . . . er . . . I'm fine," she answered, her cheeks growing hot with embarrassment. "I . . . I was just thinking about the question."

"Well, don't think quite so hard, Miss Ellison," Dr. Thompson chuckled, pointing down at her blank test book. "Half of your allotted time is up, and you haven't written a single word, except your name, of course."

The tall, stoop-shouldered professor bent over

farther and stared at the name on Kathi's blue book. "What's this?" He frowned. "Sheri Walker?"

"Oh!" For a moment Kathi's mind was totally blank, swimming with terror. When had she written that? In those wobbly block letters! How could she ever explain this to Professor Thompson?

"You forgot to get a blue book for the exam, so you had to borrow one from this girl, Sheri Walker, right?" Professor Thompson guessed, winking at Kathi. "Well, that's all right, Miss Ellison. Just cross out her name and put in your own. And you'd better start writing, or you'll never finish. I expect an A paper from you, my dear."

The gaunt, silver-haired instructor took several steps toward his desk at the front of the room and then turned abruptly and walked back to Kathi's desk.

"Your friend has atrocious penmanship!" he whispered, patting her on the shoulder. "Simply atrocious!"

Kathi nodded, not trusting herself to speak. She bent over the exam and reread the question, breathing a sigh of relief as Professor Thompson walked away from her and proceeded straight up to the podium this time, taking his seat behind the desk. What had got into her? She'd been daydreaming, and now only half the time remained to answer Dr. Thompson's involved question. Daydreaming, that was all it was.

But even as Kathi began to write in her clear, even hand, she knew that it hadn't been a simple daydream. The voices she'd heard were too frighteningly real to be a daydream. Right after this exam was over, she was going to go home and take a nap. She never should have stayed up all night last night.

For a moment, Kathi considered calling Vivian

again. Her stepmother might be able to clear up the whole mystery. But if she started asking questions of Vivian, she'd have to tell her about the nightmares and headaches. Then Vivian would worry about her, and that wouldn't do at all. Dad and Vivian had so much to worry about with the election.

Kathi wrote automatically, but her mind was not on her exam. The voices she had just heard were the same voices in her nightmares, and now she was beginning to remember what they said. She wasn't quite sure whether the remembering was a good sign or a bad sign, but things just couldn't go on this way. She simply had to find out who Sheri Walker was, but there didn't seem to be anyone to ask.

CHAPTER 7

Kathi gripped her hands tightly in her lap and made a conscious effort to listen to Rich Davies's latest joke. Her mind felt like fuzzy, gray cotton, and it was hard to make sense out of anything that was happening. They were in Rich's living room—about twenty of them—weary from their battle with midterm exams, and the wine was making everyone gay and loud. She knew she should be enjoying this party. The pressure of exams was off now, and there should be a release of tension. But instead of feeling carefree like everyone else, Kathi felt like an outsider, listening to the bursts of laughter and wishing that she were somewhere else . . . anywhere where she could be alone and think.

She had called the health center this morning, right after David left for one of his exams. She hadn't actually been surprised when Dr. Jackson told her the test was positive. In fact, she had been very calm and rational over the phone, promising the doctor that she'd get in touch with the women's group right after the break. Actually, Kathi wasn't planning on calling the hot-line number or setting up an appointment at all. For now, she would keep her pregnancy a secret, and when the time was right she would tell David. There'd be no danger of any leak of information from the doctor. He didn't even know her real name.

It was only now, in the midst of the crowd, that panic started to set in. She had responsibilities now, responsibilities that scared her. She had to make sure she got plenty of rest and ate the right foods. She had to plan out her life to make a good home for David's child. In the middle of this laughing, carefree college group, Kathi felt like an impostor.

David had urged her to come to the party, telling her that getting away from it all and enjoying an evening with friends would do her good. He went to parties so seldom that she couldn't refuse him. She was almost obligated to go, no matter how tired and upset she was. She had hoped that everyone else's gay mood would be contagious . . . at least, that had been her hope when she'd first entered the room with David. Now she knew better. The antics of the other students were making her even more depressed. As the minutes ticked by, she was feeling more and more removed from them, and sinking deeper and deeper into herself.

The burst of laughter that greeted the punch line of Rich's joke almost made Kathi wince. She forced a laugh that sounded weak even to her own ears, and looked around desperately for David. The stale air in the smoke-filled room was about to choke her, and she could feel the perspiration break out on her neck and trickle down between her breasts. They'd been here an hour already, and Kathi was more than ready to leave.

David was over near the kitchen doorway talking to a slim redhead in tight jeans, someone from his abnormal-psych class. Kathi felt an unreasonable stab of jealousy, but she forced herself to relax and act unconcerned. She couldn't ask him to leave now; everyone would think she was jealous. She'd have to wait until he finished his conversation.

Kathi picked up her wine and sipped at it, watching David out of the corner of her eye. He looked like he was having such a good time. He and his friend were gesturing wildly and laughing now, and tears of guilt sprang to Kathi's eyes as she saw how relaxed and happy he was with the other girl. She hadn't been very good company for him lately, with her withdrawn moods and her frightening nightmares. If she wanted to keep him happy, she'd better start acting more like her old self again. David wouldn't be content with someone who was frightened and self-absorbed when there were so many less complicated and more exciting women to choose from.

I'll die if I lose him. I've got to smile and laugh even if I'm not having a good time. He can't guess how desperate and afraid I feel, or it'll change our whole relationship, and then he'll want out. I couldn't stand to lose him like I lost—who? Who? What am I thinking? I haven't lost anyone before!

Kathi blinked and looked at David again. Now his head was tipped back and he was laughing again at something his friend had said. His hand moved up to stroke his beard, a gesture that made him look thoughtful, intense. He was so damned attractive that other girls were always throwing themselves at him, but so far, he hadn't ever looked twice at them. Would he decide that one of those beautiful, smiling girls was more fun than she was? Would he leave her if she told him the depth of her fears?

"He's gone! He's gone! Everyone's gone and now there's nobody!"

"I'm still here, Sheri Bear. You can't see me, but I'm here. I'll always be here, anytime you want me."

Kathi gripped her wineglass so hard she was almost afraid it would shatter. She knew that if she sat still for another second, she'd scream right out loud. She reached over and found her purse, rummaging through it frantically. There they were, the aspirins she carried with her everywhere now. Three with the glass of wine. That ought to help. Just the act of doing something helped a lot, even a small thing like digging through her purse. The conversation with Vivian had upset her . . . that was all it was. Talking about the accident seemed . . . dangerous somehow. It gave her a sick feeling in the pit of her stomach. And then finding out that she really was pregnant added another worry to everything else that was wrong. If only she could have asked Vivian who Sheri Walker was, there might have been some simple explanation. But she couldn't call Vivian again and ask more questions. If she did, she was bound to let something slip. There would be some hint of fear in her voice, she knew, and Vivian was very perceptive. She couldn't let Vivian know that she was upset. God, there were so many people she had to protect. She couldn't tell David, or he would worry about her. She couldn't tell Vivian or her father, or they'd worry. She couldn't tell *anyone*.

"You're all through, aren't you, Kathi?" one of the girls from the dorm asked, plunking down on the sagging couch. "How does it feel to be finished? I've still got two exams to go, one tomorrow and one Friday morning."

"I . . . I'm glad it's all over," Kathi replied, fixing a smile on her face. Talking should help. At least she couldn't let her mind wander if she had to concentrate on holding a conversation. "I thought you were dropping out this semester, Carol. Bev said you were leaving school to get married."

Carol gave a shrug of her shapely shoulders and lifted her eyebrows. "I thought better of it." She grinned. "With all the great men around here, it'd be a waste of time to tie myself down to one. How about you, Kathi? Are you and David planning anything permanent?"

Kathi's face turned pink. Her cheeks felt fiery, and she had the insane urge to blurt out everything to Carol, the biggest gossip in the dorm. She could say, "No, I'm going to have the baby, and then we'll see if we want to get married." The news would be all over school within five minutes.

"No—" Kathi answered, glancing over at David, who was still deep in conversation with the redheaded woman. "Nothing permanent, Carol, at least not yet. I never make any important decisions during midterm week."

"Good policy." Carol grinned and reached out for

the bowl of pretzels on the table. "I never make any decisions during midterm week either. I'm not even going to decide who to sleep with tonight. I figure I'll let them all fight over me, and the last one standing will have the privilege," she teased.

Kathi bit her lip to keep back her catty retort. From what she'd heard, it was a privilege quite a few of the men on campus had enjoyed and lived to tell about. What was the matter with her tonight, anyway? She had no reason to be rude. Carol was just trying to be friendly.

Kathi was still trying to think of something to say, when David broke away from his conversation and began to push through the crowd toward her.

"Oh, here comes David," Kathi said quickly, jumping to her feet. "I guess it's time to go. See you around, Carol."

She moved away from the couch and hurried to meet David, maneuvering around groups of students in her way. With every closing step, she could feel the relief grow and the smile on her face get wider and wider. David was so handsome, with his wheat-colored hair and his full beard. She remembered how she'd teased him when he started growing it, accusing him of trying to look like Papa Freud. If there was one word in the English language to describe David, it would have to be *rugged*. He always looked just as if he'd come in from chopping down a tree in the forest. He had the healthy tan of an outdoorsman, and there was something about him that was . . . well . . . she guessed the word was *virile*. That was it. David looked virile.

"Hey, what's the big smile for?" David grinned back at her. "You look like you're half-loaded. Have you been hitting the wine, Kathi?"

"Nope!" Kathi protested, shaking her head and smiling even wider. Of course he looked virile. He ought to! But that was her secret . . . the unborn child, and Sheri Walker.

"Oh!" Kathi gasped, stumbling slightly and reaching out for David's arm to steady herself. "Could we go, David? It's awfully warm in here."

"Sure," David agreed instantly, casting an anxious glance. "Another headache, honey?"

"Well . . . just a little one," Kathi admitted, clenching her fists to keep herself from clutching her head with the pain. "It's really noisy in here. The lack of sleep must be catching up with me."

She barely managed to control herself as David called out his good-byes and made a path for them to the door. Then they were outside in the cold night air, and her head began to clear. Perhaps it had only been the stuffy room and the noise that bothered her. She was feeling much better now.

Her hand snuggled in David's pocket, they began to walk the six blocks to their apartment building. It was chilly and foggy, a combination that Kathi usually loved. All the ugliness of the old buildings was shrouded by the fog, and the streetlights shimmered softly in the thick night air like a Van Gogh painting. Tonight, though, the fog seemed to chill Kathi's very bones. It was concealing too much tonight, hiding something ominous, and Kathi felt uneasy, as if she were on the verge of discovering something unpleasant.

"Cold?" David asked, pulling her a little closer to him. "You're shivering. You should have worn more than a sweater tonight, hon. It's damn cold for October."

"I'll get my warm things from the dorm on Friday," Kathi promised, hurrying a little to keep pace with David's long strides. She could feel the dampness settle on her bare head, and it was hard to keep from shivering even more.

Kathi held her breath as David pulled her closer to his warm body. The night air never seemed to chill David. He loved the cold. But even though Kathi knew she should feel comforted by David's protective gesture, being this close to him made her uneasy.

For a long moment, there was no sound except the crunch of their footsteps on the carpet of fallen leaves. Then Kathi tensed as she heard the sound she had unknowingly been waiting for, the mournful wail of a train whistle as they neared the railroad crossing halfway to their apartment.

"We can beat it if we hurry," David said, pulling Kathi along faster. "Hurry up, Kathi. I don't want you to stand out here in the cold and wait for one of those long freight trains."

A current of fear ran so strongly through Kathi's slender body that she thought she was going to faint. "No!" she gasped, pulling back on David's arm. "No! We-we'll wait! It's not that cold! I . . . I don't want to try to beat the train, David . . . really!"

"Hey, it's all right," David said softly, stepping back and hugging her. "I didn't know you were afraid of trains. We'll just stand by the tracks and wait then. We can count the cars as they go by, how's that?"

"Uh . . . fine," Kathi agreed, forcing herself to keep up with David as he walked toward the tracks. She didn't want to go any farther, but something was pulling her closer and closer to the gleaming wet tracks. She shuddered violently. After the accident, when she was very young, she had been afraid of trains for a while. But she'd got over that years ago. So why, after all this time, did she suddenly feel so frightened at the sound of a train?

Kathi concentrated on the sidewalk, stepping over the cracks in the old cement with a sense of doom. *Step on a crack, break your mother's back*. But her mother was dead, killed long ago at a train crossing just like this one.

They were almost there now . . . almost at the gleaming strands that shone in her nightmares. Kathi's legs felt like wooden sticks. She could no longer feel the sidewalk under her feet, and she moved jerkily, like a windup toy, one step after another. No, she would not look up. She was afraid to look up, afraid to see the bright light piercing through the fog as the train approached. She could look down at her shoes and the ground, even shut her eyes, but there was no way of closing her ears against the rumbling forceful sound that grew louder and louder. The train was screaming at her . . . calling her like a siren's song . . .

"I'm scared! I want my mama! The train's going to hurt me and I'm scared!"

"It's all right. I'm right here with you, Sheri Bear. See? You don't have to cry. There's nothing that can hurt you. It's just an old train, and trains can't come

off the track. You can believe me, Sheri Bear. You can always believe everything the Tiger says."

Kathi looked up suddenly, trying to break the cord of fear that the voices stirred in her. It was Sheri Walker again, and someone else—someone called the Tiger—and the shrill voices were invading her mind until there was no place for her to think on her own anymore. How could she think when they were screaming at her over the sound of the train? Her eyes were fixed on David's face, praying silently that he would find a way to silence the voices, to jolt her out of the nightmare and let her be herself again.

Now her whole body was shaking, and she had the crazy impulse to move—to run toward the oncoming train. Her knees bent slightly, as ready as a runner for the sound of the starting gun, and her hand reached forward as if it were being pulled toward the track. The only thing holding her back was the taut line of David's gaze, the lifeline that held her eyes fixed with his.

"Don't look away, David," she pleaded silently. "Please don't look away. Keep me from doing it . . . keep me safe. Please, David! Keep me—"

But he was turning, not reading the anguished plea on her lips, the terror in her eyes. He was turning toward the tracks, an eager smile on his face. He liked trains. How could he like trains when . . . when what? There had been a reason in her mind, but now it was gone, the inside of her head as cold as marble, brittle marble that would shatter into a thousand pieces if another thought stabbed it.

Suddenly, she was burning up, a burst of adrenaline

releasing the frozen cubes of her feet, and then she was moving, jerking suddenly away to rush headlong toward the tracks.

"Kathi!" Strong arms grabbed her and she struggled fiercely. Didn't he know she had to do it? Couldn't he hear the voices screaming out at her, demanding that she meet the rushing tons of metal? Why was he pulling her back when she had to go?

"Kathi!" He was dragging her now, away from the beckoning silver metal. She could feel her fists beating at his chest, but it was like trying to move a mountain. He had her trapped.

Now he was turning to look at her, staring at her with an astonished expression on his face, and she read the fear in his eyes. His whole face looked different . . . a face she'd never seen before. His mouth was moving, saying something she couldn't hear over the relentless voices in her head.

"Kathi!" All at once, David's frantic cry penetrated her mind. The train was gone. The invisible force had disappeared. She could hear him again.

"Kathi! What is it, Kathi? Tell me, baby. Tell me!"

But her mind was a blank. If she could only find the words to tell him about the stabbing, chilling horror that had seized her. But she was powerless against it, and there were no words for this . . . no words at all that anyone could understand.

Suddenly, it was cold, bone cold, the cold of death and icy glaciers glimmering around her. The voices were gone, and there was nothing in their place. An emptiness, that was all. How long had she been standing there, shivering with this terrible cold?

"Kathi!"

She heard the urgency in his voice, and her hand moved, inch by inch, to touch the bristly hair of his beard. The numbness was fading, but excruciatingly slowly. Would she ever be able to talk again?

"I-I'm all right." Her voice sounded dim and faraway, but an expression of relief washed over David's face. There was a current of warmth running down her fingers where she was touching his face, traveling to thaw the icy stillness of her mind. Now it was moving to her chest and she could breathe again . . . and down to her legs, trembling as they came alive. She drew a quick breath of relief and managed a shaky smile.

"I . . . I guess I never told you that I'm terrified of trains," she murmured, stumbling over the words. "I always have been, ever since the accident. We hit a train when I was four. My . . . my mother was killed. I should have said something before, but . . . but it never came up."

With each word she uttered, the numbness dissolved. His arms closed around her, and she accepted the lie for what it was, the only way she had of making him believe that everything was all right.

"Jesus! You were so scared you almost ran right out in front of the train!" David said, hugging her tightly. "Oh, honey . . . I wish you'd said something back there. No wonder you didn't want to try to beat the train! I never would have brought you this close if I'd known."

"I-it's all right now. I just wanted to see if I was still afraid," Kathi improvised. "I guess I am, hm? I'll never be an engineer on a train."

"Well! You sure had me scared for a minute!" David breathed. "Come on, you must be freezing. We'll go right home, and I'll make you a cup of hot chocolate."

With his arms still around her shaking body, David pulled Kathi forward and across the tracks. He'd never seen her so terrified before. She'd been so frightened that she'd run *toward* the train instead of away from it. Kathi's fear seemed way out of proportion to her explanation about the accident, but he wasn't going to ask her any more questions now. The only important thing was that it had happened again. She had left him, escaped to that dark frightening place of her nightmares—this time when she was wide awake—and there seemed to be nothing he could do to convince her to open up to him. Kathi was slipping away to a world within her own mind, and there was no way to hold her back unless she told him what was wrong. She was fighting him, struggling to make him think that everything was fine, but he knew better.

She had almost stopped shaking now. David tried to shield her slender body from the cold as they hurried toward the apartment. He wasn't going to say anything more about it to her tonight, but he planned to talk to his abnormal-psych professor tomorrow and get some advice. It was the only thing he could do without Kathi's cooperation. Ideally, he would have liked to talk Kathi into seeing Professor Kauffman herself, but she'd never agree to see a psychologist, not before the election. There was no point in even suggesting that. He'd talk to the professor right after his test tomorrow and take his advice. Then he and

Kathi would have a long talk. If Kathi didn't share her fears with someone, they'd only continue to grow, and she would slip away from him and be lost forever. That possibility was one David refused to even think about.

CHAPTER 8

She thought of it the moment she woke up. David was in the kitchen, making his coffee quietly so he wouldn't wake her. He always made much more noise when he tried to be quiet, and Kathi almost called out to him that she was awake, but quickly thought better of it. Let him leave, thinking she was still asleep. That way there wouldn't have to be any explanations. She could leave him a note and be back by tonight. It would only take an hour to fly down to Los Angeles and see Sally. Today was Thursday, Sally's day off, and if anyone knew about Sheri Walker, it would be Sally. She wished she had thought of it sooner.

It was difficult to lie quiet and immobile when she wanted to jump up and be off. Now that she knew what she had to do, she could scarcely contain herself. Sally would have all the answers, and then she would know.

Time crawled as David went through his morning ritual. There was the clatter of a spoon against the thick mug as he stirred his coffee, then a muffled exclamation as he burned his lip on the scalding liquid, which he did every morning. All was quiet for a few moments except for the rustling of the morning paper, and finally, his footsteps coming into the bedroom to gather his clothes.

Kathi shut her eyes and feigned sleep to the rattle of the hangers in the closet. Would he never finish dressing? She peeked out beneath her long eyelashes and saw David carrying his shoes, tiptoeing out of the bedroom. After what seemed like hours, the apartment door closed, and he was gone.

Kathi leaped out of bed and grabbed her robe, heading for the phone at a run. There was a flight in an hour. She could just make it if she hurried. She left a quickly scribbled note to David telling him that she was making a short trip to Los Angeles to pick up some things at her parents' house, and then she was off. For once, everything was going her way.

The taxi was prompt, a rarity in Berkeley, and the plane was on time. By noon, Kathi was in another taxi, heading toward the south side of Los Angeles and Sally's neat little house. Anxiously, she rang the bell.

"Why, Miss Kathi!" Sally gasped, her creased brown hand sweeping up to her throat. "What are you doing here? You look a little peaked, child. Does your mama know you're here?"

"No." Kathi smiled, hugging Sally's familiar full figure. "I came to see you, Sally. I think you can help me."

"Help you?" Sally questioned, pulling Kathi into the

small living room. "Whatever do you mean, Miss Kathi? You're not in some kind of trouble, are you, lamb?"

"No . . . well . . . I don't know," Kathi confessed, feeling better already. She could tell Sally. Sally was the one person who would understand.

Sally frowned, the creases in her mahogany forehead crinkling like finely carved wood. She put her comforting, heavy arm around Kathi's shoulders and led her to the couch.

"Sally . . . I've got to know something," Kathi blurted out. Suddenly, it was as if a dam had burst inside her. She couldn't keep it in anymore. "Please tell me the truth! Tell me who Sheri Walker is! I've just got to know, Sally . . . it's driving me crazy!"

"Why sure, honey," Sally soothed. "I always tell you the truth, child, but you're asking somethin' I don' know. I never knew anybody by that name. I never knew no Sheri Walker at all."

Deflated, Kathi sank back against the cushions of the couch. All the life seemed to go out of her, leaving her feeling boneless and tired. She had been so certain, so sure that Sally would know. Perhaps there wasn't any Sheri Walker. Perhaps it was all in her confused imagination.

"What's this all about?" Sally asked, still patting Kathi's nerveless fingers. "Why are you so all-fired set on knowing who that Sheri Walker is?"

"Do you remember when I used to have nightmares, Sally?" Kathi asked softly.

"I sure do, Miss Kathi! I swear you used to scare me out of a year's growth every time you had one of those spells! Why you'd be cryin' and carryin' on like your little heart would break, calling out for Mama and sayin' all sorts of stuff about trains and tigers and . . . and . . ."

Sally stopped with her mouth open. Then she sighed deeply and went on. "But that don' mean nothin', Miss Kathi. All little children have nightmares. That's just a part of growin' up."

"Wait," Kathi interrupted, staring intently at Sally's face. "You remembered something . . . I know you did! Tell me, Sally. You've got to tell me! What was it?"

The shrillness of Kathi's voice made Sally start to tremble. Her baby was all worked up over this. Sally just hoped it wasn't happening again. She'd thought it over a hundred times while Kathi was growing up, and she'd even tried to talk to Miss Vivian about it once, but all she'd got for her trouble was a sharp reminder never to mention it again. Her own mama used to say the spirits of the dead visited small children in their sleep. A child's mind was more open, but when a child like Miss Kathi grew up, she had to learn how to block out those spirits. But Sheri . . . there had been a Sheri once. Miss Kathi had had nightmares about Sheri. She remembered one night now, just as clear as if it were happening all over again. Was that what Miss Kathi wanted to know?

"Please, Sally!" Kathi was twisting her hands in her lap and her face was uncommonly white. There was nothing for Sally to do but tell her what she remembered.

"It was years past, lamb," Sally began, trying to make her voice sound soothing, the way she used to when Kathi awakened in the middle of the night, screaming and crying. "Years past, right after I started workin' for your mama and papa. You were havin' another nightmare, the screamin' kind, and I shook you but you didn't wake up . . . your eyes were open but you wasn't awake. Do you understand what I'm saying?"

Kathi nodded nervously. She understood only too well. It was the same thing that had been happening to her lately, that half-awake, half-asleep state. Now that the moment was here, Kathi had to bite her lip to keep from telling Sally that it had all been a mistake, that she didn't really want to know anything at all.

"You were sittin' up in bed with the covers twisted all around you, awake but not awake, and I tried to make you go back to sleep. I said, 'Go back to sleep, lamb . . . go back to sleep, Miss Kathi,' and then you said it."

"What?" Kathi asked, hanging onto Sally's words even though her head felt as if it would splinter into a million pieces. She was getting a headache again, the worst headache she'd ever got.

"'My name's not Kathi!' you said, and you stared right at me like I should know better. You said, 'My name's Sheri and I want my mama!' Then you started cryin', the kind of keenin' that a body does when they're grievin'. I kept tryin' to tell you to go to sleep, and finally you gave in, and laid your poor little head down on the pillow.

"'Everything's all right now,' I said. 'Everything's fine now.' And you opened your eyes and looked straight at me.

"'I know,' you said. 'I gave Baver the Tiger, and now he won't cry anymore.' And then you went straight off to sleep like a good girl. You never mentioned it again, and the spirit must have left you as you slept, 'cause the next mornin' you didn't even remember it."

"The spirit?" Kathi whispered. "The spirit . . . of Sheri Walker?" Even though there was skepticism written in her expression, another stabbing pain to her head convinced her that Sally was right. She was being haunted by the spirit of Sheri Walker! Was such a thing possible?

Sally's gaze had been focused on the bowl of feather flowers on the table as she recalled that night so long ago, and now she looked up to see Kathi's dead-white face.

"Child!" she gasped. "Miss Kathi! Don' look like that! I never should've told you. It's nothin', just the ramblin' of an old woman. Don' pay no mind to what I say, child."

"The spirit of Sheri Walker," Kathi breathed, her lips barely moving. "That's it, Sally. I thought I was going crazy, but it's something worse, isn't it? It's something much worse!"

"Now, child, that was a long time ago." Sally tried to soothe her. "You're fine now. No sense in getting all worked up 'bout somethin' that happened when you was just a child."

"It's happening again, Sally!" Kathi's voice was sharp. "And it's not just dreams now either! I hear strange voices, and they're real, Sally! Sheri Walker's back, and she's taking over my mind!"

There was a long uncomfortable silence when neither one of them spoke. Was it possible? Was that why the strange memories she had didn't belong to her? They belonged to Sheri Walker, and somehow she had to fight them off . . .

"What can I do, Sally?" Kathi spoke tightly, holding her scream of terror inside. "I understand now . . . it's all beginning to make sense, but what can I do?"

"Now, Miss Kathi, you just take it easy. I don' rightly know, child," Sally said, wincing as Kathi's fingers dug into her hands with a desperate grip. "I don' know about things like that. All I know is what my mama used to say, and some folks called her crazy."

"What would your mama say to do?" Kathi insisted. "You've got to tell me, Sally. I can't go on this way . . . I just can't!"

Sally's stomach contracted in fear as she saw the expression of desperation that shadowed Kathi's face. Should she tell Miss Kathi what her mama had always said about the spirits? Wouldn't that frighten her poor sweet lamb even more? Sally folded her arms around the shaking girl. Agonized sobs were tearing from Kathi's throat, and she was trembling violently. She had to do something. She couldn't stand to see Miss Kathi sobbing like this.

"Hush now, child," Sally soothed. "Mama always used to say that the only way to fight it off, was to find out what the spirit wanted, and do it. She said there was nothin' to be afraid of. A spirit is just a soul in torment 'cause there was somethin' they had to do, and they got killed before they could do it. Mama would've told you to find out what this Sheri wants, and let her do it. Then she'll leave you in peace again."

Even as Sally spoke in her comforting tone, she felt

the hair prickle on the back of her neck. It wasn't that easy, setting a spirit to rest, but she couldn't tell Miss Kathi that. Let her have what comfort she could. Maybe this Sheri Walker *did* want something simple, and Kathi would find out what it was. Maybe Kathi would be one of the lucky ones.

"I . . . I have to go, Sally," Kathi whispered, hugging the housekeeper again. "Please . . . please don't tell Dad or Vivian I was here. They can't know anything about this. Promise me, Sally. Promise me you won't tell."

"I promise, child," Sally said, tears rolling down her cheeks. "Take care, baby . . . and if you need me for anythin' at all, child, you won' have to ask twice."

Sally stared vacantly at the wall after Kathi left. She hoped she'd told her the right thing. Miss Kathi had seemed a little calmer when she left, but Sally couldn't help feeling a chill of foreboding. Now she wished she'd listened more carefully when her mama had rambled on about spirits and possession. She wished she'd copied down how to make the charms against evil, and the words to say to protect Miss Kathi. But she hadn't believed either. She hadn't believed until she took care of Miss Kathi. Mama was dead and buried when she'd gone to work at the Ellisons' big house in the canyon, and it was too late to ask her then. Now it was too late again . . . too late for Miss Kathi . . . too late for anything except praying, and that was what she was going to do.

Sally dropped to her knees on the worn rose-patterned rug and clasped her hands so tightly that they hurt. She looked up at the ceiling and shivered. "God, protect my little girl," she pleaded, her voice rising in desperation. “Sweet Jesus, keep her from hurt and evil. I ain’t asked for much, Lord, but I’m beggin’ you now. Keep Miss Kathi safe under your guidin’ hand and take this evil from her!” But the harder Sally prayed, the more fear she felt in her heart. Was it possible for one old woman’s prayers to save Miss Kathi?

CHAPTER 9

David bounded up the stairs, two at a time, careful to avoid the third step from the top, which was crumbling away. It was a steep staircase leading up the outside of the converted barracks building, and he didn't pause until he reached the second-floor landing where the Psychological Services Center was housed. The staircase had originally been a fire escape, but now college personnel used it as a private entrance.

The Psych Center smelled old and musty, and even though David had grown to regard it as a second home, he took a deep breath of the clean air outside before he pushed open the wooden screen door and greeted the dank, familiar aroma inside. It had been good of Dr. Kauffman to give him an appointment this afternoon, and he didn't want to be late. Dr. Kauffman was the busiest of all the staff psychologists. Everyone in the department regarded him as a brilliant therapist.

David hurried down the creaking hallway to the last

office on the left. The heavy door was shut. Perhaps Dr. Kauffman was running over on his last appointment. David checked his watch before he raised his hand to knock on the wooden door. He was exactly on time.

"Come in!" a muffled voice shouted at David's hesitant knock. David turned the knob and entered, shutting the door quickly behind him. Dr. Kauffman was alone, sitting behind his desk with his feet propped on a chair next to him. He smiled cheerfully at David and waved him to a chair.

Dr. Kauffman picked up a note pad and pen from the clutter on his desk and leaned back in his chair. "Now, what can I do for you, David? You said it was urgent."

David nodded. Now that he was actually here, he didn't know how to begin. Dr. Kaufman would probably think that he was overreacting, but he had to get some advice from someone. Someone had to help him help Kathi.

"Yes—" David took a deep breath. "At least, I think it's urgent. Of course, I'm personally involved, and it's hard to be objective about something like this." David recognized his own reluctance to talk. Now that he was here, his fears seemed out of proportion. What if it really was just stress from the election and midterm exams? How much should he tell the professor about Kathi? Did he dare mention her name and explain the whole problem honestly, including his part in it?

Dr. Kaufman raised his eyebrows and leaned forward, peering at David closely. His experienced eyes quickly scanned the young man's face and made note of the slight tightening around his eyes. David's mouth had a pinched look, and he was sitting upright on the edge of his chair, not relaxing as he usually did. Something was really bothering him today, and Dr. Kauffman recognized that this was no ordinary problem.

"Relax, David," Dr. Kauffman encouraged him. "Why don't you sit back and have a cigarette, and then tell me about it."

David took another deep breath to steady his nerves and busied himself with lighting a cigarette. He had to convince Dr. Kauffman that he wasn't just borrowing trouble or exaggerating the seriousness of Kathi's problem. He desperately needed the professor's experienced help, but he had to choose his words carefully, so that he didn't give Dr. Kauffman the impression that Kathi was just another high-strung college coed.

"I need to discuss something with you, but it's got to be confidential," David began, gripping the arms of the chair until his knuckles turned white. "I wouldn't mention this to anyone, but I can't handle it alone. I really need your advice."

"Anything you say in here is confidential," Dr. Kauffman quickly assured his young student. "No notes and no record of the appointment if that's what you want."

"Fine," David quickly agreed. There was no choice now. He had to tell Dr. Kauffman everything and trust the professor to keep it under wraps. "I-I'm worried about Kathi, Dr. Kauffman. Kathi Ellison, my girlfriend."

"Ellison?" the professor questioned, looking down

at the newspaper on his desk. "Any relation to Doug Ellison, the politician?"

"His daughter," David said, nodding. "That's why this has to be strictly confidential. If Kathi knew I'd come here and discussed her, she'd be even more worried about everything."

"What seems to be the problem, David?" Dr. Kauffman asked, assuming a relaxed pose in his chair. He'd never seen David Carter this upset before; he was usually self-contained and articulate. The young man was obviously struggling for words, and Dr. Kauffman could see what an effort it was for David to speak calmly.

David swallowed noisily and cleared his throat. "I . . . I think she's having a nervous breakdown," he confessed. "She seemed fine until a week or so ago . . . at least, if she was having problems before then, she hid them well. Now, all of a sudden, she's starting to fall apart, and I don't know what to do to help her."

"Tell me her symptoms," Dr. Kauffman encouraged him. "What makes you believe that she's having a breakdown?"

"Well . . . she . . . she's been having terrible nightmares, and they're getting worse. Last Sunday, she started crying in her sleep and I tried to wake her. Right before she opened her eyes, she started talking in a high-pitched voice, like a little kid's, and it took me almost two minutes before I could make her open her eyes."

David stopped, looking up at Dr. Kauffman with a lump in his throat. Just talking about it brought that helpless feeling back full force. She had been so terrified. Somehow he had to convey that terror to the professor.

"She's been having these nightmares on and off for a couple of weeks now, but they've never been this bad before. She was so frightened when I finally woke her up. I've never seen her that way before. I tell you, Dr. Kauffman, I was really afraid that I couldn't bring her out of it. Each time she has one of these awful dreams, it takes her longer to wake up. When she finally calmed down from this one, I insisted that she go to the health center and see the doctor."

"Yes?" Dr. Kauffman asked. "What happened then?"

"The doctor told her there was nothing to worry about and gave her some tranquilizers. At least that's what she said. I'm not sure she'd tell me if he said that something was seriously wrong. Anyway . . . the doctor seemed to think that it was just midterm nerves. That's what I was hoping too. But she's been through with her exams since yesterday morning, and it hasn't gotten any better. She's afraid to go to sleep now, Dr. Kauffman. She sleeps out on the couch and gives me some excuse, like she doesn't feel well or she wants to stay up late, but I know the reason she isn't sleeping in bed with me is because she's afraid she'll have another nightmare."

"Has she had another one?" Dr. Kauffman asked.

"Well, sort of," David said. "This was different though. It was kind of like a . . . a trance when she was wide awake. We were walking home from a party last night. She said she had a little headache, but I didn't realize that something was going to happen until we came to the railroad tracks. We could hear a train coming, and there was plenty of time to cross, but she insisted we wait. Then when the train came, she was so scared she almost ran right out in front of it. I held her, and then she froze up completely. She was still petrified by the time the train was gone, and I shook her and shouted her name for about five minutes. Thank God, she finally heard me.

"Then she tried to tell me that she's always been this afraid of trains because she was in an accident when she was a kid. The car her mother was driving hit a train, and her mother was killed. That would make sense, Dr. Kauffman, except for one thing. We've walked by that crossing for a month now, and there've been trains before. She never reacted this way before."

"And you're afraid that she's going to stay in one of these trances, and you won't be able to bring her back," Dr. Kauffman prompted. "Is that right, David?"

"That's it," David sighed, nodding jerkily. "I've tried asking what she hears and sees when she's in these trances, but she can't—or won't—tell me. I've got the feeling that she remembers, but she doesn't trust me enough to tell me. If it was anyone but Kathi, I'd bring her in to see you, but I'm afraid that would only make Kathi more disturbed. She's really involved in her father's campaign, and she'd never agree to see a psychologist until after the election's over. She'd be afraid that word of it would get out, and the press would pick up on it."

"I see," Dr. Kauffman said slowly. If this story had come from anyone other than David, he would have given the usual platitudes: things often seem more critical than they are; even the well-adjusted person has occasional nightmares; people often do bizarre things under stress, and the moment the pressure is relieved, they go right back to normal; worrying will do no good; just relax and she'll probably be fine; etc.

But David Carter was a stable young man and a brilliant student of psychology. He wouldn't be this worried if he thought his girlfriend's problem was only temporary. If David was worried, there was something to be worried about.

"Have you noticed any preceding situation that could be cueing these trances?" the professor asked, tapping his pen on the edge of his blotter. "Is there a specific incident that sets them off, David?"

"Uh . . . well . . . only one that I could discover," David admitted, twisting uncomfortably in the chair. "I . . . I noticed that she has nightmares every time after we have sex. For a while, I was positive that it was guilt, that she was feeling guilty about living with me and letting her parents think she was still in the dorm. But last night, all that changed. Last night, the train cued her trance. I just don't know what to think anymore, Dr. Kauffman."

There was a note of desperation in David's voice that made Dr. Kauffman want to pat him on the shoulder like he would a small boy. He suppressed the urge quickly. David hadn't come here for comfort; he had come for advice.

"Perhaps something here on campus is disturbing her," the professor offered thoughtfully. "Something you haven't noticed or thought about."

"Sure," David agreed readily. "It could be anything, but that doesn't really help me. I don't want to see Kathi sink down into one of her nightmares and not be able to come back. I've got to keep her from falling into the trances in the first place."

"It's quite a problem," Dr. Kauffman commiserated, nodding. "I don't know what advice I can give you, David, except to try to change her surroundings. There have been cases where an abrupt change of occupation or environment precedes a remission of these sorts of symptoms. One thing you can do to help her, is to take her mind off her problem. Get her involved in some sort of activity, something she's not used to doing. I'd suggest taking her to a different locale, if that could be arranged. How about a little vacation somewhere—well chaperoned, of course, because of the election. You wouldn't want the press to write a story about the two of you alone in the mountains, or anything like that."

"Get her involved in something new and different," David repeated, as if he were burning Dr. Kauffman's advice into his memory. "And if that doesn't work, take her away to totally different surroundings." He pulled thoughtfully at his beard.

There was a moment of silence as both of them mulled over Kathi's problem. Finally David looked up. "That's all?" he asked, grimacing. "That's all I can do for her?"

"Not quite," Dr. Kauffman continued. "Try to get her to talk about her trances, to tell you what happens and how it feels when she has one. If she has some sort of warning that a trance is coming on, she could give you a sign and perhaps you could avert it. That's another possibility. And try to gain her trust, David. That's the most important thing. Don't pressure her to tell you everything, but let her know that you're not going to censure her for behaving abnormally or for telling you bizarre things."

David nodded and moved his cigarette cautiously toward the ashtray. He had forgotten entirely about smoking it, and the ash was nearly falling, it had grown so long.

"You're really worried about her, aren't you, David?"

"Yes," David answered tersely, stubbing out his cigarette methodically. "I don't know what I'll do if something drastic happens during break. You're not going to be here, are you?"

The hopefulness on David's face was almost pathetic, and Dr. Kauffman had the urge to cancel his vacation, just to be on hand if he was needed. Unfortunately, he couldn't do that. His wife had been planning this vacation for the past three months, and he couldn't cancel it now. He'd done that too many times in the past. There wasn't much he could do for the girl anyway, not until after the election.

"I'm sorry, David," Dr. Kauffman apologized. "I'm not going to be in town. The whole family's going to San Diego to visit my in-laws. I'll give you the number, though, and I don't want you to hesitate to call if none of my suggestions work and Kathi's problem worsens."

Dr. Kauffman stared at the door long after David had left, wondering why he had given the number to

David. He had promised Marge that nothing would disturb their vacation this year. He gave a sigh and leaned back in his chair again, lacing his fingers together behind his head. Ah, well, he would just have to weather Marge's little tizzy if David needed him.

CHAPTER 10

He came in with a grin on his face, determined to be cheerful and supportive. "Kathi?" he called out, hanging his plaid jacket in the closet. "Kathi! I'm home!"

The apartment had a certain cold emptiness about it. Kathi was not here. The bright posters on the walls and the colorful throw pillows Kathi had made did not dispel David's gloom. Without Kathi's answering voice, the apartment was cold and lonely. She hadn't left for good, had she?

David rushed to the kitchen table where they always left notes for each other. He breathed a sigh of relief as he spotted Kathi's steno notebook propped up against the saltshaker. She'd left him a note written in her abbreviated style. At least she hadn't been in some sort of trance when she left, if she was rational enough to leave a note.

Qk. trip 2 L.A. Bck. early eve. U aced yr. test, right? K.

David picked up the notebook and grinned in relief. There was nothing unusual about a girl who flew to Los Angeles to have a quick visit with her parents. That was perfectly normal, wasn't it? A visit with her parents might do Kathi a lot of good. David knew that she was on edge about her father's campaign. She'd probably come back brimming with news from campaign headquarters, carrying stacks of bumper stickers and pins for them to distribute around campus.

Time crept slowly as David tried to busy himself around the apartment, straightening the bookshelves, fixing the squeaking cupboard door over the sink, doing all the little things he hadn't had time to do before his midterm exams. Finally, he settled down on the couch with a book he'd been meaning to read, with the television turned on for company. She should be home soon. There were regular flights coming in from Los Angeles, and Kathi's note had said early evening. She could be home any minute.

The instant David heard her key in the lock, he jumped up from the couch. "I'm glad you're back, baby!" he called out, rushing to the door to hug her tightly. "You should have called from the airport. I could have come to pick you up."

"Oh!" Kathi gasped, dropping her purse on the floor as David's arms closed around her. "Th-that's all right, David. I took a cab." She tried to hug him back, but his arms felt like a prison and she pulled away instinctively, her eyes darting warily around the apartment. "My goodness! You cleaned up in here!" There was a tone of dismay in her voice that she couldn't hide. "I haven't been a very good housekeeper lately, have I?"

"You've been fine, hon," David assured her, stepping back quickly as she struggled from his embrace. "I know you've got a lot on your mind, and I'm capable of doing a little housework too, you know. It won't destroy my masculinity to do the dishes once in a while."

Kathi looked down at the rug, avoiding David's gaze. She didn't dare look at him, or he would read the fear in her eyes, and he would question her. But there was no way she could begin to explain what she'd found out today. David was too rational a man to even consider the things Sally had told her.

"Um . . . I decided to go to L.A. all of a sudden," she said nervously. "I would have told you, but you were already gone. The . . . the idea just occurred to me. There were some things I had to pick up at home."

Too late, Kathi realized her mistake. She hadn't come back with anything other than her purse. David was bound to notice that, but he didn't say anything. He was humoring her. That made Kathi feel even worse.

"But . . . but I couldn't find what I was looking for," she stumbled on, unable to stop her babbling. "Anyway, the day wasn't a total waste. I got a chance to talk to Sally. I told you about Sally, didn't I, David? She's our housekeeper . . . well . . . actually she's more like a member of the family. Sally's been with us for as long as I can remember."

Kathi's voice trailed off and she stared miserably at the rug. She was acting like a complete idiot, babbling on and on this way. If only David would say something.

"I'm glad you had a good time," David responded pleasantly, almost as if he'd read her thoughts. "How about some coffee? I bet you're tired."

Oh, he was being so careful! David didn't know what to say either, and he acted as if he were walking on eggshells, afraid of saying something that might upset her. They were like strangers.

"Tired?" Kathi picked up on the word eagerly, almost desperately. "Yes, I certainly am tired!" She sank down on the couch and slid out of her coat. "Coffee would be wonderful, David. That is, if you don't mind making it."

"No trouble at all," David assured her cheerfully, disappearing into the kitchen. She could hear him running water, filling the tea kettle, and there was the sound of the match striking as he lit the stove.

Kathi sighed again and closed her eyes. This was almost unbearable. This thing, this awful thing that had come between them. Their words sounded stilted, like the careful questions and responses two people make when they first meet. But if she let down her guard, she would end up telling him what Sally had said, and she wasn't ready to tell anyone about it. Not yet. Maybe not ever. How could she explain to a man who laughed at the horoscopes in the daily paper and thought spirits were something you dressed up as on Halloween, that the spirit of Sheri Walker was . . . was what? She could hardly believe it herself. The more she thought about it, the more impossible it seemed.

"I . . . I think I'll pass on that coffee, David," Kathi called out. "I'm really tired, and the plane trip was a little rough. I guess I'll just go in and go to bed, if that's all right with you."

"Sure, honey," came David's prompt answer. "Do you want me to come in with you, or shall I watch television?"

"Um, you can watch television if you want to," Kathi responded, tears welling in her eyes. He knew! David knew that she didn't want to sleep with him tonight, although he couldn't possibly know why. He was being sweet and understanding, and it was all Kathi could do to keep from bursting into tears. *How much longer can things go on this way? What can I do to make everything all right again? Will things ever be the way they used to be?*

Kathi heard the sound of the television as she undressed and put on her college nightshirt, the least sexy of her nightgowns. He wouldn't come to bed and try to make love to her tonight anyway, not after the way she'd pulled away from him back there in the living room. She heard the volume lower, and she knew he was trying to be considerate. Kathi sank to the bed in desperation, feeling as if she were balancing on a tightrope stretched over the edge of disaster. What was to become of them?

She lay on her back with her eyes open, staring at the reflected light of the streetlamp on the ceiling. She could hear the small night sounds outside the window—the leaves rustling in the wind, a bird calling out softly—and the creaking as someone in the apartment above them walked across the floor. How she wished that she could call out to David . . . ask him to come to bed so she could tell him everything and have him hold her close. But that was the one thing she couldn't do. She was lonely and frightened, but she had to pretend a while longer, just until she found out what Sheri Walker wanted. It wouldn't be long now. Sheri Walker was coming more often, and soon the spirit would tell her what to do. Just a little longer, and it would be over. Then everything would be all right. Everything . . . would . . . be . . . all . . . over.

She was sleeping, hugging the pillow in her arms like a child. David tiptoed into the bedroom, and there was pain in his heart as he saw the traces of tears on her cheeks. Tonight she had been too tired, but tomorrow he would put Dr. Kauffman's suggestions into effect. He'd already planned the first activity to divert Kathi's attention. They were going to the Alameda County Fair, and Kathi was going to have a good time, even if he had to stand on his head and dance a jig to make her laugh again. They'd never been to a fair together, and it would be impossible for Kathi to stay anxious and depressed if they lost themselves in a crowd of excited, happy people. There would be rides and cotton candy and lots of sideshows to see. The fair would make everything seem better, and then, when they came back, they would have a long talk about her problem. He'd do everything Dr. Kauffman had said. He was going to pull Kathi out of this by the sheer force of his love. Once she realized that he was willing to move heaven and earth to help her, she'd share her nightmare with him, and between the two of them, they'd chase the terror away.

Quietly, carefully, David slipped between the sheets. Beautiful, vulnerable Kathi—she was so lovely when she slept untroubled like this. It wasn't going to happen again tonight. He wouldn't let it. Tonight was going to be a good night, and tomorrow, a beautiful day. Things were looking up.

Why was he kidding himself this way? Things weren't going to get better until Kathi talked to him—really talked to him. He had to get through to her tomorrow. He had to!

CHAPTER 11

The work was routine, and Sally went about it mechanically. She had plenty of time to think as she went about her familiar housekeeping duties, but the work that usually made her hum a little tune under her breath seemed like drudgery today. Sally's face was grim, and she attacked the dust with a fervent zeal, scowling as she did so. Miss Kathi was on her mind, and had been ever since the poor little lamb had shown up on her doorstep yesterday.

Sally attempted to marshal her thoughts and take pride in her cleaning as she usually did. *Cleanliness is next to Godliness*. Mama had been fond of saying that. She would polish and dust and wax until there wasn't a speck of dust anywhere. Putting the big house in order was easy. Putting her thoughts in order was something else.

Sally's routine was methodical. On Fridays, she cleaned Mr. Doug's study, vacuuming the rugs and dusting the big, carved-oak desk. Then, after the den was done, she would go on to the bedrooms, straightening up and changing the sheets. A load of laundry had to be done and some of Mr. Doug's shirts ironed. Then, there was dinner to prepare. Miss Vivian always planned the week's menus in advance, handing them to Sally on Sundays. Tonight was rare roast beef with those expensive little baby potatoes, broccoli with cheese sauce, and Jell-O parfait for dessert. Sally had chuckled when she'd seen the order for Jell-O parfait. Miss Vivian must have figured that Mr. Doug was eating too well at all those fancy, hundred-dollar-per-plate dinners.

As Sally started the dusting, she sighed morosely. Poor Miss Kathi! She was in trouble, deep trouble, and Sally just had to do something to ease Miss Kathi's mind. She had gone through Mama's trunk last night, searching for books, or anything to do with the spirits. But Mama had never been much of a reader. What she knew, she knew from hearing other people talk, and she kept it in her head. There had been nothing in the trunk except for a book of faded photographs, some picture postcards from Atlanta tied with a bit of red string, the velvet hat with the rose Mama had been fond of wearing, and the ring—the ring that Mama had called her good luck—the tigereye ring that showed a little cross when you held it up to the light.

It was too small for Sally, so she had never worn it, even though she knew that the jeweler could make it bigger to fit her finger. Sally wasn't sure why, but she hadn't wanted to wear the ring. It was still in the little box where she had put it after Mama's funeral. The ring was Mama's luck, and Mama was fond of saying that every person made their own luck. Sally had no doubt that Mama was right.

She sighed heavily and picked up the leather-bound books, dusting the covers and the shelf beneath. The books were thick and heavy, law books that Mr. Doug never had the time to read. They just gathered dust, but they were beautiful, dusted carefully and arranged just so on the shelves. If Mr. Doug ever needed them, they would be there and not a speck of dust on them!

Sally gave another deep sigh as she finished the bookshelves and turned toward the desk. She remembered Miss Kathi sitting on Mr. Doug's lap behind the desk, both of them laughing and making a chain of paper clips. Miss Kathi had been happy then, except for the dark dreams at night. The child used to like to sit at her father's desk and draw pictures on the long yellow legal pads that Mr. Doug kept in his drawer. There had been a drawer just for Miss Kathi then, with paper clips, blunt-tipped scissors, Scotch tape, and a box of crayons. Sally still had the picture Miss Kathi had made for her—a wobbly house with smoke coming out of the chimney. It made her feel sad to think of it now.

Sally patted her apron pocket where Mama's ring was resting, solid and heavy and reassuring. It was true that each person had to make his own luck, but Sally didn't think Mama would mind sharing a little bit of hers with Miss Kathi. She was going to send the ring to Miss Kathi today, take it right down to the post office and mail it off to her. Maybe it would change her luck.

Remembering Miss Kathi's white face made Sally's hands tremble as she pulled out Mr. Doug's desk drawers and dusted inside. She was going to give this desk an extra-good cleaning today, just to keep her hands busy. Mr. Doug didn't like his papers rearranged, so she would just stack the drawers on the top and oil the wooden slats under them so they'd slide nice and smooth.

She squatted on her heels and wiped out the spaces where the drawers fit, fishing out some paper clips and a book of matches that had fallen out. This desk had never had such a good cleaning! Mr. Doug might not notice, but she'd know that she'd done a good job in his den.

"What's this?" Sally muttered, pulling out a crinkled ball of paper that had fallen out of the center drawer and been shoved back underneath—a newspaper clipping. She straightened it out, hoping that it wasn't something important. Then a name—one name out of a list—caught her eye and made her gasp in surprise. Sharon Elizabeth Walker! Miss Kathi's Sheri Walker! Her name was right here in black and white!

Sally looked around furtively, the clipping clutched in her hand. She knew she should straighten it out and put it right back where she'd found it. A good housekeeper never snooped through her family's private things. But . . . wasn't this different? Would she really be snooping if she just read the clipping? It wasn't really private like a letter or some such thing. Newspapers were printed for everyone to read. Would it be so wrong just to take a little peek?

Sally wrestled with her conscience for a moment and then sat down heavily behind the desk. Her hands shook as she scanned the article, coming again to the familiar name. Then her breath caught in her throat, and she gave a wail of despair. Sheri was dead. What they had feared was true! Now Miss Kathi needed Mama's ring more than ever. . . .

"Sally? Are you there, Sally?" She heard Miss Vivian's voice in the hallway. "Is there anything wrong, Sally?"

Sally acted quickly, not really thinking about what she was doing. In the space of a second, the crumpled newspaper clipping had joined her mama's ring, out of sight in her apron pocket.

"Oh, Miss Vivian!" Sally gasped, her mind grasping at some excuse for her outcry. "I didn't mean for you to hear me. It's nothin' really. I . . . I was just cleanin' out the inside of Mr. Doug's drawers, and I poked my finger on one of the little nails. It's okay." She gave a little nervous laugh. "I guess I should've been more careful."

Vivian sighed, relieved. "You work too hard, Sally," she said, smiling as she surveyed the room. "You didn't have to clean out the inside of Doug's desk. No one ever sees the inside anyway."

"But I'd know it was dirty, Miss Vivian," Sally replied promptly. "I wouldn't be able to sleep nights, knowin' I left dirt in Mr. Doug's drawers!"

Vivian nodded, accepting the inevitable. When it came to Doug, Sally was almost too zealous. Any slight suggestion from Doug, and Sally would drop everything else to do his bidding. She ironed his shirts painstakingly and folded them in the best laundry style. She was fiercely loyal, and Vivian was sure that Sally would throw herself off the Flower Street overpass without a second thought, if Doug even hinted that was what he wanted.

"Well, be careful, Sally," Vivian said, turning to the bookshelves and idly touching the binding on Doug's leather law books. She had no doubt that Sally liked her too, but the elderly housekeeper wouldn't hesitate to turn on her like an avenging angel, if she ever thought that Vivian was hurting Doug or Kathi in any way.

"You got another one of those ladies' teas this afternoon?" Sally asked, quickly changing the subject. "I could find time to make up some of them little sandwiches with the crusts cut off, if you need some."

"No, there's nothing planned for this afternoon, Sally," Vivian answered, sighing lightly. "Do you realize that we've had one group or another here every afternoon for the past two weeks? It's getting to where I don't know what to do when I have any free time."

"You ought to get yourself out of the house, Miss Vivian," Sally said, replacing the drawers in the desk carefully. "Why don't you run on down to that nice beauty parlor and get your hair done? Not that it needs it, Miss Vivian, but you always look so pretty when you come back from the beauty parlor."

Vivian turned to smile at Sally, who was industriously dusting again. "So you think it would be good for me to get out of the house," Vivian said, nodding. "You're probably right, Sally. It's an excellent idea. I'll call for an appointment right now."

"No need to do that, Miss Vivian. You just run along upstairs, and I'll make the call for you while you get ready."

"Sally," Vivian said, smiling, "whatever would we do without you? You take such good care of us."

"I try, Miss Vivian. I try." Sally grinned, waiting until Miss Vivian had left the room before she picked up the phone. She was going to make that fancy hairdresser—the one with the tight pants—take Miss Vivian right in. Then, while Miss Vivian was relaxing at the beauty parlor, she could run down to the post office and mail off the ring to Miss Kathi. She might even make a copy of that clipping on one of the big machines they had down there. It wouldn't take more than a few extra minutes, and she could send it right along with the ring. She could have the real clipping back before Mr. Doug noticed it was gone. He probably wouldn't notice anyway. That clipping must have been lying under the drawer for a long time to be so old and wrinkled. Miss Kathi needed to know what the article said. Now she'd know more about Sheri Walker and who she was. No wonder her poor lamb was always dreaming about trains . . .

CHAPTER 12

There was something unusual about the man. He looked familiar, but, at the same time, she was certain she didn't really know him. He was older than the average student, and he didn't look like a professor either. Perhaps he worked somewhere on campus, in the food service or perhaps as a security guard. She turned to smile at him, sure that she recognized him from somewhere, but he turned his face away, avoiding her eyes. That was strange. Perhaps she didn't know him after all.

The dorm was filled with girls hurrying from room to room with suitcases in hand. Midterm break had officially started. Parents were sitting in groups in the reception area, waiting for their daughters. There was an air of festivity about the dorm this morning, but by nightfall these busy rooms would be deserted except for a skeleton staff of maintenance personnel. As Kathi hurried past the switchboard, she saw that the phone lines were all tied up with last-minute calls and orders for taxis. That must be why she had got a busy signal when she tried to reach Bev by phone earlier.

Kathi made her way carefully down the crowded corridors and knocked on Bev's door.

"Kathi!" Bev greeted her with a hug, and then stepped back to examine Kathi's face. "God! What happened to you? You look like death warmed over!"

"Well, I see you haven't changed any," Kathi retorted weakly, managing a sickly smile. "You're still as blunt as ever."

"Mmmmmm . . . sorry," Bev said. "But Kathi, you really don't look well. A fight with David?"

"No . . . no fight, it's just lack of sleep, that's all. There's nothing wrong with me that twenty-four hours in a bed wouldn't cure."

Bev frowned and raised her eyebrows. Instinctively, she knew that Kathi was lying. She'd never seen her look like this, and they'd stayed up all night studying for exams plenty of times before. Kathi actually looked ill, with dark circles under her eyes and a pinched look about her face. She was a beautiful girl, but today she looked almost haggard. Her jeans hung on her loosely, and Bev could tell she'd lost weight. There was definitely something wrong, but she wouldn't press it. Kathi would tell her the problem if she wanted her to know. She wasn't the type of roommate who would weep and whisper secrets in the dark of night, and that had suited Bev just fine. Until now, that is. Right now she would have welcomed Kathi's confidence, if it would have helped.

"Well!" Bev said heartily. "Come on in and have a

cup of coffee with me. I'll dig out the pot just like we used to do."

"Oh, thanks anyway, Bev," Kathi declined. "My stomach's a little upset today. I really just came to get the rest of my things out of your way. I'll pack everything up and have David come over to move it all tomorrow."

Bev sat down on the edge of her madras-covered bed and studied Kathi as she packed. Kathi's hands were trembling, and she looked preoccupied as she stuffed things in boxes and then pulled them out to examine them again, not at all like the efficient woman Bev knew. There really was something on Kathi's mind, but it wouldn't do a particle of good to ask about it again. All Bev could do was sit there and hope that Kathi would reconsider and tell her the problem. And from the way Kathi was hurrying through her packing, it didn't seem likely that she would.

Kathi felt Bev's eyes on her, and she fought the urge to confide in her friend. It was true that Bev might be just the person to understand, but how could she take that chance? What if Bev thought she was crazy and called David? Then he'd know that things weren't as she had pretended. Then she'd have to tell him everything and risk losing him. She couldn't take that risk now, not when she needed him so desperately.

"Well, I guess that just about does it." Kathi sighed, making a final circle of the room and picking up a vase of straw flowers and a scarf that she had forgotten. "If anyone asks, I'm still living here until after the election. All right?"

"Right," Bev agreed. "Are you going to spend the break campaigning for your father?"

"Well . . . I haven't really decided yet," Kathi answered evasively. "That depends on a lot of things. I'll be in touch though. I already called Viv and my dad and told them I had to stay here to work on a project. I just couldn't stand to spend the whole break in Los Angeles."

There was an undercurrent of desperation in Kathi's voice that made Bev raise her eyebrows again. Kathi seemed so anxious—almost haunted—as she stood there in the middle of the stripped room, a desolate figure with her head bowed and her eyes fixed on the tiled floor. Even though Bev's better instincts told her not to pry, she had to ask again.

"What's wrong, Kathi? Please tell me. I've never seen you look so down before, and it makes me feel like crying just to look at you. Isn't there something I could do to help? Wouldn't it at least help to talk about it?"

"I . . . I don't think so," Kathi replied. What could she say? That she was pregnant and didn't dare tell David until she knew for certain what Sheri Walker's spirit wanted with her? Just thinking it sounded so insane, that Kathi couldn't bring herself to utter the words. This was her problem, and she had to deal with it herself.

"Damn!" Bev muttered, digging in the desk drawer for a piece of paper and a pencil. "Here," she offered, scribbling a number on a scrap of paper. "Here's my parents' number in Phoenix. Call me if there's anything I can do, will you? And even if you think I can't help, call me if you need to talk to someone. Will you promise to do that?"

"It's really not that serious," Kathi answered, trying

to lie convincingly and knowing that she wasn't fooling Bev at all. "Really, Bev . . . there's nothing to worry about. I'll work it out."

"Sure you will," Bev nodded. "But take the number anyway. Sometimes it just helps to hear a friend's voice, and I'm your friend, Kathi, whether you believe it or not."

"I know you are," Kathi said softly, tears welling up in her eyes. "You're a good friend, and if I could talk about this to anyone, it would be you. I just want you to know that."

"Christ!" Bev muttered, wiping her eyes on her shirt sleeve. "Look at the two of us! You'd think we were at a funeral the way we're carrying on."

A cold chill settled in Kathi's mind at Bev's words. It wasn't exactly like they were at a funeral. It was more like she was saying good-bye to Bev for the last time, as if she had some terminal illness and wouldn't live long enough to see her friend again. The feeling was hideous.

"I-I'd better hurry," Kathi said quickly, picking up her purse and heading for the door. "I promised David I'd be home in an hour. He's set on taking me to the Alameda County Fair this afternoon, and you know how David is when he makes up his mind to do something. There's no getting out of it."

"That sounds like fun," Bev said, puzzled. "Don't you want to go, Kathi? The fair is super. They've got all sorts of rides and sideshows. Roger and I even went to a fortune-teller. That was an absolute panic. She told me that I was going to fall in love with a short, dark man with hair on his face, so for the rest of the afternoon Roger slouched, and he didn't shave for a week."

Kathi knew it was funny, but not that funny. She could feel the laughter bubble up inside her and burst out hysterically. She had to stop laughing, but her self-control was slipping by the minute, and she couldn't seem to get a grip on herself. Finally, clenching her teeth, she began to calm down, but even as the laughter subsided, the pain at her temples began. She had to get away before something happened.

"I . . . I really have to run, Bev," Kathi apologized. "The fair does sound like fun. I just didn't want to go out anywhere, but I'm sure I'll have a good time once I'm there."

Kathi hurried back down the corridor after Bev made her promise once more to call if there was anything she could do. The dorm was even more crowded now, and as she pushed her way past well-dressed groups of parents, she felt as if she were moving in place, walking on an endless treadmill. The groups of people were closing in on her, making her feel faint and light-headed. And still, that throbbing ache in her head was there, driving her forward with the pain until she burst from the front doors like a caged bird making a desperate bid for freedom.

Kathi saw the man in the plaid jacket again, but his face did not register in her mind as it had before. She rushed past him and fled toward the Child Care Center on the edge of campus. She stopped there at the playground and watched, out of breath and panting. The center was run by volunteers, freeing student mothers to attend classes. She had worked there last semester herself.

There were only a few children playing outside today, and Kathi paused, shaking three aspirins out of the bottle in her purse and sinking down on a bench, not even bothering to get a drink of water from the fountain to wash them down. The pills tasted bitter, but somehow she made her throat work noisily to swallow. She would sit right here and wait until her headache lessened a bit. Then she would go back to the apartment. David would be waiting for her, and Kathi knew that she couldn't face him in this condition. She was almost ready to burst into tears with Bev's kind words ringing in her ears.

Abruptly, her mind went blank. Kathi felt a prickling at the base of her neck, and her knees turned weak. Did she dare get up and walk the few blocks to her apartment, or . . . was Sheri Walker coming? No, it would be better to sit here for a while. At least there was no one to see her here. The children were playing so intently that they hadn't even noticed her. She would be safe here, safe from prying eyes, just in case.

A little boy was watching the swings enviously. Kathi could see the desire in his eyes. He wanted to swing, but he was too small to lift himself up and grasp the chains. If she had been feeling better, she would have gone to him and lifted him up high, teaching him how to pull himself up by the chains until he could sit on the board. She had taught someone that once . . . someone . . . sometime . . .

The older girl on the swing was pumping her feet now, swinging higher and higher, back and forth in a steadily widening rhythm. Knees back, knees straight, knees back, knees straight . . . up, down, up, down . . . over and over and over . . . the arc pulsing in time with the throbbing ache in her head . . . swinging higher and higher . . .

". . . all by myself now. I don't need you to push me and lift me up. I can do it all by myself now. Aren't I a big girl?"

The man in the plaid jacket stood by a tree and watched her intently. Harry wanted a complete report on her. It didn't seem all that important, Kathi stopping to rest on the playground bench and watch the children at play. He didn't think there was anything Harry would want to know about this, until he heard the childish giggle push past her lips.

He moved closer. Something was happening here, and he wasn't sure what. She seemed not to hear his approach at all. Her eyes were staring vacantly at the swings, and her face was completely blank.

"Looks like fun, doesn't it?" he asked, hoping that he was doing the right thing by talking to her. He figured he had blown his cover this morning anyway, when she had appeared to recognize him, but he couldn't be sure. If she said something about it now, he'd have another man take his place.

"Yes, fun!" Kathi answered, her voice as high and sweet as an excited child's. For a moment the investigator was startled, but then he thought he understood. She'd popped some kind of pill she had got at the dorm. She had to be high on something or other. He'd seen her take something right here on the bench only a few minutes earlier.

"Do you like to swing on the swings?" he asked cautiously, not quite knowing how to handle her. "Does it look like fun, Kathi?"

Now he really had thrown caution to the winds. If

she asked him how he knew her name, he'd have to think of some excuse, but it didn't matter. She seemed so stoned that he doubted she'd even think about it.

"My name's not Kathi," she said, giggling, her face splitting in a wide, guileless smile. "But I love to swing on the swings! We go to the park every Saturday, and we get to swing on the swings. The first time I went to the park, the swings were too high, and Uncle had to lift me up to sit on the board. Then he pushed me. He must have told the park men about the swings being too high, because now they're lower. Now I can jump up all by myself!"

"Did your uncle teach you how to do that?" the investigator asked, keeping his face carefully blank. Kathi Ellison had no uncle on either Doug's or Vivian's side. There were no relatives at all, according to her background file. Doug and Vivian were only children, as Doug's first wife, Roma, had been.

"Uncle didn't teach me," Kathi replied, still staring straight ahead, responding to his voice but not turning to look at him even once. She had to be on something, he decided, something like acid, probably. Harry would shit bricks when he got the report on this one!

"I can tell you how I do it," she continued. "I reach my hands up very high and grab the chains. The board bangs me sometimes, right under my arms. I jump really hard and pull with my hands and I can get up. It's hard to do, but most times I make it. Auntie says I'm getting taller, so it will get easier."

So now she had an aunt too! This whole thing was getting so bizarre, that he hardly knew what to ask next. It was like talking to a four-year-old! But he was saved from thinking of another question when she went on without prompting, the words spilling from her lips like those of an excited child.

"Baver can't get up by himself yet. Baver's just a baby. When he grows up, I can show him all the tricks the Tiger showed me."

Baver? Tiger? What the hell was she talking about?

"Do you go to school?" he asked, hoping to get more information for Harry's report. He could find out what age she thought she was by the question about school.

"Oh no! I'm not big enough yet. I have to stay home and help Auntie and listen to the growed-ups talk. The growed-ups sit in the living room and talk about big things. Baver and I have little chairs to sit on, and we're learning to be polite and listen."

"What do the grown-ups talk about?" he asked, feeling his palms grow slick with sweat. What the hell was he going to do if she really freaked out? Did he dare call a doctor? Harry would fry him in boiling oil if he made a wrong move and the press picked up on it. He'd have to be very careful.

"Sometimes they talk about us, but we don't know all the big words yet. I know when the important ladies come to visit, because Auntie gets a headache and cleans the house. They ask her lots of questions about the boy and the girl just like we're not there. When I asked her, Auntie said they were just checking to see if they were taking good care of us. She said some of the ladies were nicer than the others, but she wouldn't tell me who the bad ones were. I asked the Tiger after he kissed me good night, and he told me the trick about the bad ladies' knees. He said that all the bad ladies have black hairs on their knees."

She giggled again, a small child delighted at sharing a secret.

"I can see good from my little chair, so I'm watching for the bad ladies. The Tiger said that I should be really polite for the bad ladies, and look happy so they won't take us away. He said that he was working on a way for Baver and me to go where Mommy and Daddy are, but I have to be a little bit bigger before it will work. Then it will have to be a secret like everything else."

"Where are your Mommy and Daddy?" he asked. He was glad that he'd switched on the little pocket recorder he carried with him everywhere. Harry would have to hear this to believe it.

Suddenly, Kathi's eyes closed, and then she jerked, sitting upright on the edge of the bench. When she opened her eyes again, the blank glassy look was gone. "Oh!" she gasped, her face turning pink. "I-I'm terribly sorry. . . I . . . I guess I must have been daydreaming. What did you say?"

For a moment, he had no reply. The tone of her voice had deepened, and now her eyes were alert, watching him intensely, taking in every detail of his appearance. It was as if the drug she took had worn off completely, he thought in confusion.

"Oh . . . I just asked you if one of those kids out there was yours," he fielded quickly.

"No," she said, giving a little nervous laugh. "I used to work here last semester, and I just stopped to watch them for a while. How about you? Do you have a child out there?"

"No, not me," he replied. "I just came out for a bit of air. I work in the library, and I'm on my lunch break."

"That's where I've seen you before," Kathi said, smiling as if she'd solved a puzzle. "The library. Of course!"

"It's only part-time," the man added hastily. "Well—" He glanced openly at his watch in case she should ask more questions. "Lunch break's over," he said, standing briskly. "See you around campus, Miss . . ."

"Ellison, Kathi Ellison," she responded quickly.

He walked away so quickly that she didn't have time to ask his name, but she supposed she'd see him at the library again sometime. He seemed like a nice man, very friendly. But she really didn't have time to think about her short conversation with him. She had to get back to the apartment right away. She felt as if she'd been sitting there for a lifetime, but the aspirins had worked, thank God! Her headache was completely gone, and she felt so much better now, that she was sure she'd enjoy the fair with David. At least she hadn't made a fool of herself by blanking out in front of Bev or that nice man. She had been wrong this time. Sheri Walker wasn't going to contact her today after all.

CHAPTER 13

The weather in northern California, always unpredictable, had reversed itself. Today it was hot—actually stifling—as Kathi and David drove to the fairgrounds. The heat never bothered Kathi. She loved it and, incredibly, she felt her spirits lift with the heat of the day, until she felt so relieved that she almost broke into song. Sheri Walker wasn't coming today! Kathi was nearly sure she had been trying to come this morning at the playground, but something had happened to stop her. Kathi had been spared for this afternoon, free to enjoy the fair with David and lose her fear in the crowd.

"Hey, I think coming here was a good idea." David grinned as he maneuvered his compact car into a space that looked much too small to Kathi. David always did the difficult things so easily, and Kathi was envious. It would have taken her long minutes of arm-wrenching wrestling with the wheel to have parked the car in this space. Things were so easy for David. He could handle anything at all—or almost anything.

There were some things that no one could be expected to take in stride.

"Yep, I'm proud of myself for thinking about the fair," David said, not catching the fear that crossed Kathi's face. She quickly pushed aside her slight uneasiness and stilled it with the force of her will. She was going to be happy today—happy, happy, happy.

"You're having a good time already, aren't you, baby?" David asked, cutting the ignition and glancing at her now smiling face.

"Yes!" Kathi laughed, shaking her head as she slid across the hump between the bucket seats to snuggle up against his arm. "I'm happy today, David. It's going to be a super day!"

Thank God, David didn't question her forced gaiety. Kathi felt a pang of guilt as his face broke into a grin. He'd been worried about her, and it was all her fault. In the past few days he'd been tense and so very careful not to say anything that would disturb her. She'd done that to him—made him afraid to talk to her—and it was going to stop right now! She had no right to foist her fears on David. And really, the fears weren't as bad now. The warm noon sun had burned them away into just a hint of doubt lingering at the edge of her consciousness. She would be totally herself today, the way she used to be, and then David would be happy too. She was getting her control back at last!

Kathi's optimism grew as they wandered through the crowded fairgrounds, stopping to buy cotton candy and hot dogs. It was impossible to feel depressed now, the wispy sugar of the cotton candy melting in her mouth, staining her lips cherry pink. For the first time in weeks, Kathi was hungry, ravenously hungry, and she made David stop at every booth to sample the food, until she was so full she couldn't eat any more.

"Oh, David!" she cried, throwing her arms around his neck and kissing him. "This was such a marvelous idea! I feel wonderful!"

With the calliope music ringing like chimes in her ears, they rode the horses, around and around until they felt positively dizzy. By the time they dismounted, Kathi was staggering, but delighted, letting her tension evaporate and her eyes sparkle with the fun. There were no shades of ghosts and spirits here. It was almost as if the whole thing was only a bad dream. She was feeling marvelously content, walking hand in hand with David, stopping to examine the sideshow pictures, and trying to decide whether they should see the man who looked like a dog or the bearded lady.

"Oh! Look, honey!" Kathi giggled, pointing out a small tent removed from the others by a wide, grassy space. "There's the same fortune-teller that Bev talked about. The one she and Roger went to see last year."

"You don't really believe in that stuff, do you?" David asked, grinning down at her.

"No, if course not," Kathi responded quickly. "I . . . I don't want my fortune told anyway."

"I'll bet you do," David teased, ruffling her long blond hair with the back of his hand. "We should go in. Then you could tell Bev what Madame Xanda says about you."

"No, it's really a waste of money," Kathi hedged, feeling the small beginnings of fear knot the muscles in her stomach. "Madam Xanda probably says the same thing to everyone. I bet she'd tell me the same thing she told Bev last year."

"There's only one way to find out." David grinned, winking at her. "We'll just have to try it and see."

"No!" Kathi felt the cold spread through her body. "She's just a fake! You know that, David!"

David turned to glance at Kathi sharply. She sounded almost afraid! There was no reason in the world for her to be afraid of a sideshow fortune-teller, but he wasn't about to spoil their fun by insisting. Her face had that pinched look again, and her eyes were deep and dark with fright. If the afternoon was going to be a success, he'd better get her away from Madame Xanda's tent immediately.

"Come on, honey," David urged, grabbing her hand. "Let's go on the merry-go-round again. And then we'll try the house of mirrors."

"I'm with you!" Kathi gave a grateful smile that almost erased the fear in her eyes. "And there's the Octopus too. We haven't gone on the Octopus yet."

As David bought tickets for the merry-go-round, Kathi noticed two children tugging at their mother's hand.

"Just one more, Mommy, pleeeease?" the little girl begged, staring hopefully up into her tired-looking mother's face.

"Yes, Mommy! Yes!" her little brother added to the plea.

"I'm going to be glad when they're old enough to go on by themselves." The mother sighed, giving Kathi an exhausted smile. "You wouldn't believe these kids! They were up at six this morning, and they've been running me ragged ever since we got here. If I have to go on that merry-go-round one more time, I think I'll be ready for the undertaker!"

Kathi smiled back. The woman really did look tired, and it was obvious that the children weren't ready to stop riding yet.

"Why don't you let us take them on this time?" Kathi suggested helpfully. "My boyfriend's in line buying tickets right now. That way you could sit down on that bench over there and rest."

"Oh, would you?" The woman smiled thankfully. "I'd really appreciate it. My husband had to work today, and he usually takes them on all the rides. My feet are killing me."

"You just go sit down, and we'll take care of them," Kathi promised, taking the two excited children by the hands. "We'll bring them over to you just as soon as the ride's finished."

David came up to hear the last of the conversation, and he smiled at Kathi. This was the Kathi he knew and loved—the helpful, pleasant Kathi, always concerned about everyone and everything.

"What's your name, honey?" he asked, bending down so his head was level with the little girl's. "Anna? Well, come on, Anna. I'm David, and that's Kathi. We'll see you get another ride."

Kathi followed with Anna's little brother, his short stubby legs pumping hard to keep up. Perhaps her baby would look just like this little boy, freckled and blond, trundling along manfully after his big sister, Kathi mused.

"Up you go, honey!" Kathi grinned, lifting the little boy in her arms and placing him on the horse's back.

"Now hang on tight, and I'll climb right up behind you and hold you so you won't fall off."

The excited squeal he gave as the carousel started to move made Kathi grin. His warm body was so tiny, and she held him protectively as he chuckled when the merry-go-round picked up speed. She'd be very pleased to have a little son just like him, a dear little boy to care for and protect. The thought prompted her to pat her stomach in speculation.

As the carousel whirled around, Kathi had the feeling of having been here before, holding a little boy on a carved and painted horse. The music was loud and squawky, making her ears buzz and her heart beat faster. Yes, she had done this before, but something awful had happened to the boy . . . something she could have prevented if only she'd known . . .

"Don't worry, Baver. . . . I'll take care of you. You don't have to cry. I can take care of you all by myself!"

Her arms tightened around his chubby body. There was danger here. Some bad people were coming to take him away, and she had to hide him so they couldn't find him. She had to get off the merry-go-round right away and hide her baby brother to keep him safe.

"Come on, Baver! Come with me!" she gasped, jumping down suddenly from the horse and lifting him in her arms. "I'll take care of you! You'll see!"

Kathi didn't see the expression of astonishment on David's face as she hopped off the merry-go-round and raced toward the house of mirrors. They'd be safe there. Baver would like the house of mirrors. He loved mirrors, except when they had pictures of trains on them, like the one Auntie had made for him.

The boy looked up at her curiously, but that didn't matter. "We're going in here, Baver," she gasped. "We'll hide in here!"

"Hide!" He clapped his hands and laughed again. It was all right to let him think this was a game. Then he wouldn't be frightened. It was up to her to keep her little brother safe and happy. She was a big girl now with lots of responsibilities.

"Hey, lady! You need a ticket to get in here!"

The angry barker's voice didn't even register in her brain as she ran with the child in her arms. Straight through the entrance they rushed, and then she heard his gleeful chuckle as they saw themselves reflected over and over again in the wavy, distorted mirrors.

"Look, Baver! See all the faces? That's me, and that's you!" Her voice was high and shrill, and for a moment she thought he would cry, but then he laughed again, watching the mirrors. She was really a big girl now . . . almost a giant compared to her little brother. The mirrors were strange, making her look much bigger than she really was. She looked almost like Auntie, nearly as big, and that was way too big for a four-year-old girl.

She stared, not recognizing her own face. She looked so different now, but Baver looked just the same. How could that be? The mirror had made her grow up, but Baver was still a baby. That was wrong. These mirrors weren't funny. They were scary!

"Mama?" he said, his blue eyes peering intently into hers. "Want Mommy!"

"Mommy's all gone," she answered, hugging him tighter. "Mommy and Daddy went away . . ."

Her voice trailed off, and for a moment her mind was blank. She blinked once, and then once again. Mommy? He wanted his Mommy, and his mother was . . .

With a puzzled frown, Kathi turned to look around her. Where was she? And who was this little boy? The mirrors were confusing her, making her see double and triple, whirling her head in circles. He wanted his mother, of course. And his mother was . . .

"On the bench by the merry-go-round!" she cried, all her thoughts converging in a blinding flash. "Oh, no! Your mommy's waiting for us at the merry-go-round! We have to hurry right back before she worries!"

She scooped up the boy in her arms and ran faster than she could ever remember running before. She had to get back to the merry-go-round before the ride was over. She didn't know what had got into her, taking this little boy and going into the house of mirrors without telling his mother. If only the ride hadn't ended, she could get him back before they were missed. What had she done . . . and why?

She was out of breath by the time they got back to the carousel. It was just stopping, and David hopped off, holding the little girl in his arms. "Where were you?" he called out. "Is there something wrong, Kathi?"

"Uh . . . no," she forced herself to say. "I . . . I just got a little dizzy, and we got off. I took him to the house of mirrors instead."

"Mirrors," the little boy repeated, looking up at her trustingly. "Funny mirrors."

"Looks like he had a good time, anyway," David chuckled, tousling the little boy's hair. "Well, we'd better get these two back to their mother now. I hope she got a good rest."

"David? C-could you take them back?" Kathi stammered. "I-I'm still feeling a little dizzy. I think I'll just sit over there between those tents and wait for you."

"Sure, honey," David grinned. "Too much riding? You just sit down over there, and I'll be right back."

She could barely concentrate enough to get to the grassy space. David was taking the two children back now, and she could see him walking toward the bench. He had looked just like that little boy when he was young, she could tell that. David had the same wheat-colored hair and blue eyes. He'd had freckles too, freckles and chubby legs all skinned up from falling down.

"So tired," Kathi murmured, sitting down carefully on the grass. The sun glinted off the mirrors on the merry-go-round; it hurt her eyes, but she couldn't seem to close them. It was beginning again, the loud calliope music and the bright circles going faster and faster. Everything was getting fuzzy, and it didn't make any difference that the sun hurt her eyes. Everything hurt, and there was no stopping the pain once it started.

"Kathi? Kathi! Are you sleeping?" He knew she wasn't sleeping because her eyes were wide open, unfocused even when he held her head and shook her. She was like a lifeless mannequin. David called her name again, anguish in his voice. He was unsure whether he should slap her to bring her out of her trance, or hold her tightly in his arms. This time he had no idea what had set her off, but it was the most frightening thing he had ever seen. She was paralyzed, leaning heavily in his arms, not feeling, not seeing, not hearing.

As David struggled with his doubts and guilt for having brought her here in the first place, a little color began to come back into Kathi's cheeks. The pain gradually left her body as sounds began to register in her mind.

She had been aware of the voice for some time now. It slowly invaded her consciousness, first sounding like an insect droning, and then sharpening to tinny words like a cheap transistor radio turned just below an audible volume. She felt as if she were emerging from a fog, gradually aware of her arms and legs and the prickly spears of dry grass pressing against her skin.

She tried to open her eyes, but they were shut now—glued shut. When had she shut them? They were the eyes of a child who has slept too hard after a long ordeal of bedtime tears. Her eyelids felt scratchy and heavy. Finally, she managed to lift them open and discover where she was. The voice was clear now, and David was calling her name, calling it over and over. Now, at last, his voice registered in her hazy, cotton-clouded mind.

"Kathi, please . . . come on, honey. Talk to me. Tell me what happened. Please, baby, talk to me!"

"I-I'm all right now," Kathi stammered, eyes focusing at last on David's troubled face. "I . . . I think the heat got to me. The sun's so bright this afternoon!"

David nodded slowly, the pleading look on his face turning to weary resignation. She still wasn't going to tell him. Would she never trust him enough to share her fears? And how could he make her tell him without putting even more pressure on her? She would be afraid of him too, if he kept asking her, and that was the very thing he had to avoid. Even though every nerve in his body was begging to know what was happening to her, he had to be patient and understanding, to wait until she was ready to talk to him. She would tell him eventually. He was sure.

CHAPTER 14

It seemed as if she had just fallen asleep when she heard someone calling her. Her eyes snapped open, and she glanced at the clock. Midnight.

Kathi sat up in bed and looked at David. No, he hadn't called out her name. He was sleeping soundly, one hand thrown across his face as if to shield himself from a blow. She must have dreamed the voice.

Kathi stifled a yawn and snuggled down again, pulling the covers back up to her chin. She shut her eyes, but they snapped open again, as if her eyelids were on springs. Now that she was awake, sleep eluded her like a fickle lover, tempting her by making her body warm and drowsy, but forcing her eyes to open. Midnight. She hadn't had enough sleep, and her mind cried out for the comfort of unthinking oblivion. If only she could sleep forever. Sleep to get away from the nightmare she was living . . . sleep to block out the terror . . . sleep . . . quiet, peaceful sleep.

An exasperated sigh hissed past her lips, and she sat up again, blinking owlishly in the darkness. Perhaps she needed another of the tranquilizers the doctor had given her. If she took one pill right now, she ought to be able to get back to sleep.

Being very careful not to jiggle the bed, Kathi lifted the covers on her side and slid her feet into her slippers. Then she scooted out from under the cocoon of blankets and padded softly to the bathroom. No need to turn on the light. She knew exactly where the pills were.

The bathroom was dark, and she could hear the sound of David's soft snoring as she opened the medicine cabinet. He was breathing heavily, sleeping deeply, and she envied him.

The coldness of the porcelain washbowl seemed to penetrate her fingers as she leaned against it, traveling up her arms and freezing her in a kind of numbed despair. She was lonely, lonely except for the spirit invading her mind. For some reason, she was calm tonight, calmly accepting the inevitability of whatever was going to happen. There was no help for her, no hope for her. None at all, so why pretend? Why fight? It all seemed so useless. She was tired of pretending and making up excuses for herself. Wouldn't it be better if she could just let Sheri Walker have her way?

The mirror was slashed with moonlight, and she caught a glimpse of her black-pupiled eyes. There was a feeling of dread in the pit of her stomach, and she blinked rapidly, frightened at the madness she saw reflected back at her. There was evil around her. She had to get out before she became a part of it.

There seemed to be a tangible pull between her reflection and her body, leaving her helpless and immobile for what seemed like an eternity. Then, with all her strength, Kathi moved, turning and fleeing her own image to stumble into the living room. In the back of her mind she knew the movement had no purpose, but she couldn't stay and become the pawn of Sheri Walker's spirit. She had to fight even though the battle was already lost.

She tried to run, but her legs were heavy and leaden, as if she were pulling them through molasses, every step in slow motion until she reached the couch, exhausted. The wineglasses she and David had used that evening were still sitting on the coffee table, sparkling and fragile in the pale light that slanted in through the venetian blinds. She saw, rather than felt, her fingers reach out toward them.

"Now, darling, the time is now." The voice, for which Kathi had been waiting, called out to her. *"This time you'll make it, you'll see. This time it will be much easier to find your way home. Everyone's waiting for you."*

For a brief moment, resistance showed on Kathi's trembling face. Then her hand shot out as if it had been pushed by an invisible force, and knocked the glasses off the table, shattering them. She stared down at the jagged pieces of crystal. Her hands rose to her ears, ready to block out the voice, but then her arms dropped despairingly to her sides. She couldn't block it out by covering her ears. The voice was in her own head; she had no choice but to listen to it.

Somehow her hand moved down, and she was kneeling to pick up the sharp, jagged piece of stem that glittered on the floor. She stood again, and calmly pressed the stem to her wrist with fingers that obeyed the relentless inner voice.

"Press down . . . that's it, darling. Press down hard and deep. You mustn't stop now. It's so easy . . . so easy to come home again."

She watched as her hand moved and a bright drop of blood appeared, black and rich in the moonlight. The voice was right. It was so much easier this time. Much easier than the train . . . much, much easier . . .

A sound. A creaking. The flash of the bedroom light.

"Kathi? Where are you, Kathi?"

The moment passed, and suddenly she could see herself clearly, the crystal stem cutting into her flesh. The blood was flowing now, and she gave a small cry, dropping the glass and holding her wrist tightly. What was she doing? What was happening?

"Kathi?" David's voice again, impatient and sharp with worry. "Are you all right? What was the noise?"

"I-I'm fine, David," she called out, responding to him almost out of habit. "I . . . I was just cleaning up in here, and I dropped a wineglass."

Slowly, almost with reverence, she picked up the pieces of glass and walked to the kitchen, dropping them into the wastebasket. She ran cold water in the sink and cleaned her wrist, squeezing it tightly with her fingers until the flow of blood stopped. It was only a small cut, not deep enough to do any real damage.

She gave a shudder as she looked down at her wrist. If she told David about this, he would think she had been trying to commit suicide. Kathi knew that wasn't true. She hadn't been trying to kill herself. But someone—Sheri Walker?—had attempted to kill her, and she had almost succeeded.

CHAPTER 15

She heard the telephone ring, and David's arm brushed across her to answer it on the first ring. How could he be so alert at this time of the morning? Kathi was sure it was early, very early, judging by the way she felt.

"Sure, I'll tell Kathi she's got a package. No problem at all. We'll stop by and pick it up this afternoon."

As the hair on David's arm tickled her breasts, Kathi felt the small beginnings of desire. They hadn't made love in so long. Perhaps it would be all right in the morning with the sun shining brightly outside the window. She wouldn't feel the terror in the daylight, would she? It couldn't be the same as it was at night, when that awful rocking rhythm beckoned her to frightening dreams.

"Kathi?"

David was shaking her softly, and she could feel his gaze on her face. She felt warm and loving, still sleepy and comforted. Return to the womb. Wasn't that what the psychologists called it when you nestled in the covers, curled up securely against the world? She would have to ask David if that was the proper term. And she would ask him about the package too. Package? What had she heard about a package?

"Kathi, it's almost noon," David's voice was calling again. She felt his hand smooth the tumbled strands of hair from her cheeks. Now her face felt bare, and she wondered whether he thought she was still beautiful.

"Hmmmmmmm," Kathi responded at last, even though she wanted to sink back into the comfort of slumber. "Noon?"

"Noon," David repeated, a hint of laughter in his voice. "It's almost noon, and you've got a package at the dorm. It just came in this morning. I thought we could pick it up when we get the rest of your things."

"Oh . . . good idea," Kathi mumbled, still unwilling to relinquish her warm cocoon of covers. "Almost noon? I thought it was still early in the morning."

"You had a good night's sleep, baby." David grinned, his lips soft on her face, sweet and snuggling like the touch of petals against her skin. "How about making the trip to the dorm now, and then we can try that new Chinese place for lunch?"

"Sure," Kathi said, opening her eyes all the way and looking at him for the first time. She loved the way he looked, just awakened and tousled from the night. So capable, so strong, the man she loved here in their own bed. Perhaps if she just reached out and let him know that the time was right, he would—

"Come on then," David laughed, hopping out of bed with a leap that set the lumpy mattress bouncing. "I bet you got a care package from home. Sally must have made fudge for you. Remember that last package?"

Too late, but it didn't matter. He was out of bed already. Later then, she would show him how much she loved him. Later in the afternoon would be wonderful too, the sun still warm and shining.

Kathi smiled, and then laughed as she remembered the last box of fudge that had come in the mail. David had raved about it, and they'd gorged themselves until they were almost sick. He was right; it was probably a package from home. Sally would do something like that to make her feel better. And now that she thought about it, she was hungry, her mouth watering at the memory of that delicious fudge.

All of Sally's cooking was fantastic, but Kathi liked her breakfasts best of all. Bacon—crunchy and crisp—with sleepy-eyed eggs the way only Sally could make them—yolks still soft with a tasty pepper-studded covering over them. There were the little juicy sausages and a steaming plate of French toast, amply seasoned with cinnamon and nutmeg. Pancakes . . . yes . . . fluffy and light with warmed maple sugar, and . . . and . . .

"Ooooh!" Kathi gasped, sitting bolt upright in bed. Her head was suddenly whirling, and she felt as if she'd been punched in the stomach. "I . . . I think I'm going to be sick!"

David turned to look at her quickly as she sprinted for the bathroom and slammed the door closed behind her with a loud bang. Then he grinned in understanding. Too much junk food at the fair. She'd eaten like a starving waif, and now her stomach was upset. He never should have permitted those Polish sausages with sauerkraut after the hot fudge sundae. What a combination! She'd eaten like a pregnant mother with cravings yesterday.

The thought made David stop in his tracks, and he repeated it slowly, under his breath. She couldn't be . . . but that would explain everything! Now that he thought about it, he couldn't remember her having her period last month. And some women experienced all sorts of strange emotional upsets when they were pregnant. That would certainly explain the pressure, the guilt about their relationship resulting in nightmares after they'd made love, the worry about her family's reaction and the press finding out about it before the election . . .

David let the air out of his lungs as he thought about it. Then a grin appeared on his face. It was so simple! Why the hell hadn't he thought of it earlier? David's grin grew wider. Sure enough, that might just be the whole problem. Maybe she was even afraid that he'd leave her. Didn't she know that he'd do anything for her? If Kathi was pregnant, they'd get married right away. He'd been promised that teaching assistantship in the psych department next semester, and though their finances would be strained, they could make it. Hell, they could work everything out if that was all it was.

David's mind began to race as he thought of the possibilities. He'd sign up for married-student housing. That would be cheaper than the apartment. They'd work something out so Kathi could continue her classes after the baby was born. She could put in a couple of hours a week at the Child Care Center and get care for the baby free that way. Kathi pregnant with . . . a little blond girl with ribbons in her hair, dragging a teddy bear around by the ear . . . or maybe a boy, towheaded and tough, riding a bicycle and playing baseball in the backyard.

He knew the odds against student marriages, but theirs would be an exception. They would *make* it an exception. Damn, he thought. So that's what this was all about. It wasn't really a problem after all!

David looked up as Kathi came out of the bathroom, and there was so much love in his eyes that she was caught off guard. "I . . . I guess I ate too much at the fair," she mumbled, heading for the closet.

"That's all right, baby." David grinned. Kathi looked white and shaken, and he longed to pull her into his arms and tell her that he knew. He took a step toward her, and then he stopped, hands falling back to his sides. This was not the time. He wasn't going to botch it and tell her now. They'd get her things at the dorm and go straight to that new Chinese restaurant for lunch. Then he'd ask her to marry him without letting on that he knew about the baby. That way she'd never be able to fear that he'd married her just because she was pregnant.

Pleased with himself, David turned away and stuck his hands into his jeans pockets. He felt like whistling, shouting maybe. Hell! He was feeling like a proud father already, and the baby wasn't even born yet! He was willing to bet that Kathi's nightmares and strange trances would stop in a hurry after he asked her to marry him. The heavy weight he'd been carrying around for the last few weeks was gone, and he felt so damn good it was hard to control himself.

David suddenly became aware that Kathi was staring at him oddly. He forced a calm expression onto his face, but he couldn't hide the laughter in his eyes. She probably thought he was nuts, but that was all right. At least he knew *she* wasn't nuts now, and that was what counted!

"What's got into you?" Kathi asked, frowning and smiling at the same time. "You look like it's the night before Christmas. Do you really like Sally's fudge that much?"

"I sure do," David chuckled. "Come on, Kathi. Let's hurry. I've got something very important to ask you over lunch."

The package was small, not at all what Kathi had expected. She held it in her hands and burned with curiosity as they studied the menu in the Chinese restaurant.

"Why don't you open it, hon?" David suggested, watching the way her fingers curled and uncurled around the small box. "Go ahead. I know your curiosity's killing you."

"I . . . I think I'll wait until we get home," Kathi said, placing the box on the table between them. "Will you order for me, David? I have to go to the restroom."

Once in the small pink-tiled room, Kathi leaned dizzily against the sink and stared at her face in the mirror. She looked sick, pale, and hollow-eyed again. Something about the package from Sally sent chills up and down her spine and made her hands tremble uncontrollably. There was something inside that small square box she didn't want to see—something she didn't want to know. It was another link to Sheri

Walker . . . she could feel it . . . a link that Kathi didn't want. She wished she could block Sheri out of her mind, erect a barrier that nothing could penetrate. She wanted to be strong, so strong that no ghostly force, no matter how desperate, could turn her into an unwilling receiver.

Kathi shut her eyes and then opened them quickly again, staring intently at the mirror as if she could catch a glimpse of the spirit hovering there, waiting for the moment to enter. But there was nothing in the mirror except the reflection of the pink tiles and her own fearful eyes staring back at her. Her face looked unfamiliar, slightly off-center, but everything else was the same as it had always been, the blond hair falling in waves around her face, her lips full and soft, her cheekbones high—a trait that her father claimed went back generations in their family. It was her face—and yet it was not her.

Now the mirror was moving, or perhaps she was moving? The image was blurring, becoming fuzzy around the edges, waving and weaving like the mirrors in the fun house yesterday. Then it sharpened again, growing smaller, and there were pink roses around a white border—a small mirror, for a child.

"This one's yours, honey. It has little roses on it because you're a girl. We'll hang it right here on the bathroom wall, so you can see yourself."

"For me? Just for me? But, Auntie! Baver needs one too! He's too little to see in mine. Did you get one for Baver with roses on it too?"

"Boys don't need roses on their mirrors, Sheri. We got one for him, but flowers aren't right for a boy.

See the nice little train on his mirror? Do you think he'll like it?"

"No! No trains!" Kathi gasped aloud, hands gripping the edge of the sink. "Baver hates trains! He hates trains as much as me!"

"What did you say, ma'am?" one of the green-uniformed waitresses asked, staring at Kathi curiously.

"Um . . . nothing, really. Just talking to myself, I guess." Had she said something aloud? The girl seemed puzzled. What had she said?

The waitress gave Kathi one last bewildered look, and then turned back to the mirror to smooth her dark hair. She had been hoping for a quick smoke between customers, but this woman made her uncomfortable with her intense eyes and startled expression. No telling what weird thing she'd say next. The smoke could wait for a while. With a final tug at the hem of her uniform, the dark-haired waitress hurried out the door, letting it swing closed behind her.

Now she was alone. Alone, but not alone.

"Go away!" Kathi hissed, staring into the mirror with a fierce expression. "Go away, and leave me alone!"

With a snap, she turned on the water faucet, washing her hands vigorously and toweling them off with impatient briskness, as if she could banish Sheri Walker from her mind with the force of her action. She had to hurry and get back to the booth before David guessed she wasn't feeling well again. It was the package; she knew that now. It was the package that made her feel this way. She'd have to think of some excuse to get him out of the apartment later, so she could open the box in privacy. Then, if something in it made Sheri Walker come to her again, at least she'd be alone.

Kathi forced a mouthful of food past the lump in her throat. She'd used the chopsticks on purpose, blaming the trembling of her fingers on the use of the unfamiliar utensils. She felt ready to jump out of her skin.

"Yes, delicious," Kathi responded dutifully, smiling weakly. David was watching her now, and she felt the color rush to her cheeks. Did she look normal? Was she behaving the way she usually did? It was so hard to tell, with him examining her every action this way. Was her smile too strained, her jaws working too rapidly chewing the food? Everything seemed bigger than life, yet two-dimensional, as if she were watching a videotape of herself eating.

"You seem a little nervous, honey," David remarked, expertly capturing a water chestnut between his wooden chopsticks. "I bet you're wondering what I was going to ask you." His eyebrows rose in a question.

For the space of a second, Kathi's expression was blank. Then she remembered. David had said he had something important to ask her over lunch. Of course! A prayer formed in her mind. Please, God . . . nothing about the dreams! Please!

"Y-yes, I *was* thinking about that," she said. "What was it, David?"

"Well . . ." David reached out and removed the chopsticks from her nerveless fingers, holding her hands tightly between his own. "I don't know if this is the right place or time, but, . . . well . . . let's get married, Kathi. Will you marry me?"

Kathi felt her mouth drop open, and she closed it quickly. Marry him? Marry him! Didn't he know that she couldn't possibly marry him now?

"Shocked you, huh?" David chuckled, squeezing her hands. "Look, honey, I know this is a bad time for you, right before the election. But you know I love you, and I thought we could start making plans. I want to take you home to meet my parents, and then, after your dad's elected, we'll tell your family. How does that sound?"

Kathi was incapable of speech. This was a total surprise to her. She had no idea at all that David was planning to propose. The thought hadn't even entered her mind.

"Kathi?" David questioned, beginning to get a little nervous himself. He had figured that his proposal would be a shock, but her face was dead white, and there was a look of panic flickering in her eyes. Didn't she want to marry him?

"Oh . . . y-you did take me by surprise." Kathi forced a tense little laugh. Under any other circumstances, she would have blossomed with joy. He wanted to marry her! Of course, she wanted to marry David. They could be married, and her baby would have a father. But now?

For a moment, Kathi thought she was going to scream in anger. No! It wasn't fair! Nothing was going to take David away from her! She would fight to keep the man she loved, and somehow she would do it! She'd marry David, and nothing would stop her.

"Kathi? What's the matter, baby?" David asked, reacting to the fierce, determined expression on her face. She looked as if she were waging a battle within herself.

"Kathi?" he asked again, frowning. "What's the matter? Don't you want to marry me?" He tried to keep the hurt out of his voice, but it was there all the same. He had been so sure Kathi would be overjoyed by his proposal. "I thought you'd be happy."

"Oh! I . . . I am!" Kathi stammered, willing her hands to stop shaking. "I am, David!" Was that too loud? Was her voice too desperate? Could he guess how confused and frightened she was right now? Confused and frightened and relieved, all at the same time. He wanted to marry her! He *did* love her, even now!

"Well?" David prompted, relief beginning to show in his face. "Shall we start making plans?"

"I . . . I . . . yes!" Kathi faltered, hating the weak, thin sound of her voice. "Yes, David." That was better. Her voice was growing stronger now. "Let's start making plans. Of course I want to marry you! I just thought that . . . well . . . I haven't exactly been fun to live with lately and . . . and . . . I didn't think you'd want to marry me."

"For two people in love, we don't understand each other very well," David said seriously. "I know you've been nervous and upset lately, and that's all right. Everyone goes through bad times. I want you to share them with me, Kathi, good times *and* bad times.

Maybe you didn't really know that before, but I want you to know it now. That's why now I hope you'll tell me what's bothering you. It doesn't make any difference what it is. I want to marry you, and I love you. Nothing could ever change that."

"Oh, David!" Kathi murmured, tears welling in her eyes. "I . . . I guess you're right. Maybe I've been a fool, keeping everything to myself. I . . . I just thought you wouldn't understand, but I haven't been giving you very much credit, have I?"

"No," David answered quickly, stroking her cold hands. Now she could tell him about the baby, and then he'd tell her that he was delighted. That would make her feel much better. "Let's go back to the apartment, and then we can really talk. I promise you, I'll understand. That's a solemn promise from the guy who loves you."

Kathi looked down at the table. The love in David's eyes was almost too much to bear. Her eyes rested on the fortune cookies in their white bowl, untouched. Usually she loved to read the fortunes, but today she wasn't going to suggest they even open one. Sheri Walker wasn't going to give her any message through any medium today. The fortune cookies could stay right there, and she would tell David everything the minute they got back to the apartment. Maybe he could chase her fears away.

She watched him as he paid the bill, his strong, straight back, and those kind, gentle hands handling the money. His hair was growing down in a line from the back of his neck. It would have to be trimmed. She could do that. Somehow the thought of trimming

David's hair, doing something that personal for him, was much more intimate than anything she'd ever done before. It made her feel like crying. He *would* understand. He had solemnly promised that he'd understand. But, did he have any idea what it was that he had to hear?

CHAPTER 16

"But don't you see, David?" Kathi heard her voice grow shrill and frightened. He wasn't looking at her at all. Instead, David was staring mutely at the rug, tracing the design with his eyes, his eyebrows knotted in concentration.

"It's the only thing that makes any sense!" Kathi cried. She had promised to tell him, and he had promised to understand. "I told you what Sally said. She remembered what I had dreamed all these years." Kathi stifled a sob. "Sally and I know, David. Can't you see it? Sheri Walker is trying to possess me!"

Now the shameful confession was past her lips, hanging still and cold in the air between them. David still hadn't raised his eyes, and Kathi was afraid that when he did, doubt would appear on his face, the pitying look that meant he didn't believe. She would be able to see that he felt compassion for her, but there would be no belief.

How could she have been so stupid, so misguided?

Her explanation sounded like the ravings of a madwoman, even to her own ears, now that the words were spoken. He would think she was crazy, and any minute, he would jump up and run to phone the doctor or the state mental hospital to cart her away.

Kathi's heart pounded, her throat dry. She could feel the pulse pounding in her temples, waiting . . . waiting for some reaction from David. How could he sit there, immobile, when she was in an agony of waiting?

At last, David looked up. "Yes," he said slowly. "I can see why you believe you're possessed. I understand, honey. Really, I do."

But, no, he was only mouthing the words. Perhaps he did understand, but he didn't believe. She could see it in his eyes. She could tell that he thought she was deluded, the victim of a psychosis. He didn't believe her at all.

"All right, honey," David said calmly, hoping the sorrow didn't show in his voice. "You're right, you know. All the symptoms point to a classic case of possession."

Symptoms? David shuddered. A bad choice of words. He would have to be very careful how he worded what he was about to say. He didn't want to alienate her when she had, at last, confided in him. Kathi was much more disturbed than he had imagined. A well-systematized pattern of delusions. Jesus!

"Look, honey," David tried again. "You know me pretty well, and you've got to know how hard it is for me to accept something like possession. I understand why you believe that Sheri Walker is possessing you, but there's got to be some other explanation that fits the pattern equally well. Will you let me try to find that explanation? Just let me try. And if there isn't any other explanation that fits, I'll just have to agree with you. Does that make sense?"

"Yes." Kathi sighed, letting out her breath with relief. He didn't believe it, but this wasn't quite as bad as she had expected. At least David hadn't ruled out the possibility of possession. He hadn't accused her of imagining the whole thing. That was a good sign. And when he couldn't find another reasonable explanation, then he'd know too. He didn't believe her yet, but he wasn't *unwilling* to believe her.

"All right, Kathi, let me ask you one thing," David went on. "Are you sure you didn't have a friend named Sheri Walker? Someone you might have known when you were young, and now you've forgotten?"

"I'm sure. I talked to Sally right after I knew the name," Kathi explained. "She didn't remember anyone named Sheri Walker. There was just the Sheri in my dreams. That's not the explanation, David. I thought it might be, but it's not."

"An imaginary playmate, then?" David pursued. "When you were young, you might have been lonely and invented another little girl to play with. Kids do it all the time. Have you thought about that?"

Of course she'd thought about it, but David's face was so hopeful that she couldn't bear to tell him. She shook her head silently and let him hope. Someone had to hope. Let David do it for both of them. All her hopes were dead and buried.

"Hey," David said, grinning suddenly. "We forgot

all about that package from Sally. Why don't you open it now and see what she sent? Let's get our minds off this thing, honey. It won't do any good to dwell on it." He moved to the couch and slipped his arm around her cold shoulders. "And this whole thing doesn't change the way I feel about you at all. I want you to believe that. Now, let's see a smile on your pretty face. Girls who get engaged are traditionally happy."

"Right," Kathi said shortly, resisting the impulse to pull away from him as her lips twisted into the smile he had demanded. How could he expect her to smile and be happy when he didn't believe her?

"That's better." David grinned, apparently satisfied. "Now let's see what Sally sent. It's too small for a box of fudge."

Kathi's hands were shaking so badly, she could barely manage to unwrap the small parcel. There was a sheet of paper inside, folded neatly in fourths, and a small box, which she opened immediately.

A ring? What on earth?

"Look!" said Kathi, slipping the ring on her finger. It fit perfectly. "Look, David! Sally sent me a ring! Isn't it beautiful?"

David could see that the ring was very old. It was a thoughtful gift that obviously meant something to Kathi. Thank God, Sally hadn't sent some superstitious nonsense in her package. That was all Kathi needed.

"Read the letter with it," David suggested, smiling at Kathi's happy expression. "That's a tigereye, isn't it?"

As David was examining the ring, Kathi read the note quickly.

Here's Mama's ring. It always brought her luck, and she won't mind if my baby shares some of it. I found something else for you too, but don't tell no one. It fell out of your Daddy's desk, and I shouldn't have, but I read it. I'm praying for you and so is Preacher Mason. Faith, child. Sally.

"What does she say?" David asked, still watching the way the tigereye picked up the light. "It really is a beautiful ring!"

"Um, she says that this is her mother's lucky ring, and she wants me to have it," Kathi replied, carefully refolding the note and putting it back in the box. She saw another piece of paper under the note, but that she would save to read later. She had shared enough with David for today. She wasn't going to press her luck. Things were bad enough.

"Kathi?" David questioned, trying to keep his tone light. "Are you sure there's nothing else you want to tell me?"

"No," Kathi answered slowly. "I . . . I don't think so, David."

Could he have been wrong about the baby? He wondered. Maybe she wasn't pregnant after all. Of course, it didn't make any difference; they'd get married just the same. But he'd been so sure that her pregnancy was the catalyst for all her problems. He really needed to get out and walk around a little to think this thing out. Surely there was something he could do to help Kathi, if he could just think of it.

"Hey, what do you say I walk over to the liquor store and get a bottle of champagne?"

"Sure," Kathi agreed, hoping that she sounded properly delighted. "I'll be fine, David. I feel much better now that I've told you. We can have a party, just the two of us."

Kathi shivered. Even the most innocent comments sounded ominous to her now. There would be three of them—if Sheri Walker returned. She wanted David to leave the apartment for a few minutes. His absence would give her time to compose herself, and, most important of all, she could hide the rest of Sally's package from him. She wasn't going to look at it now. That would only be tempting fate. She would read that other piece tomorrow, when she was calmer. With Sally's mama's ring she could get through tonight, and tomorrow she could face the rest of it.

As the door closed behind David, Kathi stared down at the ring on her finger and tried a small smile. She was glad she hadn't told David about the baby yet. She would wait, wait to see if she could lay the ghost of Sheri Walker to rest before she even mentioned the baby. David would be doubly worried about her if he knew that she was carrying his child.

Kathi's smile grew a little wider. It was helping already, wearing the lucky ring. Some of the panic seemed to have subsided, and she imagined a link that stretched past the grave to join her with Sally's mama. The ring was her luck, too. She needed to believe that. She desperately needed to believe in something, now that she knew David would be no real help. Joining forces with Sally's mama might give her some ancient wisdom, some way of controlling Sheri Walker. Sally's prayers and her mama's ring just had to help!

CHAPTER 17

Church bells pealed in the distance as Harry Adams shifted to an upright position. He had fallen asleep working again, and there were crease marks on his cheek from the paper clip on the batch of reports he'd been trying to read.

Harry opened his mouth wide and yawned. He scratched his leg idly and then grinned. For the past two weeks, he'd been working close to eighteen hours a day, barely taking time for an occasional shower. Only sixteen days until the election now—sixteen days left to ensure that Doug would be the new senator. Harry picked up his red marker and crossed another day off his wall calendar.

He yawned again and stretched, then padded across the floor to his swivel chair. His legs found their habitual position on top of his desk. He should really do something about losing some of the flab around his middle. Not that he cared how he looked, but it was getting to be an effort, lifting his legs up there. He wiggled his toes impatiently, thinking of the candy bars he snatched for quick energy, and the way he munched continually when he was nervous. It was impossible to even plan a diet until he got through this election and Doug was safely installed at the nation's capital. Then he could relax and eat well-balanced, healthy meals. Until that time, he would just have to continue existing on candy bars, quick, fattening snacks, and the occasional meals he managed to catch at the greasy spoon around the corner.

The church bells pealed again, and Harry took a second glance at the calendar. It was Sunday! With his work schedule, he'd lost track of which day of the week it was. They were all the same—work, work, work. Harry was not what most people would regard as a religious man, but right now he hungered for the cool, air-conditioned interior of a church, and especially the Christian concept of a day of rest.

"A day of rest." Harry sighed, grinning wryly. He was lucky to get five hours of rest. He wouldn't know what a day of rest was if it came up and bit him on the ankle. Christ! He wouldn't have the slightest idea what to do with a day off, but he sure would like to try.

"Damn," Harry groaned mildly, pulling out the operative reports that had come in last night. He'd been too tired to read them, and he sighed mournfully as he picked up the file on Kathi Ellison. Doug would surely fire him if he found out that she was being tailed. It was a pretty sneaky thing for Harry to do, but that was political life. His job meant taking chances like that, and Harry accepted all the risks. If there was anything wrong with Kathi, Harry was going to be the first to know about it.

* * *

"Jesus!" Harry said as he finished the thick report and glanced at the enclosed cassette. If he hadn't known the investigator personally, he'd think someone was playing a rotten practical joke on him. "Jesus H. Christ!" Harry slammed his fists on the desk. If this was on the level, Kathi was going to blow the whole goddamn campaign.

Harry located his cassette recorder under a pile of Nut Goodie wrappers in his center desk drawer, and slipped the tape into place. He almost hoped that the investigator *was* playing a crude, rotten joke. Or maybe Kathi had caught on that she was being tailed and staged this whole thing to shake him up. Did she have that weird of a sense of humor? If he was lucky, she was putting both of them on.

When he'd heard the entire tape, Harry sat back and rubbed the heels of his hands into his eyes. What was going on? This couldn't be real, but the end of the tape had clearly been Kathi's voice. That other voice—the little girl's voice that said all the weird things—it couldn't be Kathi!

Harry thumped his fist down the desk, imagining the worse. Either Kathi was ready for a straitjacket, or she was some kind of junkie. The investigator had seen her take some pills—it said so right in the report. This was a hell of a mess!

"That's all I need!" Harry bellowed, his face turning purple. Why the hell hadn't Doug sent her to a nice girls' school in the East? Dope! Jesus!

Harry's eyes shut, visualizing headlines announcing

that Doug's own daughter had been carried off, kicking and screaming, to a private sanitarium, to recover from what they called "mental illness." It would be the same sort of slander that had killed Eagleton's chance for vice-president, and it could happen all over again in this election if he didn't find out how to stop it.

"Wait a second," Harry muttered, forcing himself to stay calm. "She could be putting us on. There's always that. She could have recognized Dan and made this whole thing up to see us sweat. I wouldn't put it past her. I wouldn't put it past her at all!"

That had to be it. Harry shook his head and grinned at himself. All this was ridiculous! Kathi wasn't the type to use drugs and act crazy, but she *was* the type to warn him with a stunt like this, if she thought her privacy was being threatened. He'd catch a plane up there this afternoon and have a talk with her. They'd straighten out the whole thing then. Jesus! She really had him going there for a minute. Kathi was a reasonable girl. He'd pull off the tail, and she could stop this silly retaliation of hers. It was simple.

Harry removed the tape from the machine and dropped it into Kathi's file. He supposed they'd laugh about this someday, but he'd had a nasty scare, all the same. The cover on the recorder snapped shut with a click, and Harry shoved it back into the center desk drawer, ignoring the mess inside. The drawer closed with difficulty, and Harry mopped the sweat from his forehead. It was this damn heat. Heat made people do strange things, like Kathi's silly stunt with the investigator. He would level with her this afternoon, tell her exactly why he'd had her followed, and she would understand. Kathi was a bright girl. She'd appreciate his efforts for her father.

Harry sighed heavily and lit up one of the small, smelly cigars that were his secret vice, despite strict orders from his doctor. Harry was a philosophical man. If he stopped smoking, he wouldn't get lung cancer, but he'd die of a heart attack because he'd be so damn nervous. He was supposed to stop smoking because it was dangerous, quit the spicy foods and alcohol because of his ulcer, and lose weight to boot. Even with all those restrictions, he was ordered to stay calm and get plenty of sleep. He supposed he could do it, but who wanted to live another year or so without any of life's small pleasures? He would go out in a blaze of glory—a cigar in his mouth, a drink in his hand, and a bag of tortilla chips on his desk.

Harry leaned back in his chair and pondered the campaign. So far, so good. The women voters loved Doug. He was at the top of the polls again this week. There was a quality of boyish charm that made the ladies' hearts palpitate every time Doug made a speech. The men listened to his speeches and liked his logical, honest approach to issues; the women all fantasized about sleeping with him.

Harry blew a cloud of dark smoke at the ceiling fan that sounded like a backfiring motorcycle. Sixteen days, and it would be over. The major groundwork was long since done. The finish would be hectic, but all they had to do was maintain the status quo with plenty of good publicity. There was no reason to be so worried. Doug was a perfect candidate.

Harry nodded and winced. Perfect? If he could find

one unethical thing Doug had ever done, no matter how trivial, maybe then he could relax. It was impossible for a man to be so perfect. In all of his other campaigns, Harry had found at least one thing to hush up. He kept thinking that there must be something here too. A corner of his mind was prickling. Call it a hunch, or intuition, or whatever, but Harry had found that this uneasy feeling always preceded the discovery of a real whopper of a problem. His little inkling never failed him. Something about Doug didn't quite ring true.

He leaned back and closed his eyes. The office felt like the inside of a steam room already, and it was only ten in the morning. His sharp mind ran through the history of Doug's life from birth to the present, and he shrugged his shoulders. Then he opened his eyes and stared at the fly-specked ceiling. Something would turn up. It always did. He'd keep his eyes open, and he'd find it. Then he'd give Doug holy hell and cover it up for him. He'd never run into any problem he couldn't cover up with a few bucks in the right places. This would be no exception. All it took was the moxie to find it before the opponent did.

CHAPTER 18

The day was so smoggy, it was difficult to breathe. David had gone to the library, presumably to return some books, but Kathi knew he was going to search through the psychology journals to discover the treatment and prognosis for people who believed they were possessed. This morning, it had been even more clear that he didn't believe her. He was humoring her, and, while she was grateful for the concern, it didn't change a thing. Why couldn't he just believe her?

Now was the time, but she had to hurry. David would probably be gone for an hour or so, but she might need that long if . . . if Sheri Walker . . . if anything happened. She was terrified, but she had to read the second sheet of paper Sally had sent. It might be something to help her.

She sat on the couch, in the same spot where she had sat last night when she and David celebrated their engagement. Kathi gave a slight shudder as she remembered the ordeal. Somehow she'd got through it.

With shaky fingers, Kathi unfolded the paper and started to read. It was a newspaper clipping.

> GALLOPING GOOSE DERAILS: The Galloping Goose, Northern Pacific's small passenger line, derailed at approximately nine PM Thursday night, killing three local residents. The accident occurred at Carlson's Crossing, one-half mile north of Swanville. Among the dead are Mr. and Mrs. Irvin Miller and their foster daughter, Sharon Elizabeth Walker, who were passengers on the train. The engineer states that the train collided with a car driven by Mrs. Roma Ellison of Little Falls. The Morrison County Sheriff's Office reports that Mrs. Ellison was killed on impact, and her daughter, Kathleen, was thrown out of the vehicle. Miss Ellison is in a coma in critical condition at St. Gabriel's Hospital in Little Falls. Services for Irvin and Dorothy Miller will be held on Monday at St. Steven's Catholic Church in Swanville with interment at Brookside Cemetery. Arrangements for the funeral of Sharon Walker are being handled by the Catholic Adoption Home in Little Falls.

"Oh, God!" Kathi moaned, covering her face with her shaking hands. "We were in the same accident!"

It was what she feared. She had been right there, in a coma, when Sheri Walker died. And if Sheri's spirit had entered her unconscious body—Oh, God! It was real now, and that made it even more frightening. What did Sheri Walker want? What sort of terrifying thing would the spirit make her do?

Kathi moved automatically, hands fumbling in her haste. Now the paper was folded and back in the box, hidden in the very bottom of her dresser drawer. She closed the drawer and looked up, her heart in her throat. The walls of the apartment were closing in on her, like a huge trap. Kathi felt a scream rise in her throat, and, with great difficulty, she held it back. She had to be calm now, everything depended on that. She had to wait . . . to trust that Sally's mama was right. If she could do what the spirit asked, Sheri Walker would leave her in peace.

Kathi shivered involuntarily and walked quickly to the window, standing directly in the bright sunlight. It was hot, but not even the golden stream of heat could warm her. She had to pull herself together before David came home.

With visible effort, Kathi forced her arms and legs to move. She walked into the sunny kitchen and stared at the sink full of dirty dishes. She had to pretend that there was nothing wrong, and convince David that she was fine now. If she didn't, she might be endangering David's life. Sheri Walker had already tried to kill her, and she might try to kill David, too, if he interfered. She would never forgive herself if anything happened to him because of her. Once David was safely out of the way, she would wait, in her moments of privacy, for the spirit to tell her what to do.

Kathi turned on the water full force and tried to think of what to fix for dinner as she squirted soap into the dishpan. She was usually a very good housekeeper. David would think that she was feeling much better if he came home to find the dishes done and dinner on the stove. But as the water ran noisily into the dishpan, Kathi began to feel the familiar dull ache at her temples, the rhythmic throbbing behind her eyes. It was time.

Shimmering droplets of water splashed out of the sink and dripped to the floor, forming a puddle at her feet. The terrified girl watched the puddle grow with a sinking feeling. She was coming now. The inevitable terror was creeping over her in numbing waves. She stared fixedly at the puddle, frozen with fear as her mind whirled back . . .

Harry heard the water running before he knocked on the door of the apartment. Someone was here. At least he hadn't wasted his time coming up here.

Harry tried the door after minutes of fruitless knocking. It was unlocked. The door swung inward, and he hesitated for a moment, and then entered. Kathi and David weren't very careful about locking their doors.

The sound of water was coming from the kitchen, and Harry set down his briefcase on the couch, noting the size and furnishings of the apartment. Brick and board bookcases, slipcovered couch, posters on the wall. The traditional student apartment.

"Hello, Kathi!" Harry called out politely, hesitating at the kitchen doorway. Then he poked his head around and drew a sharp breath. The moment he set eyes on her, he knew that there was something drastically wrong. She was standing in front of the sink, her hand over her mouth, staring at the pool of water growing at her feet. She seemed to be withdrawn completely, as if in a trance, and Harry quickly reached around her to shut off the water. For the first time, he began to believe that the investigative report wasn't some sort of joke. Kathi was clearly not herself at all.

"Kathi?" Harry's voice was quiet. "Kathi? Are you all right?"

Her eyes were wide and vacant, and her body was rigid. He could hear her quickened breathing.

"Kathi?" Harry tried again, a little louder. "Kathi, honey, it's Harry. I've come to visit you."

There was a long silence, and Harry felt his uneasiness grow. What the hell was he going to do now? She didn't seem to hear him at all. He sure didn't want to call in a doctor, but what if the kid was really sick? Where the hell was that guy she was living with? Why wasn't he here taking care of her?

"Kathi!" Harry repeated, much louder. Her body quivered slightly, and she gave a petulant sigh, not taking her eyes away from the pool of water at her feet.

"I'm not Kathi!" she answered in a high, childish voice. "Why do you call me Kathi? My name is Sheri!"

Harry felt the dread grow as he recognized that

girlish voice. It was the voice on the tape, and now Harry knew the tape had been real.

"I did it again," Kathi said, before Harry could think of anything at all to say. "She's going to be sad again. They try to make it so nice for us, but things are too big for me, and for Baver too. My arms are sore from trying to reach the squirter. And Auntie says I'm too big for the chair. If I stand on the chair, the water goes on the floor, no matter how careful I am. She got me this little stool. It's all painted white, with little roses on it because I'm a girl."

Harry was speechless. At first, it seemed as if Kathi were dreaming about her own childhood, but that was impossible. She didn't have an aunt. He had to think of something to say to bring her out of it, but Harry was so shocked, he couldn't think at all. For a moment, he was tempted to grab Kathi and shake her, but he was afraid that would frighten her into doing something even more bizarre.

"Who's this Baver you're talking about, Kathi?" Harry asked softly, hoping to draw her into reality. He hoped that if he got her talking, then she wouldn't freak out.

"You know who Baver is!" Kathi said, in a shocked sort of voice.

"Sure . . . sure," Harry soothed. "I know who Baver is, all right. I just forgot. Why don't you tell me again."

"Silly!" Kathi giggled. "Baver's my brother. He's my little baby brother, and he's awful scared of trains. It's 'cause of the Galloping Goose. When the Galloping Goose comes in, right after the noon whistle blows, Baver runs in the house. Auntie says he's scared of trains because the loud noise hurts his ears. She can't remember though. Growed-ups never can remember what it's like to be scared."

Without blinking, Kathi giggled again. "I used to be scared of the Galloping Goose too," she confided. "That was when I was little. You can feel the ground moving, and then you hear the whistle. Baver cries because he thinks it will get him. He doesn't believe that it can't come off the tracks."

Harry felt the skin prickle at the back of his neck. This was incredible! Dan had been entirely accurate in his report. She was talking about relatives she'd never had, and now a brother! Now he hoped the hell she *was* on drugs! At least that could be cured. If she was flipping out—really going crazy—it would be the end of Doug's career unless they could hush it up.

"It's like an animal, you know?" Kathi continued, her face impassive even with the changing inflections of her voice. It seemed as if another voice, not Kathi's, was moving her lips.

"You can feel it coming after you, and it breathes louder and louder, like just before someone catches you. Sometimes the whistle screams, and your feet stick right there even if you tell them to run. I stuck one time, and I saw it coming, all shiny and blasting, but the Tiger was there, so I knew it couldn't get me."

"The tiger?" Harry questioned, keeping his voice even and quiet. "Is the tiger a toy?"

His question elicited a flood of giggles. The childish laughter bubbled out, even though Kathi herself was not smiling. There was something eerie about the childish emotion in Kathi's voice and the immobility of her face. It gave Harry a creepy sensation in the pit of his stomach.

"The Tiger's not just a toy!" Kathi giggled, her voice merry and rich with untold secrets. "He's real. He's real, but he's not people. The Tiger's my secret." For a moment Kathi was silent, and then she gave another long, heartfelt sigh. "The Tiger says that if Auntie finds out about him, she'll make him go away, and then he can't bring me messages from Mommy and Daddy anymore."

"Where are Mommy and Daddy?" Harry asked quietly, hoping that she'd wakeup from this delusion of hers the way she had on the tape, when Dan had asked the same question.

"I don't know," Kathi answered, her voice sounding puzzled. "Only the Tiger knows where they really are. But I'm glad they're not where Auntie said, down in the ground with the dead people. Mommy and Daddy wouldn't like that at all!"

Harry shuddered. He found that he didn't really want to hear any more, but it made sense to get all the information he could from her. He didn't know how it all tied together. Doug and Vivian, a little girl named Sheri, relatives they didn't have, and a tiger! But Harry had to ask one more question. What had happened to Sheri's brother?

"Where is your baby brother, K—Sheri? Where's Baver?"

Her whole body trembled, and all the color vanished from her cheeks. Two glistening tears dropped from her wide, unfocused eyes, and a small sob shook her shoulders.

"Gone!" she whispered at last. "He's gone! The bad ladies came and took him away. He didn't want to go, and he cried awful hard, so I gave him the Tiger so he wouldn't be all alone. Auntie and Uncle cried too, and then . . . then . . ."

Harry watched Kathi's grip tighten on the cup that she was holding. Then her fingers relaxed and her face went slack as the cup dropped to shatter on the tile floor.

"Oh!" Kathi gasped, whirling to face Harry. Her eyes were wide awake, and her voice had returned to normal.

"Oh, Harry! What are *you* doing here?"

Just as Harry was about to answer, Kathi cried out again, looking down at the shards of pottery and water on the floor. "Harry! You . . . you scared me! What a mess!"

She gave a little self-conscious laugh and bent down to pick up the pieces of the cup, looking back over her shoulder at him.

"I left the door open again, didn't I? You must think I'm a ninny! Anyway, I'm glad to see you. How about having a cup of coffee, and then you can tell me all about Dad's campaign."

"Sure," Harry agreed quickly, glad now that he hadn't called the doctor. She seemed to be fine now, embarrassed about breaking the cup and about the water on the floor, but very much the self-confident young woman he knew. At least her episode, or trance, or whatever it was, was over for now, but Harry knew that he had to do something fast. He'd have a little talk with Kathi's boyfriend before he left. They had to get Kathi away from here before she wrecked Doug's chance for election. They could hide her someplace until after the election was over, and then they could figure out a way to get some help for her. Kathi was going to be a first-class problem if she stayed anywhere in the state. If the voters found out about this, Doug didn't have a chance.

CHAPTER 19

"Holy shit!" Harry moaned, staring at David in consternation. "She thinks she's possessed? That's the craziest thing I've ever heard! Are you really serious?"

David nodded, taking a sip of his beer. David had walked into the apartment no more than five minutes after Kathi had snapped out of her trance; after a half hour of polite conversation, Harry asked if David would show him the nearest bar, so he could have a quick drink before catching his plane back to Los Angeles. They'd left Kathi at the apartment fixing dinner, and she had seemed completely normal, but Harry didn't want David to leave her alone for long. This could be a real disaster, and he wanted the boy to know it.

"Now look, David . . ." Harry stared at the young man seated across from him. He didn't look like a radical or a doper, but you couldn't be sure about anything nowadays. "You can talk to me straight. I'm not going to turn you in or give you a lecture, or anything like that, as long as you play straight with me. What's she on anyway? Some kind of pills?"

David's eyes narrowed, and his face blotched with anger. He gripped his beer glass so tightly that Harry could see his knuckles turn white.

"No!" he denied vehemently. Then his glance wavered, and his fingers trembled visibly. Was she? He stared at Harry with a strange, pleading look on his face.

"Jesus . . . I don't know! I don't think she is. I don't know what the hell's the matter."

"Okay, take it easy," Harry said. "Sorry about that. I guess you can understand, I just had to ask. I don't think Kathi's the type to take drugs or anything like that either. So she's just plain crazy?"

"I . . . I guess so," David admitted, hating the admission, the pleading look still on his face. It seemed strange to be asking this short, quick-spoken man for help when he was a relative stranger. It was somehow disloyal to Kathi, but David was at his wit's end. He really didn't know what to do.

"Do you think I ought to take her to the hospital?" David asked, fearing Harry's answer.

"Jesus no, kid! We can't do that! We've got to keep this whole thing under wraps until after the election."

Harry frowned for a moment, and then his face relaxed as an idea came to him. "Hey, how about taking her on a skiing trip or something? Anywhere that's out of state. Somewhere nice and quiet and private, where you could take her and sort of babysit her until after the seventh. It's only a little over two weeks away, and then we can make some concrete planes. I don't dare tell Doug about this, or he'll blow the whole campaign.

I figure maybe we could sort of hide her out. A little vacation might do her good. Can you think of anywhere to take her?"

David frowned, thinking. Then he nodded slowly. "Sure, I can think of a couple of places. Somewhere out of state and somewhere quiet, right?"

Harry nodded. He was beginning to like David very much. The young man was mature, and he obviously cared for Kathi. Beard or not, David was all right in Harry's book.

"Well?" Harry prompted, glancing at his watch unobtrusively. He still had plenty of time to catch his plane back to Los Angeles, and David looked like he had decided on a place. Between the two of them, they might be able to pull this off just fine.

"How about a little town in Arizona?" David asked, still looking thoughtful. "Kathi's old roommate lives in a little town outside of Phoenix. Would that be all right?"

"Sounds good to me." Harry grinned. Sure enough! The kid had a good head on his shoulders. A little town in the Arizona desert, that was the ticket. There wouldn't be any nosy reporters there, and Kathi could be as loony as a jaybird; no one would be the wiser. It was a hell of a lot better than sticking her in some private sanitarium under an assumed name and taking a chance that the press would pick it up. "Yeah," Harry said. "That's perfect, David. I'll pick up the tab for the trip. We'll write it off as a campaign expense, and you'll both get a vacation out of the deal."

Harry snapped open his briefcase and took out a pen and checkbook. "Yeah, this trip's a legitimate campaign expense, the way I figure it. If Kathi sticks around here, we don't have a snowball's chance in hell of winning. This is probably the best investment that the People for Ellison ever made!

"Now look, kid . . ." Harry continued, tearing off the check and handing it to David. "I want you to call if there's any problem at all. Here's my card and my office number. Don't talk to anyone but me, got it? We'll keep this whole thing hushed up until after the seventh, and then we'll tell Doug."

David nodded, and then his eyes widened as he glanced at the check. "Harry, this is way too much!" he exclaimed. "We'll only need part of this."

"You never know. Just keep it, David. And get Kathi everything she needs. This is a hell of a big favor you're doing for me, and Doug'll be grateful too, when he finds out about it. You're helping to win the election for him and don't you forget it!"

Harry finished his drink in one gulp, glanced at his watch, snapped his briefcase shut, and slid from the booth, seemingly in one hurried motion. He had things to do, now that he'd averted this disaster.

"You'd better get back to Kathi, and I'd better hustle out to the airport to catch that plane. You don't have to tell Kathi where this money came from. Just say you saved it or something." He turned and started to leave, then made a complete circle, frowning. "You're sure you can get her to go?"

"I'm sure." David nodded confidently. "Bev is Kathi's best friend, and she's visited there before. It shouldn't be too hard to convince her, especially if I call Bev and set it up."

After Harry left, David stared down at the check and then folded it carefully, placing it in his billfold.

He supposed that Harry knew what he was doing, writing this off as a campaign expense. He was helping the Ellison campaign by helping Kathi. It made him feel vaguely guilty though, taking all this money for something he'd wanted to do anyway. He'd been thinking of taking Kathi away from Berkeley ever since Dr. Kauffman mentioned it. Of course, he could spend valuable time sitting here feeling guilty, but that wouldn't accomplish a thing. He had to get back and convince Kathi to go.

A moment later, David was in a phone booth, calling Bev in Arizona. His face fell as he listened to her mother's voice on the other end of the connection. Bev wasn't home. She'd left yesterday to visit her sister and wouldn't be back for a week.

"What now?" David mumbled softly, frowning outside the phone booth. Where could he take Kathi now? Harry had said it had to be someplace quiet and out of state.

The wrinkles smoothed out on David's forehead as he thought of it. The perfect solution. Why hadn't he thought of it sooner? He didn't have to take Kathi to Arizona. They had enough money to go much farther than that. They had enough money to fly back to visit his parents, and it would be much better for Kathi there.

As David walked slowly toward the apartment, he considered everything. Of course he wanted Kathi to meet his parents, but he'd hoped that it would be under better circumstances. Still, his mother and father could be trusted, especially if he explained the problem. He wouldn't tell them the whole truth—that was a little too heavy for them to handle. He'd just say that the strain of her father's campaign was getting to her.

A brief smile flashed across David's face, almost erasing the worry there. He knew exactly what would happen when he took Kathi home. Mom would feed her chicken soup and dumplings, and it would be good for Kathi to spend a little time in the Midwest, away from the fast pace of living in California. She could relax there, go for walks, and maybe even do a little fishing with them. There was a trout stream only two miles from the house, and the sleepy little town might be just what Kathi needed. His parents didn't own a television, and he could keep her away from the newspapers. They didn't even have to mention her dad's campaign. And then there was what Dr. Kauffman had said. If something in Berkeley was setting off Kathi's obsession, it might buy them some time if he could remove her from the whole situation. Life was very different in his home town, and it could be just what Kathi needed.

Unconsciously, he stepped up his pace as he made up his mind. That's exactly what they were going to do. Of course, it would take most of the money that Harry had given him, but Harry had told him to use it for anything Kathi needed.

David's vague sense of guilt about using the money disappeared as he walked faster. It was hot again this afternoon—muggy and miserable. The sun was low in the sky now, and the smog was rolling in from San Francisco. This weather was enough to drive anyone crazy. Dr. Kauffman was absolutely right! Getting Kathi out of this lousy heat and away from the pressure was bound to have a beneficial effect. And it would be great to see Mom and Dad again!

David whistled as he walked the last block. Harry was an all right guy, and because of him, Kathi was going to be all right too. He was already feeling hopeful about this whole trip. His parents would coddle Kathi, treat her like a regular princess. His mother would cook all sorts of home-baked goodies, and his dad would show her the woods and the trout stream. Everything was going to be fine now. Kathi would love it in Swanville.

CHAPTER 20

"Kathi?" David called out as he let himself into the apartment. "Hey, baby? I'm going to make you an offer you can't refuse!"

"In the kitchen," Kathi called out, smiling a little at the excitement in David's voice. "You already made me an offer I couldn't refuse, remember?"

"Well, that too." David grinned, coming up behind her to give her a big hug. She looked fine, thank God. He'd half expected to find her in another trance, and the relief he felt made him almost weak. Harry was absolutely right. Neither one of them could stand this kind of pressure for much longer. He was going to make her go to Swanville, even if he had to force her.

"My parents want to meet you," he said, nibbling at the side of her neck. "I just called them, and they insisted we fly back so they can get a chance to meet the girl I'm going to marry. How about it, Kathi? I think a trip back east is just what you need. A change of scene might do you a lot of good."

"You mean now?" Kathi questioned, turning to

look into David's earnest eyes. "Now? I . . . I can't, David! What if . . . I mean . . . oh, you know why I can't go now!"

"I told them all about you," David explained softly, kissing her neck again. "They know you've been under a strain, and that's all they have to know. I really think we ought to get away from here, Kathi. You'll feel a lot better once we get to Swanville. I'll personally guarantee it. It's just a small town, very rural, with woods all around it, and the kind of old houses you love. Just trust me, honey. I made all the arrangements, and we leave in the morning."

"Swanville? Your parents live in *Swanville?"* It wasn't possible. Swanville was the town where Sheri Walker was killed, where the accident took place! David's parents lived in Swanville!

"Yeah," David chuckled. "I know that's a strange name for a town, but wait until you hear the names of the other towns around there. Upsala, Little Falls, Sobieski, Grey Eagle . . . Kathi? What's the matter?"

"Nothing!" Kathi said hastily, turning toward the stove again. "Nothing at all, David. It's just a small world, I guess. Before we moved here, my dad had a law office in Little Falls. I know where Swanville is. It's funny that we never talked about it before. But anyway, I guess the idea of visiting your parents kind of shocked me. I . . . I don't really feel prepared to meet them right now. After the election . . . maybe . . ."

With great effort, Kathi gripped the spoon and stirred the macaroni and cheese on the stove. What could she say? She couldn't let David know about Swanville!

"Please, honey . . . just trust me," David reassured

her. "My parents are great, and you don't have to be worried about meeting them. My mom'll feed you within an inch of your life, and my dad'll bend your ear with all his stories about hunting and fishing. You'll love it, honey. I think going to Swanville is just what you need."

"My name is Sharon Elizabeth Walker, and I live at four-oh-two Elm in Swanville. Did I do that right, Auntie? Was that good?"

Kathi took a deep breath to steady herself. "I-I'll think about it, David," she promised. Didn't he know that she couldn't think about anything now? Swanville! Sheri Walker had arranged this. Somehow, she had arranged the whole thing! If she went to Swanville, Sheri would do something dreadful! She was sure of it! Everything was moving too fast now; Sheri Walker was pulling her to Swanville with David's help! Did she have to go? Would she be forced to return to the town where Sheri had lived—and died?"

"I-I'll go, David," Kathi whispered, the words pushing past her trembling lips. Let him draw his own conclusions. He would think that she was nervous about meeting his parents, afraid that she'd black out in front of them. But Kathi knew that there was a reason she had to go to Swanville, and she was powerless to fight it. She was being drawn like a fluttering moth to a flame. There was no escape at all for her. It was starting now, and nothing would stop it until the end. She would go to Swanville, and she would do Sheri Walker's bidding.

"I'm scared! I want my mommy! I'm all alone, and I'm scared!"

"Don't cry, Sheri Bear. I'm here. The Tiger's right here, and I'll take care of you. Don't worry . . . I'll always take care of you."

"Mama used to always say that the only way to fight was to find out what the spirit wanted, and do it. She said there was nothin' to be afraid of. Find out what this Sheri wants, and do it. Then she'll leave you in peace again."

The voices hurt Kathi's ears, and she almost reached up to block her ears with her hands. They were all talking at once, whispering and screaming and crying in her head. When would this end? She couldn't take much more! Kathi's hands shook so hard she could barely hold the spoon. The ring glinted on her finger, the mark of the cross to keep her from harm. Would it be enough? Would the ring be enough to save her?

"Why . . . why don't you start packing, David?" Kathi suggested in a trembling voice. "I'll finish dinner and call you when it's ready."

"Sure," David grinned, giving her tense body another hug. "And don't worry about anything, honey. A trip to Swanville is just what you need!"

Kathi glanced down at the ring on her finger again, trying to find an answer. It would happen in Swanville. There was no escape.

CHAPTER 21

"Come on in, Viv," Harry shouted, not taking his feet from the top of his desk. Vivian would think something was up if he acted any differently than he always had. He didn't dare let her know he was fishing for information, or she'd clam up on him.

"Hi, Harry!" Vivian breezed into the office and smiled charmingly as always. She was dressed in a dark red three-piece suit with a hat to match, and she looked stylish and very much the successful politician's wife. He could always count on Vivian to look the part. She was a far cry from some of the dumpy candidates' wives he'd been forced to make over.

"You said you wanted a report on the women's groups," Vivian said briskly, marching over to the chair next to Harry's desk and dusting it off carefully before she sat down. "I don't think there'll be any problem with the women, Harry. The League of Women Voters is behind Doug one hundred percent and so are the Women for Democratic Action."

"That's good," Harry mumbled, taking his feet off

the desk at last, and leaning forward to face Vivian. God, she was a beautiful woman. What a perfect wife for Doug.

"I took a little trip up to San Francisco yesterday," Harry said, stringing the hook. "While I was there, I stopped by to see how Kathi was getting along."

"Oh?"

"At first, I was a little worried about her." Harry cast out the line. "She looked a little under the weather."

Harry took time to light his cigar, carefully considering his next words. He had to be very careful how he phrased this. He didn't want to alarm Vivian; he only wanted to see if she reacted to his precisely phrased comments.

"She said she hadn't been sleeping too well. Nightmares over midterms and stuff like that," Harry went on, watching Vivian through half-lidded eyes. "You know how it is with college girls. She's probably been running around all night and trying to study all day."

He definitely had Vivian's full attention now. She was hanging on his every word.

"Anyway . . . she decided not to stick around Berkeley during the break," Harry continued. "She said she was going to visit a girlfriend of hers, Sheri something or other. Said you'd know who she meant."

The moment the words left Harry's mouth, he wished that he could call them back. There was near panic in Vivian's eyes now, and he could see the effort she was making to control herself.

"Sh-Sheri?" Vivian repeated, choking over the name. "Oh! Well . . . perhaps it'll do her good to get away for the break. Of course, Doug and I are disappointed that she's not coming home, but things are pretty hectic around here. She'll be better off getting away from things . . . getting away from anything connected with politics. Kathi's been under a strain lately, helping out with the campaign on campus and being involved with that Child Care Center. She's getting a 4.0 this semester so far, and that takes a lot of work too. She's working too hard, Harry. I-I'm glad she's spending the break with a f-friend."

Vivian's mind was whirling a million miles an hour. Sheri? Surely Kathi couldn't mean what it had seemed at first! Perhaps Harry had got the name wrong. He must have! Either that, or she'd met a new friend named Sheri. She had to get to a phone right away to call Kathi!

"You know . . . I must be getting old or something." Harry sighed, reeling in the line. "Doug called just a couple of minutes ago, and I completely forgot to tell him I'd seen Kathi. I should have told him."

"Oh! I-I'll tell him, Harry!" Vivian said hastily. She had to keep Harry from discussing Kathi with Doug! This had to be handled very carefully, and her mind spun crazy circles as she grasped for an excuse that would sound reasonable to Harry. "I really wouldn't mention that you'd seen Kathi, Harry," Vivian said. "He'd get very upset that Kathi hadn't called him herself to say she was going to visit a friend." Vivian gave a little laugh that sounded terribly hollow to her. "You know how Doug's been lately," she went on. "He's making mountains out of molehills, and he gets so terribly nervous when Kathi travels. You should have seen him when Kathi and I went to Europe a few years ago. He spent a fortune making transatlantic calls to make sure we were all right. He's simply on pins and needles when it comes to Kathi, and it's worse now that the pressure's on. I'll tell him, Harry. He might think there was something wrong if you mentioned that you saw Kathi. You know how worried he can get about her."

The words rushed past Vivian's lips so quickly, that Harry could tell she was almost hysterical. He'd better drop this one in a hurry. He didn't want Vivian to go off the deep end on him, too. He needed her for the campaign. It might have been a big mistake, mentioning Sheri, but at least he'd found out something. Vivian was hiding something from him, and she obviously was hiding it from Doug too.

"Yeah, you're right." Harry sighed, leaning back in his chair again, seemingly accepting the wisdom of Vivian's words. "You're absolutely right, Viv. Maybe it's best that I don't even mention I saw Kathi. He might think there's something wrong when there's not."

"Exactly!" Vivian replied, a little too vehemently. "I think it was very nice of you to stop by to see her, but if you mentioned that she looked in the least bit tired or run-down, Doug would be convinced that she was really ill. Kathi will be fine, Harry, with a little rest at her friend's house. She's probably just been studying too hard. She knows how important her grades are to Doug."

"My lips are sealed." Harry grinned, giving Vivian a conspiratorial wink. "The two of us are going to have to treat Doug with kid gloves, Vivian. He's under a lot of pressure right now, and it's up to us to make things as easy as possible on him, don't you think?"

"Yes," Vivian said shortly. Pressure? She could tell

Harry a thing or two about pressure right now! Doug wasn't under half the pressure she was, but that was the way it would have to be. She could handle it . . . she'd always handled it. Doug would be protected from anything that might upset him.

Vivian could feel the scream building up inside her as she sat in the cracked vinyl chair. She had to get away from Harry and go home where she could be alone and think. Sitting here with Harry made her desperately nervous. He looked different today, far different from the short, balding man she'd known for the better part of a year. His eyes were too wise, burning into hers like a bird of prey. He looked more like a detective on a homicide squad than a campaign manager. She had to leave. Her hands were shaking dreadfully, even though she willed them to be still. More than anything in the world, she wanted a tranquilizer.

"Well, I've really got to run," Vivian said, glancing at her watch pointedly, but not even noting the time. "I have an appointment in fifteen minutes. Was there anything else, Harry?"

"No, but I'll be in touch, Viv. Keep up the good work on those women's groups. You've been more help than any other candidate's wife I've ever handled."

Ordinarily, Vivian would have glowed at the unaccustomed praise. Today, she didn't even seem to hear it. His mention of Sheri had really upset her. Now all he had to do was figure out why.

CHAPTER 22

Vivian climbed out of her car, leaving the keys absentmindedly in the ignition, a complete reversal of her usual caution. She had to get to a phone immediately and find out whom Kathi was visiting. Her legs were trembling as she let herself into the cool, air-conditioned house and listened for Sally.

Vivian let out her breath in relief as she heard the reassuring sound of the vacuum cleaner coming from the family room. Sally was busy cleaning. She could slip upstairs and call Kathi, avoiding Sally completely. If she so much as let Sally see her face, the elderly maid would know that something was wrong, and then Vivian would be forced to lie about it.

She didn't even bother to take off her hat as she sat at the dressing table and dialed. Of course, Vivian knew she was overreacting, imagining that Kathi's message had been some sort of signal that she had remembered. If Kathi had remembered any more about the accident, she would have called home personally.

This would all be cleared up in a few seconds, just as soon as she got Kathi on the line.

"I'm sorry, ma'am, there's no answer," the operator said. "Most of the girls have left already for the break. Is there a message I can leave for Miss Ellison?"

"No, no message." Vivian sighed. "I'll try again later, thank you."

Vivian longed to stretch out on the bed and sleep off her tension, but the way her heart was pounding, it would be impossible to take a refreshing nap now. She had to do something to calm herself down, and there was only one thing that would work.

Vivian cast one glance at the large, soft bed and went on to the dresser, reaching for her bottle of pills. She shook two of the little blue pills out of the bottle and replaced it carefully in the drawer. Doug couldn't find out that she was taking them again. It would be a dead giveaway that something was terribly wrong.

She willed herself to be calm as she swallowed the pills with a small glass of water. Everything was going to be fine now. She would sleep for the rest of the day, but it was preferable to this damn nervousness. Vivian had just stretched out on the bed and closed her eyes when a knock sounded on the door.

"Yes?" Vivian called out, pressing both hands to her forehead. Perhaps Sally just wanted to see if she was all right. She should have checked in with Sally immediately after returning to the house.

"Mr. Doug called," Sally reported, her words muffled through the heavy door. "He wants you to have dinner out tonight."

Vivian groaned. She couldn't possibly make it now.

She'd have to think of some excuse. Could she say she was too tired?

"What time is he coming home?" she asked, holding her head a little tighter. "Did he say?"

"He said about seven," Sally replied. "He wanted to know if you had time to go out with an old boyfriend of yours, and then he laughed when I didn't catch on right away that he was talkin' about himself."

"All right," Vivian answered, trying to make her voice sound normal. That did it! She really couldn't refuse a special invitation like that. Obviously, Doug was counting on it.

"I'm going to take a little rest before he comes, Sally," Vivian said, grimacing slightly. "Will you take all my calls and wake me at six-thirty?"

"Sure will, Miss Vivian," Sally answered promptly. "Is there anythin' I can get for you now?"

"Nothing, thank you," Vivian replied, struggling to a sitting position. She had to get out of bed before the pills started working. She waited until Sally's footsteps had receded, and then rushed back to the bathroom to try to find the old bottle of pills that must be in there somewhere. Doug had been after her for years to throw out all the old prescriptions, but she never had. And now it was a good thing she hadn't.

Vivian searched until she found it: DEXEDRINE 15 MG. There were only five left, and she doubted that she could get any more. From what she'd heard, Dexedrine was one of the drugs being investigated by the federal narcotics people. The date on the bottle was six years old. If only they were still strong enough to pull her out of the fast-gathering numbness induced by the tranquilizers!

Vivian sighed. She just had to be herself at dinner. Doug would have accepted an excuse, of course, but during the past few months he'd had so little time for her. When he arrived home he was usually exhausted, and their private life together had fallen off to nothing. This dinner date was a real occasion. The least she could do was sparkle!

Her hand was shaking as she rolled two of the pills from the bottle. She hoped there would be no adverse reaction from taking the two different drugs at once, but she didn't think such a small quantity would hurt. She just needed a little boost to wake her up and let her be witty and charming, the way Doug expected her to be.

After the bottle of Dexedrine was safely replaced in the back of the cabinet, Vivian flopped down on the bed again. She had a few hours before Sally would wake her. If she was lucky, she could get a little rest so that she could manage to be herself tonight.

Vivian sighed. The blue pills were beginning to work, and she felt drowsy. The Dexedrine probably wouldn't have any effect for a while. She could enjoy her dreamlike relaxation until the Dexedrine jolted her awake.

Even though Vivian's body felt heavy and drowsy, her mind refused to stay quiet. There was something very pressing she had to do—something she'd tried to do earlier and failed to complete. What was it? Ah, yes, now she remembered. She had to get in touch with Kathi. She would try again right before dinner.

"Later." Vivian sighed, sinking a little deeper into her relaxed state. Right now, she didn't want to think about anything unpleasant . . . anything frightening. In a few hours she would be Vivian again—strong and competent—the Vivian who had gumption.

She closed her eyes and saw a long, white-tiled corridor stretching out in front of her eyelids. Shadowy figures in white were floating and whispering in muted tones.

"Not yet, ma'am. There's no word. The doctor expects some change in the very near future."

Doug's voice now. "Has she come out of it yet, Viv? Can we see her now?"

"Not yet, darling," Vivian answered, her own voice fuzzy in her mind. "Soon . . . the doctor promised. Soon everything will be all right."

But it wasn't all right. It would never be all right now. They had been so sure, or rather, *she* had been so sure. She had convinced Doug, and now she had only herself to blame if everything went wrong.

"Miss Vivian? It's six-thirty, Miss Vivian, and you have to get dressed for dinner," Sally called out cheerfully. "Just open those pretty eyes of yours and splash some water on your face, so you can be beautiful when Mr. Doug gets home!"

"Yes, Sally . . . I'm awake," Vivian answered groggily. She pushed her legs over the side of the bed and sat up blinking. She *did* feel better now, but not quite good enough. Doug would probably want to stay out late and talk to the right people at the club.

There were still three of the little green and white Dexedrine capsules left in her bottle. Vivian hesitated for a moment, and then swallowed another. That left only two for emergencies. She would be fine tonight, a credit to Doug. The Dexedrine would see to that.

Excitement rose like a tide in Vivian's mind as she showered quickly and started to apply her careful makeup. She could handle anything as long as she felt this good. There was nothing too big for her to tackle. She'd have to see Dr. Connors in the morning and get another prescription for the Dexedrine capsules. He wouldn't have the gall to refuse. After all, she was going to be the wife of one of the nation's senators!

CHAPTER 23

Vivian would have preferred to make the call from a place more private than the lobby of the country club, but it couldn't be helped. She had to contact Kathi.

"I'm sorry, ma'am." The switchboard operator sounded bored and a trifle irritated. "Miss Ellison doesn't answer her ring. I can leave a message for her, but most of our girls won't be back until after the break. Are you sure she was planning on staying at the dorm over the break?"

"No, I'm not sure," Vivian admitted. "I'll try again later, operator. Thank you for being so helpful."

"That's quite all right, ma'am." The operator seemed mollified by Vivian's thanks. Now there was a hint of friendliness in her voice. "Would you like me to send one of the staff up to check her room, ma'am? There might be a note or something."

"No, that's not necessary," Vivian answered quickly. It would never do to have Kathi find out that she had checked up on her. "I'll try to reach her tomorrow, and thank you again."

Vivian hung up the phone and sighed. She could hear the music floating softly from the piano bar, but her favorite songs did nothing to elevate her spirits. She had to pull herself together before she went back to Doug. He was having a good time, chatting with friends, but she was still upset about Kathi. Why hadn't she called home herself, instead of giving that scanty message to Harry? Was there really something wrong, or was it all in her imagination?

"Viv!" Jerry Rasmussen lurched toward her, and Vivian stifled a groan. Jerry was feeling his drinks tonight.

"Hello, Jerry." Vivian managed a smile. "How are things at the bank?"

"Auditors are due tomorrow," Jerry mumbled, slipping a beefy arm around Vivian's shoulder, which she couldn't quite avoid. "You certainly look pretty tonight, Viv. If that old man of yours ever kicks you out, you know where you can go to get warm."

"Thanks, Jerry," Vivian said sarcastically. "I needed that!"

Jerry gave her a sharp look and cocked his head, but Vivian was already smiling again. He shook his head slightly and backed off, ambling away toward the piano bar again.

Vivian frowned. Now what had got into her? She was never sharp with Jerry, even though he disgusted her. Jerry was one of Doug's staunchest supporters, but tonight she simply couldn't be bothered with fat drunks making passes. Thank God, she wasn't married to a man like Jerry! Lord knew what Marge Rasmussen had to put up with.

There was one more thing to try, and Vivian dialed the number quickly, knowing that if she was gone too much longer, Doug would decide to come looking for her. The phone was answered on the third ring, just as she had instructed.

"Ellison residence, Sally speaking."

"Sally? This is Vivian. Have any important calls come in?"

"No, Miss Vivian," Sally answered promptly. "Leastwise there wasn't any calls that were really important. Mr. Taylor called to confirm your reservation at the Heart Fund luncheon, and Mary rang up a couple minutes ago to say she was havin' bridge at her house on Wednesday, and could I go and help her out a little. That was all, Miss Vivian."

"Thank you, Sally." Vivian sighed. She felt curiously deflated, as if all the sparkle had gone out of her, leaving her as limp as a punctured balloon, despite the pills she'd taken. She had been hoping that Kathi would call from her friend's house, even though that was unlikely. Kathi didn't call home often, but still, Vivian had been hoping.

"Anything wrong, Miss Vivian?" Sally asked. "Were you expectin' a special call?"

"Oh . . . no, Sally," Vivian said. "Nothing special. I just wondered, that was all. If you don't mind helping Mary on Wednesday, you can call her back and tell her it's fine with me."

"Oh, I don't mind at all," Sally quickly assured her. "I like helpin' Miss Mary. Do you want me to call the club if any real important messages come in?"

"Only if it's a call from Kathi," Vivian replied. "Then you can have me paged. Take her number, and I'll call her right back. Have you got that, Sally?"

"Yes, Miss Vivian," Sally answered quickly. "If Miss Kathi calls, I'll take a number and page you at the club."

"That's right," Vivian said. She felt a little foolish as she hung up the phone. Sally would know that she was concerned about Kathi now, but that didn't matter. Sally knew more about her moods and troubles than anyone else, anyway. Of course she never pried, but it was comforting to know that Sally understood. Whenever she was upset, Sally would somehow know and bring her a cup of her favorite tea or a freshly picked bouquet from the garden. She had an uncanny knack for knowing things. Vivian just hoped that Sally didn't know the real reason she was upset. Of course, she couldn't know anything about that. Sally hadn't started working for them until it was all over. And she'd been marvelously patient with the little girl who had nightmares and attacks of sudden fear. She'd have to speak to Doug about a special bonus for Sally this year, something extra to show their appreciation for her loyalty. Sally deserved everything they could give her.

"Say there, lady, don't I know you from somewhere?" A familiar voice spoke in her ear, and Vivian whirled around, startled, to face Doug who was grinning widely.

"I seem to have lost my wife, and I thought the two of us could get together for a few drinks," he teased. "How about it, beautiful?"

"Well, if you're sure your wife won't mind," Vivian

laughed. “I hear she’s been a terrible crab lately, and you certainly look like you could use a little fun.”

“My wife is never a crab.” Doug grinned, draping his arm around her shoulders. Then an expression of concern crossed his face, and he abruptly dropped his teasing game. “Is there anything wrong, Viv? You were gone for quite a while.”

“No, nothing. I was just checking in with Sally, and I got tied up returning some calls. Bridge club, meetings, that sort of thing. I’m all through now.”

She slipped her arm through Doug’s. “Come on, Mr. Senator, sir. Let’s go watch Jerry make a fool of himself with the new cocktail waitress.”

CHAPTER 24

Kathi had never been nervous about flying before, but she found herself clutching David's hand tightly as they circled in a holding pattern over the Minneapolis-St. Paul International Airport. David had explained that they would rent a car and drive the rest of the way to Swanville, a little over a hundred miles.

"You're going to love it there, honey," David promised cheerfully, throwing their suitcases into the trunk of the rented car and starting the engine. "We came at just the right time. The snow hasn't hit yet, and it's pretty warm for this time of year. Wait until you see the woods! We can pick up some pinecones to take back with us."

He looked over at Kathi, who was huddled up against the door of the car. She was looking out the window, but David had the feeling that she was seeing nothing, lost in one of her strange dreams. Well . . . that would soon be over. He was counting on the change of scene and his friendly parents to draw her out of this. It wouldn't be long before Kathi would be herself again.

"I . . . I think I'll take a little nap, David," Kathi said, closing her eyes against the brightness of the sun. "I'm a little tired from the plane trip."

"Sure, hon. That's a good idea," David agreed gratefully. At least he wouldn't have to make one-sided conversation with Kathi sleeping. Besides, the nap would do her good. She'd be rested and relaxed when she met his parents.

The moment her eyes closed, Kathi knew it had been a mistake. The voices were louder with her eyes closed, as if by blocking out the sense of sight, they gathered strength.

"Take it, Baver . . . take the Tiger. You can talk to the Tiger, and then you won't cry. Here, the Tiger's your very good friend."

"But Baver has a home! Baver lives here with me! He doesn't need a new home, Auntie! Tell them! Tell those bad ladies that!"

"You're too little to understand now, honey. Just stop crying. He'll be just fine. He'll have a new Mommy and Daddy who will love him, and he'll be just fine."

"No! He doesn't need a new Mommy and Daddy! Don't you know? Mommy and Daddy are coming back! They're coming back to get us!"

"The trip would do her good, Irv. She's been sitting here staring out the window. Poor little tyke. I don't think she's ever going to get over it. I know it was best for the boy, but they should have considered her!"

"Shhhh! She might hear you. Can't question the workings of the Lord, Dorothy. I'll arrange it, though.

She'll like the train, and we'll both go. Maybe it'll get her mind off him. We've got to do something, or the poor little thing'll just waste away."

"You're coming home, Sheri Bear . . . home again, where you belong. Home with Mommy and Daddy and Baver."

At last the voices stopped, and there was only the sound of the motor, a comforting humming that made Kathi feel secure. She felt David's hand on her cheek, the tenderness in his touch, and she almost opened her eyes. Just a little longer, and she would pretend to wake. She had to convince him that everything was just fine. She didn't want David to worry about her. Things would be much easier if he thought she was getting better. How could she ever get him to leave her alone, if he was worried about her? She needed time alone in Swanville. . . .

Her eyes opened against her will. They were almost there now, and she could feel the tension claim her body even more tightly than before. She knew instinctively that it was only a matter of minutes before they came to the town. Everything was frighteningly familiar as she gazed out at the rolling fields spread out on either side of the road like giant muted-brown checkerboards. There was an aura of death in the air, the death of summer, and Kathi shivered.

"Well, sleepyhead!" David's voice was determinedly cheerful. "I was wondering if you'd ever wake up. We're almost there. Why don't you roll down that window and sniff some air that isn't smoggy? That should be a real treat for your lungs."

Kathi obediently reached for the handle, cranking down the window and inhaling deeply. The air smelled warm and rich, leaves drying in the sun with a hint of a passing stream and its cool humid scent. David was right. This air smelled nothing like California smog. Here, things were grown without irrigation, fed by underground streams and rich soil. And now, in the late fall, the leaves were swirling in the wind, blowing up against the wooden snow fences, gathering in piles. She could see the woods by the side of the narrow road, the carpet of fallen leaves and the lovely, deep darkness behind the bordering trees. It was beautiful—beautiful and frightening—and Kathi gave a little shiver of apprehension.

"Be careful of the tracks!" she warned suddenly, leaning forward to peer out of the windshield.

"What tracks?" David asked, glancing at her curiously out of the corner of his eye.

"The ones right up there!" Kathi said, pointing ahead where the road curved sharply to the left.

David made the turn before he saw the tracks, stretching out like a converging triangle in the distance. There was a sign on the shoulder of the road and David drove on, bumping across the tracks.

He glanced at her sharply, but she was staring out the side window again, seeming to enjoy the scenery. How had she known about that crossing? There must have been a sign earlier that he'd missed. He wasn't used to taking this road into town. He'd only done it to show Kathi more of the countryside. It was a back road, seldom used now that the new highway had gone through. It used to be the main road, but now it had fallen into disrepair.

"Here we are, hon!" David announced, pulling up into a wide driveway at the top of a hill. "My dad just built this house three years ago. They're a little secluded up here, but they like it that way. Look at that view!"

"Yes!" Kathi breathed, clenching her fingers into a ball. "Just look at it!"

She had been here before, many times. They'd brought a big basket of food up here for picnics, but there hadn't been a house then. Just the view of the roofs below, looking like colored building blocks in the sun.

"There's ours, Auntie! The brown one right down there!"

"Where? Where? I don't see!"

"You're too little, Baver. I'll show you next time. You can see it real good when you're bigger. Do you want me to get you a sandwich? A nice peanut-butter sammie?"

There had been the woods then, and the lake with fierce underwater monsters in the shape of minnows that nibbled at their toes. And something else too . . . something much more terrifying than pretend monsters. Close by, right over that hill, were the railroad tracks—the gleaming silver bands of her nightmares.

CHAPTER 25

Harry flung the operative report into the corner with disgust. “Oh, hell,” he groaned, flipping his glasses off onto the desk so hard they bounced. It was a feeble attempt to dispel the gathering anxiety he felt. The only answer for this kind of feeling was work, and Harry attacked the files on his desk with a vengeance, searching for some sort of answer.

The coffee-stained folder at the very bottom of the pile was the one Harry was set to examine tonight. He’d already been over the file several times, but his uneasiness grew as he pulled it out of the stack and started to read. Somewhere in this huge collection of files, he’d seen the name Sheri, but he’d be damned if he could remember where.

All the documents in this file were old, including Doug’s application for a marriage license in the state of Minnesota, listing Roma Haight as his intended bride. Roma was dead now, and had been for nearly twenty years. She was a part of Doug’s past though, and Harry examined the photostats carefully, searching for something, although he wasn't sure what.

It was the normal pattern. Roma and Doug had gone through high school together and married while Doug was still in law school. Kathi had been born the year before he graduated, and the couple had settled in Little Falls where Doug set up his own small practice. There was absolutely nothing out of the ordinary in these reports.

Harry paged through the will that Roma's parents had left when they died. The elder Haights had provided handsomely for Roma and Kathi, setting aside a large sum of money for their daughter and grandchild. There was no mention of Doug in the will, but that wasn't really unusual. It was a straight family legacy handed down in strict bloodlines. In the event of Roma's death, the remaining Haight estate was to be liquidated, and the money deposited into an account for Kathi, naming Doug and the First American National Bank of St. Cloud as coexecutors. It was material that Harry had read before, and there were no surprises forthcoming. Reports from the bank indicated that Doug had made large withdrawals from the account after Roma's death, apparently to pay for Kathi's extended hospitalization and medical care, an expense that the bank had accepted without question.

A deep furrow spread across Harry's receding hairline as he frowned in concentration. Now that he thought about it, the situation was a bit unusual. The money hadn't been left to Doug in the case of Roma's death. It had been carefully set up so that Doug would never directly inherit any of the Haight money.

The first seed of worry started to germinate as Harry

kicked his chair over to the bookcase and located the Minnesota statutes on inheritance. He had simply assumed that Minnesota was a community property state.

Suspicion grew as Harry flipped pages in the legal volume. Minnesota had not been a community property state at the time of Roma's death. The Haights had been explicit about the property settlement. Doug was carefully excluded from the will, except to act as coexecutor with the bank after Roma's death.

Harry found the passage he was searching for and frowned again as he refreshed his memory. His expression was pained as he pushed himself back to the desk and pulled out the file on the accident. If Kathi had died in the wreck, Doug would have been left penniless as far as the Haight inheritance was concerned. The money would have reverted back to the bank and been bequeathed to the Christ Lutheran Church of St. Cloud.

"So what?" Harry muttered, realizing that he was probably grasping at straws, being so suspicious of the Haight will. Kathi had not died in the accident. This was a fruitless exercise on his part. He was wasting his time hypothesizing about a situation that had not occurred.

"What ifs," Harry groaned, paging through the accident report. "I should know better than to get hung up on what ifs."

Doug was taking a shower, and Vivian knew he wouldn't be able to hear her over the sound of the water. Quickly, she found her personal phone directory and located Bev Smith's home number. Kathi was probably with Bev in Arizona. Harry must have got the name wrong.

"Kathi?" Mrs. Smith sounded puzzled. "No, Kathi's not here. We weren't expecting her. Bev's gone to spend a week in Taos with her sister, and she didn't say anything about Kathi before she left. Did you want the number, Mrs. Ellison?"

"Oh, no, thank you," Vivian said. "That's really not necessary. I just tried to call Kathi at the dorm today and got no answer, so I assumed she went with Bev."

Vivian replaced the receiver with a quick gesture and shook her head. Perhaps it hadn't been wise calling Bev's mother. Now Mrs. Smith would tell Bev that she had been looking for Kathi, and Kathi would undoubtedly hear about it. Kathi accused her of being overprotective anyway. Now Vivian was glad that she hadn't got Bev's sister's number. Calling Bev to check up on Kathi was going a little too far. She didn't want to give Kathi the impression that she didn't trust her.

Resolutely, Vivian picked up the jar of cold cream and began to get ready for bed. And she had just told Harry that Doug made mountains out of molehills! There was absolutely nothing wrong with Kathi. She was just being overprotective again.

Sally flicked off the television in her room and settled heavily on the edge of the bed. Miss Vivian had been awful worried about Miss Kathi tonight, and she'd be even more worried if she knew what trouble her little lamb was in. Sally just hoped that the prayin' and her mama's ring had helped. She couldn't do any more to help Miss Kathi unless she called. Sally had been waiting for a call all night, but none had come. She hoped that was a good sign. Perhaps Miss Kathi had discovered what the spirit wanted, and had already done it. In any event, it wouldn't hurt to pray some more. She was going to pray all night tonight if she could stay awake. Sally had the terrible feeling that this was the time Miss Kathi needed her prayers the most.

Harry had read the newspaper report of the accident before, and he almost passed over it in his search. He was about to set it aside when a name caught his eye. Sharon Walker! Sharon . . . Sheri . . . could they be one and the same? She had been a passenger on the train and been killed in the accident. This couldn't possibly have any bearing on Kathi . . . or could it?

Harry blinked rapidly as he skimmed the admitting physician's report, including a description of Kathi's multiple injuries. There was an outline of a child's body with additions written in pen, where the physician had noted Kathi's identifying features and marks.

Harry grinned slightly when he saw the star-shaped birthmark on the drawing. What a birthmark! He bet she'd got plenty of teasing from the boys at the beach when she wore a swimsuit.

"High on the left upper thigh," Harry read aloud. He chuckled appreciatively. A star meant first class, and Kathi's thighs were certainly that!

Harry smiled even wider as he realized that he was acting like a dirty old man. Maybe that was what David and Kathi were doing right now, examining the birthmark on her thigh.

Suddenly Harry stopped grinning and pulled out another file drawer. That small seed of suspicion had begun to flower, and he scattered files all over the floor as he searched for Kathi's birth records. This was it. He was right again, and this one was a beaut!

CHAPTER 26

Vivian sat upright in bed as she heard the front doorbell. Her eyes automatically sought the luminous dial of the clock, and she sat up even straighter, wiping the sleep from her eyes. It was close to midnight. Who in the world would be ringing the doorbell at this hour?

There were voices in the downstairs hallway. She recognized Sally's disgruntled tones and the deeper, angry voice of a man. She snapped on the light over her side of the bed and slid her feet into slippers as Sally's footsteps plodded up the stairs.

"Miss Vivian?" Sally called out, knocking softly. "Miss Vivian? Mr. Adams is downstairs, and he wants to see you and Mr. Doug right away. I told him you was sleepin', but he says it can't wait. He sounds awful mad, Miss Vivian, so I put him in the den to wait for you."

"All right, Sally," Vivian answered. "Tell him we'll be right down."

Doug was sitting up in bed by this time, yawning

widely. Vivian put her hand on his arm and smiled. "If you're really tired, dear, I can go down and talk to Harry," she offered. "I could just tell him that you're too tired. I'm sure it's nothing that can't wait until morning. Harry probably doesn't even realize what time it is."

"No," Doug protested, swinging his feet over the side of the bed. He looked puzzled as he noticed the time. "Even Harry draws the line at midnight. Just throw me my robe, will you?"

Vivian tossed Doug his robe and slippers, and zipped up her long housecoat. She ran a quick comb through her hair while Doug was tying his robe, and they went down the stairs together.

Harry whirled around angrily when Doug and Vivian appeared in the doorway. He had been pacing the floor, growing more and more impatient and incensed with each passing second.

"Shut the door!" he snapped. "We sure as hell don't want any witnesses to this conversation!"

Vivian had her mouth open, about to ask Harry if he wanted coffee or a drink. She closed it quickly as she noticed his flushed face and the way his hands were balled into fists. She crossed to a chair as her knees grew weak, and she sank down quickly. Something was terribly wrong, and she had the feeling that she knew exactly what it was. Somehow, Harry had found out! He knew!

Doug shut the door and walked steadily to the couch. He looked completely calm, but Vivian recognized the nearly imperceptible tightening at the corners of his mouth. Doug was sure that something was wrong, but he was going to remain composed until he found out exactly what it was.

"I can see that something's got you riled, Harry," Doug remarked evenly. "Suppose you let us in on it, too?"

"What the hell!" Harry sputtered. He stood in the middle of the floor, glaring fiercely at Doug.

"I must have asked you a hundred times if there was anything in your past that the press could pick up on!" Harry exploded. "You just shook your head and said no, like some kind of fucking saint! Jesus H. Christ! Didn't you know I'd find out about it? What kind of goddamned fool do you take me for?"

Vivian watched Doug as the blood left his face. He was still composed, but she noticed that his hands had started to tremble. Doug was afraid, but he would brave it out.

"You'd better tell me what you're talking about, Harry," Doug said calmly. "I don't appreciate you coming here at this hour and waking us up with threats."

"You know exactly what the hell I'm talking about!" Harry yelled.

"Sorry, Harry," Doug said calmly, reaching for a cigarette. "It's past midnight, and I don't feel like playing guessing games. You'd better tell me why you're so upset. It's much too late for games like this."

Harry's pacing stopped abruptly at Doug's icy tones. For a second he wondered if he could be mistaken, but the proof was right in his briefcase. He had to admit a grudging respect for Doug, though. He was trying to brazen it out. The man was as cool as a cucumber.

"You're really something!" Harry sighed, dropping into the nearest chair. "All right, Doug. If I have to spell the whole thing out for you, here it is."

There was a tense moment as Harry snapped open his briefcase, removing the incriminating file he'd hastily thrown together. He placed it on the small table next to his chair, and his lips tightened.

"This file contains a copy of Kathi's birth records and the complete records of her hospital admission after the accident in which she was supposedly injured . . . *including* a physical description of her identifying marks and features. I think you'd better tell me the whole story, Doug. I know that the girl you call Kathi Ellison isn't your real daughter."

Doug's steadiness crumbled suddenly, as if he were a marionette and someone let go of the strings. He nodded jerkily and attempted to light his cigarette with hands that trembled openly now.

"I should have leveled with you." He sighed deeply and managed to bring the match close enough to the end of the cigarette to light it. "I know I should have leveled with you." His voice was barely a whisper.

Vivian waited. She knew that once Doug started talking, there would be no stopping him. He would blurt out the whole thing. But maybe it was time to tell the truth. After all these years, she was finally beginning to value peace—and peace of mind—above prosperity, success, and status. Or maybe she was just getting too old to play the game.

"We . . . we thought we were doing the right thing. A hurt little girl . . . an orphan like that. She needed a good home. And I needed a daughter. It all seemed so simple then."

Doug's voice faltered and broke off, and for once Harry did not interrupt. He watched Doug relight his dead cigarette, and he felt a stirring of sympathy that he quickly quelled. Doug had lied to him, and that was one thing Harry would not tolerate. He wanted this whole story with nothing held back.

"From the beginning," Harry ordered, leaning back in his chair. He'd scared the hell out of Doug, and he was rather pleased with himself. This whole thing could still be hushed up, but he wasn't about to tell Doug that now. Harry wanted to see Mr. Perfect Candidate sweat a little. That way Doug would listen to him the next time he ordered him to level. Harry had sweated blood, digging out this whole damn thing, and Doug was going to pay for that. He wouldn't be caught lying to Harry Adams again. You could bet on that!

They had been naked together on the couch when Roma burst into the office. She tugged the badly frightened child by the hand, and held Kathi back when she made a move to run toward her father. A look of shocked fury distorted Roma's face, and she stood there glaring for a timeless moment.

"Oh, my God!" Vivian gasped, as Roma pulled Kathi out of the room and slammed the door behind her. She turned to Doug who was hastily pulling on his clothes.

"We've got to catch her!" he shouted. "She's drunk again. There's no telling what she'll do!"

Frantic moments later, they were speeding down Highway 10 in Vivian's car. She was at the wheel, insisting that Doug was too upset to drive. He peered through the windshield, urging Vivian on. There she was! Stopped by the signal light in the center of town!

"She's taking Route 28!" Doug breathed, watching intently as Roma's car turned left at the signal. "Hurry up Viv! You can catch her! Just stay behind her, and I'll jump out when she stops. Look at that! She's in no condition to drive!"

The white convertible swerved on the two-lane highway, barely missing the shoulder of the road. Vivian deliberately dropped back a bit, until she could barely see the taillights of the car in the distance. Roma would just speed up if she knew that they were following her, and she seemed barely able to control the car at her present speed.

Vivian turned at the crossroads, heading southwest toward Swanville. Roma was quite a distance ahead of them, but there was no other traffic. This was all farming land, and most people were in bed by dusk, getting ready for the long days of harvesting ahead. The road was deserted, and Roma's taillights were clearly visible in the distance.

Vivian drove carefully. She knew the road well, its winding curves and hills. She had grown up in this area, and it was a mystery why Roma had chosen this particular direction. There was nothing ahead in this direction except small villages. It was really a back road, poorly maintained, and scattered with potholes that appeared with the ice and snow of winter.

Doug leaned closer to the open window and listened for a moment. "There's a train coming," he announced shakily. "We'll catch her when she stops at Carlson's Crossing."

Vivian saw the train as she came over the top of the steep hill. Roma's brake lights flashed briefly, and then the white convertible surged forward again in an impossible race.

"She's trying to beat the train! She'll never make it!"

Doug cried out as Vivian pulled onto the shoulder, scattering loose gravel as the car slowed and stopped. They watched in mute shock as the train's brakes locked and squealed loudly.

In the next few seconds, a thousand questions and thoughts whirled through Doug's mind in a crazy pattern. Why? Why had he let himself be caught on his office couch with Vivian? For Doug was now sure that he had been the one who had forgotten to lock the office door. Why hadn't he gone to Roma's parents sooner? Why hadn't they believed him when he told them that Roma was an alcoholic? Why hadn't he insisted that she get some kind of treatment, even committed her to a hospital to dry out? He'd been afraid—afraid of the gossip that would ruin his law practice, afraid of his own pride—sinking into the delusion that everything would be all right once he was established and could spend more time with Roma. And then it had been too late. Then she was drunk every night, and he had left her, alone and miserable, to carry on his affair with Vivian. He had caused this disaster, and he had only himself to blame. Please . . . dear God, please! If Roma could only get across the crossing in time, things would be different. He would change his whole life and devote it to her.

There was a deafening crash and the white convertible spun crazily, bursting into flames almost instantaneously. Vivian heard a thin, high scream over the thundering crash, and then she covered her eyes as the train tipped and left the tracks in a wake of brilliant light and hurtling pieces of sharp metal.

There was a cry of unbearable anguish from Doug, and at last Vivian looked, seeing the inferno of flames and wreckage where only a moment before, the night had been peaceful. They were dead . . . both of them. . . . They had to be dead.

"Kathi!" Doug screamed, snapping out of his frozen shock at last. He was halfway out of the car as Vivian came to her senses and caught his arm, pulling him back sharply.

"No!" she shouted, struggling with all of her might against his desperate strength. "No, Doug! It won't do any good! There's nothing you can do now!"

Somehow, she managed to pull him back into the car and bang the door shut. They had to get out of here! Didn't he realize what would happen if they were found here together, at the scene of the wreck? She had to think clearly for both of them now. Doug was in a state of shock, and he couldn't possibly know what was best for him.

"There's nothing you can do now, Doug. No one could have survived that," Vivian repeated, hammering the words into Doug's shocked, numb mind.

"Leave everything to me. Just leave everything to me, darling!"

She put the car into motion frantically, surging forward with a sudden stomp on the accelerator and making a screeching U-turn on the narrow road. They were dead, and she had to protect herself and Doug now. She was all he had. Roma and Kathi were dead.

Vivian drove back to the office with the sound of Doug's anguished sobs ringing in her ears. She glanced over to see his crumpled face by the dim glow of the interior lights, and she knew that she would have to help him now. Doug was numb . . . beaten . . . shocked. She would take care of everything. Sooner or later, he would have left Roma anyway. Now he was all hers, and she would take care of him. Only she could make him whole again.

Vivian pulled up in back of the office and cut the lights. She knew what she had to do, and somehow, she had to convince Doug that she was right. She opened the door and helped him inside the building, half-dragging him into the office, and pushing him down on the couch.

"You were here all evening!" she hissed fiercely, holding his face between her hands, so he was forced to meet her eyes. "Do you hear me? You were here working all night! No one came in! You know nothing about it. Nothing at all!"

"No," Doug groaned, his eyes glassy. "Vivian! I . . . I have to . . . oh, God! I just don't know!"

"Roma and Kathi are dead, Doug!" Vivian said savagely, her eyes burning into Doug's. "Don't you understand? There's nothing you can do for them now! Do something for yourself! It's too late for them!"

Doug started to protest again and then, slowly, he nodded. She was right. Vivian was right again, as always. There was nothing to be gained by admitting they had been following Roma and Kathi. If he admitted that, then he would, in turn, have to admit that Roma had been drinking. He couldn't ruin her reputation now that she couldn't defend herself. It would be ugly if people knew that Roma had come to the office drunk, caught him and Vivian together, and raced off in her car. Then he'd be ruining Vivian's reputation too. It was too late for Roma and Kathi, but he didn't want to hurt Vivian. She was right.

"Get a hold of yourself!" Vivian spoke sharply, to try to jolt his mind into functioning again. "Here's the file on the Schumacker case. You've got to pull yourself together before the sheriff comes."

It was a full hour before the anticipated knock came on the door. Vivian had peeked in at Doug many times during that tense hour, and he had been sitting at his desk, staring blankly at the file she had given him. She still didn't know what he was going to do when the sheriff gave him the news. He looked outwardly calm, but that was a part of his lawyer's training. Vivian knew that Doug was shaking inside, as scared and shocked as she was. But this was an opportunity she had to try for, a chance she had to take.

Vivian crossed the room. She slid open the little window in the door and looked out at Jim Lester's grim countenance.

"It's Sheriff Lester," Vivian called out to Doug, opening the door with a polite smile on her face.

"Jim," Vivian greeted him warmly, stepping aside so he could enter the office. "What are you doing up here so late? I thought Marion said you were working days now."

Sheriff Lester looked a little uncertain. His face was pale, and it was clear that he disliked the news he had to bring. He cleared his throat and swallowed with difficulty.

"I'm glad you're still here, Viv," he muttered. "I-I've got some pretty bad news for your boss."

Vivian managed to look puzzled. "Doug's in his office," she said, knocking once, and then opening the oak-paneled door.

"Sheriff," Doug greeted him, looking up from his stack of papers. He smiled and made a move to rise. Vivian almost sighed audibly with relief. He was going to be just fine now.

"No," Sheriff Lester said, motioning Doug down again. "No need to get up, Counselor. I'm afraid I've got some bad news for you."

Doug looked curious, but not overly alarmed. Vivian was proud of the control he was showing. She turned to leave the two of them alone, but Jim's strained voice stopped her.

"I think you'd better stay, Viv," he suggested. "The counselor might need you." He turned to Doug. "You don't mind if Viv stays, do you?"

Doug shook his head, and Vivian crossed in front of Jim to the chair against the wall. She sat down primly, arranging her skirts and looking up expectantly.

"There's been a bad accident," Sheriff Lester began. Then he cleared his throat and dropped his eyes to the floor. There weren't words to make his duty

easier. He'd have to just come right out and say it, with the counselor staring at him apprehensively.

"I-it's your wife, Counselor," Sheriff Lester faltered. "She's . . . well . . . she's dead."

Doug groaned, and his face blanched white. His mouth opened and closed as he gasped for breath. "Dead?" he repeated, shaking his head. "Roma? Are you sure?"

"I'm sorry," Sheriff Lester said, making a tentative move toward Doug, and then backing off again, unsure of exactly what to do. He was taking it well, Sheriff Lester thought. Thank God, he wasn't the hysterical kind of man he ran into every now and then.

"What . . . what happened?" Doug asked, his voice a shocked croak. "An accident, you say? Where?"

"It happened right outside of Swanville," Sheriff Lester explained, looking as if he hated this gruesome duty. "The car she was driving collided with a train. I'm sorry, Counselor. Your wife was killed on impact."

"Oh, God!" Doug cried, a pained expression on his face. Then, when the expected news didn't follow he leaned forward, suddenly alert. "Kathi?" he gasped. "Was Kathi with her?"

Sheriff Lester nodded. "I'm afraid so," he said. "She's at St. Gabriel's now. It doesn't look good though, Counselor. She was thrown from the car, and she's hurt pretty bad."

"She's alive?"

Vivian squeezed her hands together tightly. It wasn't possible!

Doug leaped from his chair and tried to brush past Sheriff Lester, whose big brawny hand shot out and grabbed him.

"Hold on a minute, Counselor," he advised. He shot Vivian a warning glance. "I don't think you should go down there by yourself. You'll drive the counselor, won't you, Viv?"

"Of course!" Vivian exclaimed, disbelief in her voice. Kathi was alive? It was inconceivable! "I'll stay with him too, Jim. My God! I just can't believe it!"

Sheriff Lester nodded as Vivian took Doug's arm and started to lead him out of the office. Vivian Sundquist was a good girl in a pinch. She looked mighty upset herself, but she had gumption. She'd make sure the counselor didn't do anything foolish.

"I'll lock up for you here," Sheriff Lester offered, snapping off the lights. "Just get over there as fast as you can, Viv. The hospital may need some papers signed in a hurry."

Neither Vivian nor Doug uttered a word as they drove the short distance to the hospital. There was nothing to say. The impossible had happened, and by some miracle of mercy, Kathi had survived.

"Hurry!" Doug muttered, leaping out of the car before it was fully stopped. "Hurry, Viv! She's alive! Kathi's alive!"

They were met at the entrance by a nurse who ushered them right into the administrator's office. Sheriff Lester had called to say they were on their way.

"They're prepping her for surgery now, Mr. Ellison," said the charge nurse, a starched white model of efficiency and decorum as she pushed a release form in front of Doug. "This form authorizes the surgery and any procedures the physician feels are necessary."

Doug's hand was shaking as he signed the paper. He still couldn't believe that his miracle had happened.

Kathi must have been thrown from the car as it hit, and the flames had obscured their view. He had been so certain that no one could live through a hideous wreck like that. They had both been so certain!

"Mr. Ellison is here," the nurse called, pushing a button on the intercom unit. "Inform Dr. Mielke that the release form is signed."

"I'll send Dr. Merrill in with something to calm you down," she said gently, taking Doug's hand with a practiced motion, feeling for his pulse.

"No," Doug choked. "Just coffee, please. That's all I need. I'll be fine." He shook his head as the nurse frowned. "I want to be alert when Kathi comes out of the operating room," he explained. "She's going to need me. She's going to need me now, more than ever!"

"It may be hours, Mr. Ellison," the nurse explained kindly. "You should rest now. You're going to need all your strength later."

"Just coffee, Miss Jacobs," Vivian urged, reading the nurse's name tag. "Mr. Ellison will be all right, and I'll stay right here with him."

The nurse nodded. She too, had noticed the stubborn set of Doug's jaw. "I'll send Dr. Merrill in with the admission reports," she said, turning to leave. "He'll be able to answer any questions you have."

Vivian watched Doug's tense face as Dr. Merrill explained the surgery. Kathi had a ruptured spleen, which would have to be removed by immediate surgery. Her left femur was broken and had to be pinned. Kathi would spend a minimum of four weeks in traction. She had also suffered second-degree burns on her body and face, although Dr. Merrill anticipated that the burns would heal with no noticeable scars.

"She's a lucky little girl, Mr. Ellison," Dr. Merrill remarked. "Her injuries are relatively uncomplicated, although recovery time will be slow. I think she'll pull through just fine."

Vivian squeezed Doug's cold hand as Dr. Merrill left to check on Kathi's progress. "Everything's going to be just fine," she whispered. "Everything's going to be just fine, Doug."

In just a few minutes, Dr. Merrill came back with a hopeful smile on his face. "It's going well, Mr. Ellison," he reported. "They're just closing now, and your daughter should be in the recovery room in a few minutes. You can take a quick peek through the window, but I warn you not to expect much. She's still unconscious, and you won't be able to talk to her until tomorrow."

Doug nodded. He staggered a bit as he tried to get to his feet, and Vivian quickly slipped her arm around his shoulders to hold him steady.

"We've reserved a room for you right next to the recovery wing," Dr. Merrill informed him. "It might be a good idea for you to get as much rest as you can. It'll be at least ten hours before you can talk to your daughter."

Vivian saw the tears slip down his cheeks as Doug peeked in the glass window of the recovery room. Kathi was such a small bundle on the high white bed. Most of her body was encased in bandages—including her head and face—and she looked pathetically tiny, lying there, barely lifting the sheet with her shallow breathing.

The ensuing night was a blur in Vivian's memory. She remembered Dr. Merrill giving Doug a shot that made him collapse into a deep slumber. She sat in a chair by his bed, alternately dozing and thinking, her mind a jumble of images. Again and again she saw the crash and explosion, and she woke up from her naps with her heart beating wildly.

During Vivian's vigil, soft-spoken nurses brought her coffee, and she stepped outside in the corridor for an occasional cigarette, pulling the smoke into her lungs in rapid puffs, alert for any sound from Doug's room. Thank God, he was asleep! At least he didn't have to live this nightmare over and over the way she was doing. It seemed as if the long, anxious night would never end, but at last a gray dawn light seeped through the windows, and Vivian quickly washed her face and splashed water on her puffy eyes.

Dr. Merrill had been overly optimistic. Three days of waiting passed while Kathi lay unconscious. Vivian stayed at Doug's side the entire time, afraid to leave him for more than a hurried minute. Her mother made all the arrangements for Roma's funeral and helped them through the difficult days of waiting, bringing changes of clothing for Vivian, and packing a bag for Doug with clothes she got from his house. She stayed with them for part of the time, bringing in thermoses of coffee and sandwiches she had made. She was proud of her daughter for helping Mr. Ellison through this trying time. Hadn't she always claimed that her daughter was loyal and dedicated?

Doug and Vivian spent long hours alternately pacing

the quiet corridors and sitting on the stiff plastic benches that lined the waiting room, looking up hopefully every time a nurse or doctor passed. Still, there was no word until the afternoon of the fourth day.

"Dr. Mielke would like to talk to both of you in his office," a nurse informed them at last. She patted Doug's shoulder as the fear grew in his eyes.

"Your daughter's just fine, Mr. Ellison. Her condition has stabilized. It'll take a while, but she's going to be all right."

Vivian had to run to keep up with Doug as he rushed down the corridor to Dr. Mielke's office. His back had stiffened at the good news, and the tortured grief on his face was lessened. She was going to be all right! Kathi would be all right!

"Sit down, Mr. Ellison." Dr. Mielke smiled. "You too, Miss Sundquist. I've got some good news for you."

Doug's legs buckled in relief as he sank into the nearest chair. "The nurse said that Kathi's going to be all right," he whispered, leaning forward for confirmation from Dr. Mielke himself.

"That's essentially correct," Dr. Mielke agreed. "She'll need some physical therapy for her leg, of course, but young children like Kathi have great recuperative powers. There will be no permanent disability, and in six months to a year, you won't even be able to notice a limp. On the whole, her physical condition should be completely normal by that time."

"Physical condition?" Doug questioned, picking up Dr. Mielke's stress on the words. "Is there something else wrong, Doctor? Something you haven't told me?"

"There's a condition we hadn't anticipated," Dr. Mielke answered carefully. "I don't see any cause

for alarm, though. As you know, Kathi suffered a concussion in the accident, and I felt that I should discuss it with you before you see her. There is a slight problem, Mr. Ellison. Kathi is amnesic."

"You . . . you mean she doesn't remember anything?" Doug stammered, his face turning gray.

Dr. Mielke nodded. "This condition occurs occasionally when a young child experiences a traumatic shock," he continued. "There appears to be no problem with her cognitive processes. Apparently, the shock had no effect on her ability to learn and assimilate information. Try to think of memory as a slate, Mr. Ellison. Facts are written on this slate as the child matures. The information is filed in order—a description of the child's parents, the child's own name, the memory of a birthday party, the child's playmates, pets, family members, teachers, and so on. In Kathi's case, the slate has been erased. She remembers nothing at all before the accident. The slate is blank."

"Nothing?" Doug asked, leaning forward even farther to peer at Dr. Mielke in shock. "Nothing at all?" he asked again, suddenly remembering Kathi's shocked reaction when she saw Vivian and him in the office.

"That's correct," Dr. Mielke nodded. "I wanted to give you time to adjust to this new development. Kathi won't remember you, Mr. Ellison. You'll be a complete stranger to her."

"That . . . that's awful!" Vivian gasped, twisting her hands in her lap. "Will Kathi's memory come back in time, Dr. Mielke?"

"It's not likely in a child of Kathi's age, Miss Sundquist," Dr. Mielke continued. "In similar cases,

the loss of memory has generally been permanent. Of course, I'm not saying it couldn't happen, but the odds are very much against a full return of her memory."

Dr. Mielke turned to look at Doug, who was leaning back with an anguished expression on his face.

"It's not as bad as all that, Mr. Ellison," he said kindly. "The only thing missing is Kathi's memory of past events. You can help her duplicate the memory all over again by talking with her. There's nothing wrong with her mind. Her memory has just been erased."

"I see," Doug said slowly. "She . . . she's not retarded or anything like that?"

"Gracious, no!" Dr. Mielke chuckled. "Shortly after she regained consciousness, she kept the nurses hopping, demanding an explanation of why her leg was in the air, and asking questions about the monitors in her room. She was watching the heart monitor when I left, trying to regulate it with her breathing. There's no question about her ability to learn, Mr. Ellison. She'll probably know the name of every piece of equipment and how it works before we discharge her."

Doug began to smile as the full implications of Dr. Mielke's words sank into his consciousness. Kathi didn't remember seeing him with Vivian. She didn't remember the accident, or anything Roma might have said in her anger. She didn't remember her mother as an alcoholic or any of the fights they'd had. He certainly wouldn't tell her. Let all those unpleasant memories be erased. He would help to fill in the blanks, but only with pleasant memories.

Vivian waited in the corridor as Doug took a quick peek at Kathi. Dr. Mielke had told him he could stay only five minutes today. He could see her again tomorrow morning for a longer period of time.

When Doug came out of Kathi's room, he was smiling happily. "Dr. Mielke was right," he nodded. "Kathi didn't recognize me, but she was fine the moment I told her who I was. The nurses explained it to her. She asked me so many questions I felt like I was on a quiz show."

Vivian smiled, and, for the first time since the accident, the smile reached her eyes. A feeling of elation swept through her. It was all working out perfectly. Of course the price had been high, but now she had Doug, and Doug had Kathi. She could be a good mother to Kathi, a better mother than Roma had been. Once Doug saw what a good mother she could be to his child, he would love her even more. She gave a deep sigh of relief and slipped her arm through Doug's. It was a relief to be able to do it openly now.

"She doesn't remember a thing about you and me?" Vivian whispered, hardly daring to hope that things could be this perfect.

"No," Doug answered happily. "That's one secret we'll keep from her—that, and Roma's drinking. She's really going to be all right, Viv! She asked me when she could come home!" Then he shook his head slowly. "But somehow she doesn't look the same. She seems older, and her eyes have changed. Remember how they used to sparkle when she laughed?"

"They'll sparkle again," Vivian said, comforting him. "Kathi's still a sick little girl. She's not going to look like herself until she's completely well."

Doug grinned. "Yes, that must be it," he said softly. Then he took Vivian's arm and helped her out to the car.

CHAPTER 27

It was the morning of the fourth week after the accident. Doug was there outside Kathi's door, but instead of going into the room, he watched through the small square window in the door. This was the morning the doctors were going to remove his daughter's bandages.

They were working slowly and carefully, unwrapping gauze and snipping with surgical scissors. Kathi had been waiting for this moment eagerly. Last night she had been so excited that her eyes had sparkled again, almost the way they used to. Four weeks in bandages was a long time for an active little girl. And after the bandages were removed, Kathi could begin the exercises and physical therapy she needed to become fully active again. Her leg would be stiff for a while, but the doctors had told Doug that the damage she had suffered was reversible through a long program of physical therapy. They were thankful for that.

It wasn't as bad as he had expected. There was a

long, red, angry-looking scar on Kathi's leg that would fade in time, and some tender pink patches on her arms. Now they were working on the facial bandages, unwrapping her small body from its mummy-like trappings. Dr. Mielke bent down close to Kathi and said something to her that made everyone in the room laugh. The glass was soundproof, but Doug could see Kathi's mouth curve upward in a smile. He could hardly wait to see her when all this was done.

Now they had turned her away from him, cutting away the last of the bandages, and Dr. Mielke stepped back with a proud look on his face. One of the nurses in the room got a mirror and handed it to the doctor, who held it so that Kathi could see. Doug wished that they would turn her around so he could see too.

Just then, Kathi looked up at the nurse who stood closest to the door. Doug drew in his breath sharply as he saw her face. In shock, he bolted from the door and ran down the hospital corridor, his mind racing as he fled the building. He had to tell Vivian! Everything had gone wrong. As he drove back to the office, his hands shook violently against the steering wheel.

"Viv!" he gasped, barging into the office frantically. "Oh, my God, Viv, Kathi's dead! She's dead, Vivian!"

"Oh, no!" Vivian cried, rushing toward him. "Oh, Doug . . . Darling! What happened? Dr. Mielke said she was doing so well!"

"The girl in the hospital is fine," Doug choked, emotion contorting in his face. "But, Viv, she's not Kathi! They made a mistake! She's not Kathi!"

"What do you mean? How could they make a mistake like that?"

"I . . . I don't know," Doug faltered. "It must have happened at the scene of the accident. Oh, hell, Vivian! It doesn't make any difference how they made the mistake. They took the bandages off today, and that girl isn't Kathi!"

"Oh, darling! All this time you thought she was. . . . How awful, Doug! What did the doctors say?"

Doug looked at her blankly. "I . . . I didn't tell them," he mumbled. "I was so shocked, I didn't tell anyone. I just had to get right back here and tell you."

Vivian pushed Doug down on the leather couch and locked the outside door. She got a glass of water from the cooler and stroked his forehead as he gulped it down. It took at least five minutes for the color to come back to Doug's face. Then he groaned again and held his head in his hands.

"The money," he said. "Oh, God, Vivian! I used some of Kathi's money to pay for the hospital bills. I'll never be able to pay it all back now!"

"You mean the Haight money?" Vivian asked, trying to remember the stipulations of Roma's parents' will.

"The money goes to the Christ Lutheran Church of St. Cloud now," Doug said tonelessly. "Roma's parents set it up that way purposely. They knew I was thinking about leaving her when she started drinking so heavily. It was their way of providing for her if I did. They always blamed me for Roma's drinking.

She used to run and cry to them every time we had a fight about it."

Vivian pressed her hands to her temples as her mind began to work. She had to be calm now, calm and rational. Doug was still shaking like a leaf, and Vivian knew he was in no condition to make any decisions. Surely there was something they could do, if only she could think of it!

Vivian's eyes closed as she struggled to sort out the facts. "You mean when the bank finds out that Kathi is dead, they'll give the money to charity?"

"Every penny," Doug groaned. "And I'll have to pay back what I've already used, or I'll be accused of fraud! Jesus, Vivian! What am I going to do?"

"Just be quiet and let me think," Vivian said, more sharply than she had intended.

"There's no way, Vivian. I'm guilty of fraud, even though I didn't mean to do it. The whole story'll come out now, and I'll lose my law practice. But what does it matter? Kathi's dead, and nothing's important any more, Viv! Nothing!"

Vivian didn't know what she was going to do, until her hand streaked out to smack against the side of Doug's cheek. Then she set her face in a fierce expression as he looked up at her blankly.

"Listen to me!" she hissed. "I won't hear any more talk like that! If there's anything I can't stand, it's a quitter, and I refuse to listen if you're going to say things like that!"

Vivian felt her mind spin, off balance with a deluge of thoughts. She wasn't going to stand by and see everything ruined now. Doug had a promising career in front of him, and she was about to obtain her dreams. This couldn't stop her. She had to think of something to do! She wasn't going to give up her chance for happiness, and neither was Doug.

Vivian gazed at him, and gradually her eyes narrowed. The girl in the hospital, the totally amnesic little girl in the hospital, must be Sharon Walker, the orphan who was on the train. No one knew she wasn't Kathi—no one except Doug and her. The little girl didn't have any family. She had been living with her foster parents, the Millers, and they were killed in the accident. The girl had a brother, but he had been adopted weeks ago. Who would ever guess that the girl in the hospital was Sharon Walker? Who would care?

Vivian held up a warning hand as Doug opened his mouth to speak. That was it! No one knew! And what they were going to do would only be for Sharon Walker's benefit. There was a way to get out of this terrible mess, and she had to convince Doug to do it.

She took a deep breath and organized her thoughts. "Think for a minute, Doug, and don't say one word until I'm finished. I don't want any arguments or protests. I just want you to listen and think."

Doug nodded mutely, and Vivian gave him a tight smile. That was better. He seemed calmer now. Perhaps he was ready to listen to reason.

"I'm not going to stand by and watch you blurt out the truth, when it could ruin your life and Sharon Walker's too," Vivian said in a calmly determined voice. "You're in no condition to make any decisions right now. For once, you don't have all the facts."

Vivian stood straighter and marshaled her arguments.

Then she ticked them off, one by one on her fingers as she stated them clearly.

"Let's consider Sharon for a minute. What does she have to look forward to for the rest of her life? Another couple of years in the Catholic Adoption Home? Perhaps adoption if there are enough parents to go around? And if any of those parents will take a child with a crippled leg?"

Vivian stopped for a moment and made sure that Doug was listening before she continued.

"Don't you think a little girl as bright as Sharon deserves more than that, Doug? She's an orphan. She lost her mother and father when she was three. She lost her brother less than two months ago, when he was adopted. Now she's lost her foster parents too. Of course, she doesn't remember that, but the pain is still there. That poor child has lost everyone dear to her, and now she's going to lose you too!"

Doug nodded. What Vivian said was true. Sharon Walker had got a hell of a raw deal from life thus far. But—

"Now she has amnesia. Her past is a blank slate. Because of you, she's had the best medical care that money could buy. That's only because everyone—you, me, everyone—assumed she was Kathi. You heard Dr. Mielke say that she'll have to continue with physical therapy for a while to regain the use of her leg. Do you really think that the Catholic Adoption Home could raise the money for that?"

Doug shook his head. Everyone knew that the home was in financial trouble regularly, and just barely managed to provide facilities for the homeless children they took in.

"I . . . I could help . . ." he faltered. "I could offer to pay for her therapy."

"With what?" Vivian asked ruthlessly. "If you admit that she's not Kathi, the Haight money will go to charity. You can't afford the medical bills without Kathi's inheritance. You know that."

Doug nodded painfully. "You're right," he said slowly. "I won't even be able to afford the office rental without the Haight money. You know how long it takes for a law practice to come out of the red."

"Exactly," Vivian breathed. "Maybe it's not the most ethical thing in the world, Doug, but what I'm proposing is the most humane. If you tell the truth now, little Sharon Walker is never going to fully recover. The money is going to charity anyway, and I'm sure the Christ Lutheran Church of St. Cloud wouldn't even consider footing the bill for her physical therapy. They'll use the money for their own charities, and it won't include a poor Catholic orphan."

Doug nodded again. The whole thing was so confusing. What Vivian said made sense, all right. If he told the truth now, he'd be hurting poor Sharon Walker. He didn't want to do that, not if there was any way he could help it. The poor girl had suffered enough.

"I-I'll have to think about it," he finally conceded. "I . . . I don't know, Vivian. Before, when I really thought she was Kathi, it wasn't really fraud. It was an honest mistake. But this way—"

"Just think of what will happen when that poor girl

finds out that you're not her father," Vivian prodded. "Just when she's beginning to recover, her whole world is going to explode again. I wouldn't like to be the person responsible for that!"

"No," Doug said slowly. "I . . . I couldn't do that. She's so sweet . . . such a sweet little girl. I couldn't do that to her."

Vivian sighed. She had said enough.

CHAPTER 28

"Yeah," Harry said, nodding when Doug had finished his halting story. "Yeah . . . it's okay, Doug. Your secret's safe with me. It's a hell of a lot different than I thought."

He sighed again and looked down at the papers spread out on the table. "All right, Doug. I'm sorry I flew off the handle before. I guess I might have done the same thing myself, if I'd been in your place."

Vivian stared at Harry hopefully. Would he keep their secret? Would Harry help them out of this mess?

"What can we do now?" Doug asked, his hands still shaking. "Shall I try to explain everything that happened, make a clean breast of it and hope the people will understand?"

"Not on your life!" Harry exclaimed vehemently. "One little hint of scandal, no matter how good of an excuse you had, and they'll rip you to shreds. You'd better let me take care of it. If I found out, someone else could find out too. I'll fix it for you."

Doug shook his head in wonder. And he thought

they had covered everything up so thoroughly! He couldn't help but gaze at Harry with new respect. "What are you going to do?" he asked doubtfully. "How can you fix it?"

Harry grinned. He was in his element now. "Relax." He shrugged, crossing his legs. "No one's going to find out after I get through. It's just a matter of a little addition to Kathi's birth records. All we have to do is write in a few things, so her records and Sheri Walker's records will match. Then nobody'll ever be the wiser."

Doug nodded slowly. That made sense. But how did one go about altering permanent records? "How?" he asked.

Harry waved his hand nonchalantly. "I've got some friends in the right places," he explained vaguely. "I'll take care of it for you. The less you know about it, the better. Just remember . . . no more secrets from me."

Doug cringed. What Harry was implying was illegal. He opened his mouth to protest, then shut it again quickly. What he and Vivian had done was illegal too. Harry's suggestion was no worse. They had to alter the records of Kathi's birth so they matched the accident records. There was no other way.

"All right, Harry," Doug agreed, adding another brick of guilt to the wall he'd built around him. "All right. . . . And no more secrets." He reached out to shake Harry's hand.

"I'll walk Harry to the door." Vivian came up quickly behind Doug. "You just go right upstairs and get some sleep. I'll be up in a minute."

"We've got to reach Kathi, Harry! I think she's

starting to remember the accident, and she could be trouble!"

Harry gazed down into Vivian's beautiful face and saw fear there, but it wasn't fear for Kathi. She had said that Kathi could *be* trouble, not be *in* trouble. It seemed she was more worried about Doug losing the election than she was about Kathi.

"I'll handle it, Vivian," Harry said gruffly, shaking her hand off his arm. "You handle Doug, and I'll handle Kathi."

Vivian breathed a sigh of relief. "Thank you, Harry," she said, turning stiffly and stepping back. "Can you let yourself out? I'll go right upstairs to Doug."

"Sure, Vivian," Harry said to Vivian's back. He gave a shake of his head as he stepped out into the dark night. It was a damn good thing he got Bev's home phone and address from the college records. He'd give Kathi a call first thing in the morning and make a quick trip to Arizona to explain this whole thing to her. Kathi was confused and frightened now that her memory was starting to come back to her. No wonder the poor kid thought she was possessed!

CHAPTER 29

It was as if an alarm had gone off in her head. Kathi sat up in bed suddenly, blinking at the light of early dawn. There were no sounds of life in the house, no one moving about. She could tell it was very early, but she wasn't tired at all. Instead, there was a sense of urgency running through her. She had to get up. She had to get dressed without waking David or his parents and get away on her own.

Quietly, almost stealthily, Kathi pushed back the patchwork quilt that David's mother had made. She dressed methodically, donning a pair of faded blue jeans and a warm wooly sweater. There was paper and pen in her purse, and she took time to scribble a note to David saying that she had gone off exploring on her own. That would buy her some time.

They would probably sleep late. David had been up until early morning, talking with his parents. By the time they thought to look for her, it would all be over. Then she would be truly free. . . .

* * *

It wasn't until she was halfway down the hill that she remembered the ring. She had taken it off last night and placed it on the table next to her bed.

Kathi's step faltered. Perhaps she should go back and retrieve it. It was Sally's mama's lucky ring, but hadn't Sally said that each person made their own luck? It was time to trust her own. She would be okay without it. Already her feet seemed to trace a remembered path, breaking into a run of their own accord.

"Come on, Baver . . . let's run! I won't run too fast for you this time. I promise. We'll run all the way to the swings, okay?"

Left at the bottom of the hill, then two blocks. There was the park. She was running harder now, her legs moving automatically . . . left . . . right . . . left . . . right . . . one foot in front of the other, in step with her brother.

The park. Different now. The swings lower and smaller than she remembered. Everything in miniature . . . the metal merry-go-round painted orange now, instead of green. Baver had been afraid to go too fast.

"See, look, Baver . . . grab like this and jump really hard. You can do it! You can get up all by yourself!"

His lower lip was quivering . . . tears starting to roll down his cheeks . . . soft baby cheeks. "I'm not big yet! I want to be big!"

"Don't cry, Baver . . . you'll get even bigger than me someday. I'll make it go around. You like to go around don't you, Baver?"

A squeal and a chuckle. Now he wasn't crying anymore. She knew how to stop Baver from crying.

Every time, she knew how. The Tiger told her. The Tiger helped her, and she helped Baver, just like Mommy and Daddy used to do before they went away.

Time to go home now, down the cement sidewalk carefully . . . *step on a crack, break your mother's back* . . . past the tall hedge . . .

There it was! The house stood before her—big and familiar—the wooden boards shaped like a sunburst beneath the bedroom windows. It was deserted. In the front porch window was a small sign, FOR RENT, and penciled in beneath it, CHECK INSIDE AND INQUIRE NEXT DOOR IF INTERESTED. Kathi glanced quickly at the house next door. For a moment, she thought she saw a curtain slide hastily back into place, but the sign said to go right in. She didn't even have to ask for a key.

As Kathi stared, unblinking, at the front porch door, she saw the interior of the house as clearly as if she were inside. There was another door inside the first one, and then a hallway, steps leading upstairs to the room under the eaves—the room with yellow flowers on the walls and crisp white curtains, a picture of a ballet dancer on one wall and another one over the bed, a smiling bear that glowed in the dark. She remembered . . .

Kathi felt eyes on her back as she put her foot on the red brick step. Someone was watching her. But she had to go inside. Sheri was here . . . stronger than she'd ever been before.

"Home! Oh yes . . . I'm home!"

The voice broke inside her head as she opened the front door and gazed around the glass-windowed porch. For a moment, she saw clearly. The house was empty—cold and deserted—without curtains or furniture to relieve the square, box-like rooms. But her focus kept slipping. The image of the bare, lifeless rooms faded away, and she saw the old cane rocker in the corner, a braided rug beneath it, and the heavy stand filled with magazines. It was just as she knew it would be.

"Rock me, Auntie! Rock Baver too! We love it when you rock us! Please?"

"Not too big a girl for rocking, honey? Come here, then, you two little wild Indians. Here, there's room for both of you. This chair's rocked many a child, and now it'll rock my two favorite wild Indians."

The air was rich with the smell of fresh bread baking in the kitchen. Auntie baked bread every afternoon. Oh, she loved it here! It was almost as nice as living with Mommy and Daddy.

"Yes, you can have a cookie, honey, and get one out for your brother too. Just be careful not to drop the lid of the cookie jar."

"I'll be very careful! Don't worry, Auntie! I won't drop it!"

The cookies had chocolate chips in them. She could taste the crunchy bits of sweetness, and she smiled. It was warm in the kitchen from the stove, warm and friendly, and a happy place for two children to be.

The kitchen table still had crumbs from lunch. Auntie had been too busy to wipe it off. She would do it for Auntie. That would show that she was a big girl, and so helpful. Auntie would be pleased.

Her own stool was pushed under the cupboard

and she lifted it up and carried it to the table. There. Now she could reach to wipe it off. Her stool was so pretty with little roses. Uncle had made the stool just yesterday.

The table was clean now, the place mats piled neatly in the center. Auntie would say that she was a good girl for helping, and she hadn't dropped the lid of the cookie jar either. Oh, she was being good today. The bad ladies couldn't take them away if she was this good. Auntie wouldn't let them.

"Time to wash your hands for supper, honey. Take your stool with you and help your brother wash too. And don't forget your faces. We don't want any dirty faces at the supper table."

Suppertime already, and Baver squealed when she tried to lift him up to his high chair. Oh, he wasn't mad. He loved it when she tried to pick him up. Sometimes they fell to the floor and laughed until their tummies hurt.

"Let me, Sheri. He's too heavy for you. Our little boy's getting so big. He'll be able to climb up by himself one of these days. Isn't that right, son?"

She smiled and turned to look at her baby brother in his chair. The lights in the room seemed to flicker and fade, and when her eyes adjusted to the darkness, she saw that the high chair was empty, pushed back against the wall. He was gone!

"I want Baver! I want Baver to come back, Auntie!"

"I know you do, darling." The voice was soft with unshed tears. "But things don't always happen the way we want them to. Baver's got a new mommy and daddy, and I bet he's not crying like you are. You have to be a big girl, honey."

"I'm not a big girl! I'm just a little girl, and I want my Baver! He doesn't need a new mommy and daddy! All he needs is me and you and Uncle! Please, Auntie, please go tell the bad ladies to bring Baver back!"

"Oh, baby . . . come here and sit on Auntie's lap. You can cry if you want to. I think I'm going to cry too."

With one hand, Sheri reached around Auntie's neck, hugging her close, and with the other she felt for the soft, fuzzy tiger that was always beside her. But it wasn't there. The Tiger was gone too.

"Hush, child, don't you remember? You gave your toy to your brother. Do you remember now?"

Yes, she remembered. She had given the Tiger to Baver. The Tiger promised to keep him safe and tell him all the nice things he had told her. Baver needed the Tiger. She had Auntie and Uncle, but Baver had nobody.

"I'm here, Sheri Bear. . . . I'm very close to you. All you have to do is find me. It's a game, Sheri. . . . A nice game to play. Find me. . . . If you find me, everything will be all right. If you find me, I'll take you to Mommy and Daddy."

She flew down the stairs. She had to find the Tiger. It was time! Now, at last, he would take her to Mommy and Daddy! All she had to do was listen, and she would find him.

CHAPTER 30

"Here! I'm over here!" The whispering voice called her. *"Come here, Sheri! Hurry now! I can't wait for long. You'll have to hurry!"*

She hurried, running toward the hill. With the Tiger to lead her, she retraced her steps past the hedges and the park, up the hill to the solitary house. The Tiger was here . . . right here in this new house. She wasn't sure how he'd got here, but his voice was calling her up the stairs.

There were people in the kitchen. She could hear them talking—David's voice and his mother's. They didn't even know she had gone out. She had fooled them . . . she and the Tiger. But where was he? Not in the hallway. Not on David's bed. Not on the dresser. Where?

"In here, Sheri Bear! Let me out! Open the door, and let me out!"

And there he was, high on the closet shelf, above David's clothes and books. She could reach him now.

She had grown so much since the last time she had seen him.

"You found me, Sheri! You found me, and you found Baver. Didn't you know he was your own baby brother? Run now! Run fast! You know where to go . . . you've always known where to go."

Ah! He was the same! Just the same! David had taken good care of him. Of course, the Tiger was David's now, but she'd just borrow him. She needed him for a little while, and then David could have him back. The Tiger would help her now, and then the Tiger would help David.

She didn't hear them calling her as she flew from the house and into the woods, clutching the Tiger tightly against her breasts. She heard nothing except the whispering . . . whispering . . . whispering of the Tiger, and she laughed happily. He was going to take her back to Mommy and Daddy. He had promised! And later, when Baver was ready, he would take Baver too! Then they could all be together, not like now, with Mommy and Daddy gone, but all together in some secret place.

The sharp bushes tore at her face and hands as she ran, stumbling a little on the uneven ground. They weren't following her any longer. She had lost them, just as the Tiger wanted her to. A light rain had started to fall, but it didn't matter. Nothing mattered except to run fast . . . run like a big girl with the Tiger, straight to Mommy and Daddy.

"Here?" she stopped, surprised. "Where? Are Mommy and Daddy here?"

The railroad crossing stretched out before her, its

gleaming silver strands wet in the mist. She peered in first one direction, and then the other. She didn't see Mommy and Daddy anywhere. Could the Tiger be playing a trick on her?"

"Where are you?" she called out, feeling butterflies of fright dart in her veins. "I'm scared!"

"I'm right here, Sheri Bear. You're old enough to know the secret now, and it's time. Your Mommy and Daddy are waiting for you. Hurry, Sheri . . . you mustn't keep them waiting any longer."

There was no one to see as she knelt on the wooden ties of the tracks and pressed her ear down, listening . . . listening for Mommy and Daddy to come. The Tiger had promised. Soon the rails would sing a welcome home song.

She remained motionless for a time and then nodded, rising gracefully to her feet. She was careful to stand straight and tall the way Mommy and Daddy wanted her to. She was a good girl. She was a very good girl and all grown up now.

There was a peaceful smile on her face as the lights started to blink and the wooden arm lowered. She could hear the Tiger's voice even though the ringing bells were loud in her ears.

"You're almost there, Sheri Bear . . . almost there. Just a little longer, and you'll be home again."

CHAPTER 31

They heard the heavy pounding of her footsteps as she hurtled down the stairs, eyes wild, clutching the toy tiger in her arms. The heavy front door slammed behind her before David could even move. He raced for his shoes with a feeling of dread that made his fingers fumble as he pulled them on.

"I'll get her!" he called out to his astonished parents, the sight of their shocked faces fixed in his mind as he raced toward the woods, hoping to catch sight of her red sweater through the trees.

David stopped and listened, the instincts of an outdoorsman sharpened by fear, but there was no sound. Only the wind rustling the leaves and a far-off rumbling of distant thunder. A sharp gust of wind made his eyes water as he plunged forward in the direction he thought she would take, but it was only when he heard the train whistle that he knew for sure. Kathi had gone to the crossing—the train crossing in the clearing. He wondered, fleetingly, why she had taken his old toy tiger from the closet.

He saw the flashing lights through the trees as he raced toward the edge of the woods, breaking through the bushes like a crazed animal. It was raining now and he brushed his arm across his forehead, bursting into the clearing. Then he saw her, poised on the tracks like a living statue, rooted there behind the wooden warning arms and the clanging signals.

"Kathi!" he shouted, his voice a shocked croak. "Kathi! Run! The train's coming! Run!"

Even as he started to run toward her, he knew that he couldn't reach her in time. The train was approaching too fast. The whistle sounded a piercing squeal, and a sweet high voice carried over the shrill blast.

"Baver!" she called out, holding the tiger up toward David. "Don't worry, Baver, the Tiger's with me. I'm going home now . . . home to our Mommy and Daddy"

There was the rending of metal against metal as the train's brakes squealed. Then a small thud as Kathi's body lifted into the air. It was chillingly graceful, an aerial ballet setting her free to fly.

David was not aware of moving. Somehow he found himself standing protectively over Kathi's body and watching numbly as the engineer felt for a pulse. A heavy glance passed between the two men. They both knew it was useless. Kathi's neck was twisted at an impossible angle.

"Christ!" the engineer muttered. "She must have been crazy! I know she saw me. She just stood there, waiting for the train to hit her!"

David nodded slowly, and the engineer turned to face him. "Did you know her?" he asked, still shaking his head as if he couldn't quite believe what had happened.

"Yes," David answered. His voice came out in a strained sob. He had known her . . . known her for years.

"Christ!" the engineer repeated. "It was the craziest thing, mister. Right before the train hit her, I could've sworn she had a smile on her face."

David could not speak past the lump in his throat. She looked so small and defenseless lying there on the cold ground. He started to struggle out of his coat, trying to protect her even in death. The day was growing colder, and there was a chill wind blowing.

Then he stopped, squaring his shoulders. With fingers that were numb, he turned up his shirt collar to shield himself from the rising wind and picked up the Tiger lying beside her. The Tiger that she had given him so long ago. His sister, Sheri . . . his beloved, Kathi. There was nothing he could do for her now. It had all been done so long ago, he had almost forgotten. She was gone, and he had no one . . . no one but the Tiger.

CHAPTER 32

They were huddled together at the funeral. Harry had an awful feeling of inevitability about everything that had happened. Kathi Ellison, as everyone knew her, had been living on borrowed time. She had really died in the same accident that had killed her mother, nearly twenty years ago. Now the words would be spoken to lay her to final rest.

Doug was sobbing openly, Vivian's arm around him in a protective gesture. Their life was not over. No one knew. All the records had been altered, and this was Kathi, their daughter, whom they had come to bury today. Doug would be elected now. There was no question about it in Harry's mind. The sympathy vote would ensure that.

Sally had refused to come to the funeral, and Doug and Vivian had not urged her too strongly. Curiously enough, Sally seemed to feel that Kathi's death was her doing. It had been a shock for her, the poor dear. Doug had given her a week off, in the hope that she could come to grips with Kathi's death. It seemed as if the elderly housekeeper would never be herself again, with her grief-stricken cries and frantic mumblings.

David was in his room at home in Swanville, lying motionless on his bed . . . thinking . . . remembering. Pressed to his ear was the battered Tiger, comforting still. David was not sure, but he thought he could hear a faint whisper.

A romantic seven-day cruise is the perfect start to bakery owner Hannah Swensen's marriage. However, with a murder mystery heating up in Lake Eden, Minnesota, it seems the newlywed's homecoming won't be as sweet as she anticipated . . .

After an extravagant honeymoon, Hannah's eager to settle down in Lake Eden and turn domestic day-dreams into reality. But when her mother's neighbor is discovered murdered in the condo downstairs, reality becomes a nightmarish investigation. Victoria Bascomb, once a renowned stage actress, was active in the theater community during her brief appearance in town . . . and made throngs of enemies along the way. Did a random intruder murder the woman as police claim, or was a deadlier scheme at play? As Hannah peels through countless suspects and some new troubles of her own, solving this crime—and living to tell about it—might prove trickier than mixing up the ultimate banana cream pie . . .

Please turn the page for an exciting sneak peek of Joanne Fluke's newest Hannah Swensen mystery

BANANA CREAM PIE MURDER

now on sale wherever print and e-books are sold!

CHAPTER 1

Delores Swensen typed THE END and gave a smile of satisfaction as she leaned back in her desk chair. She'd finished the manuscript for her newest Regency romance novel. She was just about to get up and open the bottle of Perrier Jouet she'd been saving for this occasion when she heard a loud crack and she fell to the floor backwards.

For one stunned moment, she stared up at the ceiling in her office in disbelief, unable to move or make a sound. She blinked several times and moved her head tentatively. Nothing hurt. She was still alive. But what had happened? And why had she fallen over backwards?

When the obvious solution occurred to her, Delores started to giggle. The loud crack had sounded when the cushioned seat of her desk chair had sheared off from its base. It was something Doc had warned her would happen someday if she didn't get around to replacing it. And she hadn't. And it had. And here she was on her back, her body effectively swaddled by soft, stuffed leather, barely able to move a muscle.

As she realized that she was in the same position as a turtle flipped over on its back, Delores began to laugh even harder. It was a good thing no one was here to see her! She must look ridiculous. That meant she *had* to figure out some way to get up before Doc came home. If he saw her like this, she'd never hear the end of it. And she wouldn't put it past him to take a photo of her stuck in the chair, on her back, and show it to everyone at the hospital.

Unsure of exactly how to extricate herself, Delores braced her hands on the cushioned arms of the chair and pushed. This didn't work the way she'd thought it, but it *did* work. Instead of moving her body backwards, her action pushed the chair forward. The part of her body that Doc referred to as her gluteus maximus was now several inches away from the seat of the chair, far enough for her to bend her legs, hook her heels on the edge of the chair seat and push it even farther away.

She was getting there! Delores pushed with her heels again and the chair slid several more inches away. By repeating this motion and squirming on her back at the same time, she somehow managed to free herself from her cushioned prison and roll over on hands and knees. She got to her feet by grasping the edge of her desk and pulling herself upright. When she was in a standing position, Delores gave a sigh of relief and promised herself that she'd buy a new desk chair in the morning.

Now that she was on her feet again and none the worse for wear, she decided that celebratory champagne was a necessity. She took the prized bottle from the dorm refrigerator Doc had insisted she install in her office, and opened it with a soft pop. Loud pops were for movie scenes. She'd learned to remove the cork slowly so that not even a drop would escape.

Delores set the open bottle on the desk and went to close the window. She liked fresh air and she always opened it when she worked in the office. She was about to close it when she heard a blood-curdling scream from the floor below.

For a moment Delores just stood there, a shocked expression on her face. Then she glanced at the clock and realized it was a few minutes past eight in the evening. The scream must have come from one of Tori's acting students.

The luxury condo immediately below the penthouse Doc had given her as a wedding present was owned by Victoria Bascomb, Mayor Bascomb's sister. Tori, as she preferred to be called, had been a famous Broadway actress. She'd recently retired and moved to Lake Eden to be closer to the only family she had left, her brother Richard, and his wife Stephanie. Unable to completely divorce herself from the life she loved, Tori had volunteered to direct their local theater group, to teach drama at Jordan High, and to give private acting lessons to any Lake Edenite who aspired to take the theater world by storm. If not the richest, Tori Bascomb was undeniably the most famous person in town. Just yesterday, Tori had told Delores that she had won the lifetime achievement award from STAG, the Stage and Theater Actors Guild and she would receive her award, a gold statuette that resembled a male deer, at a nationally televised award ceremony soon.

Delores gave a little laugh. How silly she'd been to forget that Tori gave acting lessons in her home studio! The scream she'd heard was obviously part of an acting lesson. Smiling a bit at her foolishness, Delores reached out again, intending to close and lock the window, but a loud cry made her pause in mid-motion.

"No!" a female voice screamed. "Don't! Please don't!"

Whoever the aspiring actress was, she was very good! Delores began to push the window closed when she heard a sound unlike any other. A gunshot. That was a gunshot! She was sure of it!

The gunshot was followed by a second gunshot, and then a crash from the floor below. Something was wrong! No acting student could be that realistic. This was really happening!

Delores didn't think. She just reacted. She raced for the doorway that led to the back stairway that had been used by hotel employees before the Albion Hotel had been converted into luxury condos. The old stairway had been completely refurbished and accessible exclusively to the penthouse residents.

When Delores arrived at the landing of the floor below, she unlocked the door and rushed out into the narrow lobby that separated the two condos on the floor below the penthouse. She raced to Tori's door and only then did the need for caution cross her mind.

Delores stood there, the key Tori had given her in her hand, and listened. All was quiet inside Tori's condo, no sounds at all. If what she'd heard had been an acting lesson, Tori should be speaking to the would-be actress, critiquing the scene she'd just performed.

As Delores continued to listen for sounds, she considered her options. She'd look very foolish if she unlocked the door and stepped inside to find that Tori and her student were perfectly fine. On the other hand, she could be walking into danger if what she'd heard was a real murder and the intruder was still there. If she called the police before she went in, they'd advise her to wait until they got there. But what if someone needed immediate medical attention?

Delores hesitated for another moment or two and then she decided to knock. She might feel foolish if Tori came to the door and said that everything was fine, but it couldn't hurt to check. She raised her hand and knocked sharply three times.

There was no answer and she heard no rushing footfalls as the intruder hurried to a hiding place. There were no sounds from inside at all. Delores hesitated for another moment and then she made a decision. She reached into her pocket, pulled out her cell phone, and dialed the emergency number for the Winnetka County Sheriff's Station.

"Sheriff's station. Detective Kingston speaking."

Delores took a deep breath. She'd been hoping to contact her son-in-law, Bill Todd, but instead she'd gotten Mike. He was a by-the-book cop and he'd tell her to stay outside the door and wait for him to get there.

"Mike. It's Delores," she said, thinking fast. "Stay on the line, will you, please? I heard a sound from

Tori Bascomb's condo and I'm going in to make sure everything's all right."

"Delores. I want you to wait until . . ."

Delores unlocked the door with one hand and pushed it open. Then, holding the phone away from her ear so she wouldn't hear Mike's objections, she glanced around Tori's living room. Nothing was out of place, no overturned chairs, no strangers lurking in corners, no sign of anything unusual. But the scream she'd heard hadn't come from the living room. It had come from the room directly below her office and that was the room that Tori had converted into her acting studio.

Delores moved toward the studio silently, holding the phone in her left hand. It was still sputtering and squawking, but she ignored it. As she prepared to open the door, she spotted a piece of artwork on a table in the hallway. It was made of a heavy metal, probably silver, and it resembled a thin but curvaceous lady holding her arms aloft. Delores grabbed it. It was just as heavy as it looked and it would serve as a weapon if the occasion warranted.

The door to the studio was slightly open and Delores peeked in. The focus of the room was the U-shaped couch facing a low platform handcrafted of cherry wood. The platform was one step high and ran the length of the opposite wall, forming a stage for Tori's would-be actors and actresses. The couch served as Tori's throne. It was where she sat to observe her students. Delores had sat there one afternoon and she knew it was made of baby-soft, butterscotch-colored leather. A fur throw was draped over the back of the couch. Delores hadn't asked Tori which particular animals had given their lives to create the fur throw, but she suspected that it had been very expensive and was probably made from Russian sable.

The scene that presented itself did not look threatening, so Delores stepped into the studio. The indirect lighting that covered the ceiling bathed the studio in a soft glow. Delores glanced at the round coffee table in front of the couch and drew in her breath sharply. A bottle of champagne was nestled in a silver wine bucket next to the table and a crystal flute filled with champagne sat on the table next to a distinctive bakery box that Delores immediately recognized. It was a bakery box from The Cookie Jar, the bakery and coffee shop that her eldest daughter owned. The lid was open and Delores could tell that it contained one of Hannah's Banana Cream Pies. It was Tori's favorite pie and she'd told Delores that she often served it when she had guests.

The flute filled with champagne was interesting. Clouds of tiny bubbles were rising to the surface and that meant it had been poured quite recently. Delores knew, through personal experience, that the bubbles slowed and eventually stopped as time passed.

Two crystal dessert plates were stacked on the coffee table, along with two silver dessert forks. It was obvious that Tori had been expecting a guest.

Delores set the phone down on the couch and stared at the coffee table. The puzzle it presented was similar to the homework that her daughters had brought home from kindergarten, a photo-copied sheet of paper with a picture drawn in detail. The caption had been *What is wrong with this picture?* Something was wrong with Tori's coffee table. What was it?

The answer occurred to Delores almost immediately. Tori had set out two dessert plates and two dessert forks, but only one flute of champagne. That was a puzzling omission. Delores knew that Tori loved champagne and judging by the label that was peeking out of the ice bucket, this was very good champagne. Did this mean that Tori was imbibing, but her anticipated guest was not? Or had Tori filled her own champagne glass and carried it away to drink someplace else in the condo? And that question was followed by an even more important question. Where *was* Tori?

Delores was dimly aware that hissing and crackling sounds were coming from her phone. Mike was still talking to her, but his words were undecipherable, muffled by the fact she'd placed her cell phone down on the cushions of the couch. Delores ignored it and glanced around the studio again. Her gaze reached the floor near the back of the couch and halted, focusing on that area. The white plush wall-to-wall carpet looked wet. Something had been spilled there.

Delores moved toward the wet carpet. She rounded the corner of the couch and stopped, reaching out to steady herself as she saw a sight that she knew would haunt her dreams for years to come. Tori was sprawled on the rug, a sticky red stain on one of the beautiful silk caftans she wore on evenings that she worked at home.

The stain on the caftan glistened in the light from the tiny bulbs in the ceiling. Delores shuddered as she saw the crystal champagne flute tipped on its side on the floor, its expensive contents now permanently embedded in the plush white fibers. Thank goodness the blood hadn't gotten on the carpet! That could have permanently ruined it. She'd have to give Tori the name of a good carpet cleaning firm so that they could remove the champagne stain.

"Ohhhh!" Delores gave a cry that ended in a sob. Tori wouldn't need the name of a carpet cleaner. Tori would never need anything again. Tori was dead! Her friend was dead!

Tears began to fall from her eyes, but Delores couldn't seem to look away. Her friend's eyes seemed fixed on the ceiling and her mouth was slightly open, as if she were protesting the cruel twist of fate that had befallen her.

"It's okay, Delores. We're here."

The sound of a calm male voice released Delores from her horrid fixation and she managed to turn to face the sound. It was Mike, and he had brought Lonnie with him. They had both come to help her. She wanted to thank them, but she couldn't seem to find the words.

"Lonnie's going to take you back upstairs and stay with you until Michelle comes."

"Michelle's still here?" Delores recovered enough to ask about her youngest daughter. "I thought she was going back to college tonight."

"She was, but she decided to stay until Hannah and Ross get back. I'll be up later to take your statement."

As Lonnie took her arm, Delores began to shake. It was as if she had been hit with a blast of icy winter wind. She leaned heavily on Lonnie's arm as he led her from the room, from the awful sight of the friend she'd never see again, the friend who wouldn't come over for coffee in the morning, the downstairs neighbor who would no longer sit by the pool under the climate-controlled dome in Delores and Doc's penthouse garden, and chat about her career on the stage. Tori would never collect her lifetime achievement award and hear the applause of her peers. Victoria Bascomb's stellar life had ended, and Delores was overwhelmed with grief and sadness.

As she entered the penthouse on Lonnie's arm and sank onto the soft cushions of the couch, another emotion began to grow in her mind. It replaced the heaviness of her sadness, at least for the moment. That emotion was anger, anger that her friend had died in such a senseless manner. How dare someone come into Tori's home and hurt her!

As Delores sat there waiting for Michelle to arrive, she was filled with a fiery resolve. She had to tell Hannah that Tori had been murdered. The moment that Michelle arrived, they had to try to reach Hannah. They needed her and she had to help them. Her eldest daughter would know where to start and what to do. Hannah had to come home to Lake Eden immediately so that they could find Tori's killer and make him pay for the horrible crime he had committed!

Connect with
Us

THE LOEB CLASSICAL LIBRARY

FOUNDED BY JAMES LOEB, LL.D.

QUINTILIAN

II

125

THE INSTITUTIO ORATORIA OF
QUINTILIAN

WITH AN ENGLISH TRANSLATION BY

H. E. BUTLER, M.A.,
PROFESSOR OF LATIN IN LONDON UNIVERSITY

IN FOUR VOLUMES

II

CAMBRIDGE, MASSACHUSETTS
HARVARD UNIVERSITY PRESS
LONDON
WILLIAM HEINEMANN LTD
MCMLXXXV

American ISBN 0-674-99139-7
British ISBN 0 434 99125 2

First printed 1921
Reprinted 1939, 1953, 1960, 1966, 1977, 1985

Printed in Great Britain

TABLE OF CONTENTS

SIGLA

A = Codex Ambrosianus, 11th century.

B = Agreement of Codices Bernensis, Bambergensis and Nostradamensis, 10th century.

G = Codex Bambergensis where gaps in B have been supplied by an 11th-century hand.

QUINTILIAN

BOOK IV

M. FABII QUINTILIANI INSTITUTIONIS ORATORIAE

LIBER IV

Prooemium

Perfecto, Marcelle Victori, operis tibi dedicati tertio libro et iam quarta fere laboris parte transacta, nova insuper mihi diligentiae causa et altior sollicitudo, quale iudicium hominum emererer, accessit. Adhuc enim velut studia inter nos conferebamus, et si parum nostra institutio probaretur a ceteris, contenti fore domestico usu videbamur, ut tui meique
2 filii formare disciplinam satis putaremus. Cum vero mihi Domitianus Augustus sororis suae nepotum delegaverit curam, non satis honorem iudiciorum caelestium intelligam, nisi ex hoc oneris quoque
3 magnitudinem metiar. Quis enim mihi aut mores excolendi sit modus, ut eos non immerito probaverit sanctissimus censor? aut studia, ne fefellisse in iis

THE INSTITUTIO ORATORIA OF QUINTILIAN

BOOK IV

Preface

I HAVE now, my dear Marcellus Victorius, completed the third book of the work which I have dedicated to you, and have nearly finished a quarter of my task, and am confronted with a motive for renewed diligence and increased anxiety as to the judgment it may be found to deserve. For up to this point we were merely discussing rhetoric between ourselves and, in the event of our system being regarded as inadequate by the world at large, were prepared to content ourselves with putting it into practice at home and to confine ourselves to the
education of your son and mine. But now Domiti- 2
anus Augustus has entrusted me with the education of his sister's grandsons, and I should be undeserving of the honour conferred upon me by such divine appreciation, if I were not to regard this distinction as the standard by which the greatness
of my undertaking must be judged. For it is 3
clearly my duty to spare no pains in moulding the character of my august pupils, that they may earn the deserved approval of the most righteous of censors. The same applies to their intellectual

videar principem ut in omnibus, ita in eloquentia
4 quoque eminentissimum? Quodsi nemo miratur
poetas maximos saepe fecisse, ut non solum initiis
operum suorum Musas invocarent, sed provecti
quoque longius, cum ad aliquem graviorem venissent
locum, repeterent vota et velut nova precatione
5 uterentur, mihi quoque profecto poterit ignosci, si,
quod initio, quo primum hanc materiam inchoavi,
non feceram, nunc omnes in auxilium deos ipsumque
in primis, quo neque praesentius aliud nec studiis
magis propitium numen est, invocem, ut, quantum
nobis exspectationis adiecit, tantum ingenii adspiret
dexterque ac volens adsit et me qualem esse credidit
6 faciat. Cuius mihi religionis non haec sola ratio,
quae maxima est, sed alioqui sic procedit ipsum
opus, ut maiora praeteritis ac magis ardua sint,
quae ingredior. Sequitur enim, ut iudicialium
causarum, quae sunt maxime variae ac multiplices,
ordo explicetur: quod prooemii sit officium, quae
ratio narrandi, quae probationum fides, seu proposita confirmamus sive contra dicta dissolvimus,
quanta vis in perorando, seu reficienda brevi repetitione rerum memoria est iudicis sive adfectus
7 (quod est longe potentissimum) commovendi. De
quibus partibus singulis quidam separatim scribere
maluerunt velut onus totius corporis veriti, et sic

training, for I would not be found to have disappointed the expectations of a prince pre-eminent in eloquence as in all other virtues. But no one 4
is surprised at the frequency with which the greatest poets invoke the Muses not merely at the commencement of their works, but even further on when they have reached some important passage and repeat their vows and utter fresh prayers for
assistance. Assuredly therefore I may ask indulgence 5
for doing what I omitted to do when I first entered on this task and calling to my aid all the gods and Himself before them all (for his power is unsurpassed and there is no deity that looks with such favour upon learning), beseeching him to inspire me with genius in proportion to the hopes that he has raised in me, to lend me propitious and ready aid and make me even such as he has believed me to be.
And this, though the greatest, is not the only 6
motive for this act of religious devotion, but my work is of such a nature that, as it proceeds, I am confronted with greater and more arduous obstacles than have yet faced me. For my next task is to explain the order to be followed in forensic causes, which present the utmost complication and variety. I must set forth the function of the *exordium*, the method of the *statement of facts*, the cogency of *proofs*, whether we are confirming our own assertions or refuting those of our opponents, and the force of the *peroration*, whether we have to refresh the memory of the judge by a brief recapitulation of the facts, or to do
what is far more effective, stir his emotions. Some 7
have preferred to give each of these points separate treatment, fearing that if they undertook them as a whole the burden would be greater than they

quoque complures de unaquaque earum libros ediderunt; quas ego omnes ausus contexere prope infinitum laborem prospicio et ipsa cogitatione suscepti muneris fatigor. Sed durandum est, quia coepimus, et si viribus deficiemur, animo tamen perseverandum.

I. Quod principium Latine vel exordium dicitur, maiore quadam ratione Graeci videntur προοίμιον nominasse, quia a nostris initium modo significatur, illi satis clare partem hanc esse ante ingressum rei
2 de qua dicendum sit, ostendunt. Nam sive propterea quod οἴμη cantus est et citharoedi pauca illa, quae, antequam legitimum certamen inchoent, emerendi favoris gratia canunt, prooemium cognominaverunt, oratores quoque ea quae, priusquam causam exordiantur, ad conciliandos sibi iudicum animos
3 praeloquuntur eadem appellatione signarunt; sive, quod οἶμον iidem Graeci viam appellant, id quod ante ingressum rei ponitur sic vocare est institutum: certe prooemium est, quod apud iudicem dici, priusquam causam cognoverit, possit; vitioseque in scholis facimus, quod exordio semper sic utimur, quasi
4 causam iudex iam noverit. Cuius rei licentia ex hoc est, quod ante declamationem illa velut imago litis exponitur. Sed in foro quoque contingere istud

could bear, and consequently have published several books on each individual point. I have ventured to treat them altogether and foresee such infinite labour that I feel weary at the very thought of the task I have undertaken. But I have set my hand to the plough and must not look back. My strength may fail me, but my courage must not fail.

I. The commencement or *exordium* as we call it in Latin is styled a *proem* by the Greeks. This seems to me a more appropriate name, because whereas we merely indicate that we are beginning our task, they clearly show that this portion is designed as an introduction to the subject on which the orator has to
speak. It may be because οἴμη means a tune, and 2
players on the lyre have given the name of *proem* to the prelude which they perform to win the favour of the audience before entering upon the regular contest for the prize, that orators before beginning to plead make a few introductory remarks to win the indulgence of the judges. Or it may be because οἶμος 3
in Greek means a *way*, that the practice has arisen of calling an introduction a *proem*. But in any case there can be no doubt that by *proem* we mean the portion of a speech addressed to the judge before he has begun to consider the actual case. And it is a mistaken practice which we adopt in the schools of always assuming in our *exordia* that the judge is
already acquainted with the case. This form of 4
licence arises from the fact that a sketch of the case is always given before actual declamation.[1] Such kinds of *exordia* may, however, be employed in the

[1] *i.e.* the statement of the "hard case" with which the declaimer has to deal. *cp.* IV. ii. 98.

principiorum genus secundis actionibus potest;
primis quidem raro unquam, nisi forte apud eum,
cui res iam aliunde nota sit, dicimus.

5 Causa principii nulla alia est, quam ut auditorem,
quo sit nobis in ceteris partibus accommodatior, prae-
paremus. Id fieri tribus maxime rebus inter
auctores plurimos constat, si benevolum, attentum,
docilem fecerimus, non quia ista non per totam
actionem sint custodienda, sed quia initiis praecipue
necessaria, per quae in animum iudicis, ut procedere
ultra possimus, admittimur.

6 Benevolentiam aut a personis ducimus aut a causis
accipimus. Sed personarum non est, ut plerique
crediderunt, triplex ratio, ex litigatore et adversario
7 et iudice. Nam exordium duci nonnunquam etiam
ab actore causae solet. Quanquam enim pauciora
de se ipso dicit et parcius, plurimum tamen ad omnia
momenti est in hoc positum, si vir bonus creditur.
Sic enim continget, ut non studium advocati videatur adferre sed paene testis fidem. Quare in primis
existimetur venisse ad agendum ductus officio vel
cognationis vel amicitiae maximeque, si fieri poterit,
reipublicae aut alicuius certe non mediocris exempli.
Quod sine dubio multo magis ipsis litigatoribus

courts, when a case comes on for the second time, but never or rarely on the first occasion, unless we are speaking before a judge who has knowledge of the case from some other source.

The sole purpose of the *exordium* is to prepare our audience in such a way that they will be disposed to lend a ready ear to the rest of our speech. The majority of authors agree that this is best effected in three ways, by making the audience well-disposed, attentive and ready to receive instruction. I need hardly say that these aims have to be kept in view throughout the whole speech, but they are especially necessary at the commencement, when we gain admission to the mind of the judge in order to penetrate still further. 5

As regards good-will, we secure that either from persons connected with the case or from the case itself. Most writers have divided these persons into three classes, the plaintiff, the defendant and the judge. This classification is wrong, for the *exordium* may sometimes derive its conciliatory force from the person of the pleader. For although he may be modest and say little about himself, yet if he is believed to be a good man, this consideration will exercise the strongest influence at every point of the case. For thus he will have the good fortune to give the impression not so much that he is a zealous advocate as that he is an absolutely reliable witness. It is therefore pre-eminently desirable that he should be believed to have undertaken the case out of a sense of duty to a friend or relative, or even better, if the point can be made, by a sense of patriotism or at any rate some serious moral consideration. No doubt it is even more 6 7

faciendum est, ut ad agendum magna atque honesta ratione aut etiam necessitate accessisse videantur.
8 Sed ut praecipua in hoc dicentis auctoritas, si omnis in subeundo negotio suspicio sordium aut odiorum aut ambitionis afuerit, ita quaedam in his quoque commendatio tacita, si nos infirmos, imparatos, impares agentium contra ingeniis dixerimus, qualia
9 sunt pleraque Messalae prooemia. Est enim naturalis favor pro laborantibus, et iudex religiosus libentissime patronum audit, quem iustitiae suae minime timet. Inde illa veterum circa occultandam eloquentiam simulatio multum ab hac nostrorum
10 temporum iactatione diversa. Vitandum etiam, ne contumeliosi, maligni, superbi, maledici in quemquam hominem ordinemve videamur praecipueque eorum, qui laedi nisi adversa iudicum voluntate non
11 possunt. Nam in iudicem ne quid dicatur non modo palam sed quod omnino intelligi possit, stultum erat monere, nisi fieret. Etiam partis adversae patronus dabit exordio materiam, interim cum honore, si eloquentiam eius et gratiam nos timere fingendo, ut ea suspecta sint iudici, fecerimus, interim per contumeliam, sed hoc perquam raro, ut Asinius pro Urbiniae[1] heredibus Labienum adversarii patronum inter argumenta causae malae posuit.

[1] *cp.* VII. ii. 4 and 26.

necessary for the parties themselves to create the impression that they have been forced to take legal action by some weighty and honourable reason or even
by necessity. But just as the authority of the speaker 8
carries greatest weight, if his undertaking of the case is free from all suspicion of meanness, personal spite or ambition, so also we shall derive some silent support from representing that we are weak, unprepared, and no match for the powerful talents arrayed against us,
a frequent trick in the *exordia* of Messala. For 9
men have a natural prejudice in favour of those who are struggling against difficulties, and a scrupulous judge is always specially ready to listen to an advocate whom he does not suspect to have designs on his integrity. Hence arose the tendency of ancient orators to pretend to conceal their eloquence, a practice exceedingly unlike the ostentation of our
own times. It is also important to avoid giving the 10
impression that we are abusive, malignant, proud or slanderous toward any individual or body of men, especially such as cannot be hurt without
exciting the disapproval of the judges. As to the 11
judge, it would be folly for me to warn speakers not to say or even hint anything against him, but for the fact that such things do occur. Our opponent's advocate will sometimes provide us with material for our *exordium*: we may speak of him in honorific terms, pretending to fear his eloquence and influence with a view to rendering them suspect to the judge, or occasionally, though very seldom, we may abuse him, as Asinius did in his speech on behalf of the heirs of Urbinia, where he includes among the proofs of the weakness of the plaintiff's case the fact that he has secured Labienus as his advocate.

12 Negat haec esse prooemia Cornelius Celsus, quia sint extra litem. Sed ego cum auctoritate summorum oratorum magis ducor, tum pertinere ad causam puto quidquid ad dicentem pertinet, cum sit naturale, ut iudices iis, quos libentius audiunt, etiam
13 facilius credant. Ipsius autem litigatoris persona tractanda varie est. Nam tum dignitas eius adlegatur, tum commendatur infirmitas. Nonnunquam contingit relatio meritorum, de quibus verecundius dicendum erit sua quam aliena laudanti. Multum agit sexus, aetas, condicio, ut in feminis, senibus, pupillis, liberos, parentes, coniuges adlegantibus.
14 Nam sola rectum quoque iudicem inclinat miseratio. Degustanda tamen haec prooemio, non consumenda. Adversarii vero persona prope iisdem omnibus, sed e contrario ductis impugnari solet. Nam et potentes sequitur invidia et humiles abiectosque contemptus et turpes ac nocentes odium, quae tria sunt ad
15 alienandos iudicum animos potentissima. Neque haec dicere sat est, quod datur etiam imperitis; pleraque augenda aut minuenda, ut expediet. Hoc enim oratoris est, illa causae.

16 Iudicem conciliabimus nobis non tantum laudando eum, quod et fieri cum modo debet et est tamen

Cornelius Celsus denies that such remarks can be 12
considered as belonging to the *exordium* on the ground that they are irrelevant to the actual case. Personally I prefer to follow the authority of the greatest orators, and hold that whatever concerns the pleader is relevant to the case, since it is natural that the judges should give readier credence to those to
whom they find it a pleasure to listen. The character 13
of our client himself may, too, be treated in various ways: we may emphasise his worth or we may commend his weakness to the protection of the court. Sometimes it is desirable to set forth his merits, when the speaker will be less hampered by modesty than if he were praising his own. Sex, age and situation are also important considerations, as for instance when women, old men or wards are pleading in the character of wives, parents or children.
For pity alone may move even a strict judge. 14
These points, however, should only be lightly touched upon in the *exordium,* not run to death. As regards our opponent he is generally attacked on similar lines, but with the method reversed. For power is generally attended by envy, abject meanness by contempt, guilt and baseness by hatred, three emotions which are powerful factors to alienate the
good-will of the judges. But a simple statement will 15
not suffice, for even the uneducated are capable of that: most of the points will require exaggeration or extenuation as expediency may demand: the method of treatment belongs to the orator, the points themselves belong to the case.

We shall win the good-will of the judge not 16
merely by praising him, which must be done with tact and is an artifice common to both parties, but

parti utrique commune, sed si laudem eius ad utilitatem causae nostrae coniunxerimus, ut adlegemus pro honestis dignitatem illi suam, pro humilibus iustitiam, pro infelicibus misericordiam, pro
17 laesis severitatem et similiter cetera. Mores quoque, si fieri potest, iudicis velim nosse. Nam prout asperi, lenes, iucundi, graves, duri, remissi erunt, aut adsumere in causam naturas eorum, qua competent, aut mitigare, qua repugnabunt, oportebit.
18 Accidit autem interim hoc quoque, ut aut nobis inimicus aut adversariis sit amicus qui iudicat; quae res utrique parti tractanda est ac nescio an etiam ei magis, in quam videatur propensior. Est enim nonnunquam pravis hic ambitus adversus amicos aut pro iis, quibuscum simultates gerant, pronuntiandi faciendique iniuste, ne fecisse videantur.
19 Fuerunt etiam quidam rerum suarum iudices. Nam et in libris Observationum a Septimio editis adfuisse Ciceronem tali causae invenio, et ego pro regina Berenice apud ipsam eam causam dixi. Similis hic quoque superioribus ratio est. Adversarius enim fiduciam partis suae iactat, patronus

by linking his praise to the furtherance of our own case. For instance, in pleading for a man of good birth we shall appeal to his own high rank, in speaking for the lowly we shall lay stress on his sense of justice, on his pity in pleading the cause of misfortune, and on his severity when we champion the victims
of wrong, and so on. I should also wish, if possible, 17
to be acquainted with the character of the judge. For it will be desirable to enlist their temperaments in the service of our cause, where they are such as are like to be useful, or to mollify them, if they are like to prove adverse, just according as they are harsh, gentle, cheerful, grave, stern, or easy-going.
It will, however, sometimes happen that the judge 18
is hostile to us and friendly to our adversaries. Such cases demand the attention of both parties and I am not sure that the party favoured by the judge does not require to handle the situation with even more care than his opponent. For perverse judges have sometimes a preposterous tendency to give judgment against their friends or in favour of those with whom they have a quarrel, and of committing injustice merely to avoid the appearance of partiality.
Again some have been judges in cases where their 19
own interests were involved. I note, for instance, in the books of observations published by Septimius that Cicero appeared in such a case, while I myself, when I appeared on behalf of Queen Berenice, actually pleaded before her. In such cases we must be guided by the same principles that I have laid down above. The opponent of the judge will emphasise his confidence in the justice of his client's cause, while the advocate of his interests will express the fear that the judge may be influenced

20 timet cognoscentis verecundiam. Praeterea detra-
henda vel confirmanda opinio, praecipue si quam
domo videbitur iudex attulisse. Metus etiam nonnunquam est amovendus, ut Cicero pro Milone, ne
arma Pompeii disposita contra se putarent, laboravit;
nonnunquam adhibendus, ut idem in Verrem facit.
21 Sed adhibendi modus alter ille frequens et favorabilis: ne male sentiat populus Romanus, ne iudicia
transferantur; alter autem asper et rarus, quo
minatur corruptis accusationem, et id quidem in
consilio ampliore utcunque tutius; nam et mali
inhibentur et boni gaudent; apud singulos vero
22 nunquam suaserim, nisi defecerint omnia. Quod
si necessitas exigit, non erit iam ex arte oratoria,
non magis quam appellare, etiamsi id quoque saepe
utile est, aut, antequam pronuntiet, reum facere;
nam et minari et deferre etiam non orator potest.

23 Si causa conciliandi nobis iudicis materiam dabit,
ex hac potissimum aliqua in usum principii, quae
maxime favorabilia videbuntur, decerpi oportebit.

---

[1] i. 15.

[2] *e.g.* in the *Verrines* Cicero points out to the jury, then drawn entirely from senators, that they are on their trial. If they fail in their duty, the constitution of the panels will be altered and the *equites* be admitted as well.

by a quixotic delicacy. Further, if the judge is 20
thought to have come into court with a prejudice in favour of one side, we must try to remove or strengthen that prejudice as circumstances may demand. Again occasionally we shall have to calm the judges' fears, as Cicero does in the *pro Milone*, where he strives to persuade them not to think that Pompey's soldiers have been stationed in the court as a threat to themselves. Or it may be necessary to frighten them, as Cicero does in the *Verrines*.[1]
There are two ways of bringing fear to bear upon 21
the judges. The commonest and most popular is to threaten them with the displeasure of the Roman people or the transference of the juries to another class[2]; the second is somewhat brutal and is rarely employed, and consists in threatening them with a prosecution for bribery: this is a method which is fairly safe with a large body of judges, since it checks the bad and pleases the good members of the jury, but I should never recommend its employment with a single judge[3] except in the very last
resort. But if necessity should drive us to such a 22
course, we must remember that such threats do not come under the art of oratory, any more than appeals from the judgment of the court (though that is often useful), or the indictment of the judge before he gives his decision. For even one who is no orator can threaten or lay an information.

If the case affords us the means of winning the 23
favour of the judge, it is important that the points which seem most likely to serve to our purpose should be selected for introduction into the *exordium*.

[3] It must be borne in mind that *iudex* may be a juryman forming one of a large panel, or a single judge trying a civil action.

Quo in loco Verginius fallitur, qui Theodoro placere tradit, ut ex singulis quaestionibus singuli sensus
24 in prooemium conferantur. Nam ille non hoc dicit, sed ad potentissimas quaestiones iudicem praeparandum; in quo vitii nihil erat, nisi in universum id praeciperet, quod nec omnis quaestio patitur nec omnis causa desiderat. Nam protinus a petitore primo loco, dum ignota iudici lis est, quomodo ex quaestionibus ducemus sententias? nimirum res erunt indicandae prius. Demus aliquas (nam id exiget ratio nonnunquam); etiamne potentissimas omnes, id est totam causam? sic erit in prooemio
25 peracta narratio. Quid vero? si, ut frequenter accidit, paulo est durior causa, non benevolentia iudicis petenda ex aliis partibus erit, sed non ante conciliato eius animo nuda quaestionum committetur asperitas? Quae si recte semper initio dicendi
26 tractarentur, nihil prooemio opus esset. Aliqua ergo nonnunquam, quae erunt ad conciliandum nobis iudicem potentissima, non inutiliter interim ex quaestionibus in exordio locabuntur. Quae sint

On this subject Verginius falls into error, for he asserts that Theodorus lays down that some one reflexion on each individual question that is involved by the case should be introduced into the *exordium*.
As a matter of fact Theodorus does not say this, 24
but merely that the judge should be prepared for the most important of the questions that are to be raised. There is nothing to object to in this rule, save that he would make it of universal application, whereas it is not possible with every question nor desirable in every case. For instance, seeing that the plaintiff's advocate speaks first, and that till he has spoken the judge is ignorant of the nature of the dispute, how is it possible for us to introduce reflexions relating to all the questions involved? The facts of the case must be stated before that can be done. We may grant that some questions may be mentioned, for that will sometimes be absolutely necessary; but can we introduce all the most important questions, or in other words the whole case? If we do we shall have completed our *statement of facts* within the limits of the *exordium*.
Again if, as often happens, the case is somewhat 25
difficult, surely we should seek to win the good-will of the judge by other portions of our speech sooner than thrust the main questions upon him in all their naked harshness before we have done anything to secure his favour. If the main questions ought always to be treated at the beginning of a speech,
we might dispense with the *exordium*. We shall 26
then occasionally introduce certain points from the main questions into the *exordium*, which will exercise a valuable influence in winning the judge to regard us with favour. It is not necessary to enumerate

porro in causis favorabilia, enumerare non est necesse, quia et manifesta erunt cognita cuiusque
controversiae condicione et omnia colligi in tanta
27 litium varietate non possunt. Ut autem haec invenire et augere, ita quod laedit aut omnino re-
pellere aut certe minuere ex causa est. Miseratio
quoque aliquando ex eadem venit, sive quid passi
28 sumus grave sive passuri. Neque enim sum in hac
opinione, qua quidam, ut eo distare prooemium ab
epilogo credam, quod in hoc praeterita, in illo futura
dicantur, sed quod in ingressu parcius et modestius
praetemptanda sit iudicis misericordia, in epilogo
vero liceat totos effundere adfectus et fictam orationem induere personis et defunctos excitare et
pignora reorum producere; quae minus in exordiis
29 sunt usitata. Sed haec, quae supra dixi, non movere
tantum, verum ex diverso amoliri quoque prooemio
opus est. Ut autem nostrum miserabilem, si vin-
camur, exitum, ita adversariorum superbum, si
vicerint, utile est credi.

30 Sed ex iis quoque, quae non sunt personarum nec
causarum, verum adiuncta personis et causis, duci

the points which are likely to gain us such favour, because they will be obvious as soon as we have acquainted ourselves with the circumstances of each dispute, while in view of the infinite variety presented by cases it is out of the question to specify
them here. Just, however, as it is in the interest 27
of our case to note and amplify these points, so it is also to rebut or at any rate lessen the force of anything that is damaging to our case. Again our case may justify an appeal to compassion with regard to what we have suffered in the past or are
likely to suffer. For I do not share the opinion 28
held by some, that the *exordium* and the *peroration* are to be distinguished by the fact that the latter deals with the past, the former with the future. Rather I hold that the difference between them is this: in our opening any preliminary appeal to the compassion of the judge must be made sparingly and with restraint, while in the peroration we may give full rein to our emotions, place fictitious speeches in the mouths of our characters, call the dead to life, and produce the wife or children of the accused in court, practices which are less usual in
exordia. But it is the function of the *exordium* not 29
merely to excite the feelings to which I have alluded, but to do all that is possible to show that our opponent's case is not deserving of them. It is advantageous to create the impression not merely that our fate will be deserving of pity, if we lose, but that our adversary will be swollen with outrageous insolence if he prove successful.

But exordia are often drawn from matters which 30
do not, strictly speaking, concern either cases or the persons involved, though not unrelated to either.

prooemia solent. Personis applicantur non pignora modo, de quibus supra dixi, sed propinquitates, amicitiae, interim regiones etiam civitatesque, et si quid aliud eius quem defendimus casu laedi potest.
31 Ad causam extra pertinent tempus, unde principium pro Caelio; locus, unde pro Deiotaro; habitus, unde pro Milone; opinio, unde in Verrem; deinceps, ne omnia enumerem, infamia iudiciorum, exspectatio vulgi; nihil enim horum in causa est, ad causam
32 tamen pertinent. Adiicit Theophrastus ab oratione principium, quale videtur esse Demosthenis pro Ctesiphonte, ut sibi dicere suo potius arbitrio liceat rogantis quam eo modo, quem actione accusator praescripserit.

33 Fiducia ipsa solet opinione arrogantiae laborare. Faciunt favorem et illa paene communia non tamen omittenda, vel ideo ne occupentur, optare, abominari, rogare, sollicitum agere; quia plerumque attentum iudicem facit, si res agi videtur nova, magna, atrox, pertinens ad exemplum, praecipue tamen, si iudex aut sua vice aut reipublicae commovetur, cuius animus

---

[1] In the *pro Caelio* (c. 1) Cicero calls attention to the fact that the trial is taking place during a festival, all other legal business being suspended. In the *pro Deiotaro* (c. 2) he calls attention to the unusual surroundings, the speech being delivered in a private house. For the *pro Milone* see § 20 of this chapter. In the first *Verrine* (c. 1) he remarks that

In such relation to persons stand not only wives and children of whom I have just spoken, but also relations, friends, and at times districts and states together with anything else that is like to suffer injury from the fall of the client whom we defend.
As regards external circumstances[1] which have a 31
bearing on the case, I may mention time, which is introduced in the exordium of the *pro Caelio*, place (in the *pro Deiotaro*), the appearance of the court (in the *pro Milone*), public opinion (in the *Verrines*), and finally, as I cannot mention all, the ill-repute of the law courts and the popular expectation excited by the case. None of these actually belong to the case, but all have some
bearing on it. Theophrastus adds that the *exordium* 32
may be drawn from the speech of one's opponent, as that of the *pro Ctesiphonte* of Demosthenes appears to be, where he asks that he may be allowed to speak as he pleases and not to be restricted to the form laid down by the accuser in his speech.

Confidence often labours under the disadvantage 33
of being regarded as arrogance. But there are certain tricks for acquiring good-will, which though almost universal, are by no means to be neglected, if only to prevent their being first employed against ourselves. I refer to rhetorical expressions of wishing, detestation, entreaty, or anxiety. For it keeps the judge's attention on the alert, if he is led to think the case novel, important, scandalous, or likely to set a precedent, still more if he is excited by concern for himself or the common weal, when

it is generally believed that the corruption of the courts is such that it is practically impossible to secure the condemnation of a wealthy man.

spe, metu, admonitione, precibus, vanitate denique,
34 si id profuturum credimus, agitandus est. Sunt et illa excitandis ad audiendum non inutilia, si nos neque diu moraturos neque extra causam dicturos existiment. Docilem sine dubio et haec ipsa praestat attentio; sed et illud, si breviter et dilucide summam rei, de qua cognoscere debeat, indicaverimus, quod Homerus atque
35 Vergilius operum suorum principiis faciunt. Nam is eius rei modus est, ut propositioni similior sit quam expositioni, nec quomodo quidque sit actum, sed de quibus dicturus sit orator ostendat. Nec video, quod huius rei possit apud oratores reperiri melius exemplum
36 quam Ciceronis pro A. Cluentio: *Animadverti, iudices, omnem accusatoris orationem in duas divisam esse partes; quarum altera mihi inniti et magnopere confidere videbatur invidia iam inveterata iudicii Iuniani, altera tantummodo consuetudinis causa timide et diffidenter attingere rationem veneficii criminum, qua de re lege est haec quaestio constituta.* Id tamen totum respondenti facilius est quam proponenti, quia hic admonendus iudex, illic
37 docendus est. Nec me quanquam magni auctores in hoc duxerint, ut non semper facere attentum ac

his mind must be stirred by hope, fear, admonition, entreaty and even by falsehood, if it seems to us
that it is likely to advance our case. We shall also 34
find it a useful device for wakening the attention of our audience to create the impression that we shall not keep them long and intend to stick closely to the point. The mere fact of such attention undoubtedly makes the judge ready to receive instruction from us, but we shall contribute still more to this effect if we give a brief and lucid summary of the case which he has to try; in so doing we shall be following the method adopted by Homer and
Virgil at the beginning of their poems. For as regards 35
the length of the *exordium,* it should propound rather than expound, and should not describe how each thing occurred, but simply indicate the points on which the orator proposes to speak. I do not think a better example of this can be found than the
exordium to the *pro Cluentio* of Cicero. "I have 36
noted, judges, that the speech for the prosecution was divided into two parts: of these, the first seemed to rest and in the main to rely on the odium, now inveterate, arising from the trial before Junius, while the other appeared to touch, merely as a matter of form, and with a certain timidity and diffidence, on the question of the charge of poisoning, though it is to try this point that the present court has been constituted in accordance with the law." All this, however, is easier for the defender than the prosecutor, since the latter has merely to remind the judge, while the former has to instruct him.
Nor shall any authority, however great, induce me 37
to abandon my opinion that it is always desirable to render the judge attentive and ready to receive

docilem iudicem velim; non quia nesciam, id quod ab illis dicitur, esse pro mala causa, qualis ea sit non intelligi, verum quia istud non negligentia iudicis con-
38 tingit, sed errore. Dixit enim adversarius et fortasse persuasit; nobis opus est eius diversa opinione, quae mutari non potest, nisi illum fecerimus ad ea quae dicemus docilem et intentum. Quid ergo est? Imminuenda quaedam et levanda et quasi contemnenda esse consentio ad remittendam intentionem iudicis, quam adversario praestat, ut fecit pro Ligario
39 Cicero. Quid enim agebat aliud ironia illa, quam ut Caesar minus se in rem tanquam non novam intenderet? Quid pro Caelio, quam ut res exspectatione minor videretur?

Verum ex iis, quae proposuimus, aliud in alio
40 genere causae desiderari palam est. Genera porro causarum plurimi quinque fecerunt, honestum, humile, dubium vel anceps, admirabile, obscurum: id est ἔνδοξον, ἄδοξον, ἀμφίδοξον, παράδοξον, δυσπαρακολούθητον. Sunt quibus recte videtur adiici turpe,
41 quod alii humili, alii admirabili subiiciunt. Admirabile autem vocant, quod est praeter opinionem hominum constitutum. In ancipiti maxime benevolum iudicem, in obscuro docilem, in humili

---

[1] *pro Cael.* 31.

instruction. I am well aware that those who disagree with me urge that it is to the advantage of a bad case that its nature should not be understood; but such lack of understanding arises not from inattention on the part of the judge, but from his being deceived. Our opponent has spoken and 38
perhaps convinced him; we must alter his opinion, and this we cannot do unless we render him attentive to what we have to say and ready to be instructed. What are we to do then? I agree to the view that we should cut down, depreciate and deride some of our opponent's arguments with a view to lessening the attention shown him by the judge, as Cicero did in the *pro Ligario.* For what was the purpose of 39
Cicero's irony save that Caesar should be induced to regard the case as presenting only old familiar features and consequently to give it less attention? What was his purpose in the *pro Caelio*[1] save to make the case seem far more trivial than had been anticipated?

It is, however, obvious that of the rules which I have laid down, some will be applicable to one case and some to another. The majority of writers 40
consider that there are five kinds of causes, the *honourable,* the *mean,* the *doubtful* or *ambiguous,* the *extraordinary* and the *obscure,* or as they are called in Greek, ἔνδοξον, ἄδοξον, ἀμφίδοξον, παράδοξον and δυσπαρακολούθητον. To these some would add a sixth, the *scandalous,* which some again include under the heading of the *mean,* others under the *extraordinary.* The latter name is given to cases which are contrary 41
to ordinary expectation. In *ambiguous* cases it is specially important to secure the good-will of the judge, in the *obscure* to render him ready to receive

attentum parare debemus. Nam honestum quidem ad conciliationem satis per se valet, admirabili et turpi remediis opus est.

42 Eo quidam exordium in duas dividunt partes, principium et insinuationem, ut sit in principiis recta benevolentiae et attentionis postulatio; quae quia esse in turpi causae genere non possit, insinuatio surrepat animis, maxime ubi frons causae non satis honesta est, vel quia res sit improba vel quia hominibus parum probetur, aut si facie quoque ipsa premitur vel invidiosa consistentis ex diverso patroni
43 aut patris vel miserabili senis, caeci, infantis. Et quidem quibus adversus haec modis sit medendum, verbosius tradunt materiasque sibi ipsi fingunt et ad morem actionum persequuntur; sed hae cum oriantur ex causis, quarum species consequi omnes non possumus, nisi generaliter comprehenduntur, in infinitum
44 sunt extrahendae. Quare singulis consilium ex propria ratione nascetur. Illud in universum praeceperim, ut ab his quae laedunt ad ea quae prosunt refugiamus. Si causa laborabimus, persona subveniat;

instruction, in the *mean* to excite his attention. As regards the *honourable* the very nature of the case is sufficient to win the approval of the judge; in the *scandalous* and *extraordinary* some kind of palliation is required.

Some therefore divide the *exordium* into two parts, 42
the *introduction* and the *insinuation*, making the former contain a direct appeal to the good-will and attention of the judge. But as this is impossible in scandalous cases, they would have the orator on such occasions insinuate himself little by little into the minds of his judges, especially when the features of the case which meet the eye are discreditable, or because the subject is disgraceful or such as to meet with popular disapproval, or again if the outward circumstances of the case are such as to handicap it or excite odium (as for instance when a patron appears against a client or a father against a son), or pity (as when our opponent
is an old or blind man or a child). To save the situa- 43
tion the rhetoricians lay down a number of rules at quite inordinate length: they invent fictitious cases and treat them realistically on the lines which would be followed in actual pleading. But these peculiar circumstances arise from such a variety of causes as to render classification by species impossible, and their enumeration save under the most general heads
would be interminable. The line to be adopted will 44
therefore depend on the individual nature of each case. As a general principle, however, I should advise the avoidance of points which tell against us and concentrate on those which are likely to be of service. If the case itself is weak, we may derive help from the character of our client; if his character is doubtful, we may find salvation in the nature of

si persona, causa; si nihil quod nos adiuvet erit,
quaeramus quid adversarium laedat; nam ut optabile
45 est plus favoris mereri, sic proximum odii minus. In
iis, quae negari non potuerint, elaborandum, ut aut
minora quam dictum est aut alia mente facta aut
nihil ad praesentem quaestionem pertinere aut
emendari posse paenitentia aut satis iam punita
videantur. Ideoque agere advocato quam litigatori
facilius, quia et laudat sine arrogantiae crimine et
46 aliquando utiliter etiam reprehendere potest. Nam
se quoque moveri interim finget, ut pro Rabirio
Postumo Cicero, dum aditum sibi ad aures faciat et
auctoritatem induat vera sentientis, quo magis
credatur vel defendenti eadem vel neganti. Ideoque
hoc primum intuebimur, litigatoris an advocati persona
sit utendum, quotiens utrumque fieri potest; nam id in
schola liberum est, in foro rarum, ut sit idoneus
47 suae rei quisque defensor. Declamaturus autem
maxime positas in adfectibus causas propriis personis
debet induere. Hi sunt enim, qui mandari non

---

[1] *pro Rab.* i. 1.

the case. If both are hopeless, we must look out for something that will damage our opponent. For though it is desirable to secure as much positive good-will as possible, the next best thing is to incur the minimum of actual dislike. Where we cannot 45
deny the truth of facts that are urged against us, we must try to show that their significance has been exaggerated or that the purpose of the act was not what is alleged or that the facts are irrelevant or that what was done may be atoned for by penitence or has already been sufficiently punished. It is consequently easier for an advocate to put forward such pleas than for his client, since the former can praise without laying himself open to the charge of arrogance and may sometimes even reprove him with advantage to the case. At times, like Cicero in his 46
defence of Rabirius Postumus,[1] he will pretend that he himself is strongly moved, in order to win the ear of the judge and to give the impression of one who is absolutely convinced of the truth of his cause, that so his statements may find all the readier credence whether he defends or denies the actions attributed to his client. Consequently it is of the first importance, wherever the alternative is open to us, to consider whether we are to adopt the character of a party to the suit or of an advocate. In the schools, of course, we have a free choice in the matter, but it is only on rare occasions that a man is capable of pleading his own case in the actual courts. When 47
we are going to deliver a declamation on a theme that turns largely on its emotional features, we must give it a dramatic character suited to the persons concerned. For emotions are not transferable at will, nor can we give the same forcible ex-

possunt, nec eadem vi profertur alieni animi qua sui
48 motus. His etiam de causis insinuatione videtur opus
esse, si adversarii actio iudicum animos occupavit, si
dicendum apud fatigatos est; quorum alterum promittendo nostras probationes et adversas eludendo
vitabimus, alterum et spe brevitatis et iis, quibus
49 attentum fieri iudicem docuimus. Et urbanitas
opportuna reficit animos et undecunque petita
iudicis voluptas levat taedium. Non inutilis etiam
est ratio occupandi quae videntur obstare, ut Cicero
dicit, scire se mirari quosdam, quod is, qui per
tot annos defenderit multos, laeserit neminem,
ad accusandum Verrem descenderit; deinde ostendit,
hanc ipsam esse sociorum defensionem; quod schema
50 πρόληψις dicitur. Id cum sit utile aliquando, nunc a
declamatoribus quibusdam paene semper adsumitur,
qui fas non putant nisi a contrario incipere.

Negant Apollodorum secuti tris esse, de quibus supra diximus, praeparandi iudicis partes; sed multas species enumerant, ut ex moribus iudicis, ex opinioni-

[1] *Div. in Caec.* i. 1.

pression to another man's emotions that we should give to our own. The circumstances which call for 48
insinuation arise also in cases where the pleading of our opponent has made a powerful impression on the minds of the judges, or where the audience whom we have to address are tired. The first difficulty we shall evade by promising to produce our own proofs and by eluding the arguments of our opponents, the second by holding out hopes that we shall be brief and by the methods already mentioned for capturing the attention of the judges. Again an opportune 49
display of wit will often restore their flagging spirits and we may alleviate their boredom by the introduction of entertaining matter derived from any source that may be available. It will also be found advantageous to anticipate the objections that may be raised by our opponent, as Cicero[1] does when he says "I know that some persons are surprised that one, who for such a number of years has defended so many and attacked none, should have come forward as the accuser of Verres," he then goes on to show that the accusation which he has undertaken is really a defence of the allies, an artifice known as πρόληψις or anticipation. Although this is at times 50
a useful device, some of our declaimers employ it on practically every occasion, on the assumption that one should always start with the order thus reversed.

The adherents of Apollodorus reject the view stated above to the effect that there are only three respects in which the mind of the judge requires to be prepared, and enumerate many others, relating to the character of the judge, to opinions regarding matters which though outside the case have still

bus ad causam extra pertinentibus, ex opinione de ipsa causa, quae sunt prope infinitae, tum iis, ex quibus omnes controversiae constant, personis, factis, dictis, causis, temporibus, locis, occasionibus, ceteris.
51 Quas veras esse fateor, sed in haec genera recidere. Nam si iudicem benevolum, attentum, docilem habeo, quid amplius debeam optare, non reperio ; cum metus ipse, qui maxime videtur esse extra haec, et attentum iudicem faciat et ab adverso favore deterreat.

52 Verum quoniam non est satis demonstrare discentibus, quae sint in ratione prooemii, sed dicendum etiam, quomodo perfici facillime possint, hoc adiicio, ut dicturus intueatur, quid, apud quem, pro quo, contra quem, quo tempore, quo loco, quo rerum statu, qua vulgi fama dicendum sit, quid iudicem sentire credibile sit, antequam incipimus, tum quid aut desideremus aut deprecemur. Ipsa illum natura eo ducet,
53 ut sciat, quid primum dicendum sit. At nunc omne, quo coeperunt, prooemium putant et, ut quidque succurrit, utique si aliqua sententia blandiatur, exordium. Multa autem sine dubio sunt et aliis partibus causae communia, nihil tamen in quaque melius dicitur, quam quod aeque bene dici alibi non possit.

some bearing on it, to the opinion current as to the case itself, and so on *ad infinitum:* to these they add others relating to the elements of which every dispute is composed, such as persons, deeds, words, motives, time and place, occasions and the like.
Such views are, I admit, perfectly correct, but are 51
covered by one or other of the three classes which I have mentioned. For if I can secure good-will, attention and readiness to learn on the part of my judge, I cannot see what else I ought to require; even fear, which perhaps may be thought more than anything else to lie outside the considerations I have mentioned, secures the attention of the judge and deters him from favouring our opponent.

It is not, however, sufficient to explain the nature 52
of the *exordium* to our pupils. We must also indicate the easiest method of composing an *exordium.* I would therefore add that he who has a speech to make should consider what he has to say; before whom, in whose defence, against whom, at what time and place, under what circumstances he has to speak; what is the popular opinion on the subject, and what the prepossessions of the judge are likely to be; and finally of what we should express our deprecation or desire. Nature herself will give him
the knowledge of what he ought to say first. Now- 53
adays, however, speakers think that anything with which they choose to start is a *proem* and that whatever occurs to them, especially if it be a reflexion that catches their fancy, is an *exordium.* There are, no doubt, many points that can be introduced into an *exordium* which are common to other parts of a speech, but the best test of the appropriateness of a point to any part of a speech is to consider whether it would

54 Multum gratiae exordio est, quod ab actione diversae partis materiam trahit, hoc ipso, quod non compositum domi, sed ibi atque ex re natum, et facilitate famam ingenii auget et facie simplicis sumptique ex proximo sermonis fidem quoque adquirit; adeo ut, etiamsi reliqua scripta atque elaborata sint, tamen plerumque videatur tota extemporalis oratio, cuius initium nihil praeparati habuisse manifestum est.
55 Frequentissime vero prooemium decebit et sententiarum et compositionis et vocis et vultus modestia, adeo ut in genere causae etiam indubitabili fiducia se ipsa nimium exserere non debeat. Odit enim iudex fere litigantis securitatem, cumque ius suum intelli-
56 gat, tacitus reverentiam postulat. Nec minus diligenter ne suspecti simus illa parte vitandum est, propter quod minime ostentari debet in principiis cura, quia videtur ars omnis dicentis contra iudicem
57 adhiberi. Sed ipsum istud evitare summae artis est. Nam id sine dubio ab omnibus et quidem optime praeceptum est, verum aliquatenus temporum condicione mutatur, quia iam quibusdam in iudiciis maximeque capitalibus aut apud centumviros ipsi iudices exigunt sollicitas et accuratas actiones, con-

[1] The court of the *centumviri* was specially concerned with cases of inheritance.

lose effect by being placed elsewhere. A most attractive form of *exordium* is that which draws its material from the speech of our opponent, if only for the reason that the fact of its not having been composed at home, but having been improvised on the spot to meet the needs of the case increases the orator's reputation for natural talent by the readiness with which it is produced and carries conviction owing to the simple and ordinary language in which it is clothed. As a result, even although the rest of the speech has been committed to writing and carefully elaborated, the whole of the speech will often be regarded as extempore, simply because its commencement is clearly not the result of previous study. Indeed a certain simplicity in the thoughts, style, voice and look of the speaker will often produce so pleasing an effect in the *exordium* that even in a case where there is no room for doubt the confidence of the speaker should not reveal itself too openly. For as a rule the judge dislikes self-confidence in a pleader, and conscious of his rights tacitly demands the respectful deference of the orator. No less care must be taken to avoid exciting any suspicion in this portion of our speech, and we should therefore give no hint of elaboration in the *exordium*, since any art that the orator may employ at this point seems to be directed solely at the judge. But to avoid all display of art in itself requires consummate art: this admirable canon has been insisted on by all writers, though its force has been somewhat impaired by present conditions, since in certain trials, more especially those brought on capital charges or in the centumviral[1] court, the judges themselves demand the most finished and

54 55 56 57

temnique se, nisi in dicendo etiam diligentia appareat,
credunt, nec doceri tantum sed etiam delectari volunt.
58 Et est difficilis huius rei moderatio, quae tamen tem-
perari ita potest, ut videamur accurate non callide
dicere. Illud ex praeceptis veteribus manet, ne quod
insolens verbum, ne audacius translatum, ne aut ab
obsoleta vetustate aut poetica licentia sumptum in
59 principio deprehendatur. Nondum enim recepti
sumus, et custodit nos recens audientium intentio;
magis conciliatis animis et iam calentibus haec libertas
feretur, maximeque cum in locos fuerimus ingressi,
quorum naturalis ubertas licentiam verbi notari cir-
60 cumfuso nitore non patitur. Nec argumentis autem
nec locis nec narrationi similis esse in prooemio debet
oratio, neque tamen deducta semper atque circumlita,
sed saepe simplici atque illaboratae similis, nec verbis
vultuque nimia promittens. Dissimulata enim et,
ut Graeci dicunt, ἀνεπίφατος actio melius saepe sur-
repit. Sed haec, prout formari animum iudicum
expediet.

61 Turbari memoria vel continuandi verba facultate
destitui nusquam turpius, cum vitiosum prooemium

---

[1] *i.e.* unobtrusive.

elaborate speeches, think themselves insulted, unless the orator shows signs of having exercised the utmost diligence in the preparation of his speech, and desire not merely to be instructed, but to be
charmed. It is difficult to preserve the happy mean 58
in carrying this precept into effect: but by a skilful compromise it will be possible to give the impression of speaking with care but without elaborate design. The old rule still holds good that no unusual word, no overbold metaphor, no phrase derived from the lumber-rooms of antiquity or from poetic licence
should be detected in the *exordium.* For our position 59
is not yet established, the attention of the audience is still fresh and imposes restraint upon us: as soon as we have won their good-will and kindled their interest, they will tolerate such freedom, more especially when we have reached topics whose natural richness prevents any licence of expression being noticed in the midst of the prevailing
splendour of the passage. The style of the *exordium* 60
should not resemble that of our purple patches nor that of the argumentative and narrative portions of the speech, nor yet should it be prolix or continuously ornate: it should rather seem simple and unpremeditated, while neither our words nor our looks should promise too much. For a method of pleading which conceals its art and makes no vain display, being as the Greeks say ἀνεπίφατος,[1] will often be best adapted to insinuate its way into the minds of our hearers. But in all this we must be guided by the extent to which it is expedient to impress the minds of the judges.

There is no point in the whole speech where con- 61
fusion of memory or loss of fluency has a worse effect,

possit videri cicatricosa facies, et pessimus certe
gubernator qui navem, dum portu egreditur, im-
62 pegit. Modus autem principii pro causa. Nam
breve simplices, longius perplexae suspectaeque et
infames desiderant. Ridendi vero, qui velut legem
prooemiis omnibus dederunt, ut intra quattuor sensus
terminarentur. Nec minus evitanda est immodica
eius longitudo, ne in caput excrevisse videatur et
63 quo praeparare debet fatiget. Sermonem a persona
iudicis aversum, quae ἀποστροφή dicitur, quidam in
totum a prooemio summovent, nonnulla quidem in
hanc persuasionem ratione ducti. Nam prorsus esse
hoc magis secundum naturam confitendum est, ut
eos alloquamur potissimum, quos conciliare nobis
64 studemus. Interim tamen et est prooemio necessarius sensus aliquis, et hic acrior fit atque vehemen-
tior ad personam derectus alterius. Quod si accidat,
quo iure aut qua tanta superstitione prohibeamur
65 dare per hanc figuram sententiae vires? Neque
enim istud scriptores artium, quia non liceat, sed
quia non putent utile, vetant. Ita si vincet utilitas,
propter eandem causam facere debebimus propter
66 quam vetamur. Et Demosthenes autem ad Aeschi-

for a faulty *exordium* is like a face seamed with scars;
and he who runs his ship ashore while leaving port
is certainly the least efficient of pilots. The length 62
of the *exordium* will be determined by the case;
simple cases require a short introduction only,
longer *exordia* being best suited to cases which are
complicated, suspect or unpopular. As for those
who have laid it down as a law applying to all
exordia that they should not be more than four
sentences long, they are merely absurd. On the
other hand undue length is equally to be avoided,
lest the head should seem to have grown out of all
proportion to the body and the judge should be
wearied by that which ought to prepare him for
what is to follow. The figure which the Greeks 63
call *apostrophe*, by which is meant the diversion of
our words to address some person other than the
judge, is entirely banned by some rhetoricians as
far as the *exordium* is concerned, and for this they
have some reason, since it would certainly seem to
be more natural that we should specially address
ourselves to those whose favour we desire to win.
Occasionally however some striking expression of 64
thought is necessary in the *exordium* which can be
given greater point and vehemence if addressed to
some person other than the judge. In such a case
what law or what preposterous superstition is to
prevent us from adding force to such expression
of our thought by the use of this figure? For the 65
writers of text-books do not forbid it because they
regard it as illicit, but because they think it useless.
Consequently if its utility be proved, we shall have
to employ it for the very reason for which we are
now forbidden to do so. Moreover Demosthenes 66

nen orationem in prooemio convertit, et M. Tullius,
cum pro aliis quibusdam, ad quos ei visum est, tum
67 pro Ligario ad Tuberonem; nam erat multo futura
languidior, si esset aliter figurata. Quod facilius
cognoscet, si quis totam illam partem vehementis-
simam, cuius haec forma est, *Habes igitur, Tubero,
quod est accusatori maxime optandum,* et cetera con-
vertat ad iudicem; tum enim vere aversa videatur
oratio et languescat vis omnis, dicentibus nobis *Habet
igitur Tubero, quod est accusatori maxime optandum.*
68 Illo enim modo pressit atque institit, hoc tantum
indicasset. Quod idem in Demosthene, si flexum
illum mutaveris, accidit. Quid? non Sallustius de-
recto ad Ciceronem, in quem ipsum dicebat, usus est
principio, et quidem protinus? *Graviter et iniquo
animo maledicta tua paterer, Marce Tulli,* sicut Cicero
69 fecerat in Catilinam: *Quousque tandem abutere?* Ac,
ne quis apostrophen miretur, idem Cicero pro Scauro
ambitus reo, quae causa est in commentariis (nam
bis eundem defendit), prosopopoeia loquentis pro reo
utitur, pro Rabirio vero Postumo eodemque Scauro

---

[1] *de Cor.* § 11. [2] i. 2.
[3] This speech is lost: the existing speech in his defence is on the charge of extortion.

turns to address Aeschines in his *exordium*,[1] while Cicero adopts the same device in several of his speeches, but more especially in the *pro Ligario*,[2] where he turns to address Tubero. His speech 67
would have been much less effective, if any other figure had been used, as will be all the more clearly realised, if the whole of that most vigorous passage "You are, then, in possession, Tubero, of the most valuable advantage that can fall to an accuser etc." be altered so as to be addressed to the judge. For it is a real and most unnatural diversion of the passage, which destroys its whole force, if we say "Tubero is then in possession of the most valuable advantage that can fall to an accuser." In the 68
original form Cicero attacks his opponent and presses him hard, in the passage as altered he would merely have pointed out a fact. The same thing results if you alter the turn of the passage in Demosthenes. Again did not Sallust when speaking against Cicero himself address his *exordium* to him and not to the judge? In fact he actually opens with the words "I should feel deeply injured by your reflexions on my character, Marcus Tullius," wherein he followed the precedent set by Cicero in his speech against Catiline where he opens with the words "How long will you continue to abuse our patience?" Finally to remove all reason for 69
feeling surprise at the employment of *apostrophe*, Cicero in his defence of Scaurus,[3] on a charge of bribery (the speech is to be found in his Notebooks; for he defended him twice) actually introduces an imaginary person speaking on behalf of the accused, while in his *pro Rabirio* and his speech in defence of this same Scaurus on a charge of extortion he

reo repetundarum etiam exemplis, pro Cluentio (ut
70 modo ostendi) partitione. Non tamen haec, quia
possunt bene aliquando fieri, passim facienda sunt,
sed quotiens praeceptum vicerit ratio; quomodo et
similitudine, dum brevi, et translatione atque aliis
tropis (quae omnia cauti illi ac diligentes prohibent)
utemur interim, nisi cui divina illa pro Ligario ironia,
71 de qua paulo ante dixeram, displicet. Alia exordio-
rum vitia verius tradiderunt. Quod in plures causas
accommodari potest, vulgare dicitur; id minus favorabile aliquando tamen non inutiliter adsumimus,
magnis saepe oratoribus non evitatum. Quo et
adversarius uti potest, commune appellatur; quod
adversarius in suam utilitatem deflectere potest, com-
mutabile; quod causae non cohaeret, separatum;
quod aliunde trahitur, tralatum; praeterea quod
longum, quod contra praecepta est; quorum pleraque
non principii modo sunt vitia sed totius orationis.

72 Haec de prooemio, quotiens erit eius usus, non
semper autem est; nam et supervacuum aliquando
est, si sit praeparatus satis etiam sine hoc iudex, aut

employs illustrations, and in the *pro Cluentio,* as I have already pointed out, introduces division into heads. Still such artifices, although they may be 70
employed at times to good effect, are not to be indulged in indiscriminately, but only when there is strong reason for breaking the rule. The same remark applies to *simile* (which must however be brief), *metaphor* and other *tropes,* all of which are forbidden by our cautious and pedantic teachers of rhetoric, but which we shall none the less occasionally employ, unless indeed we are to disapprove of the magnificent example of irony in the *pro Ligario* to which I have already referred a few pages back. The rhetoricians 71
have however been nearer the truth in their censure of certain other faults that may occur in the *exordium.* The stock *exordium* which can be suited to a number of different cases they style *vulgar;* it is an unpopular form but can sometimes be effectively employed and has often been adopted by some of the greatest orators. The *exordium* which might equally well be used by our opponent, they style *common.* That which our opponent can turn to his own advantage, they call *interchangeable,* that which is irrelevant to the case, *detached,* and that which is drawn from some other speech, *transferred.* In addition to these they censure others as *long* and others as *contrary to rule.* Most of these faults are however not peculiar to the *exordium,* but may be found in any or every portion of a speech.

Such are the rules for the *exordium,* wherever it 72
is employed. It may however sometimes be dispensed with. For occasionally it is superfluous, if the judge has been sufficiently prepared for our speech without it or if the case is such as to render

si res praeparatione non egeat. Aristoteles quidem
in totum id necessarium apud bonos iudices negat.
Aliquando tamen uti nec si velimus eo licet, cum
iudex occupatus, cum angusta sunt tempora, cum
73 maior potestas ab ipsa re cogit incipere. Contraque
est interim prooemii vis etiam non exordio. Nam
iudices et in narratione nonnunquam et in argumentis ut attendant et ut faveant rogamus, quo
Prodicus velut dormitantes eos excitari putabat, quale
74 est: *Tum C. Varenus, is qui a familia Anchariana occisus
est—hoc, quaeso, iudices, diligenter attendite.* Utique
si multiplex causa est, sua quibusque partibus danda
praefatio est, ut *Audite nunc reliqua,* et *Transeo nunc*
75 *illuc.* Sed in ipsis etiam probationibus multa funguntur
prooemii vice, ut facit Cicero pro Cluentio dicturus
contra censores, pro Murena, cum se Servio excusat.
Verum id frequentius est, quam ut exemplis con-
firmandum sit.

76 Quotiens autem prooemio fuerimus usi, tum sive
ad expositionem transibimus sive protinus ad probationem, id debebit in principio postremum esse,
cui commodissime iungi initium sequentium poterit.
77 Illa vero frigida et puerilis est in scholis adfectatio,

---

[1] *Rhet.* iii. 14. [2] Cic. *pro Var.* fr. 8.
[3] xlii. 117. [4] iii. 7.

such preparation unnecessary. Aristotle[1] indeed says that with good judges the *exordium* is entirely unnecessary. Sometimes however it is impossible to employ it, even if we desire to do so, when, for instance, the judge is much occupied, when time is short or superior authority forces us to embark upon the subject right away. On the other hand 73
it is at times possible to give the force of an *exordium* to other portions of the speech. For instance we may ask the judges in the course of our *statement of the facts* or of our *arguments* to give us their best attention and good-will, a proceeding which Prodicus recommended as a means of wakening them when they begin to nod. A good example is the following:[2] "Gaius Varenus, he who was killed 74
by the slaves of Ancharius—I beg you, gentlemen, to give me your best attention at this point." Further if the case involves a number of different matters, each section must be prefaced with a short introduction, such as "Listen now to what follows," or "I now pass to the next point." Even in the 75
proof there are many passages which perform the same function as an *exordium*, such as the passage in the *pro Cluentio*[3] where Cicero introduces an attack on the censors and in the *pro Murena*[4] when he apologises to Servius. But the practice is too common to need illustration.

However on all occasions when we have employed 76
the *exordium*, whether we intend to pass to the *statement of facts* or direct to the *proof*, our intention should be mentioned at the conclusion of the introduction, with the result that the transition to what follows will be smooth and easy. There is indeed a pedantic 77
and childish affectation in vogue in the schools of

ut ipse transitus efficiat aliquam utique sententiam et huius velut praestigiae plausum petat, ut Ovidius lascivire in Metamorphosesin solet, quem tamen excusare necessitas potest res diversissimas in speciem
78 unius corporis colligentem. Oratori vero quid est necesse surripere hanc transgressionem et iudicem fallere, qui, ut ordini rerum animum intendat, etiam commonendus est? Peribit enim prima pars exposi-
79 tionis, si iudex narrari nondum sciet. Quapropter, ut non abrupte cadere in narrationem, ita non obscure transcendere est optimum. Si vero longior sequetur ac perplexa magis expositio, ad eam ipsam praeparandus erit iudex, ut Cicero saepius, sed et hoc loco fecit: *Paulo longius exordium rei demonstrandae repetam, quod, quaeso, iudices, ne moleste patiamini; principiis enim cognitis multo facilius extrema intelligetis.* Haec fere sunt mihi de exordio comperta.

II. Maxime naturale est et fieri frequentissime debet, ut praeparato per haec, quae supra dicta sunt, iudice res, de qua pronuntiaturus est, indicetur.
2 Haec est narratio. In qua sciens transcurram subtiles nimium divisiones quorundam plura eius genera

[1] *pro Cluent.* iv. 11.

marking the transition by some epigram and seeking to win applause by this feat of legerdemain. Ovid is given to this form of affectation in his *Metamorphoses,* but there is some excuse for him owing to the fact that he is compelled to weld together subjects of the most diverse nature so as to form a continuous
whole. But what necessity is there for an orator to 78
gloss over his transitions or to attempt to deceive the judge, who requires on the contrary to be warned to give his attention to the sequence of the various portions of the speech? For instance the first part of our *statement of the facts* will be wasted, if the judge does not realise that we have reached that
stage. Therefore, although we should not be too 79
abrupt in passing to our *statement of facts,* it is best to do nothing to conceal our transition. Indeed, if the *statement of fact* on which we are about to embark is somewhat long and complicated, we shall do well to prepare the judge for it, as Cicero often does, most notably in the following passage:[1] "The introduction to my exposition of this point will be rather longer than usual, but I beg you, gentlemen, not to take it ill. For if you get a firm grasp of the beginning, you will find it much easier to follow what comes last." This is practically all that I can find to say on the subject of the *exordium.*

II. It is a most natural and frequently necessary proceeding, that after preparing the mind of the judge in the manner described above we should indicate the nature of the subject on which he will have
to give judgment: that is the *statement of facts.* In 2
dealing with this question I shall deliberately pass over the divisions made by certain writers, who make too many classes and err on the side of subtlety. For

facientium. Non enim solam volunt esse illam negotii, de quo apud iudices quaeritur, expositionem, sed personae, ut *M. Lollius Palicanus, humili loco Picens, loquax magis quam facundus;* loci, ut *Oppidum est in Hellesponto Lampsacum, iudices;* temporis ut

Vere novo, gelidus canis cum montibus humor
Liquitur;

causarum, quibus historici frequentissime utuntur, cum exponunt, unde bellum, seditio, pestilentia.
3 Praeter haec alias perfectas, alias imperfectas vocant; quod quis ignorat? Adiiciunt expositionem et praeteritorum esse temporum, quae est frequentissima, et praesentium, qualis est Ciceronis de discursu amicorum Chrysogoni, postquam est nominatus, et futurorum, quae solis dari vaticinantibus potest;
4 nam ὑποτύπωσις non est habenda narratio. Sed nos potioribus vacemus.

Plerique semper narrandum putaverunt, quod falsum esse pluribus coarguitur. Sunt enim ante omnia quaedam tam breves causae, ut propositionem
5 potius habeant quam narrationem. Id accidit aliquando utrique parti, cum vel nulla expositio est,

---

[1] Sall. *Hist.* iv. 25. [2] Cic. *Verr.* I. xxiv. 63.
[3] Verg. *G.* i. 43. [4] *pro Rosc. Am.* xxii. 60.

they demand an explanation dealing not only with the facts of the case which is before the court, but with the person involved (as in the sentence,[1] "Marcus Lollius Palicanus, a Picentine of humble birth, a man gifted with loquacity rather than eloquence") or of the place where an incident occurred (as in the sentence[2] "Lampsacus, gentlemen, is a town situated on the Hellespont"), or of the time at which something occurred (as in the verse[3]

> "In early spring, when on the mountains hoar
> The snows dissolve"),

or of the causes of an occurrence, such as the historians are so fond of setting forth, when they explain the origin of a war, a rebellion or a pestilence.
Further they style some *statements of fact* "*complete,*" 3
and others "*incomplete,*" a distinction which is self-evident. To this they add that our explanation may refer to the past (which is of course the commonest form), the present (for which compare Cicero's[4] remarks about the excitement caused among the friends of Chrysogonus when his name was mentioned), or of the future (a form permissible only to prophets): for *hypotyposis* or picturesque description
cannot be regarded as a *statement of facts.* However 4
let us pass to matters of more importance.

The majority regard the *statement of facts* as being indispensable: but there are many considerations which show that this view is erroneous. In the first place there are some cases which are so brief, that they require only a brief summary rather than a full
statement of the facts. This may apply to both 5
parties to a suit, as for instance in cases where there is no necessity for explanation or where the facts are

vel de re constat, de iure quaeritur, ut apud centumviros, filius an frater debeat esse intestatae heres, pubertas annis an corporis habitu aestimetur: aut cum est quidem in re narrationi locus, sed aut ante iudici nota sunt omnia aut priore loco recte exposita.
6 Accidit aliquando alteri et saepius ab actore, vel quia satis est proponere vel quia sic magis expedit. Satis est dixisse, *Certam creditam pecuniam peto ex stipulatione; Legatum peto ex testamento.* Diversae
7 partis expositio est, cur ea non debeantur. Et satis est actori et magis expedit sic indicare: *Dico ab Horatio sororem suam interfectam.* Namque et propositione iudex crimen omne cognoscit, et ordo et
8 causa facti pro adversario magis est. Reus contra tunc narrationem subtrahet, cum id, quod obiicitur, neque negari neque excusari poterit, sed in sola iuris quaestione consistet; ut in eo, qui, cum pecuniam privatam ex aede sacra surripuerit, sacrilegii reus est, confessio verecundior quam expositio: *Non negamus*

admitted and the whole question turns on a point of
law, as it so often does in the centumviral court, as
for example when we discuss, whether the heir of a
woman who has died intestate should be her son or
brother, or whether puberty is to be reckoned by age
or by physical development. The same situation
arises also in cases where the facts admit of full
statement, but are well known to the judge or have
been correctly set forth by a previous speaker.
Sometimes again the statement of facts can be 6
dispensed with only by one party, who is generally
the plaintiff, either because it is sufficient for him to
make a simple summary of his case or because it is
more expedient for him to do so. It may, for instance, suffice to say, "I claim repayment of a
certain sum of money which was lent on certain
conditions" or "I claim a legacy in accordance with
the terms of the will." It is for the other party to
explain why these sums are not due to the plaintiff.
Again it is sometimes sufficient and expedient to 7
summarise a case in one sentence such as "I say
that Horatius killed his sister." For the judge will
understand the whole charge from this simple
affirmation: the sequence of events and the motive
for the deed will be matters for the defence to expound. On the other hand in some cases the 8
accused may dispense with the *statement of facts*,
when for instance the charge can neither be denied
nor palliated, but turns solely on some point of law:
the following case will illustrate my meaning. A
man who has stolen from a temple money belonging
to a private individual is accused of sacrilege: in
such a case a confession will be more seemly than
a full *statement of facts*: "We do not deny that the

de templo pecuniam esse sublatam, calumniatur tamen
accusator actione sacrilegii, cum privata fuerit non
sacra; vos autem de hoc cognoscetis, an sacrilegium
sit admissum.

9 Sed ut has aliquando non narrandi causas puto, sic
ab illis dissentio, qui non existimant esse narrationem,
cum reus quod obiicitur tantum negat; in qua est
opinione Cornelius Celsus, qui condicionis huius esse
arbitratur plerasque caedis causas et omnes ambitus
10 ac repetundarum. Non enim putat esse narrationem,
nisi quae summam criminis de quo iudicium est
contineat, deinde fatetur ipse pro Rabirio Postumo
narrasse Ciceronem; atque ille et negavit pervenisse
ad Rabirium pecuniam, qua de re erat quaestio
constituta, et in hac narratione nihil de crimine ex-
11 posuit. Ego autem magnos alioqui secutus auctores,
duas esse in iudiciis narrationum species existimo,
alteram ipsius causae, alteram rerum ad causam
12 pertinentium expositionem. *Non occidi hominem,*
nulla narratio est; convenit; sed erit aliqua et interim
etiam longa contra argumenta eius criminis de anteacta vita, de causis, propter quas innocens in periculum deducatur, aliis, quibus incredibile id quod
13 obiicitur fiat. Neque enim accusator tantum hoc

money was taken from the temple; but the accuser is bringing a false accusation in charging my client with sacrilege, since the money was not consecrated, but private property: it is for you to decide whether under these circumstances sacrilege has been committed."

While however I think that there are occasional 9
cases where the *statement of facts* may be dispensed with, I disagree with those who say that there is no *statement of facts* when the accused simply denies the charge. This opinion is shared by Cornelius Celsus who holds that most cases of murder and all of bribery and extortion fall into this class. For he 10
thinks that the only *statement of facts* is that which gives a general account of the charge before the court. Yet he himself acknowledges that Cicero employed the *statement of facts* in his defence of Rabirius Postumus, in spite of the fact that Cicero denies that any money came into the hands of Rabirius (and this was the question at issue) and gives no explanations relating to the actual charge in his *statement of facts*. For my part I follow the very 11
highest authorities in holding that there are two forms of *statement of facts* in forensic speeches, the one expounding the facts of the case itself, the other setting forth facts which have a bearing on the case. I agree that a sentence such as "I did not kill 12
the man" does not amount to a *statement of facts*: but there will be a *statement of facts*, occasionally, too, a long one, in answer to the arguments put forward by the accuser: it will deal with the past life of the accused, with the causes which have brought an innocent man into peril, and other circumstances such as show the charge to be incredible. For the 13

dicit, *occidisti*; sed, quibus id probet narrat. Ut in
tragoediis, cum Teucer Ulixen reum facit Aiacis
occisi dicens inventum eum in solitudine iuxta
exanime corpus inimici cum gladio cruento, non id
modo Ulixes respondet non esse a se id facinus
admissum, sed sibi nullas cum Aiace inimicitias
fuisse, de laude inter ipsos certatum; deinde sub-
iungit, quomodo in eam solitudinem venerit, iacentem
exanimem sit conspicatus, gladium e vulnere ex-
14 traxerit. His subtexitur argumentatio. Sed ne
illud quidem sine narratione est, dicente accusatore,
*Fuisti in eo loco, in quo tuus inimicus occisus est: Non
fui;* dicendum enim, ubi fuerit. Quare ambitus
quoque causae et repetundarum hoc etiam plures
huiusmodi narrationes habere poterunt, quo plura
crimina; in quibus ipsa quidem neganda sunt, sed
argumentis expositione contraria resistendum est
15 interdum singulis interdum universis. An reus
ambitus male narrabit, quos parentes habuerit, quemadmodum ipse vixerit, quibus meritis fretus ad petitionem descenderit? Aut qui repetundarum crimine
insimulabitur, non et anteactam vitam, et quibus de
causis provinciam universam vel accusatorem aut
16 testem offenderit, non inutiliter exponet? Quae si
narratio non est, ne illa quidem Ciceronis pro Cluentio
prima, cuius est initium: *A. Cluentius Habitus.* Nihil

---

[1] v. 11.

accuser does not merely say "You killed him," but
sets forth the facts proving his assertion: tragedy will
provide an example, where Teucer accuses Ulysses
of murdering Ajax, and states that he was found in a
lonely place near the lifeless body of his enemy with
a blood-stained sword in his hands. To this Ulysses
does not merely reply that he did not do the deed,
but adds that he had no quarrel with Ajax, the
contest between them having been concerned solely
with the winning of renown: he then goes on to
say how he came to be in the lonely place, how he
found Ajax lying lifeless and drew the sword from
the wound. Then follow arguments based on these
facts. But even when the accuser says "You were 14
found on the spot where your enemy was killed"
and the accused says "I was not," a *statement of facts*
is involved; for he must say where he was. Consequently cases of bribery and extortion will require
as many statements of this kind as there are
charges: the charges themselves will be denied, but
it will be necessary to counter the arguments of the
accuser either singly or all together by setting forth
the facts in quite a different light. Is it, I ask you, 15
irrelevant for one accused of bribery to set forth
his parentage, his past life and the services on which
he relied for success in his candidature? And if a
man is indicted for extortion, will it not be to his
advantage to set forth not merely his past record,
but also the reasons which have made the whole
province or the accuser or a witness hostile to
himself? If these are not *statements of facts*, neither 16
is the first portion of Cicero's[1] defence of Cluentius,
beginning with the words "Aulus Cluentius Habitus." For there he says nothing about the charge

enim hic de veneficio, sed de causis, quibus ei mater
17 inimica sit, dicit. Illae quoque sunt pertinentes ad causam sed non ipsius causae narrationes : vel exempli gratia ut in Verrem de L. Domitio, qui pastorem, quod is aprum, quem ipsi muneri obtulerat, exceptum esse a se venabulo confessus esset, in crucem sustulit;
18 vel discutiendi alicuius extrinsecus criminis, ut pro Rabirio Postumo: *Nam ut ventum Alexandriam est, iudices, haec una ratio a rege proposita Postumo est servandae pecuniae, si curationem et quasi dispensationem regiam suscepisset;* vel augendi, ut describitur iter Verris.

19 Ficta interim narratio introduci solet, vel ad concitandos iudices ut pro Roscio circa Chrysogonum, cuius paulo ante habui mentionem; vel ad resolvendos aliqua urbanitate, ut pro Cluentio circa fratres Caepasios; interdum per digressionem decoris gratia, qualis rursus in Verrem de Proserpina, *In his quondam locis mater filiam quaesisse dicitur.* Quae omnia eo pertinent, ut appareat non utique non narrare eum qui negat, sed illud ipsum narrare quod negat.

---

[1] v. 3. The shepherd was crucified because the carrying of arms was forbidden.

[2] x. 28. The charge in question was that Rabirius had worn the Greek *pallium* instead of the Roman *toga*. But as an official of the king he was forced to wear Greek dress.

[3] *Verr.* v. 10. [4] xxii. 60. [5] xx. 57 *sqq.*

[6] iv. 48. The words quoted do not occur in our MSS of Cicero.

of poisoning, but confines himself entirely to setting forth the reasons for the hostility of Cluentius' mother to her son. There are also statements 17
which do not set forth the facts of the case itself, but facts which are none the less relevant to the case: the speaker's purpose may be to illustrate the case by some parallel, as in the passage in the *Verrines*[1] about Lucius Domitius who crucified a shepherd because he admitted that he had used a hunting spear to kill the boar which he had brought him as a present; or he may desire to dispel some 18
charge that is irrelevant to the case as in the passage of the speech for Rabirius Postumus,[2] which runs as follows: "For when he came to Alexandria, gentlemen, the only means of saving his money which the king suggested to Postumus was that he should take charge of the royal household and act as a kind of steward." Or the orator may desire to heighten the effect of his charges, as Cicero[3] does in his description of the journey of Verres.

Sometimes a fictitious statement is employed 19
either to stir the emotions of the judges, as in that passage of the *pro Roscio Amerino*[4] dealing with Chrysogonus to which I referred just recently, or to entertain them with a show of wit, as in the passage of the *pro Cluentio*[5] describing the brothers Caepasius: sometimes again a digression may be introduced to add beauty to the speech, as in the passage about Proserpine in the *Verrines*,[6] beginning "It was here that a mother is once said to have sought her daughter." All these examples serve to show that he who denies a charge may not necessarily refrain from stating, but may actually state that very fact which he denies.

20 Ne hoc quidem simpliciter accipiendum, quod est a me positum, esse supervacuam narrationem rei, quam iudex noverit; quod sic intelligi volo, si non modo quid factum sit sciet, sed ita factum etiam, ut
21 nobis expedit, opinabitur. Neque enim narratio in hoc reperta est, ut tantum cognoscat iudex, sed aliquanto magis, ut consentiat. Quare, etiamsi non erit docendus, sed aliquo modo adficiendus, narrabimus cum praeparatione quadam: scire quidem eum in summam, quid acti sit, tamen rationem quoque facti cuiusque cognoscere ne gravetur.
22 Interim propter aliquem in consilium adhibitum nos repetere illa simulemus, interim, ut rei, quae ex adverso proponatur, iniquitatem omnes etiam circumstantes intelligant. In quo genere plurimis figuris erit varianda expositio ad effugiendum taedium nota audientis, sicut *Meministi*, et *Fortasse supervacuum fuerit hic commorari. Sed quid ego diutius, cum tu optime*
23 *noris? Illud quale sit, tu scias,* et his similia. Alioqui si apud iudicem, cui nota causa est, narratio semper videtur supervacua, potest videri non semper esse etiam ipsa actio necessaria.

24 Alterum est, de quo frequentius quaeritur, an sit utique narratio prooemio subiicienda; quod qui

---

[1] *i.e.* introduced to fill the place of a juror who had had to leave the jury.

Even the assertion which I made above to the 20
effect that a *statement* of facts familiar to the judge is superfluous, is not to be taken too literally. My meaning is that it may be dispensed with, if the judge knows not merely what has been done, but takes a view of the facts which is favourable to our case. For the purpose of the *statement of facts* is 21
not merely to instruct, but rather to persuade the judge. Therefore, when we desire to influence him in some way or other, although he may require no instruction, we shall preface our statement with some such remarks as these: "I know that you are aware of the general nature of the case, but I trust you will not take it ill if I ask you to consider each point in detail." At times again we may pretend 22
that we are repeating the facts for the benefit of some new member of the jury,[1] at times that we do so with a view to letting every bystander as well realise the gross unfairness of our opponents' assertions. Under these circumstances our statement must be diversified by a free use of figures to avoid wearying those to whom the facts are familiar: we shall for instance use phrases such as "You remember," "It may perhaps be superfluous to dwell on this point," "But why should I say more, as you are well acquainted with the fact?", "You are not ignorant how this matter stands" and so on. Besides, if we are always to 23
regard as superfluous a *statement of facts* made before a judge who is familiar with the case, we may even go so far as to regard it as superfluous at times to plead the case at all.

There is a further question which is still more 24
frequently raised, as to whether the *statement of facts* should always follow immediately on the

opinantur, non possunt videri nulla ratione ducti.
Nam cum prooemium idcirco comparatum sit, ut
iudex ad rem accipiendam fiat conciliatior, docilior,
intentior, et probatio nisi causa prius cognita non
possit adhiberi, protinus iudex notitia rerum instruen-
25 dus videtur. Sed hoc quoque interim mutat condicio
causarum; nisi forte M. Tullius in oratione pulcher-
rima, quam pro Milone scriptam reliquit, male distulisse narrationem videtur tribus praepositis quaestionibus; aut profuisset exponere, quomodo insidias
Miloni fecisset Clodius, si reum, qui a se hominem
occisum fateretur, defendi omnino fas non fuisset,
aut si iam praeiudicio senatus damnatus esset Milo,
aut si Cn. Pompeius, qui praeter aliam gratiam
iudicium etiam militibus armatis clauserat, tanquam
26 adversus ei timeretur. Ergo hae quoque quaestiones
vim prooemii obtinebant, cum omnes iudicem prae-
pararent. Sed pro Vareno quoque postea narravit
quam obiecta diluit. Quod fiet utiliter, quotiens
non repellendum tantum erit crimen, sed etiam
transferendum, ut his prius defensis velut initium
sit alium culpandi narratio, ut in armorum ratione

exordium. Those who hold that it should always do so must be admitted to have some reason on their side. For since the purpose of the *exordium* is to make the judge more favourably disposed and more attentive to our case and more amenable to instruction, and since the *proof* cannot be brought forward until the facts of the case are known, it seems right that the judge should be instructed in the facts without delay. But the practice may be 25
altered by circumstances, unless it is contended that Cicero in his magnificent published defence of Milo delayed his *statement* too long by placing three questions before it; or unless it is argued that, if it had been held to be impermissible to defend a man at all who acknowledged that he had killed another, or if Milo's case had already been prejudged and condemnation passed by the senate, or if Gnaeus Pompeius, who in addition to exerting his influence in other ways had surrounded the court with an armed guard, had been regarded with apprehension as hostile to the accused, it would have served his case to set forth how Clodius had set an ambush for Milo. These three questions, then, served the 26
purpose of an exordium, since they all of them were designed to prepare the minds of the judges. Again in the *pro Vareno* Cicero delayed his statement of facts until he had first rebutted certain allegations put forward by the prosecution. This may be done with advantage whenever we have not merely to rebut the charge, but to turn the tables on our opponents: thus after first rebutting the charge, we make *our statement of facts* the opening of an incrimination of the other party just as in actual fighting we are most

antiquior cavendi quam ictum inferendi cura est.
27 Erunt quaedam causae (neque id raro) crimine quidem, de quo cognitio est, faciles ad diluendum sed multis anteactae vitae flagitiis et gravibus oneratae; quae prius amovenda sunt, ut propitius iudex defensionem ipsius negotii, cuius propria quaestio est, audiat: ut, si defendendus sit M. Caelius, nonne optime patronus occurrat prius conviciis luxuriae, petulantiae, impudicitiae quam veneficii, in quibus solis omnis Ciceronis versatur oratio; tum deinde narret de bonis Pallae totamque de vi explicet causam, quae est ipsius actione defensa?
28 Sed nos ducit scholarum consuetudo, in quibus certa quaedam ponuntur, quae themata dicimus, praeter quae nihil est diluendum, ideoque prooemio narratio semper subiungitur. Inde libertas declamatoribus, ut etiam secundo partis suae loco narrare videantur.
29 Nam cum pro petitore dicunt et expositione, tanquam priores agant, uti solent et contradictione, tanquam respondeant, idque fit recte. Nam cum sit declamatio forensium actionum meditatio, cur non in

concerned to parry our adversary's blows before we strike him ourselves. There will also not 27
infrequently be certain cases, in which it is easy to rebut the charge that is under trial, but the conduct of which is hampered by the past life of our client and the many and serious crimes which he has committed. We must dispose of these first, in order that the judge may give a favourable hearing to our defence of the actual facts which form the question at issue. For example, if we have to defend Marcus Caelius, the best course for his advocate to adopt will be to meet the imputations of luxury, wantonness and immorality which are made against him before we proceed to the actual charge of poisoning. It is with these points that the speech of Cicero in his defence is entirely concerned. Is he then to go on to make a statement about the property of Palla and explain the whole question of rioting, a charge against which Caelius has already defended himself in the speech which he delivered on his own
behalf? We however are the victims of the practice 28
of the schools in accordance with which certain points or themes as we call them are put forward for discussion, outside which our refutation must not go, and consequently a *statement of facts* always follows the *exordium.* It is this too that leads declaimers to take the liberty of inserting a *statement of facts* even
when they speak second for their side. For when 29
they speak for the prosecution they introduce both a *statement of facts,* as if they were speaking first, and a refutation of the arguments for the defence, as if they were replying: and they are right in so doing. For since declamation is merely an exercise in forensic pleading, why should they not qualify themselves to

utrumque protinus locum se exerceat? Cuius rationis
ignari ex more, cui adsueverunt, nihil in foro putant
30 esse mutandum. Sed in scholasticis quoque nonnunquam evenit, ut pro narratione sit propositio. Nam
quid exponet, quae zelotypum malae tractationis
accusat, aut qui Cynicum apud censores reum de
moribus facit? cum totum crimen uno verbo in qualibet actionis parte posito satis indicetur. Sed haec
hactenus.

31 Nunc, quae sit narrandi ratio, subiungam. Narratio
est rei factae aut ut factae utilis ad persuadendum
expositio, vel (ut Apollodorus finit) oratio docens
auditorem, quid in controversia sit. Eam plerique
scriptores, maxime qui sunt ab Isocrate, volunt esse
lucidam, brevem, verisimilem. Neque enim refert,
an pro lucida perspicuam, pro verisimili probabilem
32 credibilemve dicamus. Eadem nobis placet divisio;
quanquam et Aristoteles ab Isocrate parte in
una dissenserit praeceptum brevitatis irridens, tanquam necesse sit longam esse aut brevem expositionem nec liceat ire per medium, Theodorei quoque
solam relinquant ultimam partem, quia nec breviter
33 utique nec dilucide semper sit utile exponere. Quo

---

[1] See note prefixed to Index.
[2] See Index, *s.v.* Cynicus. [3] *Rhet.* iii. 16.

speak either first or second[1]? Those however who do not understand the reason for such a practice, think that when they appear in the courts they should stick to the custom of the schools with which they have become familiar. But even scholastic 30
rhetoricians occasionally substitute a brief summary for the full statement of the facts. For what statement of the case can be made when a wife is accusing a jealous husband of maltreating her, or a father is indicting his son turned Cynic before the censors for indecent behaviour[2]? In both cases the charge can be sufficiently indicated by one word placed in any part of the speech. But enough of these points.

I will now proceed to the method to be adopted 31
in making our *statement of facts*. The *statement of facts* consists in the persuasive exposition of that which either has been done, or is supposed to have been done, or, to quote the definition given by Apollodorus, is a speech instructing the audience as to the nature of the case in dispute. Most writers, more especially those of the Isocratean school, hold that it should be lucid, brief and plausible (for it is of no importance if we substitute clear for lucid, or credible or probable for plausible). I agree with 32
this classification of its qualities, although Aristotle[3] disagrees with Isocrates on one point, and pours scorn on his injunction to be brief, as though it were necessary that a statement should be either long or short and it were impossible to hit the happy mean. The followers of Theodorus on the other hand recognise only plausibility on the ground that it is not always expedient that our exposition should be either short or clear. It will be necessary 33

diligentius distinguenda sunt singula, ut quid quoque loco prosit ostendam.

Narratio est aut tota pro nobis aut tota pro adversariis aut mixta ex utrisque. Si erit tota pro nobis, contenti sumus his tribus partibus per quas efficitur, quo facilius iudex intelligat, meminerit,
34 credat. Nec quisquam reprehensione dignum putet, quod proposuerim eam, quae sit tota pro nobis, debere esse verisimilem, cum vera sit. Sunt enim plurima vera quidem, sed parum credibilia, sicut falsa quoque frequenter verisimilia. Quare non minus laborandum est, ut iudex, quae vere dicimus quam quae fingimus,
35 credat. Sunt quidem hae, quas supra retuli, virtutes aliarum quoque partium. Nam et per totam actionem vitanda est obscuritas et modus ubique custodiendus, et credibilia esse omnia oportet quae dicuntur. Maxime tamen haec in ea parte custodienda sunt, quae prima iudicem docet; in qua si acciderit, ut aut non intelligat aut non meminerit aut non credat, frustra in reliquis laborabimus.

36 Erit autem narratio aperta atque dilucida, si fuerit primum exposita verbis propriis et significantibus et non sordidis quidem, non tamen exquisitis et ab usu

therefore for me to devote some care to the differentiation of the various features of this portion of a speech, in order that I may show under what circumstances each is specially useful.

The *statement* will be either wholly in our favour or wholly in that of our opponent or a mixture of both. If it is entirely in our own favour, we may rest content with the three qualities just mentioned, the result of which is to make it easier for the judge to understand, remember and believe what we say.
Now I should regret that anyone should censure my 34
conduct in suggesting that a *statement* which is wholly in our favour should be *plausible,* when as a matter of fact it is *true.* There are many things which are true, but scarcely credible, just as there are many things which are plausible though false. It will therefore require just as much exertion on our part to make the judge believe what we say
when it is true as it will when it is fictitious. These 35
good qualities, which I have mentioned above, do not indeed cease to be virtues in other portions of the speech; for it is our duty to avoid obscurity in every part of our pleading, to preserve due proportion throughout and to say nothing save what is likely to win belief. But they require special observance in that portion of the speech which is the first from which the judge can learn the nature of the case: if at this stage of the proceedings he fails to understand, remember or believe what we say, our labour is but lost in the remainder of the speech.

We shall achieve lucidity and clearness in our 36
statement of facts, first by setting forth our story in words which are appropriate, significant and free from any taint of meanness, but not on the other

remotis, tum distincta rebus, personis, temporibus, locis, causis, ipsa etiam pronuntiatione in hoc accommodata, ut iudex quae dicentur quam facillime
37 accipiat. Quae quidem virtus negligitur a plurimis, qui ad clamorem dispositae vel etiam forte circumfusae multitudinis compositi non ferunt illud intentionis silentium nec sibi diserti videntur, nisi omnia tumultu et vociferatione concusserint; rem indicare sermonis cotidiani et in quemcunque etiam indoctorum cadentis existimant, cum interim, quod tanquam facile contemnunt, nescias, praestare minus
38 velint an possint. Neque enim aliud in eloquentia, cuncta experti, difficilius reperient quam id, quod se fuisse dicturos omnes putant, postquam audierunt, quia non bona iudicant esse illa, sed vera. Tum autem optime dicit orator, cum videtur vera dicere.
39 At nunc, velut campum nacti expositionis, hic potissmum et vocem flectunt et cervicem reponunt et brachium in latus iactant totoque et rerum et verborum et compositionis genere lasciviunt; deinde, quod sit monstro simile, placet actio, causa non intelligitur. Verum haec omittamus, ne minus

hand farfetched or unusual, and secondly by giving a distinct account of facts, persons, times, places and causes, while our delivery must be adapted to our matter, so that the judge will take in what we say with the utmost readiness. This latter virtue is 37
disregarded by the majority of speakers who are used to the noisy applause of a large audience, whether it be a chance gathering or an assembly of *claqueurs,* and consequently are unnerved by the attentive silence of the courts. They feel that they have fallen short of eloquence, if they do not make everything echo with noise and clamour; they think that to state a matter simply is suited only to everyday speech such as falls within the capacity of any uneducated man, while all the time it is hard to say whether they are less willing or less capable of performing a task which they despise on account of its supposed easiness. For even when they have 38
tried everything, they will never find anything more difficult in the whole range of oratory than that which, once heard, all think they would have said,—a delusion due to the fact that they regard what has been said as having no merit save that of truth. But it is just when an orator gives the impression of absolute truth that he is speaking best. As it is, 39
when such persons as these get a fair field for stating their case, they select this as the precise occasion for affected modulations of the voice, throwing back their heads, thumping their sides and indulging in every kind of extravagance of statement, language and style. As a result, while the speech, from its very monstrosity, meets with applause, the case remains unintelligible. However, let us pass to another subject; my aim is to win favour for

gratiae praecipiendo recta quam offensae reprehendendo prava mereamur.

40 Brevis erit narratio ante omnia, si inde coeperimus rem exponere, unde ad iudicem pertinet; deinde, si nihil extra causam dixerimus; tum etiam, si reciderimus omnia, quibus sublatis neque cognitioni quid-
41 quam neque utilitati detrahatur. Solet enim quaedam esse partium brevitas, quae longam tamen efficit summam. *In portum veni, navem prospexi, quanti veheret interrogavi, de pretio convenit, conscendi, sublatae sunt ancorae, solvimus oram, profecti sumus.* Nihil horum dici celerius potest, sed sufficit dicere *e portu navigavi.* Et quotiens exitus rei satis ostendit priora, debemus hoc esse contenti, quo reliqua intelliguntur.
42 Quare, cum dicere liceat, *Est mihi filius iuvenis,* omnia illa supervacua: *Cupidus ego liberorum uxorem duxi, natum filium sustuli, educavi, in adolescentiam perduxi.* Ideoque Graecorum aliqui aliud circumcisam expositionem, id est σύντομον, aliud brevem putaverunt, quod illa supervacuis careret, haec posset aliquid ex
43 necessariis desiderare. Nos autem brevitatem in hoc ponimus, non ut minus, sed ne plus dicatur quam oporteat. Nam iterationes quidem et ταυτολογίας et περισσολογίας, quas in narratione vitandas quidam scriptores artium tradiderunt, transeo; sunt enim

pointing out the right road rather than to give offence by rebuking such perversity.

The *statement of facts* will be brief, if in the first 40
place we start at that point of the case at which it
begins to concern the judge, secondly avoid irrelevance, and finally cut out everything the removal
of which neither hampers the activities of the judge
nor harms our own case. For frequently conciseness 41
of detail is not inconsistent with length in the
whole. Take for instance such a statement as the
following: "I came to the harbour, I saw a ship, I
asked the cost of a passage, the price was agreed, I
went on board, the anchor was weighed, we loosed
our cable and set out." Nothing could be terser
than these assertions, but it would have been quite
sufficient to say "I sailed from the harbour." And
whenever the conclusion gives a sufficiently clear
idea of the premisses, we must be content with
having given a hint which will enable our audience
to understand what we have left unsaid. Con- 42
sequently when it is possible to say "I have a young
son," it is quite superfluous to say, "Being desirous of
children I took a wife, a son was born whom I
acknowledged and reared and brought up to manhood." For this reason some of the Greeks draw a
distinction between a concise statement (the word
they use is σύντομος) and a brief statement, the
former being free from all superfluous matter, while
the latter may conceivably omit something that
requires to be stated. Personally, when I use the 43
word brevity, I mean not saying less, but not saying
more than occasion demands. As for repetitions
and tautologies and diffuseness, which some writers
of textbooks tell us we must avoid, I pass them by;

haec vitia non tantum brevitatis gratia refugienda.
44 Non minus autem cavenda erit, quae nimium corripientes omnia sequitur, obscuritas, satiusque est aliquid narrationi superesse quam deesse. Nam supervacua cum taedio dicuntur, necessaria cum
45 periculo subtrahuntur. Quare vitanda est etiam illa Sallustiana, quanquam in ipso virtutis obtinet locum, brevitas et abruptum sermonis genus, quod otiosum fortasse lectorem minus fallat, audientem transvolat nec dum repetatur exspectat, cum praesertim lector non fere sit nisi eruditus, iudicem rura plerumque in decurias mittant de eo pronuntiaturum quod intellexerit; ut fortasse ubicunque, in narratione tamen praecipue, media haec tenenda sit via dicendi quan-
46 tum opus est et quantum satis est. Quantum opus est autem non ita solum accipi volo, quantum ad indicandum sufficit, quia non inornata debet esse brevitas, alioqui sit indocta; nam et fallit voluptas et minus longa quae delectant videntur, ut amoenum ac molle iter, etiamsi est spatii amplioris, minus fatigat quam
47 durum aridumque compendium. Neque mihi unquam tanta fuerit cura brevitatis, ut non ea, quae credibilem faciunt expositionem, inseri velim. Simplex enim et undique praecisa non tam narratio vocari potest quam confessio. Sunt porro multae condicione ipsa

they are faults which we should shun for other reasons beside our desire for brevity. But we must be 44 equally on our guard against the obscurity which results from excessive abridgment, and it is better to say a little more than is necessary than a little less. For though a diffuse irrelevance is tedious, the omission of what is necessary is positively dangerous. We must therefore avoid even the famous terseness 45 of Sallust (though in his case of course it is a merit), and shun all abruptness of speech, since a style which presents no difficulty to a leisurely reader, flies past a hearer and will not stay to be looked at again; and whereas the reader is almost always a man of learning, the judge often comes to his panel from the country side and is expected to give a decision on what he can understand. Consequently we must aim, perhaps everywhere, but above all in our *statement of facts*, at striking the happy mean in our language, and the happy mean may be defined as saying just what is necessary and just what is sufficient. By "just 46 what is necessary" I mean not the bare minimum necessary to convey our meaning; for our brevity must not be devoid of elegance, without which it would be merely uncouth: pleasure beguiles the attention, and that which delights us ever seems less long, just as a picturesque and easy journey tires us less for all its length than a difficult short cut through an arid waste. And I would never carry my desire 47 for brevity so far as to refuse admission to details which may contribute to the plausibility of our narrative. Simplify and curtail your statement of facts in every direction and you will turn it into something more like a confession. Moreover, the

rei longae narrationes, quibus extrema (ut praecepi) prooemii parte ad intentionem praeparandus est iudex; deinde curandum, ut omni arte vel ex spatio
48 eius detrahamus aliquid vel ex taedio. Ut minus longa sit, efficiemus quae poterimus differendo, non tamen sine mentione eorum, quae differemus: *Quas causas occidendi habuerit, quos adsumpserit conscios, quemadmodum disposuerit insidias, probationis loco*
49 *dicam.* Quaedam vero ex ordine praetermittenda, quale est apud Ciceronem: *Moritur Fulcinius; multa enim, quae sunt in re, quia remota sunt a causa, praetermittam.* Et partitio taedium levat: *Dicam quae acta sint ante ipsum rei contractum, dicam quae in re*
50 *ipsa, dicam quae postea.* Ita tres potius modicae narrationes videbuntur quam una longa. Interim expediet expositiones brevi interfatione distinguere: *Audistis quae ante acta sunt, accipite nunc quae insequuntur.* Reficietur enim iudex priorum fine et se
51 velut ad novum rursus initium praeparabit. Si tamen adhibitis quoque his artibus in longum exierit ordo rerum, erit non inutilis in extrema parte commonitio;

---

[1] *pro Caec.* iv. 11.

circumstances of the case will often necessitate a long *statement of facts*, in which case, as I have already enjoined, the judge should be prepared for it at the conclusion of the *exordium*. Next we must put forth all our art either to shorten it or to render
it less tedious. We must do what we can to make 48
it less long by postponing some points, taking care however to mention what it is that we propose to postpone. Take the following as an example. "As regards his motives for killing him, his accomplices and the manner in which he disposed his ambush,
I will speak when I come to the *proof*." Some 49
things indeed may be omitted altogether from our marshalling of the facts, witness the following example from Cicero,[1] "Fulcinius died; there are many circumstances which attended that event, but as they have little bearing on this case, I shall pass them by." Division of our statement into its various heads is another method of avoiding tedium: for example, "I will tell you first what preceded this affair, then what occurred in its actual development,
and finally you shall hear its sequel." Such a 50
division will give the impression of three short statements rather than of one long one. At times it will be well to interrupt our narrative by interjecting some brief remark like the following: "You have heard what happened before: now learn what follows." The judge will be refreshed by the fact that we have brought our previous remarks to a close and will prepare himself for what may be regarded as a fresh
start. If however after employing all these artifices 51
our array of facts is still long, it will not be without advantage to append a summary at the end of it as a reminder: Cicero does this even at the close of a

quod Cicero etiam in brevi narratione fecit: *Adhuc,*
Caesar, Q. Ligarius omni culpa caret; domo est egressus
non modo nullum ad bellum sed ne ad minimam quidem
belli suspicionem et cetera.

52 Credibilis autem erit narratio ante omnia, si prius
consuluerimus nostrum animum, ne quid naturae
dicamus adversum, deinde si causas ac rationes factis
praeposuerimus, non omnibus sed de quibus quaeritur, si personas convenientes iis, quae facta credi
volemus, constituerimus, ut furti reum cupidum,
adulterii libidinosum, homicidii temerarium, vel his
contraria, si defendemus; praeterea loca, tempora
53 et similia. Est autem quidam et ductus rei credibilis,
qualis in comoediis etiam et in mimis. Aliqua enim
naturaliter sequuntur et cohaerent ut, si priora bene
narraveris, iudex ipse quod postea sis narraturus
54 exspectet. Ne illud quidem fuerit inutile, semina
quaedam probationum spargere, verum sic ut narrationem esse meminerimus non probationem. Nonnunquam tamen etiam argumento aliquo confirmabi-
mus, quod proposuerimus, sed simplici et brevi, ut
in veneficiis: *Sanus bibit, statim concidit, livor ac tu-*
55 *mor confestim est insecutus.* Hoc faciunt et illae prae-

---

[1] *pro Lig.* ii. 4.

brief *statement of facts* in the *pro Ligario*[1]: "To this day, Caesar, Quintus Ligarius is free from all blame: he left his home not merely without the least intention of joining in any war, but when there was not the least suspicion of any war etc."

The *statement of fact* will be credible, if in the first 52 place we take care to say nothing contrary to nature, secondly if we assign reasons and motives for the facts on which the inquiry turns (it is unnecessary to do so with the subsidiary facts as well), and if we make the characters of the actors in keeping with the facts we desire to be believed: we shall for instance represent a person accused of theft as covetous, accused of adultery as lustful, accused of homicide as rash, or attribute the opposite qualities to these persons if we are defending them: further we must do the same with place, time and the like. It is also possible to treat the subject in such a way 53 as to give it an air of credibility, as is done in comedy and farce. For some things have such natural sequence and coherence that, if only the first portion of your *statement* is satisfactory, the judge will himself anticipate what you have got to say in the later part. It will also be useful to 54 scatter some hints of our proofs here and there, but in such a way that it is never forgotten that we are making a *statement of facts* and not a proof. Sometimes, however, we must also support our assertions by a certain amount of argument, though this must be short and simple: for instance in a case of poisoning we shall say, "He was perfectly well when he drank, he fell suddenly to the ground, and blackness and swelling of the body immediately supervened." The same result is produced by pre- 55

parationes, cum reus dicitur robustus, armatus contra infirmos, inermes, securos. Omnia denique, quae probatione tractaturi sumus, personam, causam, locum, tempus, instrumentum, occasionem, narratione
56 delibabimus. Aliquando, si destituti fuerimus his, etiam fatebimur vix esse credibile, sed verum et hoc maius habendum scelus; nescire nos quomodo factum
57 sit aut quare, mirari sed probaturos. Optimae vero praeparationes erunt quae latuerint, ut a Cicerone sunt quidem utilissime praedicta omnia, per quae Miloni Clodius non Clodio Milo insidiatus esse videatur; plurimum tamen facit illa callidissima simplicitatis imitatio: *Milo autem, cum in senatu fuisset eo die, quoad senatus est dimissus, domum venit, calceos et vestimenta mutavit, paulisper, dum se uxor, ut fit, comparat,*
58 *commoratus est.* Quam nihil festinato, nihil praeparato fecisse videtur Milo! Quod non solum rebus ipsis vir eloquentissimus, quibus moras et lentum profectionis ordinem ducit, sed verbis etiam vulgaribus et cotidianis et arte occulta consecutus est; quae si aliter dicta essent, strepitu ipso iudicem ad custo-
59 diendum patronum excitassent. Frigere videntur ista plerisque, sed hoc ipso manifestum est, quomodo iudi-

[1] *pro Mil.* x. 28.

paratory remarks such as the following: "The accused is a strong man and was fully armed, while his opponents were weak, unarmed and suspecting no evil." We may in fact touch on everything that we propose to produce in our *proof*, while making our statement of facts, as for instance points connected with persons, cause, place, time, the instrument and occasion employed. Sometimes, when this resource 56
is unavailable, we may even confess that the charge, though true, is scarcely credible, and that therefore it must be regarded as all the more atrocious; that we do not know how the deed was done or why, that we are filled with amazement, but will prove our case. The best kind of preparatory remarks are 57
those which cannot be recognised as such: Cicero,[1] for instance, is extraordinarily happy in the way he mentions in advance everything that shows that Clodius lay in wait for Milo and not Milo for Clodius. The most effective stroke of all is his cunning feint of simplicity: "Milo, on the other hand, having been in the senate all day till the house rose, went home, changed his shoes and clothes, and waited for a short time, while his wife was getting ready, as is the way with women." What an absence of haste 58
and premeditation this gives to Milo's proceedings. And the great orator secures this effect not merely by producing facts which indicate the slow and tardy nature of Milo's departure, but by the use of the ordinary language of everyday speech and a careful concealment of his art. Had he spoken otherwise, his words would by their very sound have warned the judge to keep an eye on the advocate. The majority of readers regard this passage as lack- 59
ing in distinction, but this very fact merely serves

cem fefellerit, quod vix a lectore deprehenditur. Haec
60 sunt quae credibilem faciant expositionem. Nam id quidem, ne qua contraria aut sibi repugnantia in narratione dicamus, si cui praecipiendum est, is reliqua frustra docetur, etiamsi quidam scriptores artium hoc quoque tanquam occultum et a se prudenter erutum tradunt.

61 His tribus narrandi virtutibus adiiciunt quidam magnificentiam, quam μεγαλοπρέπειαν vocant, quae neque in omnes causas cadit (nam quid in plerisque iudiciis privatis, de certa credita, locato et conducto, interdictis habere loci potest supra modum se tollens oratio?) neque semper est utilis, velut proximo
62 exemplo Miloniano patet. Et meminerimus multas esse causas, in quibus confitendum, excusandum, summittendum sit quod exponimus; quibus omnibus aliena est illa magnificentiae virtus. Quare non magis proprium narrationis est magnifice dicere quam miserabiliter, invidiose, graviter, dulciter, urbane; quae, cum suo quoque loco sint laudabilia, non sunt huic parti proprie adsignata et velut dedita.

63 Illa quoque ut narrationi apta, ita ceteris quoque partibus communis est virtus, quam Theodectes huic uni proprie dedit; non enim magnificam modo vult esse, verum etiam iucundam expositionem. Sunt

to show how the art which is scarce detected by a reader succeeded in hoodwinking the judge. It is qualities of this kind that make the *statement of facts* credible. If a student requires to be told that we 60 must avoid contradiction and inconsistency in our *statement of facts,* it will be vain to attempt to instruct him on the remaining points, although some writers of text-books produce this precept as if it were a mystery only discovered by their own personal penetration.

61 To these three qualities some add magnificence of diction or μεγαλοπρέπεια as they call it this quality is not, however, suitable to all cases. For what place has language that rises above the ordinary level in the majority of private suits dealing with loans, letting and hiring and interdicts? Nor yet is it always expedient, as may be inferred from the passage just cited from the *pro Milone.* We must 62 remember, too, that there are many cases in which confession, excuse or modification are necessary with regard to our statements: and magnificence is a quality wholly out of keeping with such procedure. Magnificence of diction is therefore no more specially appropriate to the statement of facts than language calculated to excite pity or hatred, or characterised by dignity, charm or wit. Each of these qualities is admirable in its proper place, but none can be regarded as the peculiar and inalienable property of this portion of the speech.

63 Theodectes asserts that the *statement of facts* should not merely be magnificent, but attractive in style. But this quality again though suitable enough to the statement of facts, is equally so in other portions of the speech. There are others

qui adiiciant his evidentiam, quae ἐνάργεια Graece
64 vocatur. Neque ego quemquam deceperim, ut dissimulem Ciceroni quoque plures partes placere. Nam praeterquam planam et brevem et credibilem vult esse evidentem, moratam cum dignitate. Sed in oratione morata debent esse omnia cum dignitate, quae poterunt. Evidentia in narratione, quantum ego intelligo, est quidem magna virtus, cum quid veri non dicendum, sed quodammodo etiam ostendendum est; sed subiici perspicuitati potest, quam quidam etiam contrariam interim putaverunt, quia in quibusdam causis obscuranda veritas esset; quod
65 est ridiculum. Nam qui obscurare vult, narrat falsa pro veris, et in iis quae narrat debet laborare, ut videantur quam evidentissima.

66 Et quatenus etiam forte quadam pervenimus ad difficilius narrationum genus, iam de iis loquamur, in quibus res contra nos erit, quo loco nonnulli praetereundam narrationem putaverunt. Et sane nihil est facilius, nisi prorsus totam causam omnino non agere. Sed si aliqua iusta ratione huiusmodi susceperis litem, cuius artis est malam esse causam silentio confiteri? nisi forte tam hebes futurus est iudex, ut secundum id pronuntiet, quod sciet narrare
67 te noluisse. Neque infitias eo in narratione, ut aliqua neganda, aliqua adiicienda, aliqua mutanda,

---

[1] *Top.* xxvi. 97.

who add palpability, which the Greeks call ἐνάργεια. And I will not conceal the fact that Cicero[1] himself 64 holds that more qualities are required. For in addition to demanding that it should be plain, brief and credible, he would have it clear, characteristic and worthy of the occasion. But everything in a speech should be characteristic and worthy of the occasion as far as possible. Palpability, as far as I understand the term, is no doubt a great virtue, when a truth requires not merely to be told, but to some extent obtruded, still it may be included under lucidity. Some, however, regard this quality as actually being injurious at times, on the ground that in certain cases it is desirable to obscure the truth. This contention is, however, absurd. For he who 65 desires to obscure the situation, will state what is false in lieu of the truth, but must still strive to secure an appearance of palpability for the facts which he narrates.

A chance turn of the discussion has led us to a 66 difficult type of *statement of facts*. I will therefore proceed to speak of those in which the facts are against us. Under such circumstances some have held that we should omit the *statement of facts* altogether. Nothing can be more easy, except perhaps to throw up the case altogether. But suppose you undertake a case of this kind with some good reason. It is surely the worst art to admit the badness of the case by keeping silence. We can hardly hope that the judge will be so dense as to give a decision in favour of a case which he knows we were unwilling to place before him. I do not of course deny that just as there may be 67 some points which you should deny in your *statement*

sic aliqua etiam tacenda; sed tacenda, quae tacere
oportebit et liberum erit. Quod fit nonnunquam
brevitatis quoque gratia, quale illud est, *Respondit*
68 *quae ei visum est.* Distinguamus igitur genera
causarum. Namque in iis, in quibus non de culpa
quaeretur sed de actione, etiamsi erunt contra nos
themata, confiteri nobis licebit: *Pecuniam de templo*
sustulit sed privatam, ideoque sacrilegus non est.
69 *Virginem rapuit, non tamen optio patri dabitur. In-*
genuum stupravit et stupratus se suspendit, non tamen
ideo stuprator capite ut causa mortis punietur, sed decem
milia, quae poena stupratori constituta est, dabit. Verum
in his quoque confessionibus est aliquid, quod de
invidia, quam expositio adversarii fecit, detrahi
possit, cum etiam servi nostri de peccatis suis mol-
70 lius loquantur. Quaedam enim quasi non narrantes
mitigabimus: *Non quidem, ut adversarius dicit, con-*
silium furti in templum attulit nec diu captavit eius rei
tempus; sed occasione et absentia custodum corruptus et
pecunia, quae nimium in animis hominum potest, victus
est. Sed quid refert? peccavit et fur est; nihil attinet

[1] The victim can claim either that the ravisher should marry her or be put to death. Her father cannot however make either of these demands on her behalf.

of facts, others which you should add, and yet again others that you should alter, so there may be some which you should pass over in silence. But still only those points should be passed over which we ought and are at liberty to treat in this way. This is sometimes done for the sake of brevity, as in the
phrase "He replied as he thought fit." We 68
must therefore distinguish between case and case. In those where there is no question of guilt but only of law, we may, even though the facts be against us, admit the truth. "He took money from the temple, but it was private property, and therefore he is not guilty of sacrilege. He abducted a maiden, but the father[1] can have no option as to
his fate. He assaulted a freeborn boy, and the 69
latter hanged himself, but that is no reason for the author of the assault to be awarded capital punishment as having caused his death; he will instead pay 10,000 sesterces, the fine imposed by law for such a crime." But even in making these admissions we may to some extent lessen the odium caused by the statement of our opponent. For even
our slaves extenuate their own faults. In some 70
cases, too, we may mitigate a bad impression by words which avoid the appearance of a *statement of facts.* We may say, for instance, "He did not, as our opponent asserts, enter the temple with the deliberate intention of theft nor seek a favourable occasion for the purpose, but was led astray by the opportunity, the absence of custodians, and the sight of the money (and money has always an undue influence on the mind of man), and so yielded to temptation. What does that matter? He committed the offence and is a thief. It is

71 *id defendere, cuius poenam non recusamus.* Interim quasi damnemus ipsi: *Vis te dicam vino impulsum? errore lapsum? nocte deceptum? vera sunt ista fortasse; tu tamen ingenuum stuprasti, solve decem milia.* Nonnunquam praepositione praemuniri potest causa,
72 deinde exponi. Contraria sunt omnia tribus filiis, qui in mortem patris coniurarant: sortiti nocte singuli per ordinem cum ferro cubiculum intrarunt patre dormiente; cum occidere eum nemo potuisset,
73 excitato omnia indicarunt. Si tamen pater, qui divisit patrimonium et reos parricidii defendit, sic agat: *Quod contra legem sufficit, parricidium obiicitur iuvenibus, quorum pater vivit atque etiam liberis suis adest. Ordinem rei narrare quid necesse est, cum ad legem nihil pertineat? sed si confessionem culpae meae exigitis, fui pater durus et patrimonii, quod iam melius*
74 *ab his administrari poterat, tenax custos;* deinde subiiciat stimulatos ab iis, quorum indulgentiores parentes erant, semper tamen habuisse eum animum, qui sit eventu deprehensus, ut occidere patrem non

useless to defend an act to the punishment of which we can raise no objection." Again we may 71
sometimes go near condemning our client ourselves. "Do you wish me to say that you were under the influence of wine? that you made a mistake? that the darkness deceived you? That may be true. But still you committed an assault on a freeborn boy; pay your 10,000 sesterces." Sometimes we may fortify our case in advance by a preliminary summary, from which we proceed to the full *statement of facts.* All the evidence points to 72
the guilt of three sons who had conspired against their father. After drawing lots they entered their father's bedroom while he slept, one following the other in the order predetermined and each armed with a sword. None of them had the heart to kill him, he woke and they confessed all. If, 73
however, the father, who has divided his estate among them and is defending them when accused of parricide, pleads as follows: "As regards my defence against the law, it suffices to point out, that these young men are charged with parricide in spite of the fact that their father still lives and is actually appearing on behalf of his children. What need is there for me to set forth the facts as they occurred since the law does not apply to them? But if you desire me to confess my own guilt in the matter, I was a hard father to them and watched over my estate, which would have been better managed by them, with miserly tenacity." And if he then should 74
add, "they were spurred to attempt the crime by others who had more indulgent fathers; but their real feelings towards their father have been proved by the result; they could not bring themselves to

possent; neque enim iureiurando opus fuisse, si
alioqui hoc mentis habuissent, nec sorte, nisi quod
se quisque eximi voluerit, omnia haec qualiacunque
placidioribus animis accipientur, illa brevi primae
75 propositionis defensione mollita. At cum quaeritur
an factum sit vel quale factum sit, licet omnia
contra nos sint, quomodo tamen evitare expositionem
salva causae ratione possumus? Narravit accusator
neque ita ut, quae essent acta, tantum indicaret, sed
adiecit invidiam, rem verbis exasperavit, accesserunt
probationes, peroratio incendit et plenos irae reli-
76 quit Exspectat naturaliter iudex, quid narretur a
nobis. Si nihil exponimus, illa esse quae adversarius dixit et talia qualia dixit credat necesse est.
Quid ergo? eadem exponemus? Si de qualitate
agitur, cuius tum demum quaestio est, cum de re
constat, eadem sed non eodem modo; alias causas,
77 aliam mentem, aliam rationem dabo. Verbis elevare
quaedam licebit; luxuria liberalitatis, avaritia parsi-

kill him. It would have been quite unnecessary for them to take an oath to kill him, if they had really had the heart to do the deed, while the only explanation of their drawing lots is that each of them wished to avoid the commission of the crime." If such were his pleading, all these pleas would, such as they are, find the judges all the more disposed to mercy, since the brief defence offered in the first summary statement would have paved the way for them. But if the question is whether 75
an act has been committed or what its nature may be, even though everything be against us, how can we avoid a *statement of facts* without gross neglect of our case? The accuser has made a *statement of facts,* and has done so not merely in such a way as to indicate what was done, but has added such comments as might excite strong prejudice against us and made the facts seem worse than they are by the language which he has used. On the top of this have come the *proofs,* while the *peroration* has kindled the indignation of the judges and left them full of anger against us. The judge naturally 76
waits to hear what we can state in our behalf. If we make no statement, he cannot help believing that our opponent's assertions are correct and that their tone represents the truth. What are we to do then? Are we to restate the same facts? Yes, if the question turns on the nature of the act, as it will if there is no doubt about the commission, but we must restate them in a different way, alleging other motives and another purpose and putting a different complexion on the case. Some 77
imputations we may mitigate by the use of other words; luxury will be softened down into generosity,

moniae, negligentia simplicitatis nomine lenietur;
vultu denique, voce, habitu vel favoris aliquid vel
miserationis merebor. Solet nonnunquam movere
lacrimas ipsa confessio. Atque ego libenter interro-
gem, sint illa defensuri, quae non narraverint,
78 necne? Nam si neque defenderint neque narraverint, tota causa prodetur; at si defensuri sunt,
proponere certe plerumque id, quod confirmaturi
sumus, oportet. Cur ergo non exponamus, quod et
dilui potest et, ut hoc contingat, utique indicandum
79 est? Aut quid inter probationem et narrationem
interest, nisi quod narratio est probationis continua
propositio, rursus probatio narrationi congruens confirmatio? Videamus ergo, num haec expositio
longior demum debeat esse et paulo verbosior praeparatione et quibusdam argumentis (argumentis dico,
non argumentatione), cui tamen plurimum confert
frequens adfirmatio effecturos nos quod dicimus;
non posse vim rerum ostendi prima expositione;
exspectent et opiniones suas differant et bene
80 sperent. Denique utique narrandum est, quidquid
aliter quam adversarius exposuit narrari potest, aut
etiam prooemia sunt in his causis supervacua; quae
quid magis agunt, quam ut cognitioni rerum accom-

avarice into economy, carelessness into simplicity, and I shall seek to win a certain amount of favour or pity by look, voice and attitude. Sometimes a frank confession is of itself sufficient to move the jury to tears. And I should like to ask those who differ from me whether they are prepared to defend what they have refused to state, or no. For if 78
they refuse either to defend or to state the facts, they will be giving away their whole case. If, on the other hand, they do propose to put in a defence, they must at least, as a rule, set forth what they intend to justify. Why then not state fully facts which can be got rid of and must in fact be pointed out to make that possible? Or again what 79
difference is there between a *proof* and a *statement of facts* save that the latter is a *proof* put forward in continuous form, while a *proof* is a verification of the facts as put forward in the *statement*? Let us consider therefore whether under such circumstances the *statement* should not be somewhat longer and fuller than usual, since we shall require to make some preliminary remarks and to introduce certain special arguments (note that I say arguments, and not argumentation), while it will add greatly to the force of our defence if we assert not once nor twice that we shall prove what we say is true and that the significance of the facts cannot be brought out by one opening statement, bidding them wait, delay forming their opinions and hope for the best. Finally it is important to include in our 80
statement anything that can be given a different complexion from that put upon it by our opponent. Otherwise even an *exordium* will be superfluous in a case of this kind. For what is its purpose if

modatiorem iudicem faciant? Atque constabit, nusquam esse eorum maiorem usum, quam ubi animus
iudicis ab aliqua contra nos insita opinione flectendus
81 est. Coniecturales autem causae, in quibus de facto
quaeritur, non tam saepe rei, de qua iudicium est,
quam eorum, per quae res colligenda est, expositionem habent. Quae cum accusator suspiciose
narret, reus levare suspicionem debeat, aliter ab hoc
82 atque ab illo ad iudicem perferri oportet. At enim
quaedam argumenta turba valent, diducta leviora
sunt. Id quidem non eo pertinet, ut quaeratur an
narrandum, sed quomodo narrandum sit. Nam et
congerere plura in expositione quid prohibet, si id
utile est causae, et promittere, sed et dividere
narrationem et probationes subiungere partibus
83 atque ita transire ad sequentia? Nam ne iis quidem accedo, qui semper eo putant ordine, quo quid
actum sit, esse narrandum, sed eo malo narrare, quo
expedit. Quod fieri plurimis figuris licet. Nam et
aliquando nobis excidisse simulamus, cum quid

---

[1] For this technical term = cases turning on questions of fact, see III. vi. 30 *sqq.*

not to make the judge better disposed for the investigation of the case? And yet it will be agreed that the *exordium* is never more useful than when it is necessary to divert the judge from some prejudice that he has formed against us. Con- 81
jectural[1] cases, on the other hand—that is to say questions of fact—require a statement, which will more often deal with the circumstances from which a knowledge of the point at issue may be derived than with the actual point which is under trial. When the accuser states these circumstances in such a manner as to throw suspicion on the case for the defence, and the accused has consequently to dispel that suspicion, the facts must be presented to the judge in quite a different light by the latter. But, 82
it may be urged, some arguments are strong when put forward in bulk, but far less effective when employed separately. My answer is that this remark does not affect the question whether we ought to make a statement of fact, but concerns the question how it should be made. For what is there to prevent us from amassing and producing a number of arguments in the *statement*, if that is likely to help our cause? Or from subdividing our statement of facts and appending the proofs to their respective sections and so passing on to what remains to be said? Neither do I agree with those who assert that 83
the order of our *statement of facts* should always follow the actual order of events, but have a preference for adopting the order which I consider most suitable. For this purpose we can employ a variety of figures. Sometimes, when we bring up a point in a place better suited to our purpose, we may pretend that it had escaped our notice;

utiliore loco reducimus, et interim nos reddituros reliquum ordinem testamur, quia sic futura sit causa lucidior; interim re exposita subiungimus causas
84 quae antecesserunt. Neque enim est una lex defensionis certumque praescriptum; pro re, pro tempore intuenda quae prosint, atque ut erit vulnus, ita vel curandum protinus vel, si curatio differri potest,
85 interim deligandum. Nec saepius narrare duxerim nefas, quod Cicero pro Cluentio fecit; estque non concessum modo, sed aliquando etiam necessarium, ut in causis repetundarum omnibusque quae simplices non sunt. Amentis est enim superstitione
86 praeceptorum contra rationem causae trahi. Narrationem ideo ante probationes ponere est institutum, ne iudex, qua de re quaeratur, ignoret. Cur igitur, si singula probanda aut refellenda erunt, non singula etiam narrentur? Me certe, quantacunque nostris experimentis habenda est fides, fecisse hoc in foro, quotiens ita desiderabat utilitas, probantibus et eruditis et iis, qui iudicabant, scio; et (quod non arroganter dixerim, quia sunt plurimi, quibuscum egi, qui me refellere possint, si mentiar) fere ponendae
87 a me causae officium exigebatur. Neque ideo tamen non id saepius facere oportebit, ut rerum ordinem sequamur. Quaedam vero etiam turpiter conver-

occasionally, too, we may inform the judge that we shall adhere to the natural order for the remainder of our statement, since by so doing we shall make our case clearer, while at times after stating a fact, we may append the causes which preceded it. For 84
there is no single law or fixed rule governing the method of defence. We must consider what is most advantageous in the circumstances and nature of the case, and treat the wound as its nature dictates, dressing at once or, if the dressing can be delayed, applying a temporary bandage. Again I 85
do not regard it as a crime to repeat a statement of a fact more than once, as Cicero does in the *pro Cluentio.* It is not merely permissible, but sometimes necessary, as in trials for extortion and all complicated cases; and only a lunatic will allow a superstitious observance of rules to lead him counter to the interests of his case. The reason for placing 86
the statement of facts before the proof is to prevent the judge from being ignorant of the question at issue. Why then, if each individual point has to be proved or refuted, should not each individual point be stated as well? If my own experience may be trusted, I know that I have followed this practice in the courts, whenever occasion demanded it, and my procedure has been approved both by learned authorities and the judges themselves, while the duty of setting forth the case was generally entrusted to me. I am not boasting, for there are many with whom I have been associated as counsel, who can bring me to book if I lie. On the other hand this is no reason 87
for not following the order of events as a general rule. Indeed inversion of the order has at times a most unhappy effect, as for example if you should mention

tuntur, ut si peperisse narres, deinde concepisse; apertum testamentum, deinde signatum; in quibus si id, quod posterius est, dixeris, de priore tacere optimum; palam est enim praecessisse.

88 Sunt quaedam et falsae expositiones, quarum in
foro duplex genus est: alterum, quod instrumentis adiuvatur, ut P. Clodius fiducia testium, qua nocte incestum Romae commiserat, Interamnae se fuisse dicebat; alterum, quod est tuendum dicentis ingenio. Id interim ad solam verecundiam pertinet, unde etiam mihi videtur dici color, interim ad quae-
89 stionem. Sed utrumcunque erit, prima sit curarum,
ut id quod fingemus fieri possit; deinde, ut et personae et loco et tempori congruat et credibilem rationem et ordinem habeat; si continget, etiam verae alicui rei cohaereat aut argumento, quod sit in causa, confirmetur. Nam quae tota extra rem petita
90 sunt, mentiendi licentiam produnt. Curandum prae-
cipue, (quod fingentibus frequenter excidit) ne qua inter se pugnent; quaedam enim partibus blandiuntur, sed in summam non consentiunt; praeterea,

---

[1] *color* is a technical term for "the particular aspect given to a case by the skilful manipulation of the facts—the 'gloss' or 'varnish' put on them by the accused or accuser."—Peterson on Quint. x. i. 116.

first that a woman has brought forth and then that she has conceived, or that a will has been read and then that it has been signed. In such cases, if you should happen to have mentioned the later incident, it is better to say nothing about the former, which must quite obviously have come first.

Sometimes, too, we get false statements of facts; 88
these, as far as actual pleading in the courts is concerned, fall into two classes. In the first case the statement depends on external support; Publius Clodius, for instance, relied on his witnesses when he stated that he was at Interamna on the night when he committed abominable sacrilege at Rome. The other has to be supported by the speaker's native talent, and sometimes consists simply in an assumption of modesty, which is, I imagine, the reason why it is called a gloss,[1] while at other times it will be concerned with
the question at issue. Whichever of these two forms 89
we employ, we must take care, first that our fiction is within the bounds of possibility, secondly that it is consistent with the persons, dates and places involved and thirdly that it presents a character and sequence that are not beyond belief: if possible, it should be connected with something that is admittedly true and should be supported by some argument that forms part of the actual case. For if we draw our fictions entirely from circumstances lying outside the case, the liberty which we have taken in resorting to falsehood will stand revealed.
Above all we must see that we do not contradict 90
ourselves, a slip which is far from rare on the part of spinners of fiction: for some things may put a most favourable complexion on portions of our case, and yet fail to agree as a whole. Further, what we say

ne iis, quae vera esse constabit, adversa sint; in
schola etiam, ne color extra themata quaeratur.
91 Utrobique autem orator meminisse debebit actione
tota, quid finxerit, quoniam solent excidere quae
falsa sunt, verumque est illud, quod vulgo dicitur,
92 mendacem memorem esse oportere. Sciamus autem,
si de nostro facto quaeratur, unum nobis aliquid esse
dicendum; si de alieno, mittere in plura suspiciones
licere. Est tamen quibusdam scholasticis controversiis, in quibus ponitur aliquem non respondere
quod interrogatur, libertas omnia enumerandi, quae
93 responderi potuissent. Fingenda vero meminerimus
ea, quae non cadant in testem. Sunt autem haec,
quae a nostro dicuntur animo, cuius ipsi tantum
conscii sumus; item quod a defunctis, nec hoc enim
est qui neget; itemque ab eo cui idem expediet, is
enim non negabit; ab adversario quoque, quia non
94 est habiturus in negando fidem. Somniorum et
superstitionum colores ipsa iam facilitate auctoritatem perdiderunt. Non est autem satis in narratione uti coloribus, nisi per totam actionem con-
sentiant, cum praesertim quorundam probatio sola
95 sit in adseveratione et perseverantia; ut ille para-
situs, qui ter abdicatum a divite iuvenem et abso-

must not be at variance with the admitted truth. Even in the schools, if we desire a *gloss,* we must not look for it outside the facts laid down by our theme. In 91
either case the orator should bear clearly in mind throughout his whole speech what the fiction is to which he has committed himself, since we are apt to forget our falsehoods, and there is no doubt about the truth of the proverb that a liar should have a good memory. But whereas, if the question turns on some 92
act of our own, we must make one statement and stick to it, if it turns on an act committed by others, we may cast suspicion on a number of different points. In certain controversial themes of the schools, however, in which it is assumed that we have put a question and received no reply, we are at liberty to enumerate all the possible answers that might have been given. But we must remember only to invent 93
such things as cannot be checked by evidence: I refer to occasions when we make our own minds speak (and we are the only persons who are in their secret) or put words in the mouth of the dead (for what they say is not liable to contradiction) or again in the mouth of someone whose interests are identical with ours (for he will not contradict), or finally in the mouth of our opponent (for he will not be believed if he does deny). *Glosses* drawn from 94
dreams and superstitions have long since lost their value, owing to the very ease with which they can be invented. But it will avail us little to use *glosses* in a *statement of fact,* unless they are consistent throughout the whole of our speech, more especially as certain things can only be proved by persistent assertion. Take for instance the case of the parasite 95
who claims as his son a young man who has been

lutum tanquam suum filium asserit, habebit quidem colorem, quo dicat et paupertatem sibi causam exponendi fuisse et ideo a se parasiti personam esse susceptam, quia in illa domo filium haberet; et ideo illum ter innocentem abdicatum, quia filius abdi-
96 cantis non esset. Nisi tamen in omnibus verbis et amorem patrium atque hunc quidem ardentissimum ostenderit et odium divitis et metum pro iuvene, quem periculose mansurum in illa domo, in qua tam invisus sit, sciat, suspicione subiecti petitoris non carebit.

97 Evenit aliquando in scholasticis controversiis, quod in foro an possit accidere dubito, ut eodem colore utraque pars utatur, deinde eum pro se quaeque
98 defendat, ut in illa controversia: Uxor marito dixit, appellatam se de stupro a privigno et sibi constitutum tempus et locum; eadem contra filius detulit de noverca, edito tantum alio tempore ac loco; pater in eo, quem uxor praedixerat, filium invenit, in eo, quem filius, uxorem; illam repudiavit, qua tacente filium abdicat. Nihil dici potest pro iuvene, quod
99 non idem sit pro noverca. Ponentur tamen etiam communia; deinde ex personarum comparatione et

thrice disinherited by a wealthy father and thrice restored to his own. He will be able to put forward as a *gloss* or plea that poverty was the reason why he exposed the child, that he assumed the rôle of a parasite because his son was in the house in question and, lastly, that the reason why the young man was thrice disinherited was simply that he was not the
son of the man who disinherited him. But unless 96
every word that he utters reveals an ardent paternal affection, hatred for his wealthy opponent and anxiety on behalf of the youth, who will, he knows, be exposed to serious danger if he remains in the house where he is the victim of such dislike, he will be unable to avoid creating the suspicion that he has been suborned to bring the action.

It sometimes happens in the controversial themes 97
of the schools, though I doubt whether it could ever occur in the courts, that both sides employ the same
gloss and support it on their own behalf. An 98
example of this may be found in the theme which runs as follows. "A wife has stated to her husband that her stepson has attempted to seduce her and that a time and place have been assigned for their meeting: the son has brought the same charge against his stepmother, with the exception that a different time and place are mentioned. The father finds the son in the place mentioned by the wife, and the wife in the place mentioned by the son. He divorces her, and then, as she says nothing in her own defence, disinherits the son." No defence can be put forward for the son which is not also a
defence of the stepmother. However, what is com- 99
mon to both sides of the case will be stated, and then arguments will be drawn from a comparison of

indicii ordine et silentio repudiatae argumenta
100 ducentur. Ne illud quidem ignorare oportet, quaedam esse quae colorem non recipiant, sed tantum
defendenda sint, qualis est ille dives, qui statuam
pauperis inimici flagellis cecidit et reus est iniuriarum;
nam factum eius modestum esse nemo dixerit, fortasse
ut sit tutum obtinebit.

101 Quodsi pars expositionis pro nobis, pars contra nos
erit, miscenda sit an separanda narratio, cum ipsa
condicione causae deliberandum est. Nam si plura
sunt quae nocent, quae prosunt obruuntur. Itaque
tunc dividere optimum erit, et iis, quae partem
nostram adiuvabunt, expositis et confirmatis, adversus
reliqua uti remediis, de quibus supra dictum est.
102 Si plura proderunt, etiam coniungere licebit, ut quae
obstant in mediis velut auxiliis nostris posita minus
habeant virium. Quae tamen non erunt nuda ponenda, sed ut et nostra aliqua argumentatione
firmemus et diversa cur credibilia non sint adiicia-
mus; quia, nisi distinxerimus, verendum est, ne bona
nostra permixtis malis inquinentur.

103 Illa quoque de narratione praecipi solent, ne qua

the characters of the two parties, from the order in which they laid information against each other and from the silence of the divorced wife. Still we 100
must not ignore the fact that there are some cases which do not admit of any form of *gloss*, but must be defended forthright. An example is provided by the case of the rich man who scourged the statue of a poor man who was his enemy, and was subsequently indicted for assault. Here no one can deny that the act was outrageous, but it may be possible to maintain that it is not punishable by law.

If, however, part of the statement of facts tells in 101
our favour and part against us, we must consider whether in view of the circumstances of the case the parts in question should be blent or kept apart. If the points which are damaging to our case be in the majority, the points which are in its favour will be swamped. Under those circumstances it will be best to keep them apart and, after setting forth and proving the points which help our case, to meet the rest by employing the remedies mentioned above. If, on the other hand, it be the 102
points in our favour which predominate, we may even blend them with the others, since thus the traitors in our camp will have less force. None the less these points, both good and bad, must not be set forth naked and helpless: those in our favour must be supported by some argument, and then reasons must be added why the points which tell against us should not be believed; since if we do not distinguish clearly between the two, it is to be feared that those which are favourable may suffer from their bad company.

Further rules are laid down with regard to the 103

ex ea fiat excursio, ne avertatur a iudice sermo, ne
alienae personae vocem demus, ne argumentemur;
adiiciunt quidam etiam, ne utamur adfectibus;
quorum pleraque sunt frequentissime custodienda,
104 immo nunquam, nisi ratio coegerit, mutanda. Ut
sit expositio perspicua et brevis, nihil quidem tam
raro poterit habere rationem quam excursio; nec
unquam debebit esse nisi brevis et talis, ut vi quadam
videamur adfectus velut recto itinere depulsi, qualis
105 est Ciceronis circa nuptias Sasiae: *O mulieris scelus
incredibile et praeter hanc unam in omni vita inauditum!
O libidinem effrenatam et indomitam! O audaciam
singularem! nonne timuisse, si minus vim deorum hominumque famam, at illam ipsam noctem facesque illas
nuptiales! non limen cubiculi! non cubile filiae! non
parietes denique ipsos, superiorum testes nuptiarum!*
106 Sermo vero aversus a iudice et brevius indicat interim et coarguit magis, de qua re idem, quod in
prooemio dixeram, sentio, sicut de prosopopoeia
quoque; qua tamen non Servius modo Sulpicius
utitur pro Aufidia: *Somnone te languidum an gravi*

---

[1] *pro Clu.* vi. 15.

statement of fact, forbidding us to indulge in digression, apostrophe or argumentation or to put our words into the mouths of others. Some even add that we should make no appeal to the passions. These rules should for the most part be observed, indeed they should never be infringed unless the circumstances absolutely demand it. If our state- 104
ment is to be clear and brief, almost anything can be justified sooner than digression. And if we do introduce a digression, it must always be short and of such a nature that we give the impression of having been forced from our proper course by some uncontrollable emotion. The passage in Cicero[1] about the marriage of Sasia is a good example of this. "What incredible wickedness in a 105
woman! Unheard of in the history of mankind till she dared the sin! What unbridled and unrestrained lust, what amazing daring! One might have thought that, even if she had no regard for the vengeance of heaven and the opinion of man, she would at least have dreaded that night of all nights and those torches that lighted her to the bridal bed: that she would have shrunk in horror from the threshold of her chamber, from her daughter's room and the very walls that had witnessed her former
marriage." As to addressing another in place of 106
the judge, it may be a means of making a point with greater brevity and give it greater force. On this subject I hold the same view that I expressed in dealing with the *exordium*, as I do on the subject of impersonation. This artifice however is employed not only by Servius Sulpicius in his speech on behalf of Aufidia, when he cries "Am I to suppose that you were drowsed with sleep or weighed down by some

lethargo putem pressum? sed M. quoque Tullius
circa nauarchos, (nam ea quoque rei expositio est)
107 *Ut adeas, tantum dabis,* et reliqua. Quid? pro
Cluentio, Staieni Bulbique colloquium nonne ad
celeritatem plurimum et ad fidem confert? Quae
ne fecisse inobservantia quadam videatur, quanquam
hoc in illo credibile non est, in Partitionibus praecepit, ut habeat narratio suavitatem, admirationes,
exspectationes, exitus inopinatos, colloquia persona-
108 rum, omnes adfectus. Argumentabimur, ut dixi,
nunquam; argumentum ponemus aliquando; quod
facit pro Ligario Cicero, cum dicit sic eum provinciae
praefuisse, ut illi pacem esse expediret. Inseremus
expositioni et brevem, cum res poscet, defensionem
109 et rationem factorum. Neque enim narrandum est
tanquam testi sed tanquam patrono. Rei ordo per se
talis est: *Q. Ligarius legatus cum C. Considio profectus.*
Quid ergo M. Tullius? *Q. enim,* inquit, *Ligarius,*
cum esset nulla belli suspicio, legatus in Africam cum
110 *C. Considio profectus est.* Et alibi: *Non modo ad*
bellum sed ne ad minimam quidem suspicionem belli.

---

[1] *Verr.* v. xlv. 118. [2] *pro Clu.* xxvi. [3] ix. 31.
[4] ii. 4. Ligarius was accused of having fought for the Pompeians in Africa. Cicero points out that he went out to Africa before the outbreak of war was dreamed of and that his whole attitude was discreet.

heavy lethargy?" but by Cicero[1] as well, when in a passage which, like the above, belongs to the statement of facts, in speaking of the ships' captains he says, "You will give so much to enter, etc." Again 107
in the *pro Cluentio*[2] does not the conversation between Staienus and Bulbus conduce to speed and enhance the credibility of the statements? In case it should be thought that Cicero did this without design (quite an incredible supposition in his case), I would point out that in the *Partitiones*[3] he lays it down that the *statement of facts* should be characterised by passages which will charm and excite admiration or expectation, and marked by unexpected turns, conversations between persons and appeals to every kind of emotion. We shall, as I 108
have already said, never argue points in the *statement of facts*, but we may sometimes introduce arguments, as for example Cicero does in the *pro Ligario*,[4] when he says that he ruled his province in such a way that it was to his interest that peace should continue. We shall sometimes also, if occasion demand, insert a brief defence of the facts in the statement and trace the reasons that led up to them. For we must state our facts like advocates, 109
not witnesses. A statement in its simplest form will run as follows, "Quintus Ligarius went out as legate to C. Considius." But how will Cicero[5] put it? "Quintus Ligarius," he says, "set out for Africa as legate to Gaius Considius at a time when there was no thought of war." And again elsewhere[6] 110
he says, "Not only not to war, but to a country where there was no thought of war." And when the sense would have been sufficiently clear had he

[5] *pro Lig.* i. 2. *ib.* ii. 4.

Et cum esset indicaturo satis, *Q. Ligarius nullo se implicari negotio passus est*, adiecit, *domum spectans, ad suos redire cupiens.* Ita quod exponebat, et ratione fecit credibile et adfectu quoque implevit.

111 Quo magis miror eos, qui non putant utendum in narratione adfectibus. Qui si hoc dicunt, *non diu neque ut in epilogo*, mecum sentiunt; effugiendae sunt enim morae. Ceterum cur ego iudicem nolim, dum
112 eum doceo, etiam movere? Cur, quod in summa parte sum actionis petiturus, non in primo statim rerum ingressu, si fieri potest, consequar? cum praesertim etiam in probationibus faciliorem sim animum eius habiturus occupatum vel ira vel misera-
113 tione. An non M. Tullius circa verbera civis Romani omnes brevissime movet adfectus, non solum condicione ipsius, loco iniuriae, genere verberum, sed animi quoque commendatione? Summum enim virum ostendit qui, cum virgis caederetur, non ingemuerit, non rogaverit, sed tantum civem Romanum esse se cum invidia caedentis et fiducia iuris clama-
114 verit. Quid? Philodami casum nonne cum per totam expositionem incendit invidia, tum in sup-

[1] *pro Lig.* i. 3.
[2] *Verr.* v. 62. A Roman citizen might not be scourged. *cp.* St. Paul. [3] *ib.* i. 30.

said no more than "Quintus Ligarius would not suffer himself to be entangled in any transaction,"[1] he adds "for he had his eyes fixed on home and wished to return to his own people." Thus he made what he stated credible by giving a reason for it and at the same time coloured it with emotion.

I am therefore all the more surprised at those 111
who hold that there should be no appeal to the emotions in the *statement of facts.* If they were to say "Such appeals should be brief and not on the scale on which they are employed in the *peroration,*" I should agree with them; for it is important that the statement should be expeditious. But why, while I am instructing the judge, should I refuse to
move him as well? Why should I not, if it is 112
possible, obtain that effect at the very opening of the case which I am anxious to secure at its conclusion, more especially in view of the fact that I shall find the judge far more amenable to the cogency of my proof, if I have previously filled his
mind with anger or pity? Does not Cicero,[2] in his 113
description of the scourging of a Roman citizen, in a few brief words stir all the emotions, not merely by describing the victim's position, the place where the outrage was committed and the nature of the punishment, but also by praising the courage with which he bore it? For he shows us a man of the highest character who, when beaten with rods, uttered not a moan nor an entreaty, but only cried that he was a Roman citizen, thereby bringing shame on his oppressor and showing his confidence
in the law. Again does he not throughout the 114
whole of his statement excite the warmest indignation at the misfortunes of Philodamus[3] and move

plicio ipso lacrimis implevit, cum flentes non tam
narraret quam ostenderet patrem de morte filii, filium
115 de patris? Quid ulli epilogi possunt magis habere
miserabile? Serum est enim advocare iis rebus
adfectum in peroratione, quas securus narraveris;
adsuevit illis iudex iamque eas sine motu mentis
accipit, quibus commotus novis non est, et difficile
est mutare animi habitum semel constitutum.

116 Ego vero (neque enim dissimulabo iudicium meum,
quanquam id, quod sum dicturus, exemplis magis
quam praeceptis ullis continetur) narrationem, ut si
ullam partem orationis, omni qua potest gratia et
venere exornandam puto. Sed plurimum refert,
117 quae sit natura eius rei quam exponemus. In parvis
ergo, quales sunt fere privatae, sit ille pressus et
velut applicitus rei cultus, in verbis summa diligentia;
quae in locis impetu feruntur et circumiectae orationis copia latent, hic expressa et, ut vult Zeno, *sensu
tincta* esse debebunt; compositio dissimulata quidem
118 sed tamen quam iucundissima; figurae non illae
poeticae et contra rationem loquendi auctoritate
veterum receptae (nam debet esse quam purissimus
sermo), sed quae varietate taedium effugiant et

us even to tears when he speaks of his punishment
and describes, or rather shows us as in a picture,
the father weeping for the death of his son and the
son for the death of his father? What can any 115
peroration present that is more calculated to stir
our pity? If you wait for the *peroration* to stir your
hearer's emotions over circumstances which you
have recorded unmoved in your *statement of facts*,
your appeal will come too late. The judge is
already familiar with them and hears their mention
without turning a hair, since he was unstirred when
they were first recounted to him. Once the habit
of mind is formed, it is hard to change it.

For my own part (for I will not conceal my 116
opinion, though it rests rather on actual examples
than on rules), I hold that the *statement of fact* more
than any portion of the speech should be adorned
with the utmost grace and charm. But much will
depend on the nature of the subject which we have
to set forth. In slighter cases, such as are the 117
majority of private suits, the decoration must be
restrained and fit close to the subject, while the
utmost care must be exercised in choice of words.
The words which in our purple passages are swept
along by the force of our eloquence and lost in the
profusion of our language, must in cases such as
these be clear and, as Zeno says, "steeped with meaning." The rhythm should be unobtrusive, but as
attractive as possible, while the figures must neither 118
be derived from poetry nor such as are contrary to
current usage, though warranted by the authority of
antiquity (for it is important that our language should
be entirely normal), but should be designed to relieve
tedium by their variety and should be frequently

mutationibus animum levent, ne in eundem casum, similem compositionem, pares elocutionum tractus incidamus. Caret enim ceteris lenociniis expositio et, nisi commendetur hac venustate, iaceat necesse
119 est. Nec in ulla parte intentior est iudex, eoque nihil recte dictum perit. Praeterea nescio quomodo etiam credit facilius, quae audienti iucunda sunt, et
120 voluptate ad fidem ducitur. Ubi vero maior res erit, et atrocia invidiose et tristia miserabiliter dicere licebit, non ut consumantur adfectus, sed ut tamen velut primis lineis designentur, ut plane, qualis futura
121 sit imago rei, statim appareat. Ne sententia quidem velut fatigatum intentione stomachum iudicis reficere dissuaserim, maxime quidem brevi interiectione, qualis est illa, *Fecerunt servi Milonis, quod suos quisque servos in tali re facere voluisset,* interim paulo liberiore, qualis est illa, *Nubit genero socrus, nullis auspicibus,*
122 *nullis auctoribus, funestis ominibus omnium.* Quod cum sit factum iis quoque temporibus, quibus omnis ad utilitatem potius quam ad ostentationem componebatur oratio, et erant adhuc severiora iudicia, quanto

[1] *pro Mil.* x. 29. [2] *pro Clu.* v. 14.

changed to relax the strain of attention. Thus we shall avoid repeating the same terminations and escape monotony of rhythm and a stereotyped turn of phrase. For the *statement of facts* lacks all the other allurements of style and, unless it is characterised by this kind of charm, will necessarily fall flat.
Moreover there is no portion of a speech at which 119
the judge is more attentive, and consequently nothing that is well said is lost. And the judge is, for some reason or other, all the more ready to accept what charms his ear and is lured by pleasure to belief.
When on the other hand the subject is on a larger 120
scale, we have a chance to excite horror by our narration of abominable wrongs or pity by a tale of woe: but we must do so in such a way as not to exhaust our stock of emotions on the spot, but merely to indicate our harrowing story in outline so that it may at once be clear what the completed
picture is like to be. Again I am far from dis- 121
approving of the introduction of some striking sentence designed to stimulate the judge's jaded palate. The best way of so doing is the interposition of a short sentence like the following: "Milo's slaves did what everyone would have wished his own slaves to do under similar circumstances"[1]: at times we may even be a little more daring and produce something like the following: "The mother-in-law wedded her son-in-law: there were no witnesses, none to sanction the union, and
the omens were dark and sinister."[2] If this was 122
done in days when every speech was designed for practical purposes rather than display and the courts were far stricter than to-day, how much more should we do it now, when the passion for producing a

nunc faciendum magis, cum in ipsa capitis aut for-
tunarum pericula inrupit voluptas? cui hominum
desiderio quantum dari debeat alio loco dicam. In-
123 terim aliquid indulgendum esse confiteor. Multum
confert adiecta veris credibilis rerum imago, quae
velut in rem praesentem perducere audientes videtur,
qualis est illa M. Caelii in Antonium descriptio:
Namque ipsum offendunt temulento sopore profligatum,
totis praecordiis stertentem, ructuosos spiritus geminare,
praeclarasque contubernales ab omnibus spondis trans-
124 *versas incubare et reliquas circumiacere passim. Quae*
tamen exanimatae terrore, hostium adventu percepto, ex-
citare Antonium conabantur, nomen inclamabant, frustra
a cervicibus tollebant, blandius alia ad aurem invocabat,
vehementius etiam nonnulla feriebat; quarum cum omnium
vocem tactumque noscitaret, proximae cuiusque collum
amplexu petebat, neque dormire excitatus neque vigilare
ebrius poterat, sed semisomno sopore inter manus centuri-
onum concubinarumque iactabatur. Nihil his neque
credibilius fingi neque vehementius exprobrari
neque manifestius ostendi potest.

125 Neque illud quidem praeteribo, quantam adferat
fidem expositioni narrantis auctoritas; quam mereri
debemus ante omnia quidem vita, sed et ipso

thrill of pleasure has forced its way even into cases where a man's life or fortunes are in peril? I shall say later to what extent I think we should indulge popular taste in this respect: in the meantime I shall admit that some such indulgence is necessary.
A powerful effect may be created if to the actual 123
facts of the case we add a plausible picture of what occurred, such as will make our audience feel as if they were actual eyewitnesses of the scene. Such is the description introduced by Marcus Caelius in his speech against Antonius. "For they found him lying prone in a drunken slumber, snoring with all the force of his lungs, and belching continually, while the most distinguished of his female companions sprawled over every couch, and the rest of
the seraglio lay round in all directions. They 124
however perceived the approach of the enemy and, half-dead with terror, attempted to arouse Antonius, called him by name, heaved up his head, but all in vain, while one whispered endearing words into his ear, and another slapped him with some violence. At last he recognised the voice and touch of each and tried to embrace her who happened to be nearest. Once wakened he could not sleep, but was too drunk to keep awake, and so was bandied to and fro between sleeping and waking in the hands of his centurions and his paramours." Could you find anything more plausible in imagination, more vehement in censure or more vivid in description?

There is another point to which I must call atten- 125
tion, namely the credit which accrues to the *statement of facts* from the authority of the speaker. Now such authority should first and foremost be the reward of our manner of life, but may also be conferred

genere orationis, quod quo fuerit gravius ac sanctius, hoc plus habeat necesse est in adfirmando
126 ponderis. Effugienda igitur in hac praecipue parte omnis calliditatis suspicio, neque enim se usquam custodit magis iudex; nihil videatur fictum, nihil sollicitum; omnia potius a causa quam ab oratore
127 profecta credantur. At hoc pati non possumus et perire artem putamus, nisi appareat, cum desinat ars esse, si apparet. Pendemus ex laude atque hanc laboris nostri ducimus summam. Ita, quae circumstantibus ostentare volumus, iudicibus prodimus.

128 Est quaedam etiam repetita narratio, quae ἐπιδιήγησις dicitur, sane res declamatoria magis quam forensis, ideo autem reperta, ut, quia narratio brevis esse debet, fusius et ornatius res possit exponi; quod fit vel invidiae gratia vel miserationis. Id et raro faciendum iudico neque sic unquam, ut totus ordo repetatur; licet enim per partes idem consequi. Ceterum, qui uti ἐπιδιηγήσει volet, narrationis loco rem stringat et contentus indicare, quod factum sit, quo sit modo factum plenius se loco suo expositurum esse promittat.

129 Initium narrationis quidam utique faciendum a

by our style of eloquence. For the more dignified and serious our style, the greater will be the weight that it will lend to our assertions. It is therefore 126
specially important in this part of our speech to avoid anything suggestive of artful design, for the judge is never more on his guard than at this stage. Nothing must seem fictitious, nought betray anxiety; everything must seem to spring from the case itself rather than the art of the orator. But our modern orators 127
cannot endure this and imagine that their art is wasted unless it obtrudes itself, whereas as a matter of fact the moment it is detected it ceases to be art. We are the slaves of applause and think it the goal of all our effort. And so we betray to the judges what we wish to display to the bystanders.

There is also a kind of repetition of the *statement* 128
which the Greeks call ἐπιδιήγησις. It belongs to declamation rather than forensic oratory, and was invented to enable the speaker (in view of the fact that the statement should be brief) to set forth his facts at greater length and with more profusion of ornament, as a means of exciting indignation or pity. I think that this should be done but rarely and that we should never go to the extent of repeating the *statement* in its entirety. For we can attain the same result by a repetition only of parts. Anyone, however, who desires to employ this form of repetition, should touch but lightly on the facts when making his *statement* and should content himself with merely indicating what was done, while promising to set forth how it was done more fully when the time comes for it.

Some hold that the *statement of facts* should always 129
begin by referring to some person, whom we must

persona putant, eamque, si nostra sit, ornandam, si aliena, infamandam statim. Hoc sane frequentis-
130 simum est, quia personae sunt inter quas litigatur. Sed hae quoque interim cum suis accidentibus ponendae, cum id profuturum est: ut *A. Cluentius Habitus fuit pater huiusce, iudices, homo non solum municipii Larinatis, ex quo erat, sed regionis illius et vicinitatis virtute, existimatione, nobilitate princeps*; interim sine his ut *Q. enim*
131 *Ligarius cum esset*; frequenter vero et a re, sicut pro Tullio Cicero *Fundum habet in agro Thurino M. Tullius paternum*; Demosthenes pro Ctesiphonte Τοῦ γὰρ Φωκικοῦ συστάντος πολέμου.

132 De fine narrationis cum iis contentio est, qui perduci expositionem volunt eo, unde quaestio oritur: *His rebus ita gestis, P. Dolabella praetor interdixit, ut est consuetudo, de vi, hominibus armatis, sine ulla exceptione, tantum ut unde deiecisset restitueret; deinde restituisse se dixit. Sponsio facta est; hac de sponsione vobis iudicandum est.* Id a petitore semper fieri potest, a defensore non semper.

III. Ordine ipso narrationem sequitur confirmatio.

---

[1] *pro Cluent.* v. 11. [2] *pro Lig.* i. 2.
[3] *pro Tull.* vi. 14. [4] § 18. [5] Cic. *pro Caec.* viii. 23.

praise if he is on our side, and abuse if he is on the side of our opponents. It is true that this is very often done for the good reason that a law-suit must take place between persons. Persons may however 130
also be introduced with all their attendant circumstances, if such a procedure is likely to prove useful. For instance, "The father of my client, gentlemen, was Aulus Cluentius Habitus, a man whose character, reputation and birth made him the leading man not only in his native town of Larinum, but in all the surrounding district."[1] Or again they may be in- 131
troduced without such circumstances, as in the passage beginning "For Quintus Ligarius etc."[2] Often, too, we may commence with a fact as Cicero does in the *pro Tullio*[3]: "Marcus Tullius has a farm which he inherited from his father in the territory of Thurium," or Demosthenes in the speech in defence of Ctesiphon,[4]—"On the outbreak of the Phocian war."

As regards the conclusion of the *statement of facts,* 132
there is a controversy with those who would have the statement end where the issue to be determined begins. Here is an example. "After these events the praetor Publius Dolabella issued an interdict in the usual form dealing with rioting and employment of armed men, ordering, without any exception, that Aebutius should restore the property from which he had ejected Caecina. He stated that he had done so. A sum of money was deposited. It is for you to decide to whom this money is to go."[5] This rule can always be observed by the prosecutor, but not always by the defendant.

III. In the natural order of things the *statement of fact* is followed by the *verification.* For it

Probanda sunt enim quae propter hoc exposuimus. Sed priusquam ingrediar hanc partem, pauca mihi de quorundam opinione dicenda sunt. Plerisque moris est prolato rerum ordine protinus utique in aliquem laetum ac plausibilem locum quam maxime
2 possint favorabiliter excurrere. Quod quidem natum ab ostentatione declamatoria iam in forum venit, postquam agere causas non ad utilitatem litigatorum, sed ad patronorum iactationem repertum est, ne, si pressae illi, qualis saepius desideratur, narrationis gracilitati coniuncta argumentorum pugnacitas fuerit, dilatis diutius dicendi voluptatibus oratio refrigescat
3 In quo vitium illud est, quod sine discrimine causarum atque utilitatis hoc, tanquam semper expediat aut etiam necesse sit, faciunt, eoque sumptas ex iis partibus, quarum alius erat locus, sententias in hanc congerunt, ut plurima aut iterum dicenda sint aut, quia alieno loco dicta sunt, dici suo non possint.
4 Ego autem confiteor, hoc exspatiandi genus non modo narrationi sed etiam quaestionibus vel universis vel

is necessary to prove the points which we stated with the proof in view. But before I enter on this portion, I have a few words to say on the opinions held by certain rhetoricians. Most of them are in the habit, as soon as they have completed the *statement of facts,* of digressing to some pleasant and attractive topic with a view to securing the utmost amount of favour from their audience. This practice 2
originated in the display of the schools of declamation and thence extended to the courts as soon as causes came to be pleaded, not for the benefit of the parties concerned, but to enable the advocates to flaunt their talents. I imagine that they feared that if the slender stream of concise statement, such as is generally required, were followed by the pugnacious tone inevitable in the arguing of the case, the speech would fall flat owing to the postponement of the pleasures of a more expansive eloquence. The ob- 3
jection to this practice lies in the fact that they do this without the slightest consideration of the difference between case and case or reflecting whether what they are doing will in any way assist them, on the assumption that it is always expedient and always necessary. Consequently they transfer striking thoughts from the places which they should have occupied elsewhere and concentrate them in this portion of the speech, a practice which involves either the repetition of a number of things that they have already said or their omission from the place which was really theirs owing to the fact that they have already been said. I admit however that this 4
form of digression can be advantageously appended, not merely to the *statement of facts,* but to each of the different questions or to the questions as a whole,

interim singulis opportune posse subiungi, cum res
postulat aut certe permittit, atque eo vel maxime
illustrari ornarique orationem, sed si cohaeret et
sequitur, non si per vim cuneatur et quae natura
5 iuncta erant distrahit. Nihil enim tam est consequens quam narrationi probatio, nisi excursus ille
vel quasi finis narrationis vel quasi initium probationis
est. Erit ergo illi nonnunquam locus, ut, si expositio
circa finem atrox fuerit, prosequamur eam velut
6 erumpente protinus indignatione. Quod tamen ita
fieri oportebit, si res dubitationem non habebit.
Alioqui prius est quod obiicias verum efficere quam
magnum, quia criminum invidia pro reo est, priusquam probabitur; difficillima est enim gravissimi
7 cuiusque sceleris fides. Item fieri non inutiliter
potest ut, si merita in adversarium aliqua exposueris,
in ingratum inveharis, aut, si varietatem criminum
narratione demonstraveris, quantum ob ea periculum
8 intentetur, ostendas. Verum haec breviter omnia.
Iudex enim ordine audito festinat ad probationem
et quam primum certus esse sententiae cupit.
Praeterea cavendum est, ne ipsa expositio

so long as the case demand, or at any rate permit it. Indeed such a practice confers great distinction and adornment on a speech, but only if the digression fits in well with the rest of the speech and follows naturally on what has preceded, not if it is thrust in like a wedge parting what should naturally come
together. For there is no part of a speech so closely 5
connected with any other as the *statement* with the *proof*, though of course such a digression may be intended as the conclusion of the *statement* and the beginning of the *proof*. There will therefore sometimes be room for digression; for example if the end of the *statement* has been concerned with some specially horrible theme, we may embroider the theme as though our indignation must find immediate
vent. This, however, should only be done if 6
there is no question about the facts. Otherwise it is more important to verify your charge than to heighten it, since the horrible nature of a charge is in favour of the accused, until the charge is proved. For it is just the most flagrant crimes that
are the most difficult to prove. Again a digression 7
may be advantageous if after setting forth the services rendered by your client to his opponent you denounce the latter for his ingratitude, or after producing a variety of charges in your statement, you point out the serious danger in which the advancement of such
charges is likely to involve you. But all these di- 8
gressions should be brief. For as soon as he has heard the facts set forth in order, the judge is in a hurry to get to the proof and desires to satisfy himself of the correctness of his impressions at the earliest possible moment. Further, care must be taken not to nullify the effect of the *statement* by

vanescat, aversis in aliud animis et inani mora
fatigatis.

9 Sed ut non semper est necessaria post nárrationem
illa procursio, ita frequenter utilis ante quaestionem
praeparatio, utique si prima specie minus erit favorabilis, si legem asperam ac poenarias actiones tuebimur.
Est hic locus velut sequentis exordii[1] ad conciliandum
probationibus nostris iudicem, mitigandum, concitandum.[2] Quod liberius hic et vehementius fieri
10 potest, quia iudici nota iam causa est. His igitur
velut fomentis, si quid erit asperum, praemolliemus,
quo facilius aures iudicum quae post dicturi erimus
admittant, ne ius nostrum oderint. Nihil enim facile
11 persuadetur invitis. Quo loco iudicis quoque noscenda
natura est, iuri magis an aequo sit appositus; proinde
enim magis aut minus erit hoc necessarium.

Ceterum res eadem et post quaestionem perora-
12 tionis vice fungitur. Hanc partem παρέκβασιν vocant
Graeci, Latini egressum vel egressionem. Sed hae
sunt plures, ut dixi, quae per totam causam varios
habent excursus, ut laus hominum locorumque, ut
descriptio regionum, expositio quarundam rerum
13 gestarum, vel etiam fabulosarum. Quo ex genere est
in orationibus contra Verrem compositis Siciliae laus,

[1] exordii, *B*: exordium, *A and Victor*.
[2] mitigandum, concitandum *omitted by B*.

diverting the minds of the court to some other theme and wearying them by useless delay.

But, though such digressions are not always neces- 9
sary at the end of the *statement*, they may form a very useful preparation for the examination of the main question, more especially if at first sight it presents an aspect unfavourable to our case, if we have to support a harsh law or demand severe punishment. For this is the place for inserting what may be regarded as a second *exordium* with a view to exciting or mollifying the judge or disposing him to lend a favouring ear to our proofs. Moreover we can do this with all the greater freedom and vehemence at this stage of the proceedings
since the case is already known to the judge. We 10
shall therefore employ such utterances as emollients to soften the harder elements of our statement, in order that the ears of the jury may be more ready to take in what we have to say in the sequel and to grant us the justice which we ask. For it is hard to persuade a man to do anything
against the grain. It is also important on such 11
occasions to know whether the judge prefers equity or a strict interpretation of the law, since the necessity for such digression will vary accordingly.

Such passages may also serve as a kind of peroration after the main question. The Greeks call 12
this παρέκβασις, the Romans *egressus* or *egressio* (digression). They may however, as I have said, be of various kinds and may deal with different themes in any portion of the speech. For instance we may extol persons or places, describe regions,
record historical or even legendary occurrences. As 13
examples I may cite the praise of Sicily and the rape

Proserpinae raptus; pro C. Cornelio popularis illa virtutum Cn. Pompei commemoratio, in quam ille divinus orator, velut nomine ipso ducis cursus dicendi teneretur, abrupto quem inchoaverat sermone devertit
14 actutum. Παρέκβασις est, ut mea quidem fert opinio, alicuius rei, sed ad utilitatem causae pertinentis extra ordinem excurrens tractatio. Quapropter non video cur hunc ei potissimum locum adsignent, qui rerum ordinem sequitur, non magis quam illud, cur hoc nomen ita demum proprium putent, si aliquid in digressu sit exponendum, cum tot modis a recto itinere
15 declinet oratio. Nam quidquid dicitur praeter illas quinque quas fecimus partes, egressio est, indignatio, miseratio, invidia, convicium, excusatio, conciliatio, maledictorum refutatio. Similia his, quae non sunt in quaestione, omnis amplificatio, minutio, omne adfectus genus, et quae [1] maxime iucundam et ornatam faciunt orationem, de luxuria, de avaritia, religione, officiis; quae cum sint argumentis subiecta similium
16 rerum, quia cohaerent, egredi non videntur. Sed plurima sunt, quae rebus nihil secum cohaerentibus inseruntur, quibus iudex reficitur, admonetur, placatur, rogatur, laudatur. Innumerabilia sunt haec,

[1] et quae, *Spalding*: atque ea, *MSS*.

---

[1] *Verr.* I vii. 27. [2] See note on IV. iv. 8.

of Proserpine[1] in the *Verrines*, or the famous recital of the virtues of Gneius Pompeius in the *pro Cornelio*,[2] where the great orator as though the course of his eloquence had been broken by the mere mention of the general's name, interrupts the topic on which he had already embarked and digresses forthwith to sing his praises. Παρέκβασις may, I think, be defined as the 14
handling of some theme, which must however have some bearing on the case, in a passage that involves digression from the logical order of our speech. I do not see therefore why it should be assigned a special position immediately following on the *statement of facts* any more than I understand why they think that the name is applicable only to a digression where some statement has to be made, when there are so many different ways in which a speech may leave the direct route. For whatever we say that falls 15
outside the five divisions of the speech already laid down is a digression, whether it express indignation, pity, hatred, rebuke, excuse, conciliation or be designed to rebut invective. Other similar occasions for digression on points not involved by the question at issue arise when we amplify or abridge a topic, make any kind of emotional appeal or introduce any of those topics which add such charm and elegance to oratory, topics that is to say such as luxury, avarice, religion, duty : but these would hardly seem to be digressions as they are so closely attached to arguments on similar subjects that they form part of the texture of the speech. There are however a 16
number of topics which are inserted in the midst of matter which has no connexion with them, when for example we strive to excite, admonish, appease, entreat or praise the judge. Such passages are

quorum alia sic praeparata adferimus, quaedam ex occasione vel necessitate ducimus, si quid nobis agentibus novi accidit, interpellatio, interventus alicuius,
17 tumultus. Unde Ciceroni quoque in prooemio, cum diceret pro Milone, digredi fuit necesse, ut ipsa oratiuncula qua usus est patet. Potest autem paulo longius exire, qui praeparat aliquid ante quaestionem et qui finitae probationi velut commendationem adiicit At qui ex media erumpit, cito ad id redire debet unde devertit.

IV. Sunt qui narrationi propositionem subiungant tanquam partem iudicialis materiae, cui opinioni respondimus. Mihi autem propositio videtur omnis confirmationis initium, quod non modo in ostendenda quaestione principali, sed nonnunquam etiam in singulis argumentis poni solet maximeque in iis quae ἐπιχειρήματα vocantur. Sed nunc de priore loquimur.
2 Ea non semper uti necesse est. Aliquando enim sine propositione quoque satis manifestum est quid in quaestione versetur, utique si narratio ibi finem habet, ubi initium quaestio, adeo, ut aliquando subiungatur expositioni, quae solet in argumentis esse summa collectio: *Haec, sicut exposui, ita gesta sunt, iudices; in-*

---

[1] The speech actually delivered, not the long speech which has come down to us, but was never delivered.

[2] III. ix. 5; xi. 27. [3] III. ix. 2. [4] See V. xiv. 14.

innumerable. Some will have been carefully prepared beforehand, while others will be produced to suit the occasion or the necessity of the moment, if anything extraordinary should occur in the course of our pleading, such as an interruption, the interven-
tion of some individual or a disturbance. For example, 17
this made it necessary for Cicero to digress even in the *exordium* when he was defending Milo, as is clear from the short speech[1] which he made on that occasion. But the orator who makes some preface to the main question or proposes to follow up his proofs with a passage designed to commend them to the jury, may digress at some length. On the other hand, if he breaks away in the middle of his speech, he should not be long in returning to the point from which he departed.

IV. After the *statement of facts* some place the *proposition*[2] which they regard as forming a division of a forensic speech. I have already expressed my opinion of this view.[3] But it seems to me that the beginning of every *proof* is a *proposition*, such as often occurs in the demonstration of the main question and sometimes even in the enunciation of individual arguments, more especially of those which are called ἐπιχειρήματα.[4] But for the moment I shall speak of the first kind. It is not always necessary to employ it. The nature of the main question 2
is sometimes sufficiently clear without any *proposition*, especially if the *statement of facts* ends exactly where the question begins. Consequently the recapitulation generally employed in the case of arguments is sometimes placed immediately after the statement of facts. "The affair took place, as I have described, gentlemen: he that laid the ambush was defeated,

sidiator superatus est, vi victa vis vel potius oppressa vir-
3 *tute audacia est.* Nonnunquam vero valde est utilis, ubi res defendi non potest et de fine quaeritur, ut pro eo, qui pecuniam privatam de templo sustulit, *Sacrilegii agitur, de sacrilegio cognoscitis,* ut iudex intelligat id unum esse officii sui, quaerere an id quod
4 obiicitur sacrilegium sit. Item in causis obscuris aut multiplicibus, nec semper propter hoc solum ut sit causa lucidior, sed aliquando etiam ut magis moveat. Movet autem, si protinus subtexantur aliqua, quae prosint. *Lex aperte scripta est ut peregrinus qui murum ascenderit morte multetur; peregrinum te esse certum est; quin ascenderis murum, non quaeritur; quid superest, nisi ut te puniri oporteat?* Haec enim propositio confessionem adversarii premit et quodammodo iudicandi moram tollit, nec indicat quaestionem sed adiuvat.

5 Sunt autem propositiones et simplices et duplices vel multiplices, quod accidit non uno modo. Nam et plura crimina iunguntur, ut cum Socrates accusatus est, quod corrumperet iuventutem et novas superstitiones introduceret; et singula ex pluribus colliguntur, ut cum legatio male gesta obiicitur Aeschini, quod mentitus sit, quod nihil ex mandatis fecerit, quod

---

[1] *pro Mil.* xi. 30.

violence was conquered by violence, or rather I should say audacity was crushed by valour."[1]
Sometimes *proposition* is highly advantageous, more 3
especially when the fact cannot be defended and the question turns on the definition of the fact; as for example in the case of the man who has taken the money of a private individual from a temple: we shall say, "My client is charged with sacrilege. It is for you to decide whether it *was* sacrilege," so that the judge may understand that his sole duty is to decide whether the charge is tantamount to sacrilege. The same method may be employed 4
in obscure or complicated cases, not merely to make the case clearer, but sometimes also to make it more moving. This effect will be produced, if we at once support our pleading with some such words as the following: "It is expressly stated in the law that for any foreigner who goes up on to the wall the penalty is death. You are undoubtedly a foreigner, and there is no question but that you went up on to the wall. The conclusion is that you must submit to the penalty." For this *proposition* forces a confession upon our opponent and to a certain extent accelerates the decision of the court. It does more than indicate the question, it contributes to its solution.

Propositions may be single, double or manifold: 5
this is due to more than one reason. For several charges may be combined, as when Socrates was accused of corrupting the youth and of introducing new superstitions; while single *propositions* may be made up of a number of arguments, as for instance when Aeschines is accused of misconduct as an ambassador on the ground that he lied, failed to

6 moratus sit, quod munera acceperit. Recusatio quoque plures interim propositiones habet, ut contra petitionem pecuniae: *Male petis, procuratorem enim tibi esse non licuit, sed neque illi, cuius nomine litigas, habere procuratorem; sed neque est heres eius, a quo*
7 *accepisse mutuam dicor nec ipsi debui.* Multiplicari haec in quantum libet possunt, sed rem ostendisse satis est. Hae si ponantur singulae subiectis probationibus, plures sunt propositiones; si coniungantur, in partitionem cadunt.

8 Est et nuda propositio, qualis fere in coniecturalibus, *Caedis ago, furtum obiicio;* est ratione subiecta, ut *Maiestatem minuit C. Cornelius; nam codicem tribunus plebis ipse pro contione legit.* Praeter haec utimur propositione aut nostra, ut *Adulterium obiicio;* aut adversarii, ut *Adulterii mecum agitur,* aut communi, ut *Inter me et adversarium quaestio est, uter sit intestato propior.* Nonnunquam diversas quoque iungimus: *Ego hoc dico, adversarius hoc.*

---

[1] The speech is lost. In 67 B.C. Cornelius as tribune of the plebs proposed a law enacting that no man should be released from the obligations of a law save by decree of the people. This struck at a privilege usurped by the senate, and Servilius Globulus, another tribune, forbade the herald to read out the proposal. Cornelius then read it himself. He was accused of *maiestas,* defended by Cicero in 65 B.C. and acquitted.

carry out his instructions, wasted time and accepted bribes. The defence may also contain several *propositions*: for instance against a claim for money we may urge, "Your claim is invalid; for you had no right to act as agent nor had the party whom you represent any right to employ an agent: further, he is not the heir of the man from whom it is asserted that I borrowed the money, nor am I his debtor." 6
These *propositions* can be multiplied at pleasure, but it is sufficient to give an indication of my meaning. If *propositions* are put forward singly with the proofs appended, they will form several distinct *propositions*: if they are combined, they fall under the head of *partition*. 7

A *proposition* may also be put forward unsupported, as is generally done in conjectural cases: "The formal accusation is one of murder, but I also charge the accused with theft." Or it may be accompanied by a reason: "Gaius Cornelius is guilty of an offence against the state; for when he was tribune of the plebs, he himself read out his bill to the public assembly."[1] In addition to these forms of *proposition* we can also introduce a *proposition* of our own, such as "I accuse him of adultery," or may use the *proposition* of our opponent, such as "The charge brought against me is one of adultery," or finally we may employ a *proposition* which is common to both sides, such as "The question in dispute between myself and my opponent is, which of the two is next-of-kin to the deceased who died intestate." Sometimes we may even couple contradictory *propositions*, as for instance "I say this, my opponent says that." 8

9 Habet interim vim propositionis, etiamsi per se non est propositio, cum exposito rerum ordine subiicimus: *De his cognoscetis*, ut sit haec commonitio iudicis, quo se ad quaestionem acrius intendat et velut quodam tactu resuscitatus finem esse narrationis et initium probationis intelligat, et nobis confirmationem ingredientibus ipse quoque quodammodo novum audiendi sumat exordium.

V. Partitio est nostrarum aut adversarii propositionum aut utrarumque ordine collocata enumeratio. Hac quidam utendum semper putant, quod ea fiat causa lucidior et iudex attentior ac docilior, si scierit et de quo dicamus et de quo dicturi postea simus.
2 Rursus quidam periculosum id oratori arbitrantur duabus ex causis: quod nonnunquam et excidere soleant quae promisimus et, si qua in partiendo praeterimus, occurrere; quod quidem nemini accidet, nisi qui plane vel nullo fuerit ingenio vel ad agendum
3 nihil cogitati praemeditatique detulerit. Alioqui quae tam manifesta et lucida est ratio quam rectae partitionis? Sequitur enim naturam ducem adeo ut memoriae id maximum sit auxilium via dicendi non decedere. Quapropter ne illos quidem probaverim, qui partitionem vetant ultra tres propositiones extendere. Quae sine dubio, si nimium sit multiplex,

We may at times produce the effect of a *proposition*, even though it is not in itself a *proposition*, by adding after the *statement of facts* some phrase such as the following: "These are the points on which you will give your decision," thereby reminding the judge to give special attention to the question and giving him a fillip to emphasise the point that we have finished the *statement of facts* and are beginning the *proof*, so that when we start to verify our statements he may realise that he has reached a fresh stage where he must begin to listen with renewed attention. 9

V. *Partition* may be defined as the enumeration in order of our own *propositions*, those of our adversary or both. It is held by some that this is indispensable on the ground that it makes the case clearer and the judge more attentive and more ready to be instructed, if he knows what we are speaking about and what we are going subsequently to speak about.
Others, on the contrary, think that such a course is 2
dangerous to the speaker on two grounds, namely that sometimes we may forget to perform what we have promised and may, on the other hand, come upon something which we have omitted in the *partition*. But this will never happen to anyone unless he is either a fool or has come into court without
thinking out his speech in detail beforehand. Be- 3
sides, what can be simpler or clearer than a straightforward *partition*? It follows nature as a guide and the adhesion to a definite method is actually of the greatest assistance to the speaker's memory. Therefore I cannot approve the view even of those who lay down that *partition* should not extend beyond the length of three *propositions*. No doubt there is a danger, if our *partition* is too complicated, that it

fugiet memoriam iudicis et turbabit intentionem; hoc
tamen numero velut lege non est alliganda, cum
4 possit causa plures desiderare. Alia sunt magis,
propter quae partitione non semper sit utendum:
primum, quia pleraque gratiora sunt, si inventa subito
nec domo adlata, sed inter dicendum ex re ipsa nata
videantur, unde illa non iniucunda schemata, *Paene
excidit mihi*, et *Fugerat me*, et *Recte admones*. Propo-
sitis enim probationibus omnis in reliquum gratia no-
5 vitatis praecerpitur. Interim vero etiam fallendus
est iudex et variis artibus subeundus, ut aliud agi
quam quod petimus putet. Nam est nonnunquam
dura propositio, quod iudex si providit, non aliter
praeformidat quam qui ferrum medici priusquam
curetur aspexit; at si re non ante proposita securum
ac nulla denuntiatione in se conversum intrarit oratio,
6 efficiet, quod promittenti non crederetur. Interim
refugienda non modo distinctio quaestionum est, sed
omnino tractatio; adfectibus turbandus et ab intentione auferendus auditor. Non enim solum oratoris

may slip the memory of the judge and disturb his
attention. But that is no reason why it should be
tied down to a definite number of *propositions,* since
the case may quite conceivably require more. There 4
are further reasons why we should sometimes dispense with *partition.* In the first place there are
many points which can be produced in a more
attractive manner, if they appear to be discovered on
the spot and not to have been brought ready made
from our study, but rather to have sprung from the
requirements of the case itself while we were speaking. Thus we get those not unpleasing figures such
as "It has almost escaped me," "I had forgotten,"
or "You do well to remind me." For if we set forth
all that we propose to prove in advance, we shall
deprive ourselves of the advantage springing from
the charm of novelty. Sometimes we shall even 5
have to hoodwink the judge and work upon him by
various artifices so that he may think that our aim is
other than what it really is. For there are cases
when a *proposition* may be somewhat startling : if the
judge foresees this, he will shrink from it in advance,
like a patient who catches sight of the surgeon's
knife before the operation. On the other hand, if
we have given him no preliminary notice and our
words take him unawares, without his interest in
them having been previously roused by any warning,
we shall gain a credence which we should not have
secured had we stated that we were going to raise
the point. At times we must not merely avoid 6
distinguishing between the various questions, but must
omit them altogether, while our audience must be
distracted by appeals to the emotion and their attention diverted. For the duty of the orator is not

est docere, sed plus eloquentia circa movendum valet. Cui rei contraria est maxime tenuis illa et scrupulose in partes secta divisionis diligentia eo tempore quo
7 cognoscenti iudicium conamur auferre. Quid quod interim, quae per se levia sunt et infirma, turba valent? Ideoque congerenda sunt potius et velut eruptione pugnandum; quod tamen rarum esse debet et ex necessitate demum, cum hoc ipsum quod dissi-
8 mile rationi est coegerit ratio. Praeter haec in omni partitione est utique aliquid potentissimum, quod cum audivit iudex cetera tanquam supervacua gravari solet. Itaque si plura vel obiicienda sunt vel diluenda, et utilis et iucunda partitio est ut, quid quaque de re dicturi simus, ordine appareat; at si unum crimen
9 varie defendemus, supervacua. Ut si illa partiamur, *Dicam non talem esse hunc quem tueor reum, ut in eo credibile videri possit homicidium; dicam occidendi causam huic non fuisse; dicam hunc eo tempore quo homo occisus est trans mare fuisse*, omnia, quae ante id quod ultimum est exsequeris, inania videri necesse est.
10 Festinat enim iudex ad id quod potentissimum est, et velut obligatum promisso patronum, si est pa-

merely to instruct: the power of eloquence is greatest in emotional appeals. Now there is no room for passion if we devote our attention to minute and microscopic division at a time when we are seeking to mislead the judgment of the person who is trying
the case. Again, there are certain arguments which 7
are weak and trivial when they stand alone, but which have great force when produced in a body. We must, therefore, concentrate such arguments, and our tactics should be those of a sudden charge in mass. This, however, is a practice which should be resorted to but rarely and only under extreme necessity when reason compels us to take a course
which is apparently irrational. In addition it must 8
be pointed out that in any *partition* there is always some one point of such special importance, that when the judge has heard it he is impatient with the remainder, which he regards as superfluous. Consequently if we have to prove or refute a number of points *partition* will be both useful and attractive, since it will indicate in order what we propose to say on each subject. On the other hand, if we are defending one point on various grounds *partition* will
be unnecessary. If you were to make a *partition* such 9
as the following, "I will not say that the character of my client is such as to render him incapable of murder, I will only say that he had no motive for murder and that at the time when the deceased was killed he was overseas," in that case all the proofs which you propose to bring before this, the final proof, must needs seem superfluous to the judge.
For the judge is always in a hurry to reach the most 10
important point. If he has a patient disposition he will merely make a silent appeal to the advocate,

tientior, tacitus appellat; si vel occupatus vel in aliqua potestate vel etiam si moribus incompositus,
11 cum convicio efflagitat. Itaque non defuerunt, qui Ciceronis illam pro Cluentio partitionem improbarent, qua se dicturum esse promisit primum, neminem maioribus criminibus, gravioribus testibus, in iudicium vocatum quam Oppianicum; deinde praeiudicia esse facta ab ipsis iudicibus, a quibus condemnatus sit; postremo, iudicium pecunia temptatum non a Cluentio, sed contra Cluentium; quia, si probari posset, quod
12 est tertium, nihil necesse fuerit dicere priora. Rursus nemo tam erit iniustus aut stultus, quin eum fateatur optime pro Murena esse partitum: *Intelligo, iudices, tris totius accusationis fuisse partes, et earum unam in reprehensione vitae, alteram in contentione dignitatis, tertiam in criminibus ambitus esse versatam.* Nam sic et ostendit lucidissime causam et nihil fecit altero supervacuum.

13 De illo quoque genere defensionis plerique dubitant: *Si occidi, recte feci; sed non occidi;* quo enim prius pertinere, si sequens firmum sit? haec invicem obstare, et utroque utentibus in neutro haberi fidem. Quod sane in parte verum est, et illo sequenti, si

---

[1] iv. 9. Oppianicus had been indicted by Cluentius for an attempt upon his life and condemned. The "previous judgments" referred to were condemnations of his accomplices, which made Oppianicus' condemnation inevitable. Oppianicus was condemned, and it was alleged that this was due to bribery by Cluentius. Cluentius was now on his trial for the alleged murder of various persons.

whom he will treat as bound by his promise. On the other hand, if he is busy, or holds exalted position, or is intolerant by nature, he will insist in no very courteous manner on his coming to the point. For these reasons there are some who disapprove of 11
the *partition* adopted by Cicero in the *pro Cluentio*,[1] where he premises that he is going to show, first, "that no man was ever arraigned for greater crimes or on stronger evidence than Oppianicus," secondly, "that previous judgments had been passed by those very judges by whom he was condemned," and finally, "that Cluentius made no attempt to bribe the jury, but that his opponent did." They argue that if the third point can be proved, there is no need to have urged the two preceding. On the 12
other hand you will find no one so unreasonable or so foolish as to deny that the *partition* in the *pro Murena*[2] is admirable. "I understand, gentlemen, that the accusation falls into three parts, the first aspersing my client's character, the second dealing with his candidature for the magistracy, and the third with charges of bribery." These words make the case as clear as possible, and no one division renders any other superfluous.

There are also a number who are in doubt as to 13
a form of defence which I may exemplify as follows: "If I murdered him, I did right; but I did not murder him."[3] What, they ask, is the value of the first part, if the second can be proved, since they are mutually inconsistent, and if anyone employs both arguments, we should believe neither? This contention is partially justified; we should employ the

[2] v. 11. [3] See III. vi. 10.

14 modo indubitabile est, sit solo utendum. At si quid
in eo, quod est fortius, timebimus, utraque probatione nitemur. Alius enim alio moveri solet, et qui
factum putavit, iustum credere potest; qui tanquam
iusto non movebitur, factum fortasse non credet. Ut
certa manus uno telo possit esse contenta, incerta
15 plura spargenda sunt, ut sit et fortunae locus. Egregie
vero Cicero pro Milone insidiatorem primum Clodium
ostendit, tum addidit ex abundanti, etiamsi id non
fuisset, talem tamen civem cum summa virtute inter-
16 fectoris et gloria necari potuisse. Neque illum tamen
ordinem, de quo prius dixi, damnaverim; quia quaedam, etiamsi ipsa sunt dura, in id tamen valent, ut
ea molliant quae sequuntur. Nec omnino sine ratione
est quod vulgo dicitur: *Iniquum petendum, ut aequum*
17 *feras.* Quod tamen nemo sic accipiat ut omnia credat
audenda. Recte enim Graeci praecipiunt, *Non
temptanda, quae effici omnino non possint.* Sed quotiens
hac, de qua loquor, duplici defensione utemur, id
laborandum est, ut in illam partem sequentem fides
ex priore ducatur. Potest enim videri, qui tuto etiam
confessurus fuit, mentiendi causam in negando non
habere.

---

[1] § 13.

[2] The proverb would seem originally to refer to bargaining in the market: the salesman, knowing he will be beaten down, sets his original price too high. But it would equally apply to claims for damages in the courts.

second alone only if the fact can be proved without
a doubt. But if we have any doubts as to being able 14
to prove the stronger argument, we shall do well to rely on both. Different arguments move different people. He who thinks that the act was committed may regard it as a just act, while he who is deaf to the plea that the act was just may perhaps believe that it was never committed: one who is confident of his powers as a marksman may be content with one shaft, whereas he who has no such confidence will do well to launch several and give fortune a chance to
come to his assistance. Cicero in the *pro Milone* 15
reveals the utmost skill in showing first that Clodius laid an ambush for Milo and then in adding as a supernumerary argument that, even if he had not done so, he was nevertheless so bad a citizen that his slaying could only have done credit to the patriotism of the slayer and redounded to his glory.
I would not however entirely condemn the order 16
mentioned above,[1] since there are certain arguments which, though hard in themselves, may serve to soften those which come after. The proverb, "If you want to get your due, you must ask for something
more,"[2] is not wholly unreasonable. Still no one 17
should interpret it to mean that you must stop short of nothing. For the Greeks are right when they lay it down as a rule that we should not attempt the impossible. But whenever the double-barrelled defence of which I am speaking is employed, we must aim at making the first argument support the credibility of the second. For he who might without danger to himself have confessed to the commission of the act, can have no motive for lying when he denies the commission.

18 Et illud utique faciendum est, ut, quotiens sus-
picabimur a iudice aliam probationem desiderari
quam de qua loquimur, promittamus nos plene et
statim de eo satis esse facturos, praecipueque si de
19 pudore agetur. Frequenter autem accidit, ut causa
parum verecunda iure tuta sit; de quo ne inviti
iudices audiant et aversi, frequentius sunt admonendi,
secuturam defensionem probitatis et dignitatis; ex-
20 spectent paulum et agi ordine sinant. Quaedam
interim nos invitis litigatoribus simulandum est
dicere, quod Cicero pro Cluentio facit circa iudicia-
riam legem; nonnunquam, quasi interpellemur ab
iis, subsistere; saepe convertenda ad ipsos oratio;
hortandi ut sinant nos uti nostro consilio. Ita sur-
repetur animo iudicis et, dum sperat probationem
21 pudoris, asperioribus illis minus repugnabit. Quae
cum receperit, etiam verecundiae defensioni facilior
erit. Sic utraque res invicem iuvabit, eritque iudex
circa ius nostrum spe modestiae attentior, circa
modestiam iuris probatione proclivior.

22 Sed ut non semper necessaria aut utilis est partitio,[1] ita opportune adhibita plurimum orationi

[1] utilis est partitio, *Victor*: utilis etiam partitio est, *A*: etiam supervacua partitio est, *B*.

Above all it is important, whenever we suspect 18 that the judge desires a proof other than that on which we are engaged, to promise that we will satisfy him on the point fully and without delay, more especially if the question is one of our client's honour. But it will often happen that a discredit- 19 able case has the law on its side, and to prevent the judges giving us only a grudging and reluctant hearing on the point of law, we shall have to warn them with some frequency that we shall shortly proceed to defend our client's honour and integrity, if they will only wait a little and allow us to follow the order of our proofs. We may also at times 20 pretend to say certain things against the wishes of our clients, as Cicero[1] does in the *pro Cluentio* when he discusses the law dealing with judicial corruption. Occasionally we may stop, as though interrupted by our clients, while often we shall address them and exhort them to let us act as we think best. Thus we shall make a gradual impression on the mind of the judge, and, buoyed up by the hope that we are going to clear our client's honour, he will be less ill-disposed toward the harder portions of our proof. And when he has accepted these, he will be all the 21 readier to listen to our defence of our client's character. Thus the two points will render mutual assistance to each other; the judge will be more attentive to our legal proofs owing to his hope that we shall proceed to a vindication of character and better disposed to accept that vindication because we have proved our point of law.

But although *partition* is neither always necessary 22 nor useful, it will, if judiciously employed, greatly

[1] lii.

lucis et gratiae confert. Neque enim solum id efficit, ut clariora fiant, quae dicuntur, rebus velut ex turba extractis et in conspectu iudicum positis; sed reficit quoque audientem certo singularum partium fine, non aliter quam facientibus iter multum detrahunt fatigationis notata inscriptis lapidibus spatia.
23 Nam et exhausti laboris nosse mensuram voluptati est, et hortatur ad reliqua fortius exsequenda scire quantum supersit. Nihil enim longum videri necesse
24 est, in quo, quid ultimum sit, certum est. Nec immerito multum ex diligentia partiendi tulit laudis Q. Hortensius, cuius tamen divisionem in digitos diductam nonnunquam Cicero leviter eludit. Nam est suus et in gestu modus, et vitanda, utique maxime, concisa nimium et velut articulosa partitio.
25 Nam et auctoritati plurimum detrahunt minuta illa nec iam membra sed frusta, et huius gloriae cupidi, quo subtilius et copiosius divisisse videantur, et supervacua adsumunt et quae natura singularia sunt secant, nec tam plura faciunt quam minora; deinde cum fecerunt mille particulas, in eandem incidunt obscuritatem, contra quam partitio inventa est.

add to the lucidity and grace of our speech. For it not only makes our arguments clearer by isolating the points from the crowd in which they would otherwise be lost and placing them before the eyes of the judge, but relieves his attention by assigning a definite limit to certain parts of our speech, just as our fatigue upon a journey is relieved by reading the distances on the milestones which we
pass. For it is a pleasure to be able to measure how 23
much of our task has been accomplished, and the knowledge of what remains to do stimulates us to fresh effort over the labour that still awaits us. For nothing need seem long, when it is definitely known
how far it is to the end. Quintus Hortensius 24
deserves the high praise which has been awarded him for the care which he took over his *partitions*, although Cicero more than once indulges in kindly mockery of his habit of counting his headings on his fingers. For there is a limit to gesture, and we must be specially careful to avoid excessive minuteness and any suggestion of articulated structure in our *partition*.
If our divisions are too small, they cease to be limbs 25
and become fragments, and consequently detract not a little from the authority of our speech. Moreover, those who are ambitious of this sort of reputation, in order that they may appear to enhance the nicety and the exhaustive nature of their division, introduce what is superfluous and subdivide things which naturally form a single whole. The result of their labours is, however, not so much to increase the number of their divisions as to diminish their importance, and after all is done and they have split up their argument into a thousand tiny compartments, they fall into that very obscurity which the *partition* was designed to eliminate.

26 Et divisa autem et simplex propositio, quotiens utiliter adhiberi potest, primum debet esse aperta atque lucida (nam quid sit turpius, quam id esse obscurum ipsum, quod in eum solum adhibetur usum, ne sint cetera obscura?), tum brevis nec ullo supervacuo onerata verbo. Non enim, quid dicamus, sed
27 de quo dicturi simus ostendimus. Obtinendum etiam, ne quid in ea desit, ne quid supersit. Superest autem sic fere, cum aut in species partimur, quod in genera partiri sit satis, aut genere posito subiicitur species, ut *dicam de virtute, iustitia, continentia,* cum iustitia
28 atque continentia virtutis sint species. Partitio prima est, quid sit de quo conveniat, quid de quo ambigatur. In eo, quod convenit, quid adversarius fateatur, quid nos; in eo, de quo ambigitur, quae nostrae propositiones, quae partis adversae. Pessimum vero, non eodem ordine exsequi, quo quidque proposueris.

The *proposition*, whether single or multiple, must, 26
on every occasion when it can be employed with
profit, be clear and lucid; for what could be more
discreditable than that a portion of the speech,
whose sole purpose is to prevent obscurity elsewhere, should itself be obscure? Secondly it must
be brief and must not be burdened with a single
superfluous word; for we are not explaining what
we *are* saying, but what we are going to say. We 27
must also ensure that it is free alike from omissions
and from redundance. Redundance as a rule occurs
through our dividing into *species* when it would be
sufficient to divide into *genera*, or through the addition of *species* after stating the *genus*. The following
will serve as an example: "I will speak of virtue,
justice and abstinence." But justice and abstinence
are *species* of the *genus* virtue. Our first *partition* 28
will be between admitted and disputed facts.
Admitted facts will then be divided into those
acknowledged by our opponent and those acknowledged by ourselves. Disputed facts will be divided
into those which we and those which our opponents
allege. But the worst fault of all is to treat your
points in an order different from that which was
assigned them in your *proposition*.

BOOK V

LIBER V

Prooemium

Fuerunt et clari quidem auctores, quibus solum videretur oratoris officium docere; namque et adfectus duplici ratione excludendos putabant, primum quia vitium esset omnis animi perturbatio, deinde quia iudicem a veritate depelli misericordia gratia similibusque non oporteret, et voluptatem audientium petere, cum vincendi tantum gratia diceretur, non modo agenti supervacuum, sed vix etiam viro dignum
2 arbitrabantur; plures vero, qui nec ab illis sine dubio partibus rationem orandi summoverent, hoc tamen proprium atque praecipuum crederent opus, sua confirmare et quae ex adverso proponerentur refutare.
3 Utrumcunque est (neque enim hoc loco meam interpono sententiam), hic erit liber illorum opinione maxime necessarius, quia toto haec sola tractantur; quibus sane et ea, quae de iudicialibus causis iam
4 dicta sunt, serviunt. Nam neque prooemii neque narrationis est alius usus, quam ut iudicem huic praeparent; et status nosse atque ea, de quibus

---

[1] *cp.* Ar. *Rhet.* I. i. 4 Also Quint. IV. v. 6.
[2] See III. vi.

BOOK V

Preface

There have been certain writers of no small authority[1] who have held that the sole duty of the orator was to instruct: in their view appeals to the emotions were to be excluded for two reasons, first on the ground that all disturbance of the mind was a fault, and secondly that it was wrong to distract the judge from the truth by exciting his pity, bringing influence to bear, and the like. Further, to seek to charm the audience, when the aim of the orator was merely to win success, was in their opinion not only superfluous for a pleader, but hardly worthy of
a self-respecting man. The majority however, while 2
admitting that such arts undoubtedly formed part of oratory, held that its special and peculiar task is to make good the case which it maintains and refute
that of its opponent. Whichever of these views is 3
correct (for at this point I do not propose to express my own opinion), they will regard this book as serving a very necessary purpose, since it will deal entirely with the points on which they lay such stress, although all that I have already said on the subject of judicial causes is subservient to the same
end. For the purpose of the *exordium* and the *state-* 4
ment of facts is merely to prepare the judge for these points, while it would be a work of supererogation to know the *bases*[2] of cases or to consider the other

supra scripsimus, intueri supervacuum foret, nisi ad
5 hanc perveniremus. Denique ex quinque quas iudicialis materiae fecimus partibus, quaecunque alia
potest aliquando necessaria causae non esse; lis
nulla est, cui probatione opus non sit. Eius praecepta sic optime divisuri videmur, ut prius, quae in
commune ad omnes quaestiones pertinent, ostendamus; deinde, quae in quoque causae genere propria
sint, exsequamur.

I. Ac prima quidem illa partitio ab Aristotele
tradita consensum fere omnium meruit, alias esse
probationes, quas extra dicendi rationem acciperet
orator, alias, quas ex causa traheret ipse et quodam
modo gigneret. Ideoque illas ἀτέχνους, id est inarti-
ficiales, has ἐντέχνους, id est artificiales, vocaverunt.
2 Ex illo priore genere sunt praeiudicia, rumores, tor-
menta, tabulae, iusiurandum, testes, in quibus pars
maxima contentionum forensium consistit. Sed ut
ipsa per se carent arte, ita summis eloquentiae viribus
et adlevanda sunt plerumque et refellenda. Quare
mihi videntur magnopere damnandi, qui totum hoc
3 genus a praeceptis removerunt. Nec tamen in animo
est omnia, quae aut pro his aut contra dici solent,
complecti. Non enim communes locos tradere de-
stinamus, quod esset operis infiniti, sed viam quandam

---

[1] III. xi. [2] III. ix. 1; IV. iii. 15.
[3] *Rhet.* I. ii. 2.

points dealt with above,[1] unless we intend to proceed
to the consideration of the *proof*. Finally, of the 5
five parts [2] into which we divided judicial cases, any single one other than the *proof* may on occasion be dispensed with. But there can be no suit in which the *proof* is not absolutely necessary. With regard to the rules to be observed in this connexion, we shall, I think, be wisest to follow our previous method of classification and show first what is common to all cases and then proceed to point out those which are peculiar to the several kinds of cases.

I. To begin with it may be noted that the division laid down by Aristotle [3] has met with almost universal approval. It is to the effect that there are some proofs adopted by the orator which lie outside the art of speaking, and others which he himself deduces or, if I may use the term, begets out of his case. The former therefore have been styled ἄτεχνοι or *inartificial* proofs, the latter ἔντεχνοι or *artificial*.
To the first class belong decisions of previous courts, 2
rumours, evidence extracted by torture, documents, oaths, and witnesses, for it is with these that the majority of forensic arguments are concerned. But though in themselves they involve no art, all the powers of eloquence are as a rule required to disparage or refute them. Consequently in my opinion those who would eliminate the whole of this class of proof from their rules of oratory, deserve the strongest
condemnation. It is not, however, my intention to 3
embrace all that can be said for or against these views. I do not for instance propose to lay down rules for commonplaces, a task requiring infinite detail, but merely to sketch out the general lines and method

atque rationem. Quibus demonstratis, non modo in exsequendo suas quisque vires debet adhibere, sed etiam inveniendo similia, ut quaeque condicio litium poscet. Neque enim de omnibus causis dicere quisquam potest saltem praeteritis, ut taceam de futuris.

II. Iam praeiudiciorum vis omnis tribus in generibus versatur: rebus, quae aliquando ex paribus causis sunt iudicatae, quae exempla rectius dicuntur, ut de rescissis patrum testamentis vel contra filios confirmatis; iudiciis ad ipsam causam pertinentibus, unde etiam nomen ductum est, qualia in Oppianicum facta dicuntur et a senatu adversus Milonem; aut cum de eadem causa pronuntiatum est, ut in reis deportatis et assertione secunda et partibus cen-
2 tumviralium, quae in duas hastas divisae sunt. Confirmantur praecipue duobus: auctoritate eorum, qui pronuntiaverunt, et similitudine rerum, de quibus quaeritur; refelluntur autem raro per contumeliam

---

[1] *pro Cluent.* xvii. *sqq.* [2] *pro Mil.* v.

[3] Banished persons who have been accused afresh after their restoration.

[4] When a slave claimed his liberty by *assertio* through a representative known as *assertor*, his case was not disposed of once and for all by a first failure, but the claim might be presented anew.

to be followed by the orator. The method once indicated, it is for the individual orator not merely to employ his powers on its application, but on the invention of similar methods as the circumstances of the case may demand. For it is impossible to deal with every kind of case, even if we confine ourselves to those which have actually occurred in the past without considering those which may occur in the future.

II. As regards decisions in previous courts, these fall under three heads. First, we have matters on which judgment has been given at some time or other in cases of a similar nature: these are, however, more correctly termed precedents, as for instance where a father's will has been annulled or confirmed in opposition to his sons. Secondly, there are judgments concerned with the case itself; it is from these that the name *praeiudicium* is derived: as examples I may cite those passed against Oppianicus [1] or by the senate against Milo.[2] Thirdly, there are judgments passed on the actual case, as for example in cases where the accused has been deported,[3] or where renewed application is made for the recognition of an individual as a free man,[4] or in portions of cases tried in the centumviral court which come before two different panels of judges.[5] Such previous decisions are as a rule 2
confirmed in two ways: by the authority of those who gave the decision and by the likeness between the two cases. As for their reversal, this can rarely be

[5] The meaning is not clear. The Latin suggests that portions of a case might be tried by two panels sitting separately, while the case as a whole was tried by the two panels sitting conjointly. The *hasta* (spear) was the symbol of the centumviral court. *cp.* XI. i. 78.

iudicum, nisi forte manifesta in iis culpa erit. Vult enim cognoscentium quisque firmam esse alterius sententiam, et ipse pronuntiaturus, nec libenter
3 exemplum, quod in se fortasse recidat, facit. Confugiendum ergo est in duobus superioribus, si res feret, ad aliquam dissimilitudinem causae; vix autem ulla est per omnia alteri similis. Si id non continget aut eadem causa erit, actionum incusanda negligentia aut de infirmitate personarum querendum, contra quas erit iudicatum, aut de gratia, quae testes corruperit, aut de invidia aut de ignorantia, aut viden-
4 dum, quid[1] causae postea accesserit. Quorum si nihil erit, licet tamen dicere multos iudiciorum casus ad inique pronuntiandum valere ideoque damnatum Rutilium, absolutos Clodium atque Catilinam. Rogandi etiam iudices, ut rem potius intueantur ipsam,
5 quam iuriiurando alieno suum donent. Adversus consulta autem senatus et decreta principum vel magistratuum remedium nullum est, nisi aut inventa quantulacunque causae differentia aut aliqua vel eorundem vel eiusdem potestatis hominum posterior constitutio, quae sit priori contraria; quae si deerunt, lis non erit.

[1] videndum quid, *Victor*: inveniendum quod, *MSS.*

---

[1] Publius Rutilius Rufus condemned for extortion while governor of Asia, owing to a conspiracy of the publicans against him. He went into voluntary exile at Mitylene and was highly honoured by the people of Asia. 91 B.C.

obtained by denouncing the judges, unless they have been guilty of obvious error. For each of those who are trying the case wishes the decision given by another to stand, since he too has to give judgment and is reluctant to create a precedent that may recoil upon himself. Consequently, as regards the 3
first two classes, we must, if possible, take refuge in some dissimilarity between the two cases, and two cases are scarcely ever alike in all their details. If, however, such a course is impossible and the case is the same as that on which the previous decision was given, we must complain of the negligence shown in the conduct of the previous case or of the weakness of the parties condemned, or of undue influence employed to corrupt the witnesses, or again of popular prejudice or ignorance which reacted unfavourably against our client; or else we must consider what has occurred since to alter the aspect of the case. If none of these courses 4
can be adopted, it will still be possible to point out that the peculiar circumstances of many trials have led to unjust decisions; hence condemnations such as that of Rutilius[1] and acquittals such as those of Clodius and Catiline. We must also ask the judges to consider the facts of the case on their merits rather than make their verdict the inevitable consequence of a verdict given by others. When, how- 5
ever, we are confronted by decrees of the senate, or ordinances of emperors or magistrates, there is no remedy, unless we can make out that there is some difference, however small, between the cases, or that the same persons or persons holding the same powers have made some subsequent enactment reversing the former decision. Failing this, there will be no case for judgment.

III. Famam atque rumores pars altera consensum civitatis et velut publicum testimonium vocat, altera sermonem sine ullo certo auctore dispersum, cui malignitas initium dederit, incrementum credulitas; quod nulli non etiam innocentissimo possit accidere fraude inimicorum falsa vulgantium. Exempla utrinque non deerunt.

IV. Sicut in tormentis quoque, qui est locus frequentissimus, cum pars altera quaestionem vera fatendi necessitatem vocet, altera saepe etiam causam falsa dicendi, quod aliis patientia facile mendacium faciat, aliis infirmitas necessarium. Quid attinet de his plura? Plenae sunt orationes veterum ac novo-
2 rum. Quaedam tamen in hac parte erunt propria cuiusque litis. Nam sive de habenda quaestione agetur, plurimum intererit, quis et quem postulet aut offerat et in quem et ex qua causa; sive iam erit habita, quis ei praefuerit, quis et quomodo sit tortus, incredibilia dixerit an inter se constantia, perseveraverit in eo quod coeperat, an aliquid dolore mutarit, prima parte quaestionis an procedente cruciatu.

III. With regard to rumour and common report, one party will call them the verdict of public opinion and the testimony of the world at large; the other will describe them as vague talk based on no sure authority, to which malignity has given birth and credulity increase, an ill to which even the most innocent of men may be exposed by the deliberate dissemination of falsehood on the part of their enemies. It will be easy for both parties to produce precedents to support their arguments.

IV. A like situation arises in the case of evidence extracted by torture: one party will style torture an infallible method of discovering the truth, while the other will allege that it also often results in false confessions, since with some their capacity of endurance makes lying an easy thing, while with others weakness makes it a necessity. It is hardly worth my while to say more on the subject, as the speeches both of ancient and modern orators are full of this topic. Individual cases may however involve special 2
considerations in this connexion. For if the point at issue is whether torture should be applied, it will make all the difference who it is who demands or offers it, who it is that is to be subjected to torture, against whom the evidence thus sought will tell, and what is the motive for the demand. If on the other hand torture has already been applied, it will make all the difference who was in charge of the proceedings, who was the victim and what the nature of the torture, whether the confession was credible or consistent, whether the witness stuck to his first statement or changed it under the influence of pain, and whether he made it at the beginning of the torture or only after it had continued some time. The

Quae utrinque tam infinita sunt quam ipsa rerum varietas.

V. Contra tabulas quoque saepe dicendum est, cum eas non solum refelli sed etiam accusari sciamus esse usitatum. Cum sit autem in his aut scelus signatorum aut ignorantia, tutius ac facilius id, quod secundo
2 loco diximus, tractatur, quod pauciores rei fiunt. Sed hoc ipsum argumenta ex causa trahit, si forte aut incredibile est id actum esse, quod tabulae continent, aut, ut frequentius evenit, aliis probationibus aeque inartificialibus solvitur; si aut is in quem signatum est, aut aliquis signator dicitur afuisse vel prius esse defunctus; si tempora non congruunt; si vel antecedentia vel insequentia tabulis repugnant. Inspectio etiam ipsa saepe falsum deprehendit.

VI. Iusiurandum litigatores aut offerunt suum aut non recipiunt oblatum, aut ab adversario exigunt aut recusant, cum ab ipsis exigatur. Offerre suum sine illa condicione, ut vel adversarius iuret, fere impro-
2 bum est. Qui tamen id faciet, aut vita se tuebitur,

---

[1] An oath might be taken by one of the parties as an alternative to evidence. In court such an oath might be taken only on the proposal of the adversary; the litigant might not swear on his own initiative, although an oath might be taken voluntarily before the case came into court. The matter of the oath rested with the profferer, and the taking of such a proffered oath meant victory for the swearer.

variety of such questions is as infinite as the variety of actual cases.

V. It is also frequently necessary to speak against documents, for it is common knowledge that they are often not merely rebutted, but even attacked as forgeries. But as this implies either fraud or ignorance on the part of the signatories, it is safer and easier to make the charge one of ignorance, because by so doing we reduce the number
of the persons accused. But our proceedings as a 2
whole will draw their arguments from the circumstances of the case at issue. For example, it may be incredible that an incident occurred as stated in the documents, or, as more often happens, the evidence of the documents may be overthrown by other proofs which are likewise of an *inartificial* nature; if, for example, it is alleged that the person, whose interests are prejudiced by the document, or one of the signatories was absent when the document was signed, or deceased before its signature, or if the dates disagree, or events preceding or following the writing of the document are inconsistent with it. Even a simple inspection of a document is often sufficient for the detection of forgery.

VI. With regard to oaths,[1] parties either offer to take an oath themselves, or refuse to accept the oath of their opponent, demand that their opponent should take an oath or refuse to comply with a similar demand when proffered to themselves. To offer to take an oath unconditionally without demanding that one's opponent should likewise take
an oath is as a rule a sign of bad faith. If, however, 2
anyone should take this course, he will defend his action by appealing to the blamelessness of his life

ut eum non sit credibile peieraturum; aut ipsa vi religionis, in qua plus fidei consequetur, si id egerit, ut non cupide ad hoc descendere sed ne hoc quidem recusare videatur; aut, si causa patietur, modo litis, propter quam devoturus se ipse non fuerit; aut praeter alia causae instrumenta adiicit ex abundanti
3 hanc quoque conscientiae suae fiduciam. Qui non recipiet, et iniquam condicionem et a multis contemni iurisiurandi metum dicet, cum etiam philosophi quidam sint reperti, qui deos agere rerum humanarum curam negarent; eum vero, qui nullo deferente iurare sit paratus, et ipsum velle de causa sua pronuntiare et, quam id quod offert leve ac facile credat, osten-
4 dere. At is, qui defert, agere modeste videtur, cum litis adversarium iudicem faciat, et eum cuius cognitio est onere liberat, qui profecto alieno iureiurando stari
5 quam suo mavult. Quo difficilior recusatio est, nisi forte res est ea, quam credibile sit notam ipsi non esse. Quae excusatio si deerit, hoc unum relinque-

as rendering perjury on his part incredible, or by the solemn nature of the oath, with regard to which he will win all the greater credence, if without the least show of eagerness to take the oath he makes it clear that he does not shrink from so solemn a duty. Or again, if the case is such as to make this possible, he will rely on the trivial nature of the point in dispute to win belief, on the ground that he would not incur the risk of the divine displeasure when so little is at stake. Or, finally, he may in addition to the other means which he employs to win his case offer to take an oath as a culminating proof of a clear conscience. The man who refuses to accept his 3
opponent's offer to take an oath, will allege that the inequality of their respective conditions are not the same for both parties and will point out that many persons are not in the least afraid of committing perjury, even philosophers having been found to deny that the gods intervene in human affairs; and further that he who is ready to take an oath without being asked to do so, is really proposing to pass sentence on his own case and to show what an easy and trivial thing he thinks the oath which he offers to take. On the other hand the man who proposes to put 4
his opponent on oath appears to act with moderation, since he is making his adversary a judge in his own case, while he frees the actual judge from the burden of coming to a decision, since the latter would assuredly prefer to rest on another man's oath than on his own. This fact makes the refusal to take an 5
oath all the more difficult, unless indeed the affair in question be of such a nature that it cannot be supposed that the facts are known to the person asked to take the oath. Failing this excuse, there

tur, ut invidiam sibi quaeri ab adversario dicat atque id agi, ut in causa, in qua vincere non possit, queri possit; itaque hominem quidem malum occupaturum hanc condicionem fuisse, se autem probare malle quae adfirmet, quam dubium cuiquam relin-
6 quere, an peierarit. Sed nobis adolescentibus seniores in agendo facti praecipere solebant, ne temere unquam iusiurandum deferremus, sicut neque optio iudicis adversario esset permittenda nec ex advocatis partis adversae iudex eligendus; nam, si dicere contraria turpe advocato videretur, certe turpius habendum, facere quod noceat.

VII. Maximus tamen patronis circa testimonia sudor est. Ea dicuntur aut per tabulas aut a praesentibus. Simplicior contra tabulas pugna. Nam et minus obstitisse videtur pudor inter paucos signatores, et pro diffidentia premitur absentia. Si reprehensionem non capit ipsa persona, infamare signatores
2 licet. Tacita praeterea quaedam cogitatio refragatur his omnibus, quod nemo per tabulas dat testimonium nisi sua voluntate; quo ipso non esse amicum ei se,

---

[1] The choice of the single *iudex* in civil cases rested with the plaintiff, though the defendant had the right to refuse the person proposed.

[2] Not an actual advocate, but a supporter and adviser on points of law.

is only one course open to him: he must say that his opponent is trying to excite a prejudice against him and is endeavouring to give the impression that he has real ground for complaint though he is not in a position to win his case; consequently, though a dishonest man would eagerly have availed himself of the proposal, he prefers to prove the truth of his statements rather than leave a doubt in anyone's mind as to whether he has committed perjury or no.
But in my young days advocates grown old in plead- 6
ing used to lay it down as a rule that we should never be in a hurry to propose that our opponent should take an oath, just as we should never allow him the choice of a judge[1] nor select our judge from among the supporters of the opposite side: for if it is regarded as a disgrace to such a supporter[2] to say anything against his client, it is surely a still worse disgrace that he should do anything that will harm his client's case.

VII. It is, however, the evidence that gives the greatest trouble to advocates. Evidence may be given either in writing or orally by witnesses present in court. Documentary evidence is easier to dispose of. For it is likely that the deponent was less ashamed of himself in the presence of a small number of witnesses, and his absence from court is attacked as indicating a lack of confidence. If we cannot call the character of the deponent in question, we may attack the witnesses to his signature.
Further there is always a certain tacit prejudice 2
against documentary evidence, since no one can be forced to give such evidence save of his own free will, whereby he shows that he harbours unfriendly feelings towards the person against whom he bears

contra quem dicit, fatetur. Neque tamen protinus cesserit orator, quo minus et amicus pro amico et inimicus contra inimicum possit verum, si integra sit ei fides, dicere. Sed late locus uterque tractatur.

3 Cum praesentibus vero ingens dimicatio est, ideoque velut duplici contra eos proque iis acie confligitur actionum et interrogationum. In actionibus primum generaliter pro testibus atque in testes dici solet.
4 Et hic communis locus, cum pars altera nullam firmiorem probationem esse contendit, quam quae sit hominum scientia nixa; altera ad detrahendam illis fidem omnia, per quae fieri soleant falsa testimonia,
5 enumerat. Sequens ratio est cum specialiter quidem, sed tamen multos pariter invadere patroni solent. Nam et gentium simul universarum elevata testimonia ab oratoribus scimus et tota genera testimoniorum: ut de auditionibus; non enim ipsos esse testes sed iniuratorum adferre voces; ut in causis repetundarum, qui se reo numerasse pecunias iurant, litigatorum non
6 testium habendos loco. Interim adversus singulos dirigitur actio; quod insectationis genus et per-

---

[1] *Interrogatio* includes both the examination in chief and cross-examination.

[2] *e.g.* in cases of extortion, where a whole province might give evidence against the accused.

witness. On the other hand an advocate should be chary of denying that a friend may give true evidence against a friend or an enemy against an enemy, provided they are persons of unimpeachable credit. But the subject admits of copious discussion, from whichever side it be regarded.

The task of dealing with the evidence of witnesses 3
present in court is, however, one of great difficulty, and consequently whether defending or impugning them the orator employs a twofold armoury in the shape of a set speech and examination.[1] In set speeches it is usual to begin with observations either
on behalf of or against witnesses in general. In so 4
doing we introduce a commonplace, since one side will contend that there can be no stronger proof than that which rests on human knowledge, while the other, in order to detract from their credibility, will enumerate all the methods by which false evidence
is usually given. The next procedure is the common 5
practice of making a special attack, which all the same involves impugning the validity of evidence given by large numbers of persons. We know, for instance, that the evidence of entire nations[2] and whole classes of evidence have been disposed of by advocates. For example, in the case of hearsay evidence, it will be urged that those who produce such evidence are not really witnesses, but are merely reporting the words of unsworn persons, while in cases of extortion, those who swear that they paid certain sums to the accused are to be regarded not
as witnesses, but as parties to the suit. Sometimes 6
however the advocate will direct his speech against single individuals. Such a form of attack may be found in many speeches, sometimes embedded in

mixtum defensioni legimus in orationibus plurimis et
7 separatim editum, sicut in Vatinium testem. Totum igitur excutiamus locum, quando universam institutionem aggressi sumus. Sufficiebant alioqui libri duo a Domitio Afro in hanc rem compositi, quem adolescentulus senem colui, ut non lecta mihi tantum ea, sed pleraque ex ipso sint cognita. Is verissime praecepit primum esse in hac parte officium oratoris, ut totam causam familiariter norit; quod sine dubio ad
8 omnia pertinet. Id quomodo contingat, explicabimus, cum ad destinatum huic parti locum venerimus. Ea res suggeret materiam interrogationi et veluti tela ad manum subministrabit; eadem docebit, ad quae iudicis animus actione sit praeparandus. Debet enim vel fieri vel detrahi testibus fides oratione perpetua, quia sic quisque dictis movetur, ut est ad credendum vel non credendum ante formatus.

9 Et quoniam duo genera sunt testium, aut voluntariorum aut eorum, quibus in iudiciis publicis lege denuntiari solet, quorum altero pars utraque utitur, alterum accusatoribus tantum concessum est, separemus officium dantis testes et refellentis.

10 Qui voluntarium producit, scire quid is dicturus

---

[1] Vatinius had appeared as a witness against Sestius, who was defended by Cicero.

[2] XII. viii.

[3] In civil cases evidence was as a rule voluntary; in criminal cases the accuser might *subpoena* witnesses, while the defence was restricted to voluntary testimony.

the speech for the defence and sometimes published separately like the speech against the evidence of
Vatinius.[1] The whole subject, therefore, demands a 7
thorough investigation, as the task which we have in hand is the complete education of an orator. Otherwise the two books written on this subject by Domitius Afer would suffice. I attended his lectures when he was old and I was young, and consequently have the advantage not merely of having read his book, but of having heard most of his views from his own lips. He very justly lays down the rule that in this connexion it is the first duty of an orator to make himself thoroughly acquainted with the case, a remark which of course applies to all portions of
a speech. How such knowledge may be acquired I 8
shall explain when I come to the appropriate portion of this work.[2] This knowledge will suggest material for the examination and will supply weapons ready to the speaker's hand: it will also indicate to him the points for which the judge's mind must be prepared in the set speech. For it is by the set speech that the credit of witnesses should be established or demolished, since the effect of evidence on the individual judge depends on the extent to which he has been previously influenced in the direction of believing the witness or the reverse.

And since there are two classes of witnesses,[3] 9
those who testify of their own free will and those who are summoned to attend in the public courts of whom the former are available to either party, the latter solely to the accusers, we must distinguish between the duties of the advocate who produces witnesses and the advocate who refutes them.

He who produces a voluntary witness is in a 10

sit potest; ideoque faciliorem videtur in rogando habere rationem. Sed haec quoque pars acumen ac vigilantiam poscit, providendumque, ne timidus, ne
11 inconstans, ne imprudens testis sit; turbantur enim et a patronis diversae partis inducuntur in laqueos et plus deprehensi nocent quam firmi et interriti profuissent. Multum igitur domi ante versandi, variis percontationibus, quales haberi ab adversario possint, explorandi sunt. Sic fit, ut aut constent sibi aut, si quid titubaverint, opportuna rursus eius a quo producti sunt interrogatione velut in gradum reponantur.
12 In iis quoque adhuc, qui constiterint sibi, vitandae insidiae; nam frequenter subiici ab adversario solent et omnia profutura polliciti diversa respondent et auctoritatem habent non arguentium illa, sed con-
13 fitentium. Explorandum igitur, quas causas laedendi adversarium adferant; nec id sat est inimicos fuisse, sed an desierint, an per hoc ipsum reconciliari velint, ne corrupti sint, ne poenitentia propositum muta-

position to know what he is likely to say: consequently the task of examining him would seem to be rendered easier. But even here such cases make a great demand on the acumen and watchfulness of the advocate, who must see that his witness is neither timid, inconsistent nor imprudent. For the opposing 11
counsel have a way of making a witness lose his head or of leading him into some trap; and once a witness trips, he does more harm to his own side than he would have done good, had he retained his composure and presence of mind. The advocate must therefore put his witnesses through their paces thoroughly in private before they appear in court and must test them by a variety of questions such as may well be put to them by his opponent. The result will be that they will not contradict themselves or, if they do make some slip, can be set upon their feet again by a timely question from the advocate who produces them. Still, even in the case 12
of witnesses whose evidence is consistent, we must be on our guard against treachery. For such witnesses are often put up by one's opponent and, after promising to say everything that will help our case, give answers of exactly the opposite character and carry more weight by the admission of facts which tell against us than they would have done had they disproved them. We must therefore discover 13
what motives they have for doing our opponent a hurt, and the fact that they were once his enemies will not suffice our purpose: we must find out whether they have ceased to be ill-disposed to him or whether they desire by means of their evidence to effect a reconciliation with him, in order to assure ourselves that they have not been bribed or repented of

verint. Quod cum in iis quoque, qui ea, quae dicturi videntur, re vera sciunt, necessarium est praecavere; multo magis in iis, qui se dicturos, quae falsa sunt,
14 pollicentur. Nam et frequentior eorum poenitentia est et promissum suspectius et, si perseverarint, reprehensio facilior.

15 Eorum vero, quibus denuntiatur, pars testium est quae reum laedere velit, pars quae nolit, idque interim scit accusator interim nescit. Fingamus in praesentia scire; in utroque tamen genere summis
16 artibus interrogantis opus est. Nam si habet testem cupidum laedendi, cavere debet hoc ipsum, ne cupiditas eius appareat, nec statim de eo, quod in iudicium venit, rogare, sed aliquo circuitu ad id pervenire, ut illi, quod maxime dicere voluit, videatur expressum; nec nimium instare interrogationi, ne ad omnia respondendo testis fidem suam minuat, sed in tantum evo-
17 care eum, quantum sumere ex uno satis sit. At in eo, qui verum invitus dicturus est, prima felicitas interrogantis extorquere quod is noluerit. Hoc non alio modo fieri potest quam longius interrogatione repetita. Respondebit enim, quae nocere causae non arbitra-

their previous attitude and changed their purpose. Such precautions are necessary even with witnesses who know that what they propose to say is true; but it is still more necessary with those who promise to give false evidence. For experience shows that 14
they are more likely to repent of their purpose, their promises are less to be relied on, and, if they do keep their promise, their evidence is easier to refute.

Witnesses appearing in answer to a subpoena may 15
be divided into two classes: those who desire to harm the accused, and those who do not. The accuser sometimes is aware of their disposition, sometimes unaware. For the moment let us assume that he is aware of their disposition, although I must point out that in either case the utmost skill is required in their examination. For if an advocate is 16
producing a witness who is desirous of harming the accused, he must avoid letting this desire become apparent, and must not at once proceed to question him on the point at issue. On the contrary this point must be approached by a circuitous route in such a manner as to make it seem that the statement which the witness is really desirous of making has been forced from him. Again he should not press the witness too much, for fear he should impair his credit by the glibness with which he answers every question, but should draw from him just so much as may seem reasonable to elicit from a single witness On the other hand in the case of a witness 17
who is reluctant to tell the truth, the essential for successful examination is to extort the truth against his will This can only be done by putting questions which have all the appearance of irrelevance. If this be done, he will give replies which he

bitur; ex pluribus deinde, quae confessus erit, eo
perducetur ut quod dicere non vult negare non possit.
18 Nam, ut in oratione sparsa plerumque colligimus argumenta, quae per se nihil reum aggravare videantur,
congregatione deinde eorum factum convincimus, ita
huiusmodi testis multa de anteactis, multa de inse-
cutis, loco, tempore, persona, ceteris est interrogandus, ut in aliquod responsum incidat, post quod
illi vel fateri quae volumus necesse sit vel iis quae
19 iam dixerit repugnare. Id si non contingit, reliquum
erit, ut eum nolle dicere manifestum sit, protrahen-
dusque, ut in aliquo, quod vel extra causam sit, deprehendatur; tenendus etiam diutius, ut omnia ac
plura quam res desiderat pro reo dicendo suspectus
iudici fiat; quo non minus nocebit, quam si vera in
20 reum dixisset. At si (quod secundo loco diximus)
nesciet actor, quid propositi testis attulerit, paulatim
et, ut dicitur, pedetentim interrogando experietur
animum eius et ad id responsum quod eliciendum
21 erit per gradus ducet. Sed, quia nonnunquam sunt
hae quoque testium artes, ut primo ad voluntatem
respondeant, quo maiore fide diversa postea dicant,

thinks can do no harm to the party which he favours, and subsequently will be led on from the admissions which he has made to a position which renders it impossible for him to deny the truth of the facts which he is reluctant to state. For just as 18
in a set speech we usually collect detached arguments which in themselves seem innocuous to the accused, but taken together prove the case against him, so we must ask the reluctant witness a number of questions relative to acts antecedent or subsequent to the case, places, dates, persons, etcetera, with a view to luring him into some reply which will force him to make the admissions which we desire or to contradict his previous evidence. If this fails, we 19
must content ourselves with making it clear that he is reluctant to tell what he knows, and lead him with a view to tripping him up on some point or other, even though it be irrelevant to the case; we must also keep him in the witness-box for an unusual length of time, so that by saying everything that can be said and more than is necessary on behalf of the accused, he may be rendered suspect to the judge. Thus he will do the accused no less harm than if he had told the truth against him. But if (to proceed to 20
our second supposition) the advocate does not know what the intentions of the witness may be, he must advance gradually inch by inch and sound him by examination and lead him step by step to the particular reply which it is desired to elicit. But since 21
these witnesses are sometimes so artful that their first replies are designed to meet the wishes of the questioner, in order to win all the greater credit when subsequently they answer in a very different way, it will be the duty of the advocate to dismiss

est actoris[1] suspectum testem, dum prodest, dimittere.

22 Patronorum in parte expeditior, in parte difficilior interrogatio est. Difficilior hoc, quod raro unquam possunt ante iudicium scire, quid testis dicturus sit; expeditior, quod, cum interrogandus est, sciunt quid
23 dixerit. Itaque, quod in eo incertum est, cura et inquisitione opus est, quis reum premat, quas et quibus ex causis inimicitias habeat: eaque in oratione praedicenda atque amolienda sunt, sive odio conflatos testes sive invidia sive gratia sive pecunia videri volumus. Et si deficietur numero pars diversa, paucitatem; si abundabit, conspirationem; si humiles producet, vilitatem; si potentes, gratiam oportebit
24 incessere. Plus tamen proderit causas, propter quas reum laedant, exponere; quae sunt variae et pro condicione cuiusque litis aut litigatoris. Nam contra illa, quae supra diximus, simili ratione responderi locis communibus solet, quia ut in paucis atque humilibus accusator simplicitate gloriari potest, quod neminem praeter eos, qui possint scire, quaesierit

[1] actoris, *Regius*; oratoris, *MSS.*

a suspect witness while he can still do so with advantage.

In the case of advocates for the defence exam- 22
ination is in some respects easier, in some more
difficult. It is more difficult because it is rarely
possible for them to have any previous knowledge of
what the witness is likely to say, and easier because,
when they come to cross-examine, they know what
he has already said. Consequently in view of the 23
uncertainty involved, there is need for careful inquiry with a view to discovering the character of the
witness against the accused and what are his motives
for hostility and what its extent: and all such points
about the witness should be set forth in advance
and disposed of, whether we desire to represent the
evidence against the accused as instigated by hatred,
envy, bribery or influence. Further, if our opponents
bring forward only a small number of witnesses, we
must attack them on that head; if on the other
hand they produce an excessive number, we must
accuse them of conspiracy: if the witnesses are
persons of inconspicuous rank, we must minimise
their importance, while if they are powerful, we shall
accuse our adversaries of bringing undue influence to
bear. It will, however, be still more helpful if we 24
expose the motives which they have for desiring to
injure the accused, and these will vary according to
the nature of the case and the parties concerned.
For the other lines of argument mentioned above
are often answered by the employment of commonplaces on similar lines, since the prosecutor, if he
produce but few witnesses of inconspicuous rank, can
parade the simple honesty of his methods on the
ground that he has produced none save those who

et multos atque honestos commendare aliquanto est
25 facilius. Verum interim et singulos ut exornare, ita
destruere contingit, aut recitatis in actione testimoniis[1] aut testibus nominatis. Quod iis temporibus, quibus testis non post finitas actiones rogabatur,
et facilius et frequentius fuit. Quid autem in quem-
que testium dicendum sit, sumi nisi ex ipsorum
personis non potest.

26 Reliquae interrogandi sunt partes. Qua in re
primum est nosse testem. Nam timidus terreri,
stultus decipi, iracundus concitari, ambitiosus inflari
potest; prudens vero et constans vel tanquam inimicus et pervicax dimittendus statim vel non interrogatione, sed brevi interlocutione patroni refutandus
est aut aliquo, si continget, urbane dicto refrigerandus
aut, si quid in eius vitam dici poterit, infamia crimi-
27 num destruendus. Probos quosdam et verecundos
non aspere incessere profuit; nam saepe, qui adversus insectantem pugnassent, modestia mitigantur.
Omnis autem interrogatio aut in causa est aut extra
causam. In causa, sicut accusatori praecepimus,

[1] testimoniis *added by Halm, some such word having been omitted by the MSS.*

---

[1] It is not clear to what Quintilian refers. There are, it is true, passages in Cicero where the orator speaks of evidence as already given, but the speeches where these references are found are all second pleadings.

are in a position to know the real facts, while if he produce a number of distinguished witnesses, it is even easier to commend them to the court. But at 25
times, just as we have to praise individual witnesses, so we may have to demolish them, whether their evidence has been given in documentary form or they have been summoned to appear in person. This was easier and of more frequent occurrence in the days when the examination of the witnesses was not deferred till after the conclusion of the pleading.[1] With regard to what we should say against individual witnesses, no general rules can be laid down: it will depend on the personality of the witness.

It remains to consider the technique to be followed 26
in the examination of witnesses. The first essential is to know your witness. For a timid witness may be terrorised, a fool outwitted, an irascible man provoked, and vanity flattered. The shrewd and self-possessed witness, on the other hand, must be dismissed at once as being malicious and obstinate; or refuted, not by cross-examination, but by a brief speech from the counsel for the defence; or may be put out of countenance by some jest, if a favourable opportunity presents itself; or, if his past life admits of criticism, his credit may be overthrown by the scandalous charges which can be brought against him.
It has been found advantageous at times when con- 27
fronted with an honest and respectable witness to refrain from pressing him hard, since it is often the case that those who would have defended themselves manfully against attack are mollified by courtesy. But every question is either concerned with the case itself or with something outside the case. As regards the first type of question counsel for the

patronus quoque altius et unde nihil suspecti sit repetita percontatione, priora sequentibus applicando saepe eo perducit homines, ut invitis quod prosit
28 extorqueat. Eius rei sine dubio neque disciplina ulla in scholis neque exercitatio traditur, et naturali magis acumine aut usu contingit haec virtus. Si quod tamen exemplum ad imitationem demonstrandum sit, solum est, quod ex dialogis Socraticorum maximeque Platonis duci potest; in quibus adeo scitae sunt interrogationes, ut, cum plerisque bene respondeatur, res tamen ad id quod volunt efficere
29 perveniat. Illud fortuna interim praestat, ut aliquid, quod inter se parum consentiat, a teste dicatur; interim, quod saepius evenit, ut testis testi diversa dicat. Acuta autem interrogatio ad hoc, quod casu
30 fieri solet, etiam ratione perducet. Extra causam quoque multa, quae prosint, rogari solent, de vita testium aliorum, de sua quisque, si turpitudo, si humilitas, si amicitia accusatoris, si inimicitiae cum reo, in quibus aut dicant aliquid quod prosit, aut in

---

[1] Above, § 17, 18.

defence may, by adopting a method which I have
already recommended for the prosecutor,[1] namely by
commencing his examination with questions of an
apparently irrelevant and innocent character and
then by comparing previous with subsequent replies,
frequently lead witnesses into such a position that
it becomes possible to extort useful admissions from
them against their will. The schools, it is true, give 28
no instruction either as to theory or practice in this
subject, and skill in examination comes rather
from natural talent or practice. If, however, I am
asked to point out a model for imitation, I can
recommend but one, namely that which may be
found in the dialogues of the Socratics and more
especially of Plato, in which the questions put are
so shrewd that although individually as a rule the
answers are perfectly satisfactory to the other side,
yet the questioner reaches the conclusion at which
he is aiming. Fortune sometimes is so kind that a 29
witness gives an answer involving some inconsistency,
while at times (and this is a more frequent occurrence)
one witness contradicts another. But acute examination methodically conducted will generally reach
the same result which is so often reached by chance.
There are also a number of points strictly irrelevant 30
to the case on which questions may be put with
advantage. We may for example ask questions about
the past life of other witnesses or about the witness'
own character, with a view to discovering whether
they can be charged with some disgraceful conduct,
or degrading occupation, with friendship with the
prosecutor or hostility toward the accused, since
in replying to such questions they may say something which will help our cause or may be convicted

mendacio vel cupiditate laedendi deprehendantur.
31 Sed in primis interrogatio cum debet esse circumspecta, quia multa contra patronos venuste testis saepe respondet, eique praecipue vulgo favetur; tum verbis quam maxime ex medio sumptis, ut qui rogatur (is autem est saepius imperitus) intelligat aut ne intelligere se neget, quod interrogantis non leve frigus
32 est. Illae vero pessimae artes, testem subornatum in subsellia adversarii mittere, ut inde excitatus plus noceat vel dicendo contra reum cum quo sederit, vel, cum adiuvisse testimonio videbitur, faciendo ex industria multa immodeste atque intemperanter, per quae non a se tantum dictis detrahat fidem, sed ceteris quoque, qui profuerant, auferat auctoritatem; quorum mentionem habui, non ut fierent, sed ut vitarentur.

Saepe inter se collidi solent inde testatio hinc testes; locus utrinque; haec enim se pars iureiu-
33 rando, illa consensu signantium tuetur. Saepe inter testes et argumenta quaesitum est. Inde scientiam

---

[1] An over-statement, since in many cases the signatories could only testify that the statement was that actually made by the deponent; with its truth they were not necessarily concerned.

of falsehood or of a desire to injure the accused. But above all our examination must be circumspect, since a witness will often launch some smart repartee in answering counsel for the defence and thereby win marked favour from the audience in general. Secondly, we must put our questions as far as possible in the language of everyday speech that the witness, who is often an uneducated man, may understand our meaning, or at any rate may have no opportunity of saying that he does not know what we mean, a statement which is apt to prove highly disconcerting to the examiner. I must however express the strongest disapproval of the practice of sending a suborned witness to sit on the benches of the opposing party, in order that on being called into the witness-box from that quarter he may thereby do all the more damage to the case for the accused by speaking against the party with whose adherents he was sitting or, while appearing to help him by his testimony, deliberately giving his evidence in such an extravagant and exaggerated manner, as not only to detract from the credibility of his own statements, but to annul the advantage derived from the evidence of those who were really helpful. I mention this practice not with a view to encourage it, but to secure its avoidance.

31

32

Documentary evidence is not frequently in conflict with oral. Such a circumstance may be turned to advantage by either side. For one party will rest its case on the fact that the witness is speaking on oath, the other on the unanimity of the signatories.[1]
Again there is often a conflict between the evidence 33
and the arguments. One party will argue that the witnesses know the facts and are bound by the

in testibus et religionem, ingenia esse in argumentis dicitur; hinc testem gratia, metu, pecunia, ira, odio, amicitia, ambitu fieri; argumenta ex natura duci, in
34 his iudicem sibi, in illis alii credere. Communia haec pluribus causis, multumque iactata sunt et semper tamen iactabuntur. Aliquando utrinque sunt testes, et quaestio sequitur ex ipsis, utri meliores viri; ex causis, utri magis credibilia dixerint; ex
35 litigatoribus, utri gratia magis valuerint. His adiicere si qui volet ea, quae divina testimonia vocant, ex responsis, oraculis, ominibus, duplicem sciat esse eorum tractatum; generalem alterum, in quo inter Stoicos et Epicuri sectam secutos pugna perpetua est, regaturne providentia mundus; specialem alterum circa partes divinationis, ut quaeque in quaestionem
36 cadit. Aliter enim oraculorum aliter aruspicum, augurum, coniectorum, mathematicorum fides confirmari aut refelli potest, cum sit rerum ipsarum ratio diversa. Circa eiusmodi quoque instrumenta firmanda vel destruenda multum habet operis oratio, si quae sint voces per vinum, somnum, dementiam

sanctity of their oath, while the arguments are nought but ingenious juggling with the facts. The other party will argue that witnesses are procured by influence, fear, money, anger, hatred, friendship, or bribery, whereas arguments are drawn from nature; in giving his assent to the latter the judge is believing the voice of his own reason, in accepting the
former he is giving credence to another. Such 34
problems are common to a number of cases, and are and will always be the subject of vehement debate. Sometimes there are witnesses on both sides and the question arises with regard to themselves as to which are the more respectable in character, or with regard to the case, which have given the more credible evidence, with regard to the parties to the case, which has brought the greater influence to bear on the
witnesses. If to this kind of evidence anyone should 35
wish to add evidence of the sort known as supernatural, based on oracles, prophecies and omens, I would remind him that there are two ways in which these may be treated. There is the general method, with regard to which there is an endless dispute between the adherents of the Stoics and the Epicureans, as to whether the world is governed by providence. The other is special and is concerned with particular departments of the art of divination, according as they may happen to affect the question at issue.
For the credibility of oracles may be established 36
or destroyed in one way, and that of soothsayers, augurs, diviners and astrologers in another, since the two classes differ entirely in nature. Again the task of establishing or demolishing such evidence as the following will give the orator plenty to do; as for example if certain words have been uttered under

emissae, vel excepta parvulorum indicia, quos pars altera nihil fingere, altera nihil iudicare dictura est.
37 Nec tantum praestari hoc genus potenter, sed etiam, ubi non est, desiderari solet: *Pecuniam dedisti; quis numeravit? ubi? unde? Venenum arguis; ubi emi? a quo? quanti? per quem dedi? quo conscio?* Quae fere omnia pro Cluentio Cicero in crimine veneficii excutit. Haec de inartificialibus quam brevissime potui.

VIII. Pars altera probationum, quae est tota in arte constatque rebus ad faciendam fidem appositis, plerumque aut omnino negligitur aut levissime attingitur ab iis, qui argumenta velut horrida et confragosa vitantes amoenioribus locis desident, neque aliter quam ii, qui traduntur a poetis gustu cuiusdam apud Lotophagos graminis et Sirenum cantu deleniti voluptatem saluti praetulisse, dum laudis falsam imaginem persequuntur, ipsa, propter quam dicitur,
2 victoria cedunt. Atqui cetera, quae continuo magis orationis tractu decurrunt, in auxilium atque ornamentum argumentorum comparantur, nervisque illis, quibus causa continetur, adiiciunt inducti super cor-

[1] *cp.* lx. 167.

the influence of wine, in sleep or in a fit of madness, or if information has been picked up from the mouths of children, whom the one party will assert to be incapable of invention, while the other will assert that they do not know what they are saying. The follow- 37
ing method may not merely be used with great effect, but may even be badly missed when it is not employed. *You gave me the money. Who counted it out? Where did this occur and from what source did the money come? You accuse me of poisoning. Where did I buy the poison and from whom? What did I pay for it and whom did I employ to administer it? Who was my accomplice?* Practically all these points are discussed by Cicero in dealing with the charge of poisoning in the *pro Cluentio.*[1] This concludes my observations upon inartificial proofs. I have stated them as briefly as I could.

VIII. The second class of proofs are wholly the work of art and consist of matters specially adapted to produce belief. They are, however, as a rule almost entirely neglected or only very lightly touched on by those who, avoiding arguments as rugged and repulsive things, confine themselves to pleasanter regions and, like those who, as poets tell, were bewitched by tasting a magic herb in the land of the Lotus-eaters or by the song of the Sirens into preferring pleasure to safety, follow the empty semblance of renown and are robbed of that victory which is the aim of eloquence. And yet those other forms of 2
eloquence, which have a more continuous sweep and flow, are employed with a view to assisting and embellishing the arguments and produce the appearance of superinducing a body upon the sinews, on which the whole case rests; thus if it is asserted

poris speciem: ut, si forte quid factum ira vel metu vel cupiditate dicatur, latius, quae cuiusque adfectus natura sit, prosequamur. Iisdem laudamus, incusamus, augemus, minuimus, describimus, deterremus,
3 querimur, consolamur, hortamur. Sed horum esse opera in rebus aut certis aut de quibus tanquam certis loquimur potest. Nec abnuerim esse aliquid in delectatione, multum vero in commovendis adfectibus; sed haec ipsa plus valent, cum se didicisse iudex putat, quod consequi nisi argumentatione aliaque omni fide rerum non possumus.

4 Quorum priusquam partiamur species, indicandum est esse quaedam in omni probationum genere communia. Nam neque ulla quaestio est, quae non sit aut in re aut in persona; neque esse argumentorum loci possunt nisi in iis, quae rebus aut personis
5 accidunt, eaque aut per se inspici solent aut ad aliud referri; nec ulla confirmatio nisi aut ex consequentibus aut ex repugnantibus, et haec necesse est aut ex praeterito tempore aut ex coniuncto aut ex insequenti petere; nec ulla res probari nisi ex alia potest, eaque sit oportet aut maior aut par aut minor.
6 Argumenta vero reperiuntur aut in quaestionibus, quae etiam separatae a complexu rerum personarumque spectari per se possint, aut in ipsa causa,

that some act has been committed under the influence of anger, fear or desire, we may expatiate at some length on the nature of each of these passions. It is by these same methods that we praise, accuse, exaggerate, attenuate, describe, deter,
complain, console or exhort. But such rhetorical 3
devices may be employed in connexion with matters about which there is no doubt or at least which we speak of as admitted facts. Nor would I deny that there is some advantage to be gained by pleasing our audience and a great deal by stirring their emotions. Still, all these devices are more effective, when the judge thinks he has gained a full knowledge of the facts of the case, which we can only give him by argument and by the employment of every other known means of proof.

Before, however, I proceed to classify the various 4
species of artificial proof, I must point out that there are certain features common to all kinds of proof. For there is no question which is not concerned either with things or persons, nor can there be any ground for argument save in connexion with matters concerning things or persons, which may be considered either by themselves or with reference to something
else; while there can be no proof except such as is 5
derived from things consequent or things opposite, which must be sought for either in the time preceding, contemporaneous with or subsequent to the alleged fact, nor can any single thing be proved save by reference to something else which must be
greater, less than or equal to it. As regards argu- 6
ments, they may be found either in the questions raised by the case, which may be considered by themselves quite apart from any connexion with individual

cum invenitur aliquid in ea non ex communi ratione ductum, sed eius iudicii, de quo cognoscitur, proprium. Probationum praeterea omnium aliae sunt necessariae, aliae credibiles, aliae non repugnantes.
7 Et adhuc omnium probationum quadruplex ratio est, ut vel quia est aliquid, aliud non sit; ut *Dies est, nox non est;* vel quia est aliquid, et aliud sit: *Sol est supra terram, dies est;* vel quia aliquid non est, aliud sit: *Nox non est, dies est;* vel quia aliquid non est, nec aliud sit: *Non est rationalis, nec homo est.* His in universum praedictis partes subiiciam.

IX. Omnis igitur probatio artificialis constat aut signis aut argumentis aut exemplis. Nec ignoro plerisque videri signa partem argumentorum. Quae mihi separandi ratio haec fuit prima, quod sunt paene ex illis inartificialibus; cruenta enim vestis et clamor et livor et talia sunt instrumenta, qualia tabulae, rumores, testes; nec inveniuntur ab oratore,
2 sed ad eum cum ipsa causa deferuntur; altera, quod signa, sive indubitata sunt, non sunt argumenta, quia, ubi illa sunt, quaestio non est, argumento autem nisi in re controversa locus esse non potest; sive dubia, non sunt argumenta sed ipsa argumentis egent.

3 Dividuntur autem in has duas primas species,

things or persons, or in the case itself, when anything is discovered in it which cannot be arrived at by the light of common reason, but is peculiar to the subject on which judgment has to be given. Further, all proofs fall into three classes, necessary, credible,
and not impossible. Again there are four forms of 7
proof. First, we may argue that, because one thing is, another thing is not; as *It is day and therefore not night.* Secondly, we may argue that, because one thing is, another thing is; as *The sun is risen, therefore it is day.* Thirdly, it may be argued that because one thing is not, another thing is; as *It is not night, therefore it is day.* Finally, it may be argued that, because one thing is not, another thing is not; as *He is not a reasoning being, therefore he is not a man.* These general remarks will suffice by way of introduction and I will now proceed to details.

IX. Every artificial proof consists either of indications, arguments or examples. I am well aware that many consider indications to form part of the arguments. My reasons for distinguishing them are twofold. In the first place indications as a rule come under the head of inartificial proofs: for a blood-stained garment, a shriek, a dark blotch and the like are all evidence analogous to documentary or oral evidence and rumours; they are not discovered by the orator, but are given him with the case itself.
My second reason was that indications, if indubitable, 2
are not arguments, since they leave no room for question, while arguments are only possible in controversial matters. If on the other hand they are doubtful, they are not arguments, but require arguments to support them.

The two first species into which artificial proofs 3

quod eorum alia sunt, ut dixi, quae necessaria sunt, alia quae non necessaria.[1] Priora illa sunt quae aliter habere se non possunt, quae Graeci vocant τεκμήρια, quia sunt ἄλυτα σημεῖα, quae mihi vix pertinere ad praecepta artis videntur; nam ubi est
4 signum insolubile, ibi ne lis quidem est. Id autem accidit, cum quid aut necesse est fieri factumve esse aut omnino non potest fieri vel esse factum; quo in causis posito non est lis facti. Hoc genus per omnia
5 tempora perpendi solet. Nam et coisse eam cum viro, quae peperit, quod est praeteriti, et fluctus esse, cum magna vis venti in mare incubuit, quod coniuncti, et eum mori, cuius cor est vulneratum, quod futuri, necesse est. Nec fieri potest, ut ibi messis sit, ubi satum non est, ut quis Romae sit, cum est Athenis, ut sit ferro vulneratus, qui sine
6 cicatrice est. Sed quaedam et retrorsum idem valent, ut vivere hominem qui spirat, et spirare qui vivit. Quaedam in contrarium non recurrent; nec enim, quia movetur qui ingreditur, etiam ingreditur qui
7 movetur. Quare potest et coisse cum viro, quae non peperit, et non esse ventus in mari, cum est fluctus, neque utique cor eius vulneratum esse, qui perit. Ac similiter satum fuisse potest, ubi non

[1] sunt . . . non necessaria *added by Regius.*

may be divided are, as I have already said, those which involve a conclusion and those which do not. The former are those which cannot be otherwise and are called τεκμήρια by the Greeks, because they are indications from which there is no getting away. These however seem to me scarcely to come under the rules of art. For where an indication is irrefutable, there can be no dispute as to facts. This 4
happens whenever there can be no doubt that something is being or has been done, or when it is impossible for it to be or have been done. In such cases there can be no dispute as to the fact. This kind of proof may be considered in connexion with past, present or future time. For example, a woman who is 5
delivered of a child must have had intercourse with a man, and the reference is to the past. When there is a high wind at sea, there must be waves, and the reference is to the present. When a man has received a wound in the heart, he is bound to die, and the reference is to the future. Nor again can there be a harvest where no seed has been sown, nor can a man be at Rome when he is at Athens, nor have been wounded by a sword when he has no scar. Some have the same force when reversed: a man 6
who breathes is alive, and a man who is alive breathes. Some again cannot be reversed: because he who walks moves it does not follow that he who moves walks. So too a woman, who has not been delivered 7
of a child, may have had intercourse with a man, there may be waves without a high wind, and a man may die without having received a wound in the heart. Similarly seed may be sown without a harvest resulting, a man, who was never at Athens, may

fuit messis, nec fuisse Romae, qui non fuit Athenis, nec fuisse ferro vulneratus, qui habet cicatricem.

8 Alia sunt signa non necessaria, quae εἰκότα Graeci vocant; quae etiamsi ad tollendam dubitationem sola non sufficiunt, tamen adiuncta ceteris plurimum valent.
9 Signum vocatur, ut dixi, σημεῖον, quanquam id quidam indicium quidam vestigium nominaverunt, per quod alia res intelligitur, ut per sanguinem caedes. At sanguis vel ex hostia respersisse vestem potest vel e naribus profluxisse: non utique, qui vestem
10 cruentam habuerit, homicidium fecerit. Sed ut per se non sufficit, ita ceteris adiunctum testimonii loco ducitur, si inimicus, si minatus ante, si eodem in loco fuit; quibus signum cum accessit, efficit
11 ut, quae suspecta erant, certa videantur. Alioqui sunt quaedam signa utrique parti communia, ut livores, tumores (nam videri possunt et veneficii et cruditatis) et vulnus in pectore sua manu et aliena perisse dicentibus, in quo est. Haec proinde firma habentur atque extrinsecus adiuvantur.

12 Eorum autem, quae signa sunt quidem, sed non necessaria, genus Hermagoras putat, non esse

never have been at Rome, and a man who has a scar may not have received a sword-wound.

There are other indications or εἰκότα, that is 8
probabilities, as the Greeks call them, which do not involve a necessary conclusion. These may not be sufficient in themselves to remove doubt, but may yet be of the greatest value when taken in conjunction with other indications. The Latin 9
equivalent of the Greek σημεῖον is *signum*, a sign, though some have called it *indicium*, an indication, or *vestigium*, a trace. Such signs or indications enable us to infer that something else has happened; blood for instance may lead us to infer that a murder has taken place. But bloodstains on a garment may be the result of the slaying of a victim at a sacrifice or of bleeding at the nose. Everyone who has a bloodstain on his clothes is not necessarily a murderer. But although such an indication 10
may not amount to proof in itself, yet it may be produced as evidence in conjunction with other indications, such for instance as the fact that the man with the bloodstain was the enemy of the murdered man, had threatened him previously or was in the same place with him. Add the indication in question to these, and what was previously only a suspicion may become a certainty. On the other 11
hand there are indications which may be made to serve either party, such as livid spots, swellings which may be regarded as symptoms either of poisoning or of bad health, or a wound in the breast which may be treated as a proof of murder or of suicide. The force of such indications depends on the amount of extraneous support which they receive.

Hermagoras would include among such indica- 12
tions as do not involve a necessary conclusion, an

virginem Atalantam, quia cum iuvenibus per silvas
vagetur. Quod si receperimus, vereor, ne omnia
quae ex facto ducuntur signa faciamus. Eadem
13 tamen ratione qua signa tractantur. Nec mihi videntur Areopagitae, cum damnaverint puerum cotur-
nicum oculos eruentem, aliud iudicasse quam id
signum esse perniciosissimae mentis multisque malo
futurae, si adolevisset. Unde Spurii Maelii Marcique
Manlii popularitas signum adfectati regni est existi-
14 matum. Sed vereor, ne longe nimium nos ducat
haec via. Nam si est signum adulterae lavari cum
viris, erit et convivere cum adolescentibus, deinde
etiam familiariter alicuius amicitia uti; fortasse
corpus vulsum, fractum incessum, vestem muliebrem
dixerit mollis et parum viri signa, si cui (cum signum
id proprie sit, quod ex eo, de quo quaeritur, natum
sub oculos venit) ut sanguis e caede, ita illa ex im-
15 pudicitia fluere videantur. Ea quoque quae, quia
plerumque observata sunt, vulgo signa creduntur, ut
prognostica. *Vento rubet aurea Phoebe* et *Cornix
plena pluviam vocat improba voce,* si causas ex qualitate

[1] Verg. *G.* i. 431. [2] *ib.* i. 388.

argument such as the following, "Atalanta cannot be a virgin, as she has been roaming the woods in the company of young men." If we accept this view, I fear that we shall come to treat all inferences from a fact as indications. None the less such arguments are in practice treated exactly as if they were
indications. Nor do the Areopagites, when they 13
condemned a boy for plucking out the eyes of quails, seem to have had anything else in their mind than the consideration that such conduct was an indication of a perverted character which might prove hurtful to many, if he had been allowed to grow up. So, too, the popularity of Spurius Maelius and Marcus Manlius was regarded as an indication that they were aiming at supreme
power. However, I fear that this line of reasoning 14
will carry us too far. For if it is an indication of adultery that a woman bathes with men, the fact that she revels with young men or even an intimate friendship will also be indications of the same offence. Again depilation, a voluptuous gait, or womanish attire may be regarded as indications of effeminacy and unmanliness by anyone who thinks that such symptoms are the result of an immoral character, just as blood is the result of a wound: for anything, that springs from the matter under investigation and comes to our notice, may properly
be called an indication. Similarly it is also usual 15
to give the names of signs to frequently observed phenomena, such as prognostics of the weather which we may illustrate by the Vergilian

"For wind turns Phoebe's face to ruddy gold"[1]

and

"The crow
With full voice, good-for-naught, invites the rain."[2]

16 caeli trahunt, sane ita appellentur. Nam si vento rubet luna, signum venti est rubor. Et si, ut idem poeta colligit, densatus et laxatus aer facit, ut sit inde ille avium concentus, idem sentiemus. Sunt autem signa etiam parva magnorum, ut vel haec ipsa cornix; nam maiora minorum esse, nemo miratur.

X. Nunc de argumentis. Hoc enim nomine complectimur omnia, quae Graeci ἐνθυμήματα, ἐπιχειρήματα, ἀποδείξεις vocant, quanquam apud illos est aliqua horum nominum differentia, etiamsi vis eodem fere tendit. Nam enthymema (quod nos commentum sane aut commentationem interpretemur, quia aliter non possumus, Graeco melius usuri) unum intellectum habet, quo omnia mente concepta significat (sed nunc non de eo loquimur); alterum, quo sententiam
2 cum ratione; tertium, quo certam quandam argumenti conclusionem vel ex consequentibus vel ex repugnantibus, quanquam de hoc parum convenit. Sunt enim, qui illud prius epichirema dicant, pluresque invenias in ea opinione, ut id demum, quod pugna constat, enthymema accipi velint, et ideo illud
3 Cornificius contrarium appellat. Hunc alii rhetoricum syllogismum, alii imperfectum syllogismum vocaverunt, quia nec distinctis nec totidem partibus

[1] Verg. *G.* i. 422. [2] v. viii. 5; xiv. 2. *n.*
[3] See v. xiv. 2, VIII. v. 9.

If these phenomena are caused by the state of the atmosphere, such an appellation is correct enough. For if the moon turns red owing to the wind, her 16
hue is certainly a sign of wind. And if, as the same poet infers,[1] the condensation and rarification of the atmosphere causes that "concert of bird-voices" of which he speaks, we may agree in regarding it as a sign. We may further note that great things are sometimes indicated by trivial signs, witness the Vergilian crow; that trivial events should be indicated by signs of greater importance is of course no matter for wonder.

X. I now turn to arguments, the name under which we comprise the ἐνθυμήματα, ἐπιχειρήματα, and ἀποδείξεις of the Greeks, terms which, in spite of their difference, have much the same meaning. For the *enthymeme* (which we translate by *commentum* or *commentatio*, there being no alternative, though we should be wiser to use the Greek name) has three meanings: firstly it means anything conceived in the mind (this is not however the sense of which
I am now speaking); secondly it signifies a proposi- 2
tion with a reason, and thirdly a conclusion of an argument drawn either from denial of consequents or from incompatibles[2]; although there is some controversy on this point. For there are some who style a conclusion from consequents an *epicheireme*, while it will be found that the majority hold the view that an *enthymeme* is a conclusion from incompatibles[3]: wherefore Cornificius styles it a *contrarium* or argument from contraries. Some again call it a rhetorical 3
syllogism, others an incomplete syllogism, because its parts are not so clearly defined or of the same number as those of the regular syllogism, since such

concluderetur; quod sane non utique ab oratore de-
4 sideratur. Epichirema Valgius aggressionem vocat; verius autem iudico, non nostram administrationem sed ipsam rem quam aggredimur, id est argumentum, quo aliquid probaturi sumus, etiamsi nondum verbis explanatum, iam tamen mente conceptum,
5 epichirema dici. Aliis videtur non destinata vel inchoata, sed perfecta probatio hoc nomen accipere, ultima specie; ideoque propria eius appellatio et maxime in usu est posita, qua significatur certa quaedam sententiae comprehensio, quae ex tribus
6 minimum partibus constat. Quidam epichirema rationem appellarunt, Cicero melius ratiocinationem, quanquam et ille nomen hoc duxisse magis a syllogismo videtur. Nam et statum syllogisticum ratiocinativum appellat, exemplisque utitur philosophorum. Et quoniam est quaedam inter syllogismum et epichirema vicinitas, potest videri hoc nomine
7 recte abusus. Ἀπόδειξις est evidens probatio, ideoque apud Geometras γραμμικαὶ ἀποδείξεις dicuntur. Hanc et ab epichiremate Caecilius putat differre solo genere conclusionis et esse apodixin imperfectum epichirema eadem causa, qua diximus enthymema syllogismo distare. Nam et epichirema syllogismi pars est. Quidam inesse epichiremati apodixin putant

---

[1] See III. i. 18. A rhetorician of the reign of Augustus.

[2] The last or lowest species. *cp.* § 56 and VII. i. 23.

[3] *i.e.* the major and minor premisses and the conclusion. See V. xiv. 6 *sqq.*

precision is not specially required by the orator.
Valgius[1] translates ἐπιχείρημα by *aggressio,* that is 4
an attempt. It would however, in my opinion, be
truer to say that it is not our handling of the
subject, but the thing itself which we attempt which
should be called an ἐπιχείρημα, that is to say the
argument by which we try to prove something and
which, even if it has not yet been stated in so many
words, has been clearly conceived by the mind.
Others regard it not as an attempted or imperfect 5
proof, but a complete proof, falling under the most
special[2] species of proof; consequently, according to
its proper and most generally received appellation it
must be understood in the sense of a definite conception of some thought consisting of at least three
parts.[3] Some call an ἐπιχείρημα a *reason,* but Cicero[4] 6
is more correct in calling it a *reasoning,* although he
too seems to derive this name from the syllogism
rather than anything else; for he calls the
syllogistic basis[5] a *ratiocinative basis* and quotes philosophers to support him. And since there is a certain kinship between a syllogism and an *epicheireme,*
it may be thought that he was justified in his use of
the latter term. An ἀπόδειξις is a clear proof; hence 7
the use of the term γραμμικαὶ ἀποδείξεις, "linear
demonstrations"[6] by the geometricians. Caecilius
holds that it differs from the *epicheireme* solely in the
kind of conclusion arrived at and that an *apodeixis* is
simply an incomplete *epicheireme* for the same reason
that we said an enthymeme differed from a syllogism.
For an *epicheireme* is also part of a syllogism. Some
think that an *apodeixis* is portion of an *epicheireme,*

[4] *de Inv.* I. xxxi. 34. [5] See III. vi. 43, 46, 51.
[6] See I. x. 38.

8 et esse partem eius confirmantem. Utrumque autem quanquam diversi auctores eodem modo finiunt, ut sit ratio per ea, quae certa sunt, fidem dubiis adferens; quae natura est omnium argumentorum, neque enim certa incertis declarantur. Haec omnia generaliter πίστεις appellant, quod etiamsi propria interpretatione dicere fidem possumus, apertius tamen probationem interpretabimur. Sed
9 argumentum quoque plura significat. Nam et fabulae ad actum scenarum compositae argumenta dicuntur, et orationum Ciceronis velut thema ipse exponens Pedianus, *Argumentum,* inquit, *tale est;* et ipse Cicero ad Brutum ita scribit: *Veritus fortasse, ne nos in Catonem nostrum transferremus illinc aliquid, etsi argumentum simile non erat.* Quo apparet omnem ad
10 scribendum destinatam materiam ita appellari. Nec mirum, cum id inter opifices quoque vulgatum sit, unde Vergilius, *Argumentum ingens;* vulgoque paulo numerosius opus dicitur argumentosum. Sed nunc de eo dicendum argumento est, quod probationem praestat. Celsus quidem probationem,[1] indicium, fidem, aggressionem eiusdem rei nomina facit, parum
11 distincte, ut arbitror. Nam probatio et fides efficitur non tantum per haec quae sunt rationis, sed etiam per inartificialia. Signum autem, quod ille indicium vocat, ab argumentis iam separavi. Ergo, cum sit

[1] praestat . . . probationem, *added by Meister.*

[1] In some letter now lost.
[2] *Aen.* vii. 791, with reference to the design on the shield of Turnus. [3] v. ix. 2.

namely the part containing the proof. But all 8
authorities, however much they may differ on other points, define both in the same way, in so far as they call both a method of proving what is not certain by means of what is certain. Indeed this is the nature of all arguments, for what is certain cannot be proved by what is uncertain. To all these forms of argument the Greeks give the name of πίστεις, a term which, though the literal translation is *fides* "a warrant of credibility," is best translated by *probatio* "proof." But *argument* has several other meanings. 9
For the plots of plays composed for acting in the theatre are called arguments, while Pedianus, when explaining the themes of the speeches of Cicero, says *The argument is as follows.* Cicero[1] himself in writing to Brutus says, *Fearing that I might transfer something from that source to my Cato, although the argument is quite different.* It is thus clear that all subjects for writing are so called. Nor is this to be 10
wondered at, since the term is also in common use among artists; hence the Vergilian phrase *A mighty argument.*[2] Again a work which deals with a number of different themes is called "rich in argument." But the sense with which we are now concerned is that which provides proof. Celsus indeed treats the terms, proof, indication, credibility, attempt, simply as different names for the same things, in which, to my thinking, he betrays a certain confusion of thought. For proof and credibility are not 11
merely the result of logical processes, but may equally be secured by inartificial arguments. Now I have already[3] distinguished signs or, as he prefers to call them, indications from arguments. Consequently, since an argument is a process of reasoning

argumentum ratio probationem praestans, qua colligitur aliud per aliud, et quae quod est dubium per id quod dubium non est confirmat, necesse est esse
12 aliquid in causa, quod probatione non egeat. Alioqui nihil erit quo probemus, nisi fuerit quod aut sit verum aut videatur, ex quo dubiis fides fiat. Pro certis autem habemus primum, quae sensibus percipiuntur, ut quae videmus, audimus, qualia sunt signa; deinde ea, in quae communi opinione consensum est, deos
13 esse, praestandam pietatem parentibus; praeterea, quae legibus cauta sunt, quae persuasione etiamsi non omnium hominum, eius tamen civitatis aut gentis, in qua res agitur, in mores recepta sunt, ut pleraque in iure non legibus sed moribus constant; si quid inter utramque partem convenit, si quid probatum est, denique cuicunque adversarius non contradicit.
14 Sic enim fiet argumentum, *Cum providentia mundus regatur, administranda respublica est*[1]*; sequitur ut administranda respublica sit, si liquebit mundum providentia*
15 *regi.* Debet etiam nota esse recte argumenta tractaturo vis et natura omnium rerum, et quid quaeque earum plerumque efficiat; hinc enim sunt, quae εἰκότα di-
16 cuntur. Credibilium autem genera sunt tria: unum firmissimum, quia fere accidit, ut liberos a parentibus

[1] est . . . respublica, *added by Halm after Regius.*

which provides proof and enables one thing to be inferred from another and confirms facts which are uncertain by reference to facts which are certain, there must needs be something in every case which requires no proof. Otherwise there will be nothing 12
by which we can prove anything; there must be something which either is or is believed to be true, by means of which doubtful things may be rendered credible. We may regard as certainties, first, those things which we perceive by the senses, things for instance that we hear or see, such as signs or indications; secondly, those things about which there is general agreement, such as the existence of the gods
or the duty of loving one's parents; thirdly, those 13
things which are established by law or have passed into current usage, if not throughout the whole world, at any rate in the nation or state where the case is being pleaded—there are for instance many rights which rest not on law, but on custom; finally, there are the things which are admitted by either party, and whatever has already been proved or is
not disputed by our adversary. Thus for instance it 14
may be argued that since the world is governed by providence, the state should similarly be governed by some controlling power: it follows that the state must be so governed, once it is clear that the world
is governed by providence. Further, the man who is 15
to handle arguments correctly must know the nature and meaning of everything and their usual effects. For it is thus that we arrive at probable arguments
or εἰκότα as the Greeks call them. With regard to 16
credibility there are three degrees. First, the highest, based on what usually happens, as for instance the assumption that children are loved by

amari; alterum velut propensius, eum qui recte valeat in crastinum perventurum; tertium tantum non repugnans, in domo furtum factum ab eo qui domi fuit.
17 Ideoque Aristoteles in secundo de Arte Rhetorica libro diligentissime est exsecutus, quid cuique rei et quid cuique homini soleret accidere, et quas res quosque homines quibus rebus aut hominibus vel conciliasset vel alienasset ipsa natura: ut divitias quid sequatur aut ambitum aut superstitionem, quid boni probent, quid mali petant, quid milites, quid rustici, quo quaeque modo res vitari vel appeti soleat.
18 Verum hoc exsequi mitto; non enim longum tantum, sed etiam impossibile aut potius infinitum est, praeterea positum in communi omnium intellectu. Si quis tamen desideraverit, a quo peteret, ostendi.
19 Omnia autem credibilia, in quibus pars maxima consistit argumentationis, ex huiusmodi fontibus fluunt: an credibile sit a filio patrem occisum, incestum cum filia commissum; et contra, veneficium in noverca, adulterium in luxurioso; illa quoque, an scelus palam factum, an falsum propter exiguam summam, quia suos quidque horum velut mores habet, plerumque

[1] 1–17.

their parents. Secondly, there is the highly probable, as for instance the assumption that a man in the enjoyment of good health will probably live till to-morrow. The third degree is found where there is nothing absolutely against an assumption, such as that a theft committed in a house was the work of one of the household. Consequently 17
Aristotle in the second book of his *Rhetoric*[1] has made a careful examination of all that commonly happens to things and persons, and what things and persons are naturally adverse or friendly to other things or persons, as for instance, what is the natural result of wealth or ambition or superstition, what meets with the approval of good men, what is the object of a soldier's or a farmer's desires, and by what means everything is sought or shunned. For 18
my part I do not propose to pursue this subject. It is not merely a long, but an impossible or rather an infinite task; moreover it is within the compass of the common understanding of mankind. If, however, anyone wishes to pursue the subject, I have indicated where he may apply. But all credibility, 19
and it is with credibility that the great majority of arguments are concerned, turns on questions such as the following: whether it is credible that a father has been killed by his son, or that a father has committed incest with his daughter, or to take questions of an opposite character, whether it is credible that a stepmother has poisoned her stepchild, or that a man of luxurious life has committed adultery; or again whether a crime has been openly committed, or false evidence given for a small bribe, since each of these crimes is the result of a special cast of character as a rule, though not always; if it were

tamen, non semper; alioqui indubitata essent, non
argumenta.

20 Excutiamus nunc argumentorum locos; quanquam
quibusdam hi quoque, de quibus supra dixi, videntur.
Locos appello non, ut vulgo nunc intelliguntur, in
luxuriam et adulterium et similia; sed sedes argumentorum, in quibus latent, ex quibus sunt petenda.
21 Nam, ut in terra non omni generantur omnia, nec
avem aut feram reperias, ubi quaeque nasci aut
morari soleat ignarus, et piscium quoque genera alia
planis gaudent alia saxosis, regionibus etiam litori-
busque discreta sunt, nec helopem nostro mari aut
scarum ducas, ita non omne argumentum undique
22 venit ideoque non passim quaerendum est. Multus
alioqui error est; exhausto labore, quod non ratione
scrutabimur, non poterimus invenire nisi casu. At
si scierimus, ubi quodque nascatur, cum ad locum
ventum erit, facile quod in eo est pervidebimus.

23 In primis igitur argumenta a persona ducenda
sunt; cum sit, ut dixi, divisio, ut omnia in haec duo
partiamur, res atque personas, ut causa, tempus,
locus, occasio, instrumentum, modus et cetera, rerum

---

[1] In previous chapter.
[2] See II. iv. 22, v. xii. 6 and xiii. 57.
[3] v. viii. 4.

always so, there would be no room for doubt, and no argument.

20 Let us now turn to consider the "places" of arguments, although some hold that they are identical with the topics which I have already discussed above.[1] But I do not use this term in its usual acceptance, namely, commonplaces[2] directed against luxury, adultery, and the like, but in the sense of the secret places where arguments reside, and from
which they must be drawn forth. 21
For just as all kinds of produce are not provided by every country, and as you will not succeed in finding a particular bird or beast, if you are ignorant of the localities where it has its usual haunts or birthplace, as even the various kinds of fish flourish in different surroundings, some preferring a smooth and others a rocky bottom, and are found on different shores and in divers regions (you will for instance never catch a sturgeon or wrasse in Italian waters), so not every kind of argument can be derived from every circumstance, and consequently our search requires
discrimination. 22
Otherwise we shall fall into serious error, and after wasting our labour through lack of method we shall fail to discover the argument which we desire, unless assisted by some happy chance. But if we know the circumstances which give rise to each kind of argument, we shall easily see, when we come to a particular "place," what arguments it contains.

23 Firstly, then, arguments may be drawn from persons; for, as I have already said,[3] all arguments fall into two classes, those concerned with things and those concerned with persons, since causes, time, place, occasion, instruments, means and the like are

sint accidentia. Personis autem non quidquid accidit exsequendum mihi est, ut plerique fecerunt, sed unde
24 argumenta sumi possunt. Ea porro sunt, genus, nam similes parentibus ac maioribus suis plerumque creduntur, et nonnunquam ad honeste turpiterque vivendum inde causae fluunt; natio, nam et gentibus proprii mores sunt, nec idem in barbaro, Romano,
25 Graeco probabile est; patria, quia similiter etiam civitatum leges, instituta, opiniones habent differentiam; sexus, ut latrocinium facilius in viro, veneficium in femina credas; aetas, quia aliud aliis annis magis convenit; educatio et disciplina, quoniam refert, a quibus et quo quisque modo sit institutus;
26 habitus corporis, ducitur enim frequenter in argumentum species libidinis, robur petulantiae, his contraria in diversum; fortuna, neque enim idem credibile est in divite ac paupere, propinquis amicis clientibus abundante et his omnibus destituto; condicionis etiam distantia, nam clarus an obscurus, magistratus an privatus, pater an filius, civis an peregrinus, liber an servus, maritus an caelebs, parens liberorum an orbus sit, plurimum distat;
27 animi natura, etenim avaritia, iracundia, misericordia, crudelitas, severitas aliaque his similia adferunt frequenter fidem aut detrahunt, sicut victus luxuriosus

all accidents of things. I have no intention of
tracing all the accidents of persons, as many have
done, but shall confine myself to those from which
arguments may be drawn. Such are birth, for 24
persons are generally regarded as having some
resemblance to their parents and ancestors, a resemblance which sometimes leads to their living
disgracefully or honourably, as the case may be;
then there is nationality, for races have their own
character, and the same action is not probable in the
case of a barbarian, a Roman and a Greek; country 25
is another, for there is a like diversity in the laws,
institutions and opinions of different states; sex,
since for example a man is more likely to commit a
robbery, a woman to poison; age, since different
actions suit different ages; education and training,
since it makes a great difference who were the instructors and what the method of instruction in each
individual case; bodily constitution, for beauty is 26
often introduced as an argument for lust, strength as
an argument for insolence, and their opposites for
opposite conduct; fortune, since the same acts are
not to be expected from rich and poor, or from one
who is surrounded by troops of relations, friends or
clients and one who lacks all these advantages;
condition, too, is important, for it makes a great
difference whether a man be famous or obscure, a
magistrate or a private individual, a father or a son,
a citizen or a foreigner, a free man or a slave,
married or unmarried, a father or childless. Nor 27
must we pass by natural disposition, for avarice,
anger, pity, cruelty, severity and the like may often
be adduced to prove the credibility or the reverse of
a given act; it is for instance often asked whether a

an frugi an sordidus, quaeritur; studia quoque, nam
rusticus, forensis, negotiator, miles, navigator, medicus
28 aliud atque aliud efficiunt. Intuendum etiam, quid
adfectet quisque, locuples videri an disertus, iustus
an potens. Spectantur ante acta dictaque, ex praeteritis enim aestimari solent praesentia. His adiiciunt quidam commotionem; hanc accipi volunt
temporarium animi motum, sicut iram, pavorem;
29 consilia autem et praesentis et praeteriti et futuri
temporis; quae mihi, etiamsi personis accidunt, per
se referenda tamen ad illam partem argumentorum
videntur, quam ex causis ducimus; sicut habitus
quidam animi, quo tractatur, amicus an inimicus.
30 Ponunt in persona et nomen; quod quidem ei accidere necesse est, sed in argumentum raro cadit, nisi
cum aut ex causa datum est, ut Sapiens, Magnus,
Pius; aut et ipsum alicuius cogitationis attulit
causam, ut Lentulo coniurationis, quod libris Sibyl-
linis aruspicumque responsis dominatio dari tribus
Corneliis dicebatur, seque eum tertium esse credebat
post Sullam Cinnamque, quia et ipse Cornelius erat.
31 Nam et illud apud Euripidem frigidum sane, quod
nomen Polynicis, ut argumentum morum, frater in-
cessit. Iocorum tamen ex eo frequens materia, qua

---

[1] Publius Cornelius Lentulus Sura, Catilinarian conspirator. *cp.* Sall *Cat.* c. 46.

[2] *Phoeniss.* 636. ἀληθῶς δ᾽ ὄνομα Πολυνείκη πατὴρ ἔθετό σοι θείᾳ προνοίᾳ νεικέων ἐπώνυμον, "with truth did our father call thee Polynices with divine foreknowledge naming thee after 'strife.'" [3] See VI. iii. 53.

man's way of living be luxurious, frugal or parsimonious. Then there is occupation, since a rustic, a lawyer, a man of business, a soldier, a sailor, a doctor all perform very different actions. We must also 28
consider the personal ambitions of individuals, for instance whether they wish to be thought rich or eloquent, just or powerful. Past life and previous utterances are also a subject for investigation, since we are in the habit of inferring the present from the past. To these some add passion, by which they mean some temporary emotion such as anger or fear; they also add design, which may refer to the past, 29
present or future. These latter, however, although accidents of persons, should be referred to that class of arguments which we draw from causes, as also should certain dispositions of mind, for example when we inquire whether one man is the friend or enemy of another. Names also are treated as 30
accidents of persons; this is perfectly true, but names are rarely food for argument, unless indeed they have been given for some special reasons, such as the titles of Wise, Great, Pious, or unless the name has suggested some special thought to the bearer. Lentulus[1] for instance had the idea of conspiracy suggested to him by the fact that according to the Sibylline books and the Responses of the soothsayers the tyranny was promised to three members of the Cornelian family, and he considered himself to be the third in succession to Sulla and Cinna, since he too bore the name Cornelius. On the other hand 31
the conceit employed by Euripides[2] where he makes Eteocles taunt his brother Polynices on the ground that his name is evidence of character, is feeble in the extreme. Still a name will often provide the subject for a jest,[3] witness the frequent jests of

Cicero in Verrem non semel usus est. Haec fere circa personas sunt aut his similia. Neque enim complecti omnia vel hac in parte vel in ceteris possumus, contenti rationem plura quaesituris ostendere.

32 Nunc ad res transeo, in quibus maxime sunt personis iuncta, quae agimus, ideoque prima tractanda. In omnibus porro, quae fiunt, quaeritur aut Quare? aut Ubi? aut Quando? aut Quomodo? aut Per quae
33 facta sunt? Ducuntur igitur argumenta ex causis factorum vel futurorum; quarum materiam, quam quidam ὕλην, alii δύναμιν nominaverunt, in duo genera, sed quaternas utriusque dividunt species. Nam fere versatur ratio faciendi circa bonorum adeptionem, incrementum, conservationem, usum, aut malorum evitationem, liberationem, imminutionem, toleran-
34 tiam; quae et in deliberando plurimum valent. Sed honestas[1] causas habent recta, prava contra ex falsis opinionibus veniunt. Nam est his initium ex iis, quae credunt bona aut mala; inde errores existunt et pessimi adfectus, in quibus sunt ira, odium, invidia, cupiditas, spes, ambitus, audacia, metus, cetera generis eiusdem. Accedunt aliquando fortuita, ebrietas, ignorantia, quae interim ad veniam valent, interim ad probationem criminis, ut si quis, dum alii insidia-
35 tur, alium dicitur interemisse. Causae porro non ad convincendum modo, quod obiicitur, sed ad defendendum quoque excuti solent, cum quis se recte

[1] honestas *W. Meyer*: has *B*: haec *A*

Cicero on the name of Verres. Such, then, and the like are the accidents of persons. It is impossible to deal with them all either here or in other portions of this work, and I must content myself with pointing out the lines on which further enquiry should proceed.

I now pass to things: of these actions are the most 32
nearly connected with persons and must therefore be treated first. In regard to every action the question arises either Why or Where or When or How or By what means the action is performed. Consequently 33
arguments are drawn from the causes of past or future actions. The matter of these causes, by some called ὕλη, by others δύναμις, falls into two genera, which are each divided into four species. For the motive for any action is as a rule concerned with the acquisition, increase, preservation and use of things that are good or with the avoidance, diminution, endurance of things that are evil or with escape therefrom. All these considerations carry great weight in deliberative oratory as well. But right actions have 34
right motives, while evil actions are the result of false opinions, which originate in the things which men believe to be good or evil. Hence spring errors and evil passions such as anger, hatred, envy, desire, hope, ambition, audacity, fear and others of a similar kind. To these accidental circumstances may often be added, such as drunkenness or ignorance, which serve sometimes to excuse and sometimes to prove a charge, as for instance when a man is said to have killed one person while lying in wait for another. Further, motives are often discussed not merely to 35
convict the accused of the offence with which he is charged, but also to defend him when he contends

fecisse, id est honesta causa, contendit; qua de re
36 latius in tertio libro dictum est. Finitionis quoque
quaestiones ex causis interim pendent. An tyrannicida, qui tyrannum, a quo deprehensus in adulterio fuerat, occidit? An sacrilegus, qui, ut hostes urbe
37 expelleret, arma templo adfixa detraxit? Ducuntur
argumenta et ex loco. Spectatur enim ad fidem probationis, montanus an planus, maritimus an mediterraneus, consitus an incultus, frequens an desertus, propinquus an remotus, opportunus consiliis an adversus; quam partem videmus vehementissime pro
38 Milone tractasse Ciceronem. Et haec quidem ac
similia ad coniecturam frequentius pertinent, sed interim ad ius quoque: privatus an publicus, sacer an profanus, noster an alienus; ut in persona, magistratus, pater, peregrinus. Hinc enim quaestiones
39 oriuntur: *Privatam pecuniam sustulisti; verum quia de*
templo, non furtum sed sacrilegium est. Occidisti adulterum, quod lex permittit; sed quia in lupanari, caedes est. Iniuriam fecisti; sed quia magistratui, maiestatis
40 *actio est.* Vel contra: *Licuit, quia pater eram, quia*
magistratus. Sed circa facti controversiam argumenta praestant, circa iuris lites materiam quaestionum. Ad qualitatem quoque frequenter pertinet locus,

---

[1] III. xi. 4–9. [2] *pro Mil.* xx.

that his action was right, that is to say proceeded from an honourable motive, a theme of which I have spoken more fully in the third book.[1] Questions 36
of definition are also at times intimately connected with motives. Is a man a tyrannicide if he kills a tyrant by whom he has been detected in the act of adultery? Or is he guilty of sacrilege who tore down arms dedicated in a temple to enable him to drive the enemy from the city? Arguments are also 37
drawn from place. With a view to proving our facts we consider such questions as whether a place is hilly or level, near the coast or inland, planted or uncultivated, crowded or deserted, near or far, suitable for carrying out a given design or the reverse. This is a topic which is treated most carefully by Cicero in his *pro Milone*.[2] These points and the like generally 38
refer to questions of fact, but occasionally to questions of law as well. For we may ask whether a place is public or private, sacred or profane, our own or another's, just as where persons are concerned we ask whether a man is a magistrate, a father, a foreigner. Hence arise such questions as the follow- 39
ing. "You have stolen private money, but since you stole it from a temple, it is not theft but sacrilege." "You have killed adulterers, an act permitted by law, but since the act was done in a brothel, it is murder." "You have committed an assault, but since the object of your assault was a magistrate, the crime is lèse-majesté. Similarly it may be urged in defence, 40
"The act was lawful, because I was a father, a magistrate." But such points afford matter for argument when there is a controversy as to the facts, and matter for enquiry when the dispute turns on a point of law. Place also frequently

neque enim idem ubique aut licet aut decorum est; quin etiam in qua quidque civitate quaeratur interest,
41 moribus enim et legibus distant. Ad commendationem quoque et invidiam valet. Nam et Aiax apud Ovidium: *Ante rates*, inquit, *agimus causam, et mecum confertur Ulixes?* Et Miloni inter cetera obiectum est, quod Clodius in monumentis ab eo maiorum
42 suorum esset occisus. Ad suadendi momenta idem valet, sicut tempus, cuius tractatum subiungam. Eius autem, ut alio loco iam dixi, duplex significatio est; generaliter enim et specialiter accipitur. Prius illud est:—nunc, olim, sub Alexandro, cum apud Ilium pugnatum est, denique praeteritum, instans, futurum. Hoc sequens habet et constituta discrimina:—aestate, hieme, noctu, interdiu; et fortuita:—in pestilentia,
43 in bello, in convivio. Latinorum quidam satis significari putaverunt, si illud generale tempus, hoc speciale tempora vocarent. Quorum utrorumque ratio et in consiliis quidem et in illo demonstrativo genere versatur, sed in iudiciis frequentissima est.
44 Nam et iuris quaestiones facit et qualitatem distinguit et ad coniecturam plurimum confert: ut cum interim

---

[1] *Met.* xiii. 5. Ajax had saved the ships from being burned by the Trojans. The dispute as to whether the arms of Achilles should be awarded to him or to Ulysses is being tried there. Ajax's argument is, "Can you refuse me my due reward on the very spot where I saved you from disaster?"

affects the quality of an action, for the same action is not always lawful or seemly under all circumstances, while it makes considerable difference in what state the enquiry is taking place, for they differ both in custom and law. Further arguments drawn 41 from place may serve to secure approval or the reverse. Ajax for instance in Ovid[1] says:—

"What! do we plead our cause before the ships?
And is Ulysses there preferred to me?"

Again one of the many charges brought against Milo was that he killed Clodius on the monument of his ancestors.[2] Such arguments may also carry 42 weight in deliberative oratory, as may those drawn from time, which I shall now proceed to discuss. Time may, as I have said elsewhere,[3] be understood in two different senses, general and special. The first sense is seen in words and phrases such as "now," "formerly," "in the reign of Alexander," "in the days of the siege of Troy," and whenever we speak of past, present or future. The second sense occurs when we speak either of definite periods of time such as "in summer," "in winter," "by night," "by day," or of fortuitous periods such as "in time of pestilence," "in time of war," "during a banquet." Certain Latin writers have thought it a sufficient 43 distinction to call the general sense "time," and the special "times." In both senses time is of importance in advisory speeches and demonstrative oratory, but not so frequently as in forensic. For questions of law 44 turn on time, while it also determines the quality of actions and is of great importance in questions of fact; for instance, occasionally it provides irrefragable

[2] *pro Mil.* vii. 17. *i.e.* on the Appian Way constructed by one of Clodius' ancestors. [3] III. vi. 25.

probationes inexpugnabiles adferat, quales sunt, si
dicatur (ut supra posui) signator, qui ante diem
tabularum decessit, aut commisisse aliquid, vel cum
45 infans esset vel cum omnino natus non esset; praeter
id, quod omnia facile argumenta aut ex iis, quae ante
rem facta sunt, aut ex coniunctis rei aut insequentibus ducuntur. Ex antecedentibus: *Mortem minatus
es, noctu existi, proficiscentem antecessisti;* causae quo-
46 que factorum praeteriti sunt temporis. Secundum
tempus subtilius quidam, quam necesse erat, diviserunt, ut esset iuncti *Sonus auditus est;* adhaerentis
Clamor sublatus est. Insequentis sunt illa *Latuisti,
profugisti, livores et tumores apparuerunt.* Iisdem temporum gradibus defensor utetur ad detrahendam ei
47 quod obiicitur fidem. In his omnis factorum dicto-
rumque ratio versatur, sed dupliciter. Nam fiunt
quaedam quia aliud postea futurum est, quaedam
quia aliud ante factum est: ut, cum obiicitur reo leno-
cinii, speciosae marito, quod adulterii damnatam quondam emerit; aut parricidii reo luxurioso, quod dixerit
patri, *Non amplius me obiurgabis.* Nam et ille non

[1] v. v. 2.

[2] Both cases are clearly themes from the schools of rhetoric.

proofs, which may be illustrated by a case which I have already cited,[1] when one of the signatories to a document has died before the day on which it was signed, or when a person is accused of the commission of some crime, although he was only an infant
at the time or not yet born. Further, all kinds of 45
arguments may easily be drawn either from facts previous to a certain act, or contemporary or subsequent. As regards antecedent facts the following example will illustrate my meaning; "You threatened to kill him, you went out by night, you started before him." Motives of actions may also belong to
past time. Some writers have shown themselves 46
over-subtle in their classification of the second class of circumstances, making "a sound was heard" an example of circumstances *combined* with an act and "a shout was raised" an instance of circumstances *attached* to an act. As regards subsequent circumstances I may cite accusations such as "You hid yourself, you fled, livid spots and swellings appeared on the corpse." The counsel for the defence will employ the same divisions of time to discredit the
charge which is brought against him. In these 47
considerations are included everything in connexion with words and deeds, but in two distinct ways. For some things are done because something else is like to follow, and others because something else has previously been done, as for instance, when the husband of a beautiful woman is accused of having acted as a procurer on the ground that he bought her after she was found guilty of adultery, or when a debauched character is accused of parricide on the ground that he said to his father "You have rebuked me for the last time."[2] For

quia emit leno est, sed quia leno erat emit; nec hic,
quia sic erat locutus, occidit, sed, quia erat occisurus,
48 sic locutus est. Casus autem, qui et ipse praestat
argumentis locum, sine dubio est ex insequentibus,
sed quadam proprietate distinguitur, ut si dicam:
Melior dux Scipio quam Hannibal; vicit Hannibalem.
Bonus gubernator; nunquam fecit naufragium. Bonus
agricola; magnos sustulit fructus. Et contra: *Sump-*
tuosus fuit; patrimonium exhausit. Turpiter vixit;
49 *omnibus invisus est.* Intuendae sunt praecipueque
in coniecturis et facultates; credibilius est enim
occisos a pluribus pauciores, a firmioribus imbecil-
liores, a vigilantibus dormientes, a praeparatis inopi-
50 nantes; quorum contraria in diversum valent. Haec
et in deliberando intuemur, et in iudiciis ad duas
res solemus referre, an voluerit quis, an potuerit;
nam et voluntatem spes facit. Hinc illa apud Ciceronem coniectura, *Insidiatus est Clodius Miloni, non*
Milo Clodio; ille cum servis robustis, hic cum mulierum
comitatu, ille equis, hic in raeda, ille expeditus, hic pae-
51 *nula irretitus.* Facultati autem licet instrumentum

---

[1] *pro Mil.* x. 29.

in the former case the accused is not a procurer because he bought the woman, but bought her because he was a procurer, while in the latter the accused is not a parricide because he used these words, but used them because he intended to kill his father. With regard to accidental circumstances, 48
which also provide matter for arguments, these clearly belong to subsequent time, but are distinguished by a certain special quality, as for instance if I should say, "Scipio was a better general than Hannibal, for he conquered Hannibal"; "He was a good pilot, for he was never shipwrecked"; "He was a good farmer, for he gathered in huge harvests"; or referring to bad qualities, "He was a prodigal, for he squandered his patrimony"; "His life was disgraceful, for he was hated by all." We must also 49
consider the resources possessed by the parties concerned, more especially when dealing with questions of fact; for it is more credible that a smaller number of persons were killed by a larger, a weaker party by a stronger, sleepers by men that were wide awake, the unsuspecting by the well-prepared, while the converse arguments may be used to prove the opposite. Such considerations arise both in deliber- 50
ative and forensic oratory: in the latter they occur in relation to two questions, namely, whether some given person had the will, and whether he had the power to do the deed; for hope will often create the will to act. Hence the well-known inference in Cicero:[1] "Clodius lay in wait for Milo, not Milo for Clodius, for Clodius had a retinue of sturdy slaves, while Milo was with a party of women; Clodius was mounted, Milo in a carriage, Clodius lightly clad, Milo hampered by a cloak." With resources we may 51

coniungere; sunt enim in parte facultatis et copiae. Sed ex instrumento aliquando etiam signa nascuntur,
52 ut spiculum in corpore inventum. His adiicitur modus, quem τρόπον dicunt, quo quaeritur, quemadmodum quid sit factum. Idque tum ad qualitatem scriptumque pertinet, ut si negemus adulterum veneno licuisse occidere, tum ad coniecturas quoque, ut si dicam bona mente factum, ideo palam; mala, ideo ex insidiis, nocte, in solitudine.

53 In rebus autem omnibus, de quarum vi ac natura quaeritur, quasque etiam citra complexum personarum ceterorumque ex quibus fit causa, per se intueri possumus, tria sine dubio rursus spectanda sunt, *An sit, Quid sit, Quale sit.* Sed, quia sunt quidam loci argumentorum omnibus communes, dividi haec tria genera non possunt, ideoque locis potius, ut in quos-
54 que incurrent, subiicienda sunt. Ducuntur ergo argumenta ex finitione seu fine; nam utroque modo traditur. Eius duplex ratio est; aut enim simpliciter quaeritur, sitne hoc virtus; aut praecedente finitione, quid sit virtus. Id aut universum verbis complectimur, ut *Rhetorice est bene dicendi scientia;* aut per partes, ut *Rhetorice est inveniendi recte et disponendi et eloquendi cum firma memoria et cum dignitate actionis*

[1] See § 40. Also III. v. 4, III. vi. 55 and 66.
[2] See above § 20.

couple instruments, which form part of resources and means. But sometimes instruments will provide us with indications as well, as for instance if we find a javelin sticking in a dead body. To these we may 52
add manner, the Greek τρόπος, in regard to which we ask how a thing was done. Manner is concerned sometimes with quality and the letter of the law[1] (we may for instance argue that it was unlawful to kill an adulterer by poison), sometimes with questions of fact, as for example if I argue that an act was committed with a good intent and therefore openly, or with a bad intent and therefore treacherously, by night, in a lonely place.

In all cases, however, in which we enquire into the 53
nature and meaning of an act, and which can be considered by themselves apart from all considerations of persons and all else that gives rise to the actual cause, there are clearly three points to which we must give attention, namely Whether it is, What it is and Of what kind it is. But as there are certain "places"[2] of argument which are common to all three questions, this triple division is impracticable and we must therefore consider these questions rather in connexion with those "places" in which they most naturally arise. Arguments, then, 54
may be drawn from definition, sometimes called *finitio* and sometimes *finis*. Definition is of two kinds. We may ask whether a particular quality is a virtue or make a definition precede and ask what is the nature of a virtue. Such a definition is either stated in general terms, such as *Rhetoric is the science of speaking well*, or in detail, such as *Rhetoric is the science of correct conception, arrangement and utterance, coupled with a retentive memory and a dignified delivery.*

55 *scientia.* Praeterea finimus aut vi, sicut superiora, aut ἐτυμολογίᾳ, ut si assiduum ab asse[1] dando, et locupletem a locorum, pecuniosum a pecorum copia. Finitioni subiecta maxime videntur genus, species,
56 differens, proprium; ex iis omnibus argumenta ducuntur. Genus ad probandam speciem minimum valet, plurimum ad refellendam. Itaque non, quia est arbor, platanus est, at quod non est arbor, utique platanus non est; nec quod virtus est, utique iustitia est, at quod non est virtus, utique non potest esse iustitia.[2] Itaque a genere perveniendum ad ultimam speciem: ut *Homo est animal* non est satis, id enim genus est; *mortale,* etiamsi est species, cum aliis tamen communis finitio; *rationale,* nihil supererit ad demonstrandum id quod velis.
57 Contra species firmam probationem habet generis, infirmam refutationem. Nam, quod iustitia est, utique virtus est; quod non est iustitia, potest esse virtus, si est fortitudo, constantia, continentia. Nunquam itaque tolletur a specie genus, nisi ut omnes species, quae sunt generi subiectae, removeantur, hoc modo, *Quod nec rationale nec mortale est neque animal,*

[1] asse, *Regius*: aere, *MSS.*
[2] quod virtus . . . at, *omitted by B*: iustitia est . . . est virtus, *omitted by A*: *the missing words are supplied by Victor.*

---

[1] Paulus (exc. Fest.) gives the following explanation of this absurd derivation, for which Cicero tells that Aelius Stilo was responsible: "Some think that *assiduus* was originally

Further, we may define a word by giving its content 55
as in the preceding instances, or by etymology: we may for instance explain *assiduus*[1] by deriving it from *as* and *do*, *locuples*[2] by deriving it from *copia locorum*, *pecuniosus*[3] from *copia pecorum*. *Genus*, *species*, *difference* and *property* seem more especially to afford scope for definition, for we derive arguments from all of these.
Genus is of little use when we desire to prove a 56
species, but of great value for its elimination. A tree is not necessarily a plane tree, but that which is not a tree is certainly not a plane tree; again, a virtue is not necessarily the virtue of justice, but that which is not a virtue is certainly not justice. We must proceed from the *genus* to the ultimate *species*;[4] for example, to say that man is an animal will not suffice; for animal merely gives us the *genus*: nor yet will the addition of the words "subject to death" be adequate; for although this epithet gives us a species, it is common to other animals as well. If, however, we define man as a rational animal, we need nothing further to make our meaning clear.
On the other hand *species* will give us clear proof of 57
genus, but is of little service for its elimination. For example, justice is always a virtue, but that which is not justice may still be a virtue, such as fortitude, constancy or self-control. *Genus* therefore cannot be eliminated by *species* unless all the *species* included in the *genus* be eliminated, as for instance in the following sentence: *That which is neither rational*

the epithet applied to one who served in the army at his own expense, contributing an *as*" (*i.e.* instead of receiving it)!

[2] *locuples* ("wealthy") is derived from *locus* = the possessors of many places.

[3] *pecuniosus* ("moneyed") is derived from *pecus* = "rich in herds."

[4] *cp.* § 5.

58 *homo non est.*[1] His adiiciunt propria et differentia. Propriis confirmatur finitio, differentibus solvitur Proprium autem est aut quod soli accidit, ut homini sermo, risus; aut quidquid utique accidit sed non soli, ut igni calfacere. Et sunt eiusdem rei plura propria, ut ipsius ignis lucere, calere. Itaque, quodcunque proprium deerit, solvit finitionem; non uti-
59 que, quodcunque erit, confirmat. Saepissime autem, quid sit proprium cuiusque, quaeritur: ut, si per ἐτυμολογίαν dicatur, *Tyrannicidae proprium est tyrannum occidere,* negemus; non enim, si traditum sibi eum carnifex occiderit, tyrannicida dicatur, nec si
60 imprudens vel invitus. Quod autem proprium non erit, differens erit, ut aliud est servum esse aliud servire; qualis esse in addictis quaestio solet: *Qui servus est, si manumittatur, fit libertinus, non item*
61 *addictus;* et plura, de quibus alio loco. Illud quoque differens vocant, cum, genere in species diducto, species ipsa discernitur. *Animal* genus, *mortale* species, *terrenum* vel *bipes* differens; nondum enim

[1] quod neque immortale nec mortale est animal non est (*and the like*) *MSS.* : *the text gives the conjecture of Halm.*

---

[1] VII. iii. 26. Also III. vi. 25.

nor mortal nor an animal is not a man. To these they 58
add *property* and *difference.* *Properties* serve to establish definitions, *differences* to overthrow them. A *property* is that which happens to one particular object and that alone; speech and laughter for instance are *properties* of man. Or it may be something specially belonging to an object, but not to it alone; heating for instance is a *property* of fire. The same thing may also have a number of *properties*: light and heat are both *properties* of fire. Consequently, the omission of any *property* in a definition will impair it, but the introduction of a *property*, whatever it may be, will not necessarily establish a
definition. We have, however, often to consider 59
what is a *property* of some given object; for example, if it should be asserted, on the ground of etymology, that the peculiar *property* of a tyrannicide is to kill tyrants, we should deny it: for an executioner is not *ipso facto* a tyrannicide, if he executes a tyrant who has been delivered to him for the purpose, nor again is he a tyrannicide who kills a tyrant unwittingly or
against his will. What is not a *property* will be a 60
difference: it is, for instance, one thing to be a slave, and another to be in a state of servitude; hence the distinction raised in connexion with persons assigned to their creditors for debt: *A slave, if he is manumitted becomes a freedman, but this is not the case with one who is assigned.* There are also other points of
difference which are dealt with elsewhere.[1] Again, 61
the term difference is applied in cases when the *genus* is divided into *species* and one *species* is subdivided. Animal, for instance, is a genus, mortal a *species*, while terrestrial or biped is a *difference*: for they are not actually properties, but serve to show

proprium est sed iam differt a marino vel quadripede; quod non tam ad argumentum pertinet quam ad
62 diligentem finitionis comprehensionem. Cicero genus et speciem, quam eandem formam vocat, a finitione deducit et iis, quae ad aliquid sunt, subiicit: ut, si is, cui argentum omne legatum est, petat signatum quoque, utatur genere; at si quis, cum legatum sit ei, quae viro materfamilias esset, neget deberi ei, quae in manum non convenerit, specie; quoniam
63 duae formae sint matrimoniorum. Divisione autem adiuvari finitionem docet, eamque differre a partitione, quod haec sit totius in partes, illa generis in formas; partes incertas esse, ut Quibus constet respublica; formas certas, ut Quot sint species rerumpublicarum, quas tris accepimus, quae populi, quae pauco-
64 rum, quae unius potestate regerentur. Et ille quidem non iis exemplis utitur, quia scribens ad Trebatium ex iure ducere ea maluit; ego apertiora posui. Propria vero ad coniecturae quoque pertinent partem: ut, quia proprium est boni recte facere, iracundi verbis aut manu male facere, facta haec ab ipsis[1]

[1] male facere, facta haec ab ipsis, *supplied by Halm and Kayser.*

---

[1] Cic. *Top.* iii. 13.

[2] There was the formal marriage *per coemptionem*, bringing the woman under the power (*in manum*) of her husband and giving her the title of *materfamilias*, and the informal marriage based on cohabitation without involving the wife's coming *in manum mariti*.

the difference between such animals and quadrupeds or creatures of the sea. This distinction, however, comes under the province not so much of argument
as of exact definition. Cicero[1] separates *genus* and 62
species, which latter he calls *form*, from definition and includes them under relation. For example, if a person to whom another man has left all his silver should claim all his silver money as well, he would base his claim upon *genus*; on the other hand if when a legacy has been left to a married woman holding the position of *materfamilias*, it should be maintained that the legacy is not due to a woman who never came into the power of her husband, the argument is based on *species*, since there are two
kinds of marriage.[2] Cicero[3] further shows that 63
definition is assisted by *division*, which he distinguishes from *partition*, making the latter the dissection of a whole into its parts and the former the division of a *genus* into its *forms* or *species*. The number of parts he regards as being uncertain, as for instance the elements of which a state consists; the *forms* or *species* are, however, certain, as for instance the number of forms of government, which we are told are three, democracy, oligarchy, and monarchy.
It is true that he does not use these illustrations, 64
since, as he was writing to Trebatius,[4] he preferred to draw his examples from law. I have chosen my illustrations as being more obvious. *Properties* have relation to questions of fact as well; for instance, it is the *property* of a good man to act rightly, of an angry man to be violent in speech or action, and consequently we believe that such acts are committed by persons of the appropriate character, or

[3] Cic. *Top.* v. 17. [4] A famous lawyer, *cp.* III. xi. 18.

esse credantur aut contra. Nam ut quaedam in quibusdam utique sunt, ita quaedam in quibusdam[1] utique non sunt: et ratio, quamvis sit ex diverso, eadem est.

65 Divisio et ad probandum simili via valet et ad refellendum. Probationi interim satis est unum habere, hoc modo, *Ut sit civis, aut natus sit oportet aut factus;* utrumque tollendum est, *Nec natus nec factus*
66 *est.* Fit hoc et multiplex, idque est argumentorum genus ex remotione, quo modo efficitur totum falsum, modo id, quod relinquitur, verum. Totum falsum est hoc modo, *Pecuniam credidisse te dicis; aut habuisti ipse aut ab aliquo accepisti aut invenisti aut surripuisti. Si neque domi habuisti neque ab aliquo accepisti et cetera,*
67 *non credidisti.* Reliquum fit verum sic, *Hic servus, quem tibi vindicas, aut verna tuus est aut emptus aut donatus aut testamento relictus aut ex hoste captus aut alienus;* deinde remotis prioribus supererit alienus. Periculosum et cum cura intuendum genus, quia, si in proponendo unum quodlibet omiserimus, cum risu
68 quoque tota res solvitur. Tutius, quod Cicero pro Caecina facit, cum interrogat, *Si haec actio non sit, quae sit?* simul enim removentur omnia. Vel cum duo ponentur inter se contraria, quorum tenuisse

[1] utique sunt, ita quaedam in quibusdam, *Iulius Victor: omitted by MSS.*

---

[1] *pro Caec.* xiii. 37.

not committed by persons of inappropriate character. For just as certain persons possess certain qualities, so certain others do not possess certain qualities, and the argument is of precisely the same nature, though from opposite premises.

In a similar way *division* is valuable both for proof 65
and refutation. For proof, it is sometimes enough to establish one thing. "To be a citizen, a man must either have been born or made such." For refutation, both points must be disproved : "he was neither born
nor made a citizen." This may be done in many ways, 66
and constitutes a form of argument by elimination, whereby we show sometimes that the whole is false, sometimes that only that which remains after the process of elimination is true. An example of the first of these two cases would be : "You say that you lent him money. Either you possessed it yourself, received it from another, found it or stole it. If you did not possess it, receive it from another, find or steal it,
you did not lend it to him." The residue after elimin- 67
ation is shown to be true as follows: "This slave whom you claim was either born in your house or bought or given you or left you by will or captured from the enemy or belongs to another." By the elimination of the previous suppositions he is shown to belong to another. This form of argument is risky and must be employed with care; for if, in setting forth the alternatives, we chance to omit one, our whole case will fail, and our audience will be moved to laughter.
It is safer to do what Cicero[1] does in the *pro* 68
Caecina, when he asks, "If this is not the point at issue, what is?" For thus all other points are eliminated at one swoop. Or again two contrary propositions may be advanced, either of which if established would suffice

utrumlibet sufficiat, quale Ciceronis est, *Unum quidem certe, nemo erit tam inimicus Cluentio, qui mihi non concedat; si constet corruptum illud esse iudicium, aut ab Habito aut ab Oppianico esse corruptum; si doceo non ab Habito, vinco ab Oppianico; si ostendo ab Oppianico,*
69 *purgo Habitum.* Fit etiam ex duobus, quorum necesse est alterum verum, eligendi adversario potestas, efficiturque, ut, utrum elegerit, noceat. Facit hoc Cicero pro Oppio: *Utrum, cum Cottam appetisset, an cum ipse sese conaretur occidere, telum e manibus ereptum est?* et pro Vareno: *Optio vobis datur, utrum velitis casu illo itinere Varenum usum esse an huius persuasu et inductu.* Deinde utraque facit accusatori contraria.
70 Interim duo ita proponuntur, ut utrumlibet electum idem efficiat, quale est, *Philosophandum est, etiamsi non est philosophandum.* Et illud vulgatum, *Quo schema, si intelligitur? quo, si non intelligitur?* Et, *Mentietur in tormentis, qui dolorem pati potest; mentietur, qui non potest.*

71 Ut sunt autem tria tempora, ita ordo rerum tribus momentis consertus est; habent enim omnia initium, incrementum, summam, ut iurgium deinde pugna,

---

[1] *pro Cluent.* xxiii. 64.

[2] Oppius was accused of embezzling public money and plotting against the life of M. Aurelius Cotta, governor of Bithynia, where Oppius was serving as quaestor. Cicero's defence of him is lost.

to prove the case. Take the following example from Cicero:[1] "There can be no one so hostile to Cluentius as not to grant me one thing: if it be a fact that the verdict then given was the result of bribery, the bribes must have proceeded either from Habitus or Oppianicus: if I show that they did not proceed from Habitus I prove that they proceeded from Oppianicus: if I demonstrate that
they were given by Oppianicus, I clear Habitus." Or 69
we may give our opponent the choice between two alternatives of which one must necessarily be true, and as a result, whichever he chooses, he will damage his case. Cicero does this in the *pro Oppio*:[2] "Was the weapon snatched from his hands when he had attacked Cotta, or when he was trying to commit suicide?" and in the *pro Vareno*:[3] "You have a choice between two alternatives: either you must show that the choice of this route by Varenus was due to chance or that it was the result of this man's persuasion and inducement." He then shows that either admission tells against his opponent.
Sometimes again, two propositions are stated of such 70
a character that the admission of either involves the same conclusion, as in the sentence, "We must philosophise, even though we ought not," or as in the common dilemma, "What is the use of a figure,[4] if its meaning is clear? And what is its use, if it is unintelligible?" or, "He who is capable of enduring pain will lie if tortured, and so will he who cannot endure pain."

As there are three divisions of time, so the order 71
of events falls into three stages. For everything has a beginning, growth and consummation, as for instance

[3] See IV. ii. 26. [4] See VII. iv. 28, IX. i. 14, IX. ii. 65.

tum[1] caedes. Est ergo hic quoque argumentorum locus invicem probantium. Nam et ex initiis summa colligitur, quale est, *Non possum togam praetextam sperare, cum exordium pullum videam;* et contra, non dominationis causa Sullam arma sumpsisse, argumen-
72 tum est dictatura deposita. Similiter ex incremento in utramque partem ducitur rei ratio cum in coniectura tum etiam in tractatu aequitatis, an ad initium summa referenda sit, id est, an ei caedes imputanda sit, a quo iurgium coepit.

73 Est argumentorum locus ex similibus: *Si continentia virtus, utique et abstinentia*; *Si fidem debet tutor, et procurator.* Hoc est ex eo genere, quod ἐπαγωγὴν Graeci vocant, Cicero inductionem. Ex dissimilibus: *Non, si laetitia bonum, et voluptas; Non, quod mulieri, idem pupillo.* Ex contrariis: *Frugalitas bonum, luxuria enim malum; Si malorum causa bellum est, erit emendatio pax; Si veniam meretur, qui imprudens nocuit, non*
74 *meretur praemium, qui imprudens profuit.* Ex pugnantibus: *Qui est sapiens, stultus non est.* Ex consequentibus sive adiunctis: *Si bonum iustitia, est recte iudi-*

[1] pugna, tum, *supplied by Halm.*

---

[1] *de Inv.* i. 31.

[2] It is possible that Quintilian regards *adiuncta* as = *consequentia.* The distinction made above is that made by Cicero, *Top.* xii.

a quarrel, blows, murder. Thus arise arguments which lend each other mutual support; for the conclusion is inferred from the beginnings, as in the following case: "I cannot expect a purple-striped toga, when I see that the beginning of the web is black"; or the beginning may be inferred from the conclusion: for instance the fact that Sulla resigned the dictatorship is an argument that Sulla did not take up arms with the intention of establishing a tyranny.
Similarly from the growth of a situation we may 72
infer either its beginning or its end, not only in questions of fact but as regards points of equity, such as whether the conclusion is referable to the beginning, that is, "Should the man that began the quarrel be regarded as guilty of the bloodshed with which it ended?"

Arguments are also drawn from similarities: "If 73
self-control is a virtue, abstinence is also a virtue." "If a guardian should be required to be faithful to his trust, so should an agent." To this class belongs the type of argument called ἐπαγωγή by the Greeks, *induction* by Cicero.[1] Or arguments may be drawn from unlikes: "It does not follow that if joy is a good thing, pleasure also is a good thing": "It does not follow that what applies to the case of a woman applies also to the case of a ward." Or from contraries: "Frugality is a good thing, since luxury is an evil thing": "If war is the cause of ill, peace will prove a remedy": "If he who does harm unwittingly deserves pardon, he who does
good unwittingly does not deserve a reward." Or 74
from contradictions: "He who is wise is not a fool." Or from consequences necessary or probable[2]: "If justice is a good thing, we must give

candum ; Si malum perfidia, non est fallendum. Idem
retro. Nec sunt his dissimilia ideoque huic loco
subiicienda, cum et ipsa naturaliter congruant: *Quod
quis non habuit, non perdidit ; Quem quis amat, sciens
non laedit ; Quem quis heredem suum esse voluit, carum
habuit, habet, habebit.* Sed cum sint indubitata, vim
75 habent paene signorum immutabilium. Sed haec consequentia dico, ἀκόλουθα ; est enim consequens sapien-
tiae bonitas ; illa insequentia, παρεπόμενα, quae postea
facta sunt aut futura. Nec sum de nominibus anxius ;
vocet enim, ut voluerit quisque, dum vis rerum
ipsa manifesta sit, appareatque hoc temporis, illud
76 esse naturae. Itaque non dubito haec quoque vocare [1]
consequentia, quamvis ex prioribus dent argumentum
ad ea quae sequuntur, quorum duas quidam species
esse voluerunt: actionis, ut pro Oppio, *Quos educere
invitos in provinciam non potuit, eos invitos retinere qui
potuit?* temporis, in Verrem, *Si finem praetoris edicto
adferunt Kalendae Ian., cur non initium quoque edicti*
77 *nascatur a Kalendis Ian.?* Quod utrumque exemplum

[1] vocare, *added by Spalding.*

---

[1] See ch. ix.

[2] *Verr.* I. xlii. 109. The praetor on entering office on Jan. 1 issued an *edict* announcing the principles on which his rulings would be given. This *edict* was an interpretation of

right judgment": "If breach of faith is a bad thing, we must not deceive." And such arguments may also be reversed. Similar to these are the following arguments, which must therefore be classed under this same head, since it is to this that they naturally belong: "A man has not lost what he never had": "A man does not wittingly injure him whom he loves": "If one man has appointed another as his heir, he regarded, still regards and will continue to regard him with affection." However, such arguments, being incontrovertible, are of the nature of absolute indications.[1] These, 75
however, I call *consequent* or ἀκόλουθα; goodness, for instance, is consequent on wisdom: while in regard to things which merely have taken place afterwards or will take place I use the term *insequent* or παρεπόμενα, though I do not regard the question of terminology as important. Give them any name you please, as long as the meaning is clear and it is shown that the one depends on time, the other on the nature of things. I have therefore no hesitation in 76
calling the following forms of argument also *consequential,* although they argue from the past to the future: some however divide them into two classes, those concerned with *action,* as in the *pro Oppio,* "How could he detain against their will those whom he was unable to take to the province against their will?" and those concerned with *time,* as in the *Verrines,*[2] "If the first of January puts an end to the authority of the praetor's edict, why should the commencement of its authority not likewise date from the first of January?" Both these in- 77

the law of Rome, and held good only during the praetor's year of office.

tale est, ut idem in diversum, si retro agas, valeat.
Consequens enim est, eos, qui inviti duci non
78 potuerint, invitos non potuisse retineri. Illa quoque, quae ex rebus mutuam confirmationem prae-
stantibus ducuntur (quae proprii generis videri
quidam volunt et vocant ἐκ τῶν πρὸς ἄλληλα, Cicero
ex rebus sub eandem rationem venientibus) fortiter
consequentibus iunxerim: *Si portorium Rhodiis
locare honestum est, et Hermocreonti conducere,* et
79 *Quod discere honestum, et docere.* Unde illa non hac
ratione dicta sed efficiens idem Domitii Afri sententia est pulchra: *Ego accusavi, vos damnastis.*
Est invicem consequens et quod ex diversis idem
ostendit; ut, qui mundum nasci dicit, per hoc ipsum
et deficere significet, quia deficit omne quod nascitur.

80 Simillima est his argumentatio, qua colligi solent
ex iis quae faciunt ea quae efficiuntur, aut contra,
quod genus a causis vocant. Haec interim necessario fiunt, interim plerumque sed non necessario.
Nam corpus in lumine utique umbram facit, et umbra,
81 ubicunque est, ibi esse corpus ostendit. Alia sunt,
ut dixi, non necessaria, vel utrinque vel ex altera
parte: *Sol colorat; non utique, qui est coloratus, a sole*

---

[1] Ar. *Rhet.* II. xxiii. 3.
[2] *de Inv.* I. xxx. 46. [3] *ib.* 47.

stances are of such a nature that the argument is reversible. For it is a necessary *consequence* that those who could not be taken to the province against their will could not be retained against their will. So too I feel clear that we should rank as 78
consequential arguments those derived from facts which lend each other mutual support and are by some regarded as forming a separate kind of argument, which they[1] call ἐκ τῶν πρὸς ἄλληλα, arguments from things mutually related, while Cicero[2] styles them arguments drawn from things to which the same line of reasoning applies; take the following example[3]: "If it is honourable for the Rhodians to let out their harbour dues, it is honourable likewise for Hermocreon to take the contract," or "What it is honourable to learn, it is also honourable to teach." Such also is the fine sentence of Domitius Afer, 79
which has the same effect, though it is not identical in form: "I accused, you condemned." Arguments which prove the same thing from opposites are also mutually *consequential*; for instance, we may argue that he who says that the world was created thereby implies that it is suffering decay, since this is the property of all created things.

There is another very similar form of argument, 80
which consists in the inference of facts from their efficient causes or the reverse, a process known as argument from causes. The conclusion is sometimes necessary, sometimes generally without being necessarily true. For instance, a body casts a shadow in the light, and the shadow wherever it falls indicates the presence of a body. There are other conclusions 81
which, as I have said, are not necessary, whether as regards both cause and effect or only one of the two. For instance, "the sun colours the skin, but not

est. Iter pulverulentum facit; sed neque omne iter pulverem movet nec, quisquis est pulverulentus, ex itinere
82 *est.* Quae utique fiunt, talia sunt: *Si sapientia bonum virum facit, bonus vir est utique sapiens;* itemque *Boni est honeste facere, mali turpiter;* et *Qui honeste faciunt, boni, qui turpiter, mali iudicantur;* recte. At, *Exercitatio plerumque robustum corpus facit; sed non quisquis est robustus exercitatus, nec quisquis exercitatus robustus; nec, quia fortitudo praestat ne mortem timeamus, quisquis mortem non timuerit, vir fortis erit existimandus; nec, si capitis dolorem facit, inutilis hominibus*
83 *sol est.* Haec ad hortativum maxime genus pertinent: *Virtus facit laudem, sequenda igitur; at voluptas infamiam, fugienda igitur.* Recte autem monemur, causas non utique ab ultimo esse repetendas, ut
84 Medea, *Utinam ne in nemore Pelio;* quasi vero id eam fecerit miseram aut nocentem, quod illic ceciderint *abiegnae ad terram trabes;* et Philocteta Paridi, *Si impar esses tibi, ego nunc non essem miser;* quo modo

[1] The opening of Ennius' translation of the *Medea* of Euripides.
[2] From the *Philoctetes* of Accius, Ribbeck fr. 178.

everyone that is coloured receives that colour from the sun; a journey makes the traveller dusty, but every journey does not produce dust, nor is everyone that is dusty just come from a journey." As examples 82
of necessary conclusions on the other hand I may cite the following: "If wisdom makes a man good, a good man must needs be wise"; and again, "It is the part of a good man to act honourably, of a bad man to act dishonourably," or "Those who act honourably are considered good, those who act dishonourably are considered bad men." In these cases the conclusion is correct. On the other hand, "though exercise generally makes the body robust, not everyone who is robust is given to exercise, nor is everyone that is addicted to exercise robust. Nor again, because courage prevents our fearing death, is every man who has no fear of death to be regarded as a brave man; nor is the sun useless to man because it sometimes gives him a headache." Argu- 83
ments such as the following belong in the main to the hortative department of oratory:—"Virtue brings renown, therefore it should be pursued; but the pursuit of pleasure brings ill-repute, therefore it should be shunned." But the warning that we should not necessarily search for the originating cause is just: an example of such error is provided by the speech of Medea[1] beginning

"Ah! would that never there in Pelion's grove,"

as though her misery or guilt were due to the fact 84
that there

"The beams of fir had fallen to the ground";

or I might cite the words addressed by Philoctetes to Paris,[2]

"Hadst thou been other than thou art, then I
Had ne'er been plunged in woe."

pervenire quolibet retro causas legentibus licet.
85 Illud his adiicere ridiculum putarem, nisi eo Cicero uteretur, quod coniugatum vocant, ut eos, qui rem iustam faciunt, iuste facere (quod certe non eget probatione), quod compascuum est, compascere licere.
86 Quidam haec, quae vel ex causis vel ex efficientibus diximus, alieno nomine vocant ἐκβάσεις id est exitus. Nam nec hic aliud tractatur quam quid ex quoque eveniat.

Adposita vel comparativa dicuntur, quae minora ex maioribus, maiora ex minoribus, paria ex paribus
87 probant. Confirmatur coniectura ex maiore, *Si quis sacrilegium facit, faciet et furtum;* ex minore, *Qui facile ac palam mentitur, peierabit;* ex pari, *Qui ob rem iudicandam pecuniam accepit, et ob dicendum falsum*
88 *testimonium accipiet.* Iuris confirmatio huiusmodi est: ex maiore, *Si adulterum occidere licet, et loris caedere;* ex minore, *Si furem nocturnum occidere licet, quid latronem?* ex pari, *Quae poena adversus interfectorem patris iusta est, eadem adversus matris;* quorum
89 omnium tractatus versatur in syllogismis. Illa magis

---

[1] *Top.* iii. 12. [2] See III. vi. 15, 43, 88.

By tracing back causes on lines such as these we may arrive anywhere. But for the fact that Cicero[1] 85
has done so, I should regard it as absurd to add to these what is styled the *conjugate* argument, such as "Those who perform a just act, act justly," a self-evident fact requiring no proof; or again, "Every man has a common right to send his cattle to graze in a common pasture." Some call these arguments 86
derived from causes or efficients by the Greek name ἐκβάσεις, that is, results; for in such cases the only point considered is how one thing results from another.

Those arguments which prove the lesser from the greater or the greater from the less or equals from equals are styled *apposite* or *comparative*. A con- 87
jecture as to a fact is confirmed by argument from something greater in the following sentence: "If a man commit sacrilege, he will also commit theft"; from something less, in a sentence such as "He who lies easily and openly will commit perjury"; from something equal in a sentence such as "He who has taken a bribe to give a false verdict will take a bribe to give false witness." Points of law may be 88
proved in a similar manner; from something greater, as in the sentence "If it is lawful to kill an adulterer, it is lawful to scourge him"; from something less, "If it is lawful to kill a man attempting theft by night, how much more lawful is it to kill one who attempts robbery with violence"; from something equal, "The penalty which is just in the case of parricide is also just in the case of matricide." In all these cases we follow the syllogistic method.[2] The following type of argument on the 89
other hand is more serviceable in questions turning

finitionibus aut qualitatibus prosunt, *Si robur corpori-
bus bonum est, non minus sanitas; Si furtum scelus, magis
sacrilegium; Si abstinentia virtus, et continentia; Si
mundus providentia regitur, administranda respublica;
Si domus aedificari sine ratione non potest, quid urbs
universa? Si agenda est*[1] *navalium cura, et armorum.*
90 Ac mihi quidem sufficeret hoc genus, sed in species
secatur. Nam ex pluribus ad unum et ex uno ad
plura (unde est *Quod semel, et saepius*), et ex parte
ad totum et ex genere ad speciem, et ex eo quod
continet ad id quod continetur, aut ex difficilioribus
ad faciliora et ex longe positis ad propiora et ad
omnia, quae contra haec sunt, eadem ratione argu-
91 menta ducuntur. Sunt enim et haec maiora et
minora aut certe vim similem obtinent, quae si
persequamur, nullus erit ea concidendi modus.
Infinita est enim rerum comparatio, iucundiora,
graviora, magis necessaria, honestiora, utiliora.
Sed mittamus plura, ne in eam ipsam, quam vito,
92 loquacitatem incidam. Exemplorum quoque ad haec
infinitus est numerus, sed paucissima attingam. Ex
maiore pro Caecina, *Quod exercitus armatos movet, id
advocationem togatorum non videbitur movisse?* Ex fa-

[1] urbs universa? si agenda est, *Radermacher*: agenda si, *B*: agendas, *A*.

---

[1] See iii. 6 *passim*. [2] xv. 43.

on definition or quality.[1] "If strength is good for the body, health is no less good." "If theft is a crime, sacrilege is a greater crime." "If abstinence is a virtue, so is self-control." "If the world is governed by providence, the state also requires a government." "If a house cannot be built without a plan, what of a whole city?" "If naval stores require careful supervision, so also do arms." I am 90
content to treat this type of argument as a *genus* without going further; others however divide it into *species*. For we may argue from several things to one or from one thing to several; hence arguments such as "What has happened once may happen often." We may also argue from a part to a whole, from *genus* to *species*, from that which contains to that which is contained, from the difficult to the easy, from the remote to the near, and similarly from the opposites of all these to their opposites.
Now all these arguments deal with the greater or 91
the less or else with things that are equal, and if we follow up such fine distinctions, there will be no limit to our division into species. For the comparison of things is infinite; things may be more pleasant, more serious, more necessary, more honourable, more useful. I say no more for fear of falling
into that very garrulity which I deprecate. The 92
number of examples of these arguments which I might quote is likewise infinite, but I will only deal with a very few. As an example of argument from something greater take the following example from the *pro Caecina*[2]: "Shall we suppose that that which alarms whole armies caused no alarm to a peaceful company of lawyers?" As an instance of argument from something easier, take this passage

ciliore in Clodium et Curionem, *Ac vide, an facile fieri*
93 *tu potueris, cum is factus non sit, cui tu concessisti.* Ex difficiliore, *Vide quaeso, Tubero, ut, qui de meo facto non dubitem, de Ligarii audeam dicere.* Et ibi, *An sperandi Ligario causa non sit, cum mihi apud te locus sit etiam pro altero deprecandi?* Ex minore pro Caecina, *Itane scire esse armatos sat est, ut vim factam probes;*
94 *in manus eorum incidere non est satis?* Ergo, ut breviter contraham summam, ducuntur argumenta a personis, causis, locis, tempore (cuius tres partes diximus, praecedens, coniunctum, insequens), facultatibus (quibus instrumentum subiecimus), modo (id est, ut quidque sit factum), finitione, genere, specie, differentibus, propriis, remotione, divisione, initio, incrementis, summa, similibus, dissimilibus, pugnantibus, consequentibus, efficientibus, effectis, eventis, comparatione, quae in plures diducitur species.

95 Illud adiiciendum videtur, duci argumenta non a confessis tantum sed etiam a fictione, quod Graeci καθ' ὑπόθεσιν vocant; et quidem ex omnibus iisdem

[1] A lost speech of Cicero, to which reference is made in III. vii. 2.

[2] *pro Lig.* iii. 8 and x. 31. Cicero's point is that he has been a much more bitter opponent of Caesar than Ligarius, and yet he has been pardoned while Ligarius has not.

[3] xvi. 45. Caecina had attempted to take possession of lands left him by will, but was driven off by armed force. Cicero has just pointed out that there were precedents for

from the speech against Clodius and Curio[1]: "Consider whether it would have been easy for you to secure the praetorship, when he in whose favour you withdrew failed to secure election?" The fol- 93
lowing[2] provides an example of argument from something more difficult: "I beg you, Tubero, to remark that I, who do not hesitate to speak of my own deed, venture to speak of that performed by Ligarius"; and again, "Has not Ligarius reason for hope, when I am permitted to intercede with you for another?" For an argument drawn from something less take this passage from the *pro Caecina*[3]: "Really! Is the knowledge that the men were armed sufficient to prove that violence was offered, and the fact that he fell into their hands insufficient?" Well, then, to give a brief 94
summary of the whole question, arguments are drawn from persons, causes, place and time (which latter we have divided into preceding, contemporary and subsequent), from resources (under which we include instruments), from manner (that is, how a thing has been done), from definition, genus, species, difference, property, elimination, division, beginnings, increase, consummation, likes, unlikes, contradictions, consequents, efficients, effects, results, and comparison, which is subdivided into several species.

I think I should also add that arguments are 95
drawn not merely from admitted facts, but from fictitious suppositions, which the Greeks style καθ' ὑπόθεσιν, and that this latter type of argument falls into all the same divisions as those which I have

regarding the mere sight of armed men in occupation of the property claimed as sufficient proof of violence.

locis, quibus superiora, quia totidem species esse pos-
96 sunt fictae quot verae. Nam fingere hoc loco hoc est proponere aliquid, quod, si verum sit, aut solvat quaestionem aut adiuvet; deinde id, de quo quaeritur, facere illi simile. Id quo facilius accipiant iuvenes nondum scholam egressi, primo familiaribus
97 magis ei aetati exemplis ostendam. Lex: *Qui parentes non aluerit, vinciatur.* Non alit aliquis, et vincula nihilominus recusat. Utitur fictione, si miles, si infans sit, si reipublicae causa absit. Et illa contra optionem fortium, si tyrannidem petas, si templorum
98 eversionem. Plurimum ea res virium habet contra scriptum. Utitur his Cicero pro Caecina, *unde tu aut familia aut procurator tuus. Si me villicus tuus solus deiecisset—Si vero ne habeas quidem servum praeter eum, qui me deiecerit,* et alia in eodem libro plurima.
99 Verum eadem fictio valet et ad qualitates: *Si Catilina*

[1] *cp.* VII. v. 4.

[2] xix. 55. Quintilian merely quotes fragments of Cicero's arguments. The sense of the passages omitted is supplied in brackets. The interdict of the praetor had ordered Caecina's restoration. His adversary is represented by Cicero as attempting to evade compliance by verbal quibbles.

[3] *pro Mur.* xxxix. 83. Cicero argues that Murena's election as consul is necessary to save the state from Catiline. If the jury now condemn him, they will be doing exactly what Catiline and his accomplices, now in arms in Etruria, would do if they could try him.

mentioned above, since there may be as many species of fictitious arguments as there are of true arguments. When I speak of fictitious arguments 96
I mean the proposition of something which, if true, would either solve a problem or contribute to its solution, and secondly the demonstration of the similarity of our hypothesis to the case under consideration. To make this the more readily intelligible to youths who have not yet left school, I will first of all illustrate it by examples of a kind familiar to the young. There is a law to the effect that "the 97
man who refuses to support his parents is liable to imprisonment." A certain man fails to support his parents and none the less objects to going to prison. He advances the hypothesis that he would be exempt from such a penalty if he were a soldier, an infant, or if he were absent from home on the service of the state. Again in the case where a hero is allowed to choose his reward[1] we might introduce the hypotheses of his desiring to make himself a tyrant or to overthrow the temples of the gods. Such 98
arguments are specially useful when we are arguing against the letter of the law, and are thus employed by Cicero in the *pro Caecina*[2]: "[The interdict contains the words,] 'whence you or your household or your agent had driven him.' If your steward alone had driven me out, [it would not, I suppose, be your household but a member of your household that had driven me out]. . . . If indeed you owned no slave except the one who drove me out, [you would cry, 'If I possess a household at all, I admit that my household drove you out']." Many other examples might be quoted from the same work. But fictitious 99
suppositions are also exceedingly useful when we are concerned with the quality of an act[3]: "If

cum suo consilio nefariorum hominum, quos secum eduxit, hac de re posset iudicare, condemnaret L. Murenam; et ad amplificationem: *Si hoc tibi inter cenam in illis immanibus poculis tuis accidisset.* Sic et, *Si respublica vocem haberet.*

100 Has fere sedes accepimus probationum in universum, quas neque generatim tradere sat est, cum ex qualibet earum innumerabilis argumentorum copia oriatur, neque per singulas species exsequi patitur natura rerum, quod qui sunt facere conati, duo pariter subierunt incommoda, ut et nimium dicerent nec
101 tamen totum. Inde plurimi, cum in hos inexplicabiles laqueos inciderunt, omnem, etiam quem ex ingenio suo poterant habere, conatum velut adstricti certis legum vinculis perdiderunt, et magistrum
102 respicientes naturam ducem sequi desierunt. Nam ut per se non sufficiet scire, omnes probationes aut a personis aut a rebus peti, quia utrumque in plura dividitur, ita ex antecedentibus et iunctis et insequentibus trahenda esse argumenta qui acceperit, num protinus in hoc sit instructus ut, quid in quaque
103 causa ducendum sit ex his, sciat? praesertim, cum plurimae probationes in ipso causarum complexu

[1] *Phil.* II. xxv. 63. "This" = vomiting. Cicero continues "who would not have thought it disgraceful."

[2] Probably an allusion to *Cat.* i. 7, where Cicero makes the state reproach Catiline for his conduct.

Catiline could try this case assisted by a jury composed of those scoundrels whom he led out with him he would condemn Lucius Murena." It is useful also for amplification[1]: "If this had happened to you during dinner in the midst of your deep potations"; or again,[2] "If the state could speak."

Such in the main are the usual topics of proof 100
as specified by teachers of rhetoric, but it is not sufficient to classify them generically in our instructions, since from each of them there arises an infinite number of arguments, while it is in the very nature of things impossible to deal with all their individual species. Those who have attempted to perform this latter task have exposed themselves in equal degree to two disadvantages, saying too much and
yet failing to cover the whole ground. Consequently 101
the majority of students, finding themselves lost in an inextricable maze, have abandoned all individual effort, including even that which their own wits might have placed within their power, as though they were fettered by certain rigid laws, and keeping their eyes fixed upon their master have ceased
to follow the guidance of nature. But as it is not 102
in itself sufficient to know that all proofs are drawn either from persons or things, because each of these groups is subdivided into a number of different heads so he who has learned that arguments must be drawn from antecedent, contemporary or subsequent facts will not be sufficiently instructed in the knowledge of the method of handling arguments to understand what arguments are to be drawn from
the circumstances of each particular case; especially 103
as the majority of proofs are to be found in the special circumstances of individual cases and have

reperiantur, ita ut sint cum alia lite nulla communes, eaeque sint et potentissimae et minime obviae, quia communia ex praeceptis accepimus, propria inveni-
104 enda sunt. Hoc genus argumentorum sane dicamus ex circumstantia, quia περίστασιν dicere aliter non possumus, vel ex iis quae cuiusque causae propria sunt: ut in illo adultero sacerdote, qui lege, qua unius servandi potestatem habebat, se ipse servare voluit, proprium controversiae est dicere, *Non unum nocentem servabas, quia te dimisso adulteram occidere non licebat.* Hoc enim argumentum lex facit, quae
105 prohibet adulteram sine adultero occidere. Et illa, in qua lata lex est, ut argentarii dimidium ex eo quod debebant solverent, creditum suum totum exigerent. Argentarius ab argentario solidum petit. Proprium ex materia est argumentum creditoris, idcirco adiectum esse in lege, ut argentarius totum exigeret; adversus alios enim non opus fuisse lege, cum omnes praeterquam ab argentariis totum exi-
106 gendi ius haberent. Cum multa autem novantur in omni genere materiae tum praecipue in iis quaestio-

---

[1] This law and those which follow are imaginary laws invented for the purposes of the schools of rhetoric.

[2] The argument is far from clear. The case assumes that by a species of moratorium a banker may be released from payment of his debts in full to ordinary creditors. This moratorium does not however apparently apply to debts contracted between banker and banker.

no connexion with any other dispute, and therefore while they are the strongest, are also the least obvious, since, whereas we derive what is common to all cases from general rules, we have to discover for ourselves whatever is peculiar to the case which
we have in hand. This type of argument may 104
reasonably be described as drawn from circumstances, there being no other word to express the Greek περίστασις, or from those things which are peculiar to any given case. For instance, in the case of the priest who having committed adultery desired to save *his own* life by means of the law [1] which gave him the power of saving *one* life, the appropriate argument to employ against him would run as follows: "You would save more than one guilty person, since, if you were discharged, it would not be lawful to put the adulteress to death." For such an argument follows from the law forbidding the execution of the adulteress apart from the
adulterer. Again, take the case falling under the 105
law which lays down that bankers may pay only half of what they owe, while permitted to recover the whole of what they are owed. One banker requires payment of the whole sum owed him by another banker. The appropriate argument supplied by the subject to the creditor is that there was special reason for the insertion of the clause [2] sanctioning the recovery of the whole of a debt by a banker, since there was no need of such a law as against others, inasmuch as all have the right to recover the whole of a debt from any save a banker.
But while some fresh considerations are bound to 106
present themselves in every kind of subject, this is more especially the case in questions turning on

nibus, quae scripto constant, quia vocum est in singulis ambiguitas frequens et adhuc in coniunctis
107 magis. Et haec ipsa plurium legum aliorumve scrip-
torum vel congruentium vel repugnantium complexu
varientur necesse est, cum res rei aut ius iuris quasi
signum est. *Non debui tibi pecuniam ; nunquam me
appellasti, usuram non accepisti, ultro a me mutuatus es.*
Lex est, *Qui patri proditionis reo non adfuerit, exheres
sit.* Negat filius,[1] nisi si pater absolutus sit. Quid
signi? Lex altera, *Proditionis damnatus cum advocato
108 exulet.* Cicero pro Cluentio Publium Popilium et
Tiberium Guttam dicit non iudicii corrupti sed ambitus esse damnatos. Quid signi? quod accusatores
eorum, qui erant ipsi ambitus damnati, e lege sint
109 post hanc victoriam restituti. Nec minus in hoc
curae debet adhiberi, quid proponendum quam quomodo sit quod proposuerimus probandum. Hic
immo vis inventionis, si non maior, certe prior.
Nam ut tela supervacua sunt nescienti, quid petat,
sic argumenta, nisi provideris cui rei adhibenda sint.
110 Hoc est, quod comprehendi arte non possit. Ideo-

[1] filius, *Spalding*: fit, *MSS.*

---

[1] xxxvi. 98. The *lex Iulia de ambitu* contained a provision that the penalty (loss of civil rights) incurred by conviction for *ambitus* should be annulled if the condemned man could secure the conviction of another person for the same offence.

the letter of the law, since not merely individual words, but still more whole phrases are frequently
ambiguous. And these considerations must vary 107
according to the complexity of laws and other documents, whether they are in agreement or contradictory, since fact throws light on fact and law on law as in the following argument: "I owed you no money: you never summoned me for debt, you took no interest from me, nay, you actually borrowed money from me." It is laid down by law that he who refuses to defend his father when accused of treason thereby loses his right to inherit. A son denies that he is liable to this penalty unless his father is acquitted. How does he support this contention? There is another law to the effect that a man found guilty of treason shall be banished and
his advocate with him. Cicero in the *pro Cluentio*[1] 108
says that Publius Popilius and Tiberius Gutta were not condemned for receiving bribes to give a false verdict, but for attempting to bribe the jury. What is his argument in support of this view? That their accusers, who were themselves found guilty of bribing the jury, were restored in accordance with
law after winning their case. But the consideration 109
as to what argument should be put forward requires no less care than the consideration of the manner in which we are to prove that which we have put forward. Indeed in this connexion invention, if not the most important, is certainly the first consideration. For, just as weapons are superfluous for one who does not know what his target is, so too arguments are useless, unless you see in advance to what they are to be applied. This is a task for
which no formal rules can be laid down. Conse- 110

que, cum plures eadem didicerint, generibus argumentorum similibus utentur; alius alio plura, quibus utatur, inveniet. Sit exempli gratia proposita controversia, quae communes minime cum aliis quaes-
111 tiones habet: *Cum Thebas evertisset Alexander, invenit tabulas, quibus centum talenta mutua Thessalis dedisse Thebanos continebatur. Has, quia erat usus commilitio Thessalorum, donavit his ultro; postea restituti a Cassandro Thebani reposcunt Thessalos.* Apud Amphictyonas agitur. Centum talenta et credidisse eos
112 constat et non recepisse. Lis omnis ex eo, quod Alexander ea Thessalis donasse dicitur, pendet. Constat illud quoque, non esse iis ab Alexandro pecuniam datam; quaeritur ergo, an proinde sit,
113 quod datum est, ac si pecuniam dederit? Quid proderunt argumentorum loci, nisi haec prius videro, nihil eum egisse donando, non potuisse donare, non donasse? Et prima quidem actio facilis ac favorabilis repetentium iure quod vi sit ablatum; sed hinc aspera et vehemens quaestio exoritur de iure belli, dicentibus Thessalis, hoc regna, populos, fines gen-
114 tium atque urbium contineri. Inveniendum contra

quently, though a number of orators, who have studied the same rules, will use similar kinds of arguments, one will discover a greater number of arguments to suit his case than another. Let us take as an example a controversial theme involving problems that have little in common with other
cases. "When Alexander destroyed Thebes, he 111
found documents showing that the Thebans had lent a hundred talents to the Thessalians. These documents he presented to the Thessalians as a reward for the assistance they had given him in the campaign. Subsequently the Thebans, after the restoration of their city by Cassander, demanded that the Thessalians should repay the money." The case is tried before the Amphictyonic council. It is admitted that the Thebans lent the money and
were not repaid. The whole dispute turns on the 112
allegation that Alexander had excused the Thessalians from payment of the debt. It is also admitted that the Thessalians had received no money from Alexander. The question is therefore whether his gift is equivalent to his having given them money.
What use will formal topics of argument be in such 113
a case, unless I first convince myself that the gift of Alexander made no difference, that he had not the power to make it, and that he did not make it? The opening of the Thebans' plea presents no difficulty and is likely to win the approval of the judges, since they are seeking to recover by right what was taken from them by force. But out of this point arises a violent controversy as to the right of war, since the Thessalians urge that kingdoms and peoples and the frontiers of nations and cities
depend upon these rights. To meet this argument 114

est, quo distet haec causa a ceteris, quae in potestatem victoris venirent; nec circa probationem res haeret, sed circa propositionem. Dicamus inprimis: in eo, quod in iudicium deduci potest, nihil valere ius belli nec armis erepta nisi armis posse retineri; itaque, ubi illa valeant, non esse iudicem; ubi iudex
115 sit, illa nihil valere. Hoc inveniendum est, ut adhiberi possit argumentum: ideo captivos, si in patriam suam redierint, liberos esse, quia bello parta nonnisi eadem vi possideantur. Proprium est et illud causae, quod Amphictyones iudicant (ut alia apud centumviros, alia apud privatum iudicem in iisdem quaes-
116 tionibus ratio); tum secundo gradu, non potuisse donari a victore ius, quia id demum sit eius, quod teneat; ius, quod sit incorporale, adprehendi manu non posse. Hoc reperire est difficilius quam, cum inveneris, argumentis adiuvare, ut alia sit condicio heredis, alia victoris, quia ad illum ius, ad hunc res
117 transeat. Proprium deinde materiae, ius publici

[1] *cp.* § 118. The Amphictyonic Council of Delphi in the fourth century B.C. had come to be an international council, in which the great majority of the states of Greece were represented.

[2] *i.e.* a right can only be transferred by the possessor, not by force or seizure.

it is necessary to discover in what respect this case differs from others which are concerned with property that has fallen into the hands of the victor: the difficulty moreover lies not so much in the proof as in the way it should be put forward. We may begin by stating that the rights of war do not hold good in any matter which can be brought before a court of justice, and that what is taken by force of arms can only be retained by force of arms, and consequently, wherever the rights of war hold good, there is no room for the functions of a judge, while on the contrary where the functions of the judge come into play, the rights of war cease to have any force. The reason why it is necessary 115
to discover this principle is to enable us to bring the following argument into play: that prisoners of war are free on returning to their native land just because the gains of war cannot be retained except by the exercise of the same violence by which they were acquired. Another peculiar feature of the case is that it is tried before the Amphictyonic council,[1] and you will remember that we have to employ different methods in pleading a case before the centumviral court and before an arbitrator, though the problems of the cases may be identical. Secondly 116
we may urge that the right to refuse payment could not have been conferred by the victor because he possesses only what he holds, but a right, being incorporeal, cannot be grasped by the hand.[2] It is more difficult to discover this principle than, once discovered, to defend it with arguments such as that the position of an heir and a conqueror are fundamentally different, since right passes to the one and property to the other. It is further an 117

crediti transire ad victorem non potuisse, quia, quod populus crediderit, omnibus debeatur, et, quamdiu quilibet unus superfuerit, esse eum totius summae creditorem, Thebanos autem non omnes in Alex-
118 andri manu fuisse. Hoc non extrinsecus probatur, quae vis est argumenti, sed ipsum per se valet. Tertii loci pars prior magis vulgaris, non in tabulis esse ius; itaque multis argumentis defendi potest. Mens quoque Alexandri duci debet in dubium, honorarit eos an deceperit. Illud iam rursus proprium materiae et velut novae controversiae, quia restitutione recepisse ius, etiamsi quod amiserint, Thebani videntur. Hic et, quid Cassander velit, quaeritur; sed vel potentissima apud Amphictyonas aequi tractatio est.

119 Haec non idcirco dico, quod inutilem horum locorum, ex quibus argumenta ducuntur, cognitionem putem, alioqui nec tradidissem; sed ne se, qui cognoverint ista, si cetera negligant, perfectos protinus atque consummatos putent et, nisi in ceteris, quae

[1] See v. x. 20.

argument peculiar to the subject matter of the case that the right over a public debt could not have passed to the victor, because the repayment of a sum of money lent by a whole people is due to them all, and as long as any single one of them survives, he is creditor for the whole amount: but the Thebans were never all of them to a man in Alexander's power. The force of this argument resides 118
in the fact that it is not based on any external support, but holds good in itself. Proceeding to the third line of argument we may note that the first portion of it is of a more ordinary type, namely that the right to repayment is not based on the actual document, a plea which can be supported by many arguments. Doubt may also be thrown on Alexander's purpose: did he intend to honour them or to trick them? Another argument peculiar to the subject (indeed it practically introduces a new discussion) is that the Thebans may be regarded as having in virtue of their restoration recovered the right even though it be admitted that they had lost it. Again Cassander's purpose may be discussed, but, as the case is being pleaded before the Amphictyonic council, we shall find that the most powerful plea that can be urged is that of equity.

I make these remarks, not because I think that a 119
knowledge of the "places"[1] from which arguments may be derived is useless (had I thought so, I should have passed them by) but to prevent those who have learnt these rules from neglecting other considerations and regarding themselves as having a perfect and absolute knowledge of the whole subject, and to make them realise that, unless they acquire a thorough knowledge of the

mox praecipienda sunt, elaboraverint, mutam quan-
120 dam scientiam consecutos intelligant. Neque enim artibus editis factum est, ut argumenta inveniremus, sed dicta sunt omnia, antequam praeciperentur, mox ea scriptores observata et collecta ediderunt. Cuius rei probatio est, quod exemplis eorum veteribus utuntur et ab oratoribus illa repetunt, ipsi nullum
121 novum et quod dictum non sit inveniunt. Artifices ergo illi qui dixerunt; sed habenda his quoque gratia est, per quos labor nobis est detractus. Nam, quae priores beneficio ingenii singula invenerunt, nobis et non sunt requirenda et notata[1] sunt omnia. Sed non magis hoc sat est quam palaestram didicisse, nisi corpus exercitatione, continentia, cibis, ante omnia natura iuvatur, sicut contra ne illa qui-
122 dem satis sine arte profuerint. Illud quoque studiosi eloquentiae cogitent, neque omnibus in causis, quae demonstravimus, cuncta posse reperiri; neque, cum proposita fuerit materia dicendi, scrutanda singula et velut ostiatim pulsandum,[2] ut sciant, an ad probandum id, quod intendimus, forte respondeant, nisi
123 cum discunt et adhuc usu carent. Infinitam enim faciat ista res dicendi tarditatem, si semper necesse

[1] notata, *Guelferbytanus* : notat, *B* : notant, *A*.
[2] pulsandum, *Francius* : pulsanda, *MSS*.

remaining points which I am about to discuss, they will be the possessors of what I can only call a dumb
science. For the discovery of arguments was not 120
the result of the publication of text-books, but every kind of argument was put forward before any rules were laid down, and it was only later that writers of rhetoric noted them and collected them for publication. A proof of this is the fact that the examples which they use are old and quoted from the orators, while they themselves discover nothing new
or that has not been said before. The creators of 121
the art were therefore the orators, though we owe a debt of gratitude also to those who have given us a short cut to knowledge. For thanks to them the arguments discovered by the genius of earlier orators have not got to be hunted out and noted down in detail. But this does not suffice to make an orator any more than it suffices to learn the art of gymnastic in school: the body must be assisted by continual practice, self-control, diet and above all by nature; on the other hand none of these are sufficient in
themselves without the aid of art. I would also 122
have students of oratory consider that all the forms of argument which I have just set forth cannot be found in every case, and that when the subject on which we have to speak has been propounded, it is no use considering each separate type of argument and knocking at the door of each with a view to discovering whether they may chance to serve to prove our point, except while we are in the position of mere learners without any knowledge of actual
practice. Such a proceeding merely retards the 123
process of speaking to an incalculable extent, if it is always necessary for us to try each single

sit, ut temptantes unumquodque eorum, quod sit aptum atque conveniens, experiendo noscamus; nescio an etiam impedimento futura sint, nisi et animi quaedam ingenita natura et studio exercitata velocitas recta nos ad ea, quae conveniunt causae, ferant.

124 Nam, ut cantus vocis plurimum iuvat sociata nervorum concordia, si tamen tardior manus nisi inspectis demensisque singulis, quibus quaeque vox fidibus iungenda sit, dubitet, potius fuerit esse contentum eo, quod simplex canendi natura tulerit, ita huiusmodi praeceptis debet quidem aptata esse et citharae

125 modo intenta ratio doctrinae; sed hoc exercitatione multa consequendum, ut, quemadmodum illorum artificum, etiamsi alio spectant, manus tamen ipsa consuetudine ad graves, acutos, medios nervorum[1] sonos fertur, sic oratoris cognitionem nihil moretur haec varietas argumentorum et copia, sed quasi offerat se et occurrat, et, ut litterae syllabaeque scribentium cogitationem non exigunt, sic rationem sponte quadam sequantur.

XI. Tertium genus ex iis, quae extrinsecus adducuntur in causam, Graeci vocant παράδειγμα, quo nomine et generaliter usi sunt in omni similium adpositione et specialiter in iis, quae rerum gestarum auctoritate nituntur. Nostri fere similitudinem vocari maluerunt, quod ab illis παραβολὴ dicitur, alterum exemplum, quanquam et hoc simile est et illud

[1] nervorum, *Gertz* : horum, *MSS.*

argument and thus learn by experiment what is apt and suitable to our case. In fact I am not sure that it will not be an actual obstacle to progress unless a certain innate penetration and a power of rapid divination seconded by study lead us straight to the arguments which suit our case. For just as the 124
melody of the voice is most pleasing when accompanied by the lyre, yet if the musician's hand be slow and, unless he first look at the strings and take their measure, hesitate as to which strings match the several notes of the voice, it would be better that he should content himself with the natural music of the voice unaccompanied by any instrument; even so our theory of speaking must be adapted and, like the lyre, attuned to such rules as these. But it is only by constant practice that we 125
can secure that, just as the hands of the musician, even though his eyes be turned elsewhere, produce bass, treble or intermediate notes by force of habit, so the thought of the orator should suffer no delay owing to the variety and number of possible arguments, but that the latter should present themselves uncalled and, just as letters and syllables require no thought on the part of a writer, so arguments should spontaneously follow the thought of the orator.

XI. The third kind of proof, which is drawn into the service of the case from without, is styled a *παράδειγμα* by the Greeks, who apply the term to all comparisons of like with like, but more especially to historical parallels. Roman writers have for the most part preferred to give the name of comparison to that which the Greeks style *παραβολή*, while they translate *παράδειγμα* by example, although this latter involves comparison, while the former is of

2 exemplum. Nos, quo facilius propositum explicemus, utrumque παράδειγμα esse credamus, et ipsi appellemus exemplum. Nec vereor, ne videar repugnare Ciceroni, quanquam collationem separat ab exemplo. Nam idem omnem argumentationem dividit in duas partes, inductionem et ratiocinationem, ut plerique Graecorum in παραδείγματα et ἐπιχειρήματα, dixerunt-
3 que παράδειγμα ῥητορικὴν ἐπαγωγήν. Nam illa, qua plurimum est Socrates usus, hanc habuit viam, ut cum plura interrogasset, quae fateri adversario necesse esset, novissime id, de quo quaerebatur, inferret, ut simile concessis.[1] Id est inductio. Hoc in oratione fieri non potest; sed, quod illic interrogatur, hic
4 fere sumitur. Sit igitur illa interrogatio talis: *Quod est pomum generosissimum? nonne quod optimum?* concedetur. *Quid equus? qui generosissimus? Nonne qui optimus?* et plura in eundem modum. Deinde, cuius rei gratia rogatum est, *Quid homo? Nonne is genero-*
5 *sissimus, qui optimus?* fatendum erit. Hoc in testium interrogatione valet plurimum, in oratione perpetua dissimile est; aut enim sibi ipse respondet orator aut quod illic interrogatur, hic fere sumitur.[2] *Quod*

[1] concessis, *Törnebladh*: concessisse, *MSS.*

[2] aut quod . . . sumitur, *supplied by Meister. Some such phrase must have been lost, but there can be no certainty either as regards the exact words or their precise place.*

the nature of an example. For my own part, I 2
prefer with a view to making my purpose easier of apprehension to regard both as παραδείγματα and to call them examples. Nor am I afraid of being thought to disagree with Cicero, although he does separate comparison from example.[1] For he divides all arguments into two classes, induction and ratiocination, just as most Greeks[2] divide it into παραδείγματα and ἐπιχειρήματα, explaining παράδειγμα
as a rhetorical induction. The method of argument 3
chiefly used by Socrates was of this nature: when he had asked a number of questions to which his adversary could only agree, he finally inferred the conclusion of the problem under discussion from its resemblance to the points already conceded. This method is known as induction, and though it cannot be used in a set speech, it is usual in a speech to assume that which takes the form of a
question in dialogue. For instance take the follow- 4
ing question: "What is the finest form of fruit? Is it not that which is best?" This will be admitted. "What of the horse? What is the finest? Is it not that which is the best?" Several more questions of the same kind follow. Last comes the question for the sake of which all the others were put: "What of man? Is not he the finest type who is best?" The answer can only be in the affirmative.
Such a procedure is most valuable in the examina- 5
tion of witnesses, but is differently employed in a set speech. For there the orator either answers his own questions or makes an assumption of that which in dialogue takes the form of a question. "What is

[1] *de Inv.* I. xxx. 49.
[2] *cp.* Ar. *Rh.* I. ii. 18.

pomum generosissimum? puto, quod optimum; et equus? qui velocissimus: ita hominum, non qui claritate nascendi sed qui virtute maxime excellet.

Omnia igitur ex hoc genere sumpta necesse est aut similia esse aut dissimilia aut contraria. Similitudo adsumitur interim et ad orationis ornatum; sed illa, cum res exiget, nunc ea, quae ad probationem
6 pertinent, exsequar. Potentissimum autem est inter ea quae sunt huius generis, quod proprie vocamus exemplum, id est rei gestae aut ut gestae utilis ad persuadendum id quod intenderis commemoratio. Intuendum igitur est, totum simile sit an ex parte, ut aut omnia ex eo sumamus aut quae utilia sunt. Simile est, *Iure occisus est Saturninus sicut Gracchi.*
7 Dissimile, *Brutus occidit liberos proditionem molientes; Manlius virtutem filii morte multavit.* Contrarium, *Marcellus ornamenta Syracusanis hostibus restituit; Verres eadem sociis abstulit.* Et probandorum et culpandorum ex iis confirmatio eosdem gradus habet.
8 Etiam in iis, quae futura dicemus, utilis similium admonitio est, ut si quis dicens, Dionysium idcirco petere custodes salutis suae, ut eorum adiutus armis

---

[1] VIII. iii. 72 *sqq.*

[2] Manlius had forbidden all encounters with the enemy. His son engaged in single combat and slew his man. See Liv. VIII. vii. 1.

[3] *cp. Verr.* IV. lv. 123.

the finest fruit? The best, I should imagine. What is the finest horse? The swiftest. So too the finest type of man is not he that is noblest of birth, but he that is most excellent in virtue."

All arguments of this kind, therefore, must be from things like or unlike or contrary. Similes are, it is true, sometimes employed for the embellishment of the speech as well, but I will deal with them in their proper place[1]; at present I am concerned with the use of similitude in proof. The most 6
important of proofs of this class is that which is most properly styled example, that is to say the adducing of some past action real or assumed which may serve to persuade the audience of the truth of the point which we are trying to make. We must therefore consider whether the parallel is complete or only partial, that we may know whether to use it in its entirety or merely to select those portions which are serviceable. We argue from the like when we say, "Saturninus was justly killed, as were the Gracchi"; from the unlike when we say, 7
"Brutus killed his sons for plotting against the state, while Manlius condemned his son to death for his valour";[2] from the contrary when we say, "Marcellus restored the works of art which had been taken from the Syracusans who were our enemies, while Verres[3] took the same works of art from our allies." The same divisions apply also to such forms of proof in panegyric or denunciation. It will also be found useful when we are speaking of 8
what is likely to happen to refer to historical parallels: for instance if the orator asserts that Dionysius is asking for a bodyguard that with their armed assistance he may establish himself as tyrant, he may

tyrannidem occupet, hoc referat exemplum, eadem
ratione Pisistratum ad dominationem pervenisse.
9 Sed ut sunt exempla interim tota similia ut hoc
proximum, sic interim ex maioribus ad minora, ex
minoribus ad maiora ducuntur. *Urbes violata propter
matrimonia eversae sunt; quid fieri adultero par est?
Tibicines, cum ab urbe discessissent, publice revocati sunt;
quanto magis principes civitatis viri et bene de republica
10 meriti, cum invidiae cesserint, ab exilio reducendi?* Ad
exhortationem vero praecipue valent imparia. Ad-
mirabilior in femina quam in viro virtus. Quare, si ad
fortiter faciendum accendatur aliquis, non tantum
adferent momenti Horatius et Torquatus quantum
illa mulier cuius manu Pyrrhus est interfectus, et
ad moriendum non tam Cato et Scipio quam Lucretia;
11 quod ipsum est ex maioribus ad minora. Singula
igitur horum generum ex Cicerone (nam unde potius?)
exempla ponamus. Simile est hoc pro Murena,
*Etenim mihi ipsi accidit, ut cum duobus patriciis, altero
improbissimo et audacissimo altero modestissimo atque
optimo viro, peterem; superavi tamen dignitate Catilinam,*

---

[1] *cp.* Liv. ix. 30. The flute-players employed in public worship migrated to Tibur because deprived of an old-established privilege, but were brought back by stratagem, after their hosts had made them drunk.

[2] viii. 17. Sulpicius, one of Murena's accusers and an unsuccessful candidate for the consulship, had sought to depreciate Murena's birth. Cicero urges that even if Sulpicius' statements were true they would be irrelevant and cites his own case to support his argument.

adduce the parallel case of Pisistratus who secured the supreme power by similar means.

But while examples may at times, as in the last 9
instance, apply in their entirety, at times we shall argue from the greater to the less or from the less to the greater. "Cities have been overthrown by the violation of the marriage bond. What punishment then will meet the case of adultery?" "Flute-players have been recalled by the state to the city which they had left. How much more then is it just that leading citizens who have rendered good service to their country should be recalled from that exile to which they have been driven by envy."[1]
Arguments from unlikes are most useful in exhor- 10
tation. Courage is more remarkable in a woman than in a man. Therefore, if we wish to kindle someone's ambition to the performance of heroic deeds, we shall find that parallels drawn from the cases of Horatius and Torquatus will carry less weight than that of the woman by whose hand Pyrrhus was slain, and if we wish to urge a man to meet death, the cases of Cato and Scipio will carry less weight than that of Lucretia. These are however arguments from the
greater to the less. Let me then give you separate 11
examples of these classes of argument from the pages of Cicero; for where should I find better? The following passage from the *pro Murena*[2] is an instance of argument from the like: "For it happened that I myself when a candidate had two patricians as competitors, the one a man of the most unscrupulous and reckless character, the other a most excellent and respectable citizen. Yet I defeated Catiline by force of merit and Galba by my

12 *gratia Galbam.* Maius minoris, pro Milone, *Negant intueri lucem esse fas ei qui a se hominem occisum esse fateatur. In qua tandem urbe hoc homines stultissimi disputant? nempe in ea quae primum iudicium de capite vidit M. Horatii, fortissimi viri, qui nondum libera civitate tamen populi Romani comitiis liberatus est, cum sua manu sororem esse interfectam fateretur.* Minus maioris: *Occidi, occidi, non Spurium Maelium, qui annona levanda iacturisque rei familiaris, quia nimis amplecti plebem videbatur, in suspicionem incidit regni adfectandi,* et cetera, deinde, *Sed eum (auderet enim dicere, cum patriam periculo liberasset) cuius nefandum adulterium in pulvinaribus,* et totus in Clodium locus.

13 Dissimile plures causas habet, fit enim genere, modo, tempore, loco, ceteris, per quae fere omnia Cicero praeiudicia, quae de Cluentio videbantur facta, subvertit; contrario vero exemplo censoriam notam laudando censorem Africanum, qui eum, quem peierasse conceptis verbis palam dixisset, testimonium etiam pollicitus, si quis contra diceret, nullo accu-

---

[1] iii. 7. [2] *pro Mil.* xxvii. 72.
[3] *pro Cluent.* xxxii. *sqq.*
[4] *ib.* xlviii. 134. The accused was a knight: the retention of his horse implied that he retained his status.

popularity." The *pro Milone*[1] will give us an example of argument from the greater to the less: "They say that he who confesses to having killed a man is not fit to look upon the light of day. Where is the city in which men are such fools as to argue thus? It is Rome itself, the city whose first trial on a capital charge was that of Marcus Horatius, the bravest of men, who, though the city had not yet attained its freedom, was none the less acquitted by the assembly of the Roman people, in spite of the fact that he confessed that he had slain his sister with his own hand." The following[2] is an example of argument from the less to the greater: "I killed, not Spurius Maelius, who by lowering the price of corn and sacrificing his private fortune fell under the suspicion of desiring to make himself king, because it seemed that he was courting popularity with the common people overmuch," and so on till we come to, "No, the man I killed (for my client would not shrink from the avowal, since his deed had saved his country) was he who committed abominable adultery even in the shrines of the gods"; then follows the whole invective against Clodius. 12

Arguments from unlikes present great variety, for they may turn on kind, manner, time, place, etcetera, almost every one of which Cicero employs to overthrow the previous decisions that seemed to apply to the case of Cluentius,[3] while he makes use of argument from contraries when he minimises[4] the importance of the censorial stigma by praising Scipio Africanus, who in his capacity of censor allowed one whom he openly asserted to have committed deliberate perjury to retain his horse, because no one had appeared as evidence against him, though he 13

sante, traducere equum passus esset; quae, quia erant
14 longiora, non suis verbis exposui. Breve autem apud
Vergilium contrarii exemplum est:

> *At non ille, satum quo te mentiris, Achilles*
> *Talis in hoste fuit Priamo.*

15 Quaedam autem ex iis, quae gesta sunt, tota narrabimus, ut Cicero pro Milone: *Pudicitiam cum eriperet*
militi tribunus militaris in exercitu C. Marii, propinquus
eius imperatoris, interfectus ab eo est, cui vim adferebat.
Facere enim probus adolescens periculose quam perpeti
turpiter maluit; atque hunc ille summus vir scelere solutum
16 *periculo liberavit.* Quaedam significare satis erit, ut
idem ac pro eodem: *Neque enim posset Ahala ille*
Servilius aut P. Nasica aut L. Opimius aut me consule
senatus non nefarius haberi, si sceleratos interfici nefas
esset. Haec ita dicentur, prout nota erunt vel utilitas
causae aut decor postulabit.

17 Eadem ratio est eorum, quae ex poeticis fabulis
ducuntur, nisi quod iis minus adfirmationis adhibetur;
cuius usus qualis esse deberet, idem optimus auctor
18 ac magister eloquentiae ostendit. Nam huius quoque generis in eadem oratione reperietur exemplum
Itaque hoc, iudices, non sine causa etiam fictis fabulis

---

[1] *Aen.* ii. 540.
[2] *pro Mil.* iv. 9. [3] *ib.* iii. 8.
[4] *ib.* iii. 8. The allusion is to Orestes, acquitted when tried before the Areopagus at Athens by the casting vote of Pallas Athene.

promised to come forward himself to bear witness to his guilt, if any should be found to accuse him. I have paraphrased this passage because it is too long to quote. A brief example of a similar argument is 14
to be found in Virgil,[1]

> "But he, whom falsely thou dost call thy father,
> Even Achilles, in far other wise
> Dealt with old Priam, and Priam was his foe."

Historical parallels may however sometimes be re- 15
lated in full, as in the *pro Milone*[2]: "When a military tribune serving in the army of Gaius Marius, to whom he was related, made an assault upon the honour of a common soldier, the latter killed him; for the virtuous youth preferred to risk his life by slaying him to suffering such dishonour. And yet the great Marius acquitted him of all crime and let him go scot free." On the other hand in certain 16
cases it will be sufficient merely to allude to the parallel, as Cicero does in the same speech[3]: "For neither the famous Servilius Ahala nor Publius Nasica nor Lucius Opimius nor the Senate during my consulship could be cleared of serious guilt, if it were a crime to put wicked men to death." Such parallels will be adduced at greater or less length according as they are familiar or as the interests or adornment of our case may demand.

A similar method is to be pursued in quoting from 17
the fictions of the poets, though we must remember that they will be of less force as proofs. The same supreme authority, the great master of eloquence, shows us how we should employ such quotations. For 18
an example of this type will be found in the same speech[4]: "And it is therefore, gentlemen of the jury, that men of the greatest learning have re-

doctissimi homines memoriae prodiderunt, eum, qui patris ulciscendi causa matrem necavisset, variatis hominum sententiis, non solum divina sed sapientissimae deae sententia
19 *liberatum.* Illae quoque fabellae, quae, etiamsi originem non ab Aesopo acceperunt (nam videtur earum primus auctor Hesiodus), nomine tamen Aesopi maxime celebrantur, ducere animos solent praecipue rusticorum et imperitorum, qui et simplicius, quae ficta sunt, audiunt, et capti voluptate facile iis quibus delectantur consentiunt: siquidem et Menenius Agrippa plebem cum patribus in gratiam traditur reduxisse nota illa de membris humanis adversus
20 ventrem discordantibus fabula. Et Horatius ne in poemate quidem humilem generis huius usum putavit in illis versibus, *Quod dixit vulpes aegroto cauta leoni.* Αἶνον Graeci vocant et αἰσωπείους, ut dixi, λόγους et λιβυκούς; nostrorum quidam, non sane recepto in
21 usum nomine, apologationem. Cui confine est παροιμίας genus illud, quod est velut fabella brevior et per allegorian accipitur: *Non nostrum inquit onus; bos clitellas.*

22 Proximas exempli vires habet similitudo, praecipue illa, quae ducitur citra ullam translationum mixturam ex rebus paene paribus: *Ut, qui accipere in Campo consuerunt, iis candidatis, quorum nummos suppressos esse putant, inimicissimi solent esse, sic eiusmodi iudices infesti*

---

[1] See Liv. ii. 32. [2] *Epist.* I. i. 73.
[3] In the preceding section. *cp.* Arist. *Rhet.* II. xx. 3 for "Libyan stories."

corded in their fictitious narratives that one who had killed his mother to avenge his father was acquitted, when the opinion of men was divided as to his guilt, not merely by the decision of a deity, but by the vote of the wisest of goddesses." Again those fables 19
which, although they did not originate with Aesop (for Hesiod seems to have been the first to write them), are best known by Aesop's name, are specially attractive to rude and uneducated minds, which are less suspicious than others in their reception of fictions and, when pleased, readily agree with the arguments from which their pleasure is derived. Thus Menenius Agrippa[1] is said to have reconciled the plebs to the patricians by his fable of the limbs' quarrel with the belly. Horace[2] also did not regard 20
the employment of fables as beneath the dignity even of poetry; witness his lines that narrate

"What the shrewd fox to the sick lion told."

The Greeks call such fables *αἶνοι* (tales) and, as I have already[3] remarked, Aesopean or Libyan stories, while some Roman writers term them "apologues," though the name has not found general acceptance. Similar to these is that class of proverb which may 21
be regarded as an abridged fable and is understood allegorically: "The burden is not mine to carry," he said, "the ox is carrying panniers."

Simile has a force not unlike that of *example*, more 22
especially when drawn from things nearly equal without any admixture of metaphor, as in the following case: "Just as those who have been accustomed to receive bribes in the Campus Martius are specially hostile to those whom they suspect of having withheld the money, so in the present case the judges came into court with a strong prejudice against the

23 *tum reo venerunt.* Nam παραβολή, quam Cicero collationem vocat, longius res quae comparentur repetere solet. Neque hominum modo inter se opera similia spectantur, ut Cicero pro Murena facit: *Quodsi e portu solventibus, qui iam in portum ex alto invehuntur, praecipere summo studio solent et tempestatum rationem et praedonum et locorum (quod natura adfert, ut iis faveamus, qui eadem pericula, quibus nos perfuncti sumus, ingrediantur), quo me tandem animo esse oportet, prope iam ex magna iactatione terram videntem, in hunc, cui video maximas tempestates esse subeundas?* sed et a mutis atque etiam inanimis interim simile[1] huius-
24 modi ducitur. Et quoniam similium alia facies in alia ratione, admonendum est rarius esse in oratione illud genus, quod εἰκόνα Graeci vocant (quo exprimitur rerum aut personarum imago, ut Cassius: *Quis istam faciem lanipedis senis torquens?*) quam id, quo probabilius fit quod intendimus: ut, si animum dicas excolendum, similitudine utaris terrae, quae neglecta spinas ac dumos, culta fructus creat; aut si ad curam

[1] simile, *added by Halm.*

---

[1] *pro Cluent.* xxvii. 75. [2] *de Inv.* i. 30. [3] ii. 4.
[4] Probably the epigrammatist Cassius of Parma. *lanipedis* =bandaged for the gout. Regius emended to *planipedis*, a dancer who performed barefoot.

accused."[1] For παραβολή, which Cicero[2] translates 23
by "comparison," is often apt to compare things whose resemblance is far less obvious. Nor does it merely compare the actions of men as Cicero does in the *pro Murena*[3]: "But if those who have just come into harbour from the high seas are in the habit of showing the greatest solicitude in warning those who are on the point of leaving port of the state of the weather, the likelihood of falling in with pirates, and the nature of the coasts which they are like to visit (for it is a natural instinct that we should take a kindly interest in those who are about to face the dangers from which we have just escaped), what think you should be my attitude who am now in sight of land after a mighty tossing on the sea, towards this man who, as I clearly see, has to face the wildest weather?" On the contrary, similes of this kind are sometimes drawn from dumb animals
and inanimate objects. Further, since similar objects 24
often take on a different appearance when viewed from a different angle, I feel that I ought to point out that the kind of comparison which the Greeks call εἰκών, and which expresses the appearance of things and persons (as for instance in the line of Cassius[4]—

"Who is he yonder that doth writhe his face
Like some old man whose feet are wrapped in wool?")

should be more sparingly used in oratory than those comparisons which help to prove our point. For instance, if you wish to argue that the mind requires cultivation, you would use a comparison drawn from the soil, which if neglected produces thorns and thickets, but if cultivated will bear fruit; or if you

rei publicae horteris, ostendas apes etiam formicasque,
non modo muta, sed etiam parva animalia, in commune
25 tamen laborare. Ex hoc genere dictum illud est
Ciceronis: *Ut corpora nostra sine mente, ita civitas sine
lege suis partibus, ut nervis ac sanguine et membris, uti
non potest.* Sed ut hac corporis humani pro Cluentio,
ita pro Cornelio equorum, pro Archia saxorum quoque
26 usus est similitudine. Illa (ut dixi) propiora: *ut re-
miges sine gubernatore, sic milites sine imperatore nihil
valere.* Solent tamen fallere similitudinum species,
ideoque adhibendum est iis iudicium. Neque enim,
ut navis utilior nova quam vetus, sic amicitia; vel, ut
laudanda, quae pecuniam suam pluribus largitur, ita,
quae formam. Verba sunt in his similia *vetustatis* et
largitionis, vis quidem longe diversa navis et amicitiae,[1]
27 pecuniae et pudicitiae. Itaque in hoc genere maxime
quaeritur, an simile sit, quod infertur. Etiam in illis
interrogationibus Socratis, quarum paulo ante feci
mentionem, cavendum, ne incaute respondeas; ut
apud Aeschinen Socraticum male respondit Aspasiae
Xenophontis uxor, quod Cicero his verbis transfert:
28 *Dic mihi, quaeso, Xenophontis uxor, si vicina tua melius*

[1] navis et amicitiae, *added by Spalding.*

---

[1] *pro Cluent.* liii. 146.
[2] See IV. iv. 8.
[3] *pro Arch.* viii. 19.
[4] § 3.
[5] *de Inv.* I. xxxi. 51.

are exhorting someone to enter the service of the state, you will point out that bees and ants, though not merely dumb animals, but tiny insects, still toil for the common weal. Of this kind is the saying 25
of Cicero[1]: "As our bodies can make no use of their members without a mind to direct them, so the state can make no use of its component parts, which may be compared to the sinews, blood and limbs, unless it is directed by law." And just as he draws this simile in the *pro Cluentio* from the analogy of the human body, so in the *pro Cornelio*[2] he draws a simile from horses, and in the *pro Archia*[3] from stones. As I have already said, the following type 26
of simile comes more readily to hand: "As oarsmen are useless without a steersman, so soldiers are useless without a general." Still it is always possible to be misled by appearances in the use of simile, and we must therefore use our judgment in their employment. For though a new ship is more useful than one which is old, this simile will not apply to friendship: and again, though we praise one who is liberal with her money, we do not praise one who is liberal with her embraces. In these cases there is similitude in the epithets *old* and *liberal*, but their force is different, when applied to ships and friendship, money and embraces. Consequently, it is all- 27
important in this connexion to consider whether the simile is really applicable. So in answering those Socratic questions which I mentioned above,[4] the greatest care must be taken to avoid giving an incautious answer, such as those given by the wife of Xenophon to Aspasia in the dialogue of Aeschines the Socratic: the passage is translated by Cicero[5] as follows: "Tell me, pray, wife of Xenophon, if your 28

*habeat aurum, quam tu habes: utrumne illud an tuum
malis? Illud, inquit. Quid si vestem et ceterum
ornatum muliebrem pretii maioris habeat, quam tu,
tuumne an illius malis? Respondit, Illius vero. Age sis,
inquit, si virum illa meliorem habeat, quam tu habes,*
29 *utrumne tuum virum malis an illius?* Hic mulier
erubuit, merito; male enim responderat se malle
alienum aurum quam suum; nam est hoc improbum.
At, si respondisset malle se aurum suum tale esse,
quale illud esset, potuisset pudice respondere malle
se virum suum talem esse, qualis melior esset.

30 Scio quosdam inani diligentia per minutissimas ista
partes secuisse, et esse aliquid minus simile, ut simia
homini et marmora deformata prima manu, aliquid
plus, ut illud, *Non ovum tam simile ovo;* et dissimilibus inesse simile, ut formicae et elephanto genus,
quia sunt animalia; et similibus dissimile, ut *canibus
catulos et matribus haedos,* differunt enim aetate;
31 contrariorum quoque aliter accipi opposita, ut noctem
luci, aliter noxia, ut aquam frigidam febri, aliter
repugnantia, ut verum falso, aliter disparata, ut dura
non duris; sed, quid haec ad praesens propositum
magnopere pertineant, non reperio.

---

[1] Verg. *Ecl.* i. 23.

neighbour has finer gold ornaments than you, would you prefer hers or yours?" "Hers," she replied. "Well, then, if her dress and the rest of her ornaments are more valuable than yours, which would you prefer, hers or yours?" "Hers," she replied. "Come, then," said she, "if her husband is better than yours,
would you prefer yours or hers?" At this the wife of 29
Xenophon not unnaturally blushed; for she had answered ill in replying that she would prefer her neighbour's gold ornaments to her own, since it would be wrong to do so. If on the other hand she had replied that she would prefer her ornaments to be of the same quality as those of her neighbour, she might have answered without putting herself to the blush that she would prefer her husband to be like him who was his superior in virtue.

I am aware that some writers have shown pedantic 30
zeal in making a minute classification of similes, and have pointed out that there is lesser similitude (such as that of a monkey to a man or a statue when first blocked out to its original), a greater similitude (for which compare the proverb "As like as egg to egg"), a similitude in things dissimilar (an elephant, for instance, and an ant both belong to the genus *animal*), and dissimilitude in things similar (puppies and kids, for example, are unlike the parents,[1] for
they differ from them in point of age). So too they 31
distinguish between contraries: some are opposites, as night to day, some hurtful, as cold water to a fever, some contradictory, as truth to falsehood, and some negative, as things which are not hard when contrasted with things which are hard. But I cannot see that such distinctions have any real bearing on the subject under discussion.

32 Illud est adnotandum magis, argumenta duci ex iure simili: ut Cicero in Topicis, *Eum, cui domus usus fructus relictus sit, non restituturum heredi, si corruerit, quia non restituat servum, si is decesserit;* ex contrario: *Nihil obstat quo minus iustum matrimonium sit mente coeuntium, etiamsi tabulae signatae non fuerint. Nihil enim proderit signasse tabulas, si mentem matrimonii non fuisse constabit;* ex dissimili, quale est Ciceronis pro
33 Caecina: *Ut, si qui me exire domo coegisset armis, haberem actionem, si qui introire prohibuisset, non haberem?* Dissimilia sic deprehenduntur, *Non si, qui argentum omne legavit, videri potest signatam quoque pecuniam reliquisse, ideo etiam, quod est in nominibus, dari voluisse creditur.*

34 'Αναλογίαν quidam a simili separaverunt, nos eam subiectam huic generi putamus. Nam, ut unum ad decem, ita[1] decem ad centum simile certe est; et ut hostis, sic malus civis. Quanquam haec ulterius quoque procedere solent: *si turpis dominae consuetudo*

[1] ita, *Spalding*: et, *MSS.*

---

[1] iii. 15. [2] xii. 34.
[3] *cp.* Cic. *Top.* iii. 13 and 16.

It is more important for our purpose to note that 32
arguments may be drawn from similar, opposite, and dissimilar points of law. As an example of the first, take the following passage from the *Topica* of Cicero,[1] where he argues that a man to whom the usufruct of a house has been left will not restore it in the interests of the heir if it collapses; just as he would not replace a slave if he should die. The following will provide an example of an argument drawn from opposite points of law: "The absence of a formal contract is no bar to the legality of a marriage, provided the parties cohabit by mutual consent, since the signing of a formal document will count for nothing in the absence of such mutual consent." An instance of an argument drawn from dissimilar points of law occurs in the *pro Caecina* of
Cicero[2]: "If anyone had driven me from my house 33
by armed violence, I should have ground for action against him. Have I then no ground, if he has prevented me from entering my house?" Dissimilar points may be illustrated by the following example[3]: "Because a man has bequeathed all his silver to a given person and this bequest is regarded as including silver coin as well as plate, it does not follow that he intended all outstanding debts to be paid to the legatee."

Some draw a distinction between *analogy* and 34
similarity, but personally I regard the former as included under the latter. For the statement that the relation of 1 to 10 is the same as that of 10 to 100 certainly involves similarity, just as does the statement that a bad citizen may be compared to an actual enemy. But arguments of this kind are carried still further: "If connexion with a male

cum servo, turpis domino cum ancilla; si mutis animali-
35 *bus finis voluptas, idem homini.* Cui rei facillime occurrit ex dissimilibus argumentatio: *Non idem est dominum cum ancilla coisse, quod dominam cum servo; nec, si mutis finis voluptas, rationalibus quoque;* immo ex contrario: *Quia mutis, ideo non rationalibus.*

36 Adhibebitur extrinsecus in causam et auctoritas. Haec secuti Graecos, a quibus κρίσεις dicuntur, *iudicia* aut *iudicationes* vocant, non de quibus ex causa dicta sententia est (nam ea quidem in exemplorum locum cedunt), sed si quid ita visum gentibus, populis, sapientibus viris, claris civibus, illustribus poetis
37 referri potest. Ne haec quidem vulgo dicta et recepta persuasione populari sine usu fuerint. Testimonia sunt enim quodammodo vel potentiora etiam, quod non causis accommodata, sed liberis odio et gratia mentibus ideo tantum dicta factaque, quia aut hon-
38 estissima aut verissima videbantur. An vero me de incommodis vitae disserentem non adiuvabit earum persuasio nationum, quae fletibus natos, laetitia de-

slave is disgraceful to the mistress of the house, so is the connexion of the master with a female slave. If pleasure is an end sought by dumb animals, so also must it be with men." But these arguments 35 may readily be met by arguments from dissimilars: "It is not the same thing for the master of the house to have intercourse with a female slave as for the mistress to have intercourse with a male slave; nor does it follow that because dumb animals pursue pleasure, reasoning beings should do likewise." Or they may even be met by arguments from opposites; as for instance, "Because pleasure is an end sought by dumb animals, it should not be sought by reasoning beings."

Authority also may be drawn from external sources 36 to support a case. Those who follow the Greeks, who call such arguments κρίσεις, style them *judgments* or *adjudications*, thereby referring not to matters on which judicial sentence has been pronounced (for such decisions form examples or precedents), but to whatever may be regarded as expressing the opinion of nations, peoples, philosophers, distinguished citizens, or illustrious poets. Nay, even common sayings and popular beliefs may 37 be found to be useful. For they form a sort of testimony, which is rendered all the more impressive by the fact that it was not given to suit special cases, but was the utterance or action of minds swayed neither by prejudice or influence, simply because it seemed the most honourable or honest thing to say or do. For instance, if I am speaking of the mis- 38 fortunes of this mortal life, surely it will help me to adduce the opinion of those nations who hold that we should weep over the new-born child and rejoice

functos prosequuntur? Aut si misericordiam com-
mendabo iudici, nihil proderit, quod prudentissima
civitas Atheniensium non eam pro adfectu sed pro nu-
39 mine accepit? Iam illa septem praecepta sapientium
nonne quasdam vitae leges existimamus? Si causam
veneficii dicat adultera, non M. Catonis iudicio dam-
nata videatur, qui nullam adulteram non eandem esse
veneficam dixit? Nam sententiis quidem poetarum
non orationes modo sunt refertae sed libri etiam
philosophorum, qui quanquam inferiora omnia praeceptis suis ac litteris credunt, repetere tamen auctor-
40 itatem a plurimis versibus non fastidierunt. Neque
est ignobile exemplum, Megarios ab Atheniensibus,
cum de Salamine contenderent, victos Homeri versu,
qui tamen ipse non in omni editione reperitur,
significans Aiacem naves suas Atheniensibus iunxisse.
41 Ea quoque, quae vulgo recepta sunt, hoc ipso, quod
incertum auctorem habent, velut omnium fiunt: quale
est, *Ubi amici, ibi opes*, et, *Conscientia mille testes*, et
apud Ciceronem, *Pares autem* (*ut est in vetere proverbio*)
cum paribus maxime congregantur; neque enim duras-
sent haec in aeternum, nisi vera omnibus viderentur.
42 Ponitur a quibusdam et quidem in parte prima deorum auctoritas, quae est ex responsis, ut, *Socraten*

[1] *Il.* ii. 558. "Twelve ships great Ajax brought from Salamis, And ranged them where the Athenian army stood."

[2] *Cato maj.* iii 7.

over the dead. Or if I am urging the judge to shew pity, surely my argument may be assisted by the fact that Athens, the wisest of all states, regarded pity not merely as an emotion, but even as a god.
Again, do we not regard the precepts of the Seven 39
Wise Men as so many rules of life? If an adulteress is on her trial for poisoning, is she not already to be regarded as condemned by the judgment of Marcus Cato, who asserted that every adulteress was as good as a poisoner? As for reflexions drawn from the poets, not only speeches, but even the works of the philosophers, are full of them; for although the philosophers think everything inferior to their own precepts and writings, they have not thought it beneath their dignity to quote numbers of lines from the poets to lend
authority to their statements. Again, a remark- 40
able example of the weight carried by authority is provided by the fact that when the Megarians disputed the possession of Salamis with the Athenians, the latter prevailed by citing a line from Homer,[1] which is not however found in all editions, to the effect that Ajax united his ships with those of
the Athenians. Generally received sayings also be- 41
come common property owing to the very fact that they are anonymous, as, for instance, "Friends are a treasure," or "Conscience is as good as a thousand witnesses," or, to quote Cicero,[2] "In the words of the old proverb, birds of a feather flock together." Sayings such as these would not have acquired immortality had they not carried conviction of their
truth to all mankind. Some include under this head 42
the supernatural authority that is derived from oracles, as for instance the response asserting that Socrates was the wisest of mankind: indeed, they

esse sapientissimum. Id rarum est, non sine usu tamen. Utitur eo Cicero in libro de aruspicum responsis et in contione contra Catilinam, cum signum Iovis columnae impositum populo ostendit, et pro Ligario, cum causam C. Caesaris meliorem, quia hoc dii iudicaverint, confitetur. Quae cum propria causae sunt, divina testimonia vocantur; cum aliunde arcessuntur, argumenta.
43 Nonnunquam contingit iudicis quoque aut adversarii aut eius, qui ex diverso agit, dictum aliquid aut factum adsumere ad eorum, quae intendimus, fidem. Propter quod fuerunt, qui exempla et has auctoritates inartificialium probationum esse arbitrarentur,
44 quod ea non inveniret orator, sed acciperet. Plurimum autem refert. Nam testis et quaestio et his similia de ipsa re, quae in iudicio est, pronuntiant; extra petita, nisi ad aliquam praesentis disceptationis utilitatem ingenio applicantur, nihil per se valent.

XII. Haec fere de probatione vel ab aliis tradita vel usu percepta in hoc tempus sciebam. Neque mihi fiducia est, ut ea sola esse contendam, quin immo hortor ad quaerendum et inveniri posse fateor; quae tamen adiecta fuerint, non multum ab his

---

[1] *de har. resp. passim.* The soothsayers consulted as to the significance of certain prodigies had replied that they were due to the profanation of sacred rites. Clodius interpreted this as referring to the rebuilding of Cicero's house. Cicero argued against this in a speech to the senate (56 B.C.).
[2] *in Cat.* III. ix. 21. [3] vi. 19.

rank it above all other authorities. Such authority is rare, but may prove useful. It is employed by Cicero in his speech on the Replies of the Soothsayers[1] and in the oration in which he denounced Catiline to the people,[2] when he points to the statue of Jupiter crowning a column, and again in the *pro Ligario*,[3] where he admits the cause of Caesar to be the better because the gods have decided in his favour. When such arguments are inherent in the case itself they are called supernatural evidence; when they are adduced from without they are styled supernatural arguments. Sometimes, again, it may 43
be possible to produce some saying or action of the judge, of our adversary or his advocate in order to prove our point. There have therefore been some writers who have regarded examples and the use of authorities of which I am speaking as belonging to *inartificial* proofs, on the ground that the orator does not discover them, but receives them ready-made. But the point is of great importance. For 44
witnesses and investigation and the like all make some pronouncement on the actual matter under trial, whereas arguments drawn from without are in themselves useless, unless the pleader has the wit to apply them in such a manner as to support the points which he is trying to make.

XII. Such in the main are the views about proof which I have either heard from others or learned by experience. I would not venture to assert that this is all there is to be said; indeed I would exhort students to make further researches on the subject, for I admit the possibilities of making further discoveries. Still anything that may be discovered will not differ greatly from what I have said here.

abhorrebunt. Nunc breviter, quemadmodum sit utendum iis, subiungam.

2 Traditum fere est argumentum oportere esse confessum; dubiis enim probari dubia qui possunt? Quaedam tamen, quae in alterius rei probationem ducimus, ipsa probanda sunt. *Occidisti virum, eras enim adultera.* Prius de adulterio convincendum est ut, cum id coeperit esse pro certo, fiat incerti argumentum. *Spiculum tuum in corpore occisi inventum est;* negat suum: ut probationi prosit,
3 probandum est. Illud hoc loco monere inter necessaria est, nulla esse firmiora quam quae ex dubiis facta sunt certa. *Caedes a te commissa est, cruentam enim vestem habuisti;* non est tam grave argumentum, si fatetur quam si convincitur. Nam si fatetur, multis ex causis potuit cruenta esse vestis; si negat, hic causae cardinem ponit, in quo si victus fuerit, etiam in sequentibus ruit. Non enim videtur in negando mentiturus fuisse, nisi desperasset id posse defendi, si confiteretur.

4 Firmissimis argumentorum singulis instandum, infirmiora congreganda sunt, quia illa per se fortia non oportet circumstantibus obscurare, ut qualia sunt

[1] *cp.* v. xi. 39.

I will now proceed to make a few remarks as to how proofs should be employed.

It has generally been laid down that an argument to be effective must be based on certainty; for it is obviously impossible to prove what is doubtful by what is no less doubtful. Still some things which are adduced as proof require proof themselves. "You killed your husband, for you were an adulteress."[1] Adultery must first be proved: once that is certain it can be used as an argument to prove what is uncertain. "Your javelin was found in the body of the murdered man." He denies that it was his. If this point is to serve as a proof, it must itself be proved. 2

It is, however, necessary in this connection to point out that there are no stronger proofs than those in which uncertainty has been converted into certainty. "You committed the murder, for your clothes were stained with blood." This argument is not so strong if the accused admits that his clothes were bloodstained as if the fact is proved against his denial. For if he admits it, there are still a number of ways in which the blood could have got on to his clothes: if on the other hand he denies it, he makes his whole case turn on this point, and if his contention is disproved, he will be unable to make a stand on any subsequent ground. For it will be thought that he would never have told a lie in denying the allegation, unless he had felt it a hopeless task to justify himself if he admitted it. 3

In insisting on our strongest arguments we must take them singly, whereas our weaker arguments should be massed together: for it is undesirable that those arguments which are strong in themselves should have their force obscured by the 4

appareant, haec imbecilla natura mutuo auxilio
5 sustinentur. Ita quae non possunt valere, quia
magna sint, valebunt, quia multa sunt; utique vero
ad eiusdem rei probationem omnia spectant. Ut, si
quis hereditatis gratia hominem occidisse dicatur:
*Hereditatem sperabas et magnam hereditatem, et pauper
eras et tum maxime a creditoribus appellabaris; et
offenderas eum, cuius eras heres, et mutaturum tabulas
sciebas.* Singula levia sunt et communia, universa vero
nocent etiamsi non ut fulmine, tamen ut grandine.

6 Quaedam argumenta ponere satis non est, adiuvanda sunt: *cupiditas causa sceleris fuit,* quae sit vis
eius: *ira,* quantum efficiat in animis hominum talis
adfectio; ita et firmiora erunt ipsa et plus habebunt
decoris, si non nudos et velut carne spoliatos artus
7 ostenderint. Multum etiam refert, si argumento
nitemur odii, utrum hoc ex invidia sit an ex iniuria
an ex ambitu, vetus an novum, adversus inferiorem,

surrounding matter, since it is important to show their true nature: on the other hand arguments which are naturally weak will receive mutual support if grouped together. Consequently arguments 5
which have no individual force on the ground of strength will acquire force in virtue of their number, since all tend to prove the same thing. For instance, if one man is accused of having murdered another for the sake of his property, it may be argued as follows: "You had expectations of succeeding to the inheritance, which was moreover very large: you were a poor man, and at the time in question were specially hard pressed by your creditors: you had also offended him whose heir you were, and knew that he intended to alter his will." These arguments are trivial and commonplace in detail, but their cumulative force is damaging. They may not have the overwhelming force of a thunderbolt, but they will have all the destructive force of hail.

There are certain arguments, which must not 6
merely be stated, but supported as well. If we say, "The motive for the crime was greed," we must show the force of greed as a motive: if we say that anger was the motive, we must show the sway that this passion has over the minds of men. Thus our arguments will not only be strengthened, but will be more ornamental as well, since we shall have produced something more than a mere fleshless skeleton. It also makes an enormous difference, 7
supposing that we allege hatred as the motive for a crime, whether such hatred was due to envy, injury or unlawful influence, whether it was recent or of long standing, whether it was directed against an

parem, superiorem, alienum, propinquum. Suos habent omnia ista tractatus et ad utilitatem partis
8 eius quam tuemur referenda sunt. Nec tamen omnibus semper, quae invenerimus, argumentis onerandus est iudex, quia et taedium adferunt et fidem detrahunt. Neque enim potest iudex credere satis esse ea potentia, quae non putamus ipsi sufficere qui diximus. In rebus vero apertis argumentari tam sit stultum quam in clarissimum solem mortale lumen inferre.

9 His quidam probationes adiiciunt, quas παθητικὰς vocant, ductas ex adfectibus. Atque Aristoteles quidem potentissimum putat ex eo, qui dicit, si sit vir bonus; quod ut optimum est, ita longe quidem,
10 sed sequitur tamen, videri. Inde enim illa nobilis Scauri defensio: *Q. Varius Sucronensis ait Aemilium Scaurum rem publicam populi Romani prodidisse; Aemilius Scaurus negat.* Cui simile quiddam fecisse Iphicrates dicitur, qui cum Aristophontem, quo accusante similis criminis reus erat, interrogasset, an is accepta pecunia rem publicam proditurus esset; isque id negasset: *Quod igitur,* inquit, *tu non fecisses,*
11 *ego feci?* Intuendum autem et qui sit apud quem dicimus, et id quod illi maxime probabile videatur requirendum; qua de re locuti sumus in prooemii et

---

[1] *Rhet.* I. ii. 4. [2] Ar. *Rhet.* II. xxiii. 7.

inferior, an equal or a superior, against a stranger or a relative. There are special methods for the treatment of all these arguments, and the treatment to be selected will depend on the interests of the case which we are defending. On the other hand 8
we must not always burden the judge with all the arguments we have discovered, since by so doing we shall at once bore him and render him less inclined to believe us. For he will hardly suppose those proofs to be valid which we ourselves who produce them regard as insufficient. On the other hand, where the facts are fairly obvious, it would be as foolish to argue about them as to bring some artificial light into broad sunlight.

To these proofs some authorities would add those 9
which they call *pathetic* or *emotional*. Aristotle[1] indeed holds that the strongest argument in support of a speaker is that he is a good man. This no doubt is the best support, but to seem good is also of value, though the semblance is but a bad second to the reality. Of this nature is the noble defence 10
of Scaurus. "Quintus Varius of Sucro asserts that Aemilius Scaurus has betrayed the interests of the Roman people: Aemilius Scaurus denies it." A similar defence is said to have been employed by Iphicrates[2]: he asked Aristophon who was accusing him on a similar charge of treason whether he would consent to betray his country for a bribe: when Aristophon replied in the negative, he continued, "Have I then done what you would have refused to do?" We must however take the 11
character of the judge into consideration and seek out such arguments as will appeal to him. I have already spoken of this in the rules which I laid

12 suasoriae praeceptis. Altera ex adfirmatione probatio est: *Ego hoc feci; Tu mihi hoc dixisti;* et *O facinus indignum!* et similia; quae non debent quidem deesse orationi et, si desunt, multum nocent; non tamen habenda sunt inter magna praesidia, cum hoc in eadem causa fieri ex utraque parte similiter possit.
13 Illae firmiores ex sua cuique persona probationes, quae credibilem rationem subiectam habeant: ut vulneratus aut filio orbatus non fuerit alium accusaturus quam nocentem, quando, si negotium innocenti facit, liberet eum noxa qui admiserit. Hinc et patres adversus liberos et adversus suos quisque necessarios auctoritatem petunt.

14 Quaesitum etiam, potentissima argumenta primone ponenda sint loco, ut occupent animos, an summo, ut inde dimittant, an partita primo summoque, quod Homerica dispositione in medio sint infirma, ut ab aliis[1] crescant? Quae prout ratio causae cuiusque postulabit, ordinabuntur, uno, ut ego censeo, excepto, ne a potentissimis ad levissima decrescat oratio.

15 Ego haec breviter demonstrasse contentus ita posui, ut locos ipsos et genera quam possem apertis-

[1] ab aliis, *Butler*: aut animis, *MSS*.

---

[1] IV. i. 17 *sq.*, III. viii. 36 *sq.* [2] *Il.* iv. 299.

down for the exordium and for deliberative oratory.[1] Another form of proof is provided by asseveration 12
as in "I did this," "You told me this," or "O outrageous crime!" and the like. Every pleading should contain some such asseverations; if it does not, the loss will be considerable. Still asseverations must not be regarded as supports of the first importance, since they can be produced by either party in the same case with the same emphasis. A more forcible kind of proof is that drawn 13
from character and supported by some plausible reason, as for instance, "It is not likely that a wounded man or one who has lost his son would accuse anyone who is not guilty, since if he accused an innocent man, he would free the real offender from all risk of punishment." It is from such arguments that fathers seek support when pleading against their sons or one relative against another.

The further question has been raised as to whether 14
the strongest arguments should be placed first, to take possession of the judge's mind, or last, to leave an impression on it; or whether they should be divided between the commencement and close of the proof, adopting the Homeric disposition of placing the weakest in the centre of the column,[2] so that they may derive strength from their neighbours. But in the disposition of our arguments we must be guided by the interests of the individual case: there is only one exception to this general rule in my opinion, namely, that we should avoid descending from the strongest proofs to the weakest.

I have been content to give a brief outline of my 15
views concerning these points, and have put them forward in such a way as to show as clearly as was in

sime ostenderem. Quidam executi sunt verbosius, quibus placuit, proposita locorum communium materia, quo quaeque res modo dici posset, ostendere; sed
16 mihi supervacuum videbatur. Nam et fere apparet, quid in iniuriam, quid in avaritiam, quid in testem inimicum, quid in potentes amicos dicendum sit; et de omnibus his omnia dicere infinitum est, tam hercule quam si controversiarum, quae sint quaeque futurae sint, quaestiones, argumenta, sententias tradere
17 velim. Ipsas autem argumentorum velut sedes non me quidem omnes ostendisse confido, plurimas tamen.

Quod eo diligentius faciendum fuit, quia declamationes, quibus ad pugnam forensem velut praepilatis exerceri solebamus, olim iam ab illa vera imagine orandi recesserunt atque ad solam compositae voluptatem nervis carent, non alio medius fidius vitio dicentium, quam quo mancipiorum negotiatores for-
18 mae puerorum virilitate excisa lenocinantur. Nam ut illi robur ac lacertos barbamque ante omnia et alia, quae natura proprie maribus dedit, parum existimant decora, quaeque fortia, si liceret, forent ut dura molliunt, ita nos habitum ipsum orationis virilem et illam vim stricte robusteque dicendi tenera quadam elocutionis cute operimus et, dum levia sint ac

my power the various topics and kinds of arguments. Others have dealt with the subject at greater length, preferring to deal with the whole subject of commonplaces and to show how each topic may be treated. This seems to me unnecessary, since it is as a rule 16
obvious what should be said against the injurious conduct or avarice of our opponents, or against a hostile witness or powerful friends; to say everything on all these subjects is an endless task, as endless in fact as if I were to attempt to lay down rules for dealing with every dispute that can ever occur and all the questions, arguments and opinions thereby involved. I do not venture to suppose that 17
I have pointed out all the circumstances that may give rise to arguments, but I think that I have done so in the majority of cases.

This was a task which required all the more careful handling because the declamations, which we used to employ as foils wherewith to practise for the duels of the forum, have long since departed from the true form of pleading and, owing to the fact that they are composed solely with the design of giving pleasure, have become flaccid and nerveless: indeed, declaimers are guilty of exactly the same offence as slave-dealers who castrate boys in order to increase the attractions of their beauty. For just as the 18
slave-dealer regards strength and muscle, and above all, the beard and other natural characteristics of manhood as blemishes, and softens down all that would be sturdy if allowed to grow, on the ground that it is harsh and hard, even so we conceal the manly form of eloquence and power of speaking closely and forcibly by giving it a delicate complexion of style and, so long as what we say is smooth and

nitida, quantum valeant, nihil interesse arbitramur.
19 Sed mihi naturam intuenti nemo non vir spadone
formosior erit, nec tam aversa unquam videbitur ab
opere suo providentia, ut debilitas inter optima inventa sit, nec id ferro speciosum fieri putabo, quod,
si nasceretur, monstrum erat. Libidinem iuvet ipsum effeminati sexus mendacium, numquam tamen
hoc continget malis moribus regnum ut, si qua
20 pretiosa fecit, fecerit et bona. Quapropter eloquentiam, licet hanc (ut sentio enim, dicam) libidinosam
resupina voluptate auditoria probent, nullam esse
existimabo, quae ne minimum quidem in se indicium
masculi et incorrupti, ne dicam gravis et sancti viri,
21 ostentet. An vero statuarum artifices pictoresque
clarissimi, cum corpora quam speciosissima fingendo
pingendove efficere cuperent, numquam in hunc inciderunt errorem, ut Bagoam aut Megabyzum aliquem
in exemplum operis sumerent sibi, sed Doryphoron
illum aptum vel militiae vel palaestrae, aliorum quoque iuvenum bellicosorum et athletarum corpora
decora vere existimaverunt: nos, qui oratorem studemus effingere, non arma sed tympana eloquentiae
22 demus? Igitur et ille, quem instituimus, adolescens,
quam maxime potest, componat se ad imitationem
veritatis, initurusque frequenter forensium certami-
num pugnam iam in schola victoriam spectet et ferire

[1] Eunuchs.

[2] The famous statue of Polycletus, regarded as the standard of manly beauty and proportion. Many copies have survived. Doryphorus = the Spearbearer.

polished, are absolutely indifferent as to whether our words have any power or no. But I take Nature for 19
my guide and regard any man whatsoever as fairer to view than a eunuch, nor can I believe that Providence is ever so indifferent to what itself has created as to allow weakness to be an excellence, nor again can I think that the knife can render beautiful that which, if produced in the natural course of birth, would be regarded as a monster. A false resemblance to the female sex may in itself delight lust, if it will, but depravity of morals will never acquire such ascendancy as to succeed in giving real value to that to which it has succeeded in giving a
high price. Consequently, although this debauched 20
eloquence (for I intend to speak with the utmost frankness) may please modern audiences by its effeminate and voluptuous charms, I absolutely refuse to regard it as eloquence at all: for it retains not the slightest trace of purity and virility in itself, not
to say of these qualities in the speaker. When the 21
masters of sculpture and painting desired to carve or paint forms of ideal beauty, they never fell into the error of taking some Bagoas or Megabyzus[1] as models, but rightly selected the well-known Doryphorus,[2] equally adapted either for the fields of war or for the wrestling school, and other warlike and athletic youths as types of physical beauty. Shall we then, who are endeavouring to mould the ideal orator, equip eloquence not with weapons but with
timbrels? Consequently, let the youth whom we 22
are training devote himself, as far as in him lies, to the imitation of truth and, in view of the fact that the battles of the forum that await him are not few, let him strive for victory in the schools and learn

vitalia ac tueri sciat; et praeceptor id maxime exigat, inventum praecipue probet. Nam, ut ad peiora iuvenes laude ducuntur, ita laudari in bonis malent.
23 Nunc illud male est, quod necessaria plerumque silentio transeunt, nec in dicendo videtur inter bona utilitas. Sed haec et in alio nobis tractata sunt opere et in hoc saepe repetenda. Nunc ad ordinem inceptum.

XIII. Refutatio dupliciter accipi potest. Nam et pars defensoris tota est posita in refutatione, et quae dicta sunt ex diverso debent utrinque dissolvi. Et hoc est proprie, cui in causis quartus adsignatur locus. Sed utriusque similis condicio est. Neque vero ex aliis locis ratio argumentorum in hac parte peti potest quam in confirmatione, nec locorum aut sententiarum aut verborum et figurarum alia condicio
2 est. Adfectus plerumque haec pars mitiores habet.

Non sine causa tamen difficilius semper est creditum, quod Cicero saepe testatur, defendere quam accusare. Primum, quod est res illa simplicior, proponitur enim uno modo, dissolvitur varie, cum accusatori satis sit plerumque, verum esse id, quod obiecerit, patronus neget, defendat, transferat, excuset,

---

[1] Perhaps the lost *de causis corruptae eloquentiae*.
[2] (i) exordium, (ii) statement of facts, (iii) confirmation, (iv) refutation, (v) peroration.

how to strike the vitals of his foe and protect his own; and let his instructor insist on his doing this above all else and reserve his special approval for the mastery of this art. For though young men may be lured to evil practices by praise, they still prefer to be praised for what is right. At the present time 23
the misfortune is that teachers more often than not pass over what is necessary in silence, and utility is not accounted one of the good qualities of eloquence. But I have dealt with these points in another work,[1] and shall often have to recur to them in this. I will now return to my prescribed course.

XIII. Refutation may be understood in two senses. For the duty of the defence consists wholly in refutation, while whatever is said by our opponents must be rebutted, whether we are speaking for the defence or the prosecution. It is in this sense that refutation is assigned the fourth place[2] in pleadings, but the methods required in either case are identical. For the principles of argument in refutation can only be drawn from the same sources as those used in proof, while topics and thoughts, words and figures will all be on the same lines. As a rule no strong 2
appeal to the emotions is made in refutation.

It is not, however, without reason that, as Cicero so often testifies,[3] the task of defence has always been considered harder than that of prosecution. In the first place accusation is a simpler task: for the charge is put forward in one definite form, but its refutation may take a number of different forms, since as a rule it is sufficient for the accuser that his charge should be true, whereas counsel for the defence may deny

[3] It is not clear what passages Quintilian has in his mind.

deprecetur, molliat, minuat, avertat, despiciat, deri-
deat. Quare inde recta fere atque, ut sic dixerim,
clamosa est actio; hinc mille flexus et artes deside-
3 rantur. Tum accusator praemeditata pleraque domo
adfert, patronus etiam inopinatis frequenter occurrit.
Accusator dat testem, patronus ex re ipsa refellit.
Accusator e criminum invidia, etsi falsa sit, materiam dicendi trahit, de parricidio, sacrilegio, maie-
state; quae patrono tantum neganda sunt. Ideoque
accusationibus etiam mediocres in dicendo suffe-
cerunt; bonus defensor nemo nisi qui eloquentissimus fuit. Quanquam ut, quod sentio, semel finiam,
tanto est accusare quam defendere, quanto facere
quam sanare vulnera, facilius.

4 Plurimum autem refert, et quid proposuerit[1] adversarius et quomodo. Primum igitur intuendum est,
id, cui responsuri sumus, proprium sit eius iudicii an
ad causam extra arcessitum. Nam si est proprium,
aut negandum aut defendendum aut transferendum;
5 extra haec in iudiciis fere nihil est. Deprecatio
quidem, quae est sine ulla specie defensionis, rara

[1] proposuerit, *Meister*: profuerit, *AB*.

---

[1] See III. vi. 23. No exact rendering of *translatio* is possible. Literally it means "transference of the charge": it would seem to cover cases where the charge was brought in the wrong court or by the wrong person. It is used generally to indicate a plea made by defendant in bar of plaintiff's action. [2] See VII. iv. 17.

or justify the facts, raise the question of competence,[1] make excuses, plead for mercy, soften, extenuate, or divert the charge, express contempt or derision. The task of the accuser is consequently straightforward and, if I may use the phrase, vociferous; but the defence requires a thousand arts and stratagems. Moreover the prosecutor generally produces a speech 3
which he has prepared at home, while the counsel for the defence has frequently to deal with quite unexpected points. The prosecutor brings forward his witnesses, while counsel for the defence has to refute the charge by arguments drawn from the case itself. The prosecutor draws his material from the odium excited by the charges, even though it have no justification, denouncing parricide, sacrilege, or treason, whereas counsel for the defence can only deny them. Consequently quite moderate speakers have proved adequate in prosecution, while no one can be a good counsel for the defence unless he possesses real eloquence. In a word, it is just so much easier to accuse than to defend as it is easier to inflict than to heal a wound.

The nature of the arguments put forward by our 4
opponent and the manner in which he produces them will, however, make an enormous difference to our task. We must therefore first consider what it is to which we have to reply, whether it is part and parcel of the actual case or has been introduced from circumstances lying outside the case. For in the former case we must deny or justify the facts or raise the question of competence: for these are practically the sole methods of defence available in the courts. Pleas for mercy,[2] which are not in any sense a 5
method of actual defence, can rarely be used, and

admodum et apud eos solos iudices, qui nulla certa pronuntiandi forma tenentur. Quanquam illae quoque apud C. Caesarem et triumviros pro diversarum partium hominibus actiones, etiamsi precibus utuntur, adhibent tamen patrocinia; nisi hoc non fortissime defendentis est dicere, *Quid aliud egimus, Tubero,*
6 *nisi ut, quod hic potest, nos possemus?* Quodsi quando apud principem aliumve, cui utrum velit liceat, dicendum erit, dignum quidem morte eum, pro quo loquemur, clementi tamen servandum esse vel talem, primum omnium non erit res nobis cum adversario sed cum iudice, deinde forma deliberativae magis materiae quam iudicialis utemur. Suadebimus enim ut laudem humanitatis potius quam voluptatem ulti-
7 onis concupiscat. Apud iudices quidem secundum legem dicturos sententiam de confessis praecipere ridiculum est. Ergo, quae neque negari neque transferri possunt, utique defendenda sunt, qualiacunque sunt, aut causa cedendum. Negandi duplicem ostendimus formam, aut non esse factum aut non hoc esse, quod factum sit. Quae neque defendi

[1] *e.g.* in the emperor's court as opposed to the *quaestiones perpetuae* or civil actions.

[2] As in the *pro Ligario* and *pro Deiotaro* pleaded in Caesar's house. It is not known what cases were tried before the (2nd) triumvirate. [3] Cic. *pro Lig.* iv. 10.

only before judges who are not limited to some precise form of verdict.[1] Even those speeches delivered before Gaius Caesar[2] and the triumvirs on behalf of members of the opposite party, although they do employ such pleas for mercy, also make use of the ordinary methods of defence. For I think you will agree with me that the following passage contains arguments of a strongly defensive character[3]: "What was our object, Tubero, save that we might have the power that Caesar has now?"
But if, when pleading before the emperor or any 6
other person who has power either to acquit or condemn, it is incumbent on us to urge that, while our client has committed an offence that deserves the death penalty, it is still the duty of a merciful judge to spare him despite his sins, it must be noted in the first place that we have to deal, not with our adversary, but with the judge, and secondly that we shall have to employ the deliberative rather than the forensic style. For we shall urge the judge to fix his desire rather on the glory that is won by clemency than on the pleasure that is given by
vengeance. On the other hand, when we are 7
pleading before judges who have to give their verdict in accordance with the prescriptions of law, it would be absurd to give them advice as to how they should deal with a criminal who admits his guilt. Consequently, when it is impossible either to deny the facts or to raise the question of competence, we must attempt to justify the facts as best we can, or else throw up the case. I have pointed out that there are two ways in which a fact can be denied: it can be denied absolutely, or it may be denied that a fact is of the nature alleged.

neque transferri possunt, utique neganda, nec solum
si finitio potest esse pro nobis, sed etiam si nuda
8 infitiatio superest. Testes erunt, multa in eos dicere
licet; chirographum, de similitudine litterarum dis-
seremus. Utique nihil erit peius quam confessio.
Ultima est actionis controversia, cum defendendi
9 negandive non est locus, id est translatio.[1] Atqui
quaedam sunt, quae neque negari neque defendi
neque transferri possunt. *Adulterii rea est quae, cum*
anno vidua fuisset, enixa est; lis non erit. Quare
illud stultissime praecipitur, quod defendi non possit,
silentio dissimulandum: siquidem est id, de quo
10 iudex pronuntiaturus est. At si extra causam sit
adductum et tantum coniunctum, malim quidem
dicere, nihil id ad quaestionem nec esse in iis mo-
randum et minus esse quam adversarius dicat;
tamen velut huic simulationi oblivionis ignoscam.
Debet enim bonus advocatus pro rei salute brevem
negligentiae reprehensionem non pertimescere.
11 Videndum etiam, simul nobis plura aggredienda

[1] translatio, *Regius*: relatio, *MSS.*

---

[1] *i.e.* if we cannot say "The act was right" or "This court is not competent to try it" or "The prosecutor has no *locus standi.*" See n. on § 2.

[2] *i.e.* suggest that it is a forgery.

When it is impossible to plead justification or to raise the question of competence,[1] we must deny the facts, and that not merely when a definition of the facts will serve our case, but even when nothing except an absolute denial is left for us. If wit- 8
nesses are produced, there is much that may be said to discredit them; if a document is put forward, we may hold forth on the similarity of the handwritings.[2] In any case there can be no worse course than confession of guilt. When denial and justification are both impossible, we must as a last resort base our defence on the legal point of competence.
Still, there are some cases in which none of these 9
three courses is possible. "She is accused of adultery on the ground that after a widowhood of twelve months she was delivered of a child." In this case there is no ground for dispute. Consequently I regard as the height of folly the advice that is given in such cases, that what cannot be defended should be ignored and passed over in silence, at any rate if the point in question is that on which the judge has
to give his decision. On the other hand, if the 10
allegation is irrelevant to the actual case and no more than accessory, I should prefer simply to state that it has nothing to do with the question at issue, that it is not worth our attention, and that it has not the importance given to it by our opponent, though in such a case I should be prepared to pardon a policy of ignoring the charge such as I have just mentioned. For a good advocate ought not to be afraid of incurring a trivial censure for negligence, if such apparent negligence is likely to save his client.

We must further consider whether we should 11

sint an amolienda singula. Plura simul invadimus, si aut tam infirma sunt, ut pariter impelli possint, aut tam molesta, ut pedem conferre cum singulis non expediat; tum enim toto corpore obnitendum et, ut sic dixerim, directa fronte pugnandum est.
12 Interim, si resolvere ex parte diversa dicta difficilius erit, nostra argumenta cum adversariorum argumentis conferemus, si modo haec ut valentiora videantur effici poterit. Quae vero turba valebunt, diducenda erunt, ut, quod paulo ante dixi: *Heres eras et pauper et magna pecunia appellabaris a creditoribus et offen-*
13 *deras et mutaturum tabulas testamenti sciebas.* Urgent universa; at si singula quaeque dissolveris, iam illa flamma, quae magna congerie convaluerat, diductis quibus alebatur, concidet, ut, si vel maxima flumina in rivos diducantur, qualibet transitum praebent. Itaque propositio quoque secundum hanc utilitatem accommodabitur, ut ea nunc singula ostendamus, nunc
14 complectamur universa. Nam interim quod pluribus collegit adversarius, sat est semel proponere; ut, si multas causas faciendi, quod arguit, reo dicet accusator fuisse, nos, non enumeratis singulis, semel hoc in totum [1] negemus, quia non, quisquis causam faci-

[1] hoc in totum, *Becher*: hoc intuendum, *MSS.*

attack our opponent's arguments *en masse* or dispose of them singly. We shall adopt the former course if the arguments are so weak that they can be overthrown simultaneously, or so embarrassing that it would be inexpedient to grapple with them individually. For in such a case we must fight with all the force at our disposal and make a frontal attack.
Sometimes, if it is difficult to refute the statements 12
made by our opponents, we may compare our arguments with theirs, at least if by such a procedure it is possible to prove the superiority of our own. On the other hand, those arguments which rely on their cumulative force must be analysed individually, as for example in the case which I cited above: "You were the heir, you were poor and were summoned by your creditors for a large sum: you had offended him and knew that he intended to change his will."
The cumulative force of these arguments is dam- 13
aging. But if you refute them singly, the flame which derived its strength from the mass of fuel will die down as soon as the material which fed it is separated, just as if we divert a great stream into a number of channels we may cross it where we will. We shall therefore adapt our method of refutation to the exigencies of our case, now dealing with individual arguments and now treating them in bulk.
For at times we may include in a single proposition 14
the refutation of an argument which our opponent has constructed of a number of different points. For instance, if the accuser allege that the accused had a number of motives for committing a crime, we may make a general denial of the fact without dealing singly with each alleged motive, because the fact that a man has had a motive for committing a

15 endi sceleris habuit, et fecerit. Saepius tamen accusatori congerere argumenta, reo dissolvere expediet.

Id autem, quod erit ab adversario dictum, quomodo refutari debeat, intuendum est. Nam si erit palam falsum, negare satis est, ut pro Cluentio Cicero eum, quem dixerat accusator epoto poculo concidisse,
16 negat eodem die mortuum. Palam etiam contraria et supervacua et stulta reprehendere nullius est artis, ideoque nec rationes eorum nec exempla tradere necesse est. Id quoque (quod obscurum vocant), quod secreto et sine teste aut argumento dicitur factum, satis natura sua infirmum est; sufficit enim, quod adversarius non probat; item si ad causam non
17 pertinet. Est tamen interim oratoris efficere, ut quid aut contrarium esse aut a causa diversum aut incredibile aut supervacuum aut nostrae potius causae videatur esse coniunctum. Obiicitur Oppio, quod de militum cibariis detraxerit; asperum crimen, sed id contrarium ostendit Cicero, quia iidem accusatores obiecerint Oppio, quod is voluerit exercitum largi-
18 endo corrumpere. Testes in Cornelium accusator lecti a tribuno codicis pollicetur; facit hoc Cicero

---

[1] lx. 168. [2] *cp.* § 21 and v. x. 69. [3] *cp.* iv. iii. 13.

crime does not prove that he has actually committed
it. It will however as a rule be expedient for the 15
prosecution to employ massed arguments, and for
the accused to refute them in detail.

We must, however, also consider the manner in
which we should refute the arguments of our
opponent. If his statements be obviously false, it
will be sufficient to deny them. This is done by
Cicero in the *pro Cluentio*,[1] where he denies that
the man alleged by the accuser to have fallen dead
on the spot after drinking the contents of the cup,
died on the same day. Again, it requires no skill 16
to rebut arguments which are obviously contradictory, superfluous or foolish, and consequently I
need give no examples nor instructions as to the
method to be employed. There is also the type
of charge which is known as obscure, where it is
alleged that an act was committed in secret without
witnesses or any evidence to prove it: this suffers
from an inherent weakness, since the fact that our
opponent can produce no proof is sufficient for our
purpose: the same applies to arguments which are
irrelevant to the case. It is, however, sometimes an 17
orator's duty to make it appear that some argument
of his opponent is contradictory or irrelevant or
incredible or superfluous or really favourable to his
own client. Oppius[2] is charged with having em-
bezzled the supplies intended to feed the troops.
It is a serious charge, but Cicero shows that it
contradicts other charges, since the same accusers
also charged Oppius with desiring to corrupt the
army by bribes. The accuser of Cornelius offers to 18
produce witnesses to show that he read out the law
when tribune[3]: Cicero makes this argument super-

supervacuum, quia ipse fateatur. Petit accusationem in Verrem Q. Caecilius, quod fuerat quaestor eius;
19 ipsum Cicero ut pro se videretur effecit. Cetera, quae proponuntur, communis locus habet. Aut enim coniectura excutiuntur, an vera sint; aut finitione, an propria; aut qualitate, an inhonesta, iniqua, improba, inhumana, crudelia et cetera, quae ei generi
20 accidunt. Eaque non modo in propositionibus et rationibus sed in toto genere actionis intuenda: an sit crudelis, ut Labieni in Rabirium lege perduellionis; inhumana, ut Tuberonis Ligarium exulem accusantis atque id agentis ne ei Caesar ignoscat; superba,
21 ut in Oppium ex epistola Cottae reum factum. Perinde praecipites, insidiosae, impotentes deprehenduntur. Ex quibus tamen fortissime invaseris, quod est aut omnibus periculosum, ut dicit Cicero pro Tullio: *Quis hoc statuit unquam, aut cui concedi sine summo omnium periculo potest, ut eum iure potuerit occidere, a quo metuisse se dicat, ne ipse posterius occide-*

---

[1] Cicero argues that since the relation between praetor and quaestor is almost that which should exist between father and son, a quaestor should not be allowed to prosecute his praetor.

[2] Rabirius was accused of causing the death of Saturninus forty years after the event.

[3] P. Oppius, quaestor to M. Aurelius Cotta in Bithynia, was charged by Cotta in a letter to the senate with misappropriation of supplies for the troops and with an attempt on his life. Cicero defended him in 69 B.C. The speech is lost.

fluous by admitting it. Quintus Caecilius demands to be entrusted with the task of accusing Verres on the ground that he had been the latter's quaestor: Cicero actually makes this argument tell in his own favour.[1] As regards other charges, they may all be 19
dealt with by very similar methods. For they may be demolished either by conjecture, when we shall consider whether they are true, by definition, when we shall examine whether they are relevant to the case, by quality, when we shall consider whether they are dishonourable, unfair, scandalous, inhuman, cruel, or deserve any other epithet coming under the head of quality. Such questions have to be 20
considered, not merely in connection with the statement of the charges or the reasons alleged, but with reference to the nature of the case in its entirety. For instance, the question of cruelty is considered with regard to the charge of high treason brought against Rabirius[2] by Labienus; of inhumanity in the case of Tubero who accused Ligarius when he was an exile and attempted to prevent Caesar from pardoning him; of arrogance as in the case of the charge brought against Oppius[3] on the strength of a letter of Cotta. Similarly, it may be shown that 21
charges are hasty, insidious or vindictive. The strongest argument, however, which can be brought against a charge is that it involves peril to the community or to the judges themselves; we find an example of the former in the *pro Tullio*,[4] where Cicero says "Who ever laid down such a principle as this, or who could be allowed, without grave peril to the community, to kill a man, just because he asserts that he feared that he himself might be

[4] *cp.* IV. ii. 131. The speech is lost.

retur? aut ipsis iudicibus, ut pro Oppio monet pluribus, ne illud actionis genus in equestrem ordi-
22 nem admittant. Nonnunquam tamen quaedam bene et contemnuntur vel tanquam levia vel tanquam nihil ad causam pertinentia. Multis hoc locis fecit Cicero; et haec simulatio interim hucusque procedit, ut, quae dicendo refutare non possumus, quasi fastidiendo calcemus.

23 Quoniam vero maxima pars eorum similibus constat, rimandum erit diligentissime, quid sit in quoque, quod adsumitur, dissimile. In iure facile deprehenditur. Est enim scriptum de rebus utique diversis, tantoque magis ipsarum rerum differentia potest esse manifesta. Illas vero similitudines, quae ducuntur ex mutis animalibus aut inanimis, facile est
24 eludere. Exempla rerum varie tractanda sunt, si nocebunt; quae si vetera erunt, fabulosa dicere licebit; si indubia, maxime quidem dissimilia. Neque enim fieri potest, ut paria sint per omnia, ut si Nasica post occisum Gracchum defendatur exemplo Ahalae, a quo Maelius est interfectus, Maelium regni adfectatorem fuisse, a Graccho leges modo latas esse populares, Ahalam magistrum equitum fuisse, Nasicam privatum esse dicatur. Si defecerint omnia, viden-

[1] A third of the jury were composed of *equites*.
[2] *cp.* III. vii 20, V. ix. 13.

killed by him?" An instance of the latter occurs in the *pro Oppio*, where Cicero warns the judges at some length not to permit such an action to be brought against the equestrian order.[1] On the other 22
hand there are certain arguments which at times may best be treated with contempt, as being trivial or irrelevant. This course is frequently pursued by Cicero, indeed this affectation of indifference is sometimes carried so far that we trample disdainfully under foot arguments which we should never succeed in refuting by counter-argument.

Since, however, the majority of such arguments 23
are based on similarity, we must make diligent search to discover if any discrepancy is to be found in what is put forward. It is easy to do this where points of law are concerned. For the law was drafted to cover cases quite other than the present, and consequently it is all the easier to show the difference between case and case. As to parallels drawn from dumb animals or inanimate objects, they are easy to make light of. Examples drawn from facts, if damag- 24
ing to our case, must be treated in various ways: if they are ancient history, we may call them legendary, while if they are undoubted, we may lay stress on their extreme dissimilarity. For it is impossible for two cases to be alike in every detail. For instance, if the case of Ahala,[2] by whom Maelius was killed, is quoted to justify Nasica for the slaying of Tiberius Gracchus, we may argue that Maelius was endeavouring to make himself king, while all that Gracchus had done was to bring forward laws in the interest of the people, and that while Ahala was Master of the Horse, Nasica was a private citizen. In the last resort, if all else prove unavailing, we must see if

dum erit, an obtineri possit, ne illud quidem recte factum. Quod de exemplis, idem etiam de iudicatis observandum.

25 Quod autem posui, referre, quo quidque accusator modo dixerit, huc pertinet, ut, si est minus efficaciter elocutus, ipsa eius verba ponantur; si acri et vehementi fuerit usus oratione, eandem rem nostris verbis mitioribus proferamus, ut Cicero de Cornelio, *Codicem*
26 *attigit;* et protinus cum quadam defensione, ut, si pro luxurioso dicendum sit, *Obiecta est paulo liberalior vita.* Sic et pro sordido parcum, pro maledico liberum
27 dicere licebit. Utique committendum nunquam est, ut adversariorum dicta cum sua confirmatione referamus, aut etiam loci alicuius exsecutione adiuvemus, nisi cum eludenda erunt: *Apud exercitum mihi fueris, inquit; tot annis forum non attigeris, abfueris tamdiu et, cum tam longo intervallo veneris, cum his, qui in foro*
28 *habitarunt, de dignitate contendas?* Praeterea in contradictione interim totum crimen exponitur, ut Cicero pro Scauro circa Bostarem facit veluti orationem diversae partis imitatus, aut pluribus propositionibus iunctis, ut pro Vareno, *cum iter per agros et loca sola*

---

[1] *cp.* IV. iv. 8. [2] *cp.* IV. ii. 77. [3] *pro Mur.* ix. 21.
[4] *cp.* IV. i. 69. Scaurus was accused of extortion in Sardinia, and of having murdered a certain Bostar at a banquet. [5] *cp.* V. x. 69.

we can show that the action adduced as a parallel was itself unjustifiable. These remarks as to examples apply also to previous decisions in the courts.

With regard to my statement that the manner in 25 which the accuser stated his charges was of importance, I would point out in this connexion that if he has spoken but feebly, we may repeat his actual words; while, if he has used bitter and violent language, we may restate the facts in milder terms, as Cicero does in the *pro Cornelio*, where he says, "He put his hand to the tablet containing the law"[1]: and we may do this in such a way as to 26 defend our client; for instance, if our client is addicted to luxury, we may say, "He has been charged with living in a somewhat too liberal style." So, too, we may call a mean man thrifty and a slanderous tongue free.[2] But we must never under 27 any circumstances repeat our opponent's charges together with their proofs, nor emphasise any of his points by amplifying them, unless we do so with a view to making light of them, as for instance in the following passage[3]: "You have been with the army, he says, and have not set foot in the forum for so many years, and do you now on returning after so long an interval seek to compete for a post of high dignity with those who have made the forum their home?" Again, when we are replying to the 28 accuser we may sometimes set forth the whole charge, as Cicero does in the *pro Scauro* with reference to the death of Bostar,[4] where he virtually parodies the speech of his opponent, or we may take a number of points raised in the course of the accusation and put them together as in the *pro Vareno*[5]: "They have asserted that, when he was

faceret cum Pompuleno, in familiam Ancharianam incidisse dixerunt, deinde Pompulenum occisum esse, illico Varenum vinctum asservatum, dum hic ostenderet, quid de eo fieri vellet. Quod est utile,[1] si erit incredibilis rei ordo et ipsa expositione fidem perditurus. Interim per partes dissolvitur, quod contextu nocet; et plerumque id est tutius. Quaedam contradictiones natura sunt singulae; id exemplis non eget.

29 Communia bene apprehenduntur non tantum, quia utriusque sunt partis, sed quia plus prosunt respondenti. Neque enim pigebit, quod saepe monui, referre; commune qui prior dicit, contrarium facit.
30 Est enim contrarium, quo adversarius bene uti potest: *At enim non verisimile est, tantum scelus M. Cottam esse commentum. Quid? hoc verisimile est, tantum scelus Oppium esse conatum?* Artificis autem est invenire in actione adversarii quae contra semetipsa pugnent aut pugnare videantur, quae aliquando ex rebus ipsis manifesta sunt, ut in causa Caeliana Clodia aurum se Caelio commodasse dicit, quod signum magnae familiaritatis est; venenum sibi paratum, quod summi

[1] utile, *Badius*: utique, *MSS.*

---

[1] *i.e.* are easy to make use of. [2] *pro Cael.* xiii.

journeying with Pompulenus through a lonely stretch of country, he fell in with the slaves of Ancharius, that Pompulenus was then killed and Varenus imprisoned on the spot until such time as this man should indicate what he wished to be done with him." Such a procedure is useful, if the sequence of facts alleged by the prosecution is incredible, and likely to lose its force by restatement. Sometimes, on the other hand, we may destroy the cumulative force of a number of statements by refuting them singly; in fact this is generally the safest course. Sometimes, again, the different portions of our reply will be independent of one another, a case which requires no illustration.

Common arguments[1] are readily appropriated, not 29
merely because they can be used by either party, but because they are of greater service to the speaker who is replying; for I shall not scruple to repeat the warning which I have often given already; the speaker who is first to employ such an argument makes it tell against himself. For an argument 30
must needs tell against a speaker if it be one which his opponent can use with effect. "But, you say, it is not probable that a crime of this magnitude was designed by Marcus Cotta. Is it probable then that a crime of this magnitude was attempted by Oppius?" On the other hand it is a task for a real artist to discover inconsistencies, real or apparent, in the speech of his opponent, though such inconsistencies are sometimes evident from the bare facts, as for instance in the case of Caelius,[2] where Clodia asserts on the one hand that she lent Caelius money, which is an indication of great intimacy, and on the other hand that he got poison to murder her, which

31 odii argumentum est. Tubero Ligarium accusat, quod is in Africa fuerit, et queritur, quod ab eo ipse in Africam non sit admissus. Aliquando vero praebet eius rei occasionem minus considerata ex adverso dicentis oratio; quod accidit praecipue cupidis sententiarum, ut ducti occasione dicendi non respiciant quid dixerint, dum locum praesentem non totam
32 causam intuentur. Quid tam videri potest contra Cluentium quam censoria nota? Quid tam contra eundem, quam filium ab Egnatio corrupti iudicii, quo Cluentius Oppianicum circumvenisset, crimine
33 exheredatum? At haec Cicero pugnare invicem ostendit: *Sed tu, Atti, consideres, censeo, diligenter, utrum censorium iudicium grave velis esse an Egnatii. Si Egnatii, leve est, quod censores de ceteris subscripserunt. Ipsum enim Egnatium, quem tu gravem esse vis, ex senatu eiecerunt. Sin autem censorium, hunc Egnatium, quem pater censoria subscriptione exheredavit, censores in senatu, cum patrem eiecissent, retinuerunt.*
34 Illa magis vitiose dicuntur quam acute reprehen-

---

[1] *pro Lig.* iii. [2] *pro Cluent.* xlviii. 135.

is a sign of violent hatred. Tubero similarly[1] 31
accuses Ligarius of having been in Africa, and complains that Ligarius refused to allow him to land in Africa. At times, however, some ill-advised statement by our opponent will give us an opportunity of demolishing his arguments. This is specially likely to occur with speakers who have a passion for producing impressive thoughts: for the temptation to air their eloquence is such that they take no heed of what they have said already, being absorbed by the topic immediately before them to the detriment of the interests of the case as a
whole. What is there likely to tell so heavily 32
against Cluentius as the stigma inflicted by the censors? What can be more damaging than the fact that Egnatius disinherited his son on the ground that he had been bribed to give a false verdict in the trial in which Cluentius secured the condemnation of Oppianicus? But Cicero[2] shows that the 33
two facts tell against one another. "But, Attius, I would urge you to give the closest consideration to the following problem. Which do you desire to carry the greater weight—the judgment of the censors, or of Egnatius? If the latter, you regard the judgment of the censors in other cases as counting for little, since they expelled this same Gnaeus Egnatius, on whose authority you lay such stress, from his place in the senate. On the other hand, if you attach most weight to the judgment of the censors, I must point out that the censors retained the younger Egnatius, whom his father disinherited by an act resembling a censorial decision, in his position as senator, although they had expelled his father."
As regards errors such as the following, the folly 34

duntur, argumentum dubium pro necessario, controversum pro confesso, commune pluribus pro proprio, vulgare, supervacuum, constitutum contra fidem. Nam et illa accidunt parum cautis, ut crimen augeant, quod probandum est; de facto disputent, cum de auctore quaeratur; impossibilia aggrediantur, pro effectis relinquant vixdum inchoata, de homine
35 dicere quam de causa malint; hominum vitia rebus adsignent, ut, si quis decemviratum accuset non Appium; manifestis repugnent; dicant, quod aliter accipi possit; summam quaestionis non intueantur, non ad proposita respondeant; quod unum aliquando recipi potest, cum mala causa adhibitis extrinsecus remediis tuenda est, ut cum peculatus reus Verres fortiter et industrie tuitus contra piratas Siciliam dicitur.

36 Eadem adversus contradictiones nobis oppositas praecepta sunt, hoc tamen amplius, quod circa eas multi duobus vitiis diversis laborant. Nam quidam etiam in foro tanquam rem molestam et odiosam praetereunt, et iis plerumque, quae composita domo

shown in their commission is out of all proportion to the skill required to deal with them: I refer to mistakes such as advancing a disputable argument as indisputable, a controversial point as admitted, a point common to a number of cases as peculiar to the case in hand, or the employment of trite, superfluous, or incredible arguments. For careless speakers are liable to commit a host of errors: they will exaggerate a charge which has still got to be proved, will argue about an act when the question is who committed it, will attempt impossibilities, drop an argument as if it were complete, whereas it is scarcely begun, speak of the individual in preference
to the case, and attribute personal faults to circum- 35
stances, as for instance if a speaker should attack the decemvirate instead of Appius. They will also contradict what is obvious, speak ambiguously, lose sight of the main issue of the case, or give replies which have no relation to the charges made. This latter procedure may, it is true, be occasionally employed when we have a bad case which requires to be supported by arguments drawn from matters foreign to the case. The trial of Verres provides an example; when accused of peculation it was alleged that he had shown courage and energy in his defence of Sicily against the pirates.

The same rules apply to objections which we may 36
have to meet. But there is one point which requires special attention, since in such cases many speakers fall into two very different faults. For some even in the courts will pass by such objections when raised by their opponents as troublesome and vexatious details, and, contenting themselves with the arguments which they have brought ready-made

attulerunt, contenti sine adversario dicunt; et scilicet multo magis in scholis, in quibus non solum contradictiones omittuntur, verum etiam materiae ipsae sic plerumque finguntur, ut nihil dici pro parte altera
37 possit. Alii diligentia lapsi verbis etiam vel sententiolis omnibus respondendum putant, quod est et infinitum et supervacuum; non enim causa reprehenditur sed actor; quem ego semper videri malim disertum, ut, si dixerit quod rei prosit, ingenii credatur laus esse non causae; si forte laedat,[1]
38 causae non ingenii culpa. Itaque illae reprehensiones aut obscuritatis, qualis in Rullum est, aut infantiae in dicendo, qualis in Pisonem, aut inscitiae rerum verborumque et insulsitatis etiam, qualis in Antonium est, animo dantur et iustis odiis, suntque utiles ad conciliandum iis, quos invisos facere volueris,
39 odium. Alia respondendi patronis ratio; et aliquando tamen eorum non oratio modo, sed vita etiam, vultus denique, incessus, habitus recte incusari solet; ut adversus Quintium Cicero non haec solum, sed ipsam etiam praetextam demissam ad talos insectatus est. Presserat enim turbulentis contionibus Cluentium

[1] non laedat, *MSS., corrected by Becher.*

---

[1] *de Leg. Agr.* II. v. 13. [2] *in Pis.* i. 30, etc.
[3] *Phil.* ii. 4, iii. 4, xiii. 19, etc. [4] *pro Cluent.* xl. 111.

from their study, will speak as if their opponent did not exist. This error is of course far more common in the schools, for there objections are not merely disregarded, but the subjects for declamation are generally framed in such a way that there is nothing to be said on the opposite side. On the other hand 37
there are some who suffer from excess of zeal, and think it their duty to reply to every word and even every trifling reflexion, a task which is at once endless and superfluous. For it is not the case, but the pleader, whom they are refuting. Personally I should always prefer that a speaker should reveal his eloquence in such a way that, if what he says advances his case, the credit will be given to his talent and not to the nature of his case, while if what he says damages his case the blame will attach to the case and not to his powers. Consequently 38
when we come across denunciations such as that directed against Rullus for the obscurity of his language,[1] or against Piso for his utter incapacity as a speaker,[2] or against Antony[3] for his lack of taste and his complete ignorance both of words and things, we shall give them our sanction as reasonable concessions to passion and just resentment, and as useful in stirring up hatred against those whom it is desired to render unpopular. The method of reply 39
to our opponent's counsel should be on different lines. Sometimes however we are justified in attacking, not merely their manner of speaking, but also their character, their appearance, their gait or bearing. Indeed, in his attack on Quintius, Cicero[4] does not confine himself to these topics, but even attacks his purple-bordered toga that goes trailing to his heels: for Quintius had caused Cluentius grave

40 Quintius. Nonnunquam elevandae invidiae gratia,
quae asperius dicta sunt, eluduntur, ut a Cicerone
Triarius. Nam cum Scauri columnas per urbem
plaustris vectas esse dixit, *Ego porro,* inquit, *qui
Albanas habeo columnas, clitellis eas apportavi.* Et
magis hoc in accusatores concessum est, quibus con-
41 viciari aliquando patrocinii fides cogit. Illa vero
adversus omnes et recepta et non inhumana con-
questio, si callide quid tacuisse, breviasse, obscurasse
42 distulisse dicuntur. Defensionis quoque permutatio
reprehenditur saepe, ut Attius adversus Cluentium,
Aeschines adversus Ctesiphontem facit, cum ille
Ciceronem lege usurum modo, hic minime de lege
dicturum Demosthenen queritur.

Declamatores vero inprimis sunt admonendi, ne contradictiones eas ponant, quibus facillime responderi possit, neu sibi stultum adversarium fingant. Facimus autem (quod maxime uberes loci popularesque sententiae nascuntur materiam dicendi nobis,

---

[1] *pro Scauro* xxii. 46. [2] *pro Cluent.* lii.
[3] Aesch. *in Ctes.* § 206. *cp.* also III. vi. 3.

embarrassment by his turbulent harangues. Some- 40
times, in order to dispel the unpopularity excited by
bitter criticism, the latter may be disposed of by a
jest, as for example Cicero disposes of Triarius.
For to the allegation that the pillars destined for the
house of Scaurus were carried on waggons through
the city streets he replied,[1] "I got my pillars
from the quarries of Alba, and had them brought in
panniers!" Such tactics are more readily allowed
against an accuser, for the duties of counsel for the
defence sometimes force him to make such personal
attacks. On the other hand there is no objection to 41
complaining of the conduct of the advocates on
either side, so long as our complaint follows accepted
practice and does not overstep the limits imposed by
good manners; I refer to complaints such as that
our opponents have abridged, obscured or postponed
the discussion of some point, or with deliberate
cunning have avoided discussing it at all. A change 42
in the tactics of defence is also often selected for
censure. For example, Attius[2] in his speech against
Cluentius complains that Cicero insists on the letter
of the law, and Aeschines[3] in his speech against
Ctesiphon complains that Demosthenes refuses to
consider the legal aspect of the case.

It is however necessary to issue a special warning to declaimers that they should not put forward objections that can easily be met or assume that their opponent is a fool. As it is, owing to our tendency to think that the subject-matter of our speech may be drawn from our own fancy, florid commonplaces and epigrams designed to bring down the house occur to our minds with the utmost

quod volumus, ducentibus) ut non sit ille inutilis versus:

Non male respondit, male enim prior ille rogarat.

43 Fallet haec nos in foro consuetudo, ubi adversario, non ipsi nobis respondebimus. Aiunt Accium interrogatum, cur causas non ageret, cum apud eum in tragoediis tanta vis esset optime respondendi, hanc reddidisse rationem, quod illic ea dicerentur quae ipse vellet, in foro dicturi adversarii essent quae minime
44 vellet. Ridiculum est ergo in exercitationibus, quae foro praeparant, prius cogitare quid responderi quam quid ex diverso dici possit. Et bonus praeceptor non minus laudare discipulum debet, si quid pro diversa quam si quid pro sua parte acriter ex-
45 cogitavit. Rursus aliud in scholis permittendum semper, in foro rarum. Nam loco a petitore primo contradictione uti qui possumus, ubi vera res agitur,
46 cum adversarius adhuc nihil dixerit? Incidunt tamen plerique in hoc vitium vel consuetudine declamatoria vel etiam cupiditate dicendi, dantque de se respondentibus venustissimos lusus, cum modo, se vero nihil dixisse neque tam stulte dicturos; modo, bene admonitos ab adversario et agere gratias, quod adiuti

---

[1] Origin unknown.

readiness, with the result that we should do well to bear in mind the lines:

> "A shrewd retort! Could it be otherwise?
> A foolish question makes for smart replies."[1]

But such a practice will be fatal in the courts, 43
where we have to answer our opponent and not ourselves. It is said that Accius, when asked why he did not turn advocate in view of the extraordinary skill in making apt replies which his tragedies revealed, replied that in his plays the characters said what he himself wanted them to say, whereas in the courts his adversaries would probably say just what
he least wanted them to say. It is therefore 44
ridiculous in exercises which prepare the student for the actual courts to consider what answer can be made before ever giving a thought to what the opposing counsel is likely to say. And a good teacher should commend a pupil no less for his skill in thinking out arguments that may be put forward for the opposite side than in discovering arguments
to prove his own case. Again, there is another 45
practice which is always permissible in the schools, but rarely in the courts. For when we speak first as claimants in a real case, how can we raise objections, seeing that our opponent has so far said
nothing? Still, many fall into this error either 46
because they have acquired the habit in declamation or simply owing to a passion for hearing their own voice, thereby affording fine sport to those who reply: for sometimes the latter will remark sarcastically that they never said anything of the kind and have no intention of saying anything so idiotic, and sometimes that they are grateful for the admirable

sint, iocantur; frequentissime vero, id quod firmissimum est, nunquam iis responsurum adversarium
fuisse, quae proposita non essent, nisi illa sciret vera
esse et ad fatendum conscientia esset impulsus; ut
47 pro Cluentio Cicero: *Nam hoc persaepe dixisti, tibi sic
renuntiari, me habere in animo causam hanc praesidio legis
defendere. Itane est? ab amicis imprudentes videlicet
prodimur? et est nescio quis de iis, quos amicos nobis
arbitramur, qui nostra consilia ad adversarium deferat?
Quisnam hoc tibi renuntiavit? quis tam improbus fuit;
cui ego autem narravi? Nemo, ut opinor, in culpa est;
48 nimirum tibi istud lex ipsa renuntiavit.* At quidam contradictione non contenti totos etiam locos explicant:
scire se hoc dicturos adversarios et ita persecuturos.
Quod factum venuste nostris temporibus elusit Vibius
Crispus, vir ingenii iucundi et elegantis: *Ego vero,*
inquit, *ista non dico; quid enim attinet illa bis dici?*
49 Nonnunquam tamen aliquid simile contradictioni
poni potest, si quid ab adversario testationibus com-
prehensum in advocationibus iactatum sit; respondebimus enim rei ab illis dictae, non a nobis excogi-
tatae; aut, si id genus erit causae, ut proponere

[1] lii. 143.

[2] The exact purport is not clear. The reference would seem to be to information as to the line of defence likely to be adopted, which has leaked out during a discussion of the written evidence by the *advocati* or legal advisers of the *patronus*. But see note prefixed to Index.

warnings so kindly given by their opponent: but most often they will say, and this is the strongest line that they can take, that their opponent would never have replied to objections which had never been raised had he not realised that these objections were justified and been driven to admit it by his consciousness of the fact. We may find an example 47
of this in the *pro Cluentio*[1] of Cicero: "You have frequently asserted that you are informed that I intend to base my defence on the letter of the law. Really! I suppose that my friends have secretly betrayed me, and that there is one among those whom I believe to be my friends who reports my designs to my opponent. Who gave you this information? Who was the traitor? And to whom did I ever reveal my design? No one, I think, is to blame. It must have been the law itself that told you." But there are some who, not content with raising 48
imaginary objections, develop whole passages on such themes, saying that they know their opponents will say this and will proceed to argue thus and thus. I remember that Vibius Crispus in our own day disposed of this practice very neatly, for he was a humorous fellow with a very pretty wit: "I do not make those objections which you attribute to me," he said, "for what use would it be to make them twice?" Sometimes however it may be possible to put for- 49
ward something not unlike such objections, if some point included by our opponent in the depositions which he produces has been discussed among his advocates[2]: for then we shall be replying to something which they have said and not to an objection which has been invented by ourselves; or again, this will be possible if the case is of such a nature that we

possimus certa, extra quae dici nihil possit: ut, cum
res furtiva in domo deprehensa sit, dicat necesse est
reus aut se ignorante illatam aut depositam apud se
aut donatam sibi; quibus omnibus, etiamsi proposita
50 non sunt, responderi potest. At in scholis recte et
propositionibus[1] et contradictionibus occurremus, ut
in utrumque locum, id est primum et secundum,
simul plurimum exerceamur. Quod nisi fecerimus,
nunquam utemur contradictione; non enim erit, cui
respondeamus.

51 Est et illud vitium nimium sollicite et circa omnia
momenta luctantis; suspectam enim facit iudici
causam, et frequenter, quae statim dicta omnem dubitationem sustulissent, dilata ipsis praeparationibus
fidem perdunt, quia patronus et aliis crediderit opus
fuisse. Fiduciam igitur orator prae se ferat semperque ita dicat, tanquam de causa optime sentiat; quod
52 sicut omnia in Cicerone praecipuum est. Nam illa
summa cura securitatis est similis, tantaque in oratione
auctoritas, ut probationis locum obtineat dubitare nobis
non audentibus. Porro, qui scierit, quid pars adversa,
quid nostra habeat valentissimum, facile iudicabit,

[1] propositionibus, *added by Badius.* See note prefixed to Index.

are in a position to state certain definite objections which are absolutely essential to our opponent's case: for instance, if stolen goods have been discovered in a house, the accused must of necessity allege either that they were brought there without his knowledge or deposited with him or given to him; and we may therefore answer all these points even although they have not been put forward. On the 50
other hand, in the schools we are quite justified in answering both statements and imaginary objections; for by these means we shall train ourselves at one and the same time for speaking either first or second. Unless we do this, we shall have no chance of employing objections, since there is no adversary to whom we can reply.

There is another serious fault into which pleaders 51
fall: the anxious over-elaboration of points. Such a procedure makes his case suspect to the judges, while frequently arguments which, if stated without more ado, would have removed all doubt, lose their force owing to the delay caused by the elaborate preparations made for their introduction, due to the fact that the advocate thinks that they require additional support. Our orator must therefore adopt a confident manner, and should always speak as if he thought his case admirable. This quality, like all other good qualities, is particularly evident in Cicero.
For the extraordinary care which he takes gives the 52
impression of confidence and carries such weight when he speaks that it does not permit us to feel the least doubt and has all the force of genuine proof. Further, the advocate who knows what are the strongest points in his own and his opponent's case will easily be able to decide what points it

quibus maxime rebus vel occurrendum sit vel instandum.

53 Ordo quidem in parte nulla minus adfert laboris. Nam si agimus, nostra confirmanda sunt primum, tum, quae nostris opponuntur refutanda; si respon-
54 demus, prius incipiendum est a refutatione. Nascuntur autem ex his, quae contradictioni opposuimus, aliae contradictiones, euntque interim longius; ut gladiatorum manus, quae secundae vocantur, fiunt et tertiae, si prima ad evocandum adversarii ictum prolata erat, et quartae, si geminata captatio est, ut bis cavere, bis repetere oportuerit; quae ratio et
55 ultra ducit. Sed illam etiam, quam supra ostendi, simplicem ex adfectibus atque ex adfirmatione sola probationem recipit refutatio, qualis est illa Scauri, de qua supra dixi; quin nescio an etiam frequentior, ubi quid negatur. Videndum praecipue utrique parti, ubi sit rei summa. Nam fere accidit, ut in causis multa dicantur, de paucis iudicetur.

56 In his probandi refutandique ratio est, sed adiuvanda viribus dicentis et ornanda. Quamlibet enim sint ad dicendum, quod volumus, accommodata ieiuna [1] tamen erunt et infirma, nisi maiore quodam
57 oratoris spiritu implentur. Quare et illi communes

[1] ieiuna, *Bonnell*: pecunia, *A* : *omitted by B.*

---

[1] Not enough is known of gladiatorial fighting to render this passage fully intelligible.
[2] v. xii. 12. [3] v. xii. 10.

will be most necessary for him to emphasise or to counter.

As regards order, there is no part of a case which 53
involves less trouble. For, if we are prosecuting, our first duty will be to prove our own case, our second to refute the arguments brought against it. If, on the other hand, we are defending, we must
begin by refutation. But from our answers to 54
objections fresh objections will arise, a process which may be carried to some length. The *strokes*[1] of gladiators provide a parallel. If the first stroke was intended to provoke the adversary to strike, the second will lead to the third, while if the challenge be repeated it will lead to the fourth stroke, so that there will be two parries and two attacks. And the
process may be prolonged still further. But refuta- 55
tion also includes that simple form of proof, which I described above,[2] based on an appeal to the emotions and mere assertion; for an example see the words of Scaurus which I have already quoted.[3] Nay, I am not sure that this form of proof is not actually of more frequent occurrence when something is denied. It is, however, specially important for both parties that they should see where the main issue lies. For it often happens that the points raised in pleading are many, although those on which a decision is given are few.

Such are the elements of the methods of proof 56
and refutation, but they require to be embellished and supported by the powers of the speaker. For although our arguments may be admirably adapted to express what we desire, they will none the less be slight and weak unless the orator makes a special
effort to give them life. Consequently the common- 57

loci de testibus, de tabulis, de argumentis aliisque
similibus magnam vim animis iudicum adferunt, et hi
proprii, quibus factum quodque laudamus aut contra,
iustum vel iniustum docemus, maius aut minus, asperius aut mitius. Ex iis autem alii ad comparationem
singulorum argumentorum faciunt, alii ad plurium,
58 alii ad totius causae inclinationem. Ex quibus sunt
qui praeparent animum iudicis, sunt qui confirment.
Sed praeparatio quoque aut confirmatio aliquando
totius causae est, aliquando partium, et proinde, ut
59 cuique conveniunt, subiicienda. Ideoque miror inter
duos diversarum sectarum velut duces non mediocri
contentione quaesitum, singulisne quaestionibus sub-
iiciendi essent loci, ut Theodoro placet, an prius
docendus iudex quam movendus, ut praecipit Apollodorus, tanquam perierit haec ratio media, et
nihil cum ipsius causae utilitate sit deliberandum.
Haec praecipiunt, qui ipsi non dicunt in foro,
ut artes a securis otiosisque compositae ipsa pug-
60 nae necessitate turbentur. Namque omnes fere,
qui legem dicendi quasi quaedam mysteria tradiderunt, certis non inveniendorum modo argumentorum

---

[1] *cp.* v. xiv. 27.

places on the subject of witnesses, documentary evidence, arguments and the like make a great impression on the minds of the judges, as also do those topics which are peculiar to the case, those I mean in which we praise or blame any action or show that it is just or unjust, or make it seem more or less important or more or less harsh than it really is. Of these topics some are adapted to the comparison of individual arguments, others to the comparison of a number, while others may serve to influence the success or failure of the whole case.
Some again prepare the mind of the judge, while 58
others confirm it in opinions already formed. But such preparation or confirmation will sometimes apply to the whole case, sometimes only to particular portions, and must therefore be employed with due regard to circumstances. I am 59
consequently surprised that there should be a violent dispute between the leaders of two opposite schools as to whether such commonplaces should be applied to individual questions (which is the view of Theodorus), or whether the judge should be instructed in the facts before any appeal is made to his feelings (the latter being the view of Apollodorus), as though no middle course were possible and no regard were to be had to the exigencies of the case itself. Those who lay down such rules have no experience of speaking in the actual courts, the result being that text-books composed in the calm leisure of the study are sadly upset by the neces-
sities of forensic strife. For practically all those 60
who have set forth the law of speaking as though it were a profound mystery,[1] have tied us down not merely to fixed topics for argument, but to definite

locis, sed concludendorum quoque nos praeceptis alligaverunt; de quibus brevissime praelocutus, quid ipse sentiam, id est quid clarissimos oratores fecisse videam, non tacebo.

XIV. Igitur enthymema et argumentum ipsum, id est rem, quae probationi alterius adhibetur, appellant et argumenti elocutionem, eam vero, ut dixi, duplicem: ex consequentibus, quod habet propositionem coniunctamque ei protinus probationem, quale pro Ligario, *Causa tum dubia, quod erat aliquid in utraque parte, quod probari posset; nunc melior ea iudicanda est, quam etiam dii adiuverunt;* habet enim rationem et
2 propositionem, non habet conclusionem. Ita est ille imperfectus syllogismus. Ex pugnantibus vero, quod etiam solum enthymema quidam vocant, fortior multo probatio est. Tale est Ciceronis pro Milone: *Eius igitur mortis sedetis ultores, cuius vitam si putetis per vos*
3 *restitui posse, nolitis.* Quod quidem etiam aliquando multiplicari solet, ut est ab eodem et pro eodem reo factum: *Quem igitur cum omnium gratia noluit, hunc voluit cum aliquorum querela? quem iure, quem loco,*

[1] For this chapter see note prefixed to Index. [2] *cp.* v. x. 2.
[3] vi. 19. The cause helped by heaven is that of Caesar. *cp.* Lucan's *victrix causa deis placuit, sed victa Catoni.*
[4] *cp.* v. x. 2.
[5] xxix. 79. The death is that of Clodius. [6] xvi. 41.

rules as to how we should draw our conclusions. I propose after making a few preliminary remarks on the subject to give a frank expression of my own views, or in other words to set forth what I perceive to have been the practice of the most distinguished orators.

XIV. The term *enthymeme*[1] is applied not merely to the actual argument, that is to say, the matter adduced to prove something else, but also to its expression, the nature of which, as I have already pointed out, is twofold.[2] It may be drawn from denial of *consequents,* when it will consist of a proposition immediately followed by a proof, as in the following passage from the *pro Ligario*[3]; "At that point the justice of the cause was doubtful, since there was something to be said on both sides. But now we can only regard that cause as superior, which even the gods supported." Here we have a proposition and a reason, but no formal conclusion: it is therefore the
incomplete syllogism known as an *enthymeme.* It may 2
on the other hand be drawn from *incompatibles,* in which case the proof will be much stronger; indeed some restrict the title of *enthymeme*[4] to this form of argument. The following passage from the *pro Milone*[5] of Cicero will provide a parallel: "You are then sitting there to avenge the death of a man whom you would refuse to restore to life, even if
you thought it within your power to do so." This form 3
of argument may even at times consist of a number of clauses, as in the following passage from the same speech[6]: "Was he resolved then to kill to the dissatisfaction of some a man whom he refused to kill to the satisfaction of all? Are we to believe that he did not hesitate, in defiance of the law and

quem tempore, quem impune non est ausus, hunc iniuria, iniquo loco, alieno tempore, cum periculo capitis non
4 *dubitavit occidere?* Optimum autem videtur enthymematis genus, cum propositio dissimili vel contraria ratio subiungitur, quale est Demosthenis: *Non enim, si quid unquam contra leges actum est, idque tu es imitatus, idcirco te convenit poena liberari; quin e contrario damnari multo magis. Nam ut, si quis eorum damnatus esset, tu haec non scripsisses, ita, damnatus tu si fueris, non scribet alius.*

5 Epichirematos et quattuor et quinque et sex etiam factae sunt partes a quibusdam. Cicero maxime quinque defendit, ut sit propositio, deinde ratio eius, tum adsumptio et eius probatio, quinta complexio; quia vero interim et propositio non egeat rationis et adsumptio probationis, nonnunquam etiam complexione opus non sit, et quadripertitam et tripertitam et
6 bipertitam quoque fieri posse ratiocinationem. Mihi et pluribus nihilominus auctoribus tres summum videntur. Nam ita se habet ipsa natura, ut sit, de quo quaeratur et per quod probetur; tertium adiici potest velut ex consensu duorum antecedentium. Ita erit

---

[1] *in Androt.* § 7; *in Aristocr.* § 99.
[2] *de Inv.* I. xxxvii. 67.

despite the unfavourable circumstances both of time and place and the risk involved to his own life, to kill one whom he did not venture to kill when he might have done so legally, at his own time and place and without the least danger to himself?" The 4
most effective kind of *enthymeme* seems however to be that in which a reason is subjoined to a dissimilar or contrary proposition as in the following passage from Demosthenes[1]: "For if at any time an act has been committed contrary to law and you have imitated it, it does not therefore follow that you should go scot free; on the contrary it is an additional reason why you should be condemned. For if any of those who transgressed the law had been condemned, you would not have proposed this, and further, if you are condemned, no one else will propose anything of the kind."

As regards the *epicheireme*, some authorities hold 5
that it consists of four, five, and even six parts. Cicero[2] urges that there are not more than five at most, *i.e.* the major premise and its reason, the minor premise and its proof, and fifthly the conclusion. But since at times the major premise does not require a reason nor the minor a proof, while occasionally even the conclusion is not necessary, he holds that the *epicheireme* may consist of only four, three, or even two parts. Personally however 6
I follow the majority of authorities in holding that there are not more than three parts. For it follows from the very nature of reasoning that there must be something to form the subject of enquiry and something else to provide the proof, while the third element which has to be added may be regarded as resulting from the agreement of the two previous

prima intentio, secunda adsumptio, tertia connexio.
Nam confirmatio primae ac secundae partis et exor-
7 natio eisdem cedere possunt, quibus subiiciuntur. Sumamus enim ex Cicerone quinque partium exemplum:
*Melius gubernantur ea, quae consilio reguntur quam quae
sine consilio administrantur.* Hanc primam partem
numerant; eam deinceps rationibus variis et quam
copiosissimis verbis approbari putant oportere. Hoc
ego totum cum sua ratione unum puto; alioqui si
ratio pars est, est autem varia ratio, plures partes
8 esse dicantur. Adsumptionem deinde ponit: *Nihil
autem omnium rerum melius quam omnis mundus administratur.* Huius adsumptionis quarto in loco iam porro
inducunt approbationem; de quo idem quod supra
9 dico. Quinto inducunt loco complexionem, quae aut
id infert solum quod ex omnibus partibus cogitur,
hoc modo, *Consilio igitur mundus administratur;* aut,
unum in locum cum conduxit breviter propositionem
et adsumptionem, adiungit quid ex his conficiatur, ad
hunc modum: *Quodsi melius geruntur, quae consilio
quam quae sine consilio administrantur, nihil autem
omnium rerum melius quam omnis mundus administratur, consilio igitur mundus administratur.* Cui parti
consentio.

10 In tribus autem, quas fecimus, partibus non est

---

[1] *de Inv.* I. xxxiv. 58.

elements. Thus the first part will be the major, the second the minor premise and the third the conclusion. For the confirmation and development of both premises may reasonably be included in the parts to which they belong. Let us then take 7
an example from Cicero[1] of the *epicheireme* consisting of five parts. "Those things which are controlled by reason are better governed than those which are not." This they call the first part and consider that it requires to be established by various reasons and a copious display of eloquence. Personally I hold that the whole of this together with its reason forms but one part. Otherwise, if the *reason* is to be treated as a separate part and if there are a variety of *reasons*, this will involve an addition to the number of parts. Next he produces the *minor premise*: 8
"But there is nothing better administered than the universe." The proof of this minor premise is treated as the fourth part of the *epicheireme*. My criticism of this statement is identical with my criticism of the preceding. The fifth place they 9
assign to the conclusion which either merely makes the necessary inference from the preceding parts (*i.e.* "Therefore the universe is governed by reason") or after briefly bringing major and minor premise together adds what is deduced from them with the following result: "But if on the one hand things that are controlled by reason are better governed than things which are not and on the other nothing is better administered than the universe, then it follows that the universe is governed by reason." As regards this part of the *epicheireme* I agree.

I have said that the *epicheireme* consists of three 10
parts: its form is not however invariable. There is

forma semper eadem, sed una, in qua idem concluditur quod intenditur: *Anima immortalis est. Nam quidquid ex se ipso movetur, immortale est; anima autem ex se ipsa movetur, immortalis igitur est anima.* Hoc fit non solum in singulis argumentis sed in totis causis,
11 quae sunt simplices, et in quaestionibus. Nam et hae primam habent propositionem: *Sacrilegium commisisti; Non, quisquis hominem occidit, caedis tenetur,* deinde rationem; (sed haec est in causis et quaestione longior quam in singulis argumentis) et plerumque summa complexione, vel per enumerationem vel per brevem conclusionem, testantur, quid effecerint. In hoc genere propositio dubia est, de
12 hac enim quaeritur. Altera est complexio non par intentioni sed vim habens parem: *Mors nihil ad nos, nam quod est dissolutum, sensu caret; quod autem sensu caret, nihil ad nos.* In alio genere non eadem propositio est quae connexio: *Omnia animalia meliora sunt quam inanima, nihil autem melius est mundo, mundus igitur animal.* Hic potest videri deesse intentio.[1] Potuit enim sic constitui ratiocinatio: *Animal est mundus, omnia enim animalia meliora sunt quam inanima*
13 et cetera. Haec propositio aut confessa est ut

[1] deesse, *Madvig*: de re, *MSS.*: intentio, *Spalding*: contentio, *MSS.*

---

[1] See III. vi. 9, 10.

firstly the form in which the *conclusion* is identical with what has already been stated in the *major premise.* "The soul is immortal, since whatever derives its motion from itself is immortal. But the soul derives its motion from itself. Therefore the soul is immortal." This process occurs not merely in individual arguments, but in whole *cases,* provided they are of a simple character, and also in *questions.*[1]
For cases and questions always have first a *major* 11
premise, such as "You have committed sacrilege," or "Not everyone who has killed a man is guilty of murder." Second comes a *reason,* which is stated at greater length in cases and questions than in separate arguments, while finally comes the *conclusion* in which as a rule they set forth the point they have proved either by enumeration of particulars or in the form of a hasty conclusion. In this type of *epicheireme* the *major premise* is doubtful, since
it is still under investigation. There is another 12
form of *conclusion* which is not actually identical with the *major premise,* but has the same force "Death is nothing to us, for that which is dissolved into its elements is devoid of feeling, and that which is devoid of feeling is nothing to us." There is a third form in which the *major premise* and the *conclusion* are different. "All animate things are better than inanimate, but there is nothing better than the universe, wherefore the universe is animate." It may be thought that in this case there is no real *major premise,* since it would be possible to state the reasoning in the following form: "The universe is animate, for all things animate are better
than inanimate," etcetera. This *major premise* is either 13
an admitted fact as in the last example or requires

proxima, aut probanda ut, *Qui beatam vitam vivere volet, philosophetur oportet,* non enim conceditur; cetera sequi nisi confirmata prima parte non possunt. Item adsumptio interim confessa est ut, *Omnes autem volunt beatam vitam vivere;* interim probanda ut illa, *Quod est dissolutum, sensu caret;* cum, soluta corpore anima an sit immortalis vel ad tempus certe maneat, sit in dubio. Quam adsumptionem alii, rationem alii vocant.

14 Epichirema autem nullo differt a syllogismis, nisi
quod illi et plures habent species et vera colligunt
veris, epichirematis frequentior circa credibilia est
usus. Nam si contingeret semper controversa confessis probare, vix esset in hoc genere usus oratoris.
15 Nam quo ingenio est opus, ut dicas: *Bona ad me*
pertinent, solus enim sum filius defuncti, vel *solus heres,*
cum iure bonorum possessio testati secundum tabulas tes-
16 *tamenti detur, ad me igitur pertinet.* Sed cum ipsa
ratio in quaestionem venit, efficiendum est certum id
quo probaturi sumus quod incertum est: ut si ipsa
forte intentione dicatur aut *filius non es* aut *non es*
legitimus aut *non es solus,* itemque aut *non es heres,*
aut *non iustum testamentum est,* aut *capere non potes,* aut
habes coheredes, efficiendum est iustum, propter quod

to be proved as in the following: "He who wishes to live a happy life, must be a philosopher": for this is not an acknowledged truth, and the premises must be established before we can arrive at the conclusion. Sometimes again the *minor premise* is an admitted fact, as for instance, "But all men wish to live a happy life," while sometimes it requires to be proved, as for example the statement quoted above, "That which is dissolved into its elements is devoid of feeling," since it is doubtful whether the soul is immortal after its release from the body or only continues to exist for a time. Some call this a *minor premise*, some a *reason*.

There is no difference between the *epicheireme* and 14
the *syllogism*, except that the latter has a number of forms and infers truth from truth, whereas the *epicheireme* is frequently concerned with statements that are no more than credible. For if it were always possible to prove controversial points from admitted premises, the orator would have little to
do in this connexion. For what skill does it require 15
to say, "The property is mine, for I am the only son of the deceased," or "I am the sole heir, since possession of the testator's estate is given by the law of property in accordance with the terms of his will:
the property therefore belongs to me"? But when 16
the reason given is itself disputable, we must establish the certainty of the premises by which we are proposing to prove what is uncertain. For example, if our opponent says "You are not his son" or "You are illegitimate" or "You are not his only son"; or, again, "You are not his heir" or "The will is invalid" or "You are not entitled to inherit" or "You have co-heirs," we must prove the validity

17 nobis bona adiudicari debeant. Sed tum est necessaria illa summa connexio, cum intervenit ratio longior; alioqui sufficiunt intentio ac ratio: *Silent enim leges inter arma nec se expectari iubent, cum ei, qui exspectare velit, ante iniusta poena luenda sit quam iusta repetenda.* Ideoque id enthymema, quod est ex consequentibus, rationi simile dixerunt. Sed et singula, interimque recte, ponuntur, ut ipsum illud
18 *Silent leges inter arma;* et a ratione incipere fas est, deinde concludere, ut ibidem: *Quodsi duodecim tabulae nocturnum furem quoquo modo, diurnum autem, si se telo defenderet, interfici impune voluerunt, quis est qui, quoquo modo quis interfectus sit, puniendum putet?* Variavit hic adhuc et rursus rationem tertio loco posuit, *cum videat aliquando gladium nobis ab ipsis*
19 *porrigi legibus.* Per constantem[1] partis duxit ordinem: *Insidiatori vero et latroni quae potest inferri iniusta nex?* hoc intentio; *Quid comitatus nostri, quid gladii volunt?* hoc ratio; *Quos habere certe non liceret, si uti illis nullo pacto liceret,* hoc ex ratione et intentione connexio.

[1] per constantem, *Radermacher*: prioris autem, *MSS.*

---

[1] *pro Mil.* iv. 10. [2] *ib.* iii. 9. [3] *ib.* iv. 10.

of the reason on which we base our claim that the property should be adjudicated to us. But when 17
a *reason* of unusual length intervenes, it is necessary to state the final conclusion, otherwise the *major premise* and the *reason* would suffice. "Laws are silent in the midst of arms, and do not require us to await their sanction when the circumstances are such that he who would await their sanction is certain to be the victim of an unjust penalty before ever the just penalty can be claimed."[1] Hence it has been asserted that the form of *enthymeme* which is based on denial of consequents resembles a *reason.* But sometimes, again, it is sufficient to state a single proposition as in the example just quoted, "The laws are silent in the midst of arms." We may also begin 18
with the *reason* and then proceed to the conclusion as in another passage from the same speech[2]: "But if the Twelve Tables permitted the killing of a thief by night under any circumstances, and by day if he used a weapon to defend himself, who is there who will contend that the slayer must be punished under whatever circumstances a man has been killed?" The process is still further varied by Cicero, and the *reason* placed third, as in the phrase, "When he sees that the sword is sometimes placed in our hands by the laws themselves." On the other hand, he 19
places the various parts in the regular order in the following instance: "How can it be unjust to kill a robber who lies in wait for his victim?"[3] Next comes the *reason:* "What is the object of our escorts and our swords?" Last comes the conclusion resulting from the *major premise* and the *reason:* "Which we certainly should not be permitted to have, if we were absolutely forbidden to use them."

20 Huic generi probationis tribus occurritur modis, id est per omnes partes. Aut enim expugnatur intentio aut adsumptio aut conclusio, nonnunquam omnia. Intentio expugnatur: *Iure occidi eum, qui insidiatus sit.* Nam prima statim quaestio pro Milone est, *an ei fas sit lucem intueri qui a se hominem necatum*
21 *esse fateatur.* Expugnatur adsumptio omnibus iis quae de refutatione diximus. Et ratio quidem nonnunquam[1] est vera, cum eius propositio vera non sit; interim verae propositionis falsa ratio est. *Virtus bonum est,* verum est; si quis rationem subiiciat, *quod ea locupletes faciat,* verae intentionis falsa sit ratio.
22 Conclusio autem aut vera negatur, cum aliud colligit quam id quod ex prioribus efficitur, aut nihil ad quaestionem dicitur pertinere. Non est vera sic: *Insidiator iure occiditur; nam cum vitae vim adferat ut hostis, debet etiam repelli ut hostis; recte igitur Clodius ut hostis occisus est;* non utique, nondum enim Clodium insidiatorem ostendimus. Sed fit vera connexio, *Recte igitur insidiator ut hostis occiditur;* nihil ad nos,
23 nondum enim Clodius insidiator apparet. Sed ut potest vera esse intentio et ratio et tamen falsa

[1] nonnunquam, *MSS.* : nunquam, *Victor.*

---

[1] In the preceding chapter.

This form of proof may be countered in three ways, that is to say it may be attacked in all its parts. For either the *major premise* or the *minor* or the *conclusion* or occasionally all three are refuted. The *major premise* is refuted in the following case: "I was justified in killing him, as he lay in wait for me." For the very first question in the defence of Milo is "whether it is right that he who confesses that he has killed a man should look upon the light 20
of day." The *minor premise* is refuted by all the 21
methods which we mentioned in dealing with refutation.[1] As to the *reason* it must be pointed out that it is sometimes true when the *proposition* to which it is attached is not true, but may on the other hand sometimes be false although the proposition is true. For example, "Virtue is a good thing" is true, but if the reason, "Because it brings us wealth," be added, we shall have an instance of a true *major*
premise and a false *reason.* With regard to the 22
conclusion, we may either deny its truth when it infers something which does not logically result from the premises, or we may treat it as irrelevant. The truth is denied in the following case: "We are justified in killing one who lies in wait for us; for since, like an enemy, he threatens us with violence, we ought to repulse his attack as though he were an enemy: therefore Milo was justified in killing Clodius as an enemy." The conclusion is not valid, since we have not yet proved that Clodius lay in wait for him. But the conclusion that we are therefore justified in killing one who lies in wait for us is perfectly true, though irrelevant to the case, for it is not yet clear that Clodius lay in wait
for Milo. But while the *major premise* and the *reason* 23

connexio, ita, si illa falsa sunt, nunquam est vera
connexio.

24 Enthymema ab aliis oratorius syllogismus, ab aliis
pars dicitur syllogismi, propterea quod syllogismus
utique conclusionem et propositionem habet et per
omnes partes efficit, quod proposuit, enthymema
25 tantum intelligi contentum sit. Syllogismus talis:
*Solum bonum virtus, nam id demum bonum est, quo nemo
male uti potest; virtute nemo male uti potest, bonum est
ergo virtus.* Enthymema ex consequentibus: *Bonum
est virtus, qua nemo male uti potest.* Et contra, *Non est
bonum pecunia; non enim bonum, quo quis male uti
potest; pecunia potest quis male uti, non igitur bonum est
pecunia.* Enthymema ex pugnantibus: *An bonum est
26 pecunia, qua quis male uti potest?—Si pecunia, quae
est in argento signato, argentum est, qui argentum omne
legavit, et pecuniam, quae est in argento signato, legavit;
argentum autem omne legavit, igitur et pecuniam, quae est
in argento, legavit,* habet formam syllogismi. Oratori
satis est dicere, *Cum argentum legaverit omne, pecuniam
quoque legavit, quae est in argento.*

27 Peregisse mihi videor sacra tradentium artes, sed
consilio locus superest. Namque ego, ut in oratione

may both be true and the conclusion false, yet if both are false, the conclusion can never be true.

Some call the *enthymeme* a *rhetorical syllogism,* while 24
others regard it as a part of the *syllogism,* because whereas the latter always has its premises and conclusion and effects its proof by the employment of all its parts, the *enthymeme* is content to let its
proof be understood without explicit statement. The 25
following is an example of a syllogism: "Virtue is the only thing that is good, for that alone is good which no one can put to a bad use: but no one can make a bad use of virtue; virtue therefore is good." The *enthymeme* draws its conclusion from denial of consequents. "Virtue is a good thing because no one can put it to a bad use." On the other hand take the following syllogism. "Money is not a good thing; for that is not good which can be put to a bad use: money may be put to a bad use; therefore money is not a good thing." The *enthymeme* draws its conclusion from incompatibles. "Can money be a good thing when it is possible to put it
to a bad use?" The following argument is couched 26
in syllogistic form: "If money in the form of silver coin is silver, the man who bequeathes all his silver to a legatee, includes all money in the form of coined silver: but he bequeathed all his silver: therefore he included in the bequest all money in the form of coined silver." But for the orator it will be sufficient to say, "Since he bequeathed all his silver, he included in his bequest all his silver money."

I think I have now dealt with all the precepts of 27
those who treat oratory as a mystery. But these rules still leave scope for free exercise of the judgment. For although I consider that there are occasions

syllogismo quidem aliquando uti nefas non duco, ita constare totam aut certe confertam esse aggressionum et enthymematum stipatione minime velim. Dialogis enim et dialecticis disputationibus erit similior quam nostri operis actionibus, quae quidem inter se pluri-
28 mum differunt. Namque in illis homines docti et inter doctos verum quaerentes minutius et scrupulosius scrutantur omnia, et ad liquidum confessumque perducunt, ut qui sibi et inveniendi et iudicandi vindicent partes, quarum alteram *τοπικήν* alteram
29 *κριτικήν* vocant. Nobis ad aliorum iudicia componenda est oratio, et saepius apud omnino imperitos atque illarum certe ignaros litterarum loquendum est, quos nisi et delectatione allicimus et viribus trahimus et nonnunquam turbamus adfectibus, ipsa, quae iusta ac vera sunt, tenere non possumus.
30 Locuples et speciosa et imperiosa vult esse eloquentia; quorum nihil consequetur, si conclusionibus certis et in unam prope formam cadentibus concisa et contemptum ex humilitate et odium ex quadam severitate et ex copia satietatem et ex simili-
31 tudine fastidium attulerit. Feratur ergo non semitis sed campis, non uti fontes angustis fistulis colliguntur

when the orator may lawfully employ the syllogism, I am far from desiring him to make his whole speech consist of or even be crowded with a mass of *epicheiremes* and *enthymemes.* For a speech of that character would resemble dialogues and dialectical controversies rather than pleadings of the kind with which we are concerned, and there is an enormous difference between the two. For in the former we 28
are confronted with learned men seeking for truth among men of learning; consequently they subject everything to a minute and scrupulous inquiry with a view to arriving at clear and convincing truths, and they claim for themselves the tasks of invention and judgment, calling the former τοπική or the art of selecting the appropriate material for treatment, and the latter κριτική or the art of criticism. We on the other hand have to compose our 29
speeches for others to judge, and have frequently to speak before an audience of men who, if not thoroughly ill-educated, are certainly ignorant of such arts as dialectic: and unless we attract them by the charm of our discourse or drag them by its force, and occasionally throw them off their balance by an appeal to their emotions, we shall be unable to vindicate the claims of truth and justice. Elo- 30
quence aims at being rich, beautiful and commanding, and will attain to none of these qualities if it be broken up into conclusive inferences which are generally expressed in the same monotonous form: on the contrary its meanness will excite contempt, its severity dislike, its elaboration satiety, and its sameness boredom. Eloquence therefore must not restrict 31
itself to narrow tracks, but range at large over the open fields. Its streams must not be conveyed

sed ut beatissimi amnes totis vallibus fluunt, ac sibi viam, si quando non acceperit, faciat. Nam quid illa miserius lege velut praeformatas infantibus litteras persequentium et, ut Graeci dicere solent, quem mater amictum dedit, sollicite custodientium: propositio ac conclusio ex consequentibus et repugnan-
32 tibus? Non inspiret? non augeat? non mille figuris variet ac verset? ut ea nasci et ipsa provenire natura, non manu facta et arte suspecta magistrum fateri ubique videantur? Quis unquam sic dixit orator? Nonne apud ipsum Demosthenen paucissima huius generis[1] reperiuntur? Quae apprehensa Graeci magis (nam hoc solum peius faciunt) in catenas ligant et inexplicabili serie connectunt, et indubitata colligunt et probant confessa et se antiquis per hoc similes vocant, deinde interrogati nunquam respondebunt, quem imitentur. Sed de figuris alio loco.

33 Nunc illud adiiciendum, ne iis quidem consentire me, qui semper argumenta sermone puro et dilucido et distincto ceterum minime elato ornatoque putant esse dicenda. Namque ea distincta quidem ac per-

[1] generis, *Zumpt*: veris, *A*: veris vel artis, *G*.

---

[1] The proverb which is also found in Plutarch (*de Alex. Fort.* i. 330 B) seems to refer to a child's passionate fondness for some particular garment. [2] IX. i. ii. iii.

through narrow pipes like the water of fountains, but flow as mighty rivers flow, filling whole valleys; and if it cannot find a channel it must make one for itself. For what can be more distressing than to be fettered by petty rules, like children who trace the letters of the alphabet which others have first written for them, or, as the Greeks say, insist on keeping the coat their mother gave them.[1] Are we to have nothing but premises and conclusions from consequents and incompatibles? Must not the orator breathe life into the argument and
develop it? Must he not vary and diversify it by a 32
thousand figures, and do all this in such a way that it seems to come into being as the very child of nature, not to reveal an artificial manufacture and a suspect art nor at every moment to show traces of an instructor's hand? What orator ever spoke thus? Even in Demosthenes we find but few traces of such a mechanism. And yet the Greeks of to-day are even more prone than we are (though this is the only point in which their practice is worse than ours) to bind their thoughts in fetters and to connect them by an inexorable chain of argument, making inferences where there was never any doubt, proving admitted facts and asserting that in so doing they are following the orators of old, although they always refuse to answer the question who it is that they are imitating. However of figures I shall speak elsewhere.[2]

For the present I must add that I do not even 33
agree with those who hold that arguments should always be expressed in language which is not only pure, lucid and distinct, but also as free as possible from all elevation and ornateness. I readily admit that

spicua debere esse confiteor, in rebus vero minoribus etiam sermone ac verbis quam maxime propriis et ex
34 usu; at si maior erit materia, nullum iis ornatum, qui modo non obscuret, subtrahendum puto. Nam et saepe plurimum lucis adfert ipsa translatio, cum etiam iurisconsulti, quorum summus circa verborum proprietatem labor est, litus esse audeant dicere, qua
35 fluctus eludit.[1] Quoque quid est natura magis asperum, hoc pluribus condiendum est voluptatibus; et minus suspecta argumentatio dissimulatione, et multum ad fidem adiuvat audientis voluptas. Nisi forte existimamus Ciceronem haec ipsa mala in argumentatione dixisse, *silere leges inter arma*, et *gladium nobis interim ab ipsis porrigi legibus.* Hic tamen habendus istis modus, ut sint ornamento non impedimento.

[1] elidit, *Valla.*

arguments should be distinct and clear, and further that in arguments of a minor character the language and words should be as appropriate and as familiar as possible. But if the subject be one of real im- 34
portance every kind of ornament should be employed, so long as it does nothing to obscure our meaning. For metaphor will frequently throw a flood of light upon a subject: even lawyers, who spend so much trouble over the appropriateness of words, venture to assert that the word *litus* is derived from *eludere*, because the shore is a place where the waves break
in play. Further, the more unattractive the natural 35
appearance of anything, the more does it require to be seasoned by charm of style: moreover, an argument is often less suspect when thus disguised, and the charm with which it is expressed makes it all the more convincing to our audience. Unless indeed we think that Cicero was in error when he introduced phrases such as the following into an argumentative passage: "The laws are silent in the midst of arms," and "A sword is sometimes placed in our hands by the laws themselves." However, we must be careful to observe a happy mean in the employment of such embellishments, so that they may prove a real ornament and not a hindrance.

BOOK VI

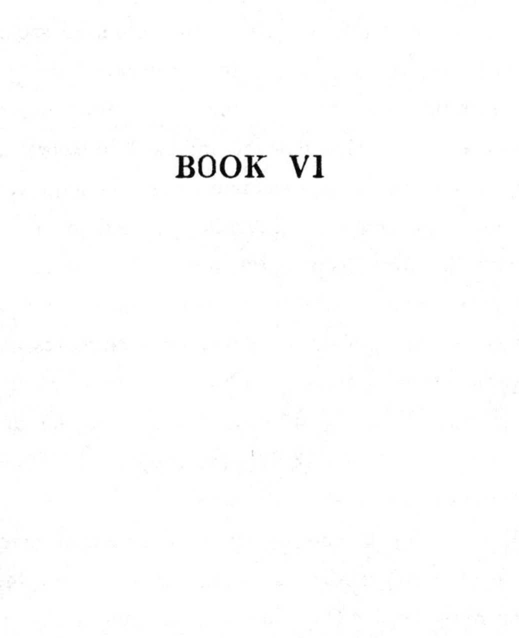

LIBER VI

Prooemium

Haec, Marcelle Victori, ex tua voluntate maxime
ingressus, tum si qua ex nobis ad iuvenes bonos pervenire posset utilitas, novissime paene etiam necessitate quadam officii delegati mihi sedulo laborabam;
respiciens tamen illam curam meae voluptatis, quod
filio, cuius eminens ingenium sollicitam quoque
parentis diligentiam merebatur, hanc optimam partem relicturus hereditatis videbar ut, si me, quod
aequum et optabile fuit, fata intercepissent, prae-
2 ceptore tamen patre uteretur. At me fortuna id
agentem diebus ac noctibus festinantemque metu
meae mortalitatis ita subito prostravit, ut laboris mei
fructus ad neminem minus quam ad me pertineret.
Illum enim, de quo summa conceperam et in quo
spem unicam senectutis reponebam, repetito vulnere
3 orbitatis amisi. Quid nunc agam? aut quem ultra

[1] *cp.* Proem, Bk. I. [2] *cp.* Proem, Bk. IV.

BOOK VI

Preface

I UNDERTOOK my present task, Marcellus Victorius, mainly to gratify your request,[1] but also with a view to assist the more earnest of our young men as far as lay in my power, while latterly the energy with which I have devoted myself to my labours has been inspired by the almost imperative necessity imposed by the office conferred on me,[2] though all the while I have had an eye to my own personal pleasure. For I thought that this work would be the most precious part of the inheritance that would fall to my son, whose ability was so remarkable that it called for the most anxious cultivation on the part of his father. Thus if, as would have been but just and devoutly to be wished, the fates had torn me from his side, he would still have been able to enjoy the benefit of
his father's instruction. Night and day I pursued 2
this design, and strove to hasten its completion in the fear that death might cut me off with my task unfinished, when misfortune overwhelmed me with such suddenness, that the success of my labours now interests no one less than myself. A second bereavement has fallen upon me, and I have lost him of whom I had formed the highest expectations, and in whom I reposed all the hopes that should solace
my old age. What is there left for me to do? Or 3

esse usum mei, diis repugnantibus, credam? Nam ita forte accidit, ut eum quoque librum, quem de causis corruptae eloquentiae emisi, iam scribere aggressus ictu simili ferirer. Nonne igitur optimum fuit, infaustum opus et quidquid hoc est in me infelicium litterarum super immaturum funus consumpturis viscera mea flammis iniicere neque hanc impiam
4 vivacitatem novis insuper curis fatigare? Quis enim mihi bonus parens ignoscat, si studere amplius possum, ac non oderit hanc animi mei firmitatem, si quis in me alius usus vocis, quam ut incusem deos superstes omnium meorum, nullam in terras despicere providentiam tester, si non meo casu, cui tamen nihil obiici, nisi quod vivam, potest, at illorum certe, quos utique immeritos mors acerba damnavit, erepta prius mihi matre eorundem, quae nondum expleto aetatis undevicesimo anno duos enixa filios, quamvis
5 acerbissimis rapta fatis, non infelix decessit? Ego vel hoc uno malo sic eram adflictus, ut me iam nulla fortuna posset efficere felicem. Nam cum omni virtute, quae in feminas cadit, functa insanabilem attulit marito dolorem, tum aetate tam puellari, praesertim meae comparata, potest et ipsa numerari
6 inter vulnera orbitatis. Liberis tamen superstitibus et, quod nefas erat, sed optabat ipsa, me salvo maxi-

what further use can I hope to be on earth, when
heaven thus frowns upon me? For it so chances
that just at the moment when I began my book on
the causes of the decline of eloquence, I was stricken
by a like affliction. Better had I thrown that ill-
omened work and all my ill-starred learning upon
the flames of that untimely pyre that was to consume
the darling of my heart, and had not sought to
burden my unnatural persistence in this wicked
world with the fatigue of fresh labours! For what 4
father with a spark of proper feeling would pardon
me for having the heart to pursue my researches
further, and would not hate me for my insensibility,
had I other use for my voice than to rail against
high heaven for having suffered me to outlive all
my nearest and dearest, and to testify that providence deigns not at all to watch over this earth of
ours? If this is not proved by my own misfortune
(and yet my only fault is that I still live), it is most
surely manifest in theirs, who were cut off thus
untimely; their mother was taken from me earlier
still, she had borne me two sons ere the completion of
her nineteenth year; but for her, though she too died
most untimely, death was a blessing. Yet for me her 5
death alone was such a blow that thereafter no good
fortune could bring me true happiness. For she had
every virtue that is given to woman to possess, and
left her husband a prey to irremediable grief; nay,
so young was she when death took her, that if her
age be compared with mine, her decease was like
the loss not merely of a wife, but of a daughter.
Still her children survived her, and I, too, lived on 6
by some unnatural ordinance of fate, which for all
its perversity was what she herself desired; and

mos cruciatus praecipiti via effugit. Mihi filius minor
quintum egressus annum prior alterum ex duobus
7 eruit lumen. Non sum ambitiosus in malis nec
augere lacrimarum causas volo, utinamque esset ratio
minuendi. Sed dissimulare qui possum, quid ille
gratiae in vultu, quid iucunditatis in sermone, quos
ingenii igniculos, quam substantiam placidae et (quod
scio vix posse credi) iam tum altae mentis ostenderit;
qualis amorem quicunque alienus infans mereretur.
8 Illud vero insidiantis, quo me validius cruciaret,
fortunae fuit, ut ille mihi blandissimus me suis nutri-
cibus, me aviae educanti, me omnibus, qui sollicitare
9 illas aetates solent, anteferret. Quapropter illi do-
lori, quem ex matre optima atque omnem laudem
supergressa paucos ante menses ceperam, gratulor.
Minus enim est, quod flendum meo nomine quam
quod illius gaudendum est.

Una post haec Quintiliani mei spe ac voluptate
10 nitebar, et poterat sufficere solacio. Non enim flos-
culos, sicut prior, sed iam decimum aetatis ingressus
annum, certos ac deformatos fructus ostenderat.
Iuro per mala mea, per infelicem conscientiam, per
illos manes, numina mei doloris, eas me in illo
vidisse virtutes ingenii, non modo ad percipiendas
disciplinas, quo nihil praestantius cognovi plurima
expertus, studiique iam tum non coacti (sciunt prae-

thus by her swift departure from this life she escaped the worst of tortures. My youngest boy was barely five, when he was the first to leave me, robbing me
as it were of one of my two eyes. I have no desire 7
to flaunt my woes in the public gaze, nor to exaggerate the cause I have for tears; would that I had some means to make it less! But how can I forget the charm of his face, the sweetness of his speech, his first flashes of promise, and his actual possession of a calm and, incredible though it may seem, a powerful mind. Such a child would have captivated
my affections, even had he been another's. Nor was 8
this all; to enhance my agony the malignity of designing fortune had willed that he should devote all his love to me, preferring me to his nurses, to his grandmother who brought him up, and all those who, as a rule, win the special affection of infancy.
I am, therefore, grateful to the grief that came to 9
me some few months before his loss in the death of his mother, the best of women, whose virtues were beyond all praise. For I have less reason to weep my own fate than to rejoice at hers.

After these calamities all my hopes, all my delight were centred on my little Quintilian, and he might
have sufficed to console me. For his gifts were not 10
merely in the bud like those of his brother: as early as his ninth birthday he had put forth sure and well-formed fruit. By my own sorrows, by the testimony of my own sad heart, by his departed spirit, the deity at whose shrine my grief does worship, I swear that I discerned in him such talent, not merely in receiving instruction, although in all my wide experience I have never seen his like, nor in his power of spontaneous application, to which his

ceptores), sed probitatis, pietatis, humanitatis, liberalitatis, ut prorsus posset hinc esse tanti fulminis metus, quod observatum fere est celerius occidere festinatam maturitatem et esse nescio quam, quae spes tantas decerpat, invidiam, ne videlicet ultra
11 quam homini datum est nostra provehantur. Etiam illa fortuita aderant omnia, vocis iucunditas claritasque, oris suavitas et in utracunque lingua, tanquam ad eam demum natus esset, expressa proprietas omnium litterarum. Sed hae spes adhuc; illa maiora, constantia, gravitas, contra dolores etiam ac metus robur. Nam quo ille animo, qua medicorum admiratione mensium octo valetudinem tulit! ut me in supremis consolatus est! quam etiam deficiens iamque non noster ipsum illum alienatae mentis
12 errorem circa scholas ac litteras habuit! Tuosne ego, o meae spes inanes, labentes oculos, tuum fugientem spiritum vidi? Tuum corpus frigidum exsangue complexus animam recipere auramque communem haurire amplius potui, dignus his cruciatibus, quos
13 fero, dignus his cogitationibus? Tene consulari nuper adoptione ad omnium spes honorum prius admotum, te avunculo praetori generum destinatum, te [omnium spes] avitae eloquentiae candidatum, super-

[1] It was customary for the next-of-kin to receive in the mouth the last breath of the dying to continue the existence of the spirit.

teachers can bear witness, but such upright, pious, humane and generous feelings, as alone might have sufficed to fill me with the dread of the fearful thunder-stroke that has smitten me down: for it is a matter of common observation that those who ripen early die young, and that there is some malign influence that delights in cutting short the greatest promise and refusing to permit our joys to pass beyond the bound allotted to mortal man. He 11
possessed every incidental advantage as well, a pleasing and resonant voice, a sweetness of speech, and a perfect correctness in pronouncing every letter both in Greek and Latin, as though either were his native tongue. But all these were but the promise of greater things. He had finer qualities, courage and dignity, and the strength to resist both fear and pain. What fortitude he showed during an illness of eight months, till all his physicians marvelled at him! How he consoled me during his last moments. How even in the wanderings of delirium did his thoughts recur to his lessons and his literary studies, even when his strength was sinking and he was no longer ours to claim! Child of my vain 12
hopes, did I see your eyes fading in death and your breath take its last flight? Had I the heart to receive your fleeting spirit,[1] as I embraced your cold pale body, and to live on breathing the common air. Justly do I endure the agony that now is mine, and the thoughts that torment me. Have I lost you at 13
the moment when adoption by a consular had given hope that you would rise to all the high offices of state, when you were destined to be the son-in-law of your uncle the praetor, and gave promise of rivalling the eloquence of your grandsire? and do I

stes parens tantum ad poenas, amisi[1]? Et si non cupido lucis, certe patientia vindicet te reliqua mea aetate. Nam frustra mala omnia ad crimen fortunae
14 relegamus. Nemo nisi sua culpa diu dolet. Sed vivimus, et aliqua vivendi ratio quaerenda est, credendumque doctissimis hominibus, qui unicum adversorum solacium litteras putaverunt. Si quando tamen ita resederit praesens impetus, ut aliqua tot luctibus alia cogitatio inseri possit, non iniuste petierim morae veniam. Quis enim dilata studia miretur, quae potius non abrupta esse mirandum est?
15 Tum, si qua fuerint minus effecta iis, quae levius adhuc adflicti coeperamus, imperitanti fortunae remittantur, quae, si quid mediocrium alioqui in nostro ingenio virium fuit, ut non exstinxerit, debilitavit tamen. Sed vel propter hoc nos contumacius erigamus, quod illam ut perferre nobis difficile est, ita facile contemnere. Nihil enim sibi adversus me reliquit et infelicem quidem, sed certissimam tamen
16 attulit mihi ex his malis securitatem. Boni autem consulere nostrum laborem vel propter hoc aequum est, quod in nullum iam proprium usum perseveramus, sed omnis haec cura alienas utilitates (si modo

[1] omnium spes, *bracketed by Spalding.* avitae, *Erasmus*: acutis *or* acutae, *MSS.*: ad poenas amisi, *Regius*: poenas, *MSS.*

your father survive only to weep? May my endurance (not my will to live, for that is gone from me)
prove me worthy of you through all my remaining
years. For it is in vain that we impute all our ills
to fortune. No man grieves long save through his
own fault. But I still live, and must find something 14
to make life tolerable, and must needs put faith in
the verdict of the wise, who held that literature
alone can provide true solace in adversity. Yet, if
ever the violence of my present grief subside and
admit the intrusion of some other thought on so
many sorrowful reflexions, I may with good cause
ask pardon for the delay in bringing my work to
completion. Who can wonder that my studies have
been interrupted, when the real marvel is that they
have not been broken off altogether? Should 15
certain portions therefore betray a lack of finish
compared with what was begun in the days when
my affliction was less profound, I would ask that the
imperfections should be regarded with indulgence,
as being due to the cruel tyranny of fortune, which,
if it has not utterly extinguished, has at any rate
weakened such poor powers of intellect as I once
possessed. But for this very reason I must rouse
myself to face my task with greater spirit, since it
is easy to despise fortune, though it may be hard
to bear her blows. For there is nothing left that
she can do to me, since out of my calamities she
has wrought for me a security which, full of sorrow
though it be, is such that nothing can shake it.
And the very fact that I have no personal interest 16
in persevering with my present work, but am moved
solely by the desire to serve others, if indeed anything that I write can be of such service, is a reason

quid utile scribimus) spectat. Nos miseri sicut facultates patrimonii nostri, ita hoc opus aliis praeparabamus, aliis relinquemus.

I. Peroratio sequebatur, quam cumulum quidam, conclusionem alii vocant. Eius duplex ratio est posita aut in rebus aut in adfectibus. Rerum repetitio et congregatio, quae Graece dicitur ἀνακεφαλαίωσις, a quibusdam Latinorum enumeratio, et memoriam iudicis reficit et totam simul causam ponit ante oculos et, etiamsi per singula minus moverat,
2 turba valet. In hac, quae repetemus, quam brevissime dicenda sunt et, quod Graeco verbo patet, decurrendum per capita. Nam, si morabimur, non iam enumeratio sed quasi altera fiet oratio. Quae autem enumeranda videntur, cum pondere aliquo dicenda sunt et aptis excitanda sententiis et figuris utique varianda; alioqui nihil est odiosius recta illa
3 repetitione velut memoriae iudicum diffidentis. Sunt autem innumerabiles species,[1] optimeque in Verrem Cicero: *Si pater ipse iudicaret, quid diceret, cum haec probarentur?* et deinde subiecit enumerationem; aut cum

[1] species, *added by Halm.*

---

[1] v. lii. 136

for regarding my labours with an indulgent eye. Alas! I shall bequeath it, like my patrimony, for others than those to whom it was my design to leave it.

I. The next subject which I was going to discuss was the peroration which some call the completion and others the conclusion. There are two kinds of peroration, for it may deal either with facts or with the emotional aspect of the case. The repetition and grouping of the facts, which the Greeks call ἀνακεφαλαίωσις and some of our own writers call the enumeration, serves both to refresh the memory of the judge and to place the whole of the case before his eyes, and, even although the facts may have made little impression on him in detail, their cumulative effect is considerable. This final recapitu- 2
lation must be as brief as possible and, as the Greek term indicates, we must summarise the facts under the appropriate heads. For if we devote too much time thereto, the peroration will cease to be an enumeration and will constitute something very like a second speech. On the other hand the points selected for enumeration must be treated with weight and dignity, enlivened by apt reflexions and diversified by suitable figures; for there is nothing more tiresome than a dry repetition of facts, which merely suggests a lack of confidence in the judges' memory. There are how- 3
ever innumerable ways in which this may be done. The finest example is provided by Cicero's prosecution of Verres.[1] "If your own father were among your judges, what would he say when these facts were proved against you?" Then follows the enumer-

idem in eundem per invocationem deorum spoliata a praetore templa dinumerat. Licet et dubitare, num quid nos fugerit, et quid responsurus sit adversarius his et his, aut quam spem accusator habeat omnibus
4 ita defensis. Illa vero iucundissima, si contingat aliquod ex adversario ducere argumentum, ut si dicas: *Reliquit hanc partem causae*, aut *invidia premere maluit*, aut *ad preces confugit merito, cum sciret haec et*
5 *haec.* Sed non sunt singulae species persequendae, ne sola videantur, quae forte nunc dixero, cum occasiones et ex causis et ex dictis adversariorum et ex quibusdam fortuitis quoque oriantur. Nec referenda modo nostra, sed postulandum etiam ab adversariis,
6 ut ad quaedam respondeant. Id autem, si et actioni supererit locus et ea proposuerimus, quae refelli non possint. Nam provocare quae inde sint fortia, non
7 arguentis est, sed monentis. Id unum epilogi genus visum est plerisque Atticorum et philosophis fere omnibus, qui de arte oratoria scriptum aliquid reli-

---

[1] *ib.* lxxii.

ation. Another admirable example[1] may be found in the same speech where the enumeration of the temples which the praetor had despoiled takes the form of invoking the various deities concerned. We may also at times pretend to be in doubt whether we have not omitted something and to wonder what the accused will say in reply to certain points or what hope the accuser can have after the manner in which we have refuted all the charges brought against
us. But the most attractive form of peroration is 4
that which we may use when we have an opportunity of drawing some argument from our opponent's speech, as for instance when we say "He omitted to deal with this portion of the case," or "He preferred to crush us by exciting odium against us," or "He had good reason for resorting to entreaty, since he
knew certain facts." But I must refrain from deal- 5
ing with the various methods individually, for fear that the instances that I produce should be regarded as exhaustive, whereas our opportunities spring from the nature of the particular case, from the statements of our opponents and also from fortuitous circumstances. Nor must we restrict ourselves to recapitulating the points of our own speech, but must call upon our opponent to reply to certain questions.
This however is only possible if there is time for him 6
to do so and if the arguments which we have put forward are such as not to admit of refutation. For to challenge points which tell in our opponent's favour is not to argue against him, but to play the
part of prompter to him. The majority of Athenians 7
and almost all philosophers who have left anything in writing on the art of oratory have held that the recapitulation is the sole form of peroration. I

querunt. Id sensisse Atticos credo, quia Athenis adfectus movere etiam per praeconem prohibebatur orator. Philosophos minus miror, apud quos vitii loco est adfici; nec boni mores videntur, sic a vero iudicem averti, nec convenire bono viro vitiis uti. Necessarios tamen adfectus fatebuntur, si aliter obtineri vera et iusta et in commune profutura non
8 possint. Ceterum illud constitit inter omnes, etiam in aliis partibus actionis, si multiplex causa sit et pluribus argumentis defensa, utiliter ἀνακεφαλαίωσιν fieri solere, sicut nemo dubitaverit multas esse causas, in quibus nullo loco sit necessaria, si breves et simplices fuerint. Haec pars perorationis accusatori patronoque ex aequo communis est.

9 Adfectibus quoque iisdem fere utuntur, sed aliis hic, aliis[1] ille saepius ac magis, nam huic concitare iudices, illi flectere convenit. Verum et accusator habet interim lacrimas ex miseratione eius rei quam ulciscitur; et reus de indignitate calumniae aut con-

[1] aliis, *Spalding*: aut, *AG*.

[1] Athenaeus (xiii. 6, 590 E) states that a law against appeals to the emotions was passed at Athens after Hyperides' defence of Phryne (see II. xv. 9.). But there is no real evidence for the existence of such a law save in cases tried before the Areopagus (see Arist. *Rhet.* I. i. 5). Appeals for pity were as freely employed in the ordinary courts of Athens during the fourth century as at Rome. When Xenophon (*Mem.* IV. iv. 4) says that Socrates refused to beg mercy of his judges contrary to the law, he seems to refer to the spirit, not the letter.

imagine that the reason why the Athenians did so was that appeals to the emotions were forbidden to Athenian orators, a proclamation to this effect being actually made by the court-usher.[1] I am less surprised at the philosophers taking this view, for they regard susceptibility to emotion as a vice, and think it immoral that the judge should be distracted from the truth by an appeal to his emotions and that it is unbecoming for a good man to make use of vicious procedure to serve his ends. None the less they must admit that appeals to emotion are necessary if there are no other means for securing the victory of truth, justice and the public interest. It 8
is however admitted by all that recapitulation may be profitably employed in other portions of the speech as well, if the case is complicated and a number of different arguments have been employed in the defence; though no one will doubt but that there are many cases, in which no recapitulation at all is necessary at any point, assuming, that is, that the cases are both brief and simple. This part of the peroration is common both to the prosecution and the defence.

Both parties as a general rule may likewise em- 9
ploy the appeal to the emotions, but they will appeal to different emotions and the defender will employ such appeals with greater frequency and fulness. For the accuser has to rouse the judge, while the defender has to soften him. Still even the accuser will sometimes make his audience weep by the pity excited for the man whose wrongs he seeks to avenge, while the defendant will at times develop no small vehemence when he complains of the injustice of the calumny or conspiracy of which

spirationis vehementius interim queritur. Dividere
igitur haec officia commodissimum, quae plerumque
sunt, ut dixi, in prooemio similia, sed hic liberiora ple-
10 nioraque. Inclinatio enim iudicum ad nos petitur initio
parcius, cum admitti satis est et oratio tota superest;
in epilogo vero est, qualem animum iudex in consilium ferat, et iam nihil amplius dicturi sumus nec
11 restat quo reservemus. Est igitur utrisque commune, conciliare sibi, avertere ab adversario iudicem,
concitare adfectus et componere. Et brevissimum
quidem hoc praeceptum dari utrique parti potest, ut
totas causae suae vires orator ponat ante oculos; et
cum viderit, quid invidiosum, favorabile, invisum,
miserabile aut sit in rebus aut videri possit, ea
dicat, quibus, si iudex esset, ipse maxime moveretur.
12 Sed certius est ire per singula.

Et quae concilient quidem accusatorem, in praeceptis exordii iam diximus. Quaedam tamen, quae
illic ostendere sat est, in peroratione implenda sunt
magis, si contra impotentem, invisum, perniciosum
suscepta causa est, si iudicibus ipsis aut gloriae dam-

---

[1] IV. i. 27, 28. [2] IV. i. 5 *sq.*

he is the victim. It will therefore be best to treat
these duties separately: as I have already said,[1] they
are much the same in the peroration as in the
exordium, but are freer and wider in scope in the
former. For our attempts to sway the judges are 10
made more sparingly at the commencement of the
speech, when it is enough that such an attempt
should gain admittance and we have the whole
speech before us. On the other hand in the peroration we have to consider what the feelings of the
judge will be when he retires to consider his verdict,
for we shall have no further opportunity to say anything and cannot any longer reserve arguments to be
produced later. It is therefore the duty of both parties 11
to seek to win the judge's goodwill and to divert it
from their opponent, as also to excite or assuage his
emotions. And the following brief rule may be laid
down for the observation of both parties, that the
orator should display the full strength of his case
before the eyes of the judge, and, when he has made
up his mind what points in his case actually deserve
or may seem to deserve to excite envy, goodwill,
dislike or pity, should dwell on those points by which
he himself would be most moved were he trying the
case. But it will be safer to discuss these consider- 12
ations in detail.

The points likely to commend the accuser to the judge have already been stated in my remarks on the exordium.[2] There are however certain things which require fuller treatment in the peroration than in the exordium, where it is sufficient merely to outline them. This fuller treatment is specially required if the accused be a man of violent, unpopular or dangerous character or if the condemna-

13 natio rei aut deformitati futura absolutio. Nam egregie in Vatinium Calvus, *Factum*, inquit, *ambitum scitis omnes et hoc vos scire omnes sciunt.* Cicero quidem in Verrem etiam emendari posse infamiam iudiciorum damnato reo dicit; quod est unum ex supra dictis. Metus etiam, si est adhibendus, ut faciat idem, hunc habet locum fortiorem quam in prooemio. Qua de re quid sentirem, alio iam libro
14 exposui. Concitare quoque invidiam, odium, iram, liberius in peroratione contingit; quorum invidiam gratia, odium turpitudo, iram offensio iudici facit, si contumax, arrogans, securus sit, quae non ex facto modo dictove aliquo sed vultu, habitu, aspectu moveri solet. Egregieque nobis adolescentibus dixisse accusator Cossutiani Capitonis videbatur, Graece quidem, sed in hunc sensum, *Erubescis Caesarem*
15 *timere.* Summa tamen concitandi adfectus accusatori in hoc est, ut id, quod obiecit, aut quam atrocissimum aut etiam, si fieri potest, quam maxime miserabile esse videatur. Atrocitas crescit ex his, quid factum sit, a quo, in quem, quo animo, quo

[1] I. xv. 43. [2] IV. i. 20, 21.

[3] See Tac. *Ann.* xiii. 33. Cossutianus was condemned for extortion in his province. His accuser is not known.

tion of the accused is likely to cover the judges with glory or his acquittal with disgrace. Calvus for 13
example in his speech against Vatinius makes an admirable remark: "You know, gentlemen, that bribery has been committed and everybody knows that you know it." Cicero again in the *Verrines*[1] says that the ill-name acquired by the courts may be effaced by the condemnation of Verres, a statement that comes under the head of the conciliatory methods mentioned above. The appeal to fear also, if it is necessary to employ it to produce a like effect, occupies a more prominent place in the peroration than in the exordium, but I have expressed my views on this subject in an earlier book.[2] The peroration 14
also provides freer opportunities for exciting the passions of jealousy, hatred or anger. As regards the circumstances likely to excite such feelings in the judge, jealousy will be produced by the influence of the accused, hatred by the disgraceful nature of his conduct, and anger by his disrespectful attitude to the court, if, for instance, he be contumacious, arrogant or studiously indifferent: such anger may be aroused not merely by specific acts or words, but by his looks, bearing and manner. In this connexion the remark made by the accuser of Cossutianus Capito[3] in my young days was regarded with great approval: the words used were Greek, but may be translated thus:—"You blush to fear even Caesar."
The best way however for the accuser to excite the 15
feelings of the judge is to make the charge which he brings against the accused seem as atrocious or, if feasible, as deplorable as possible. Its atrocity may be enhanced by considerations of the nature of the act, the position of its author or the victim, the

tempore, quo loco, quo modo; quae omnia infinitos
16 tractatus habent. Pulsatum querimur: de re primum ipsa dicendum; tum si senex, si puer, si magistratus, si probus, si bene de re publica meritus; etiam si percussus sit a vili aliquo contemptoque vel ex contrario a potente nimium vel ab eo, quo minime oportuit, et si die forte sollemni aut iis temporibus, cum iudicia eius rei maxime exercerentur, aut in sollicito civitatis statu; item in theatro, in templo,
17 in contione, crescit invidia; et si non errore nec ira vel etiam, si forte ira, sed iniqua, quod patri adfuisset, quod respondisset, quod honores contra peteret, et si plus etiam videri potest voluisse quam fecit. Plurimum tamen adfert atrocitatis modus, si graviter, si contumeliose: ut Demosthenes ex parte percussi corporis, ex vultu ferientis, ex habitu invidiam Midiae
18 quaerit. Occisus utrum ferro an igne an veneno, uno vulnere an pluribus, subito an exspectatione

---

[1] *in Mid.* 72.

purpose, time, place and manner of the act: all of which may be treated with infinite variety. Suppose 16
that we are complaining that our client has been beaten. We must first speak of the act itself; we shall then proceed to point out that the victim was an old man, a child, a magistrate, an honest man or a benefactor to the state; we shall also point out that the assailant was a worthless and contemptible fellow, or (to take the opposite case) was in a position of excessive power or was the last man who should have given the blow, or again that the occasion was a solemn festival, or that the act was committed at a time when such crimes were punished with special severity by the courts or when public order was at a dangerously low ebb. Again the hatred excited by the act will be enhanced if it was committed in the theatre, in a temple, or at
a public assembly, and if the blow was given not 17
in mistake or in a moment of passion or, if it was the result of passion which was quite unjustifiable, being due to the fact that the victim had gone to the assistance of his father or had made some reply or was a candidate for the same office as his assailant; or finally we may hint that he wished to inflict more serious injury than he succeeded in inflicting. But it is the manner of the act that contributes most to the impression of its atrocity, if, for example, the blow was violent or insulting: thus Demosthenes [1] seeks to excite hatred against Midias by emphasising the position of the blow, the attitude of the assailant and the expression
of his face. It is in this connexion that we shall 18
have to consider whether a man was killed by sword or fire or poison, by one wound or several, and

tortus, ad hanc partem maxime pertinet. Utitur frequenter accusator et miseratione, cum aut eius casum, quem ulciscitur, aut liberorum ac parentium
19 solitudinem conqueritur. Etiam futuri temporis imagine iudices movet, quae maneant eos, qui de vi et iniuria questi sunt, nisi vindicentur; fugiendum de civitate, cedendum bonis aut omnia, quaecunque
20 inimicus fecerit, perferenda. Sed saepius id est accusatoris, avertere iudicem a miseratione, qua reus sit usurus, atque ad fortiter iudicandum concitare. Cuius loci est etiam occupare, quae dicturum facturumve adversarium putes. Nam et cautiores ad custodiam suae religionis iudices facit et gratiam responsuris aufert, cum ea quae dicta sunt ab accusatore iam, si pro reo repetentur, non sint nova: ut Servium Sulpicium Messala contra Aufidiam, ne signatorum, ne ipsius discrimen obiiciatur sibi, praemonet. Nec non ab Aeschine, quali sit usurus Demosthenes actione, praedictum est. Docendi quoque interim iudices, quid rogantibus respondere debeant; quod est unum repetitionis genus.

21 Periclitantem vero commendat dignitas et studia

[1] *cp.* IV. ii. 106. See note prefixed to Index.
[2] *in Ctes.* 207.

whether he was slain on the spot or tortured by being kept in suspense. The accuser will also frequently attempt to excite pity by complaining of the fate of the man whom he is seeking to avenge or of the desolation which has fallen upon his children
or parents. The judges may also be moved by draw- 19
ing a picture of the future, of the fate which awaits those who have complained of violence and wrong, if they fail to secure justice. They must go into exile, give up their property or endure to the end whatever their enemy may choose to inflict upon them.
But it will more frequently be the duty of the 20
accuser to divert the judge from all the temptations to pity which the accused will place before him, and to incite him to give a strong and dispassionate verdict. It will also be his duty in this connexion to forestall the arguments and actions to which his opponent seems likely to have recourse. For it makes the judge more cautious in observing the sanctity of his oath and destroys the influence of those who are going to reply to us when the arguments used by the defence have already been dealt with by the prosecution, since they lose their novelty. An instance of this will be found in the speech of Messala against Aufidia,[1] where he warns Servius Sulpicius not to talk about the peril which threatens the signatories to the document and the defendant herself. Again Aeschines[2] foretells the line of defence which Demosthenes will pursue. There are also occasions when the judges should be told what answer they should make to requests on behalf of the accused, a proceeding which is a form of recapitulation.

If we turn to the defendant, we must note that 21

fortia et susceptae bello cicatrices et nobilitas et merita maiorum. Hoc, quod proxime dixi, Cicero atque Asinius certatim sunt usi, pro Scauro patre hic
22 ille pro filio. Commendat et causa periculi, si suscepisse inimicitias ob aliquod factum honestum videtur; praecipue bonitas, humanitas, misericordia. Iustius enim tunc petere ea quisque videtur a iudice, quae aliis ipse praestiterit. Referenda pars haec quoque ad utilitatem rei publicae, ad iudicum gloriam,
23 ad exemplum, ad memoriam posteritatis. Plurimum tamen valet miseratio, quae iudicem non flecti tantum cogit, sed motum quoque animi sui lacrimis confiteri. Haec petentur aut ex iis, quae passus est reus, aut iis quae cum maxime patitur, aut iis quae damnatum manent; quae et ipsa duplicantur, cum dicimus ex
24 qua illi fortuna et in quam recidendum sit. Adfert in his momentum et aetas et sexus et pignora; liberi, dico, et parentes et propinqui. Quae omnia tractari

[1] See IV. i. 69.

his worth, his manly pursuits, the scars from wounds received in battle, his rank and the services rendered by his ancestors, will all commend him to the good-will of the judges. Cicero,[1] as I have already pointed out, and Asinius both make use of this form of appeal: indeed they may almost be regarded as rivals in this respect, since Cicero employed it when defending the elder Scaurus, Asinius when defending the son. Again, the cause which has brought 22
the accused into peril may serve to produce the same effect, if, for example, it appears that he has incurred enmity on account of some honourable action: above all his goodness, humanity or pity may be emphasised with this end in view. For it adds to the apparent justice of his claim, if all that he asks of the judge is that he should grant to him what he himself has granted to others. We may also in this connexion lay stress on the interests of the state, the glory which will accrue to the judges, the importance of the precedent which their verdict will set and the place it will hold in the memory of
after generations. But the appeal which will carry 23
most weight is the appeal to pity, which not merely forces the judge to change his views, but even to betray his emotion by tears. Such appeals to pity will be based either on the previous or present sufferings of the accused, or on those which await him if condemned. And the force of our appeal will be doubled if we contrast the fortune which he now enjoys with that to which he will be reduced, if he
fail. In this connexion great play may be made by 24
reference to the age and sex of the accused, or to his nearest and dearest, that is, his children, parents and kindred, all of which topics are treated in

varie solent. Nonnunquam etiam ipse patronus has partes subit, ut Cicero pro Milone, *O me miserum! o te infelicem! Revocare me tu in patriam, Milo, potuisti per hos, ego te in patria per eosdem retinere non potero?* Maximeque, si, ut tunc accidit, non conveniunt ei qui
25 accusatur preces. Nam quis ferret Milonem pro capite suo supplicantem, qui a se virum nobilem interfectum, quia id fieri oportuisset, fateretur? Ergo et illi captavit ex ipsa praestantia animi favorem et in locum lacrimarum eius ipse successit.

His praecipue locis utiles sunt prosopopoeiae, id est fictae alienarum personarum orationes, quales litigatorum ore dicit patronus. Nudae tantum res movent; at cum ipsos loqui fingimus, ex personis
26 quoque trahitur adfectus. Non enim audire iudex videtur aliena mala deflentis, sed sensum ac vocem auribus accipere miserorum, quorum etiam mutus aspectus lacrimas movet; quantoque essent miserabiliora, si ea dicerent ipsi, tanto sunt quadam portione ad adficiendum potentiora, cum velut ipsorum ore

---

[1] xxxvii. 102.

different ways. Sometimes the advocate himself may
even assume the role of close intimacy with his
client, as Cicero does in the *pro Milone*,[1] where he
cries: "Alas, unhappy that I am! Alas, my unfortunate friend! You succeeded by the agency of
those who are now your judges in recalling me to
my native land, and cannot I through the same
agency retain you in yours?" Such a method is
especially serviceable when, as was the case with
Milo, entreaty is not in keeping with the character
of the accused. Who would have endured to hear 25
Milo pleading for his life, when he admitted that
he had killed a man of noble birth because it was
his duty to do so? Consequently Cicero sought to
win the judges' goodwill for Milo by emphasising
the staunchness of his character, and himself assumed
the role of suppliant.

Impersonation may also be employed with profit
in such passages, and by impersonations I mean
fictitious speeches supposed to be uttered, such as
an advocate puts into the mouth of his client. The
bare facts are no doubt moving in themselves; but
when we pretend that the persons concerned themselves are speaking, the personal note adds to the
emotional effect. For then the judge seems no 26
longer to be listening to a voice bewailing another's
ills, but to hear the voice and feelings of the unhappy
victims, men whose appearance alone would call
forth his tears even though they uttered never a
word. And as their plea would awaken yet greater
pity if they urged it with their own lips, so it is
rendered to some extent all the more effective when
it is, as it were, put into their mouth by their
advocate: we may draw a parallel from the stage,

dicuntur, ut scenicis actoribus eadem vox eademque pronuntiatio plus ad movendos adfectus sub persona
27 valet. Itaque idem Cicero, quanquam preces non dat Miloni, eumque potius animi praestantia commendat, accommodavit tamen ei verba, convenientes etiam forti viro conquestiones: *Frustra, inquit, mei suscepti labores! O spes fallaces! O cogitationes inanes meas!*

Nunquam tamen debet esse longa miseratio, nec sine causa dictum est, nihil facilius quam lacrimas
28 inarescere. Nam cum etiam veros dolores mitiget tempus, citius evanescat necesse est illa, quam dicendo effinximus, imago; in qua si moramur, lacrimis fatigatur auditor et requiescit et ab illo, quem
29 ceperat, impetu ad rationem redit. Non patiamur igitur frigescere hoc opus, et adfectum, cum ad summum perduxerimus, relinquamus nec speremus fore ut aliena quisquam diu ploret. Ideoque cum in aliis tum maxime in hac parte debet crescere oratio, quia, quidquid non adiicit prioribus, etiam detrahere videtur, et facile deficit adfectus qui descendit.

30 Non solum autem dicendo sed etiam faciendo quaedam lacrimas movemus, unde et producere ipsos,

---

[1] *pro Mil.* xxxiv. 94.

[2] A quotation from the rhetorician Apollonius, *cp.* Cic. *de Inv.* i. 56.

where the actor's voice and delivery produce greater emotional effect when he is speaking in an assumed role than when he speaks in his own character.
Consequently Cicero, to quote him once again, 27
although he will not put entreaties into Milo's mouth, and prefers to commend him by his staunchness of character, still lends him words in the form of such complaint as may become a brave man.[1] "Alas!" he says, "my labours have been in vain! Alas for my blighted hopes! Alas for my baffled purpose!"

Appeals to pity should, however, always be brief, and there is good reason for the saying that nothing
dries so quickly as tears.[2] Time assuages even 28
genuine grief, and it is therefore inevitable that the semblance of grief portrayed in our speech should vanish yet more rapidly. And if we spend too much time over such portrayal our hearer grows weary of his tears, takes a breathing space, and returns once more to the rational attitude from which he has
been distracted by the impulse of the moment. We 29
must not, therefore, allow the effect which we have produced to fall flat, and must consequently abandon our appeal to the emotion just when that emotion is at its height, nor must we expect anyone to weep for long over another's ills. For this reason our eloquence ought to be pitched higher in this portion of our speech than in any other, since, wherever it fails to add something to what has preceded, it seems even to diminish its previous effect, while a *diminuendo* is merely a step towards the rapid disappearance of the emotion.

Actions as well as words may be employed to 30
move the court to tears. Hence the custom of

qui periclitentur, squalidos atque deformes et liberos eorum ac parentes institutum, et ab accusatoribus cruentum gladium ostendi et lecta e vulneribus ossa et vestes sanguine perfusas videmus, et vulnera
31 resolvi, verberata corpora nudari. Quarum rerum ingens plerumque vis est velut in rem praesentem animos hominum ducentium, ut populum Romanum egit in furorem praetexta C. Caesaris praelata in funere cruenta. Sciebat interfectum eum, corpus denique ipsum impositum lecto erat, at vestis tamen illa sanguine madens ita repraesentavit imaginem sceleris, ut non occisus esse Caesar sed tum maxime
32 occidi videretur. Sed non ideo probaverim, quod factum et lego et ipse aliquando vidi, depictam in tabula sipariove[1] imaginem rei, cuius atrocitate iudex erat commovendus. Quae enim est actoris infantia, qui mutam illam effigiem magis quam orationem pro se
33 putet locuturam? At sordes et squalorem et propinquorum quoque similem habitum scio profuisse, et magnum ad salutem momentum preces attulisse. Quare et obsecratio illa iudicum per carissima pig-

[1] sipariove, *F. C. Conradus*: supra Iovem, *MSS.*

bringing accused persons into court wearing squalid and unkempt attire, and of introducing their children and parents, and it is with this in view that we see blood-stained swords, fragments of bone taken from the wound, and garments spotted with blood, displayed by the accusers, wounds stripped of their
dressings, and scourged bodies bared to view. The 31
impression produced by such exhibitions is generally enormous, since they seem to bring the spectators face to face with the cruel facts. For example, the sight of the bloodstains on the purple-bordered toga of Gaius Caesar, which was carried at the head of his funeral procession, aroused the Roman people to fury. They knew that he had been killed; they had even seen his body stretched upon the bier: but his garment, still wet with his blood, brought such a vivid image of the crime before their minds, that Caesar seemed not to have been murdered, but
to be being murdered before their very eyes. Still I 32
would not for this reason go so far as to approve a practice of which I have read, and which indeed I have occasionally witnessed, of bringing into court a picture of the crime painted on wood or canvas, that the judge might be stirred to fury by the horror of the sight. For the pleader who prefers a voiceless picture to speak for him in place of his
own eloquence must be singularly incompetent. On 33
the other hand, I know that the wearing of mourning and the presentation of an unkempt appearance, and the introduction of relatives similarly arrayed, has proved of value, and that entreaties have been of great service to save the accused from condemnation. The practice therefore of appealing to the judges by all that is near and dear to them will be

nora, utique si et reo sint liberi, coniux, parentes,
34 utilis erit; et deorum etiam invocatio velut ex bona conscientia profecta videri solet; stratum denique iacere et genua complecti, nisi si tamen persona nos et anteacta vita et rei condicio prohibebit; quaedam enim tam fortiter tuenda quam facta sunt. Verum sic habenda est auctoritatis ratio, ne sit invisa securi-
35 tas. Fuit quondam inter haec omnia potentissimum, quo L. Murenam Cicero accusantibus clarissimis viris eripuisse praecipue videtur, persuasitque nihil esse ad praesentem rerum statum utilius quam pridie Kalendas Ianuarias ingredi consulatum. Quod genus nostris temporibus totum paene sublatum est, cum omnia curae tutelaeque unius innixa periclitari nullo iudicii exitu possint.

36 De accusatoribus et reis sum locutus, quia in periculis maxime versatur adfectus. Sed privatae quoque causae utrumque habent perorationis genus, et illud quod est ex enumeratione probationum, et hoc quod ex lacrimis, si aut statu periclitari aut opinione litigator videtur. Nam in parvis quidem litibus has

[1] *i.e.* although such entreaties are effective, they cannot always be employed. Thus they would have been out of place in the case of Milo, whose character was such that it was necessary to defend him with a boldness worthy of the boldness required to perform the deed of which he was accused. Still we must not carry such methods (*e.g.* such as Cicero employs on behalf of Milo) too far.

of great service to the accused, especially if he, too, has children, a wife and parents. Invocation of the 34
gods, again, usually gives the impression that the speaker is conscious of the justice of his cause, while it may produce a good effect if the accused throws himself on the ground and embraces the knees of the judges, unless his character, his past life and station prohibit a resort to this device: for there are some acts which require to be defended with no less boldness than was required for their commission. But we must take care not to carry matters with too high a hand, for fear of creating a bad impression by an appearance of over-confidence.[1] The most 35
effective of all such methods was in times past that by which more than anything else Cicero is considered to have saved Lucius Murena[2] from the attacks of his accusers, who were men of the greatest distinction. For he persuaded the court that nothing was more necessary in view of the critical position of affairs than that Murena should assume the consulship on the thirty-first of December. This form of appeal is now, however, almost entirely obsolete, since the safety of the state is to-day dependent on the watchful care of a single ruler, and cannot conceivably be imperilled by the result of a trial.

I have spoken of accusers and accused because it 36
is in situations involving danger that the emotional appeal is most serviceable. But private cases also admit of both kinds of peroration, namely, that which consists in the recapitulation of the proofs and that which takes the form of an appeal for pity, the latter being employed when the position or reputation of the litigant seems to be in danger. For to

[2] *pro Mur.* xxxvii. 79.

tragoedias movere tale est, quasi si personam Herculis et cothurnos aptare infantibus velis.

37 Ne illud quidem indignum est admonitione, ingens in epilogis meo iudicio verti discrimen, quomodo se dicenti, qui excitatur, accommodet. Nam et imperitia et rusticitas et rigor et deformitas adferunt interim frigus, diligenterque sunt haec actori provi-
38 denda. Equidem repugnantes eos patrono et nihil vultu commotos et intempestive renidentes[1] et facto aliquo vel ipso vultu risum etiam moventes saepe vidi; praecipue vero cum aliqua velut scenice fiunt, alio
39 cadunt.[2] Transtulit aliquando patronus puellam, quae soror esse adversarii dicebatur (nam de hoc lis erat), in adversa subsellia, tanquam in gremio fratris relicturus, at is a nobis praemonitus discesserat. Tum ille, alioqui vir facundus, inopinatae rei casu obmutuit et infantem suam frigidissime reportavit.
40 Alius imaginem mariti pro rea proferre magni putavit, et ea saepius risum fecit. Nam et ii, quorum officium erat ut traderent eam, ignari, qui esset epilo-

[1] renidentes, *Spalding*: residentes, *AG*.
[2] alio, *Halm*: aliam, alia, alias, *MSS*

embark on such tragic methods in trivial cases would be like putting the mask and buskins of Hercules on a small child.

It is also worth while pointing out that, in my 37
opinion, the manner in which the client whose sorrows we parade before the court conforms his behaviour to the methods of his advocate is of the utmost importance. For sometimes our appeal falls flat owing to the ignorance, rusticity, indifference or uncouthness of our client, and it is consequently most important that the advocate should take all
necessary precautions in this connexion. I have 38
often seen clients whose behaviour was wholly out of keeping with the line adopted by their counsel, since their expression showed not the slightest emotion, while they displayed a most unseasonable cheerfulness and even aroused laughter by their looks or actions; such incongruity is especially frequent when the appeal is of a theatrical character.
On one occasion an advocate produced a girl alleged 39
to be the sister of the opposing party (for it was on this point that the dispute turned) and led her across to the benches occupied by his opponents as though to leave her in the arms of her brother: I however had given the brother timely warning and he had left his seat. The advocate, although as a rule an eloquent speaker, was struck dumb by the unexpected turn of events and took his little girl back again in
the tamest possible manner. There was another 40
advocate who was defending a woman who thought to secure a great effect by producing the portrait of her husband, but sent the court into repeated peals of laughter. For the persons entrusted with the duty of handing in the portrait had no idea

gus, quotiens respexisset patronus, offerebant palam, et prolata novissime deformitate ipsa (nam senis cadaveri cera[1] erat infusa) praeteritam quoque ora-
41 tionis gratiam perdidit. Nec ignotum, quid Glyconi, cui Spiridion fuit cognomen, acciderit. Huic puer, quem is productum quid fleret interrogabat, a paedagogo se vellicari respondit. Sed nihil illa circa Cepasios Ciceronis fabula efficacius ad pericula epi-
42 logorum. Omnia tamen haec tolerabilia iis, quibus actionem mutare facile est; at, qui a stilo non recedunt, aut conticescunt ad hos casus aut frequentissime falsa dicunt. Inde est enim, *Tendit ad genua vestra supplices manus*, et *Haeret in complexu liberorum miser*, et *Revocat ecce me*, etiamsi nihil horum is, de quo
43 dicitur, faciat. Ex scholis haec vitia, in quibus omnia libere fingimus et impune, quia pro facto est quidquid voluimus; non admittit hoc idem veritas, egregieque Cassius dicenti adolescentulo: *Quid me torvo vultu intueris, Severe? Non mehercule, inquit, faciebam, sed si sic scripsisti, ecce!* et quam potuit truculentissime
44 eum aspexit. Illud praecipue monendum, ne quis

[1] cadaveri cera, *Halm*: caduca veri, *AG.*

---

[1] *pro Cluent.* XX. *sqq.* *cp.* Quint. VI. iii. 40.

of the nature of a peroration and displayed it whenever the advocate looked their way, and when at last it was produced at the proper moment it destroyed all the good effect of his previous eloquence by its hideousness, for it was a wax cast taken from an old man's corpse. We are also familiar with the story 41
of what happened to Glycon, nicknamed Spiridion. He asked a boy whom he produced in court why he was crying; to which the boy replied, that his *paedagogus* was pinching him. But the most effective warning as to the perils which beset the peroration is the story told by Cicero[1] about the Caepasii. But all these perils may be boldly faced by those 42
who have no difficulty in changing their line of pleading. Those however who cannot get away from what they have written, are reduced to silence by such emergencies or else led into making false statements, as for instance if an advocate should say, "He stretches out suppliant hands to embrace your knees," or "The unhappy man is locked in the embrace of his children," or "See he recalls me to the point," although the person in question is doing none of these things. Such faults are due to the 43
practice of the schools, where we are free to feign what we will with impunity, because we are at liberty to invent facts. But this is impossible when we are confronted with realities, and it was an excellent remark that Cassius made to a young orator who said, "Why do you look so fiercely at me, Severus?" To which he replied, "I was doing nothing of the kind, but if it is in your manuscript, here you are!" And he fixed his eyes on him with the most ferocious scowl that he could muster. There is one point which it is specially important to 44

nisi summis ingenii viribus ad movendas lacrimas
aggredi audeat; nam ut est longe vehementissimus
hic, cum invaluit, adfectus, ita, si nihil efficit, tepet;
quem melius infirmus actor tacitis iudicum cogitatio-
45 nibus reliquisset. Nam et vultus et vox et ipsa illa
excitati rei facies ludibrio etiam plerumque sunt
hominibus, quos non permoverunt. Quare metiatur
ac diligenter aestimet vires suas actor et quantum
onus subiturus sit intelligat; nihil habet ista res
medium, sed aut lacrimas meretur aut risum.

46 Non autem commovere tantum miserationem sed
etiam discutere epilogi est proprium cum oratione
continua, quae motos lacrimis iudices ad iustitiam
reducat, tum etiam quibusdam urbane dictis, quale
est *Date puero panem, ne ploret;* et corpulento litigatori, cuius adversarius, item puer, circa iudices erat
ab advocato latus: *Quid faciam? ego te baiulare non*
47 *possum.* Sed haec tamen non debent esse mimica
Itaque nec illum probaverim, quanquam inter clarissimos sui temporis oratores fuit, qui pueris in epilo-
gum productis talos iecit in medium, quos illi diripere
coeperunt; namque haec ipsa discriminis sui igno-

remember, that we should never attempt to move our
audience to tears without drawing on all the resources
of our eloquence. For while this form of emotional
appeal is the most effective of all, when successful,
its failure results in anti-climax, and if the pleader is
a feeble speaker he would have been wiser to leave
the pathos of the situation to the imagination of the
judges. For look and voice and even the expression 45
on the face of the accused to which the attention of
the court is drawn will generally awaken laughter
where they fail to awaken compassion. Therefore
the pleader must measure and make a careful
estimate of his powers, and must have a just com-
prehension of the difficulty of the task which he
contemplates. For there is no halfway house in such
matters between tears and laughter.

The task of the peroration is not however confined 46
to exciting pity in the judges: it may also be required to dispel the pity which they feel, either by
a set speech designed to recall them from their tears
to a consideration of the justice of the case, or by a
few witticisms such as, "Give the boy some bread to
stop him crying," or the remark made by counsel
to a corpulent client, whose opponent, a mere child,
had been carried round the court by his advocate,
"What am I to do? I can't carry you!" Such 47
jests should not however descend to buffoonery.
Consequently I cannot give my approval to the
orator, although he was one of the most distinguished speakers of his day, who, when his opponent
brought in some children to enhance the effect of
his peroration, threw some dice among them, with
the result that they began to scramble for them.
For their childish ignorance of the perils with which

48 rantia potuit esse miserabilis; neque illum, qui, cum
esset cruentus gladius ab accusatore prolatus, quo is
hominem probabat occisum, subito ex subselliis ut
territus fugit et, capite ex parte velato cum ad agendum ex turba prospexisset, interrogavit, an iam ille
cum gladio recessisset. Fecit enim risum, sed ridi-
49 culus fuit. Discutiendae tamen oratione eiusmodi
scenae, egregieque Cicero, qui contra imaginem
Saturnini pro Rabirio graviter et contra iuvenem,
cuius subinde vulnus in iudicio resolvebatur, pro
Vareno multa dixit urbane.

50 Sunt et illi leniores epilogi, quibus adversario
satisfacimus, si forte sit eius persona talis, ut illi
debeatur reverentia, aut cum amice aliquid commo-
nemus et ad concordiam hortamur. Quod est genus
egregie tractatum a Passieno, cum Domitiae uxoris
suae pecuniaria lite adversus fratrem eius Ahenobar-
bum ageret; nam, cum de necessitudine multa dixisset, de fortuna quoque, qua uterque abundabat,
adiecit: *Nihil vobis minus deest, quam de quo conten-
ditis.*

51 Omnes autem hos adfectus, etiamsi quibusdam

---

[1] *cp. pro Rab.* ix. 24.

they were threatened might in itself have awakened compassion. For the same reason I cannot commend 48
the advocate who, when his opponent the accuser produced a bloodstained sword in court, fled suddenly from the benches as though in an agony of terror, and then, when his turn came to plead, peeped out of the crowd with his head half covered by his robe and asked whether the man with the sword had gone away. For though he caused a laugh, he made himself ridiculous. Still, theatrical effects of the 49
kind we are discussing can be dispelled by the power of eloquence. Cicero provides most admirable examples of the way in which this may be done both in the *pro Rabirio*[1] where he attacks the production in court of the portrait of Saturninus in the most dignified language, and in the *pro Vareno* where he launches a number of witticisms against a youth whose wound had been unbound at intervals in the course of the trial.

There are also milder kinds of peroration in which, 50
if our opponent is of such a character that he deserves to be treated with respect, we strive to ingratiate ourselves with him or give him some friendly warning or urge him to regard us as his friends. This method was admirably employed by Passienus when he pleaded in a suit brought by his wife Domitia against her brother Ahenobarbus for the recovery of a sum of money: he began by making a number of remarks about the relationship of the two parties and then, referring to their wealth, which was in both cases enormous, added, "There is nothing either of you need less than the subject of this dispute."

All these appeals to emotion, although some hold 51

videntur in prooemio atque in epilogo sedem habere,
in quibus sane sint frequentissimi, tamen aliae quoque partes recipiunt, sed breviores, ut cum ex iis
plurima sint reservanda.[1] At hic, si usquam, totos
52 eloquentiae aperire fontes licet. Nam et, si bene
diximus reliqua, possidebimus iam iudicum animos,
et e confragosis atque asperis evecti tota pandere
possumus vela, et, cum sit maxima pars epilogi
amplificatio, verbis atque sententiis uti licet magni-
ficis et ornatis. Tunc est commovendum theatrum,
cum ventum est ad ipsum illud, quo veteres tragoediae comoediaeque cluduntur, *Plodite.*

53 In aliis autem partibus tractandus erit adfectus,
ut quisque nascetur, nam neque exponi sine hoc res
atroces et miserabiles debent; cum de qualitate
alicuius rei quaestio est, probationibus uniuscuiusque
54 rei recte subiungitur. Ubi vero coniunctam ex pluribus causam agimus, etiam necesse erit uti pluribus
quasi epilogis, ut in Verrem Cicero fecit. Nam et
Philodamo et nauarchis et cruci civis Romani et aliis
55 plurimis suas lacrimas dedit. Sunt, qui hos μερικοὺς
ἐπιλόγους vocent, quo partitam perorationem signi-

[1] sint reservanda, *Early editors*: sit res eruenda, *MSS.*

that they should be confined to the exordium and the peroration, which are, I admit, the places where they are most often used, may be employed in other portions of the speech as well, but more briefly, since most of them must be reserved for the opening or the close. But it is in the peroration, if anywhere, that we must let loose the whole torrent of our eloquence. For, if we have spoken well in the rest 52
of our speech, we shall now have the judges on our side, and shall be in a position, now that we have emerged from the reefs and shoals, to spread all our canvas, while since the chief task of the peroration consists of amplification, we may legitimately make free use of words and reflexions that are magnificent and ornate. It is at the close of our drama that we must really stir the theatre, when we have reached the place for the phrase with which the old tragedies and comedies used to end, "Friends, give us your applause."

In other portions of the speech we must appeal 53
to the emotions as occasion may arise. For it would clearly be wrong to set forth facts calling for horror and pity without any such appeal, while, if the question arises as to the quality of any fact, such an appeal may justifiably be subjoined to the proofs of the fact in question. When we are pleading a 54
complicated case which is really made up of several cases, it will be necessary to introduce a number of passages resembling perorations, as Cicero does in the *Verrines*, where he laments over Philodamus, the ships' captains, the crucifixion of the Roman citizen, and a number of other tragic incidents. Some call 55
these μερικοὶ ἐπίλογοι, by which they mean a peroration distributed among different portions of a speech.

ficant. Mihi non tam partes eius quam species videntur, siquidem et epilogi et perorationis nomina ipsa aperte satis ostendunt, hanc esse consummationem orationis.

II. Quamvis autem pars haec iudicialium causarum summa praecipueque constet adfectibus, et aliqua de iis necessario dixerim, non tamen potui ac ne debui quidem istum locum in unam speciem concludere. Quare adhuc opus superest, cum ad obtinenda quae volumus potentissimum, tum supradictis multo difficilius, movendi iudicum animos atque in eum quem volumus habitum formandi et velut transfigurandi.
2 Qua de re pauca, quae postulabat materia, sic attigi, ut magis quid oporteret fieri quam quo id modo consequi possemus, ostenderem. Nunc altius omnis rei repetenda ratio est.

Nam et per totam, ut diximus, causam locus est adfectibus, et eorum non simplex natura nec in transitu tractanda, quo nihil adferre maius vis orandi
3 potest. Nam cetera forsitan tenuis quoque et angusta ingenii vena, si modo vel doctrina vel usu sit adiuta, generare atque ad frugem aliquam perducere queat; certe sunt semperque fuerunt non parum

---

[1] VI. i. 51.

I should regard them rather as *species* than as *parts* of the peroration, since the terms epilogue and peroration both clearly indicate that they form the conclusion of a speech.

II. The peroration is the most important part of forensic pleading, and in the main consists of appeals to the emotions, concerning which I have consequently been forced to say something. But I have not yet been able to give the topic specific consideration as a whole, nor should I have been justified in doing so. We have still, therefore, to discuss a task which forms the most powerful means of obtaining what we desire, and is also more difficult than any of those which we have previously considered, namely that of stirring the emotions of the judges, and of moulding and transforming them to the attitude which we
desire. The few remarks which I have already 2
made on this subject were only such as were essential to my theme, while my purpose was rather to show what ought to be done than to set forth the manner in which we can secure our aim. I must now review the whole subject in a more exhaustive fashion.

There is scope for an appeal to the emotions, as I have already said,[1] in every portion of a speech. Moreover these emotions present great variety, and demand more than cursory treatment, since it is in their handling that the power of oratory shews itself
at its highest. Even a slight and limited talent may, 3
with the assistance of practice or learning, perhaps succeed in giving life to other departments of oratory, and in developing them to a serviceable extent. At any rate there are, and have always been, a con-

multi, qui satis perite, quae essent probationibus utilia, reperirent; quos equidem non contemno, sed hactenus utiles credo, ne quid per eos iudici sit ignotum, atque (ut dicam, quod sentio) dignos, a quibus causam diserti docerentur. Qui vero iudicem rapere et, in quem vellet habitum animi, posset perducere, quo dicente[1] flendum irascendumve esset,
4 rarus fuit. Atqui hoc est quod dominetur in iudiciis, haec eloquentia regnat.[2] Namque argumenta plerumque nascuntur ex causa, et pro meliore parte plura sunt semper, ut, qui per haec vicit, tantum non
5 defuisse sibi advocatum sciat. Ubi vero animis iudicum vis adferenda est et ab ipsa veri contemplatione abducenda mens, ibi proprium oratoris opus est. Hoc non docet litigator, hoc causarum libellis non continetur. Probationes enim efficiant sane ut causam nostram meliorem esse iudices putent, adfectus praestant ut etiam velint; sed id quod volunt cre-
6 dunt quoque. Nam cum irasci, favere, odisse, misereri coeperunt, agi iam rem suam existimant; et, sicut amantes de forma iudicare non possunt, quia

[1] dicente, *Spalding*: dicto, *MSS.*
[2] eloquentia regnat, *Halm*: eloquentiam regunt, *MSS.*

siderable number of pleaders capable of discovering arguments adequate to prove their points. I am far from despising such, but I consider that their utility is restricted to providing the judge with such facts as it is necessary for him to know, and, to be quite frank, I regard them merely as suitable persons to instruct pleaders of real eloquence in the facts of a case. But few indeed are those orators who can sweep the judge with them, lead him to adopt that attitude of mind which they desire, and compel
him to weep with them or share their anger. And 4
yet it is this emotional power that dominates the court, it is this form of eloquence that is the queen of all. For as a rule arguments arise out of the case itself, and the better cause has always the larger number to support it, so that the party who wins by means of them will have no further satisfaction than that of knowing that his advocate did not
fail him. But the peculiar task of the orator arises 5
when the minds of the judges require force to move them, and their thoughts have actually to be led away from the contemplation of the truth. No instruction from the litigant can secure this, nor can such power be acquired merely by the study of a brief. Proofs, it is true, may induce the judges to regard our case as superior to that of our opponent, but the appeal to the emotions will do more, for it will make them wish our case to be the better. And what they
wish, they will also believe. For as soon as they 6
begin to be angry, to feel favourably disposed, to hate or pity, they begin to take a personal interest in the case, and just as lovers are incapable of forming a reasoned judgment on the beauty of the object of their affections, because passion forestalls

sensum oculorum praecipit animus, ita omnem veritatis inquirendae rationem iudex omittit occupatus adfectibus; aestu fertur et velut rapido flumini obse-
7 quitur. Ita argumenta ac testes quid egerint, pronuntiatio ostendit; commotus autem ab oratore iudex, quid sentiat, sedens adhuc atque audiens confitetur. An cum ille, qui plerisque perorationibus petitur, fletus erumpit, non palam dicta sententia est? Huc igitur incumbat orator, *hoc opus, hic labor est,* sine quo cetera nuda, ieiuna, infirma, ingrata sint; adeo velut spiritus operis huius atque animus est in adfectibus.

8 Horum autem, sicut antiquitus traditum accepimus, duae sunt species: alteram Graeci πάθος vocant, quod nos vertentes recte ac proprie adfectum dicimus, alteram ἦθος, cuius nomine, ut ego quidem sentio, caret sermo Romanus; mores appellantur, atque inde pars quoque illa philosophiae ἠθικὴ moralis
9 est dicta. Sed ipsam rei naturam spectanti mihi non tam mores significari videntur quam morum quaedam proprietas; nam ipsis quidem omnis habitus mentis continetur. Cautiores voluntatem complecti quam nomina interpretari maluerunt. Adfectus igi-

---

[1] *Aen.* vi. 128.

the sense of sight, so the judge, when overcome by his emotions, abandons all attempt to enquire into the truth of the arguments, is swept along by the tide of passion, and yields himself unquestioning to
the torrent. Thus the verdict of the court shows 7
how much weight has been carried by the arguments and the evidence; but when the judge has been really moved by the orator he reveals his feelings while he is still sitting and listening to the case. When those tears, which are the aim of most perorations, well forth from his eyes, is he not giving his verdict for all to see? It is to this, therefore, that the orator must devote all his powers,

"There lie the task and toil!"[1]

Without this all else is bare and meagre, weak and devoid of charm. For it is in its power over the emotions that the life and soul of oratory is to be found.

Emotions however, as we learn from ancient 8
authorities, fall into two classes; the one is called *pathos* by the Greeks and is rightly and correctly expressed in Latin by *adfectus* (emotion): the other is called *ethos*, a word for which in my opinion Latin has no equivalent: it is however rendered by *mores* (morals) and consequently the branch of philosophy known as
ethics is styled *moral* philosophy by us. But close 9
consideration of the nature of the subject leads me to think that in this connexion it is not so much *morals* in general that is meant as certain peculiar aspects; for the term *morals* includes every attitude of the mind. The more cautious writers have preferred to give the sense of the term rather than to translate it into Latin. They therefore explain *pathos*

tur πάθος concitatos, ἦθος[1] mites atque compositos esse dixerunt; in altero vehementer commotos, in altero lenes; denique hos imperare, illos persuadere; hos ad perturbationem, illos ad benivolentiam praevalere.
10 Adiiciunt quidam ἦθος perpetuum,[2] πάθος temporale esse. Quod ut accidere frequentius fateor, ita nonnullas credo esse materias, quae continuum desiderent adfectum. Nec tamen minus artis aut usus hi leniores habent, virium atque impetus non tantundem exigunt. In causis vero etiam pluribus versantur, immo secundum quendam intellectum in
11 omnibus. Nam cum ex illo ethico[3] loco nihil non ab oratore tractetur, quidquid de honestis et utilibus, denique faciendis et non faciendis dicitur, ἦθος vocari potest. Quidam commendationem atque excusationem propria huius officii putaverunt, nec abnuo esse ista in hac parte; sed non concedo ut sola sint.
12 Quin illud adhuc adiicio, πάθος atque ἦθος esse interim ex eadem natura, ita ut illud maius sit, hoc minus, ut amor πάθος, caritas ἦθος; interdum diversa inter se, sicut in epilogis, nam quae πάθος concitavit, ἦθος solet mitigare. Proprie tamen mihi huius nominis exprimenda natura est, quatenus appellatione
13 ipsa non satis significari videtur. Ἦθος, quod intelligimus quodque a dicentibus desideramus, id erit, quod ante omnia bonitate commendabitur, non solum

[1] πάθος . . ἦθος, *excerpts of Cassiodorus with slight alteration of order*: hos . . illos, *MSS.*

[2] ἦθος perpetuum, *excerpts of Cassiodorus*: hoc pertuum, *A*: aut pertuum, *G*; peritorum, *codd. dett.*

[3] ethico, *Halm*: et hoc, *MSS.*

as describing the more violent emotions and *ethos* as
designating those which are calm and gentle: in the
one case the passions are violent, in the other sub-
dued, the former command and disturb, the latter
persuade and induce a feeling of goodwill. Some 10
add that *ethos* is continuous, while *pathos* is momen-
tary. While admitting that this is usually the case,
I still hold that there are some subjects which
demand that the more violent emotion should be
continuous. But, although the gentler emotions
require less force and impetus, they call for no less
art and experience than the more vehement, and are
demanded in a greater number of cases, indeed in a
certain sense they are required in all. For as every- 11
thing treated by the orator may be regarded from
the ethical standpoint, we may apply the word *ethos*
whenever he speaks of what is honourable and expedient or of what ought or ought not to be done.
Some regard commendation and excuse as the peculiar spheres of *ethos*, but while I admit that they do
fall within its sphere, I do not regard them as being
alone in so doing. Indeed I would add that *pathos* 12
and *ethos* are sometimes of the same nature, differing
only in degree; love for instance comes under the
head of *pathos*, affection of *ethos*; sometimes however
they differ, a distinction which is important for the
peroration, since *ethos* is generally employed to calm
the storm aroused by *pathos*. I ought however to
explain what is meant by *ethos* in greater detail,
since the term is not in itself sufficiently expressive
of its meaning. The *ethos* which I have in my mind 13
and which I desiderate in an orator is commended
to our approval by goodness more than aught else
and is not merely calm and mild, but in most cases

mite ac placidum, sed plerumque blandum et humanum et audientibus amabile atque iucundum, in quo exprimendo summa virtus ea est, ut fluere omnia ex natura rerum hominumque videantur utque mores dicentis ex oratione perluceant et quodammodo ag-
14 noscantur. Quod est sine dubio inter coniunctas maxime personas, quotiens ferimus, ignoscimus, satisfacimus, monemus, procul ab ira, procul ab odio. Sed tamen alia patris adversus filium, tutoris adversus pupillum, mariti adversus uxorem moderatio est (hi enim praeferunt eorum ipsorum, a quibus laeduntur, caritatem, neque alio modo invisos eos faciunt quam quod amare ipsi videntur), alia, cum senex adolescentis alieni convicium, honestus inferioris fert; hic enim tantum concitari, illic etiam
15 adfici debet. Sunt et illa ex eadem natura, sed motus adhuc minoris, veniam petere adulescentiae, defendere amores. Nonnunquam etiam lenis caloris alieni derisus ex hac forma venit, sed his non ex locis tantum. Verum aliquanto magis propria fuit virtus simulationis, satisfaciendi rogandi εἰρωνεία, quae
16 diversum ei quod dicit intellectum petit. Hinc etiam

ingratiating and courteous and such as to excite pleasure and affection in our hearers, while the chief merit in its expression lies in making it seem that all that we say derives directly from the nature of the facts and persons concerned and in the revelation of the character of the orator in such a way that
all may recognise it. This kind of *ethos* should be 14
especially displayed in cases where the persons concerned are intimately connected, whenever we tolerate or pardon any act or offer satisfaction or admonition, in all of which cases there should be no trace of anger or hatred. On the other hand the moderation shown by a father to his son, a guardian to his ward or a husband to his wife will differ from that which is shown by an old man to a youthful stranger who has insulted him or by a man of high rank to his inferior, since in the former cases they emphasise their affection for the wrongdoer and there is no desire to do anything that will excite dislike against them save by the manifestation of the fact that they still love them; while in the one case the offended party should be no more than provoked, in the other he should be really deeply moved.
Of the same character, though less violent, is the 15
emotion to be shown when we ask pardon for the errors of the young, or apologise for some youthful amour. Sometimes again gentle raillery of another's passion may derive its tone from *ethos*, though only to a partial extent. More closely dependent on *ethos* are the skilful exercise of feigned emotion or the employment of irony in making apologies or asking questions, irony being the term which is applied to words which mean something other than they seem
to express. From the same source springs also that 16

ille maior ad concitandum odium nasci adfectus solet, cum hoc ipso, quod nos adversariis summittimus, intelligitur tacita impotentiae exprobratio. Namque eos graves et intolerabiles id ipsum demonstrat, quod cedimus, et ignorant cupidi maledicendi aut adfectatores libertatis plus invidiam quam convicium posse; nam invidia adversarios, convicium nos invisos facit.
17 Ille iam paene medius adfectus est ex amoribus et ex desideriis amicorum et necessariorum, nam et hoc maior est et illo minor. Non parum significanter etiam illa in scholis ἤθη dixerimus, quibus plerumque rusticos, superstitiosos, avaros, timidos secundum condicionem propositionum effingimus. Nam si ἤθη mores sunt cum hos imitamur, ex his ducimus orationem.

18 Denique ἦθος[1] omne bonum et comem virum poscit. Quas virtutes cum etiam in litigatore debeat orator, si fieri potest, approbare, utique ipse aut habeat aut habere credatur. Sic proderit plurimum causis, quibus ex sua bonitate faciet fidem. Nam qui, dum dicit, malus videtur, utique male dicit; non enim videtur iusta dicere, alioqui ἦθος videretur.
19 Quare ipsum etiam dicendi genus in hoc placidum debet esse ac mite; nihil superbum, nihil elatum

[1] ἦθος, *Meister*: hoc *MSS.*

---

[1] *cp.* I. ix. 3.

more powerful method of exciting hatred, when by a feigned submission to our opponents we pass silent censure on their violence. For the very fact of our yielding serves to demonstrate their insupportable arrogance, while orators who have a passion for abuse or are given to affect freedom of speech fail to realise that it is a far more effective course to make your antagonist unpopular than to abuse him. For the former course makes our antagonists disliked, the latter ourselves. The emotion of love and longing 17
for our friends and connexions is perhaps of an intermediate character, being stronger than *ethos* and weaker than *pathos*. There is also good reason for giving the name of *ethos* to those scholastic exercises[1] in which we portray rustics, misers, cowards and superstitious persons according as our theme may require. For if *ethos* denotes moral character, our speech must necessarily be based on *ethos* when it is engaged in portraying such character.

Finally *ethos* in all its forms requires the speaker to 18
be a man of good character and courtesy. For it is most important that he should himself possess or be thought to possess those virtues for the possession of which it is his duty, if possible, to commend his client as well, while the excellence of his own character will make his pleading all the more convincing and will be of the utmost service to the cases which he undertakes. For the orator who gives the impression of being a bad man while he is speaking, is actually speaking badly, since his words seem to be insincere owing to the absence of *ethos* which would otherwise have revealed itself. Consequently the 19
style of oratory employed in such cases should be calm and mild with no trace of pride, elevation or

saltem ac sublime desiderat; proprie, iucunde, credibiliter dicere sat est, ideoque et medius ille orationis modus maxime convenit.

20 Diversum est huic, quod πάθος dicitur, quodque nos adfectum proprie vocamus; et, ut proxime utriusque differentiam signem, illud comoediae, hoc tragoediae magis simile. Haec pars circa iram, odium, metum, invidiam, miserationem fere tota versatur. Quae quibus ex locis ducenda sint, et manifestum omnibus et a nobis in ratione prooemii atque epilogi dictum est.
21 Et metum tamen duplicem intelligi volo, quem patimur et quem facimus, et invidiam; namque altera invidum, altera invidiosum facit. Hoc autem hominis, illud rei est; in quo et plus habet operis oratio. Nam quaedam videntur gravia per se, parricidium, caedes,
22 veneficium; quaedam efficienda sunt. Id autem contingit, cum magnis alioqui malis gravius esse id quod passi sumus, ostenditur; quale est apud Virgilium:

O felix una ante alias Priameïa virgo,
Hostilem ad tumulum Troiae sub moenibus altis
Iussa mori—

(quam miser enim casus Andromachae, si comparata

---

[1] *i.e.* the style intermediate between the restrained (Attic) and the grand (Asiatic) style.
[2] IV. i and VI. i. [3] *Aen.* iii. 321.

sublimity, all of which would be out of place. It is enough to speak appropriately, pleasantly and persuasively, and therefore the intermediate[1] style of oratory is most suitable.

The *pathos* of the Greeks, which we correctly translate by *emotion*, is of a different character, and I cannot better indicate the nature of the difference than by saying that *ethos* rather resembles comedy and *pathos* tragedy. For *pathos* is almost entirely concerned with anger, dislike, fear, hatred and pity. It will be obvious to all what topics are appropriate to such appeals and I have already spoken on the subject in discussing the exordium and the peroration.[2] I wish however to point out that fear is of two kinds, that which we feel and that which we cause in others. Similarly there are two kinds of *invidia* (hatred, envy), to which the two adjectives *invidus* (envious) and *invidiosus* (invidious, hateful) correspond. The first supplies an epithet for persons, the second for things, and it is in this latter connexion that the orator's task is even more onerous. For though some things are hateful in themselves such as parricide, murder, poisoning, other things have to be made to seem hateful. This latter contingency arises when we attempt to shew that what we have suffered is of a more horrible nature than what are usually regarded as great evils. Vergil will provide an example in the lines[3]:—

20

21

22

"O blest beyond all maidens Priam's child,
Beneath Troy's lofty bulwarks doomed to die
Upon the tomb of him that was thy foe."

For how wretched was the lot of Andromache, if Polyxena be accounted happy in comparison with

23 ei felix Polyxena); aut cum ita exaggeramus iniuriam nostram, ut etiam quae multo minora sunt intoleranda dicamus: *Si pulsasses, defendi non poteras; vulnerasti.* Sed haec diligentius, cum de amplificatione dicemus.[1] Interim notasse contentus sum, non id solum agere adfectus, ut, quae sunt, ostendantur acerba ac luctuosa, sed etiam ut, quae toleranda haberi solent, gravia videantur: ut cum in maledicto plus iniuriae quam in manu, in infamia plus poenae
24 dicimus quam in morte. Namque in hoc eloquentiae vis est, ut iudicem non in id tantum compellat, in quod ipsa rei natura ducetur, sed aut, qui non est, aut maiorem quam est, faciat adfectum. Haec est illa, quae δείνωσις vocatur, rebus indignis, asperis, invidiosis addens vim oratio; qua virtute praeter alias plurimum Demosthenes valuit.

25 Quodsi tradita mihi sequi praecepta sufficeret satisfeceram huic parti, nihil eorum quae legi vel didici, quod modo probabile fuit, omittendo; sed eruere in animo est quae latent, et penitus ipsa huius loci aperire penetralia, quae quidem non aliquo tradente, sed experimento meo ac natura ipsa duce accepi.
26 Summa enim, quantum ego quidem sentio, circa

[1] de amplificatione dicemus, *Halm*: ad eam amplificationem dicemus, *AG*: ad eam amplificationem venerimus, dicemus, *vulgo*.

---

[1] VIII. iv. 9. [2] Lit. "making terrible."

her! Again the same problem arises when we endeavour to magnify our wrongs by saying that other far lesser ills are intolerable; *e.g.* "If you had merely struck him, your conduct would have been indefensible. But you did more, you wounded him." However I will deal with this subject more fully when I come to speak of *amplification*.[1] Meanwhile I will content myself with the observation that the aim of appeals to the emotion is not merely to shew the bitter and grievous nature of ills that actually are so, but also to make ills which are usually regarded as tolerable seem unendurable, as for instance when we represent insulting words as inflicting more grievous injury than an actual blow or represent disgrace as being worse than death. For the force of eloquence is such that it not merely compels the judge to the conclusion toward which the nature of the facts lead him, but awakens emotions which either do not naturally arise from the case or are stronger than the case would suggest. This is known as *deinosis*,[2] that is to say, language giving additional force to things unjust, cruel or hateful, an accomplishment in which Demosthenes created immense and special effect. 23 24

If I thought it sufficient to follow traditional rules, I should regard it as adequate treatment for this topic to omit nothing that I have read or been taught, provided that it be reasonably sound. But my design is to bring to light the secret principles of this art, and to open up the inmost recesses of the subject, giving the result not of teaching received from others, but of my own experience and the guidance of nature herself. The prime essential for stirring the emotions of others is, in my opinion, 25 26

movendos adfectus in hoc posita est, ut moveamur ipsi. Nam et luctus et irae et indignationis aliquando etiam ridicula fuerit imitatio, si verba vultumque tantum, non etiam animum accommodarimus. Quid enim aliud est causae, ut lugentes utique in recenti dolore disertissime quaedam exclamare videantur et ira nonnunquam indoctis quoque eloquentiam faciat, quam quod illis inest vis mentis et veritas ipsa morum?
27 Quare in iis, quae esse verisimilia volemus, simus ipsi similes eorum qui vere patiuntur adfectibus, et a tali animo proficiscatur oratio qualem facere iudicem volet. An ille dolebit, qui audiet me, qui in hoc dicam, non dolentem? irascetur, si nihil ipse, qui in iram concitat se idque exigit, similia patietur? siccis agentis
28 oculis lacrimas dabit? Fieri non potest. Nec incendit nisi ignis nec madescimus nisi humore nec res ulla dat alteri colorem quem non ipsa habet. Primum est igitur, ut apud nos valeant ea quae valere apud iudicem volumus, adficiamurque antequam adficere
29 conemur. At quomodo fiet, ut adficiamur? neque enim sunt motus in nostra potestate. Temptabo etiam de hoc dicere. Quas φαντασίας Graeci vocant, nos sane visiones appellemus, per quas imagines rerum absentium ita repraesentantur animo, ut eas cernere

first to feel those emotions oneself. It is sometimes positively ridiculous to counterfeit grief, anger and indignation, if we content ourselves with accommodating our words and looks and make no attempt to adapt our own feelings to the emotions to be expressed. What other reason is there for the eloquence with which mourners express their grief, or for the fluency which anger lends even to the uneducated, save the fact that their minds are stirred to power by the depth and sincerity of their
feelings? Consequently, if we wish to give our 27
words the appearance of sincerity, we must assimilate ourselves to the emotions of those who are genuinely so affected, and our eloquence must spring from the same feeling that we desire to produce in the mind of the judge. Will he grieve who can find no trace of grief in the words with which I seek to move him to grief? Will he be angry, if the orator who seeks to kindle his anger shows no sign of labouring under the emotion which he demands from his audience? Will he shed tears if the pleader's eyes
are dry? It is utterly impossible. Fire alone can 28
kindle, and moisture alone can wet, nor can one thing impart any colour to another save that which it possesses itself. Accordingly, the first essential is that those feelings should prevail with us that we wish to prevail with the judge, and that we should be moved ourselves before we attempt to
move others. But how are we to generate these 29
emotions in ourselves, since emotion is not in our own power? I will try to explain as best I may. There are certain experiences which the Greeks call *φαντασίαι*, and the Romans *visions*, whereby things absent are presented to our imagination with such extreme

30 oculis ac praesentes habere videamur. Has quisquis bene conceperit, is erit in adfectibus potentissimus. Hunc quidam dicunt εὐφαντασίωτον, qui sibi res, voces, actus secundum verum optime finget; quod quidem nobis volentibus facile continget. Nisi[1] vero inter otia animorum et spes inanes et velut somnia quaedam vigilantium ita nos hae de quibus loquor imagines prosequuntur, ut peregrinari, navigare, proeliari, populos alloqui, divitiarum, quas non habemus, usum videamur disponere, nec cogitare sed facere: hoc
31 animi vitium ad utilitatem non transferemus? At hominem occisum queror; non omnia, quae in re praesenti accidisse credibile est, in oculis habebo? non percussor ille subitus erumpet? non expavescet circumventus? exclamabit vel rogabit vel fugiet? non ferientem, non concidentem videbo? non animo sanguis et pallor et gemitus extremus, denique exspirantis hiatus insidet?

32 Insequitur ἐνάργεια, quae a Cicerone illustratio et evidentia nominatur, quae non tam dicere videtur quam ostendere; et adfectus non aliter, quam si

[1] nisi, *Törnebladh*: nihil, *AG*.

---

[1] Perhaps an allusion to *Part. Or.* vi. 20. ἐνάργεια = clearness.

vividness that they seem actually to be before
our very eyes. It is the man who is really sen- 30
sitive to such impressions who will have the greatest power over the emotions. Some writers describe the possessor of this power of vivid imagination, whereby things, words and actions are presented in the most realistic manner, by the Greek word *εὐφαντασίωτος*; and it is a power which all may readily acquire if they will. When the mind is unoccupied or is absorbed by fantastic hopes or day-dreams, we are haunted by these visions of which I am speaking to such an extent that we imagine that we are travelling abroad, crossing the sea, fighting, addressing the people, or enjoying the use of wealth that we do not actually possess, and seem to ourselves not to be dreaming but acting. Surely, then, it may be possible to turn this form of halluci-
nation to some profit. I am complaining that a man 31
has been murdered. Shall I not bring before my eyes all the circumstances which it is reasonable to imagine must have occurred in such a connexion? Shall I not see the assassin burst suddenly from his hiding-place, the victim tremble, cry for help, beg for mercy, or turn to run? Shall I not see the fatal blow delivered and the stricken body fall? Will not the blood, the deathly pallor, the groan of agony, the death-rattle, be indelibly impressed upon my mind?

From such impressions arises that *ἐνάργεια* which 32
Cicero[1] calls *illumination* and *actuality*, which makes us seem not so much to narrate as to exhibit the actual scene, while our emotions will be no less actively stirred than if we were present at the actual

rebus ipsis intersimus, sequentur. An non ex his visionibus illa sunt; *Excussi manibus radii, revolutaque*
33 *pensa?—Levique patens in pectore vulnus?* equus ille in funere Pallantis,—*positis insignibus?* Quid? non idem poeta penitus ultimi fati concepit imaginem, ut
34 diceret: *Et dulces moriens reminiscitur Argos?* Ubi vero miseratione opus erit, nobis ea, de quibus queremur, accidisse credamus atque id animo nostro persuadeamus. Nos illi simus, quos gravia, indigna, tristia passos queremur, nec agamus rem quasi alienam, sed adsumamus parumper illum dolorem. Ita dicemus,
35 quae in nostro simili casu dicturi fuissemus.[1] Vidi ego saepe histriones atque comoedos, cum ex aliquo graviore actu personam deposuissent, flentes adhuc egredi. Quodsi in alienis scriptis sola pronuntiatio ita falsis accendit adfectibus, quid nos faciemus, qui illa cogitare debemus ut moveri periclitantium vice
36 possimus? Sed in schola quoque rebus ipsis adfici convenit easque veras sibi fingere, hoc magis quod

[1] fuissemus, *Halm*: vidissemus, *AG*.

---

[1] *Aen.* ix. 474. [2] *ib.* xi. 40.
[3] *ib.* xi. 89. [4] *ib.* x. 782.

occurrence. Is it not from visions such as these that Vergil was inspired to write—

> "Sudden her fingers let the shuttle fall
> And all the thread was spilled,"[1]

Or,

> "In his smooth breast the gaping wound,"[2] 33

or the description of the horse at the funeral of Pallas, "his trappings laid aside"?[3] And how vivid was the image of death conceived by the poet when he wrote—

> "And dying sees his own dear Argive home"?[4]

34 Again, when we desire to awaken pity, we must actually believe that the ills of which we complain have befallen our own selves, and must persuade our minds that this is really the case. We must identify ourselves with the persons of whom we complain that they have suffered grievous, unmerited and bitter misfortune, and must plead their case and for a brief space feel their suffering as though it were our own, while our words must be such as we should use if we stood in their shoes. I have often 35
seen actors, both in tragedy and comedy, leave the theatre still drowned in tears after concluding the performance of some moving role. But if the mere delivery of words written by another has the power to set our souls on fire with fictitious emotions, what will the orator do whose duty it is to picture to himself the facts and who has it in his power to feel the same emotion as his client whose interests are at stake? Even in the schools it is desirable that 36
the student should be moved by his theme, and should imagine it to be true; indeed, it is all the more desirable then, since, as a rule in scholastic

illic ut litigatores loquimur frequentius quam ut advocati. Orbum agimus et naufragum et periclitantem, quorum induere personas quid attinet, nisi adfectus adsumimus? Haec dissimulanda mihi non fuerunt, quibus ipse, quantuscunque sum aut fui, pervenisse me ad aliquod nomen ingenii credo; frequenter motus sum, ut me non lacrimae solum deprehenderent, sed pallor et veri similis dolor.

III. Huic diversa virtus, quae risum iudicis movendo et illos tristes solvit adfectus et animum ab intentione rerum frequenter avertit et aliquando etiam reficit et a satietate vel a fatigatione renovat. Quanta sit autem in ea difficultas, vel duo maxime oratores, alter Graecae alter Latinae eloquentiae
2 principes, docent. Nam plerique Demostheni facultatem defuisse huius rei credunt, Ciceroni modum. Nec videri potest noluisse Demosthenes, cuius pauca admodum dicta nec sane ceteris eius virtutibus respondentia palam ostendunt, non displicuisse illi
3 iocos, sed non contigisse. Noster vero non solum extra iudicia, sed in ipsis etiam orationibus habitus est nimius risus adfectator. Mihi quidem, sive id recte iudico sive amore immodico praecipui in elo-

declamations, the speaker more often appears as the actual litigant than as his advocate. Suppose we are impersonating an orphan, a shipwrecked man, or one in grave peril. What profit is there in assuming such a rôle unless we also assume the emotions which it involves? I have thought it necessary not to conceal these considerations from my reader, since they have contributed to the acquisition of such reputation for talent as I possess or once possessed. I have frequently been so much moved while speaking, that I have not merely been wrought upon to tears, but have turned pale and shown all the symptoms of genuine grief.

III. I now turn to a very different talent, namely that which dispels the graver emotions of the judge by exciting his laughter, frequently diverts his attention from the facts of the case, and sometimes even refreshes him and revives him when he has begun to be bored or wearied by the case. How hard it is to attain success in this connexion is shown by the cases of the two great masters of Greek and
Roman oratory. For many think that Demosthenes 2
was deficient in this faculty, and that Cicero used it without discrimination. Indeed, it is impossible to suppose that Demosthenes deliberately avoided all display of humour, since his few jests are so unworthy of his other excellences that they clearly show that he lacked the power, not merely that he
disliked to use it. Cicero, on the other hand, was 3
regarded as being unduly addicted to jests, not merely outside the courts, but in his actual speeches as well. Personally (though whether I am right in this view, or have been led astray by an exaggerated admiration for the prince of orators, I cannot say),

quentia viri labor, mira quaedam in eo videtur fuisse
4 urbanitas. Nam et in sermone cotidiano multa et in altercationibus et interrogandis testibus plura quam quisquam dixit facete, et ipsa illa, quae sunt in Verrem dicta frigidius, aliis adsignavit et testimonii loco posuit; ut, quo sunt magis vulgaria, eo sit credibilius illa ab oratore non ficta sed passim esse
5 iactata. Utinamque libertus eius Tiro aut alius, quisquis fuit, qui tris hac de re libros edidit, parcius dictorum numero indulsissent et plus iudicii in eligendis quam in congerendis studii adhibuissent: minus obiectus calumniantibus foret, qui tamen nunc quoque, ut in omni eius ingenio, facilius, quod reiici
6 quam quod adiici possit, invenient. Adfert autem summam rei difficultatem primum, quod ridiculum dictum plerumque falsum est (hoc semper humile), saepe ex industria depravatum, praeterea nunquam honorificum; tum varia hominum iudicia in eo, quod non ratione aliqua sed motu animi quodam nescio an
7 enarrabili iudicatur. Neque enim ab ullo satis explicari puto, licet multi temptaverint, unde risus, qui non solum facto aliquo dictove, sed interdum quodam etiam corporis tactu lacessitur. Praeterea non una ratione moveri solet, neque enim acute tantum ac venuste sed stulte, iracunde, timide dicta aut facta

I regard him as being the possessor of a remarkable turn of wit. For his daily speech was full of humour, 4
while in his disputes in court and in his examination of witnesses he produced more good jests than any other, while the somewhat insipid jokes which he launches against Verres are always attributed by him to others and produced as evidence: wherefore, the more vulgar they are, the more probable is it that they are not the invention of the orator, but were current as public property. I wish, however, that 5
Tiro, or whoever it may have been that published the three books of Cicero's jests, had restricted their number and had shown more judgment in selecting than zeal in collecting them. For he would then have been less exposed to the censure of his calumniators, although the latter will, in any case, as in regard to all the manifestations of his genius, find it easier to detect superfluities than deficiencies.
The chief difficulty which confronts the orator in 6
this connexion lies in the fact that sayings designed to raise a laugh are generally untrue (and falsehood always involves a certain meanness), and are often deliberately distorted, and, further, never complimentary: while the judgments formed by the audience on such jests will necessarily vary, since the effect of a jest depends not on the reason, but on an emotion which it is difficult, if not impossible, to describe. For 7
I do not think that anybody can give an adequate explanation, though many have attempted to do so, of the cause of laughter, which is excited not merely by words or deeds, but sometimes even by touch. Moreover, there is great variety in the things which raise a laugh, since we laugh not merely at those words or actions which are smart or witty, but also

ridentur; ideoque anceps eius rei ratio est, quod a
8 derisu non procul abest risus. *Habet* enim, ut Cicero
dicit, *sedem in deformitate aliqua et turpitudine,* quae
cum in aliis demonstrantur, urbanitas, cum in ipsos
dicentes recidunt, stultitia vocatur.

Cum videatur autem res levis et quae ab scurris,
mimis, insipientibus denique saepe moveatur, tamen
habet vim nescio an imperiosissimam et cui repug-
9 nari minime potest. Erumpit etiam invitis saepe,
nec vultus modo ac vocis exprimit confessionem, sed
totum corpus vi sua concutit. Rerum autem saepe
(ut dixi) maximarum momenta vertit, ut cum odium
10 iramque frequentissime frangat. Documento sunt
iuvenes Tarentini, qui multa de rege Pyrrho sequius
inter cenam locuti, cum rationem facti reposceren-
tur et neque negari res neque defendi posset, risu
sunt et opportuno ioco elapsi. Namque unus ex iis,
Immo, inquit, *nisi lagona defecisset, occidissemus te;*
eaque urbanitate tota est invidia criminis dissoluta.

11 Verum hoc, quidquid est, ut non ausim dicere
carere omnino arte, quia nonnullam observationem
habet, suntque ad id pertinentia et a Graecis et a

---

[1] *De Or.* II. lviii. 236. [2] Where?

at those which reveal folly, anger or fear. Consequently, the cause of laughter is uncertain, since laughter is never far removed from derision. For, 8
as Cicero[1] says, "Laughter has its basis in some kind or other of deformity or ugliness," and whereas, when we point to such a blemish in others, the result is known as wit, it is called folly when the same jest is turned against ourselves.

Now, though laughter may be regarded as a trivial matter, and an emotion frequently awakened by buffoons, actors or fools, it has a certain imperious force of its own which it is very hard to resist. It 9
often breaks out against our will and extorts confession of its power, not merely from our face and voice, but convulses the whole body as well. Again, it frequently turns the scale in matters of great importance, as I have already observed:[2] for instance, it often dispels hatred or anger. A proof of this is 10
given by the story of the young men of Tarentum, who had made a number of scurrilous criticisms of Pyrrhus over the dinner table: they were called upon to answer for their statements, and, since the charge was one that admitted neither of denial nor of excuse, they succeeded in escaping, thanks to a happy jest which made the king laugh; for one of the accused said, "Yes, and if the bottle hadn't been empty, we should have killed you!" a jest which succeeded in dissipating the animosity which the charge had aroused.

11 Still, whatever the essence of humour may be, and although I would not venture to assert that it is altogether independent of art (for it involves a certain power of observation, and rules for its employment have been laid down by writers both of Greece and

Latinis composita praecepta, ita plane adfirmo, prae-
12 cipue positum esse in natura et in occasione. Porro
natura non tantum in hoc valet, ut acutior quis atque
habilior sit ad inveniendum (nam id sane doctrina
possit augeri), sed inest proprius quibusdam decor in
habitu ac vultu, ut eadem illa minus alio dicente
13 urbana esse videantur. Occasio vero et in rebus est
cuius est[1] tanta vis, ut saepe adiuti ea non indocti
modo, sed etiam rustici salse dicant, et in eo cum quis
aliquid dixerit prior. Sunt enim longe venustiora
14 omnia in respondendo quam in provocando. Accedit
difficultati, quod eius rei nulla exercitatio est, nulli
praeceptores. Itaque in conviviis et sermonibus
multi dicaces, quia in hoc usu cotidiano proficimus.
Oratoria urbanitas rara nec ex arte propria sed ad
15 hanc consuetudinem commodata. Nihil autem
vetabat et componi materias in hoc idoneas, ut
controversiae permixtis salibus fingerentur, vel res
proponi singulas ad iuvenum talem exercitationem.
16 Quin illae ipsae (*dicta* sunt ac vocantur), quas certis
diebus festae licentiae dicere solebamus, si paulum
adhibita ratione fingerentur, aut aliquid in his serium

[1] cuius est, *added by Halm following Spalding.*

---

[1] The meaning of this passage is not clear, and no satisfactory explanation or correction has been suggested.

Rome), I will insist on this much, that it depends mainly on nature and opportunity. The influence 12
of nature consists not merely in the fact that one man is quicker or cleverer than another in the invention of jests (for such a power can be increased by teaching), but also in the possession of some peculiar charm of look or manner, the effect of which is such that the same remarks would be less entertaining if uttered by another. Opportunity, on the 13
other hand, is dependent on circumstances, and is of such importance that with its assistance not merely the unlearned, but even mere country bumpkins are capable of producing effective witticisms: while much again may depend on some previous remark made by another which will provide opportunity for repartee. For wit always appears to greater advantage in reply than in attack. We are also con- 14
fronted by the additional difficulty that there are no specific exercises for the development of humour nor professors to teach it. Consequently, while convivial gatherings and conversation give rise to frequent displays of wit, since daily practice develops the faculty, oratorical wit is rare, for it has no fixed rules to guide it, but must adapt itself to the ways of the world. There has, however, never been any- 15
thing to prevent the composition of themes such as will afford scope for humour, so that our controversial declamations may have an admixture of jests, while special topics may be set which will give the young student practice in the play of wit. Nay, 16
even those pleasantries in which we indulge on certain occasions of festive licence (and to which we give the name of *mots*,[1] as, indeed, they are), if only a little more good sense were employed in their

quoque esset admixtum, plurimum poterant utilitatis adferre; quae nunc iuvenum vel sibi ludentium exercitatio est.

17 Pluribus autem nominibus in eadem re vulgo utimur; quae tamen si diducas, suam quandam propriam vim ostendent. Nam et urbanitas dicitur, qua quidem significari video sermonem praeferentem in verbis et sono et usu proprium quendam gustum urbis et sumptam ex conversatione doctorum tacitam eruditionem, denique cui contraria sit rusticitas.
18 Venustum esse, quod cum gratia quadam et venere dicatur, apparet. Salsum in consuetudine pro ridiculo tantum accipimus; natura non utique hoc est, quanquam et ridicula oporteat esse salsa. Nam et Cicero omne, quod salsum sit, ait esse Atticorum, non quia sunt maxime ad risum compositi; et Catullus, cum dicit, *Nulla est in corpore mica salis,* non
19 hoc dicit, nihil in corpore eius esse ridiculum. Salsum igitur erit, quod non erit insulsum, velut quoddam simplex orationis condimentum, quod sentitur latente iudicio velut palato, excitatque et a taedio defendit orationem. Sales enim,[1] ut ille in cibis paulo liberalius aspersus, si tamen non sit immodicus, adfert aliquid propriae voluptatis, ita hi quoque in dicendo habent quiddam, quod nobis faciat

[1] sales enim, *Spalding*: sane tamen, *MSS.*

---

[1] *Orat.* xxvi. 90. [2] *Cat.* lxxxvi. 4.

invention, and they were seasoned by a slight admixture of seriousness, might afford a most useful training. As it is, they serve merely to divert the young and merrymakers.

There are various names by which we describe 17
wit, but we have only to consider them separately to perceive their specific meaning. First, there is *urbanitas,* which I observe denotes language with a smack of the city in its words, accent and idiom, and further suggests a certain tincture of learning derived from associating with well-educated men; in a word, it represents the opposite of rusticity.
The meaning of *venustus* is obvious; it means that 18
which is said with grace and charm. *Salsus* is, as a rule, applied only to what is laughable: but this is not its natural application, although whatever is laughable should have the salt of wit in it. For Cicero,[1] when he says that whatever has the salt of wit is Attic, does not say this because persons of the Attic school are specially given to laughter; and again when Catullus says—

In all her body not a grain of salt![2]

he does not mean that there is nothing in her body to
give cause for laughter. When, therefore, we speak 19
of the salt of wit, we refer to wit about which there is nothing insipid, wit, that is to say, which serves as a simple seasoning of language, a condiment which is silently appreciated by our judgment, as food is appreciated by the palate, with the result that it stimulates our taste and saves a speech from becoming tedious. But just as salt, if sprinkled freely over food, gives a special relish of its own, so long as it is not used to excess, so in the case of those who have the salt of wit there is something about

audiendi sitim. Facetum quoque non tantum circa
20 ridicula opinor consistere. Neque enim diceret
Horatius, facetum carminis genus natura concessum
esse Vergilio. Decoris hanc magis et excultae cuiusdam elegantiae appellationem puto. Ideoque in
epistolis Cicero haec Bruti refert verba: *Ne illi sunt
pedes faceti ac delicatius ingredienti molles.* Quod convenit cum illo Horatiano, *molle atque facetum Vergilio*·
21 Iocum vero accipimus, quod est contrarium serio·
sed hoc nimis angustum,[1] nam et fingere et terrere
et promittere interim iocus est. Dicacitas sine dubio
a dicendo, quod est omni generi commune, ducta
est, proprie tamen significat sermonem cum risu ali-
quos incessentem. Ideo Demosthenen urbanum
fuisse dicunt, dicacem negant.

22 Proprium autem materiae, de qua nunc loquimur,
est ridiculum, ideoque haec tota disputatio a Graecis
περὶ γελοίου inscribitur. Eius prima divisio traditur
eadem, quae est omnis orationis, ut sit positum in
23 rebus aut in verbis. Usus autem maxime triplex;
aut enim ex aliis risum petimus aut ex nobis aut ex
rebus mediis. Aliena aut reprehendimus aut refu-
tamus aut elevamus aut repercutimus aut eludimus.

[1] sed hoc nimis angustum, *added by Halm.*

---

[1] *Sat.* I. x. 44. molle atque facetum / Vergilio adnuerunt gaudentes rure Camenae. [2] This letter is lost.

their language which arouses in us a thirst to hear. Again, I do not regard the epithet *facetus* as applicable solely to that which raises a laugh. If that 20
were so Horace[1] would never have said that nature had granted Vergil the gift of being *facetus* in song. I think that the term is rather applied to a certain grace and polished elegance. This is the meaning which it bears in Cicero's letters, where he quotes the words of Brutus,[2] "In truth her feet are graceful and soft as she goes delicately on her way." This meaning suits the passage in Horace,[1] to which I have already made reference, "To Vergil gave a soft and graceful wit." *Iocus* is usually taken to mean 21
the opposite of seriousness. This view is, however, somewhat too narrow. For to feign, to terrify, or to promise, are all at times forms of jesting. *Dicacitas* is no doubt derived from *dico,* and is therefore common to all forms of wit, but is specially applied to the language of banter, which is a humorous form of attack. Therefore, while the critics allow that Demosthenes was *urbanus,* they deny that he was *dicax.*

The essence, however, of the subject which we 22
are now discussing is the excitement of laughter, and consequently the whole of this topic is entitled περὶ γελοίου by the Greeks. It has the same primary division as other departments of oratory, that is to say, it is concerned with things and words. The 23
application of humour to oratory may be divided into three heads: for there are three things out of which we may seek to raise a laugh, to wit, others, ourselves, or things intermediate. In the first case we either reprove or refute or make light of or retort or deride the arguments of others. In the

Nostra ridicule indicamus et, ut verbo Ciceronis utar, dicimus aliqua subabsurda. Namque quaedam, quae, si imprudentibus excidant, stulta sunt, si
24 simulamus, venusta creduntur. Tertium est genus, ut idem dicit, in decipiendis exspectationibus, dictis aliter accipiendis ceterisque, quae neutram personam
25 contingunt ideoque a me media dicuntur. Item ridicula aut facimus aut dicimus. Facto risus conciliatur interim admixta gravitate: ut M. Caelius praetor, cum sellam eius curulem consul Isauricus fregisset, alteram posuit loris intentam; dicebatur autem consul a patre flagris aliquando caesus; interim sine respectu pudoris, ut in illa pyxide Caeliana, quod neque oratori neque ulli viro gravi conveniat.
26 Idem autem de vultu gestuque ridiculo dictum sit; in quibus est quidem summa gratia, sed maior, cum captare risum non videntur; nihil enim est iis, quae sicut salsa[1] dicuntur, insulsius. Quanquam autem gratiae plurimum dicentis severitas adfert, fitque ridiculum id ipsum, quod qui dicit illa non ridet, est tamen interim et aspectus et habitus oris et gestus

[1] sicut, *Gesner*: dūt, *G*: dicenti, *A*.

---

[1] *de Or.* II. lxxi. 289.
[2] *cp. pro Cael.* xxix. 69. There is no jest in this passage which lays itself open to such censure. The jest must have consisted in some action on the part of the orator.

second we speak of things which concern ourselves in a humorous manner and, to quote the words of Cicero,[1] say things which have a suggestion of absurdity. For there are certain sayings which are regarded as folly if they slip from us unawares, but as witty if uttered ironically. The 24
third kind consists, as Cicero also tells us, in cheating expectations, in taking words in a different sense from what was intended, and in other things which affect neither party to the suit, and which I have, therefore, styled intermediate. Further, things de- 25
signed to raise a laugh may either be said or done. In the latter case laughter is sometimes caused by an act possessing a certain element of seriousness as well, as in the case of Marcus Caelius the praetor, who, when the consul Isauricus broke his curule chair, had another put in its place, the seat of which was made of leather thongs, by way of allusion to the story that the consul had once been scourged by his father: sometimes, again, it is aroused by an act which passes the grounds of decency, as in the case of Caelius' box,[2] a jest which was not fit for an orator or any respectable man to make. On 26
the other hand the joke may lie in some remark about a ridiculous look or gesture; such jests are very attractive, more especially when delivered with every appearance of seriousness; for there are no jests so insipid as those which parade the fact that they are intended to be witty. Still, although the gravity with which a jest is uttered increases its attraction, and the mere fact that the speaker does not laugh himself makes his words laughable, there is also such a thing as a humorous look, manner or

27 non inurbanus, cum iis modus contingit. Id porro,
quod dicitur, aut est lascivum et hilare, qualia A.
Galbae pleraque, aut contumeliosum, qualia nuper
Iunii Bassi, aut asperum, qualia Cassii Severi, aut
28 lene, qualia Domitii Afri. Refert, his ubi quis
utatur. Nam in convictibus et cotidiano sermone
lasciva humilibus, hilaria omnibus convenient. Laedere nunquam velimus, longeque absit propositum
illud potius amicum quam dictum perdendi. In
hac quidem pugna forensi malim mihi lenibus uti
licere; quanquam [1] et contumeliose et aspere dicere
in adversarios permissum est, cum accusare etiam
palam et caput alterius iuste petere concessum sit.
Sed hic quoque tamen inhumana videri solet fortunae insectatio, vel quod culpa caret vel quod recidere etiam in ipsos, qui obiecerunt, potest. Primum
itaque considerandum est, et quis et in qua causa et
29 apud quem et in quem et quid dicat. Oratori minime
convenit distortus vultus gestusque, quae in mimis
rideri solent. Dicacitas etiam scurrilis et scenica
huic personae alienissima est. Obscenitas vero non
a verbis tantum abesse debet, sed etiam a signifi-

[1] quanquam, *Regius*: nonnunquam, *MSS.*

gesture, provided always that they observe the happy mean. Further, a jest will either be free and lively, 27
like the majority of those uttered by Aulus Galba, or abusive, like those with which Junius Bassus recently made us familiar, or bitter, like those of Cassius Severus, or gentle, like those of Domitius Afer. Much depends on the occasion on which a 28
jest is uttered. For in social gatherings and the intercourse of every day a certain freedom is not unseemly in persons of humble rank, while liveliness is becoming to all. Our jests should never be designed to wound, and we should never make it our ideal to lose a friend sooner than lose a jest. Where the battles of the courts are concerned I am always better pleased when it is possible to indulge in gentle raillery, although it is, of course, permissible to be abusive or bitter in the words we use against our opponents, just as it is permissible to accuse them openly of crime, and to demand the last penalty of the law. But in the courts as elsewhere it is regarded as inhuman to hit a man when he is down, either because he is the innocent victim of misfortune or because such attacks may recoil on those who make them. Consequently, the first points to be taken into consideration are who the speaker is, what is the nature of the case, who is the judge, who is the victim, and what is the character of the remarks that are made. It is most unbecoming 29
for an orator to distort his features or use uncouth gestures, tricks that arouse such merriment in farce. No less unbecoming are ribald jests, and such as are employed upon the stage. As for obscenity, it should not merely be banished from his language, but should not even be suggested. For even if our

catione. Nam si quando obiici potest, non in ioco
30 exprobranda est. Oratorem praeterea ut dicere
urbane volo, ita videri adfectare id plane nolo.
Quapropter ne dicet quidem salse, quotiens poterit,
et dictum potius aliquando perdet quam minuet
31 auctoritatem. Nec accusatorem autem atroci in
causa nec patronum in miserabili iocantem feret
quisquam. Sunt etiam iudices quidam tristiores
32 quam ut risum libenter patiantur. Solet interim
accidere, ut id quod in adversarium dicimus aut in
iudicem conveniat aut in nostrum quoque litiga-
torem; quanquam aliqui reperiuntur, qui ne id quidem, quod in ipsos recidere possit, evitent. Quod
fecit Longus Sulpicius, qui, cum ipse foedissimus
esset, ait eum, contra quem iudicio liberali aderat,
ne faciem quidem habere liberi hominis; cui respon-
dens Domitius Afer, *Ex tui,* inquit, *animi sententia,*
33 *Longe, qui malam faciem habet, liber non est?* Vitandum etiam, ne petulans, ne superbum, ne loco, ne
tempore alienum, ne praeparatum et domo adlatum
videatur quod dicimus. Nam adversus miseros,
sicut supra dixeram, inhumanus est iocus. Sed quidam ita sunt receptae auctoritatis ac notae verecundiae, ut nocitura sit in eos dicendi petulantia. Nam
34 de amicis iam praeceptum est. Illud non ad oratoris[1]

[1] oratoris, *Harster*: orat fori*, *A*: orā fori, *G*.

opponent has rendered himself liable to such a
charge, our denunciation should not take the form
of a jest. Further, although I want my orator to 30
speak with wit, he must not give the impression of
striving after it. Consequently he must not display
his wit on every possible occasion, but must sacrifice
a jest sooner than sacrifice his dignity. Again, no 31
one will endure an accuser who employs jests to
season a really horrible case, nor an advocate for the
defence who makes merry over one that calls for pity.
Moreover, there is a type of judge whose tempera-
ment is too serious to allow him to tolerate laughter.
It may also happen that a jest directed against an 32
opponent may apply to the judge or to our own client,
although there are some orators who do not refrain
even from jests that may recoil upon themselves.
This was the case with Sulpicius Longus, who,
despite the fact that he was himself surpassingly
hideous, asserted of a man against whom he was
appearing in a case involving his status as a free
man, that even his face was the face of a slave. To
this Domitius Afer replied, "Is it your profound
conviction, Longus, that an ugly man must be a
slave?" Insolence and arrogance are likewise to 33
be avoided, nor must our jests seem unsuitable to
the time or place, or give the appearance of studied
premeditation, or smell of the lamp, while those
directed against the unfortunate are, as I have
already said, inhuman. Again, some advocates are
men of such established authority and such known
respectability, that any insolence shown them
would only hurt the assailant. As regards the
way in which we should deal with friends I have
already given instructions. It is the duty not merely 34

consilium sed ad hominis pertinet; lacessat hoc
modo quem laedere sit periculosum, ne aut inimicitiae graves insequantur aut turpis satisfactio. Male
etiam dicitur, quod in plures convenit, si aut nationes
totae incessantur aut ordines aut condicio aut studia
35 multorum. Ea quae dicet vir bonus omnia salva
dignitate ac verecundia dicet. Nimium enim risus
pretium est, si probitatis impendio constat.

Unde autem concilietur risus et quibus ex locis
peti soleat, difficillimum dicere. Nam si species
omnes persequi velimus, nec modum reperiemus et
36 frustra laborabimus. Neque enim minus numerosi
sunt loci, ex quibus haec dicta, quam illi, ex quibus
eae, quas sententias vocamus, ducuntur, neque alii.
Nam hic quoque est inventio et elocutio, atque ipsius
37 elocutionis vis alia in verbis, alia in figuris. Risus
igitur oriuntur aut ex corpore eius, in quem dicimus,
aut ex animo, qui factis ab eo dictisque colligitur, aut
ex iis, quae sunt extra posita. Intra haec enim est
omnis vituperatio; quae si gravius posita sit, severa
est, si levius, ridicula. Haec aut ostenduntur aut
38 narrantur aut dicto notantur. Rarum est, ut oculis

of an orator, but of any reasonable human being, when attacking one whom it is dangerous to offend to take care that his remarks do not end in exciting serious enmity, or the necessity for a grovelling apology. Sarcasm that applies to a number of persons is injudicious: I refer to cases where it is directed against whole nations or classes of society, or against rank and pursuits which are common to
many. A good man will see that everything he 35
says is consistent with his dignity and the respectability of his character; for we pay too dear for the laugh we raise if it is at the cost of our own integrity.

It is, however, a difficult task to indicate the sources from which laughter may be legitimately derived or the topics where it may be naturally employed. To attempt to deal exhaustively with the subject would be an interminable task and a waste
of labour. For the topics suitable to jests are no 36
less numerous than those from which we may derive *reflexions*, as they are called, and are, moreover, identical with the latter. The powers of invention and expression come into play no less where jests are concerned, while as regards expression its force will depend in part on the choice of words, in part
on the figures employed. Laughter then will be 37
derived either from the physical appearance of our opponent or from his character as revealed in his words and actions, or from external sources; for all forms of raillery come under one or other of these heads; if the raillery is serious, we style it as severe; if, on the other hand, it is of a lighter character, we regard it as humorous. These themes for jest may be pointed out to the eye or described
in words or indicated by some *mot*. It is only on 38

subiicere contingat, ut fecit C. Iulius; qui, cum Helvio Manciae saepius obstrepenti sibi diceret, *Etiam ostendam, qualis sis*, isque plane instaret interrogatione, qualem se ostensurus esset, digito demonstravit imaginem Galli in scuto Cimbrico pictam, cui Mancia tum simillimus est visus. Tabernae autem erant circa forum, ac scutum illud signi gratia positum.

39 Narrare, quae salsa sint, inprimis est subtile et oratorium, ut Cicero pro Cluentio narrat de Caepasio atque Fabricio aut M. Caelius de illa D. Laelii collegaeque eius in provinciam festinantium contentione. Sed in his omnibus cum elegans et venusta exigitur tota expositio, tum id festivissimum est quod adiicit orator. Nam et a Cicerone sic est

40 Fabricii fuga illa condita: *Itaque cum callidissime se putaret dicere, et cum illa verba gravissima ex intimo artificio deprompsisset, Respicite, iudices, hominum fortunas, respicite C. Fabricii senectutem, cum hoc, Respicite, ornandae orationis causa saepe dixisset, respexit ipse; at Fabricius a subselliis demisso capite discesserat*, et cetera, quae adiecit (nam est notus locus), cum in re hoc

[1] Cic. *de Or*. II. lxvi. 266.
[2] *pro Cluent*. xxi. 58.

rare occasions that it is possible to make them visible to the eye, as Gaius Julius[1] did when Helvius Mancia kept clamouring against him. "I will show you what you're like!" he cried, and then, as Mancia persisted in asking him to do so, pointed with his finger at the picture of a Gaul painted on a Cimbric shield, a figure to which Mancia bore a striking resemblance. There were shops round the forum and the shield had been hung up over one
of them by way of a sign. The narration of a 39
humorous story may often be used with clever effect and is a device eminently becoming to an orator. Good examples are the story told of Caepasius and Fabricius, which Cicero tells in the *pro Cluentio,* or the story told by Caelius of the dispute between Decimus Laelius and his colleague when they were both in a hurry to reach their province first. But in all such cases the whole narrative must possess elegance and charm, while the orator's own contribution to the story should be the most humorous element. Take for instance the way in which Cicero gives a special relish to the flight of Fabricius.[2]
"And so, just at the moment when he thought his 40
speech was showing him at his best and he had uttered the following solemn words, words designed to prove a master-stroke of art, 'Look at the fortunes of mankind, gentlemen, look at the aged form of Gaius Fabricius,' just at that very moment, I say, when he had repeated the word 'look' several times by way of making his words all the more impressive, he looked himself, and found that Fabricius had slunk out of court with his head hanging down." I will not quote the rest of the passage, for it is well known. But he develops the theme

41 solum esset, Fabricium a iudicio recessisse. Et
Caelius cum omnia venustissime finxit, tum illud
ultimum, *Hic subsecutus quomodo transierit, utrum rate
an piscatorio navigio, nemo sciebat, Siculi quidem, ut sunt
lascivi et dicases, aiebant in delphino sedisse et sic tan-*
42 *quam Ariona transvectum.* In narrando autem Cicero
consistere facetias putat, dicacitatem in iaciendo.
Mire fuit in hoc genere venustus Afer Domitius,
cuius orationibus complures huiusmodi narrationes
insertae reperiuntur, sed dictorum quoque ab eodem
43 urbane sunt editi libri. Illud quoque genus est
positum non in hac veluti iaculatione dictorum et
inclusa breviter urbanitate sed in quodam longiore
actu, quod de L. Crasso contra Brutum Cicero in
secundo de Oratore libro et aliis quibusdam locis
44 narrat. Nam, cum Brutus in accusatione Cn. Planci
ex duobus lectoribus ostendi set, contraria L. Crassum
patronum eius in oratione, quam de Colonia Narbo-
nensi habuerat, suasisse iis, quae de lege Servilia
dixerat, tris excitavit et ipse lectores, hisque patris
eius dialogos dedit legendos; quorum cum in Priver-
nati unus, alter in Albano, tertius in Tiburti sermonem
habitum complecteretur, requirebat, ubi essent eae
possessiones. Omnes autem illas Brutus vendiderat;
et tum paterna emancupare praedia turpius habeba-

[1] *i.e.* D. Laelius or his colleague: see § 39.

[2] *Orat.* xxvi. 87. [3] lv. 223.

[4] Probably members of his household, employed on this occasion to read out passages from Crassus' previous speeches.

still further although the plain facts amount simply to this, that Fabricius had left the court. The 41
whole of the story told by Caelius is full of wit and invention, but the gem of the passage is its conclusion. "He followed him, but how he crossed the straits, whether it was in a ship or a fisherman's boat, no one knew; but the Sicilians, being of a lively turn of wit, said that he rode on a dolphin and effected his crossing like a second Arion."[1] Cicero[2] 42
thinks that humour belongs to narrative and wit to sallies against the speaker's antagonist. Domitius Afer showed remarkable finish in this department; for, while narratives of the kind I have described are frequent in his speeches, several books have been published of his witticisms as well. This latter form 43
of wit lies not merely in sallies and brief displays of wit, but may be developed at greater length, witness the story told by Cicero in the second book of his *de Oratore*,[3] in which Lucius Crassus dealt with Brutus, against whom he was appearing in court. Brutus was prosecuting Cnaeus Plancus and had 44
produced two readers[4] to show that Lucius Crassus, who was counsel for the defence, in the speech which he delivered on the subject of the colony of Narbo had advocated measures contrary to those which he recommended in speaking of the Servilian law. Crassus, in reply, called for three readers and gave them the dialogues of Brutus' father to read out. One of these dialogues was represented as taking place on his estate at Privernum, the second on his estate at Alba, and the third on his estate at Tibur. Crassus then asked where these estates were. Now Brutus had sold them all, and in those days it was considered somewhat discreditable to sell one's

tur. Similis in apologis quoque et quibusdam interim etiam historiis exponendi gratia consequi solet.

45 Sed acutior est illa atque velocior in urbanitate brevitas. Cuius quidem duplex forma est dicendi ac respondendi, sed ratio communis in partem; nihil enim quod in lacessendo dici potest, non etiam in
46 repercutiendo. At quaedam propria sunt respondentium; illa etiam[1] atque etiam cogitata adferri solent, haec plerumque in altercatione aut in rogandis testibus reperiuntur.[2] Cum sint autem loci plures, ex quibus dicta ridicula ducantur, repetendum est mihi non omnes eos oratoribus convenire; in primis
47 ex amphibolia neque illa obscena,[3] quae Atellani e more captant, nec qualia vulgo iactantur a vilissimo quoque, conversa in maledictum fere ambiguitate; ne illa quidem, quae Ciceroni aliquando sed non in agendo exciderunt, ut dixit, cum is candidatus, qui coqui filius habebatur, coram eo suffragium ab alio
48 peteret: *Ego quoque tibi favebo.* Non quia excludenda sint omnino verba duos sensus significantia, sed quia raro belle respondeant, nisi cum prorsus rebus ipsis

[1] etiam atque etiam, *Spalding*: etiam itaque *or* etiam ira *MSS.*: cogitata, *Becher*: concitati, *MSS.*
[2] reperiuntur, *Spalding*: requiriuntur, *A*: requirantur, *G.*
[3] obscena, *Teuffel*: obscura, *MSS.*

---

[1] The pun is untranslatable, turning as it does on the similarity of sound between *coque* and *quoque*, so that the

paternal acres. Similar attractive effects of narrative may be produced by the narration of fables or at times even of historical anecdotes.

On the other hand brevity in wit gives greater 45 point and speed. It may be employed in two ways, according as we are the aggressors, or are replying to our opponents; the method, however, in both cases is to some extent the same. For there is nothing that can be said in attack that cannot be used in riposte. But there are certain points 46 which are peculiar to reply. For remarks designed for attack are usually brought ready-made into court, after long thought at home, whereas those made in reply are usually improvised during a dispute or the cross-examination of witnesses. But though there are many topics on which we may draw for our jests, I must repeat that not all these topics are becoming to orators: above all *doubles* 47 *entendres* and obscenity, such as is dear to the Atellan farce, are to be avoided, as also are those coarse jibes so common on the lips of the rabble, where the ambiguity of words is turned to the service of abuse. I cannot even approve of a similar form of jest, that sometimes slipped out even from Cicero, though not when he was pleading in the courts: for example, once when a candidate, alleged to be the son of a cook, solicited someone else's vote in his presence, he said, *Ego quoque tibi favebo.*[1] I say 48 this not because I object absolutely to all play on words capable of two different meanings, but because such jests are rarely effective, unless they are helped out by actual facts as well as similarity of sound.

sentence might mean either *I will support you, cook,* or *I too will support you.*

adiuvantur. Quare [non hoc modo][1] paene et ipsum scurrile Ciceronis est in eundem, de quo supra dixi, Isauricum: *Miror, quid sit, quod pater tuus, homo con-*
49 *stantissimus, te nobis varium reliquit.* Sed illud ex eodem genere praeclarum; cum obiiceret Miloni accusator in argumentum factarum Clodio insidiarum, quod Bovillas ante horam nonam devertisset, ut exspectaret, dum Clodius a villa sua exiret, et identidem interrogaret, quo tempore Clodius occisus esset, respondit, *Sero;* quod vel solum sufficit, ut
50 hoc genus non totum repudietur. Nec plura modo significari solent, sed etiam diversa, ut Nero de servo pessimo dixit nulli plus apud se fidei haberi, nihil
51 ei neque occlusum neque signatum esse. Pervenit res usque ad aenigma, quale est Ciceronis in Pletorium Fonteii accusatorem, *cuius matrem,* dixit, *dum vixisset, ludum, postquam mortua esset, magistros habuisse.* Dicebantur autem, dum vixit, infames feminae convenire ad eam solitae; post mortem bona eius venierant. Quanquam hic *ludus* per translationem dictus est,
52 *magistri* per ambiguitatem. In metalepsin quoque

[1] non hoc modo, *bracketed by Halm.*

---

[1] Here again the pun is virtually untranslatable. *varium* is used in the double sense of *unstable* or *mottled,* with reference to the story that he had been scourged by his father. See above § 25.

[2] *sero* may mean *at a late hour* or *too late.*

[3] Cic. *de Or.* II. lxi. 248. Probably C. Claudius Nero victor of the Metaurus.

For example, I regard the jest which Cicero levelled against that same Isauricus, whom I mentioned above, as being little less than sheer buffoonery. "I wonder," he said, "why your father, the steadiest of men, left behind him such a stripy gentleman as yourself."[1] On the other hand, the following 49 instance of the same type of wit is quite admirable: when Milo's accuser, by way of proving that he had lain in wait for Clodius, alleged that he had put up at Bovillae before the ninth hour in order to wait until Clodius left his villa, and kept repeating the question, "When was Clodius killed?", Cicero replied, "Late!"[2] a retort which in itself justifies us in refusing to exclude this type of wit altogether. Sometimes, too, the same word may be used not 50 merely in several senses, but in absolutely opposite senses. For example, Nero[3] said of a dishonest slave, "No one was more trusted in my house: there was nothing closed or sealed to him." Such ambi- 51 guity may even go so far as to present all the appearance of a riddle, witness the jest that Cicero made at the expense of Pletorius, the accuser of Fonteius: "His mother," he said, "kept a school while she lived and masters after she was dead."[4] The explanation is that in her lifetime women of infamous character used to frequent her house, while after her death her property was sold. (I may note however that *ludus*, is used metaphorically in the sense of school, while *magistri* is used ambiguously.) A similar form of 52

[4] *magister* may mean a schoolmaster or a receiver (*magister bonorum*) placed in charge of the goods to be sold. The phrase here has the same suggestion as "having the bailiffs in the house." This passage does not occur in the portions of the *pro Fonteio* which survive.

cadit eadem ratio dictorum, ut Fabius Maximus, incusans Augusti congiariorum, quae amicis dabantur, exiguitatem, *heminaria* esse dixit; nam *congiarium* commune liberalitatis atque mensurae, a mensura
53 ducta imminutio rerum. Haec tam frigida quam est nominum fictio adiectis, detractis, mutatis litteris, ut Acisculum, quia esset pactus, *Pacisculum,* et Placidum nomine, quod is acerbus natura esset, *Acidum*, et
54 Tullium, cum fur esset, *Tollium* dictos invenio. Sed haec eadem genera commodius in rebus quam in nominibus respondent. Afer enim venuste Manlium Suram, multum in agendo discursantem, salientem, manus iactantem, togam deiicientem et reponentem, non agere, dixit, sed satagere. Est enim dictum per se urbanum satagere etiamsi nulla subsit alterius
55 verbi similitudo. Fiunt et adiecta et detracta aspiratione et divisis coniunctisque verbis similiter saepius frigida, aliquando tamen recipienda. Eademque condicio est in iis, quae a nominibus trahuntur. Multa ex hoc Cicero in Verrem, sed ut ab aliis dicta,

---

[1] See VIII. vi. 37. "Substitution" is the nearest translation.

[2] *congiarium* is derived from *congius* a measure equal to about 6 pints. It was employed to denote the largesse of wine or oil distributed to the people. Fabius coined the word *heminarium* from *hemina,* the twelfth part of the *congius.* Fabius was consul in 10 B.C. and a friend of Ovid.

[3] From *tollere* to take away.

jest may be made by use of the figure known as *metalepsis*,[1] as when Fabius Maximus complained of the meagreness of the gifts made by Augustus to his friends, and said that his *congiaria* were *heminaria*: for *congiarium*[2] implies at once liberality and a particular measure, and Fabius put a slight on the liberality of Augustus by a reference to the measure.
This form of jest is as poor as is the invention of 53
punning names by the addition, subtraction or change of letters: I find, for instance, a case where a certain Aciscullus was called Pacisculus because of some "compact" which he had made, while one Placidus was nicknamed Acidus because of his "sour" temper, and one Tullius was dubbed Tollius[3] because he was
a thief. Such puns are more successful with things 54
than names. It was, for example, a neat hit of Afer's when he said that Manlius Sura, who kept rushing to and fro while he was pleading, waving his hands, letting his toga fall and replacing it, was not merely pleading, but giving himself a lot of needless trouble.[4] For there is a spice of wit about the word *satagere* in itself, even if there were no
resemblance to any other word. Similar jests may 55
be produced by the addition or removal of the aspirate, or by splitting up a word or joining it to another: the effect is generally poor, but the practice is occasionally permissible. Jests drawn from names are of the same type. Cicero introduces a number of such jests against Verres, but always as quotations

[4] This pun cannot be reproduced. Watson attempts to express it by "doing business in pleading" and "overdoing it." But "overdoing it" has none of the neatness of *satagere*, which is said to have "a spice of wit about it," since it means *lit.* "to do enough," an ironic way of saying "to overdo it."

modo *futurum, ut omnia verreret,* cum diceretur Verres, modo *Herculi,* quem expilaverat, *molestiorem apro Erymanthio fuisse,* modo *malum sacerdotem, qui tam nequam verrem reliquisset,* quia Sacerdoti Verres suc-
56 cesserat. Praebet tamen aliquando occasionem quaedam felicitas hoc quoque bene utendi: ut pro Caecina Cicero in testem Sex. Clodium Phormionem, *Nec minus niger,* inquit, *nec minus confidens quam est ille Terentianus Phormio.*

57 Acriora igitur sunt et elegantiora, quae trahuntur ex vi rerum. In his maxime valet similitudo, si tamen ad aliquid inferius leviusque referatur; quae iam veteres illi iocabantur, qui Lentulum Spintherem et Scipionem Serapionem esse dixerunt. Sed ea non ab hominibus modo petitur verum etiam ab animalibus, ut nobis pueris Iunius Bassus, homo inprimis
58 dicax, asinus albus vocabatur; et Sarmentus Messium Cicirrum equo fero comparavit. Ducitur et ab inanimis[1] sicut P. Blaesius Iulium, hominem nigrum et macrum et pandum, *fibulam ferream* dixit. Quod
59 nunc risus petendi genus frequentissimum est. Adhi-

[1] Messium . . . inanimis, *an addition suggested by Radermacher.*

---

[1] *verres* is also the second pers. sing. of the future of *verro.*

[2] *verres* means a boar and here suggests a pig that should have been killed as a victim. For these jests see *Verr.* II. xxi. 62, IV. xliii. 95, I. xlvi. 121 respectively. Compare also IV. xxiv. 53 and xxv. 57.

[3] x. 27. The reference must be to the make-up of Phormio on the stage: there is nothing in the play to suggest the epithet "black."

from others. On one occasion he says that he would sweep[1] everything away, for his name was Verres; on another, that he had given more trouble to Hercules, whose temple he had pillaged, than was given by the Erymanthine "boar"; on another, that he was a bad "priest" who had left so worthless a pig behind him.[2] For Verres' predecessor was named Sacerdos. Sometimes, however, a lucky 56
chance may give us an opportunity of employing such jests with effect, as for instance when Cicero in the *pro Caecina*[3] says of the witness Sextus Clodius Phormio, "He was not less black or less bold than the Phormio of Terence."

We may note therefore that jests which turn on 57
the meaning of things are at once more pointed and more elegant. In such cases resemblances between things produce the best effects, more especially if we refer to something of an inferior or more trivial nature, as in the jests of which our forefathers were so fond, when they called Lentulus Spinther and Scipio Serapio.[4] But such jests may be drawn not merely from the names of men, but from animals as well; for example when I was a boy, Junius Bassus, one of the wittiest of men, was nicknamed the white ass. And Sarmentus[5] compared Messius Cicirrus 58
to a wild horse. The comparison may also be drawn from inanimate objects: for example Publius Blessius called a certain Julius, who was dark, lean and bent, the iron buckle. This method of raising a laugh is much in vogue to-day. Such resemblances 59

[4] From their resemblances to Spinther, a bad actor, and to Serapio, a dealer in sacrificial victims.

[5] Sarmentus, a favourite of Augustus, *cp.* Hor. *Sat.* I. v. 56, where the story is given.

betur autem similitudo interim palam, interim inseri solet parabolae; cuius est generis illud Augusti, qui militi libellum timide porrigenti, *Noli,* inquit, *tanquam*
60 *assem elephanto des.* Sunt quaedam vi[1] similia; unde Vatinius dixit hoc dictum, cum reus, agente in eum Calvo, frontem candido sudario tergeret, idque ipsum accusator in invidiam vocaret, *Quamvis reus sum,* inquit,
61 *et panem item*[2] *candidum edo.* Adhuc est subtilior illa ex simili translatio, cum, quod in alia re fieri solet, in aliam mutuamur. Ea dicatur sane fictio: ut Chrysippus, cum in triumpho Caesaris eborea oppida essent translata, et post dies paucos Fabii Maximi lignea, thecas esse oppidorum Caesaris dixit. Et Pedo de mirmillone, qui retiarium consequebatur nec feriebat,
62 *Vivum,* inquit, *capere vult.* Iungitur amphiboliae similitudo, ut a Galba, qui pilam negligenter petenti, *Sic,* inquit, *petis, tanquam Caesaris candidatus.*

[1] vi *is the reading of AG, but is unsatisfactory as introducing nothing new.* veri (*some later MSS.*), vitii (*Halm*), vix (*Radermacher*), *do nothing to help out the meaning.*
[2] panem item, *Haupt*: parentem, *MSS.*

---

[1] The accused habitually wore mourning. Calvus suggested that Vatinius should not therefore have a white handkerchief. Vatinius retorts, *You might as well say that I ought to have dropped eating white bread.*
[2] Legatus of Caesar in Spain. The wooden models were so worthless compared with those of ivory that Chrysippus said they must be no more than the boxes in which Caesar kept the latter.
[3] Probably Chrysippus Vettius, a freedman and architect.
[4] Presumably the poet Pedo Albinovanus.

may be put to the service of wit either openly or allusively. Of the latter type is the remark of Augustus, made to a soldier who showed signs of timidity in presenting a petition, "Don't hold it out
as if you were giving a penny to an elephant." Some 60
of these jests turn on similarity of meaning. Of this kind was the witticism uttered by Vatinius when he was prosecuted by Calvus. Vatinius was wiping his forehead with a white handkerchief, and his accuser called attention to the unseemliness of the act. Whereupon Vatinius replied, "Though I am on my trial, I go on eating white bread all the
same."[1] Still more ingenious is the application of 61
one thing to another on the ground of some resemblance, that is to say the adaptation to one thing of a circumstance which usually applies to something else, a type of jest which we may regard as being an ingenious form of fiction. For example, when ivory models of captured towns were carried in Caesar's triumphal procession, and a few days later wooden models of the same kind were carried at the triumph of Fabius Maximus,[2] Chrysippus[3] remarked that the latter were the cases for Caesar's ivory towns. And Pedo[4] said of a heavy-armed gladiator who was pursuing another armed with a net and failed to
strike him, "He wants to catch him alive." Resem- 62
blance and ambiguity may be used in conjunction: Galba for example said to a man who stood very much at his ease when playing ball, "You stand as if you were one of Caesar's candidates."[5] The

[5] A candidate recommended by the emperor was automatically elected. I have borrowed Watson's translation of the pun. *Petere* is the regular word for "standing for office." *Petere pilam* probably means "to attempt to catch the ball."

Nam illud *petis* ambiguum est, securitas similis.
63 Quod hactenus ostendisse satis est. Ceterum frequentissima aliorum generum cum aliis mixtura est, eaque optima, quae ex pluribus constat. Eadem dissimilium ratio est. Hinc eques Romanus, ad quem in spectaculis bibentem cum misisset Augustus, qui ei diceret, *Ego si prandere volo, domum eo: Tu*
64 *enim,* inquit, *non times, ne locum perdas.* Ex contrario non una species. Neque enim eodem modo dixit Augustus praefecto, quem cum ignominia mittebat, subinde interponenti precibus, *Quid respondebo patri meo? Dic, me tibi displicuisse;* quo Galba penulam roganti: *Non possum commodare, domi maneo,* cum cenaculum eius perplueret. Tertium adhuc illud: (nisi quod,[1] ut ne auctorem ponam, verecundia ipsius facit) *Libidinosior es quam ullus spado;* quo sine dubio et opinio decipitur sed ex contrario. Et hoc ex eodem loco est sed nulli priorum simile, quod dixit M. Vestinus, cum ei nuntiatum esset... necatum esse,[2]
65 *Aliquando desinet putere.* Onerabo librum exemplis similemque iis, qui risus gratia componuntur, efficiam, si persequi voluero singula veterum.

[1] nisi quod, *Becher*: si quod, *AG*.
[2] necatum esse, *supplied by Spalding.*

ambiguity lies in the word *stand*, while the indifference shewn by the player supplies the resemblance. I 63
need say no more on this form of humour. But the practice of combining different types of jest is very common, and those are best which are of this composite character. A like use may be made of dissimilarity. Thus a Roman knight was once drinking at the games, and Augustus sent him the following message, "If I want to dine, I go home." To which the other replied, "Yes, but you are not afraid of losing your seat." Contraries give rise to more than 64
one kind of jest. For instance the following jests made by Augustus and Galba differ in form. Augustus was engaged in dismissing an officer with dishonour from his service: the officer kept interrupting him with entreaties and said, "What shall I say to my father?" Augustus replied, "Tell him that I fell under your displeasure." Galba, when a friend asked him for the loan of a cloak, said, "I cannot lend it you, as I am going to stay at home," the point being that the rain was pouring through the roof of his garret at the time. I will add a third example, although out of respect to its author I withhold his name: "You are more lustful than a eunuch," where we are surprised by the appearance of a word which is the very opposite of what we should have expected. Under the same heading, although it is quite different from any of the preceding, we must place the remark made by Marcus Vestinus when it was reported to him that a certain man was dead. "Some day then he will cease to stink," was his reply. But I shall overload this book with illustrations and 65
turn it into a common jest-book, if I continue to quote each jest that was made by our forefathers.

Ex omnibus argumentorum locis eadem occasio est. Nam et finitione usus est Augustus de pantomimis duobus, qui alternis gestibus contendebant, cum eorum alterum *saltatorem* dixit alterum *interpella-*
66 *torem;* et partitione Galba, cum paenulam roganti respondit, *Non pluit, non opus est tibi; si pluit, ipse utar.* Proinde genere, specie, propriis, differentibus, iugatis, adiunctis, consequentibus, antecedentibus, repugnantibus, causis, effectis, comparatione parium, maiorum, minorum similis materia praebetur; sicut
67 in tropos quoque omnes cadit. An non plurima per hyperbolen[1] dicuntur? quale refert Cicero de homine praelongo, *caput eum ad fornicem Fabium offendisse;* et quod P. Oppius dixit de genere Lentulorum, cum assidue minores parentibus liberi essent, *nascendo*
68 *interiturum.* Quid ironia? nonne etiam quae severissime fit, ioci prope genus est? Qua urbane usus est Afer, cum Didio Gallo, qui provinciam ambitiosissime petierat, deinde, impetrata ea, tanquam coactus querebatur, *Age,* inquit, *aliquid et rei publicae causa.* Metaphora[2] quoque Cicero lusit, cum, Vatinii morte nuntiata, cuius parum certus dicebatur auctor, *Inte-*

[1] per hyperbolen, *added by Regius.*
[2] metaphora, *Halm*: et abora, et labora, etc., *MSS.*

---

[1] See v. x. 85. [2] See v. x. 55 *sqq.*
[3] *cp. de Orat.* II. lxvi. 267, where the jest is attributed to Crassus.

All forms of argument afford equal opportunity for jests. Augustus for example employed *definition* when he said of two ballet-dancers who were engaged in a contest, turn and turn about, as to who could make the most exquisite gestures, that one was a dancer and the other merely interrupted the dancing. Galba on 66
the other hand made use of *partition* when he replied to a friend who asked him for a cloak, "It is not raining and you don't need it; if it does rain, I shall wear it myself." Similar material for jests is supplied by genus, species, property, difference, conjugates,[1] adjuncts, antecedents, consequents, contraries, causes, effects, and comparisons of things greater, equal, or less,[2] as it is also by all forms of trope. Are 67
not a large number of jests made by means of *hyperbole?* Take for instance Cicero's[3] remark about a man who was remarkable for his height, "He bumped his head against the Fabian arch," or the remark made by Publius Oppius about the family of the Lentuli to the effect, that since the children were always smaller than their parents, the race would "perish by propagation." Again, what of *irony?* Is not 68
even the most severe form of irony a kind of jest? Afer made a witty use of it when he replied to Didius Gallus, who, after making the utmost efforts to secure a provincial government, complained on receiving the appointment that he had been forced into accepting, "Well, then, do something for your country's sake."[4] Cicero also employed *metaphor* to serve his jest, when on receiving a report of uncertain authorship to the effect that Vatinius was dead, he remarked, "Well, for the meantime I shall

[4] *i.e.* sacrifice your own interests and serve your country for its own sake.

69 *rim,* inquit, *usura fruar.* Idem per allegorian M.
Caelium, melius obiicientem crimina quam defen-
dentem, bonam dextram, malam sinistram habere
dicebat. Emphasi A. Villius dixit, *ferrum in Tuc-*
70 *cium incidisse.* Figuras quoque mentis, quae σχήματα
διανοίας dicuntur, res eadem recipit omnes, in quas
nonnulli diviserunt species dictorum. Nam et in-
terrogamus et dubitamus et adfirmamus et minamur
et optamus, quaedam ut miserantes, quaedam ut
irascentes dicimus. Ridiculum est autem omne,
71 quod aperte fingitur. Stulta reprehendere facilli-
mum est, nam per se sunt ridicula; sed rem urbanam
facit aliqua ex nobis adiectio. Stulte interrogaverat
exeuntem de theatro Campatium Titius Maximus, an
spectasset? fecit Campatius dubitationem eius stulti-
orem dicendo, *Non, sed in orchestra pila lusi.*

72 Refutatio cum sit in negando, redarguendo, defen-
dendo, elevando, ridicule negavit Manius Curius;
nam, cum eius accusator in sipario omnibus locis aut
nudum eum in nervo aut ab amicis redemptum ex
73 alea pinxisset: *Ergo ego,* inquit, *nunquam vici?* Re-

---

[1] The report may be false, but I will enjoy the hope it arouses in me. The capital on which I receive a dividend may be non-existent, but I will enjoy the interest.

[2] The right being the sword arm, the left carrying the shield.

[3] Tuccius was clearly a coward who committed suicide. Villius suggested that he would never have had the courage

make use of the interest."[1] He also employed 69
allegory in the witticism that he was fond of making about Marcus Caelius, who was better at bringing charges than at defending his client against them, to the effect that he had a good right hand, but a weak left.[2] As an example of the use of *emphasis* I may quote the jest of Aulus Villius, that Tuccius was
killed by his sword falling upon him.[3] Figures of 70
thought, which the Greeks call σχήματα διανοίας, may be similarly employed, and some writers have classified jests under their various headings. For we ask questions, express doubts, make assertions, threaten, wish and speak in pity or in anger. And everything
is laughable that is obviously a pretence. It is easy 71
to make fun of folly, for folly is laughable in itself; but we may improve such jests by adding something of our own. Titius Maximus put a foolish question to Campatius, who was leaving the theatre, when he asked him if he had been watching the play. "No," replied Campatius, "I was playing ball in the stalls," whereby he made the question seem even more foolish than it actually was.

Refutation consists in denying, rebutting, defend- 72
ing or making light of a charge, and each of these affords scope for humour. Manius Curius, for example, showed humour in the way in which he denied a charge that had been brought against him. His accuser had produced a canvas, in every scene of which he was depicted either as naked and in prison or as being restored to freedom by his friends paying off his gambling debts. His only comment was,
"Did I never win, then?" Sometimes we rebut a 73

to fall upon his sword, and that therefore the sword must have fallen on him.

darguimus interim aperte, ut Cicero Vibium Curium multum de annis aetatis suae mentientem, *Tum ergo, cum una declamabamus, non eras natus;* interim et simulata assensione, ut idem Fabia Dolabellae dicente triginta se annos habere, *Verum est*, inquit; *nam*
74 *hoc illam iam viginti annis audio.* Belle interim subiicitur pro eo, quod neges, aliud mordacius: ut Iunius Bassus, querente Domitia Passieni, quod incusans eius sordes calceos eam veteres diceret vendere solere, *Non mehercules*, inquit, *hoc unquam dixi; sed dixi emere te solere.* Defensionem imitatus est eques Romanus, qui obiicienti Augusto, quod patrimonium
75 comedisset, *Meum*, inquit, *putavi.* Elevandi ratio est duplex, ut aut nimiam quis[1] iactantiam minuat: quemadmodum C. Caesar Pomponio ostendenti vulnus ore exceptum in seditione Sulpiciana, quod is se passum pro Caesare pugnantem gloriabatur, *Nunquam fugiens respexeris*, inquit; aut crimen obiectum, ut Cicero obiurgantibus, quod sexagenarius Publiliam
76 virginem duxisset, *Cras mulier erit*, inquit. Hoc genus dicti consequens vocant quidam, atque illi

[1] nimiam quis, *Deffner*: veniam quis aut, *MSS.*

---

[1] See VI. i. 50.
[2] A cousin of the father of C. Julius Caesar.

charge openly, as Cicero did when he refuted the extravagant lies of Vibius Curius about his age: "Well, then," he remarked, "in the days when you and I used to practise declamation together, you were not even born." At other times we may rebut it by pretending to agree. Cicero, for example, when Fabia the wife of Dolabella asserted that her age was thirty, remarked, "That is true, for I have heard it for the last twenty years." Sometimes too it is 74
effective to add something more biting in place of the charge which is denied, as was done by Junius Bassus when Domitia the wife of Passienus[1] complained that by way of accusing her of meanness he had alleged that she even sold old shoes. "No," he replied, "I never said anything of the sort. I said you bought them." A witty travesty of defence was once produced by a Roman knight who was charged by Augustus with having squandered his patrimony. "I thought it was my own," he answered. As regards making light of a charge, there 75
are two ways in which this may be done. We may throw cold water on the excessive boasts of our opponent, as was done by Gaius Caesar,[2] when Pomponius displayed a wound in his face which he had received in the rebellion of Sulpicius and which he boasted he had received while fighting for Caesar: "You should never look round," he retorted, "when you are running away." Or we may do the same with some charge that is brought against us, as was done by Cicero when he remarked to those who reproached him for marrying Publilia, a young unwedded girl, when he was already over sixty, "Well, she will be a woman to-morrow." Some style this 76
type of jest *consequent* and, on the ground that both

simile, quod Cicero Curionem, semper ab excusatione aetatis incipientem, facilius cotidie prooemium habere dixit, quia ista natura sequi et cohaerere
77 videantur. Sed elevandi genus est etiam causarum relatio, qua Cicero est usus in Vatinium. Qui pedibus aeger, cum vellet videri commodioris valetudinis factus et diceret, se iam bina milia passuum ambulare, *Dies enim,* inquit, *longiores sunt.* Et Augustus nuntiantibus Tarraconensibus palmam in ara eius
78 enatam, *Apparet,* inquit, *quam saepe accendatis.* Transtulit crimen Cassius Severus. Nam cum obiurgaretur a praetore, quod advocati eius L. Varo Epicureo, Caesaris amico, convicium fecissent, *Nescio,* inquit, *qui conviciati sint, et puto Stoicos fuisse.*

Repercutiendi multa sunt genera, venustissimum, quod etiam similitudine aliqua verbi adiuvatur: ut Trachalus dicenti Suelio, "*Si hoc ita est, is in exilium,*"
79 "*Si non est ita, redis,*" inquit. Elusit Cassius Severus obiiciente quodam, quod ei domo sua Proculeius interdixisset, respondendo, *Numquid ergo illuc accedo?* Sic eluditur et ridiculum ridiculo: ut divus Augustus, cum ei Galli torquem aureum centum pondo dedissent, et Dolabella per iocum, temptans tamen

---

[1] The point is obscure; we have no key to the circumstances of the jest.

jests seem to follow so naturally and inevitably, class it with the jest which Cicero levelled against Curio, who always began his speeches by asking indulgence for his youth: "You will find your exordium easier every day," he said. Another method of making 77
light of a statement is to suggest a reason. Cicero employed this method against Vatinius. The latter was lame and, wishing to make it seem that his health was improved, said that he could now walk as much as two miles. "Yes," said Cicero, "for the days are longer." Again Augustus, when the inhabitants of Tarraco reported that a palm had sprung up on the altar dedicated to him, replied, "That shows how often you kindle fire upon it." Cassius Severus 78
showed his wit by transferring a charge made against himself to a different quarter. For when he was reproached by the praetor on the ground that his advocates had insulted Lucius Varus, an Epicurean and a friend of Caesar, he replied, "I do not know who they were who insulted him, I suppose they were Stoics."

Of retorts there are a number of forms, the wittiest being that which is helped out by a certain verbal similarity, as in the retort made by Trachalus to Suelius. The latter had said, "If that is the case, you go into exile": to which Trachalus replied, "And if it is not the case, you go back into exile." [1]
Cassius Severus baffled an opponent who reproached 79
him with the fact that Proculeius had forbidden him to enter his house by replying, "Do I ever go there?" But one jest may also be defeated by another: for example, Augustus of blessed memory, when the Gauls gave him a golden necklet weighing a hundred pounds, and Dolabella, speaking in jest but with an

ioci sui eventum, dixisset, "*Imperator, torque me dona,*"
80 "*Malo,* inquit, *te civica donare*": mendacium quoque mendacio, ut Galba, dicente quodam, victoriato se uno in Sicilia quinque pedes longam murenam emisse: *Nihil,* inquit, *mirum; nam ibi tam longae nascuntur, ut*
81 *iis piscatores pro restibus cingantur.* Contraria est neganti confessionis simulatio, sed ipsa quoque multum habet urbanitatis. Sic Afer, cum ageret contra libertum Claudii Caesaris, et ex diverso quidam condicionis eiusdem, cuius erat litigator, exclamasset, "*Praeterea tu semper in libertos Caesaris dicis,*" "*Nec mehercule,* inquit, *quicquam proficio.*" Cui vicinum est non negare quod obiicitur, cum et id palam falsum est et inde materia bene respondendi datur: ut Catulus dicenti Philippo, "*Quid latras?*" "*Furem*
82 *video,*" inquit. In se dicere non fere est nisi scurrarum et in oratore utique minime probabile, quod fieri totidem modis quot in alios potest. Ideoque hoc,
83 quamvis frequens sit, transeo. Illud vero, etiamsi ridiculum est, indignum tamen est homine liberali,[1] quod aut turpiter aut potenter dicitur; quod fecisse

[1] liberali, *early edd.*: tolerabili, *MSS.*

---

[1] The civic crown of oak leaves was given as a reward for saving the life of a fellow-citizen in war. The *torquis* was often given as a reward for valour, and Augustus pretends to believe that Dolabella had asked for a military decoration. The point lies in the contrast between the intrinsic value and

eye to the success of his jest, said, "General, give me your necklet," replied, "I had rather give you the crown of oak leaves."[1] So, too, one lie may be 80
defeated by another: Galba, for instance, when someone told him that he once bought a lamprey five feet long for half a denarius in Sicily, replied, "There is nothing extraordinary in that: for they grow to such a length in those seas that the fishermen tie them round their waists in lieu of ropes!"
Then there is the opposite of denial, namely a feigned 81
confession, which likewise may show no small wit. Thus Afer, when pleading against a freedman of Claudius Caesar and when another freedman called out from the opposite side of the court, "You are always speaking against Caesar's freedmen," replied, "Yes, but I make precious little headway." A similar trick is not to deny a charge, though it is obviously false and affords good opportunity for an excellent reply. For example, when Philippus said to Catulus, "Why do you bark so?" the latter replied,[2]
"I see a thief." To make jokes against oneself is 82
scarcely fit for any save professed buffoons and is strongly to be disapproved in an orator. This form of jest has precisely the same varieties as those which we make against others and therefore I pass it by,
although it is not infrequently employed. On the 83
other hand scurrilous or brutal jests, although they may raise a laugh, are quite unworthy of a gentleman. I remember a jest of this kind being made by

weight of the two decorations. Further, Augustus was very parsimonious in bestowing military decorations and had himself received the crown of oak leaves from the senate as the saviour of Rome, a fact which must have rendered its bestowal on others rare, if not non-existent.

[2] *cp.* Cic. *de Or.* II. liv. 220.

quendam scio, qui humiliori libere adversus se loquenti, *Colaphum,* inquit, *tibi ducam et formulam scribam,*[1] *quod caput durum habeas.* Hic enim dubium est, utrum ridere audientes an indignari debuerint.

84 Superest genus decipiendi opinionem aut dicta aliter intelligendi, quae sunt in omni hac materia vel venustissima. Inopinatum et a lacessente poni solet, quale est, quod refert Cicero, *Quid huic abest nisi res et virtus?* aut illud Afri, *Homo in agendis causis optime vestitus;* et in occurrendo, ut Cicero, audita falsa Vatinii morte, cum obvium libertum eius interrogasset, "*Rectene omnia?*" dicenti, "*Recte,*"
85 "*Mortuus est?*" inquit. Plurimus autem circa simulationem et dissimulationem[2] risus est, quae sunt vicina et prope eadem; sed simulatio est certam opinionem animi sui imitantis, dissimulatio aliena se parum intelligere fingentis. Simulavit Afer, cum in causa subinde dicentibus Celsinam de re cognovisse, quae erat potens femina: *Quis est,* inquit, *iste?*
86 Celsinam enim videri sibi virum finxit. Dissimulavit Cicero, cum Sex. Annalis testis reum laesisset, et instaret identidem accusator ei, *Dic, M. Tulli,*

[1] scribam, *Badius*: scribes, *A*: scribe, *G.*
[2] et dissimulationem, *added by Regius.*

[1] See IX. ii. 22. [2] *de Or.* II. lxx. 281. [3] *cp.* § 68.

a certain man against an inferior who had spoken with some freedom against him: "I will smack your head, and bring an action against you for having such a hard skull!" In such cases it is difficult to say whether the audience should laugh or be angry.

84 There remains the prettiest of all forms of humour, namely the jest which depends for success on deceiving anticipations[1] or taking another's words in a sense other than he intended. The unexpected element may be employed by the attacking party, as in the example cited by Cicero,[2] "What does this man lack save wealth and—virtue?" or in the remark of Afer, "For pleading causes he is most admirably—dressed." Or it may be employed to meet a statement made by another, as it was by Cicero[3] on hearing a false report of Vatinius' death: he had met one of the latter's freedmen and asked him, "Is all well?" The freedman answered, "All is well." To which Cicero replied, "Is he dead, then?"
But the loudest laughter of all is produced by simula- 85
tion and dissimulation, proceedings which differ but little and are almost identical; but whereas simulation implies the pretence of having a certain opinion of one's own, dissimulation consists in feigning that one does not understand someone else's meaning. Afer employed simulation, when his opponents in a certain case kept saying that Celsina (who was an influential lady) knew all about the facts, and he, pretending to believe that she was a man, said, "Who
is he?" Cicero on the other hand employed dissimu- 86
lation when Sextus Annalis gave evidence damaging to the client whom he was defending, and the accuser kept pressing him with the question, "Tell me, Marcus Tullius, what have you to say about Sextus Annalis?"

numquid[1] *potes de Sex. Annali?* versus enim dicere coepit de libro Ennii annali sexto:

Quis potis ingentis causas evolvere belli?

87 Cui sine dubio frequentissimam dat occasionem ambiguitas: ut Cascellio, qui consultatori dicenti, "*Navem dividere volo,*" "*Perdes,*" inquit. Sed averti intellectus et aliter solet, cum ab asperioribus ad leniora deflectitur: ut qui interrogatus, quid sentiret de eo, qui in adulterio deprehensus esset, *Tardum*
88 *fuisse* respondit. Ei confine est, quod dicitur per suspicionem: quale illud apud Ciceronem querenti, quod uxor sua ex fico sese suspendisset, *Rogo, des mihi surculum ex illa arbore, ut inseram*; intelligitur
89 enim quod non dicitur. Et hercule omnis salse dicendi ratio in eo est, ut aliter quam est rectum verumque dicatur: quod fit totum fingendis aut nostris aut alienis persuasionibus aut dicendo quod
90 fieri non potest. Alienam finxit Iuba, qui querenti, quod ab equo suo esset aspersus, *Quid? Tu,* inquit, *me Hippocentaurum putas?* suam C. Cassius, qui militi

[1] Tulli numquid, *cod. Parisinus* 7723: Tullius inquid, *AG*.

---

[1] Enn. 174 (with *oras* for *causas*). The question (*numquid*, etc.) is treated by Cicero as meaning "Can you quote anything from the sixth book of the Annals?" *ingentis* is acc. plural.

[2] A famous lawyer mentioned by Horace, *A.P.* 371. Cascellius pretends to take *dividere* literally (*i.e.* cut in two); his client had meant "to sell half his ship," *i.e.* take a partner in the venture.

To which he replied by beginning to recite the Sixth book of the Annals of Ennius, which commences with the line,

"Who may the causes vast of war unfold?"[1]

This kind of jest finds its most frequent opportunity in ambiguity, as for example, when Cascellius,[2] on being consulted by a client who said, "I wish to divide my ship," replied, "You will lose it then." But there are also other ways of distorting the meaning; we may for instance give a serious statement a comparatively trivial sense, like the man who, when asked what he thought of a man who had been caught in the act of adultery, replied that he had been too slow in his movements.[3] Of a similar nature are jests whose point lies in insinuation. Such was the reply which Cicero[4] quotes as given to the man who complained that his wife had hung herself on a fig-tree. "I wish," said someone, "you would give me a slip of that tree to plant." For there the meaning is obvious, though it is not expressed in so many words. Indeed the essence of all wit lies in the distortion of the true and natural meaning of words: a perfect instance of this is when we misrepresent our own or another's opinions or assert some impossibility. Juba misrepresented another man's opinion, when he replied to one who complained of being bespattered by his horse, "What, do you think I am a Centaur?"[5] Gaius Cassius misrepresented his own, when he said to a soldier whom he

87

88

89

90

[3] *de Or.* II. lxviii. 275. [4] *ib.* lxix. 278.

[5] The point of the jest, such as it is, is that Juba disclaims forming part of his horse. The reference is to Juba, historian and king of Mauretania, captured by Julius Caesar and restored by Augustus.

sine gladio decurrenti, *Heus, commilito, pugno bene uteris,* inquit. Et Galba de piscibus, qui cum pridie ex parte adesi et versati postera die appositi essent, *Festinemus, alii subcenant,* inquit. Tertium illud Cicero, ut dixi, adversus Curium; fieri enim certe non pote-
91 rat ut, cum declamaret, natus non esset. Est et illa ex ironia fictio, qua usus est C. Caesar. Nam cum testis diceret a reo femina sua ferro petita, et esset facilis reprehensio, cur illam potissimum partem corporis vulnerare voluisset: *Quid enim faceret,* inquit,
92 *cum tu galeam et loricam haberes?* Vel optima est simulatio contra simulantem, qualis illa Domitii Afri fuit: vetus habebat testamentum, et unus ex amicis recentioribus, sperans aliquid ex mutatione tabularum, falsam fabulam intulerat, consulens eum, an primipilari seni iam testato rursus[1] suaderet ordinare suprema iudicia. *Noli,* inquit, *facere; offendis illum.*
93 Iucundissima sunt autem ex his omnibus lenia et, ut sic dixerim, boni stomachi: ut Afer idem ingrato litigatori conspectum eius in foro vitanti per nomenclatorem missum ad eum, *Amas me,* inquit, *quod te non vidi?* Et dispensatori, qui, cum reliqua non

[1] primipilari . . . rursus, *Spalding*: primipilaris enim intestator, *AG*.

---

[1] § 73.
[2] Lit. the slave employed to name persons to his master.

saw hurrying into battle without his sword, "Shew yourself a handy man with your fists, comrade." So too did Galba, when served with some fish that had been partially eaten the day before and had been placed on the table with the uneaten sides turned uppermost: "We must lose no time," he said, "for there are people under the table at work on the other side." Lastly there is the jibe that Cicero made against Curius, which I have already cited;[1] for it was clearly impossible that he should be still unborn at a time when he was already declaiming.
There is also a form of misrepresentation which has 91
its basis in irony, of which a saying of Gaius Caesar will provide an example. A witness asserted that the accused attempted to wound him in the thighs, and although it would have been easy to ask him why he attacked that portion of his body above all others, he merely remarked, "What else could he have done, when you had a helmet and breast-
plate?" Best of all is it when pretence is met by 92
pretence, as was done in the following instance by Domitius Afer. He had made his will long ago, and one of his more recent friends, in the hopes of securing a legacy if he could persuade him to change it, produced a fictitious story and asked him whether he should advise a senior centurion who, being an old man, had already made his will to revise it; to which Afer replied, "Don't do it: you will offend him."

But the most agreeable of all jests are those which 93
are good humoured and easily digested. Take another example from Afer. Noting that an ungrateful client avoided him in the forum, he sent his servant[2] to him to say, "I hope you are obliged to me for not having seen you." Again when his

responderent, dicebat subinde, "*Non comedi; pane et aqua vivo*,"[1] "*Passer, redde quod debes.*" Quae ὑπὸ τὸ
94 ἦθος vocant. Est gratus iocus, qui minus exprobrat quam potest, ut idem dicenti candidato, *Semper domum tuam colui*, cum posset palam negare, *Credo*, inquit, *et verum est.* Interim de se dicere ridiculum et quod in alium si absentem diceretur urbanum non erat,
95 quoniam ipsi palam exprobratur, movet risum: quale Augusti est, cum ab eo miles nescio quid improbe peteret et veniret contra Marcianus, quem suspicabatur et ipsum aliquid iniuste rogaturum: *Non magis*, inquit, *faciam, commilito, quod petis, quam quod Marcianus a me petiturus est.*

96 Adiuvant urbanitatem et versus commode positi, seu toti ut sunt (quod adeo facile est, ut Ovidius ex tetrastichon Macri carmine librum in malos poetas composuerit), quod fit gratius, si qua etiam ambiguitate conditur: ut Cicero in Lartium, hominem callidum et versutum, cum is in quadam causa sus-
97 pectus esset, *Nisi si qua Ulixes intervasit Lartius;* seu verbis ex parte mutatis, ut in eum qui, cum antea

[1] responderet *MSS. corr. Salmasius.* pane et aqua, *A*: panem et aquam, *remaining MSS.* vivo, *Haupt*: bibo, *MSS.*

---

[1] The meaning is dubious and the phrase cannot be paralleled and is probably corrupt.

[2] Aemilius Macer, a contemporary of Virgil and Horace. The work presumably consisted of epigrams, four lines long.

[3] The author, presumably a tragic poet, is unknown. *Lartius* = *Laertius*, son of Laertes.

steward, being unable to account for certain sums of money, kept saying, "I have not eaten it: I live on bread and water," he replied, "Master sparrow, pay what you owe." Such jests the Greeks
style ὑπὸ τὸ ἦθος[1] or adapted to character. It is a 94
pleasant form of jest to reproach a person with less than would be possible, as Afer did when, in answer to a candidate who said, "I have always shown my respect for your family," he replied, although he might easily have denied the statement, "You are right, it is quite true." Sometimes it may be a good joke to speak of oneself, while one may often raise a laugh by reproaching a person to his face with things that it would have been merely bad-mannered to bring
up against him behind his back. Of this kind was the 95
remark made by Augustus, when a soldier was making some unreasonable request and Marcianus, whom he suspected of intending to make some no less unfair request, turned up at the same moment: "I will no more grant your request, comrade, than I will that which Marcianus is just going to make."

Apt quotation of verse may add to the effect of 96
wit. The lines may be quoted in their entirety without alteration, which is so easy a task that Ovid composed an entire book against bad poets out of lines taken from the quatrains of Macer.[2] Such a procedure is rendered specially attractive if it be seasoned by a spice of ambiguity, as in the line which Cicero quoted against Lartius, a shrewd and cunning fellow who was suspected of unfair dealing in a certain case,

"Had not Ulysses Lartius intervened."[3]

Or the words may be slightly altered, as in the line 97
quoted against the senator who, although he had

stultissimus esset habitus, post acceptam hereditatem primus sententiam rogabatur, *Hereditas est, quam vocant sapientiam,* pro illo, *facilitas est;* seu ficti notis
98 versibus similes, quae παρῳδία dicitur. Et proverbia opportune aptata: ut homini nequam lapso et, ut allevaretur, roganti, *Tollat te qui non novit.* Ex historia etiam ducere urbanitatem eruditum est: ut Cicero fecit, cum ei testem in iudicio Verris roganti dixisset Hortensius, "*Non intelligo haec aenigmata.*" "*Atqui debes,* inquit, *cum Sphingem domi habeas*"; acceperat autem ille a Verre Sphingem aeneam magnae pecuniae.

99 Subabsurda illa constant stulti simulatione; quae,[1] nisi fingantur, stulta sunt: ut, qui mirantibus, quod humile candelabrum emisset, *Pransorium erit,* inquit. Sed illa similia absurdis sunt acria, quae tanquam sine ratione dicta feruntur: ut servus Dolabellae, cum interrogaretur an dominus eius auctionem proposuisset, *Domum,* inquit, *vendidit.*

[1] stulti simulatione; quae, *Spalding*: stultissimi imitatione et quae, *MSS.*

---

[1] Probably from a lost comedy.
[2] Hor. *Ep.* I. xvii. 62, where the passers by reply *Quaere peregrinum* to an imposter who, having fallen down and broken his leg, implores them to pick him up, crying *Credite, non ludo: crudeles, tollite claudum.*

always in previous times been regarded as an utter fool, was, after inheriting an estate, asked to speak first on a motion—

"What men call wisdom is a legacy,"[1]

where *legacy* is substituted for the original *faculty*. Or again we may invent verses resembling well-known lines, a trick styled parody by the Greeks.
A neat application of proverbs may also be effective, 98
as when one man replied to another, a worthless fellow, who had fallen down and asked to be helped to his feet, "Let someone pick you up who does not know you."[2] Or we may shew our culture by drawing on legend for a jest, as Cicero did in the trial of Verres, when Hortensius said to him as he was examining a witness, "I do not understand these riddles." "You ought to, then," said Cicero, "as you have got the Sphinx at home." Hortensius had received a bronze Sphinx of great value as a present from Verres.

Effects of mild absurdity are produced by the 99
simulation of folly and would, indeed, themselves, be foolish were they not fictitious. Take as an example the remark of the man who, when people wondered why he had bought a stumpy candlestick, said, "It will do for lunch."[3] There are also sayings closely resembling absurdities which derive great point from their sheer irrelevance, like the reply of Dolabella's slave, who, on being asked whether his master had advertised a sale of his property, answered, "He has sold his house."[4]

[3] Lunch requiring a less elaborate service, but being in broad daylight.

[4] *i.e.* how can he? he has nothing left to sell.

100 Deprehensi interim pudorem suum ridiculo aliquo explicant: ut, qui testem dicentem se a reo vulneratum interrogaverat an cicatricem haberet, cum ille ingentem in femine ostendisset, *Latus*, inquit, *oportuit.* Contumeliis quoque uti belle datur: ut Hispo obiicienti atrociora[1] crimina accusatori, *Me ex te metiris,*[2] inquit. Et Fulvius Propinquus legato interroganti an in tabulis, quas proferebat, chirographus esset, *Et verus*, inquit, *domine.*

101 Has aut accepi species aut inveni frequentissimas, ex quibus ridicula ducerentur; sed repetam necesse est, infinitas esse tam salse dicendi quam severe, quas praestat persona, locus, tempus, casus denique,
102 qui est maxime varius. Itaque haec, ne omisisse viderer, attigi; illa autem, quae de usu ipso et modo iocandi complexus sum, audeo confirmare[3] esse plane necessaria.

His adiicit Domitius Marsus, qui de urbanitate diligentissime scripsit, quaedam non ridicula, sed cuilibet severissimae orationi convenientia eleganter dicta et proprio quodam lepore iucunda; quae sunt
103 quidem urbana sed risum tamen non habent. Neque

[1] contumeliis *Badius*: umis *AG*: atrociora, *Halm*: arbore, *MSS.*
[2] me ex te metiris, *Burmann*: mentis, mentiris, *MSS.*
[3] audeo confirmare, *Radermacher*: adeo infirmare, infirmarem, infirma sed, *MSS.*

---

[1] *sc.* because then he would have killed you.
[2] Presumably the *legatus* had been suspected of forgery.

Sometimes you may get out of a tight corner by 100
giving a humorous explanation of your embarrassment, as the man did who asked a witness, who alleged that he had been wounded by the accused, whether he had any scar to show for it. The witness proceeded to show a huge scar on his thigh, on which he remarked, "I wish he had wounded you in the side."[1] A happy use may also be made of insult. Hispo, for example, when the accuser charged him with scandalous crimes, replied, "You judge my character by your own"; while Fulvius Propinquus, when asked by the representative of the emperor whether the documents which he produced were autographs, replied, "Yes, Sir, and the handwriting is genuine, too!"[2]

Such I have either learned from others or dis- 101
covered from my own experience to be the commonest sources of humour. But I must repeat that the number of ways in which one may speak wittily are of no less infinite variety than those in which one may speak seriously, for they depend on persons,
place, time and chances, which are numberless. I 102
have, therefore, touched on the topics of humour that I may not be taxed with having omitted them; but with regard to my remarks on the actual practice and manner of jesting, I venture to assert that they are absolutely indispensable.

To these Domitius Marsus, who wrote an elaborate treatise on *Urbanity*, adds several types of saying, which are not laughable, but rather elegant sayings with a certain charm and attraction of their own, which are suitable even to speeches of the most serious kind: they are characterised by a certain
urbane wit, but not of a kind to raise a laugh. And 103

enim ei de risu sed de urbanitate est opus institutum, quam propriam esse nostrae civitatis et sero sic intelligi coeptam, postquam Urbis appellatione, etiamsi nomen proprium non adiiceretur, Romam
104 tamen accipi sit receptum. Eamque sic finit: *Urbanitas est virtus quaedam in breve dictum coacta et apta ad delectandos movendosque homines in omnem adfectum animi, maxime idonea ad resistendum vel lacessendum, prout quaeque res aut persona desiderat.* Cui si brevitatis exceptionem detraxeris, omnes orationis virtutes complexa sit. Nam si constat rebus et personis, quod in utrisque oporteat dicere perfectae eloquentiae est. Cur autem brevem esse
105 eam voluerit, nescio, cum idem atque[1] in eodem libro dicat fuisse in multis narrandi urbanitatem. Paulo post ita finit, Catonis (ut ait) opinionem secutus, *Urbanus homo erit, cuius multa bene dicta responsaque erunt, et qui in sermonibus, circulis, conviviis, item in contionibus, omni denique loco ridicule commodeque dicet. Risus erunt, quicunque haec faciet*
106 *orator.* Quas si recipimus finitiones, quidquid bene dicetur, et urbane dicti nomen accipiet. Ceterum illi, qui hoc proposuerat, consentanea fuit illa divisio, ut dictorum urbanorum alia seria, alia iocosa, alia

[1] cum idem atque, *Halm*: cumidem ad quem, *A*: cuidem ad quem, *G*; quidem at quam, *codd. litt.*

as a matter of fact his work was not designed to deal with humour, but with *urbane wit,* a quality which he regards as peculiar to this city, though it was not till a late period that it was understood in this sense, after the word *Urbs* had come to be accepted as indicating Rome without the addition of any proper
noun. He defines it as follows: "Urbanity is a 104
certain quality of language compressed into the limits of a brief saying and adapted to delight and move men to every kind of emotion, but specially suitable to resistance or attack according as the person or circumstances concerned may demand." But this definition, if we except the quality of brevity, includes all the virtues of oratory. For it is entirely concerned with persons and things to deal with which in appropriate language is nothing more nor less than the task of perfect eloquence. Why he insisted on brevity being essential I do not know,
since in the same book he asserts that many speakers 105
have revealed their *urbanity* in narrative. And a little later he gives the following definition, which is, as he says, based on the views expressed by Cato: "Urbanity is the characteristic of a man who has produced many good sayings and replies, and who, whether in conversation, in social or convivial gatherings, in public speeches, or under any other circumstances, will speak with humour and appropriateness. If any orator do this, he will undoubtedly
succeed in making his audience laugh." But if we 106
accept these definitions, we shall have to allow the title of *urbane* to anything that is well said. It was natural therefore that the author of this definition should classify such sayings under three heads, serious, humorous and intermediate, since all good

media faceret. Nam est eadem omnium bene dictorum. Verum mihi etiam iocosa quaedam videntur
107 posse in non satis urbana referri. Nam meo quidem iudicio illa est urbanitas, in qua nihil absonum, nihil agreste, nihil inconditum, nihil peregrinum neque sensu neque verbis neque ore gestuve possit deprehendi; ut non tam sit in singulis dictis quam in toto colore dicendi, qualis apud Graecos ἀττικισμὸς ille
108 reddens Athenarum proprium saporem. Ne tamen iudicium Marsi, hominis eruditissimi, subtraham, seria partitur in tria genera, honorificum, contumeliosum, medium. Et honorifici ponit exemplum Ciceronis pro Ligario apud Caesarem, *Qui nihil soles*
109 *oblivisci nisi iniurias;* et contumeliosi, quod Attico scripsit de Pompeio et Caesare, *Habeo, quem fugiam; quem sequar, non habeo;* et medii, quod ἀποφθεγματικὸν vocat et est ita, cum dixerit, *Nec gravem mortem accidere viro forti posse nec immaturam consulari neque miseram sapienti.* Quae omnia sunt optime dicta; sed cur proprie nomen urbanitatis accipiant,
110 non video. Quod si non totius, ut mihi videtur, orationis color meretur, sed etiam singulis dictis tribuendum est, illa potius urbana dixerim, quae sunt generis eiusdem, quo ridicula dicuntur et tamen

---

[1] xii. 35. [2] *Ad. Att.* VIII. vii. 2. [3] IV. ii. 3.

sayings may be thus classified. But, in my opinion, there are certain forms of humorous saying that may be regarded as not possessing sufficient *urbanity*. For 107
to my thinking *urbanity* involves the total absence of all that is incongruous, coarse, unpolished and exotic whether in thought, language, voice or gesture, and resides not so much in isolated sayings as in the whole complexion of our language, just as for the Greeks *Atticism* means that elegance of taste which was peculiar to Athens. However, out of respect to 108
the judgment of Marsus, who was a man of the greatest learning, I will add that he divides serious utterances into three classes, the honorific, the derogatory and the intermediate. As an example of the honorific he quotes the words uttered by Cicero in the *pro Ligario*[1] with reference to Caesar, "You who forget nothing save injuries." The 109
derogatory he illustrates by the words used by Cicero of Pompey and Caesar in a letter to Atticus:[2] "I know whom to avoid, but whom to follow I know not." Finally, he illustrates the intermediate, which he calls apophthegmatic (as it is), by the passage from Cicero's speech against Catiline[3] where he says, "Death can never be grievous to the brave nor premature for one who has been consul nor a calamity to one that is truly wise." All these are admirable sayings, but what special title they have to be called *urbane* I do not see. If it is 110
not merely, as I think, the whole complexion of our oratory that deserves this title, but if it is to be claimed for individual sayings as well, I should give the name only to those sayings that are of the same general character as humorous sayings, without actually being humorous. I will give an

ridicula non sunt, ut de Pollione Asinio seriis iocisque pariter accommodato dictum est esse eum omnium
111 horarum; et de actore facile dicente ex tempore, ingenium eum in numerato habere; etiam Pompeii, quod refert Marsus, in Ciceronem diffidentem partibus, *Transi ad Caesarem, me timebis.* Erat enim, si de re minore aut alio animo aut denique non ab ipso dictum fuisset, quod posset inter ridicula nume-
112 rari. Etiam illud, quod Cicero Caerelliae scripsit reddens rationem, cur illa C. Caesaris tempora tam patienter toleraret, *Haec aut animo Catonis ferenda sunt aut Ciceronis stomacho;* stomachus enim ille habet aliquid ioco simile. Haec, quae movebant, dissimulanda mihi non fuerunt; in quibus ut erraverim, legentes tamen non decepi, indicata et diversa opinione, quam sequi magis probantibus liberum est.

IV. Altercationis praecepta poterant videri tunc inchoanda, cum omnia, quae ad continuam orationem pertinent, peregissem, nam est usus eius ordine ultimus; sed, cum sit posita in sola inventione neque habere dispositionem possit nec elocutionis ornamenta magnopere desideret aut circa memoriam et pronuntiationem laboret, prius quam secundam quinque partium, hanc quae tota ex prima pendet tractaturus

---

[1] Now lost. Caerellia was a literary lady.

[2] *i.e.* he must "stomach" it.

[3] The *altercatio*, which followed the set speeches, took the form of a number of brief arguments *pro* and *con*.

[4] See v. Pr. 5.

illustration of what I mean. It was said of Asinius Pollio, who had equal gifts for being grave or gay,
that he was "a man for all hours," and of a pleader 111
who was a fluent speaker extempore, that "his ability was all in ready money." Of the same kind, too, was the remark recorded by Marsus as having been made by Pompey to Cicero when the latter expressed distrust of his party: "Go over to Caesar and you will be afraid of me." Had this last remark been uttered on a less serious subject and with less serious purpose, or had it not been uttered by Pompey himself, we might have counted it among examples
of humour. I may also add the words used by 112
Cicero in a letter[1] to Caerellia to explain why he endured the supremacy of Caesar so patiently: "These ills must either be endured with the courage of Cato or the stomach[2] of Cicero," for here again the word "stomach" has a spice of humour in it. I felt that I ought not to conceal my feelings on this point. If I am wrong in my views, I shall not, at any rate, lead my readers astray, since I have stated the opposite view as well, which they are at liberty to adopt if they prefer it.

IV. With regard to the principles to be observed in forensic debate,[3] it might seem that I should delay such instructions until I had finished dealing with all the details of continuous speaking, since such debates come after the set speeches are done. But since the art of debate turns on invention alone, does not admit of arrangement, has little need for the embellishments of style, and makes no large demand on memory or delivery, I think that it will not be out of place to deal with it here before I proceed to the second of the five parts,[4] since it is

non alieno loco videor; quam scriptores alii fortasse ideo reliquerunt, quia satis ceteris praeceptis in hanc
2 quoque videbatur esse prospectum. Constat enim ex intentione ac depulsione, de quibus satis traditum est; quia, quidquid in actione perpetua circa probationes utile est, idem in hac brevi atque concisa prosit necesse est. Neque alia dicuntur in altercatione, sed aliter, aut interrogando aut respondendo. Cuius rei fere omnis observatio in illo testium loco
3 excussa nobis est. Tamen quia latius hoc opus aggressi sumus neque perfectus orator sine hac virtute dici potest, paululum impendamus huic quoque peculiaris operae, quae quidem in quibusdam causis
4 ad victoriam vel plurimum valet. Nam ut in qualitate generali, in qua rectene factum quid an contra sit quaeritur, perpetua dominatur oratio, et quaestionem finitionis actiones plerumque satis explicant et omnia paene, in quibus de facto constat aut coniectura artificiali ratione colligitur, ita in iis causis, quae sunt frequentissimae, quae vel solis extra artem probationibus vel mixtis continentur, asperrima in hac parte dimicatio est, nec alibi dixeris magis mucrone
5 pugnari. Nam et firmissima quaeque memoriae iudicis inculcanda sunt et praestandum quidquid in

---

[1] See v. vii. [2] See III. vi.
[3] See v. i. [4] See v. i.

entirely dependent on the first. Other writers have omitted to deal with it on the ground perhaps that they thought the subject had been sufficiently covered by their precepts on other topics. For debate con- 2
sists in attack and defence, on which enough has already been said, since whatever is useful in a continuous speech for the purpose of proof must necessarily be of service in this brief and discontinuous form of oratory. For we say the same things in debate, though we say them in a different manner, since debate consists of questions and replies, a topic with which we have dealt fairly exhaustively in connexion with the examination of witnesses.[1] But 3
since this work is designed on an ample scale and since no one can be called a perfect orator unless he be an expert debater, we must devote a little special attention to this accomplishment as well, which as a matter of fact is not seldom the deciding factor in a forensic victory. For just as the continuous speech 4
is the predominant weapon in general questions of quality (where the inquiry is as to whether an act was right or wrong), and as a rule is adequate to clear up questions of definition and almost all those in which the facts are ascertained or inferred by conjecture[2] from artificial proof,[3] so on the other hand those cases, which are the most frequent of all and depend on proofs which are either entirely inartificial[4] or of a composite character, give rise to the most violent debates; in fact I should say that there is no occasion when the advocate has to come to closer grips with his adversary. For all the 5
strongest points of the argument have to be sharply impressed on the memory of the judge, while we have also to make good all the promises we may

actione promisimus et refellenda mendacia. Nusquam est denique qui cognoscit intentior. Nec immerito quidam quanquam in dicendo mediocres hac tamen altercandi praestantia meruerunt nomen patro-
6 norum. At quidam litigatoribus suis illum modo ambitiosum declamandi sudorem praestitisse contenti cum turba laudantium destituunt subsellia pugnamque illam decretoriam imperitis ac saepe pullatae
7 turbae relinquunt. Itaque videas alios plerumque iudiciis privatis ad actiones advocari alios ad probationem. Quae si dividenda sunt officia, hoc certe magis necessarium est, pudendumque dictu, si plus litigantibus prosunt minores. In publicis certe iudiciis vox illa praeconis praeter patronos ipsum, qui egerit, citat.

8 Opus est igitur inprimis ingenio veloci ac mobili, animo praesenti et acri. Non enim cogitandum, sed dicendum statim est et prope sub conatu adversarii manus exigenda. Quare cum in omni parte huiusce officii plurimum facit, totas non diligenter modo sed etiam familiariter nosse causas, tum in altercatione maxime necessarium est, omnium personarum, instrumentorum, temporum, locorum habere notitiam;

---

[1] The allusion is obscure. But Quintilian's point seems to be merely that the pleader is officially regarded as being of at least equal importance with the other advocates.

have made in the course of our speech and to refute the lies of our opponents. There is no point of a trial where the judge's attention is keener. And even mediocre speakers have not without some reason acquired the reputation of being good advocates simply by their excellence in debate. Some on the 6
other hand think they have done their duty to their clients by an ostentatious and fatiguing display of elaborate declamation and straightway march out of court attended by an applauding crowd and leave the desperate battle of debate to uneducated performers who often are of but humble origin. As a result 7
in private suits you will generally find that different counsel are employed to plead and to prove the case. If the duties of advocacy are to be thus divided, the latter duty must surely be accounted the more important of the two, and it is a disgrace to oratory that inferior advocates should be regarded as adequate to render the greater service to the litigants. In public cases at any rate the actual pleader is cited by the usher as well as the other advocates.[1]

For debate the chief requisites are a quick and 8
nimble understanding and a shrewd and ready judgment. For there is no time to think; the advocate must speak at once and return the blow almost before it has been dealt by his opponent. Consequently while it is most important for every portion of the case that the advocate should not merely have given a careful study to the whole case, but that he should have it at his fingers' ends, when he comes to the debate it is absolutely necessary that he should possess a thorough acquaintance with all the persons, instruments and circumstances of time and place involved: otherwise he will often be reduced

alioqui et tacendum erit saepe et aliis subiicientibus (plerumque autem studio loquendi fatue modo) accedendum; quo nonnunquam accidit, ut nostra creduli-
9 tate aliena stultitia erubescamus. Neque tantum cum his ipsis monitoribus clam res erit[1]; quidam faciunt aperte ut quoque rixentur.[2] Videas enim plerosque ira percitos exclamantes, ut iudex audiat contrarium id esse, quod admoneatur, sciatque ille, qui pronun-
10 tiaturus est in causa, malum quod tacetur. Quare bonus altercator vitio iracundiae careat; nullus enim rationi magis obstat adfectus et fert extra causam plerumque et deformia convicia facere ac mereri cogit et in ipsos nonnunquam iudices incitat. Melior moderatio ac nonnunquam etiam patientia. Neque enim refutanda tantum quae ex contrario dicuntur, sed contemnenda, elevanda, ridenda sunt; nec usquam plus loci recipit urbanitas. Hoc, dum ordo est et pudor; contra turbantes audendum et impu-
11 dentiae fortiter resistendum. Sunt enim quidam praeduri in hoc oris, ut obstrepant ingenti clamore

[1] tantum . . . clam res erit, *Halm* : tam cum . . . clarescit, *MSS.*

[2] ut quoque rixentur, *Madvig* : quod (*or* quae) rixemur, *MSS.*

to silence and forced to give a hurried assent to those who prompt him as to what he should say, suggestions which are often perfectly fatuous owing to excess of zeal on the part of the prompter. As a result it sometimes happens that we are put to the blush by too ready acceptance of the foolish suggestions of another. Moreover, we have to deal with 9
others beside these prompters who speak for our ear alone. Some go so far as to turn the debate into an open brawl. For you may sometimes see several persons shouting angrily at the judge and telling him that the arguments thus suggested are contrary to the truth, and calling his attention to the fact that some point which is prejudicial to the case has been deliberately
passed over in silence. Consequently the skilled 10
debater must be able to control his tendency to anger; there is no passion that is a greater enemy to reason, while it often leads an advocate right away from the point and forces him both to use gross and insulting language and to receive it in return; occasionally it will even excite him to such an extent as to attack the judges. Moderation, and sometimes even longsuffering, is the better policy, for the statements of our opponents have not merely to be refuted: they are often best treated with contempt, made light of or held up to ridicule, methods which afford unique opportunity for the display of wit. This injunction, however, applies only so long as the case is conducted with order and decency: if, on the other hand, our opponents adopt turbulent methods we must put on a bold front and resist
their impudence with courage. For there are some 11
advocates so brazen-faced that they bluster and bellow at us, interrupt us in the middle of a sentence

et medios sermones intercipiant et omnia tumultu
confundant, quos ut non imitari sic acriter propulsare
oportebit, et ipsorum improbitatem retundendo, et
iudices vel praesidentes magistratus appellando fre
quentius, ut loquendi vices serventur. Non est res
animi iacentis et mollis supra modum frontis, fallit-
que plerumque, quod probitas vocatur, quae est im-
12 becillitas. Valet autem in altercatione plurimum
acumen, quod sine dubio ex arte non venit (natura
13 enim non docetur), arte tamen adiuvatur. In qua
praecipuum est, semper id in oculis habere, de quo
quaeritur et quod volumus efficere; quod propositum
tenentes nec in rixam ibimus nec causae debita tempora conviciando conteremus gaudebimusque, si hoc
adversarius facit.

14 Omni tempore fere parata sunt meditatis diligenter, quae aut ex adverso dici aut responderi a nobis
possunt. Nonnunquam tamen solet hoc quoque esse
artis genus, ut quaedam in actione dissimulata subito
in altercando proferantur; est inopinatis eruptioni-
bus aut incursioni ex insidiis factae simillimum. Id
autem tum faciendum, cum est aliquid, cui responderi non statim possit, potuerit autem, si tempus ad
disponendum fuisset. Nam quod fideliter firmum

and try to throw everything into confusion. While, then, it would be wrong to pay them the compliment of imitation, we must none the less repel their onslaughts with vigour by crushing their insolence and making frequent appeals to the judges or presiding magistrates to insist on the observance of the proper order of speaking. The debater's task is not one that suits a meek temper or excessive modesty, and we are apt to be misled because that which is really weakness is dignified by the name of
honesty. But the quality which is the most service- 12
able in debate is acumen, which while it is not the result of art (for natural gifts cannot be taught),
may none the less be improved by art. In this 13
connexion the chief essential is never for a moment to lose sight either of the question at issue or the end which we have in view. If we bear this in mind, we shall never descend to mere brawling nor waste the time allotted to the case by indulging in abuse, while we shall rejoice if our adversary does so.

Those who have given a careful study to the ar- 14
guments that are likely to be produced by their opponents or the replies which may be made by themselves are almost always ready for the fray. There is, however, a further device available which consists in suddenly introducing into the debate arguments which were deliberately concealed in our set speech: it is a procedure which resembles a surprise attack or a sally from an ambush. The occasion for its employment arises when there is some point to which it is difficult to improvise an answer, though it would not be difficult to meet if time were allowed for consideration. For solid and irrefutable

est a primis statim actionibus arripere optimum est,
15 quo saepius diutiusque dicatur. Illud vix saltem
praecipiendum videtur, ne turbidus et clamosus tantum sit altercator, et quales faceti sunt, qui litteras
nesciunt. Nam improbitas, licet adversario molesta
sit, iudici invisa est. Nocet etiam diu pugnare in
16 iis quae obtinere non possis. Nam, ubi vinci necesse
est, expedit cedere; quia, sive plura sunt de quibus
quaeritur, facilior erit in ceteris fides, sive unum,
mitior solet poena irrogari verecundiae. Nam cul-
pam praesertim deprehensam pertinaciter tueri
culpa altera est.

17 Dum stat acies, multi res consilii atque artis est,
ut errantem adversarium trahas et ire quam longis-
sime cogas, ut vana interim spe exultet. Ideo quaedam bene dissimulantur instrumenta. Instant enim
et saepe discrimen omne committunt, quod deesse
nobis putant, et faciunt probationibus nostris aucto-
18 ritatem postulando. Expedit etiam dare aliquid
adversario quod pro se putet, quod apprehendens
maius aliquid cogatur dimittere; duas interim res

arguments are best produced at once in the actual
pleading in order that they may be repeated and
treated at greater length. I think I need hardly 15
insist on the necessity for the avoidance in debate of
mere violence and noise and such forms of pleasantry
as are dear to the uneducated. For unscrupulous
violence, although annoying to one's antagonist,
makes an unpleasant impression on the judge. It is
also bad policy to fight hard for points which you
cannot prove. For where defeat is inevitable, it is 16
wisest to yield, since, if there are a number of other
points in dispute, we shall find it easier to prove
what remains, while if there is only one point at
issue, surrender with a good grace will generally
secure some mitigation of punishment. For obstinacy
in the defence of a fault, more especially after detection, is simply the commission of a fresh fault.

While the battle still rages, the task of luring on 17
our adversary when he has once committed himself
to error, and of forcing him to commit himself as
deeply as possible, even to the extent at times of
being puffed up with extravagant hopes of success,
requires great prudence and skill. It is, therefore,
wise to conceal some of our weapons: for our
opponents will often press their attack and stake
everything on some imagined weakness of our own,
and will give fresh weight to our proofs by the
instancy with which they demand us to produce
them. It may even be expedient to yield ground 18
which the enemy thinks advantageous to himself:
for in grasping at the fancied advantage he may
be forced to surrender some greater advantage: at
times, too, it may serve our purpose to give him a
choice between two alternatives, neither of which

proponere quarum utramlibet male sit electurus; quod in altercatione fit potentius quam in actione, quia in illa nobis ipsi respondemus, in hac adver-
19 sarium quasi confessum tenemus. Est inprimis acuti videre, quo iudex dicto moveatur, quid respuat; quod et vultu saepissime et aliquando etiam dicto aliquo factove eius deprehenditur. Et instare proficientibus et ab iis, quae non adiuvent, quam mollissime pedem oportet referre. Faciunt hoc medici quoque, ut remedia proinde perseverent adhibere vel desinant,
20 ut illa recipi vel respui vident. Nonnunquam, si rem evolvere propositam facile non sit, inferenda est alia quaestio, atque in eam iudex, si fieri potest, avocandus. Quid enim, cum respondere non possis, agendum est, nisi ut aliud invenias, cui adversarius
21 respondere non possit? In plerisque idem est, ut dixi, qui circa testes locus et personis modo distat, quod hic patronorum inter se certamen, illic pugna inter testem et patronum.

Exercitatio vero huius rei longe facilior. Nam est utilissimum, frequenter cum aliquo, qui sit studiorum eorundem, sumere materiam vel verae vel etiam fictae controversiae, et diversas partes altercationis modo tueri; quod idem etiam in simplici genere quaestio-
22 num fieri potest. Ne illud quidem ignorare advoca-

---

[1] We propound the dilemma and ourselves point out that whichever answer our opponent gives must tell against him.
[2] § 2. [3] *cp.* II. i. 9 and V. x. 53.

he can select without damage to his cause. Such a course is more effective in debate than in a set speech, for the reason that in the latter we reply to ourselves,[1] while in the former our opponent replies, and thereby delivers himself into our hands.
It is, above all, the mark of a shrewd debater to 19
perceive what remarks impress the judge and what he rejects: this may often be detected from his looks, and sometimes from some action or utterance. Arguments which help us must be pressed home, while it will be wise to withdraw as gently as possible from such as are of no service. We may take a lesson from doctors who continue or cease to administer remedies according as they note that they are received or rejected by the stomach.
Sometimes, if we find difficulty in developing our 20
point, it is desirable to raise another question and to divert the attention of the judge to it if this be feasible. For what can you do, if you are unable to answer an argument, save invent another to which
your opponent can give no answer? In most re- 21
spects the rules to be observed in debate are, as I have said,[2] identical with those for the cross-examination of witnesses, the only difference lying in the fact that the debate is a battle between advocates, whereas cross-examination is a fight between advocate and witness.

To practise the art of debate is, however, far easier. For it is most profitable to agree with a fellow-student on some subject, real or fictitious, and to take different sides, debating it as would be done in the courts. The same may also be
done with the simpler class of questions.[3] I 22
would further have an advocate realise the order in

tum volo, quo quaeque ordine probatio sit apud iudicem proferenda; cuius rei eadem quae in argumentis ratio est, ut potentissima prima et summa ponantur. Illa enim ad credendum praeparant iudicem, haec ad pronuntiandum.

V. His pro nostra facultate tractatis non dubitassem transire protinus ad dispositionem, quae ordine ipso sequitur, nisi vererer ne, quoniam fuerunt qui iudicium inventioni subiungerent, praeterisse hunc locum quibusdam viderer, qui mea quidem opinione adeo partibus operis huius omnibus connexus ac mixtus est, ut ne a sententiis quidem aut verbis saltem singulis possit separari, nec magis arte tra-
2 ditur quam gustus aut odor. Ideoque nos, quid in quaque re sequendum cavendumque sit, docemus ac deinceps docebimus, ut ad ea iudicium dirigatur. Praecipiam igitur, ne, quod effici non potest, aggrediamur, ut contraria vitemus et communia, ne quid in eloquendo corruptum, obscurum sit? Referatur oportet ad sensus, qui non docentur.

3 Nec multum a iudicio credo distare consilium, nisi quod illud ostendentibus se rebus adhibetur, hoc latentibus et aut omnino nondum repertis aut dubiis. Et iudicium frequentissime certum est, consilium

---

[1] See III. iii. 5 and 6.

which his proofs should be presented to the judge: the method to be followed is the same as in arguments: the strongest should be placed first and last. For those which are presented first dispose the judge to believe us, and those which come last to decide in our favour.

V. Having dealt with these points to the best of my ability, I should have had no hesitation in proceeding to discuss arrangement, which is logically the next consideration, did I not fear that, since there are some who include judgment[1] under the head of invention, they might think that I had deliberately omitted all discussion of judgment, although personally I regard it as so inextricably blent with and involved in every portion of this work, that its influence extends even to single sentences or words, and it is no more possible to teach it than it is to instruct the powers of taste and smell. Consequently, all I can do is now and 2
hereafter to show what should be done or avoided in each particular case, with a view thereby to guide the judgment. What use then is it for me to lay down general rules to the effect that we should not attempt impossibilities, that we should avoid whatever contradicts our case or is common to both, and shun all incorrectness or obscurity of style? In all these cases it is common sense that must decide, and common sense cannot be taught.

There is no great difference, in my opinion, 3
between judgment and sagacity, except that the former deals with evident facts, while the latter is concerned with hidden facts or such as have not yet been discovered or still remain in doubt. Again judgment is more often than not a matter of

vero est ratio quaedam alte petita et plerumque plura perpendens et comparans habensque in se et
4 inventionem et iudicationem. Sed ne de hoc quidem praecepta in universum exspectanda sunt. Nam ex re sumitur cuius locus ante actionem est frequenter; nam Cicero summo consilio videtur in Verrem vel contrahere tempora dicendi maluisse quam in eum annum, quo erat Q. Hortensius consul futurus, in-
5 cidere. Et in ipsis actionibus primum ac potentissimum obtinet locum; nam, quid dicendum, quid tacendum, quid differendum sit, exigere consilii est; negare sit satis an defendere, ubi prooemio utendum et quali, narrandumne et quomodo, iure prius pugnandum an aequo, qui sit ordo utilissimus, tum omnes colores, aspere an leniter an etiam summisse
6 loqui expediat. Sed haec quoque, ut quisque passus est locus, monuimus, idemque in reliqua parte faciemus; pauca tamen exempli gratia ponam, quibus manifestius appareat quid sit, quod demonstrari
7 posse praeceptis non arbitror. Laudatur consilium Demosthenis, quod, cum suaderet bellum Athenien-

---

[1] *Phil.* i. 2.

certainty, while sagacity is a form of reasoning from deep-lying premises, which generally weighs and compares a number of arguments and in itself
involves both invention and judgment. But here 4
again you must not expect me to lay down any general rules. For sagacity depends on circumstances and will often find its scope in something preceding the pleading of the cause. For instance in the prosecution of Verres Cicero seems to have shown the highest sagacity in preferring to cut down the time available for his speech rather than allow the trial to be postponed to the following year when Quintus
Hortensius was to be consul. And again in the 5
actual pleading sagacity holds the first and most important place. For it is the duty of sagacity to decide what we should say and what we should pass by in silence or postpone; whether it is better to deny an act or to defend it, when we should employ an exordium and on what lines it should be designed, whether we should make a statement of facts and if so, how, whether we should base our plea on law or equity and what is the best order to adopt, while it must also decide on all the nuances of style, and settle whether it is expedient to speak harshly,
gently or even with humility. But I have already 6
given advice on all these points as far as each occasion permitted, and I shall continue to do the same in the subsequent portions of this work. In the meantime, however, I will give a few instances to make my meaning clearer, since it is not possible, in my opinion, to do so by laying down general rules.
We praise Demosthenes[1] for his sagacity because 7
when he urged a policy of war upon the Athenians after they had met with a series of reverses, he

sibus parum id prospere expertis, nihil adhuc factum esse ratione monstrat. Poterat enim emendari neglegentia; at, si nihil esset erratum, melioris in pos-
8 terum spei non erat ratio. Idem, cum offensam vereretur, si obiurgaret populi segnitiam in asserenda libertate rei publicae, maiorum laude uti maluit, qui rem publicam fortissime administrassent. Nam et faciles habuit aures, et natura sequebatur, ut
9 meliora probantes peiorum poeniteret. Ciceronis quidem vel una pro Cluentio quamlibet multis exemplis sufficiet oratio. Nam quod in eo consilium maxime mirer? primamne expositionem, qua matri, cuius filium premebat auctoritas, abstulit fidem? an quod iudicii corrupti crimen transferre in adversarium maluit quam negare propter inveteratam, ut ipse dicit, infamiam? an quod in re invidiosa legis auxilio novissime est usus, quo genere defensionis etiam offendisset nondum praemollitas iudicum mentes? an quod se ipsum invito Cluentio facere testatus
10 est? Quid pro Milone? quod non ante narravit, quam praeiudiciis omnibus reum liberaret? quod

---

[1] *Phil.* i. 1. [2] vi. 17. [3] i. 4. [4] lii. 143 *sqq.*
[5] lii. 144, 148, 149. [6] *cp.* Quint. III. vi. 93.

pointed out that so far their action had been entirely irrational. For they might still make amends for their negligence, whereas, if they had made no mistakes, they would have had no ground for hopes of better success in the future. Again,[1] since he feared to 8
give offence if he taxed the people with lack of energy in defending the liberties of their country, he preferred to praise their ancestors for their courageous policy. Thus he gained a ready hearing, with the natural result that the pride which they felt in the heroic past made them repent of their own degenerate behaviour. If we turn to Cicero, we 9
shall find that one speech alone, the *pro Cluentio*, will suffice to provide a number of examples. The difficulty is to know what special exhibition of sagacity to admire most in this speech. His opening statement of the case, by which he discredited the mother whose authority pressed so hardly on her son?[2] The fact that he preferred to throw the charge of having bribed the jury back upon his opponents rather than deny it on account of what he calls the notorious infamy of the verdict?[3] Or his recourse, last of all, to the support of the law in spite of the odious nature of the affair, a method by which he would have set the judges against him but for the fact that he had already softened their feelings towards him?[4] Or the skill which he shows in stating that he has adopted this course in spite of the protests of his client?[5] What again am I to select as 10
an outstanding instance of his sagacity in the *pro Milone*? The fact that he refrains from proceeding to his statement of facts until he has cleared the ground by disposing of the previous verdicts against the accused?[6] The manner in which he turns the

insidiarum invidiam in Clodium vertit, quanquam revera fuerat pugna fortuita? quod factum et laudavit et tamen voluntate Milonis removit? quod illi preces non dedit et in earum locum ipse successit? Infinitum est enumerare, ut Cottae detraxerit auctoritatem, ut pro Ligario se opposuerit, Cornelium

11 ipsa confessionis fiducia eripuerit. Illud dicere satis habeo, nihil esse non modo in orando, sed in omni vita prius consilio, frustraque sine eo tradi ceteras artes, plusque vel sine doctrina prudentiam quam sine prudentia facere doctrinam. Aptare etiam orationem locis, temporibus, personis est eiusdem virtutis. Sed hic quia latius fusus est locus mixtusque cum elocutione, tractabitur cum praecipere de apte dicendo coeperimus.

---

[1] See above i. 25 and 27.
[2] *cp.* above v. xiii. 30. The reference is to the *pro Oppio.*
[3] See above v. x. 93. [4] See above v. xiii. 18 and 26.
[5] In XI. i. *cp.* I. v. 1.

odium of the attempted ambush against Clodius, although as a matter of fact the encounter was a pure chance? The way in which he at one and the same time praised the actual deed and showed that it was forced upon his client? Or the skill with which he avoided making Milo plead for consideration and undertook the rôle of suppliant himself?[1] It would be an endless task to quote all the instances of his sagacity, how he discredited Cotta,[2] how he put forward his own case in defence of Ligarius[3] and saved Cornelius[4] by his bold admission of the facts.
It is enough, I think, to say that there is nothing 11
not merely in oratory, but in all the tasks of life that is more important than sagacity and that without it all formal instruction is given in vain, while prudence unsupported by learning will accomplish more than learning unsupported by prudence. It is sagacity again that teaches us to adapt our speech to circumstances of time and place and to the persons with whom we are concerned. But since this topic covers a wide field and is intimately connected with eloquence itself, I shall reserve my treatment of it till I come to give instructions on the subject of appropriateness in speaking.[5]

NOTES

IV. ii. 28, *secundo partis suae loco.* There seems to have been nothing in the schools of rhetoric which corresponded with the mock trials employed to-day for the training of law students. It would have needed little to adapt the *controversiae* to this more practical form, but it seems not to have been done. The declaimer dealt both with the case for the prosecution and that for the defence, as stated in section 29. But more than one declamation might be made on the same theme. The declamation which is described as being delivered *secundo loco* would appear to be, not a declamation for the defence, though this is conceivable, but rather a second speech in answer to the defence. The declaimer refutes the arguments which he alleges have been made by the defence, but that he may not miss the opportunity of practice in making a statement of facts, preludes his refutation with a statement of facts, inserted in the usual position immediately following the exordium. For the whole of this obscure passage *cp.* v. xiii. 50.

V. xiii. 49. An alternative interpretation is that certain depositions have been communicated to the prosecution by the defence and are used to supply material for *contradictiones* after discussion among the prosecutor's *advocati.*

V. xiii. 50. The reading is uncertain. Cod. Bern. reads *et * * et*; Cod. Bamb. *et et*; Cod. Ambr. *enaribus.* It is clear that something is lost. *propositionibus* is a harmless rather than a probable emendation. *propositionibus* and *contradictionibus* have been translated as datives. It would also be possible to treat them as ablatives: "meet our imaginary opponent's case both by statements and by objections."

NOTES

V. xiv. 1 *sqq.* I am indebted for this note to my colleague, Dr. A. Wolf, Reader in Logic and Ethics in the University of London.

§ 1. *ex consequentibus.* If S is M, it is P; S is not P; therefore S is not M (a Destructive syllogism). The argument is: [If Caesar's cause were not superior the gods would not support it;] the gods have supported Caesar's cause; therefore our cause is superior. The Major is omitted, thereby converting the syllogism into an enthymeme. The conclusion is stated, though it does *not* follow the premise, as it should do *formally.*

§ 2. *ex pugnantibus.* The usual form would be: It would be inconsistent for S to be M and not also to be P; S is M; therefore S is also P. Quintilian's form of Minor and Conclusion is: S is not P; therefore S is not M. The argument is: [It would be inconsistent to hold that someone's death should be avenged and not also that his life should be restored, if possible;] you hold that his life was not worth restoring, even if possible; therefore you cannot hold that his death should be avenged. The Major is omitted.

§ 3. The argument is: [It would be inconsistent to hold that a man would commit a murder under unfavourable circumstances, and not to hold that he would do so under favourable circumstances;] but you know that he did not commit murder under favourable circumstances; therefore, you cannot hold that he did so under unfavourable circumstances.

§ 4. The original argument is: If a man is guilty of an illegality which others have committed with impunity, he should not be punished; S is guilty of such an illegality; therefore he should not be punished. The counter-argument (in the text) uses the same reason (*i.e.* the fact that the illegality in question has been frequently committed with impunity) to establish a contrary conclusion (*i.e.* that special punishment should be administered).

§ 5. The epicheireme is a syllogism in which either premise is supported by a reason. The reason is a premise of another syllogism, so that the reason taken together with the premise which it supports is really an enthymeme; *e.g.* M is P, because it is Q [and Q is P];

S is M, because it is R [and R is M]; therefore S is P.

§§ 7–9. The argument is confused. It may be expressed thus: *Major.* [If the universe were not controlled by reason, something could be found better governed than it is.] *Reason.* Because things that are governed by reason are better governed than those which are not. *Minor.* But nothing is better administered than the universe. *Conclusion.* Therefore the universe is governed by reason. (The argument is at once an enthymeme (*ex consequentibus*) and an epicheireme.)

§ 10. The *Conclusion* here is *not* identical with the *Major*, it is only expressed in the same sentence: viz. *Major.* Whatever derives its motion from itself is immortal. *Minor and Conclusion.* The soul derives its motion from itself; therefore the soul is immortal.

§ 11. The proposition is doubtful because it is a hasty inference based on mere enumeration of instances.

§ 12. 1st Ex. The argument is: *Major.* That which is devoid of feeling is nothing to us. *Minor* (omitted). Death is a state devoid of feeling. *Reason.* Because a state of dissolution is a state devoid of feeling. Here we have an epicheireme with *Reason* substituted for *Minor*, and *Major* is misunderstood as in § 10 (*q.v.*).

2nd Ex. *Major* (omitted). If the universe were not animate, there would be something better. *Reason.* Because all animate things are better than inanimate. *Minor.* But there is nothing better than the universe. *Conclusion.* Therefore the universe is animate. The *Major* is really omitted as Quintilian suspects.

§ 13 (last sentence). What he calls the *Minor* is only its *Reason.*

§ 17. The argument is: *Major.* If in the midst of arms laws were not silent, then he who would await their sanction is certain to be the victim, etc. *Minor* (omitted). But he who awaits their sanction should not be the victim, etc. *Conclusion.* Therefore in the midst of arms laws are silent. Here we have an enthymeme *ex consequentibus.* There is still no *Reason* for either premise. The *Major* is the *Reason* for the *Conclusion*, which is a different matter.

§ 18. *Major* (omitted). If the Twelve Tables permit the killing of a man under certain circumstances, it cannot be maintained that a slayer must be killed whatever the circumstances. *Minor.* The Twelve Tables do permit the killing, etc. *Conclusion.* Therefore it cannot be maintained that a slayer, etc. Here also what is given is a *Reason* for the *Conclusion* (*i.e.* itself a premise) and not for the *Premise.*

§ 19. The Real argument is: *Major.* If it were wrong to kill robbers, etc., we should not be allowed escorts and swords. *Reason.* For escorts and swords are intended to enable us to fight robbers. *Minor.* But we are allowed escorts and swords. *Conclusion.* Therefore it is not wrong to kill robbers, etc.

§ 20. *Major.* If a man confesses, etc., he should be condemned. *Objection.* If a man confesses that he has killed someone who lay in wait for him he should *not* be condemned.

§ 21. The *Reason* is one of the premises for the proposition. If the other *Reason* be false, the proposition will be false, but the first *Reason* will still be true.

§ 23. The doctrine is false. If both premises are true, the conclusion, *if valid,* is true, while if both premises or either be false, the conclusion may still be true. *Cp.* Ar. An. Pr. ii. 2.

§ 25. *Enthymema ex consequentibus . . . ex pugnantibus* See on § 10. Both these enthymemes omit the major premise.

VI. I. 20. Servium Sulpicium Messala is the reading of Scholl. The MSS. give Servius Sulpicius.

INDEX

INDEX

(Only those names are included which seem to require some explanation ; a complete index will be contained in Vol. IV.)

INDEX

Consul with Marius 102 B.C. and with him victor over the Cimbri at Vercellae. One of the characters in Cicero's *de Oratore*.
Celsus, Cornelius, IV. i. 12; ii. 9. Writer on rhetoric, medicine and many other subjects: flourished under Augustus and Tiberius.
Chrysogonus, IV. ii. 3. A powerful freedman of Sulla.
Clodia, V. xiii. 30. Sister of Clodius, mistress of Catullus, Caelius and many others.
Clodius, IV. ii. 25, 57, 88; V. ii. 4; V. x. 41; V. xiv. 22. Demagogue and inveterate enemy of Cicero; killed by Milo.
Cornificius, V. x. 2. Rhetorician contemporary with Cicero, probably author of the rhetorical treatise *ad Herennium*.
Crassus, L., VI. iii. 43, 44. With L. Antonius the chief Roman orator prior to Cicero of whom he was an elder contemporary.
Curio, VI. iii. 76. Younger contemporary of Cicero, a turbulent politician and supporter of Caesar.
Cynicus, IV. ii. 30. The reference seems to be to a rhetorical theme which occurs in the declamations of the Pseudo-Quintilian (283) where a father disinherits his son for turning Cynic and denounces the indecency of his garb.

Deiotarus, IV. i. 31. A Galatian King defended by Cicero.
Dionysius, V. xi. 8. Tyrant of Syracuse.
Dolabella (i), IV. ii. 132. Praetor 67 B.C.
Dolabella (ii), VI. iii. 73 and 99. A disreputable politician and follower of Caesar. Fabia appears to have been his first wife. He later married Cicero's daughter.
Dolabella (iii), VI. iii. 79. Son of (ii); friend of Augustus.
Domitius Afer, V. vii. 7; V. x. 79; VI. iii. 27 and 91. A brilliant orator of the reigns of Tiberius, Caligula, Claudius and Nero.
Domitius, L., IV. ii. 17. Governor of Sicily *circ.* 97 B.C.

Fontieus, VI. iii. 51. Defended by Cicero on a charge of extortion as governor of Gaul in 69 B.C.

Galba, A., VI. iii. 27, 62 and 80. Unknown humorist. The name should perhaps be Gabba.
Galba, P. Sulpicius, V. xi. 11. Unsuccessful candidate for the consulship in 64 B.C.
Glyco, VI. i. 41. A Greek rhetorician, *fl. circ.* 40 A.D.

Hermagoras, V. ix. 12. Famous rhetorician of the Rhodian school, contemporary with Cicero.
Hispo, VI. iii. 100. A rhetorician prominent from the time of Tiberius to that of Nero. Notorious as an informer.
Horatius, M. (i), IV. ii. 7; V. xi. 12. The survivor of the three Horatii who defeated the three Curiatii, champions of Alba. He slew his sister for bewailing the death of one of the Curiatii to whom she was betrothed.
Horatius (ii), V. xi. 10. Perhaps Horatius Cocles, defender of the bridge against the Etruscans; perhaps identical with (i).
Hortensius, IV. v. 24; VI. iv. 4. The leading orator at Rome when Cicero first made his appearance at the bar, and the latter's most serious rival.

Iphicrates, V. xii. 10. Athenian general prosecuted for refusing to engage the enemy: according to one account the speech in question was written by Lysias.
Isocrates, IV. ii. 31. Famous orator and founder of the science and technique of Greek rhetoric, 436–338 B.C.
Iulius Caesar Strabo Vopiscus, C., VI. iii. 38. A distinguished orator, one of the characters of Cicero's dialogue, the *de Oratore*; was put to death by Marius.

INDEX

INDEX

Printed in Great Britain by
Fletcher & Son Ltd, Norwich

THE LOEB CLASSICAL LIBRARY

VOLUMES ALREADY PUBLISHED

Latin Authors

AMMIANUS MARCELLINUS. Translated by J. C. Rolfe. 3 Vols.

APULEIUS: THE GOLDEN ASS (METAMORPHOSES). W. Adlington (1566). Revised by S. Gaselee.

ST. AUGUSTINE: CITY OF GOD. 7 Vols. Vol. I. G. E. McCracken. Vols. II and VII. W. M. Green. Vol. III. D. Wiesen. Vol. IV. P. Levine. Vol. V. E. M. Sanford and W. M. Green. Vol. VI. W. C. Greene.

ST. AUGUSTINE, CONFESSIONS OF. W. Watts (1631). 2 Vols.

ST. AUGUSTINE, SELECT LETTERS. J. H. Baxter.

AUSONIUS. H. G. Evelyn White. 2 Vols.

BEDE. J. E. King. 2 Vols.

BOETHIUS: TRACTS and DE CONSOLATIONE PHILOSOPHIAE. Rev. H. F. Stewart and E. K. Rand. Revised by S. J. Tester.

CAESAR: ALEXANDRIAN, AFRICAN and SPANISH WARS. A. G. Way.

CAESAR: CIVIL WARS. A. G. Peskett.

CAESAR: GALLIC WAR. H. J. Edwards.

CATO: DE RE RUSTICA. VARRO: DE RE RUSTICA. H. B. Ash and W. D. Hooper.

CATULLUS. F. W. Cornish. TIBULLUS. J. B. Postgate. PERVIGILIUM VENERIS. J. W. Mackail.

CELSUS: DE MEDICINA. W. G. Spencer. 3 Vols.

CICERO: BRUTUS and ORATOR. G. L. Hendrickson and H. M. Hubbell.

[CICERO]: AD HERENNIUM. H. Caplan.

CICERO: DE ORATORE, etc. 2 Vols. Vol. I. DE ORATORE, Books I and II. E. W. Sutton and H. Rackham. Vol. II. DE ORATORE, Book III. DE FATO; PARADOXA STOICORUM; DE PARTITIONE ORATORIA. H. Rackham.

CICERO: DE FINIBUS. H. Rackham.

CICERO: DE INVENTIONE, etc. H. M. Hubbell.

CICERO: DE NATURA DEORUM and ACADEMICA. H. Rackham.

CICERO: DE OFFICIIS. Walter Miller.

CICERO: DE REPUBLICA and DE LEGIBUS. Clinton W. Keyes.

Cicero: De Senectute, De Amicitia, De Divinatione. W. A. Falconer.

Cicero: In Catilinam, Pro Flacco, Pro Murena, Pro Sulla. New version by C. Macdonald.

Cicero: Letters to Atticus. E. O. Winstedt. 3 Vols.

Cicero: Letters to His Friends. W. Glynn Williams, M. Cary, M. Henderson. 4 Vols.

Cicero: Philippics. W. C. A. Ker.

Cicero: Pro Archia, Post Reditum, De Domo, De Haruspicum Responsis, Pro Plancio. N. H. Watts.

Cicero: Pro Caecina, Pro Lege Manilia, Pro Cluentio, Pro Rabirio. H. Grose Hodge.

Cicero: Pro Caelio, De Provinciis Consularibus, Pro Balbo. R. Gardner.

Cicero: Pro Milone, In Pisonem, Pro Scauro, Pro Fonteio, Pro Rabirio Postumo, Pro Marcello, Pro Ligario, Pro Rege Deiotaro. N. H. Watts.

Cicero: Pro Quinctio, Pro Roscio Amerino, Pro Roscio Comoedo, Contra Rullum. J. H. Freese.

Cicero: Pro Sestio, In Vatinium. R. Gardner.

Cicero: Tusculan Disputations. J. E. King.

Cicero: Verrine Orations. L. H. G. Greenwood. 2 Vols.

Claudian. M. Platnauer. 2 Vols.

Columella: De Re Rustica. De Arboribus. H. B. Ash, E. S. Forster and E. Heffner. 3 Vols.

Curtius, Q.: History of Alexander. J. C. Rolfe. 2 Vols.

Florus. E. S. Forster.

Frontinus: Stratagems and Aqueducts. C. E. Bennett and M. B. McElwain.

Fronto: Correspondence. C. R. Haines. 2 Vols.

Gellius. J. C. Rolfe. 3 Vols.

Horace: Odes and Epodes. C. E. Bennett.

Horace: Satires, Epistles, Ars Poetica. H. R. Fairclough.

Jerome: Selected Letters. F. A. Wright.

Juvenal and Persius. G. G. Ramsay.

Livy. B. O. Foster, F. G. Moore, Evan T. Sage, and A. C. Schlesinger and R. M. Geer (General Index). 14 Vols.

Lucan. J. D. Duff.

Lucretius. W. H. D. Rouse. Revised by M. F. Smith.

Manilius. G. P. Goold.

Martial. W. C. A. Ker. 2 Vols. Revised by E. H. Warmington.

Minor Latin poets: from Publilius Syrus to Rutilius Namatianus, including Grattius, Calpurnius Siculus, Nemesianus, Avianus and others, with "Aetna" and the "Phoenix." J. Wight Duff and Arnold M. Duff. 2 Vols.

MINUCIUS FELIX. Cf. TERTULLIAN.

NEPOS CORNELIUS. J. C. Rolfe.

OVID: THE ART OF LOVE and OTHER POEMS. J. H. Mosley. Revised by G. P. Goold.

OVID: FASTI. Sir James G. Frazer

OVID: HEROIDES and AMORES. Grant Showerman. Revised by G. P. Goold

OVID: METAMORPHOSES. F. J. Miller. 2 Vols. Revised by G. P. Goold.

OVID: TRISTIA and EX PONTO. A. L. Wheeler.

PERSIUS. Cf. JUVENAL.

PERVIGILIUM VENERIS. Cf. CATULLUS.

PETRONIUS. M. Heseltine. SENECA: APOCOLOCYNTOSIS. W. H. D. Rouse. Revised by E. H. Warmington.

PHAEDRUS and BABRIUS (Greek). B. E. Perry.

PLAUTUS. Paul Nixon. 5 Vols.

PLINY: LETTERS, PANEGYRICUS. Betty Radice. 2 Vols.

PLINY: NATURAL HISTORY. 10 Vols. Vols. I–V and IX. H. Rackham. VI.–VIII. W. H. S. Jones. X. D. E. Eichholz.

PROPERTIUS. H. E. Butler.

PRUDENTIUS. H. J. Thomson. 2 Vols.

QUINTILIAN. H. E. Butler. 4 Vols.

REMAINS OF OLD LATIN. E. H. Warmington. 4 Vols. Vol. I. (ENNIUS AND CAECILIUS) Vol. II. (LIVIUS, NAEVIUS PACUVIUS, ACCIUS) Vol. III. (LUCILIUS and LAWS OF XII TABLES) Vol. IV. (ARCHAIC INSCRIPTIONS)

RES GESTAE DIVI AUGUSTI. Cf. VELLEIUS PATERCULUS.

SALLUST. J. C. Rolfe.

SCRIPTORES HISTORIAE AUGUSTAE. D. Magie. 3 Vols.

SENECA, THE ELDER: CONTROVERSIAE, SUASORIAE. M. Winterbottom. 2 Vols.

SENECA: APOCOLOCYNTOSIS. Cf. PETRONIUS.

SENECA: EPISTULAE MORALES. R. M. Gummere. 3 Vols.

SENECA: MORAL ESSAYS. J. W. Basore. 3 Vols.

SENECA: TRAGEDIES. F. J. Miller. 2 Vols.

SENECA: NATURALES QUAESTIONES. T. H. Corcoran. 2 Vols.

SIDONIUS: POEMS and LETTERS. W. B. Anderson. 2 Vols.

SILIUS ITALICUS. J. D. Duff. 2 Vols.

STATIUS. J. H. Mozley. 2 Vols.

SUETONIUS. J. C. Rolfe. 2 Vols.

TACITUS: DIALOGUS. Sir Wm. Peterson. AGRICOLA and GERMANIA. Maurice Hutton. Revised by M. Winterbottom, R. M. Ogilvie, E. H. Warmington.

TACITUS: HISTORIES and ANNALS. C. H. Moore and J. Jackson. 4 Vols.

Terence. John Sargeaunt. 2 Vols.

Tertullian: Apologia and De Spectaculis. T. R. Glover. Minucius Felix. G. H. Rendall.

Tibullus. Cf. Catullus.

Valerius Flaccus. J. H. Mozley.

Varro: De Lingua Latina. R. G. Kent. 2 Vols.

Velleius Paterculus and Res Gestae Divi Augusti. F. W. Shipley.

Virgil. H. R. Fairclough. 2 Vols.

Vitruvius: De Architectura. F. Granger. 2 Vols.

Greek Authors

Achilles Tatius. S. Gaselee.

Aelian: On the Nature of Animals. A. F. Scholfield. 3 Vols.

Aeneas Tacticus. Asclepiodotus and Onasander. The Illinois Greek Club.

Aeschines. C. D. Adams.

Aeschylus. H. Weir Smyth. 2 Vols.

Alciphron, Aelian, Philostratus: Letters. A. R. Benner and F. H. Fobes.

Andocides, Antiphon. Cf. Minor Attic Orators.

Apollodorus. Sir James G. Frazer. 2 Vols.

Apollonius Rhodius. R. C. Seaton.

Apostolic Fathers. Kirsopp Lake. 2 Vols.

Appian: Roman History. Horace White. 4 Vols.

Aratus. Cf. Callimachus.

Aristides: Orations. C. A. Behr. Vol. I.

Aristophanes. Benjamin Bickley Rogers. 3 Vols. Verse trans.

Aristotle: Art of Rhetoric. J. H. Freese.

Aristotle: Athenian Constitution, Eudemian Ethics, Vices and Virtues. H. Rackham.

Aristotle: Generation of Animals. A. L. Peck.

Aristotle: Historia Animalium. A. L. Peck. Vols. I.–II.

Aristotle: Metaphysics. H. Tredennick. 2 Vols.

Aristotle: Meteorologica. H. D. P. Lee.

Aristotle: Minor Works. W. S. Hett. On Colours, On Things Heard, On Physiognomies, On Plants, On Marvellous Things Heard, Mechanical Problems, On Indivisible Lines, On Situations and Names of Winds, On Melissus, Xenophanes, and Gorgias.

Aristotle: Nicomachean Ethics. H. Rackham.

Aristotle: Oeconomica and Magna Moralia. G. C. Armstrong (with Metaphysics, Vol. II).

Aristotle: On the Heavens. W. K. C. Guthrie.

Aristotle: On the Soul, Parva Naturalia, On Breath. W. S. Hett.

Aristotle: Categories, On Interpretation, Prior Analytics. H. P. Cooke and H. Tredennick.

Aristotle: Posterior Analytics, Topics. H. Tredennick and E. S. Forster.

Aristotle: On Sophistical Refutations.

On Coming to be and Passing Away, On the Cosmos. E. S. Forster and D. J. Furley.

Aristotle: Parts of Animals. A. L. Peck; Motion and Progression of Animals. E. S. Forster.

Aristotle: Physics. Rev. P. Wicksteed and F. M. Cornford. 2 Vols.

Aristotle: Poetics and Longinus. W. Hamilton Fyfe; Demetrius on Style. W. Rhys Roberts.

Aristotle: Politics. H. Rackham.

Aristotle: Problems. W. S. Hett. 2 Vols.

Aristotle: Rhetorica Ad Alexandrum (with Problems. Vol. II). H. Rackham.

Arrian: History of Alexander and Indica. Rev. E. Iliffe Robson. 2 Vols. New version P. Brunt.

Athenaeus: Deipnosophistae. C. B. Gulick. 7 Vols.

Babrius and Phaedrus (Latin). B. E. Perry.

St. Basil: Letters. R. J. Deferrari. 4 Vols.

Callimachus: Fragments. C. A. Trypanis. Musaeus: Hero and Leander. T. Gelzer and C. Whitman.

Callimachus, Hymns and Epigrams, and Lycophron. A. W. Mair; Aratus. G. R. Mair.

Clement of Alexandria. Rev. G. W. Butterworth.

Colluthus. Cf. Oppian.

Daphnis and Chloe. Thornley's Translation revised by J. M. Edmonds: and Parthenius. S. Gaselee.

Demosthenes I.: Olynthiacs, Philippics and Minor Orations I.–XVII. and XX. J. H. Vince.

Demosthenes II.: De Corona and De Falsa Legatione. C. A. Vince and J. H. Vince.

Demosthenes III.: Meidias, Androtion, Aristocrates, Timocrates and Aristogeiton I. and II. J. H. Vince.

Demosthenes IV.–VI: Private Orations and In Neaeram. A. T. Murray.

Demosthenes VII: Funeral Speech, Erotic Essay, Exordia and Letters. N. W. and N. J. DeWitt.

Dio Cassius: Roman History. E. Cary. 9 Vols.

Dio Chrysostom. J. W. Cohoon and H. Lamar Crosby. 5 Vols.

Diodorus Siculus. 12 Vols. Vols. I.–VI. C. H. Oldfather. Vol. VII. C. L. Sherman. Vol. VIII. C. B. Welles. Vols. IX. and X. R. M. Geer. Vol. XI. F. Walton. Vol. XII. F. Walton. General Index. R. M. Geer.

Diogenes Laertius. R. D. Hicks. 2 Vols. New Introduction by H. S. Long.

Dionysius of Halicarnassus: Roman Antiquities. Spelman's translation revised by E. Cary. 7 Vols.

Dionysius of Halicarnassus: Critical Essays. S. Usher. 2 Vols. Vol. I.

Epictetus. W. A. Oldfather. 2 Vols.

Euripides. A. S. Way. 4 Vols. Verse trans.

Eusebius: Ecclesiastical History. Kirsopp Lake and J. E. L. Oulton. 2 Vols.

Galen: On the Natural Faculties. A. J. Brock.

Greek Anthology. W. R. Paton. 5 Vols.

Greek Bucolic Poets (Theocritus, Bion, Moschus). J. M. Edmonds.

Greek Elegy and Iambus with the Anacreontea. J. M. Edmonds. 2 Vols.

Greek Lyric. D. A. Campbell. 4 Vols. Vol. I.

Greek Mathematical Works. Ivor Thomas. 2 Vols.

Herodes. Cf. Theophrastus: Characters.

Herodian. C. R. Whittaker. 2 Vols.

Herodotus. A. D. Godley. 4 Vols.

Hesiod and The Homeric Hymns. H. G. Evelyn White.

Hippocrates and the Fragments of Heracleitus. W. H. S. Jones and E. T. Withington. 4 Vols.

Homer: Iliad. A. T. Murray. 2 Vols.

Homer: Odyssey. A. T. Murray. 2 Vols.

Isaeus. E. W. Forster.

Isocrates. George Norlin and LaRue Van Hook. 3 Vols.

[St. John Damascene]: Barlaam and Ioasaph. Rev. G. R. Woodward, Harold Mattingly and D. M. Lang.

Josephus. 10 Vols. Vols. I.–IV. H. Thackeray. Vol. V. H. Thackeray and R. Marcus. Vols. VI.–VII. R. Marcus. Vol. VIII. R. Marcus and Allen Wikgren. Vols. IX.–X. L. H. Feldman.

Julian. Wilmer Cave Wright. 3 Vols.

Libanius. A. F. Norman. 3 Vols. Vols. I.–II.

Lucian. 8 Vols. Vols. I.–V. A. M. Harmon. Vol. VI. K. Kilburn. Vols. VII.–VIII. M. D. Macleod.

Lycophron. Cf. Callimachus.

LYRA GRAECA, J. M. Edmonds. 2 Vols.

LYSIAS. W. R. M. Lamb.

MANETHO. W. G. Waddell.

MARCUS AURELIUS. C. R. Haines.

MENANDER. W. G. Arnott. 3 Vols. Vol. I.

MINOR ATTIC ORATORS (ANTIPHON, ANDOCIDES, LYCURGUS, DEMADES, DINARCHUS, HYPERIDES). K. J. Maidment and J. O. Burtt. 2 Vols.

MUSAEUS: HERO AND LEANDER. Cf. CALLIMACHUS.

NONNOS: DIONYSIACA. W. H. D. Rouse. 3 Vols.

OPPIAN, COLLUTHUS, TRYPHIODORUS. A. W. Mair.

PAPYRI. NON-LITERARY SELECTIONS. A. S. Hunt and C. C. Edgar. 2 Vols. LITERARY SELECTIONS (Poetry). D. L. Page.

PARTHENIUS. Cf. DAPHNIS and CHLOE.

PAUSANIAS: DESCRIPTION OF GREECE. W. H. S. Jones. 4 Vols. and Companion Vol. arranged by R. E. Wycherley.

PHILO. 10 Vols. Vols. I.–V. F. H. Colson and Rev. G. H. Whitaker. Vols. VI.–IX. F. H. Colson. Vol. X. F. H. Colson and the Rev. J. W. Earp.

PHILO: two supplementary Vols. (*Translation only.*) Ralph Marcus.

PHILOSTRATUS: THE LIFE OF APOLLONIUS OF TYANA. F. C. Conybeare. 2 Vols.

PHILOSTRATUS: IMAGINES; CALLISTRATUS: DESCRIPTIONS. A. Fairbanks.

PHILOSTRATUS and EUNAPIUS: LIVES OF THE SOPHISTS. Wilmer Cave Wright.

PINDAR. Sir J. E. Sandys.

PLATO: CHARMIDES, ALCIBIADES, HIPPARCHUS, THE LOVERS, THEAGES, MINOS and EPINOMIS. W. R. M. Lamb.

PLATO: CRATYLUS, PARMENIDES, GREATER HIPPIAS, LESSER HIPPIAS. H. N. Fowler.

PLATO: EUTHYPHRO, APOLOGY, CRITO, PHAEDO, PHAEDRUS, H. N. Fowler.

PLATO: LACHES, PROTAGORAS, MENO, EUTHYDEMUS. W. R. M. Lamb.

PLATO: LAWS. Rev. R. G. Bury. 2 Vols.

PLATO: LYSIS, SYMPOSIUM, GORGIAS. W. R. M. Lamb.

PLATO: Republic. Paul Shorey. 2 Vols.

PLATO: STATESMAN, PHILEBUS. H. N. Fowler; ION. W. R. M. Lamb.

PLATO: THEAETETUS and SOPHIST. H. N. Fowler.

PLATO: TIMAEUS, CRITIAS, CLITOPHO, MENEXENUS, EPISTULAE. Rev. R. G. Bury.

PLOTINUS: A. H. Armstrong. 7 Vols. Vols. I.–V.

Plutarch: Moralia. 16 Vols. Vols I.–V. F. C. Babbitt. Vol. VI. W. C. Helmbold. Vols. VII. and XIV. P. H. De Lacy and B. Einarson. Vol. VIII. P. A. Clement and H. B. Hoffleit. Vol. IX. E. L. Minar, Jr., F. H. Sandbach, W. C. Helmbold. Vol. X. H. N. Fowler. Vol. XI. L. Pearson and F. H. Sandbach. Vol. XII. H. Cherniss and W. C. Helmbold. Vol. XIII 1–2. H. Cherniss. Vol. XV. F. H. Sandbach.

Plutarch: The Parallel Lives. B. Perrin. 11 Vols.

Polybius. W. R. Paton. 6 Vols.

Procopius. H. B. Dewing. 7 Vols.

Ptolemy: Tetrabiblos. F. E. Robbins.

Quintus Smyrnaeus. A. S. Way. Verse trans.

Sextus Empiricus. Rev. R. G. Bury. 4 Vols.

Sophocles. F. Storr. 2 Vols. Verse trans.

Strabo: Geography. Horace L. Jones. 8 Vols.

Theocritus. Cf. Greek Bucolic Poets.

Theophrastus: Characters. J. M. Edmonds. Herodes, etc. A. D. Knox.

Theophrastus: Enquiry into Plants. Sir Arthur Hort, Bart. 2 Vols.

Theophrastus: De Causis Plantarum. G. K. K. Link and B. Einarson. 3 Vols. Vol. I.

Thucydides. C. F. Smith. 4 Vols.

Tryphiodorus. Cf. Oppian.

Xenophon: Cyropaedia. Walter Miller. 2 Vols.

Xenophon: Hellencia. C. L. Brownson. 2 Vols.

Xenophon: Anabasis. C. L. Brownson.

Xenophon: Memorabilia and Oeconomicus. E. C. Marchant. Symposium and Apology. O. J. Todd.

Xenophon: Scripta Minora. E. C. Marchant. Constitution of the athenians. G. W. Bowersock.